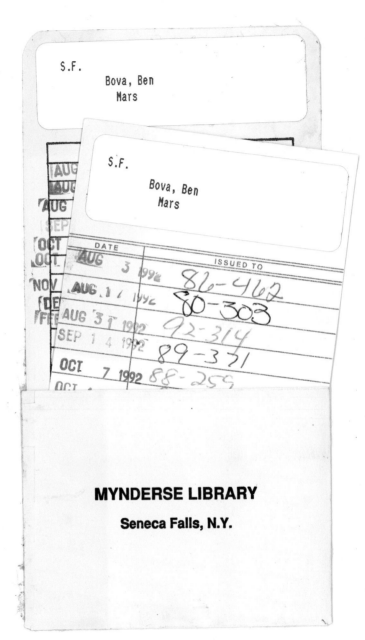

FICTION BY BEN BOVA

THE TRIKON DECEPTION (with Bill Pogue)
ORION IN THE DYING TIME
FUTURE CRIME*
VOYAGERS III: STAR BROTHERS
CYBERBOOKS
PEACEKEEPERS
VENGEANCE OF ORION
THE KINSMAN SAGA
BATTLE STATION*
VOYAGERS II: THE ALIEN WITHIN
PROMETHEANS*
PRIVATEERS
THE ASTRAL MIRROR*
ORION
ESCAPE PLUS*
THE WINDS OF ALTAIR
TEST OF FIRE
VOYAGERS
THE EXILES TRILOGY
KINSMAN
MAXWELL'S DEMONS*
COLONY
THE MULTIPLE MAN
MILLENIUM
CITY OF DARKNESS
THE STARCROSSED
GREMLINS, GO HOME! (with Gordon R. Dickson)
FORWARD IN TIME*
WHEN THE SKY BURNED
AS ON A DARKLING PLAIN
THX 1138 (with George Lucas)
ESCAPE!
THE DUELING MACHINE
OUT OF THE SUN
THE WEATHERMAKERS
STAR WATCHMAN
THE STAR CONQUERORS

*collection

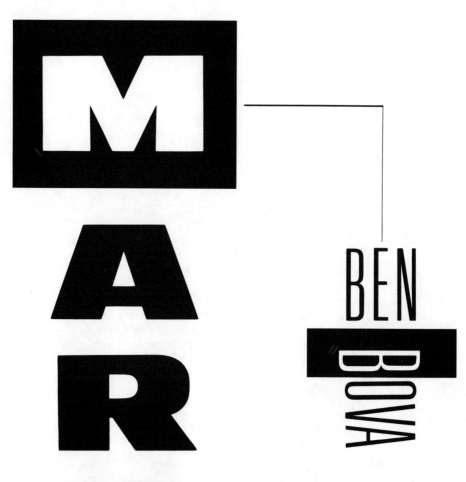

MARS

BEN BOVA

BANTAM BOOKS

NEW YORK · TORONTO · LONDON · SYDNEY · AUCKLAND

M A R S

A BANTAM SPECTRA BOOK/JULY 1992

ALL RIGHTS RESERVED

COPYRIGHT © 1992 BY BEN BOVA

BOOK DESIGN BY JAYA DAYAL

LIBRARY OF CONGRESS CATALOGING-IN-PUBLICATION DATA

BOVA, BEN, 1932–
   MARS / BEN BOVA.
    P. CM.
   ISBN 0-553-07892-5.
   ISBN 0-553-08330-9 (SPECIAL LIMITED ED.)
   I. TITLE.
  PS 3552.082M37 1992
  813'.54—DC20   91-29466
                            CIP

PUBLISHED SIMULTANEOUSLY IN THE UNITED STATES AND CANADA

BANTAM BOOKS ARE PUBLISHED BY BANTAM BOOKS, A DIVISION
OF BANTAM DOUBLEDAY DELL PUBLISHING GROUP, INC. ITS TRADE-
MARK, CONSISTING OF THE WORDS "BANTAM BOOKS" AND
THE PORTRAYAL OF A ROOSTER, IS REGISTERED IN U. S. PATENT
AND TRADEMARK OFFICE AND IN OTHER COUNTRIES. MARCA
REGISTRADA. BANTAM BOOKS, 666 FIFTH AVENUE, NEW YORK,
NEW YORK 10103.

PRINTED IN THE UNITED STATES OF AMERICA

RRH 0 9 8 7 6 5 4 3 2 1

TO FLORENCE AND JERRY NELSON

ACKNOWLEDGMENTS

This novel could not have been written without the generous help of Mark Chartrand, Stephen L. Gillet, Tony Hillerman, William R. Pogue, Kenneth Jon Rose, and Paul Soderberg. Fred Doyle and R. M. Batson of the United States Geological Survey kindly provided beautifully detailed maps of Mars. My deepest thanks to them and to all the countless others who, over the years, provided many valuable insights and ideas.

They have helped to make this novel as accurate a depiction as possible of the planet Mars, of the hardware that the first explorers of Mars will use, and of the mythology of the Navaho people. I have taken poetic liberties with the basic facts, here and there, as every author must. The authenticity of this novel is thanks to them; any inaccuracies are entirely my own doing.

Finally, my heartfelt thanks also to Edgar Rice Burroughs, Stanley G. Weinbaum, and most especially Ray Bradbury. The different versions of Mars that they wrote about exist only in the imagination— but that is more than enough.

BEN BOVA
West Hartford
and Marco Island

MARS

T H E   R E D   W O R L D
A N D   T H E   B L U E

Listen to the wisdom of the Old Ones:

The red world and the blue are brothers. They were born together in the seething maelstrom of dust and gas spinning out from the heart of the vast cloud that was to become Father Sun.

For uncountable time each world was engulfed in endless violence. Monsters roared down out of the sky, pounding the worlds mercilessly in a holocaust of terrible explosions. Under such awesome bombardment there could be no solid ground; the rocks themselves were liquid bubbling magma as the fiery rain from the sky went on and on, blotting out the radiance of the newly bright Father Sun with steaming clouds that covered each world from pole to pole.

Slowly, with the godlike patience of the stars themselves, slowly their surfaces cooled. Solid land took form, bare rock, hard and harsh and lifeless. Worse than the desert where The People live; much worse. There was no tree, no blade of grass, not even a drop of water.

Deep below their crusts both worlds were still liquid-hot with the energy of their violent creation. Water trapped beneath the ground boiled up, sweated from the depths like droplets beading a gourd in the heat of summer. The water evaporated into the thin film of atmosphere swaddling each newborn world. Cooling rain began to spatter onto the naked rocks, running into rivulets, streams, raging torrents that gouged the rocks out of their paths and tore huge gashes in the land.

On the bigger of the two worlds mighty oceans grew, filling deep rocky basins with water. The smaller world formed broad shallow lakes, but gradually they faded away into the thin, cold atmosphere or sank out of sight below the surface of the land.

Because of its glistening wide oceans the larger of the two worlds took on a deep blue tint. The smaller world slowly turned into a dusty, windblown desert as its waters sank into its ground. It turned rust-red.

Life arose on the blue world, first in the seas and later on dry land. Gigantic beasts roamed forests and marshes, only to disappear forever. At last The People came to the blue world—First Man and First Woman emerged, standing tall and proud in the bright sunlight. Their children multiplied. Some of them wondered about the world in which they lived and about the stars that dotted the night.

They turned their intelligent eyes to the red gleam in the sky that marked their brother world and wondered what it was. They watched it carefully, and the other stars too, and tried to understand the workings of the heavens.

To The People, the stars spoke of the endless cycles of the seasons, the time to plant, the time of the rains. The red world held no special fascination for them. They called it merely "Big Star."

But to the Anglos, steeped in conquest and killing, whenever their pale eyes turned to the red gleam in the sky that marked their brother world they trembled with thoughts of blood and death. They named the red world after their god of war.

Mars.

S O L 1: MORNING

"Touchdown."

It was said in Russian first and then immediately repeated in English.

Jamie Waterman never felt the actual moment when they touched the surface of Mars. The descent vehicle was lowering so gently that when it finally set down on the ground Jamie and the others realized it only because the vibration of the rocket thrusters ceased. Beyond everything else, Vosnesensky was a superb pilot.

All sense of motion stopped. There was no sound. Through the thick insulation of his pressure suit helmet Jamie could hear nothing except his own excited breathing.

Then Joanna Brumado's voice came through his earphones, hushed, awed: "We're here."

Eleven months ago they had been on Earth. Half an hour ago they had been in orbit around the planet Mars. Then came the terrifying ride down, shaking and bumping and burning their way through the thin atmosphere, an artificial meteor blazing across the empty Martian sky. A journey of more than a hundred million kilometers, a quest that had already taken four years of their lives, had at last reached its destination.

Now they sat in numb silence on the surface of a new world, four scientists encased in bulky, brightly colored pressure suits that made them look as if they had been swallowed alive by oversized robots.

Abruptly, without a word of command from the cockpit above them, the four scientists began to unstrap their safety harnesses and get up stiffly, awkwardly from their chairs. Jamie slid his helmet visor up as he squeezed between Ilona Malater and Tony Reed to get to the small round observation port, the only window in their cramped compartment.

He reached the window and looked out. The other three pressed

4 around him, their hard-shell pressure suits butting and sliding against one another like a quartet of awkward tortoises trying to dip their beaks into the same tiny life-giving puddle.

A red dusty desert stretched out as far as the eye could see, rust-colored boulders scattered across the barren gently rolling land like toys left behind by a careless child. The uneven horizon seemed closer than it should be. The sky was a delicate salmon pink. Small wind-shaped dunes heaped in precise rows, and the reddish sand piled against some of the bigger rocks.

Jamie catalogued the scene professionally: ejecta from impacts, maybe volcanic eruptions but more likely meteor hits. No bedrock visible. The dunes look stable, probably been there since the last dust storm, maybe longer.

"Mars," breathed Joanna Brumado, her helmet practically touching his as they peered through the window.

"Mars," Jamie agreed.

"It looks so desolate," said Ilona Malater, sounding disappointed, as if she had expected a welcoming committee or at least a blade of grass.

"Exactly like the photos," said Antony Reed.

To Jamie, the red desert world beyond the window looked just as he had expected it to look. Like home.

The first member of the team to leave the landing ship was the sturdy construction robot. Crowding against the small observation window with the three other scientists, Jamie Waterman watched the bulbous, blue-gray metal vehicle roll across the rusty red sand on its six springy wheels, stopping abruptly about fifty meters from where their lander stood.

Watching the square-sided machine with the bulky liquefied air tanks atop it, Jamie thought to himself, Russian design, Japanese electronics, and American software. Just like everything else on this expedition.

A pair of gleaming metal arms unfolded from the truck's front like a giraffe climbing to its feet and began to pull a shapeless heap of plastic from the big storage bin on its side. The robot spread the plastic out on the sand as precisely as a grandmother spreading a picnic tablecloth. Then it seemed to stop, as if to inspect the shiny, rubbery-looking material. Slowly, the lifeless plastic began to stir, filling with air from the big tanks on the robot's top. The plastic heap grew and took form: a bubble, a balloon, finally a rigid hemispherical dome that completely hid the robot from view.

Ilona Malater, pressing close, murmured, "Our home on Mars."

Tony Reed replied, "If it doesn't leak."

For more than an hour they watched the industrious little robot building their inflated dome, fixing its rim firmly to the dusty Martian soil, trundling back and forth through a man-tall flap to get reinforcing metal ribs and a complete airlock assembly from the landing vehicle's cargo bay and then weld them into place.

They were all anxious to go outside and plant their booted feet on the rust-red soil of Mars, but Vosnesensky insisted that they follow the mission plan to the letter. "The braking structure must cool," he called down to them from the cockpit, by way of legitimizing his decision. "The dome structure must be finished and fully pressurized."

Vosnesensky, of course, was too busy to stand by the observation port and watch with the rest of them. As commander of the ground team he was up in the cockpit, checking out all the lander's systems while he reported to the mission leader in the spacecraft orbiting overhead and, through him, to the mission controllers back on Earth, more than a hundred million kilometers away.

Pete Connors, the American astronaut who copiloted the lander, sat at Vosnesensky's side and monitored the construction robot and the sensors that were sampling the thin air outside. Only the four scientists were free to watch the machine erect the first human habitation on the surface of Mars.

"We should be getting into our backpacks," said Joanna Brumado.

"Plenty of time for that," Tony Reed said.

Ilona Malater gave a wicked little laugh. "You wouldn't want him to become angry with us, would you, Tony?" She pointed upward, toward the cockpit level.

Reed cocked an eyebrow and smiled back at her. "I don't suppose it would do to upset him on the very first day, would it?"

Jamie took his eyes from the hard-working robot, now fitting a second heavy metal airlock into the dome's curving structure. Without a word he squeezed past the three others and reached for the backpack to his pressure suit, hanging on its rack against the far bulkhead. Like their suits, the backpacks were color coded: Jamie's was sky-blue. He backed against it and felt the latches click into place against the back of his hard suit. The suit itself still felt stiff, like a new pair of Levis, only worse. It took real effort to move its shoulder joints.

In the jargon of the Mars Project their vehicle was called an L/AV:

landing/ascent vehicle. It had been designed for efficiency, not comfort. It was large, but most of its space was given to capacious cargo bays housing equipment and supplies for the six explorers. Atop the cargo bays, on the airlock level, the hard suits and backpacks for outside work were stored. There were four fold-down seats in the airlock level, but the compartment felt terribly crowded to Jamie when he and the three other scientists were jammed into it, especially when they were bundled inside their cumbersome hard-shell suits. Above the airlock level sat the cockpit with the cosmonaut commander and astronaut second-in-command.

If they had to, the six men and women could live for days inside this landing vehicle. The mission plan called for them to set up their base in the inflated dome that the robot was building. But they could survive in the lander, if it came to that.

Maybe. Jamie thought that if they had to spend just a few more hours cooped up in this cramped claustrophobic compartment, somebody would commit murder. It had been bad enough during the nine-month flight from Earth in the much roomier modules of the parent spacecraft. This little descent vehicle would quickly turn into a lunatic asylum if they had to live in it for days on end.

They donned the backpacks using the buddy system, as they had been trained to do, one scientist helping the other to check out all the connections to the suit batteries, heater, and air regenerator. Then check it all again. The backpacks were designed to connect automatically to ports in the pressure suit, but one tiny misalignment could kill you out on the surface of Mars.

Then they began to check the suits themselves, from the heavy boots to the marvelously thin and flexible gloves. What passed for air outside was rarer than the highest stratosphere of Earth, an unbreathable mix of mainly carbon dioxide. An unprotected human would die in an explosive agony of ruptured lungs and blood that would literally boil at such low pressure.

"What! Not ready yet!"

Vosnesensky's deep voice grated. The Russian tried to make it sound mildly humorous, but it was clear that he had no patience with his scientific underlings. He was fully encased in his blazing red suit, backpack riding like a hump behind his shoulders, ready to go, as he clumped down the ladder from the cockpit. Connors, right behind him, was also in his clean white hard suit and backpack. Jamie wondered which genius among the administrators and psychologists back home had assigned the black astronaut to a gleaming white suit.

Jamie had helped Tony Reed and now the Englishman turned away from him to face their flight commander.

"We'll be ready in a few moments, Mikhail Andreivitch. Please be patient with us. We're all a bit nervous, you know."

It was not until that exact moment that the enormity of it hit Jamie. They were about to step outside this metal canister and plant their booted feet on the red soil of Mars. They were about to fulfill a dream that had haunted humankind for all the ages of existence.

And I'm a part of it, Jamie said to himself. Maybe by accident, but still I'm here. On Mars!

"You want my honest opinion? It's crazy."

Jamie and his grandfather Al were hiking along the crest of the wooded ridge that overlooked the freshly whitewashed mission church and the clustered adobe houses of the pueblo. The first snow had dusted the mountains and the Anglo tourists would soon be arriving for the ski season. Al wore his bulky old sheepskin coat and droop-brimmed hat with the silver coin band. Jamie felt so warm in the morning sun that he had already unzipped his dark-blue NASA-issue windbreaker.

Al Waterman looked like an ancient totem pole, tall and bone-lean, his craggy face the faded tan color of weathered wood. Jamie was shorter, more solidly built, his face broader, his skin tanned an almost coppery brown. The two men shared only one feature in common: eyes as black and deep as liquid jet.

"Why is it crazy?" Jamie asked.

Al puffed out a breath of steam and turned to squint at his grandson, standing with his back to the sun.

"The Russians are runnin' the show, right?"

"It's an international mission, Al. The U.S., the Russians, Japanese, lots of other countries."

"Yeah, but the Russians are callin' most of the shots. They been shootin' at Mars for twenty years now. More."

"But they need our help."

"And the Japs."

Jamie nodded. "But I don't see what that's got to do with it."

"Well, it's like this, son. Here in the good old U.S. of A. you can get on the first team because you're an Indian—now don't get mad at me, sonny. I know you're a smart geologist and all that. But being a red man hasn't hurt you with NASA and those other government whites, has it? Equal opportunity and all that."

Jamie found himself grinning at his grandfather. Al ran a trinket shop on the plaza in Santa Fe and milked the tourists shamelessly. He harbored no ill will for the Anglos, no hostility or even bitterness. He simply used his wits and his charm to get along in the world, the same as any Yankee trader or Florida real estate agent.

"Okay," Jamie admitted, "being a Native American hasn't hurt. But I am the best damned geologist they've got." That wasn't entirely true, he knew. But close enough. Especially for family.

"Sure you are," his grandfather agreed, straight-faced. "But those Russians aren't going to take you all the way to Mars on their ship just because you're a red man. They'll pick one of their own people and you'll have spent two-three years training for nothing."

Jamie unconsciously rubbed at his nose. "Well, maybe. That's a possibility. There are plenty of good geologists from other countries applying for the mission."

"So why break your heart? Why give them years of your life when the chances are a hundred to one against you?"

Jamie looked out past the darkly green ponderosa pines toward the rugged, weather-seamed cliffs where his ancestors had built their dwellings a thousand years ago. Turning back to his grandfather he realized that Al's face was weathered and lined just as those cliffs were. His skin was almost the same bleached tan color.

"Because it draws me," he said. His voice was low but as firm as the mountains themselves. "Mars is drawing me to it."

Al gave him a puzzled, almost troubled look.

"I mean," Jamie tried to explain, "who am I, Al? What am I? A scientist, a white man, a Navaho—I don't really know who I am yet. I'm nearly thirty years old and I'm a nobody. Just another assistant professor digging up rocks. There's a million guys just like me."

"Helluva long way to go, all the way to Mars."

Jamie nodded. "I have to go there, though. I have to find out if I can make something of my life. Something real. Something important."

A slow smile crept across his grandfather's leathery face, a smile that wrinkled the corners of his eyes and creased his cheeks.

"Well, every man's got to find his own path in life. You've got to live in balance with the world around you. Maybe your path goes all the way out to Mars."

"I think it does, Grandfather."

Al clasped his grandson's shoulder. "Then go in beauty, son."

Jamie smiled back at him. He knew his grandfather would understand. Now he had to break the news to his parents, back in Berkeley.

Vosnesensky personally checked each scientist's hard suit and backpack. Only when he was satisfied did he slide the transparent visor of his own helmet down and lock it in place.

"At last the time has come," he said in almost accentless English, like a computer's voice synthesis.

All the others locked their visors down. Connors, standing by the heavy metal hatch, leaned a gloved finger against the stud that activated the air pumps. Through the thick soles of his boots Jamie felt them start chugging, saw the light on the airlock control panel turn from green to amber.

Time seemed to stand still. For eternity the pumps labored while the six explorers stood motionless and silent inside their brightly colored hard suits. With their visors down Jamie could not see their faces, but he knew each of his fellow explorers by the color of their suits: Joanna was dayglo orange; Ilona vivid green; Tony Reed canary yellow.

The clattering of the pumps dwindled as the air was sucked out of the compartment until Jamie could hear nothing, not even his own breathing, because he was holding his breath in anticipation.

The pumps stopped. The indicator light on the panel next to the hatch went to red. Connors pulled the lever and the hatch popped open a crack. Vosnesensky pushed it all the way open.

Jamie felt light-headed. As if he had climbed to the top of a mesa too fast, or jogged a couple of miles in the thin air of the mountains. He let out his breath and took a deep gulp of his suit's air. It tasted cold and metal dry. Mars lay framed in the oval hatchway, glowing pink and red and auburn like the arid highlands where he had spent his childhood summers.

Vosnesensky was starting down the ladder, Jamie realized. Connors went down next, followed by Joanna, then Tony, Ilona, and finally himself. As if in a dream Jamie went slowly down the ladder, one booted foot at a time, gloved hands sliding along the gleaming metal rails that ran between two of the unfolded petals of the aerobrake. Its ceramic-coated alloy had absorbed the blazing heat of their fiery entry into the Martian atmosphere. The metal mesh seemed dead cold now.

Jamie stepped off the last rung of the flimsy ladder. He stood on the sandy surface of Mars.

He felt totally alone. The five human figures beside him could not truly be people; they looked like strange alien totems. Then he realized that they *were* aliens, and he was too. Here on Mars we are the alien invaders, Jamie told himself.

He wondered if there were Martians hidden among the rocks, invisible to their eyes, watching them the way red men had watched the first whites step ashore onto their land centuries ago. He wondered what they would do about this alien invasion, and what the invaders would do if they found native life forms.

In his helmet earphones Jamie could hear the Russian team leader conversing with the expedition commander up in the orbiting spacecraft, his deep voice more excited than Jamie had ever heard before. Connors was checking the TV camera perched up at the front of the stilled robot construction vehicle.

Finally Vosnesensky spoke to his five charges as they arranged themselves in a semicircle around him. "All is ready. The words we speak next will be heard by everyone on Earth."

As planned, they stood with their backs to the landing vehicle while the robot's camera focused on them. Later they would pan the vidcam around to show the newly erected dome and the desolate Martian plain on which they had set foot.

Holding up one gloved hand almost like a symphony conductor, Vosnesensky took a self-conscious half step forward and pronounced: "In the name of Konstantin Eduardovich Tsiolkovsky, of Sergei Pavlovich Korolev, of Yuri Alexeyevich Gagarin, and of all the other pioneers and heroes of space, we come to Mars in peace for the advancement of all human peoples."

He said it in Russian first and then in English. Only afterward were the others invited to recite their little prewritten speeches.

Pete Connors, with the hint of Texan drawl he had picked up during his years at Houston, recited, "This is the greatest day in the history of human exploration, a proud day for all the people of the United States, the Soviet Union, and the whole world."

Joanna Brumado spoke in Brazilian Portuguese and then in English. "May all the peoples of the Earth gain in wisdom from what we learn here on Mars."

Ilona Malater, in Hebrew and then English, "We come to Mars to expand and exalt the human spirit."

Antony Reed, in his calm, almost bored Oxfordian best, "To His Majesty the King, to the people of the United Kingdom and the British Commonwealth, to the people of the European Community and the entire world—today is your triumph. We deeply feel that we are merely your representatives on this distant world."

Finally it was Jamie's turn. He felt suddenly weary, tired of the posturings and pomposities, exhausted by the years of stress and sacrifice. The excitement he had felt only minutes ago had drained away, evaporated. A hundred million kilometers from Earth and they were still playing their games of nations and allegiances. He felt as if someone had draped an enormous weight around his shoulders.

The others all turned toward him, five faceless figures in hard suits and gold-tinted visors. Jamie saw his own faceless helmet reflected five times. He had already forgotten the lines that had been written for him a hundred million kilometers ago.

He said simply, "Ya'aa'tey."

E A R T H

R I O D E J A N E I R O : It was bigger even than Carnival. Despite the scorching midafternoon sun the crowds thronged downtown, from the Municipal Theater all the way up the mosaic sidewalks of the Avenida Rio Branco, past Praca Pio X and the magnificent old Candelaria Church, out along Avenida Presidente Vargas. Not a car or even a bicycle could get through. The streets were literally wall-to-wall with *cariocas*, dancing the samba, sweating, laughing, staggering in the heat, celebrating in the biggest spontaneous outpouring of joy that the city had ever seen.

They jammed into the tree-shaded residential square where gigantic television screens had been set up in front of high-rise glass-walled apartment buildings. They stood on the benches in the square and clambered up the trees for a better view of the screens. They cheered and cried and shouted as they watched the space-suited explorers, one by one, climb down the ladder and stand on that barren rocky desert beneath the strange pink sky.

When Joanna Brumado spoke her brief words they cheered all the louder, drowning out the little speeches of those who followed her.

Then they took up the chant: "Brumado—Brumado—Bru-ma-*do*! Bru-ma-*do*! Bru-ma-*do*!"

Inside the apartment that had been lent to him for the occasion, Alberto Brumado smiled ruefully at his friends and associates. He had watched his daughter step onto the surface of Mars with a mixture of fatherly pride and anxiety that had brought tears to the corners of his eyes.

"You must go out, Alberto," said the mayor of Rio. "They will not stop until you do."

Large TV consoles had been wheeled into the four corners of the spacious, high-ceilinged parlor. Only a dozen people had been invited to share this moment of triumph with their famous countryman, but more than forty others had squeezed into the room. Many of the men were in evening clothes; the women wore their finest frocks and jewels. Later Brumado and the select dozen would be whisked by helicopter to the airport and then on to Brasilia, to be received by the president of the republic.

Outside, the people of Rio thundered, "Bru-ma-*do!* Bru-ma-*do!*"

Alberto Brumado was a small, slight man. Well into his sixties, his dark round face was framed by a neatly clipped grizzled beard and short gray hair that seemed always tousled, as if he had just been engaged in some strenuous action. It was a kindly face, smiling, looking slightly nonplussed at the sudden insistence of the crowd outside. He was more accustomed to the quiet calm of the university classroom or the hushed intensity of the offices of the great and powerful.

If the governments of the world's industrial nations were the brain directing the Mars Project, and the multinational corporations were the muscle, then Alberto Brumado was the heart of the mission to explore Mars. No, more still: Brumado was its soul.

For more than thirty years he had traveled the world, pleading with those in power to send human explorers to Mars. For most of those years he had faced cold indifference or outright hostility. He had been told that an expedition to Mars would cost too much, that there was nothing humans could do on Mars that could not be done by automated robotic machinery, that Mars could wait for another decade or another generation or another century. There were problems to be solved on Earth, they said. People were starving. Disease and ignorance and poverty held more than half the world in their mercilessly tenacious grip.

Alberto Brumado persevered. A child of poverty and hunger himself, born in a cardboard shack on a muddy, rainswept hill overlooking the posh *residências* of Rio de Janeiro, Alberto Brumado had fought his way through public school, through college, and into a brilliant career as an astronomer and teacher. He was no stranger to struggle.

Mars became his obsession. "My one vice," he would modestly say of himself.

When the first unmanned landers set down on Mars and found no evidence of life, Brumado insisted that their automated equipment was too simple to make meaningful tests. When a series of probes from the Soviet Union and, later, the United States returned rocks and soil samples that bore nothing more complex than simple organic chemicals, Brumado pointed out that they had barely scratched a billionth of that planet's surface.

He hounded the world's scientific congresses and industrial conferences, pointing out the photos of Mars that showed huge volcanoes, enormous rift valleys, and canyons that looked as if they had been gouged out by massive flood waters.

"There must be water on Mars," he said again and again. "Where there is water there must be life."

It took him nearly twenty years to realize that he was speaking to the wrong people. It mattered not what scientists thought or what they wanted. It was the politicians who counted, the men and women who controlled national treasuries. And the people, the voters who filled those treasuries with their tax money.

He began to haunt their halls of power—and the corporate boardrooms where the politicians bowed to the money that elected them. He made himself into a media celebrity, using talented, bright-eyed students to help create television shows that filled the world's people with the wonder and awe of the majestic universe waiting to be explored by men and women of faith and vision.

And he *listened*. Instead of telling the world's leaders and decision makers what they should do, he listened to what they wanted, what they hoped for, what they feared. He listened and planned and gradually, shrewdly, he shaped a scheme that would please them all.

He found that each pressure group, each organization of government or industry or ordinary citizens, had its own aims and ambitions and anxieties.

The scientists wanted to go to Mars for curiosity's sake. To them, exploration of the universe was a goal in itself.

The visionaries wanted to go to Mars because it is there. They viewed the human race's expansion into space with religious fervor.

The military said there was no point in going to Mars; the planet was so far away that it served no conceivable military function.

The industrialists realized that sending humans to Mars would serve as a stimulus to develop new technology—on risk-free money provided by government.

The representatives of the poor complained that the billions spent on going to Mars should be spent instead on food production and housing and education.

Brumado listened to them all and then softly, quietly, he began speaking to them in terms they could understand and appreciate. He played their dreams and dreads back to them in an exquisitely manipulative feedback that focused their attention on his goal. He orchestrated their desires until they themselves began to believe that Mars was the logical objective of their own plans and ambitions.

In time, the world's power brokers began to predict that Mars would be the new century's first test of a nation's vigor, determination, and strength. Media pundits began to warn gravely that it might be more costly to a nation's competitive position in the global marketplace not to go to Mars than to go there.

Statesmen began to realize that Mars could serve as the symbol of a new era of global cooperation in peaceful endeavors that could capture the hearts and minds of all the world.

The politicians in Moscow and Washington, Tokyo and Paris, Rio and Beijing, listened carefully to their advisors and then made up their minds. Their advisors had fallen under Brumado's spell.

"We go to Mars," said the American President to the Congress, "not for pride or prestige or power. We go to Mars in the spirit of the new pragmatic cooperation among the nations of the world. We go to Mars not as Americans or Russians or Japanese. We go to Mars as human beings, representatives of the planet Earth."

The president of the Soviet Federation told his people, "Mars is not only the symbol of our unquenchable will to expand and explore the universe, it is the symbol of the cooperation that is possible between East and West. Mars is the emblem of the inexorable progress of the human mind."

Mars would be the crowning achievement of a new era of international cooperation. After a century of war and terrorism and mass murder, a cosmic irony turned the blood-red planet named after the god of war into the new century's blessed symbol of peaceful cooperation.

For the people of the rich nations, Mars was a source of awe, a goal grander than anything on Earth, the challenge of a new frontier that could inspire the young and stimulate their passions in a healthy, productive way.

For the people of the poor nations—well, Alberto Brumado told them that he himself was a child of poverty, and if the thought of Mars filled him with exhilaration why shouldn't they be able to raise their eyes beyond the squalor of their day-to-day existence and dream great dreams?

There was a price to be paid, of course. Brumado's successful wooing of the politicians meant that his cherished goal of Mars was the child of their marriage. Thus the first expedition to Mars was undertaken not as the scientists wanted it, not even as the engineers and planners of the various national space agencies wanted it. The first humans to go to Mars went as the politicians wanted them to go: as quickly and cheaply as possible.

The unspoken rationale of the first expedition was: politics first, science second—a distant second. This was to be a "flags and footprints" mission, no matter how much the scientists wanted to explore.

Efficiency was an even more distant third, as it usually is when political considerations are uppermost. The politicians found it easier to rationalize the necessary expenditures if the project were completed quickly, before an opposition party got the chance to gain power and take credit for its ultimate success. Haste did not automatically make waste, but it forced the administrators to plan a mission that was far from efficient.

Hundreds of scientists were recruited for the Mars Project. Scores of cosmonauts and astronauts. Thousands of engineers, technicians, flight controllers, and administrators. They spent ten years in planning and three more in training for the two-year-long mission. All so that twenty-five men and women could spend sixty days on Mars. Eight paltry weeks on Mars, and then back home again. That was the mission plan. That was the goal for which thousands devoted thirteen years of their lives.

To the world at large, however, the excitement of the Mars Project grew with each passing month as the chosen personnel went through their training and the spacecraft took shape at launching centers in the Soviet Union, the United States, South America, and Japan. The world made itself ready to reach out to the red planet. Alberto Brumado was the acknowledged spiritual leader of the Mars mission, although he was not entrusted with anything more concrete than moral support. But moral support was desperately needed more than once during these years, as one government or another would want to opt out of the decade-long financial burden. But none did.

Too old to fly into space himself, Brumado instead watched his daughter board the spacecraft that would take her to Mars.

Now he had watched her step out onto the surface of that distant world, while the crowd outside chanted their name.

Wondering if he had done the right thing, Alberto Brumado went to the long, sunlit windows. The crowd cheered wildly at the sight of him.

KALININGRAD: Mission control for the Mars expedition had more redundancy than the spacecraft the explorers flew in. While redundancy in the spacecraft was required for safety, at mission control it was required by politics. Each position in mission control was shared by two people at identical side-by-side consoles. Usually one was a Russian and the other an American, although at a few of the desks sat Japanese, British, French, and even an Argentine—with a Russian by the side of each one of them.

The men and women of the mission control center were just starting to celebrate. Up to the moment of touchdown they had been rigidly intent on their display screens, but now at last they could lean back, slip off their headsets, laugh together, sip champagne, and light up victory cigars. Even some of the women took cigars. Behind the rows of consoles, in the glassed-in media section, reporters and photographers toasted one another and the mission controllers with vodka in paper cups.

Only the chief of the American team, a burly balding man in his shirtsleeves, sweat stains at his armpits, unlit cigar clamped between his teeth, looked unhappy. He leaned over the chair of the American woman who bore the archaic title of CapCom.

"What did he say?"

She glanced up from her display screens. "I don't know what it was."

"It sure as hell wasn't what he was *supposed* to say!"

"Would you like to replay the tape?" asked the Russian working beside the young woman. His voice was soft, but it cut through the buzz of conversation.

The woman deftly tapped a few buttons on her keyboard and the screen once again showed the figure of James Waterman standing in his sky-blue pressure suit on the sands of Mars.

"Ya'aa'tey," said Jamie Waterman's image.

"Garbled transmission?" the chief asked.

"No way," said the woman.

The Russian turned from the screen to give the chief a piercing look. "What does it mean?"

"Damned if I know," grumbled the chief. "But we're sure as hell going to find out!"

Up in the media section, one young TV reporter noticed the two men hunched over the CapCom's seat. He wondered why they looked so puzzled.

BERKELEY: Professor Jerome Waterman and Professor Lucille Monroe Waterman had canceled their classes for the day and remained at home to watch their son step out onto the surface of Mars. No friends. No students or faculty colleagues. A battalion of reporters hovered outside the house, but the Watermans would not face them until after they had seen the landing.

They sat in their comfortably rumpled, book-lined study watching the television pictures, window blinds closed tightly against the bright morning sun and the besieging media reporters encamped outside.

"It takes almost ten minutes for the signals to reach the Earth," mused Jerry Waterman.

His wife nodded absently, her eyes focused on the sky-blue figure among the six faceless creatures on the screen. She held her breath when it was Jamie's turn at last to speak.

"Ya'aa'tey," said her son.

Lucille gasped: "Oh no!"

Jamie's father grunted with surprise.

Lucille turned accusingly to her husband. "He's starting that Indian business all over again!"

SANTA FE: Old Al always knew how to pack the store with customers even on a day like this. He had simply put a TV set prominently up on a shelf next to the Kachina dolls. People thronged in from all over the plaza to see Al's grandson on Mars.

"Ya'aa'tey," said Jamie Waterman, from a hundred million kilometers away.

"Hee-ah!" exclaimed old Al Waterman. "The boy did it!"

D A T A   B A N K

Mars.

Picture Death Valley at its worst. Barren desert. Nothing but rock and sand. Remove every trace of life: get rid of each and every cactus, every bit of scrub, all the lizards and insects and sun-bleached bones and anything else that even looks as if it might have once been alive.

Now freeze-dry the whole landscape. Plunge it down to a temperature of a hundred below zero. And suck away the air until there's not even as much as you would find on Earth a hundred thousand feet above the ground.

That is roughly what Mars is like.

Fourth planet out from the sun, Mars never gets closer to the Earth than thirty-five million miles. It is a small world, roughly half the diameter of ours, with a surface gravity just a bit more than a third of Earth's. A hundred pounds on Earth weighs only thirty-eight pounds on Mars.

Mars is known as the red planet because its surface is mainly a bone-dry desert of sandy iron oxides: rusty iron dust.

Yet there is water on Mars. The planet has bright polar caps, composed at least partially of frozen water—covered over most of the year by frozen carbon dioxide, dry ice.

For Mars is a *cold* world. It orbits roughly one and a half times farther from the sun than the Earth does. Its atmosphere is far too thin to retain solar heat. On a clear midsummer day along the Martian equator the afternoon high temperature might climb to seventy degrees Fahrenheit; that same night, however, it will plunge to a hundred below zero or lower.

The atmosphere of Mars is too thin to breathe, even if it were pure oxygen. Which it is not. More than ninety-five percent of the Martian "air" is carbon dioxide; nearly three percent nitrogen. There is a tiny amount of oxygen and even less water vapor. The rest of the atmosphere consists of inert gases such as argon, neon and such, a whiff of carbon monoxide, and a trace of ozone.

Still, Mars is the most Earthlike of any other world in the solar system. There are seasons on Mars—spring, summer, autumn, and winter. Because its orbit is farther from the sun, the Martian year is nearly twice as long as Earth's (a few minutes short of 689 Earth days) and its seasons are correspondingly much longer than Earth's.

Mars rotates about its axis in almost the same time that Earth does. A day on Earth is 23 hours, 56 minutes, and 4.09 seconds long. A day on Mars is only slightly longer: 24 hours, 37 minutes, and 22.7 seconds.

To avoid confusion, space explorers refer to the Martian day as a "sol." In one Martian year there are 669 sols, plus an untidy fourteen hours, forty-six minutes, and twelve seconds.

Is there life on Mars?

That question has haunted the human psyche for centuries. It is the primary force behind our drive to reach the red planet. We want to see for ourselves if life can exist there.

Or once did.

Or does now.

S O L 1: AFTERNOON

The first thing the scientists did, after their little arrival speeches, was collect contingency samples of the Martian rocks, soil, and atmosphere.

Just in case a sudden emergency forced them to scramble into their landing/ ascent vehicle and blast back into orbit around the planet, they spent their first two hours on the surface stuffing rocks and soil samples into airtight cases and filling vials with whiffs of air taken from ground level on up to ten meters, the latter obtained with the use of a gangling titanium pole.

Meanwhile, the construction robot trundled across the rocky ground out to the three unmanned cargo carriers that had landed the previous day, scattered over a two-kilometer-wide radius from their nominal landing site. Like an oversized mechanical ant, the robot busily hauled their cargos back to the inflated dome that would be home to the explorers for the next eight weeks.

Mikhail Andreivitch Vosnesensky, veteran of a dozen space missions, sat up in the cockpit in the commander's seat, one eye on the scientists and the other on the mission schedule. Beside him, Pete Connors monitored the robot and conversed with the expedition command in orbit around the planet. Although both men stayed in their hard suits, ready to dash outside if an emergency required their help, they had taken their helmets off.

Connors switched off the radio and turned to the Russian. "The guys in orbit confirm that we landed only a hundred thirty meters from our nominal target spot. They send their congratulations."

Vosnesensky offered a rare smile. "It would have been closer, but the boulders were too big farther south."

"You did a damned good job," said Connors. "Kaliningrad will be pleased." His voice was a rich baritone, trained in church choirs. The American had a long, almost horsey face with a complexion the color of milk chocolate and large sorrowful brown eyes rimmed with red. His hair was cropped militarily short, showing the distinct vee of a widow's peak.

"You know what the old pilots say," Vosnesensky replied.

Connors chuckled. "Any landing you can walk away from is a good landing."

"All systems are working. We are on schedule." It was Vosnesensky's way of making light of his skillful landing. The Russian did not trust flattery, even from a man he had worked with for nearly four years. A scowl was the normal expression on his broad, beefy face. His sky-blue eyes always looked suspicious.

"Yeah. And now the second team has to land where we are. Wonder how good Mironov and my old buddy Abell will be?"

"Mironov is very good. An excellent pilot. He could land on our roof, if he wanted to."

Connors laughed, light and easy. "Now that would cause a helluva problem, wouldn't it?

Vosnesensky made his lips curl upward, but it obviously took an effort.

The scientists stored their contingency samples inside the airlock section of the L/AV. In an emergency, the airlock section and the cockpit atop it would lift off the ground. The lower half of the lander—the cargo bays and aerobrake—would remain on Mars. Even if one or more of the explorers were left behind, the precious samples would make it to the expedition spacecraft riding in orbit and then back to the scientists waiting on Earth.

That first chore completed to Vosnesensky's satisfaction, he ordered the team to move supplies into the dome. They hurried to beat the oddly tiny sun as it got close to the western horizon. The construction vehicle towed the heavy pallets of equipment, while the explorers performed feats of seemingly superhuman strength, lifting man-tall green cylinders of oxygen tanks and bulky crates that would have weighed hundreds of pounds on Earth.

Sweating like a laborer inside his pressurized hard suit, Jamie smiled bitterly at the thought that the first task of the first explorers on Mars was to toil like coolies, grunting and lifting for hours in mindless drudgery. The public-relations statements and TV pictures make it all look so damned easy, he thought. Nobody ever watches a scientist at work—especially when he's doing dog labor.

Neither he nor the others paid any special attention to their low-gravity strength. Over the nine-plus months of their flight from Earth their spacecraft had spun on a five-kilometer-long tether to simulate a feeling of weight, since prolonged periods in zero gravity weakened muscles dangerously and demineralized bones. Their artificial gravity began at a normal Earthly one g, then was slowly reduced during the months of their flight to the Martian value of roughly one-third g. Now, on the surface of Mars, they could walk normally yet still lift enormous weights with their Earth-evolved muscles.

At the end of their long, exhausting day they moved at last inside the inflated dome. The tiny sun was turning the sky flame-red and the temperature outside was already fifty below zero.

The dome was filled with breathable air at normal Earth pressure and temperature, according to the gauges. The thermometer read precisely twenty-one degrees Celsius: sixty-nine point eight degrees Fahrenheit.

The six of them were still inside their pressurized hard suits, however, and would stay in them until Vosnesensky decided it was safe to breathe the dome's air. Jamie's suit felt heavy against his shoulders. It no longer had that "new car" odor of clean plastic and untouched fabric; it smelled of sweat and machine oil. The backpack regenerator replaced carbon dioxide with breathable oxygen, but the filters and miniature fans inside the suit could not remove all of the odors that accumulated from strenuous work.

"Now comes the moment of truth," he heard Ilona Malater's husky voice, sounding sexy—or maybe just tired.

Vosnesensky had spent the past few hours checking the dome for leaks, monitoring the air pressure and composition, fussing over the life-support pumps and heaters grouped together in the center of the hardened plastic flooring. One by one, the others slowly drifted to him, clumping in their thick boots, waiting for him to give the order they all awaited with a strange mixture of eagerness and dread.

Like it or not, Vosnesensky was their team leader, and years of training had drilled them to obey their leader's orders without a thought for his nationality. Everything they did on this dangerously different world would be carried out according to rules and regulations painstakingly developed on Earth. Vosnesensky's first and most important task was to see that those rules and regulations were carried out here on Mars.

Now the Russian turned from the gently humming air-circulation fans and the row of backup oxygen tanks to see that his five team members had gathered around him. It was difficult to make out his face through the helmet visor, impossible to read his expression. In his barely accented American English he said, "All the gauges are in the normal range. It appears safe to get out of our suits."

Jamie recalled a physicist at Albuquerque, frustrated over an experiment that refused to work right, telling him, "All of physics boils down to reading a goddam dial on a goddam gauge."

Vosnesensky turned to Connors, the second-in-command. "Pete, the mission plan calls for you to test the air first."

The American chuckled nervously from inside his helmet. "Yeah, I'm the guinea pig, I know."

He took an exaggeratedly sighing breath that they could all hear in their earphones. Then, "Here goes."

Connors opened his helmet visor a crack, took a sniff, then slid the visor all the way up and pulled in a deeper breath. He broke into a toothy grin. "Helluva lot better than what's outside."

They all laughed and the tension cracked. Each of them pushed up their visors, then unlocked the neck seals of their suits and lifted their helmets off altogether. Jamie's ears popped, but nothing worse happened.

Ilona shook her short-clipped blonde curls and inhaled slowly, her slim nostrils flaring slightly. "Huh! It smells just like the training module. Too dry. Bad for the skin."

Jamie took a long look around their new home, now that his vision was no longer restricted by the helmet.

He saw the dome rising into shadowed gloom over his head, ribbed with curving metal struts. It reminded him of the first time he had gone into a planetarium, back when he'd been a kid in Santa Fe. The same hushed, awed feeling. The same soft coolness to the air. To Ilona the air felt too dry; to him it felt delicious.

The dome's smooth plastic skin had been darkened by a polarizing electric current to keep the heat inside. In daylight the dome's lower section would be made transparent to take advantage of solar heating, but at night it was like an oversized igloo sitting on the frozen Martian plain, darkened to retain heat and not allow it to radiate away into the thin, frigid Martian air. Strips of sunlight-equivalent fluorescent lamps lit the floor area softly, but the upper reaches of the dome were barely visible in the darkness gathering there.

The plastic skin of the dome was double walled, like insulating windows, to keep out the cold. The topmost section was opaque, filled in with a special dense plastic that would absorb harmful radiation and even stop small meteorites, according to the engineers.

The thought of the dome getting punctured was scary. Patches and sealing compounds were placed along its perimeter, but would they have time to repair a puncture before all the air gushed out? Jamie remembered the hoary old joke of the parachute packers: "Don't worry about it. If this chute doesn't work, bring it back and we'll give you a new one."

The electric power that heated the dome came from the compact nuclear generator inside one of the cargo vehicles. Tomorrow, after the second team's landing, the construction robot was scheduled to extract the generator and bury it in the Martian soil half a kilometer from the dome.

Mustn't call it soil, Jamie reminded himself. Soil is alive with microorganisms and earthworms and other living creatures. Here on Mars it's called regolith, just like the totally dead surface of the totally dead moon.

Is Mars really dead? Jamie asked himself. He remembered the stories he had read as a youngster, wild tales of Martians battling along their planet-girdling canals, beautiful fantasies of cities built like chess pieces and houses that turned to follow the sun like flowers. There were no canals on Mars, Jamie knew. No cities. But is the planet entirely lifeless? Are there fossils to be dug out of that red sand?

IN TRAINING: KAZAKHSTAN

As they drove along the river, Yuri Zavgorodny gestured with his free hand.

"Like your New Mexico, no?" he asked in his hesitant English.

Jamie Waterman unconsciously rubbed his side. They had taken the stitches out only yesterday and the incision still felt sore.

"New Mexico," Zavgorodny repeated. "Like this? Yes?"

Jamie almost answered, "No." But the mission administrators had warned them all to be as diplomatic as possible with the Russians—and everyone else.

"Sort of," Jamie murmured.

"Yes?" asked Zavgorodny over the rush of the searing wind blowing through the car windows.

"Yes," said Jamie.

The flat brown country stretching out beyond the river looked nothing like New Mexico. The sky was a washed-out pale blue, the desert bleak and empty in every direction. This is an old, tired land, Jamie said to himself as he squinted against the baking hot wind. Used up. Dried out. Nothing like the vivid mountains and bold skies of his home. New Mexico was a new land, raw and magic and mystical. This dull dusty desert out here is ancient; it's been worn flat by too many armies riding across it.

"Like Mars," said one of the other Russians. His voice was a deep rumble, where Zavgorodny's was reedy, like a snake-charmer's flute. Jamie had been quickly introduced to all four of them but the only name that stuck was Zavgorodny's.

Christ, I hope Mars isn't this dull, Jamie said to himself.

Yesterday Jamie had been at Bethesda Naval Hospital, having the stitches from his appendectomy removed. All the Mars mission trainees had their appendixes taken out. Mission regulations. No sense risking an attack of appendicitis twenty million miles from the nearest hospital. Even though the decisions about who would actually go to Mars had not been made yet, everyone lost his or her appendix.

"Where are we going?" Jamie asked. "Where are you taking me?"

It was Sunday, supposedly a day of rest even for the men and women who were training to fly to Mars. Especially for a new arrival, jet-lagged and bearing a fresh scar on his belly. But the four cosmonauts had roused Jamie from his bed at the hotel and insisted that he come with them.

"Airport," said the deep-voiced cosmonaut on Jamie's left. He was jammed into the back seat with two of the Russians, sweaty, body odor pungent despite the sharp scent of strong soap. Two more rode up front, Zavgorodny at the wheel.

Like a gang of Mafia hit men taking me for a ride, Jamie thought. The Russians smiled at one another a lot, grinning as they talked among themselves and hiking their eyebrows significantly. Something was up. And they were not going to tell the American geologist about it until they were damned good and ready.

They were solidly built men, all four of them. Short and thickset. Like Jamie himself, although the Russians were much lighter in complexion than Jamie's half-Navaho skin.

"Is this official business?" he had asked them when they pounded on his hotel door at the crack of dawn.

"No business," Zavgorodny had replied while the other three grinned broadly. "Pleasure. Fun."

Fun for them, maybe, Jamie grumbled to himself as the car hummed along the concrete of the empty highway. The river curved off to their left. The wind carried the smell of sun-baked dust. The old town of Tyuratam and Leninsk, the new city built for the space engineers and cosmonauts, was miles behind them now.

"Why are we going to the airport?" Jamie asked.

The one on his right side laughed aloud. "For fun. You will see."

"Yes," said the one on his left. "For much fun."

Jamie had been a Mars trainee for little more than six months. This was his first trip to Russia, although his schedule had already whisked him to Australia, Alaska, French Guiana, and Spain. There had been endless physical examinations, tests of his reflexes, his strength, his eyesight, his judgment. They had probed his teeth and pronounced them in excellent shape, then sliced his appendix out of him.

And now a quartet of cosmonauts he'd never met before was taking him in the early morning hours of a quiet Sunday for a drive to Outer Nowhere, Kazakhstan.

For much fun.

There had been precious little fun in the training for Mars. A lot of competition among the scientists, since only sixteen would eventually make the flight: sixteen out of more than two hundred trainees. Jamie realized that the competition must be equally fierce among the cosmonauts and astronauts.

"Have you all had your appendixes removed?" he asked.

The grins faded. The cosmonaut beside him answered, "No. Is not necessary. We do not go to Mars."

"You're not going?"

"We are instructors," Zavgorodny said over his shoulder. "We have already been turned down for the flight mission."

Jamie wanted to ask why, but thought better of it. This was not a pleasant topic of conversation.

"Your appendix?" the man on his left asked. He ran a finger across his throat.

Jamie nodded. "They took the stitches out yesterday." He realized it had actually been Friday in Bethesda and now it was Sunday, but it felt like yesterday.

"You are an American Indian?"

"Half Navaho."

"The other half?"

"Anglo," said Jamie. He saw the word meant nothing to the Russians. "White. English."

The man sitting up front beside Zavgorodny turned to face him. "When they took out your appendix—you had a medicine man with painted face to rattle gourds over you?"

All four of the Russians burst into uproarious laughter. The car swerved on the empty highway, Zavgorodny laughed so hard.

Jamie made himself grin back at them. "No. I had anesthesia, just as you would."

The Russians chattered among themselves. Jamie got a vision of jokes about Indians, maybe about a red man wanting to go to the red planet. There was no nastiness in it, he felt. Just four beer-drinking fliers having some fun with a new acquaintance.

Wish I understood Russian, he said to himself. Wish I knew what these four clowns are up to. Much fun.

Then he remembered that none of these men could even hope to get to Mars anymore. They had been relegated to the role of instructors. I've still got a chance to make the mission. Do they hold that against me? Just what in the hell are they planning to do?

Zavgorodny swung the car off the main highway and down a two-lane dirt road that paralleled a tall wire fence. Jamie could see, far in the distance, hangars and planes parked haphazardly. So we really are going to an airport, he realized.

They drove through an unguarded gate and out to a far corner of the sprawling airport where a single small hangar stood all by itself, like an outcast or an afterthought. A high-wing, twin-engine plane sat on squat tricycle landing gear on the concrete apron in front of the hangar. To Jamie it looked like a Russian version of a twin Otter, a plane he had flown in during his week's stint in Alaska's frigid Brooks Range.

"You like to fly?" Zavgorodny asked as they piled out of the car.

Jamie stretched his arms and back, glad to be no longer squeezed into the car's back seat. It was not even nine o'clock yet, but the sunshine felt hot and good as it baked into his shoulders.

"I enjoy flying," he said. "I don't have a pilot's license, though. I'm not qualified . . ."

Zavgorodny laughed. "Good thing! We are four pilots. That is three too many."

The four cosmonauts were already wearing one-piece flight suits of faded, well-worn tan. Jamie had pulled on a white short-sleeved knit shirt and a pair of denims when they had roused him from his hotel bed. He followed the others into the sudden cool darkness of the hangar. It smelled of machine oil and gasoline. Two of the cosmonauts went clattering up a flight of metal stairs to an office perched on the catwalk above.

Zavgorodny beckoned Jamie to a long table where a row of parachute packs sat big and lumpy, with straps spread out like the limp arms of octopi.

"We must all wear parachutes," Zavgorodny said. "Regulations."

"To fly in that?" Jamie jabbed a thumb toward the plane.

"Yes. Military plane. Regulations. Must wear chutes."

"Where are we flying to?" Jamie asked.

Zavgorodny picked up one of the cumbersome chute packs and handed it to Jamie like a laborer passing a sack of cement.

"A surprise," the Russian said. "You will see."

"Much fun," said the other cosmonaut. He was already buckling the groin straps of his chute.

Much fun for who? Jamie asked silently. But he worked his arms through the shoulder straps of the chute and leaned over to pull the groin straps tight.

The other two came back down the metal steps, boots echoing in the nearly empty hangar. Jamie followed the quartet of cosmonauts out into the baking sunshine toward the plane. A wide metal hatch had been cut into its side. There were no stairs. When he hiked his foot up to the rim of the hatch, Jamie's side twinged with pain. He grabbed the sides of the hatch and pulled himself inside the plane. Without help. Without wincing.

It was like an oven inside. Two rows of bucket seats, bare, un-padded. The two men who had been sitting in the back of the car with Jamie pushed past him and went to the cockpit. The pilot's and co-pilot's chairs were thick with padding; they looked comfortable.

Zavgorodny gestured Jamie to the seat directly behind the pilot. He sat himself in the opposite seat and pulled the safety harness across his shoulders and thighs. Jamie did the same, making cer-tain the straps were tight. The parachute pack served as a sort of cushion, but it felt awkward to Jamie: like underwear that had gotten twisted.

The engines coughed, sputtered, then blasted into life. The plane shook like a palsied old man. As the propellers whirred to invisible blurs, Jamie heard all sorts of rattling noises, as if the plane was going to fall apart at any moment. Something creaked, something else moaned horribly. The plane lurched forward.

The two pilots had clamped earphones over their heads, but if they were in radio contact with the control tower, Jamie could not hear a word they spoke over the noise of the engines and the wind blowing through the cabin. The fourth cosmonaut was sitting behind Jamie. No one had shut the hatch. Jamie twisted around in his seat and realized that there was no door for the hatch; they were going to fly with it wide open.

The wind roared through as the plane hurtled down the runway, skidding slightly first one way and then the other.

Awfully long run for a plane this small, Jamie thought. He glanced across at Zavgorodny. The Russian grinned at him.

And then they were off the ground. Jamie saw the airport dwin-dling away out his window, the planes and buildings shrinking into toys. The land spread out, brown and dead-dry beneath the cloudless pale sky. The engines settled into a rumbling growl and the wind howled so loudly that Jamie had to lean across the aisle and shout into Zavgorodny's ear:

"So where are we going?"

Zavgorodny shouted back, "To find Muzhestvo."

"Moo . . . what?"

"Muzhestvo!" the cosmonaut yelled louder.

"Where is it? How far away?"

The Russian laughed. "You will see."

They climbed steadily for what seemed like an hour. Can't be much more than ten thousand feet, Jamie said to himself. It was difficult to judge vertical distances, but they would have to go on oxygen if they flew much beyond ten thousand feet, he knew. It was getting cold. Jamie wished he had brought a windbreaker. They should have told me to, he thought. They should have warned me.

The co-pilot looked back over his shoulder, staring directly at Jamie. He grinned, then put a hand over his mouth and hollered, "Hoo-hoo-hoo!" His version of an Indian war whoop. Jamie kept his face expressionless.

Suddenly the plane dipped and skidded leftward. Jamie was slammed against the curving skin of the fuselage and almost banged his head against the window. He stared out at the brown landscape beneath him, wrinkled with hills and a single sparkling lake far below, as the plane seemed to hang on its left wingtip and slowly, slowly revolve.

Then it dove and pulled upward, squeezing Jamie down into his seat. The plane climbed awkwardly, waddling in the air, then flipped over onto its back. Jamie felt all weight leaving him; he was hanging by his seat harness but he weighed practically nothing. It dived again and weight returned, heavy, crushing, as the plane hurtled toward those bare brown hills, engines screaming, wind whistling through the shaking, rattling cabin.

And then it leveled off, engines purring, everything as normal as a commuter flight.

Zavgorodny was staring at Jamie. The co-pilot glanced back over his shoulder. And Jamie understood. They were ragging him. He was the new kid on the block and they were seeing if they could scare him. Their own little version of the Vomit Comet, Jamie said to himself. See if they can make me turn green, or get me to puke. Much fun.

Every tribe has its initiation rites, he realized. He had never been properly initiated as a Navaho; his parents were too Anglicized to allow it. But these guys are going to make up for that.

Jamie made himself grin at Zavgorodny. "That was fun," he yelled, hoping that the other three could hear him over the engines and the wind. "I didn't know you could loop an old crate like this."

Zavgorodny bobbed his head up and down. "Not recommended. Maybe the wings come off."

Jamie shrugged inside the seat harness. "What's next?"

"Muzhestvo."

They flew peacefully for another quarter-hour or so, no aerobatics, no conversation. Then Jamie realized they had made one wide circling turn and were starting another. He looked out the window. The ground below was flat and empty, as desolate as Mars except for a single road running straight across the brown barren wasteland.

Zavgorodny unbuckled his safety harness and stood up. He had to crouch slightly because of the low overhead as he stepped out into the aisle and back toward the big wide-open hatch.

Jamie turned and saw that the other cosmonaut was on his feet, too, and standing at the hatch.

Christ, one lurch of this crate and he'll go ass over teakettle out the door!

Zavgorodny stood beside the other man with one hand firmly gripping a slim metal rod that ran the length of the cabin's ceiling. They seemed to be chatting, heads close together, nodding as if they were at their favorite bar holding a casual conversation. With ten thousand feet of empty air just a step away.

Zavgorodny beckoned to Jamie, gestured him to come up and join them. Jamie felt a cold knot in his stomach. I don't want to go over there. I don't want to.

But he found himself unbuckling the seat harness and walking unsteadily toward the two near the open hatch. The plane bucked slightly, and Jamie grabbed that overhead rod with both fists.

"Parachute range." Zavgorodny pointed out the hatch. "We make practice jumps here."

"Today? Now?"

"Yes."

The other cosmonaut had pulled a plastic helmet onto his head. He slid the tinted glass visor down over his eyes, yelled something in Russian, and jumped out of the plane.

Jamie gripped the overhead rod even tighter.

"Look!" Zavgorodny yelled at him, pointing. "Watch!"

Cautiously Jamie peered through the gaping hatch. The cosmonaut was falling like a stone, arms and legs outstretched, dwindling into a tiny tan dot against the deeper brown land so far below.

"Is much fun," Zavgorodny hollered into Jamie's ear.

Jamie shivered, not merely from the icy wind slicing through his lightweight shirt.

Zavgorodny pushed a helmet into his hands. Jamie stared at it. The plastic was scratched and pitted, its red and white colors almost worn off completely.

"I've never jumped," he said.

"We know."

"But I . . ." He wanted to say that he had just had the stitches removed from his side, that he knew you could break both your legs parachute-jumping, that there was absolutely no way they were going to get him to step out of this airplane.

Yet he put the helmet on and strapped it tight under his chin.

"Is easy," Zavgorodny said. "You have done gymnastics. It is on your file. Just land with knees bent and roll over. Easy."

Jamie was shaking. The helmet felt as if it weighed three hundred pounds. His left hand was wrapped around that overhead rod in a death grip. His right was fumbling along the parachute harness straps, searching blindly for the D-ring that would release the chute.

Zavgorodny looked quite serious now. The plane was banking slightly, tilting them toward the open, yawning hole in the plane's side. Jamie planted his feet on the metal flooring as solidly as he could, glad that he had worn a sturdy pair of boots.

The Russian took his right hand and placed it on the D-ring. The metal felt cold as death to Jamie.

"Not to worry," Zavgorodny shouted, his voice muffled by Jamie's helmet. "I attach static line to overhead. It opens chute automatically. No problem."

"Yeah." Jamie's voice was shaky. His insides were boiling. He could feel sweat trickling down his ribs even though he felt shivering cold.

"You step out. You count to twenty. Understand? If chute has not opened by then, you pull ring. Understand?"

Jamie nodded.

"I will follow behind you. If you die I will bury you." His grin returned. Jamie felt like puking.

Zavgorodny gave him a long probing look. "You want to go back and sit down?"

Every atom in Jamie's being wanted to answer a fervent "Yes!" But he shook his head and took a hesitant, frightened step toward the open hatch.

The Russian reached up and slid the visor over Jamie's eyes. "Count to twenty. Slowly. I will see you on ground in two minutes. Maybe three."

Jamie swallowed hard and let Zavgorodny position him squarely at the lip of the hatch. The ground looked iron-hard and very, very far below. They were in shadow, the overhead wing was shading them, the propeller too far forward to be any danger. Jamie took that all in with a single wild glance.

A tap on his shoulder. Jamie hesitated a heartbeat, then pushed off with both feet.

Nothing. No motion. No sound except the thrum of wind rushing past. Jamie suddenly felt that he was in a dream, just hanging in emptiness, floating really, waiting to wake up safe and somehow disappointed in bed. The plane had disappeared somewhere behind and above him. The ground was miles below, revolving slowly, not getting noticeably closer.

He was spinning, turning lazily as he floated in mid-air. It was almost pleasant. Fun, nearly. Just hanging in nothingness, separated from the entire world, alone, totally alone and free.

It was as if he had no body, no physical existence at all. Nothing but pure spirit, clean and light as the air itself. He remembered the old legends his grandfather had told him about Navaho heroes who had traveled across the bridge of the rainbow. Must be like this, he thought, high above the world, floating, floating. Like Coyote, when he hitched a ride on a comet.

He realized with a heart-stopping lurch that he had forgotten to count. And his hand had come off the D-ring. He fumbled awkwardly, seeing now that the hard baked dry ground was rushing up to smash him, pulverize him, kill him dead, dead, dead.

A gigantic hand grabbed him and nearly snapped his head off. He twisted in mid-air as new sounds erupted all around him. Like the snapping of a sail, his parachute unfolded and spread above him, leaving Jamie hanging in the straps floating gently down toward the barren ground.

His heart was hammering in his ears, yet he felt disappointed. Like a kid who had gone through the terrors of his first roller-coaster ride and now was sad that it had ended. Far down below he could see the tiny figure of a man gathering up a dirty-white parachute.

I did it! Jamie thought. I made the jump. He wanted to give out a real Indian victory whoop.

But the sober side of his mind warned, You've still got to land without breaking your ankles. Or popping that damned incision.

The ground was really rushing up at him now. Relax. Bend your knees. Let your legs absorb the shock.

He hit hard, rolled over twice, and then felt the hot wind tugging at his billowing chute. Suddenly Zavgorodny was at his side pulling on the cords, and the other cosmonaut was wrapping his arms around the chute itself like a man trying to get a ton of wrapping paper back inside a box.

Jamie got to his feet shakily. They helped him wriggle out of the chute harness. The plane circled lazily overhead.

"You did hokay," Zavgorodny said, smiling broadly now.

"How'd you get down so fast?" Jamie asked.

"I did free-fall, went past you. You did not see me? I was like a rocket!"

"Yuri is free-fall champion," said the other cosmonaut.

The plane was coming in to land, flaps down, engines coughing. Its wheels hit the ground and kicked up enormous plumes of dust.

"So now we go to Muzhestvo?" Jamie asked Zavgorodny.

The Russian shook his head. "We have found it already. Muzhestvo means in English courage. You have courage, James Waterman. I am glad."

Jamie took a deep breath. "Me too."

"We four," Zavgorodny said, "we will not go to Mars. But some of our friends will. We will not allow anyone who does not show courage to go to Mars."

"How can you . . .?"

"Others test you for knowledge, for health, for working with necessary equipment. We test for courage. No one without courage goes to Mars. It would make a danger for our fellow cosmonauts."

"Muzhestvo," Jamie said.

Zavgorodny laughed and slapped him on the back and they started walking across the bare dusty ground toward the waiting plane.

Muzhestvo, Jamie repeated to himself. Their version of a sacred ritual. Like a Navaho purifying rite. I'm one of them now. I've proved it to them. I've proved it to myself.

S O L 1: EVENING

The dome was neatly laid out with two airlocks on opposite sides of its circular perimeter, all the life-support equipment in the center, and precisely partitioned little cells for each of the twelve team members arranged in an arc on one side of the floor. The plastic partitions were two meters high, like a set of office cubicles in a bank staffed by basketball players. The psychologists had insisted that the tall partitions be colored in cool pastels. Jamie would have preferred the bold warm hues of his native desert. We're going to need all the warmth we can get here, he thought.

Two phonebooth-sized bathrooms stood at either end of the personnel cubicles. Scheduling would be a major headache.

Common areas were grouped around the center: a galley; a wardroom that was nothing more than a trio of tables with spindly Martian-gravity chairs of lightweight plastic; and a communications center with desktop computers and display screens. Workstations for the individual scientists were arrayed along the circular outer wall. Each scientist was responsible for unpacking his or her own equipment and setting up a workstation. Most of their equipment was still up in orbit; it was to be brought down by the second lander.

After their long day of labor, the four scientists and two astronauts began to shrug out of their backpacks and peel off the hard suits they had been wearing for more than twenty hours.

Within minutes the suits were strewn on the floor like discarded pieces of brightly colored armor, and the six team members stood in their coveralls of tan or olive green or pale aqua blue. We look like human beings again, Jamie thought.

Frightened human beings. Each staring silently at the others, as if seeing them for the first time. Each realizing with utter finality that they were more than a hundred million kilometers from home, from safety, that a single failed transistor or a slight rip in the dome's plastic skin could kill them all without warning or mercy.

They stood in silence, wide-eyed, openmouthed, hands held stiffly away from their bodies, as if testing the world on which they stood and trying to determine if it would be kind to them or not. Like children suddenly thrust into a totally new place, they held their breath and stared silently around them.

Tony Reed broke the tense silence. "I hate to bring up anything so pedestrian, but I'm rather peckish. How about some supper?"

Vosnesensky snorted, Connors laughed out loud, and the others grinned broadly. They left their discarded suits on the floor and trooped to the galley where six frozen precooked meals were speedily microwaved to steaming readiness.

Joanna Brumado disappeared into her own cubicle briefly and came back with a bottle of Spanish champagne.

"You brought that all the way from Brazil?" Pete Connors asked.

Reed said disdainfully, "Of course not. Obviously Joanna fermented the grapes on the way here."

The cork popped noisily and champagne frothed over their dining table.

"I'm afraid it's not chilled," Joanna apologized.

"That's all right. Don't worry about it."

Jamie thought, Just put it outside for a minute or so. That'll ice it down.

There was enough champagne for one drink each. Reed sat between the willowy blonde Ilona and the dark-eyed little Joanna. The Israeli had the lean, haughty look of an aristocrat, even in drab coveralls. Joanna looked like a waif, barely suppressing the anxiety that lay just behind her wide dark eyes.

Reed, sandy haired, athletically trim, seemed absolutely at ease. He was saying, ". . . so we actually have all the comforts of home, almost."

"Almost," echoed Ilona Malater.

"Food, air, good company," Reed bantered. "What more could one ask for?"

"The water is recycled," Ilona said. "Doesn't that bother you?"

Reed ran a fingertip across his pencil-slim sandy moustache. "I must admit I'd prefer to have something to purify the water. Whisky would do nicely."

"That's not allowed," Joanna said seriously. "I broke the rules with my bottle of champagne."

"Yes," said Ilona. "I'm surprised that *he*"—she tilted her head slightly toward Vosnesensky, at the head of the table—"didn't reprimand you and confiscate the bottle for himself."

"Oh, he's not that bad," Reed said. "We'll make him unbend, never fear."

The Israeli biochemist looked doubtful. Then she said, "I wish we did have some Scotch whisky here."

"Perhaps I could mix you some from my infirmary supplies."

Ilona raised an eyebrow. Joanna looked perplexed at the suggestion.

"You've got to be careful, however," Reed went on. "I once shared a bottle of whisky with a Scotsman. When I mixed a little water with my drink the man actually shuddered!"

Both women laughed.

The two pilots were at the end of the little table, talking earnestly together about flying, judging from the way they were using their hands. Pink-faced Russian and black American, their nationalities— even their races—made less difference here than the fact that they were fliers rather than scientists: engineers, at best. A clear difference in caste from the scientists. The American was lanky, lean dancer's legs and arms. The Russian was shorter, thicker, his hair the shade of auburn that had probably been brick-red when he was a child. His fleshy face, normally a dark scowl, was animated now and his bright blue eyes sparkled as he talked about flying.

Jamie knew he was the outsider. For nearly four years these men and women had trained with Father DiNardo, the Jesuit geologist who had originally been picked for the Mars expedition. Jamie had been one of the also-rans, knowing every instant of every day for nearly four years that he was going through the motions of training for a mission he would never be a part of. And then DiNardo's god struck him down with a gall bladder infection that required surgery, and his chosen backup had been swiftly chopped down by back-room politics. Suddenly, miraculously, unbelievably, James Water-man—Native American—had joined the team that would actually set foot on Mars.

A red man on the red planet, Jamie mused. I'm here, but only because of blind luck. They accept me, but DiNardo was their first choice; I'm just a substitute.

Yes, he heard the whispered voice of his grandfather. But you're *here*, on Mars, and the Anglo priest is not.

Jamie almost smiled. To his grandfather even a Jesuit from the

Vatican was an Anglo. He was glad that he was here among the first explorers, yet that very emotion stirred a latent sense of guilt. He had won this privilege at the expense of other men's pain. A true Navaho would fear retribution.

Vosnesensky pushed himself away from the table and stood up.

"Time for sleeping," he said gruffly, as if expecting an argument. "Tomorrow we must be ready for the arrival of the second team. And before we sleep we must clean the suits and store them properly."

No one argued, although Tony Reed muttered something that Jamie could not catch. They were all tired but they knew that the hard suits had to be properly maintained. Tomorrow's schedule would be just as punishing as this first day's. The tensions and hostilities that had grown during their nine-month flight had not evaporated simply because they had set foot on Mars. Maybe in the days to come, Jamie thought, when we're busy working and we can roam around outside, maybe then things will change. Maybe then.

After vacuuming the dust off his hard suit and hanging it properly in the storage rack by the airlock, Jamie passed Ilona Malater's quarters on his way to his own. The accordion-fold door to her cubicle was open. She was taping a tattered old photograph to the partition beside her bunk.

She noticed Jamie and said over her shoulder, "Come in for a moment."

Feeling slightly uncomfortable, Jamie hesitated at her doorway.

Ilona whispered throatily, "I'm not going to seduce you, red man. Not our first night on Mars."

Jamie hung by the doorway, not knowing what to say.

"Would you like to see my family album?" Ilona asked, with a wicked smile.

There was only the one photograph taped up. Jamie stepped in closer and saw a tall, tired man in a dirty soldier's uniform standing in a street choked with rubble, his hands raised over his head, half a dozen soldiers in a different uniform menacing him with submachine guns.

"That is my grandfather in 1956," Ilona said, her voice suddenly louder, brittle. "In Budapest. Those are Russian soldiers. The Russians hanged my grandfather, eventually. His crime was to defend his country against them."

"We're on Mars now," Jamie said softly.

"Yes. What of it?"

Jamie turned and left her cubicle without another word. Ilona would keep on deviling Vosnesensky, just as she had all during the long months of the flight here. She thought she had a reason to hate all Russians. All during the years of training she had cleverly hidden her hatred. And nursed it. Now it was coming out into the open. Now, when it might get us all killed.

We bring it all with us, Jamie said to himself. We come to a new world with words of peace and love, but we carry all the old fears and hatreds wherever we go

Feeling completely spent, Jamie tumbled onto his cot without bothering to undress. Nearly an hour later he lay still awake on the spindly cot in his cubicle, worrying about Ilona. The dome was dark now, but not silent. The metal and plastic creaked and groaned as the cold of the Martian night tightened its frigid grip. Pumps were chugging softly and air fans humming. The psychologists had decided that such noises would actually be comforting to the lonely explorers. If the machinery noise suddenly stopped it would alert them to a dangerous situation, just as the sudden cutoff of a plane's engine starts the adrenaline flowing immediately.

As he lay on his cot, though, Jamie heard another sound. A rhythmic sort of sighing that came and went, started and stopped. A low whispering, almost like a soft moaning, so faint that Jamie at first thought it was his imagination. But it persisted, a strange ghostly breathing just barely audible over the background chatter of the manmade equipment.

The wind.

There was a breeze blowing softly across their dome, stroking this new alien artifact with its gentle fingers. Mars was caressing them, the way a child might reach out to touch something new and inexplicable. Mars was welcoming them gently.

Jamie let his thoughts drift as he clasped his hands behind his head and listened to the soft wind of Mars until at last he fell asleep.

He dreamed of spaceships landing in New Mexico and whole tribes of Indians stepping out of them, naked, to claim the harsh barren land for their own.

I N   T R A I N I N G: ANTARCTICA

1

McMurdo Base reminded Jamie of a cross between a seedy mining town and a run-down community college campus, set on the edge of frigid McMurdo Sound between the snow-covered mountains and the Ross Ice Shelf, a quarter-mile-thick shield of ice that covered most of the Ross Sea. All the buildings looked government issue: curved-roof metal huts and square wooden barracks, even the newer cinderblock two-story administrative offices. There was a farm of oil tanks, endless rows of equipment sheds, a U.S. Coast Guard icebreaker anchored in the harbor, and an airfield literally carved out of the shelf of glittering ice that extended past the horizon, covering an area bigger than France.

The streets were plowed clear of snow, but hardly anybody ventured out into the piercing wind. The coldest temperature ever recorded on Earth had been measured in Antarctica, one hundred twenty-seven degrees below zero Fahrenheit.

A midsummer overnight low on Mars, Jamie knew.

Inside the hut provided for the Mars Project trainees it was almost comfortably warm, thanks to the new nuclear power system that had been installed the previous year. Old-style environmentalists had protested bringing nuclear power to Antarctica, while the new-style environmentalists protested against further use of fuel oil that soiled the increasingly polluted Antarctic air with its sooty emissions.

Each group of trainees for the Mars mission had to spend six weeks at the Antarctic station learning what it was like to live in a research outpost cut off from the rest of the world, crowded tensely together in barely adequate facilities with few amenities and little privacy, struggling to survive in a barren frozen world of ice and bitter cold.

As Jamie strode briskly down the narrow corridor of the half-buried hut he thought to himself, All project scientists are equal. Except that some are more equal than others. And now Dr. Li is more equal than all the rest of us.

Dressed in his usual thick red-and-black corduroy shirt and faded denim jeans, his western boots thumping against the worn wooden flooring, Jamie headed toward the office of Dr. Li Chengdu, the man who had just been designated to be the expedition commander. No other appointment had been made for the mission, not yet, not officially. But the snow-blanketed base was a buzzing beehive of rumors and speculation about who would be picked to fly to Mars and who would not. The men and women cooped up in the crowded base had set up betting pools. Some of them were even trying to hack their way into the computer's confidential personnel files.

Tomorrow Jamie and the group he was attached to would fly out of McMurdo and back to civilization, weather permitting, ending their mandatory six weeks. Jamie had spent much of his time in searches for meteorites out on the snow-covered glacier that fed into the ice pack covering the Ross Sea. Antarctica was a good place for meteorite hunting. The perpetual ice and snow of the frozen continent preserved the rocks that had fallen from the sky, keeping them relatively free of terrestrial contaminants. Some of those meteorites were in fact suspected to have come from Mars. Jamie had hoped to find one in his searches of the wind-swept glacier. If I can't get to Mars, he had told himself, maybe I can find a chunk of Mars that's come to Earth.

In six weeks he had found four meteorites in the ice, none of them Martian.

For more than three years Jamie had worked and trained with scientists from a dozen different nations in laboratories and field centers from Iceland to Australia. For most of that time he—and everyone else—had known that he would not be selected as the geologist to land on Mars. Father Fulvio DiNardo was the top choice for the mission, not only a world-class geologist but a Jesuit priest as well.

"He's what we call a 'twofer,'" one of the American mission administrators had explained cheerfully over breakfast, months earlier, when they had been at Star City, outside Moscow. "Fills two slots: geologist and chaplain."

Tony Reed had agreed, a slight smirk twitching at his lips. "Yes. He can hear confessions and baptize any babies born during the mission. No other geologist could be so useful."

Jamie reluctantly accepted the reality of DiNardo's unassailable position. The priest had been involved in planetary studies since the great second wave of space probes had been sent to Jupiter and the asteroids; he had actually helped design some of the instruments they carried. He had been the first geologist on the moon since the *Apollo 17* mission, thirty-some years ago. Even now, while the scientists trained for the first manned mission to Mars, Father DiNardo spent most of his time in the isolation laboratory up in the Soviet space station, *Mir 5*, directing the geological studies of the rock and soil samples returned by the unmanned probes sent to scout the red planet in advance of the human expedition.

It was Father DiNardo's backup who bothered Jamie. Franz Hoffman seemed to have the inside track, according to all the gossip. The Viennese had been a physicist originally, then had switched to geology only a few years ago. Jamie was certain that it was his Austrian nationality more than his work in geology that placed him in the number-two slot behind DiNardo. And ahead of Jamie.

For months Jamie had felt a simmering anger rising within him. I'm a better geologist than Hoffman, he told himself. But he'll get the nod to go to Mars as DiNardo's backup and I'll stay here on Earth. Because the politicians want a balance of nationalities and there's no other Austrian in the group. Worse yet, he knew, the politicians are trying their damnedest to keep the numbers of Americans and Russians equal. And they count me as an American.

As he approached Dr. Li's door he wondered for the thousandth time what he could do to change the situation. Why has he sent for me? Now that Li's officially been named as expedition commander is he going to act as a scientist or as a politician? Can he help me? Will he, if he can?

Jamie knocked on Dr. Li's door.

The position of expedition commander had been selected with extreme care by the politicians and administrators. He had to be a highly regarded scientist, a natural leader, an inspiration to the men and women whom he would command on another world. He had to be able to placate wounded egos and solve emotional problems among his sensitive scientists—and astronauts.

Most of all, he had to be from a neutral nation: neither East nor West, neither Arab nor Jew, neither Hindu nor Moslem.

Dr. Li Chengdu was an ascetically lean, sallow-faced man who had been born in Singapore of a Chinese merchant family, educated in Shanghai and Geneva, and was rumored to be in line for a Nobel

Prize for his research in atmospheric physics: he had found a way to reverse the depletion of the ozone layer and close the long-dreaded ozone hole in the upper atmosphere. A man in his early fifties, he was young and hale enough to make the long journey to Mars, yet old and respected enough to be the unquestioned leader of the expedition in fact as well as in name.

"Enter please," came Dr. Li's voice, only slightly muffled by the thin pressed-wood door.

Jamie stepped into the room that served as Li's office and living quarters. Li got to his feet from behind the desk that had been shoehorned in between the bunk bed and the sloping curve of the outer wall. He was so tall that he had to stoop to avoid hitting his head against the curving ceiling panels.

The room had no personality in it at all, no stamp of an individual's presence. Li had come in only a few days ago and was scheduled to leave with Jamie's group the following morning. The desk was bare except for a laptop computer that hummed softly, its screen glowing a pale orange. The bed was made with military precision, blankets meticulously tucked in under the thin mattress. The one window was blocked by the plowed snow heaped against the side of the building. A strip of fluorescent lamps ran along the low ceiling, turning Li's sallow skin tones into something almost ghastly.

When he had first met Dr. Li, two years earlier, Jamie had been surprised at the man's height. Now he felt surprised all over again. Li was almost six-five, lean to the point of gauntness, a tall scarecrow of a man, with hollow cheeks and long slim fingers. The newly named expedition commander wore a soft velour shirt of deep charcoal that hung loosely on his thin frame.

"Ah, Dr. Waterman. Please sit down." Li indicated the only other chair in the room, a government-issue piece of worn dull-gray steel with a thin plastic cushion that felt iron hard.

Li took his chair behind the desk once again. For a long moment he said nothing. He peered intently at Jamie, as if trying to see inside him. Jamie returned the gaze calmly. He had watched his grandfather conversing with other Navahos often enough; they were never in a hurry to speak. It was important to allow time for thought, for reflection, for sizing up the other man.

Jamie studied Li's face. His hair was still dark, though receding from his high domed forehead. Decidedly oriental eyes, hooded, unfathomable; with the drooping moustache they made him look like an ancient Chinese sage, or perhaps the villain in an old-fashioned tale of intrigue. He ought to be dressed in a long silk robe and be living in a palace in Beijing, not stuck in the snow down at the ass end of the world.

There was a slightly cloying odor in the tiny room. Incense? Cologne? It almost smelled like marijuana.

"I have a favor to ask of you," said Dr. Li at last. His voice had become soft, almost a whisper. Jamie found himself leaning forward slightly to catch his words over the incessant hiss of the air blowing through the heating ducts.

With an almost furtive glance at the orange display screen of the computer on his desk, Li went on, "You have done very good work here—and in your other training activities, as well."

"Thank you." Jamie bowed his head slightly.

"I wonder if you would consider staying here for another six weeks?"

"Stay? Here?"

"The group you have been working with is scheduled to go to Utah next, I believe." Another glance at the computer screen. "Yes, survival training on high desert."

Before Jamie could reply, Li added, "I would appreciate it if you would remain here at McMurdo and help the next group to acclimatize themselves to the Antarctic environment. It would be extremely helpful to me and to your fellow scientists."

Jamie's mind was racing. He's just been appointed expedition commander. It wouldn't be smart to refuse his request. But why is he asking me to do this? Why is he asking *me*?

"Uh . . . the ten of us have been training pretty much as a unit, you know."

"I realize that," said Dr. Li. "But you understand that these groupings made for training will not be the same as the teams selected for the actual flight."

Jamie nodded, wondering what was going on and why.

"Among the group due to come here next is Dr. Joanna Brumado. She is an excellent microbiologist."

"I've met her."

Li nodded slowly. In his softest voice he said, "Daughter of Alberto Brumado."

Jamie leaned back in his chair. Now he understood. Alberto Brumado's daughter would get special consideration. With the rest of the scientists it was sink or swim, survive the rigors of training or get scratched from the list of possible Mars team members. But with

Brumado's daughter the situation was different. They want to make sure she gets through her six weeks here without packing it in.

Because he did not know what else to do, Jamie said, "I see. Okay, sure. I'll stay over the next six weeks and help them all I can."

Dr. Li smiled, but to Jamie it seemed more sad than happy. "Thank you, Dr. Waterman. I am deeply grateful."

Jamie got up from the chair. Dr. Li extended his hand and wished him good fortune.

It was not until he was halfway down the corridor on the way back to his own quarters that Jamie realized the implications of Li's request. He would miss the next six weeks of training. He was being asked to act as a special teacher-guide-escort for Alberto Brumado's daughter.

They had already scratched him from the Mars mission roster. He had been relegated to the status of an instructor. They had no intention of letting him go to Mars.

2

All the scientists under consideration for the Mars expedition had met one another, of course, and often more than once, as their training took them hopscotching around the world. But it had been many months since Jamie had seen Joanna Brumado. He had barely said a dozen words to the woman.

Jamie went to the entrance area of the snow-covered base, more to say good-bye to the men and women he had been training with than to welcome the new arrivals. His group members were already looking at him with pity in their eyes, sympathy for a man who was obviously not going to make it. Some of them almost shied away from him at that last moment, as if afraid to be contaminated by the touch of a loser.

Dr. Li took off one glove and shook Jamie's hand solemnly, wordlessly, before departing. His hand felt dry and limp, like a dead lizard.

Jamie stood inside the doorway, just out of the cutting wind, wrapped in his bulky parka, and watched his ex-teammates trot out to the waiting bus that would take them to the airstrip scraped out of the ice shelf. The bus was towed by a huge earth mover with a snowplow attached to its front. Overkill, thought Jamie. The base's streets had been plowed and there had been no snowfall for days.

Ten people, bundled up in hooded parkas so that you could not tell the women from the men, sprinted from the hut's entrance to the bus, bent against the frigid wind. All of them carried silvered metal cases and floppy garment bags—their precious personal items of clothing and scientific equipment. All except the cadaverous Dr. Li, who carried only his laptop and a small duffel bag. The scarecrow travels light, Jamie thought.

Ten similarly clothed and burdened figures made their way through the snarling wind from the bus to the doorway where Jamie was standing. Jamie recognized tiny Joanna Brumado easily among the ten who trooped into the entranceway, stamping the snow off their boots after the brief run between the bus and the hut's doorway. He also saw that Antony Reed was among the newcomers.

So was Franz Hoffman.

Without a word Jamie turned toward the wooden stairs that led down into the hut's main floor and headed for his quarters.

It was not until the new group met in the dining hall, just before lunch, that Jamie worked up the strength to go out and greet them.

The dining hall was the largest room in the hut that had been donated to the Mars Project: big enough to seat fully thirty persons at its long Formica-topped tables. Joanna was sitting at the end of one of them with Tony Reed and Dorothy Loring, a Canadian biologist.

"Mind if I join you?" Jamie asked.

Reed looked up. "Waterman? What are you still doing here?"

Keeping his face impassive as he pulled up a chair, Jamie said, "I've been asked to hang around and help get you people acclimatized."

Reed glanced at Joanna, then quickly returned his focus to Jamie. "I see."

The word for Antony Reed was "suave." He looked like the average American's idea of an upper-class Englishman, which in fact he almost was. A trim, slight frame, the kind of spare figure that comes from tennis and handball and perhaps polo. Handsome face, with elegant cheekbones and a chiseled profile. Neat little moustache, sandy hair that flopped roguishly over his forehead. He wore precisely creased royal-blue coveralls over a white turtleneck and managed to look almost as if it were a jaunty yachting costume. Yet his eyes were too old for his face, Jamie thought. Ice-blue, coldly calculating eyes.

Reed was a physician who had refused to take over his father's posh practice in London, preferring to join the British astronaut corps as a flight surgeon. When the European Community joined the international Mars Project, Reed immediately applied. He exuded the calm self-confidence of a man possessed of the certain knowledge that he would be picked as the team physician for the Mars explorers.

Jamie sat between the Englishman and Joanna Brumado, who smiled her welcome to him.

"I did not know that you were going to stay on here," she said. Her voice was a whisper, like a little girl who had been trained to stay as quiet as possible.

"It was Dr. Li's idea," Jamie replied tightly. "The base commander will explain everything at the briefing, right after lunch."

"I wonder if our crafty Chinese has some sort of *mano a mano* up his sleeve," Reed mused.

Jamie kept himself from glaring at him.

"*Mano a mano?*" asked Dorothy Loring. "Like in a bullfight?" She was a big-boned blonde, completely at home in her thick sweater and heavy-duty jeans, a latter-day Valkyrie, a descendant of Vikings who had gone from her family's farm in Manitoba to a doctorate at McGill and postdoc work at the Salk Institute in La Jolla.

Reed pointed with his eyes. At the other end of the table sat Franz Hoffman, alone, intently frowning into the display screen of a computer he had set up on the tabletop.

Jamie said nothing.

Neither did Joanna, but her eyes showed that she understood Reed's implication. They were beautifully soft brown eyes, large and liquid, wide-spaced like a child's. Joanna was small and round, almost hidden inside a bulky brown sweater. Her face was heart shaped, framed by a dark mass of hair that curled thickly even though it had been cropped short. To Jamie she looked like a waif, a lost child, with her small stature and those big brown eyes that seemed troubled, almost frightened.

"Our Viennese friend," Reed said in a lower voice, "is not very well liked, I fear."

"You should not say that," Joanna whispered.

"Why not?" Reed asked. "Good lord, the man has all the charm of a Prussian drillmaster. And the eating habits to match."

Loring broke into a giggle, then quickly put her hand to her mouth to stifle it. Jamie, sitting where he looked directly down the table at Hoffman, saw that the Austrian never glanced up from his computer,

3

"I do not understand," said Franz Hoffman. "Does Dr. Li think that
I need an assistant? A Sherpa guide to carry my baggage up the
mountain?"

Jamie held onto his swooping temper, just barely. He had decided
that there would be no way to avoid Hoffman in the crowded,
snow-buried base so he would make a virtue of necessity by offering to help the Austrian to continue the meteorite search out on the
glacier.

Hoffman had been unpacking his clothes when Jamie knocked on
the half-ajar door to his quarters. It happened to be the same room
that Dr. Li had just left. But already Hoffman had turned it into his
personal domain. A five-foot-long photomosaic map of Mars was
pinned up on the flat wall above the bunk bed. On the curving wall
beside the desk the geologist had taped a smaller satellite photo of
the Markham glacier, already marked with red circles where meteorites had been located. A framed color photograph sat on the government-issue three-drawer bureau, a round-cheeked young woman
with twin babies in her arms smiling dubiously into the camera.

"Look," Jamie said, leaning against the doorjamb, "Li asked me
to help your group through your six weeks here. If you're interested
in continuing the search for meteorites I'm willing to help."

Hoffman eyed Jamie silently, then went back to taking folded
clothes out of a large suitcase on the bed and placing them in precise
stacks in the bureau drawers.

"At the very least," Jamie said, "I can show you which areas I've
already covered. Save you going over areas where nothing's been
found."

"That information is in the data bank, is it not?" Hoffman asked.

He was about Jamie's own age and height, but thin and almost
weak-looking where Jamie was solid and chunky. Hoffman was
round-shouldered and round faced. His hair was already turning
gray, and it was cropped close to his skull. His face was a picture
of darkly brooding suspicion, eyes small and squinting, narrow lips

pressed firmly together. Jamie thought, Put a monocle in his eye and he'd look like an old-time Nazi general.

"Yes, the computer has a complete file of my treks on the glacier," Jamie replied evenly. "But once you're out there on the ice the computer data loses a lot of its meaning. Even the satellite pictures aren't much help when you're actually out there."

"I have done field work," Hoffman said stiffly. "I was born in the shadow of the Alps. None of this is new to me."

"Suit yourself," Jamie said. He turned to leave.

"Wait."

"For what?"

Hoffman stood in the middle of the room, his fingers drumming unconsciously against the sides of his heavy wool slacks.

"Tell me," he said, his voice a little less sharp, "why does Dr. Li think that I need an assistant?"

"It's not . . ."

Hoffman did not let Jamie finish his sentence. "You did not have an assistant. None of the other geologists had assistants. Does Li think I'm incapable? Does he think I can't make it on my own? Is this his subtle way of getting rid of me?"

Jamie felt his mouth drop open. Hoffman was just as worried and frightened as he was. Behind the brittle facade was a man who feared he would be left behind, just as Jamie feared.

Shit! Jamie snarled to himself. It would be so much easier to hate him.

4

After lunch and the base commander's brief orientation lecture, Jamie spent the rest of the day saying hello to each of the newcomers, telling them that he was there to give them any help or advice they required. He felt awkward, more like an unwanted and unneeded accessory than a valued and trusted associate.

His insides were in turmoil over Hoffman. Walk a mile in the other guy's moccasins, he thought. Sure. Great. No wonder the Indians got swamped by the whites.

By the time he had spoken to the first three of the newcomers, Jamie had worked out a little speech that explained quickly, with a minimum of embarrassment, why he had remained at the base and what he was offering to do. The newcomers' reactions varied from Hoffman's fear of inadequacy to Tony Reed's cynical smile of understanding.

"Does little Joanna know that you're to be her personal chaperon?" Reed asked.

"I don't think anybody's spelled it out to her," Jamie replied.

Reed's lopsided grin turned almost into a sneer. "She'd be a fool if she didn't figure it out for herself."

"Maybe," said Jamie.

He had left Joanna for last, and now, feeling as frustrated and exhausted as he had the winter he had tried to sell magazine subscriptions bicycling through his Berkeley neighborhood, he tapped at the door to Joanna's room.

She opened the door, looked up at him, and smiled.

"Come in," said Joanna Brumado in her little girl's voice. "Sit down."

She still wore the sweater and jeans she had arrived in. Her room was neatly arranged, emptied suitcases stacked in the far corner, garment bag hanging behind the door. Her laptop computer was open on the desktop but its screen was dark and silent. There were no pictures on the walls, no personal items in sight.

Jamie took the chair that stood by the bunk.

"I've told all the others," Jamie began, "that Dr. Li asked me to stay here at McMurdo to help you and the rest of your group get through your six weeks here as easily and profitably as possible."

Joanna went to the desk and sat at the chair behind it, turning the desk into a protective barrier.

Her face entirely serious, she said, "We can be honest with one another, James."

"Jamie."

Her lips did not curve up into a smile. Her luminous dark eyes were somber. "You are here to make certain that I get through this part of the training. You have stayed behind because I am Alberto Brumado's daughter and for no other reason."

Well, she's no fool, Jamie said to himself. She's under no illusions. No pretensions.

"Dr. Li asked me to remain here," he said.

"Because of me."

"It was his first big decision as expedition commander."

Her eyes would not leave his. "And what about your training? Your own group is going ahead with its regular schedule, is it not?"

"They're going to Utah, yes."

"And you?"

Jamie made himself shrug. "I've spent most of my summers in New Mexico. Maybe Dr. Li figures I don't need any more time in the desert."

Joanna shook her head. "He asked you to stay here? He himself? Personally?"

"Yes."

"And you agreed to do it?"

"What choice did I have? Tell Li that I refuse to carry out his first major decision? How would that look on my record?"

She bit her lower lip. "Yes, he did not give you any real choice at all, did he?"

"Well, I'm here and you're here, so we should try to make the best of it."

"But you will be throwing away your chance for a position on the mission just for me."

"I guess that's already been decided," Jamie said, surprised at the obvious bitterness in his voice.

"I could call my father," said Joanna, tentatively, her eyes sliding away from his. "I could tell him what Dr. Li has done to you."

Jamie tried to probe beneath her words, understand what was churning inside her. She was not angry, yet something was radiating from this elfin woman as she sat behind the desk. Was it fear? Bitterness? A sense of injustice?

"Are you afraid that the others will think you're getting special treatment?" he asked.

"I am getting special treatment!"

"And you don't like it?"

"It could cost you your chance to make the mission."

"But it's important to your father that you go to Mars."

Her eyes went even wider.

"Is that important to you?" Jamie asked.

"Important? That I go to Mars?"

"Right."

"Of course it is important! Do you think I am here merely to satisfy my father's vicarious desires?"

A part of Jamie's mind was registering the fact that Joanna was beautiful. Her figure was certainly adult enough; not even the bulky sweater could hide that. It was her face that gave her the lost, defenseless look of a street urchin, vulnerable yet knowing. And that tiny, whispering voice. Her deep brown eyes were large and almost as dark as Jamie's own.

Jamie looked into those luminous eyes and saw emotions battling against one another. What is she afraid of? he wondered. She says she doesn't want to be her father's pawn, yet she certainly doesn't want to be left behind. That's unmistakable. She wants to go to Mars. Badly.

"I'll help you," he said. "That's my job assignment now."

"I will call my father and tell him what Dr. Li has done to you. It is not fair that . . ."

Jamie silenced her with an upraised hand. "You don't want to be causing trouble between Li and your father. That would be bad for everybody—and especially bad for you."

"But you. What about you?"

He made himself smile. "The Navahos believe that a man's got to keep in balance with the world around him. Sometimes that means you must accept things that you don't particularly like."

"That is stoicism."

"Yep, I suppose it is," said Jamie, trying hard to mask his real feelings.

5

I do wish Father DiNardo were here, Antony Reed said to himself for the twentieth time that morning. He's the only one who can keep that Austrian prig in his place.

Reed was at his desk in the small room that served as the base dispensary. The snow had been shoveled away from the room's only window; pale sunlight drifted in and a milky pearl-gray sky showed through its triple panes. In place of the bookshelves and equipment racks that crammed most of the offices in the half-buried base, the dispensary contained an examination table and medical equipment.

Reed shared the office with the "in-house" physician, a surgeon who looked after the routine medical needs of the base's regular staff as well as the Mars trainees. Reed's work was more concerned with the computer on the desktop than with pills and bandages. He was serving in the role of psychologist for the trainees more than medical officer.

The computer screen showed that his next appointment was with

Franz Hoffman. Reed loathed the Austrian geologist, loathed everything about him—especially his reputed successes among the
women trainees. He kept wondering how any decent, self-respecting
female could let herself be touched by that neo-Nazi.

Yet the tales were undoubtedly true. Hoffman had a way with
women. A way that Reed found himself envying.

He hunched forward in the creaking swivel chair and flicked his
fingers across the computer keyboard. All the details of each trainee's
medical and psychological records were available to him. Perhaps
there was something in Hoffman's background that could be used to
disqualify him for the mission.

Reed searched Hoffman's dossier avidly, the thought of spending
nine months in a cramped spacecraft with the Austrian depressing
him beyond measure.

Nothing. His record was immaculate. Impressive, even. Doctorates
in physics and geology. Excellent health. No psychological history
at all; as far as the records showed his only contact with psychologists
had been when he had taken standard tests as part of the Mars Project
requirements. The test results were dismally normal. Either he's just
as dull as he seems or he's a mastermind at hiding his true personality, Reed thought.

No mention of his amours, of course. That kind of information
seldom got into the record. Unless there was an incident too awful
to be hushed up.

"Ahhh!" Reed said aloud. Softly, but aloud. An incident too awful
to be hushed up. Perhaps one could be manufactured.

He needed a victim. A woman who would not only be offended
by Hoffman's advances, but who would make a stink about it. And
he thought he knew who it should be.

Flicking rapidly through the files he found the woman. Her background and her personality profile were well-nigh perfect. From what
Reed knew of her through personal contact she would be frightened
and enraged by the Austrian's boorishness.

"It's worth a try," Reed murmured, a crooked little smile spreading
across his handsome face. "I could even stand by to console the poor
wench afterward."

He cleared the computer screen and looked expectantly toward
the door. Precisely at the hour set for his appointment, Franz Hoffman knocked once, then opened the door and stepped into the dispensary. He looked as if he were ready to receive a knighthood.
Round face shaved and scrubbed pink, hair slicked back, crisp fresh

shirt and trousers with a crease that could slice bread. Even his shoes were polished.

"Come in, come in," said Reed happily.

Throughout the perfunctory physical examination Reed had difficulty keeping a straight face. He kept thinking of Browning's wonderful "Soliloquy of the Spanish Cloister," with its perfect final line: "G-r-r—you swine!"

Reed chatted affably with the Austrian, using his best bedside manner. Hoffman had only two modes of discourse, as far as Reed could tell: either scowling suspicion or smug superiority. Taking Reed's affable manner at face value, the Austrian responded with infuriating haughtiness. He doesn't even realize he's doing it, Reed thought. Which merely damned him further.

As he took Hoffman's blood pressure and laid him on the table for an EKG and tapped him here and there, Reed slowly, subtly moved their conversation to the subject of women.

"I don't know how you do it," Reed said smoothly. "I seem to be all thumbs around a pretty girl."

"It is the fault of your schooling, I think," said Hoffman. "You Englishmen are sent to boys' schools. You never see women until you are graduated from college, except for your mothers and nurses. That is why there are so many homosexuals among you."

Reed broke into a sunny smile. G-r-r—you swine! he said to himself.

"Most young women are looking for father figures," Hoffman expounded. "It is not necessary to wine and dine them; merely show them a mixture of authority and kindness and they will fall into your bed."

"Is that so?"

"It has never failed for me. The only difficulty is that sometimes they don't know when the affair is over. You must be very expert at getting rid of them. That takes more skill than screwing them in the first place."

"Hmm, I never thought of that."

"On this mission, of course, one will have to be very careful, very discreet. And pick the women carefully. There are those who know how to behave and those who don't."

"Yes, I see." Reed hesitated only long enough to prevent himself from bursting out in laughter. "How can you tell which is which?"

Hoffman smiled an oily, scheming smile, and beckoned Reed to lean closer.

"You test your subjects before the flight begins, naturally," he whispered. "What else would a good scientist do?"

"Test your subjects? Oh, of course. Are you doing that now?"

Something flickered in Hoffman's eyes. An awareness of danger, perhaps. A realization that he was talking too much.

"A gentleman does not kiss and tell," he replied, somewhat stiffly.

Reed arched an eyebrow. "Yes, I can see where it might get sticky, dabbling among the women here. And the project managers are very concerned about sex during the mission. They don't want to disrupt the efficient functioning of the team, you know."

Hoffman matched Reed's raised brow. "Perhaps the team would function more efficiently if a certain amount of lubrication was included in the operation."

"Lubrication! That's a good one!"

Hoffman looked pleased with himself, but said no more.

"You know," Reed said, lowering his voice to a conspirator's whisper, "there's one woman among the group here who's been watching you very closely."

"Oh?"

"She hasn't said anything to me, you realize, but I can see that she's fascinated by you. And if ever a young lady looked up to a father figure, it's her."

"Who?"

"Why, Joanna Brumado, of course. Didn't you know?"

6

Jamie delayed going to the dining room until he was certain most of the others had eaten and returned to their individual quarters. Most of the regular McMurdo staff and visiting researchers shared dormitory rooms, but the Mars Project's one luxury was to afford each of its members a private room. Jamie had spent the day talking with the new arrivals, embarrassing them and himself. He had no desire to speak with any of them further. Not this evening.

Sure enough, the dining room was almost empty. It had been a long day for the newcomers, he realized. The flight in from Christchurch took ten hours even when the weather was good. Unpacking, getting settled in this spartan godforsaken base—the new arrivals were already in their bunks, for the most part. Only a couple of them still sat at one of the long galley tables, tiredly huddled over the remains of their dinners, talking in whispers. Half a dozen of the base's regular technicians and maintenance personnel sat near the battered old coffee urn, playing cards.

Somebody had put a cassette in the tape player up by the snow-covered window: a softly whining old country lament: "Mamas, don't let your babies grow up to be cowboys. . . ."

Or scientists, Jamie said to himself as he took a tray and walked down the self-service counter. He found that he had no appetite, settled for a slice of soggy defrosted pie and a mug of coffee. Then he went to the farthest corner of the dining room and sat alone at the end of an empty table.

No one paid him any attention. Which suited Jamie fine. He was an outsider now, a pariah, and they all knew it.

Then Joanna came in, wearing a dark green chamois man's shirt that fit her like a tent: shoulders drooped down almost to her elbows, shirttails around her knees. She had rolled up the sleeves, and beneath it she wore a white tee shirt and nubby running pants. Dressed for comfort, Jamie saw. Yet she did not look sloppy: casual, not unkempt.

She went straight to the coffee urn and poured herself a steaming mug. Then, looking around the nearly empty dining room, she saw Jamie and came to his table.

"I could not sleep," she said, sitting at the corner of the table just to his right.

Jamie nodded toward the coffee mug. "That's not going to help you."

She laughed lightly. "Oh, caffeine never keeps me awake. I was raised on coffee."

"In Brazil."

"Yes."

As if to prove her point Joanna took a long swallow, then put the mug down on the Formica tabletop. Jamie felt as if he wanted to get away, but he did not know how.

Joanna said, "I understand that you are an Indian."

"Half Navaho."

"In Brazil you would be called a mestizo. I am a mestizo myself. My father and mother, both mestizos. There are millions of us in Brazil. Tens of millions in Latin America, from Mexico southward."

"And two here in Antarctica," Jamie said.

She laughed again, a pleasant happy sound. She seemed less tense than she had been earlier, her voice stronger. "Yes, two of us here."

Jamie smiled back at her. They began to talk, easily, quietly. He could feel himself relaxing with her.

She told him about São Paulo and Rio, how the poor farmers and villagers had streamed into the cities in such a torrent that they had swollen into a single urban megacity more than three hundred kilometers wide that stretched from the beaches to the inland hills, sparkling high-rise towers for the rich, sprawling filthy slums for the poor, and smoggy lung-corroding pollution for all.

Jamie found himself telling her about Berkeley and the Bay, beautiful, earthquake-vulnerable San Francisco and the golden fertile valleys of California. And then about New Mexico and his grandfather.

"Al thinks of himself as a Navaho, but he acts like an Anglo businessman. He can go around saying that a man can't get rich if he takes proper care of his family, yet he owns half the housing developments on the north side of Santa Fe."

Jamie lost track of the time, talking with Joanna. She asked if he had a girlfriend and he told her that he had been dating a TV anchorwoman back in Houston.

"But it's nothing serious," he quickly added. "What about you? Are you married? Engaged?"

Joanna shook her head. "No. No one. There is only my father and me. My mother died several years ago."

Then she asked, "When did you first become interested in going to Mars?"

"Oh, god, it happened so long ago I don't even remember . . . wait, yes I do." The memory came into clear clean focus. "In elementary school. They took the class on a field trip to the planetarium. The show was all about Mars."

"Ah," said Joanna. "With me, of course, it was my father. We talked about Mars every evening at dinner, every morning at breakfast."

"I started reading everything I could about Mars. Fiction, nonfiction. Pretty soon I found the scientific books much more interesting than the fiction."

"That is why you became a scientist?"

Jamie thought a moment. "Yep, I guess maybe it is."

"But why a geologist?" she asked.

With a grin, Jamie replied, "You can't spend much time in the southwest without becoming a geologist. Have you ever seen the Grand Canyon? Or the Barringer Meteor Crater?"

Joanna shook her head.

"The mountains, the rocks—they're like picture books that have the history of the planet written on them."

"And Mars?"

He shrugged. "A new world. Nobody's touched it yet."

Jamie had done a double major in school: geology and planetary sciences. He did not want to be just another rock hound or end up working for an oil company. He wanted to find out what makes the world the way it is; not just the Earth, the other planets too.

But there were no jobs in planetary sciences when he left school with his brand-new Ph.D. He accepted a postdoc at CalTech and spent a year hunting for meteorites. When the year was finished he wound up taking an assistant professorship at Albuquerque, thinking that he would have to spend the rest of his life teaching would-be oil hunters and doing field work in the summers. He was in Canada studying astroblemes, the scars from ancient meteor strikes, when the Mars Project sent out its first call for scientists.

"A new world," Joanna echoed. "Is that why you enrolled for training?"

"My parents were against it. Even my grandfather had his doubts. But I had to give it a shot, had to try. I didn't want to be just another assistant professor working toward tenure. I didn't want them going to Mars without . . ." Jamie suddenly realized where he was and what he had agreed to. ". . . without me," he finished lamely.

Joanna placed her hand atop his. A small soft feminine hand, pale against his own, roughened and darkened by years of field work.

"I will write to my father," she said softly. "Perhaps there is something he can do."

Jamie said nothing, but he thought to himself bleakly, They've already got one part-Indian set for the mission. They won't need another.

7

It was cold in the helicopter. Cold and noisy. The big chopper clattered and lurched in the gusty wind blowing down from the summit of Mount Markham. Glancing out the window of the rattling, vibrating cargo door Jamie saw the broad white expanse of the glacier stretching below them, glaring reflected sunlight into his eyes, glittering where snow had drifted into mountainous dunes.

"Several of the meteorites found in this area have been proven to be from the moon," Hoffman was telling Joanna, bellowing to be heard over the roar of the turbine engines.

She was sitting in the middle seat, safety harness buckled tightly across her shoulders and lap, her gloved hands clenched into rigid little fists, her head turned toward Hoffman so that she would not have to look out at the desolate world of ice below them.

Hoffman was lecturing at the top of his voice. To anyone else it would have sounded like the ultimate in arrogance, but Jamie knew that the Austrian was just as frightened as Joanna was. He was talking to stay in control of himself, telling Joanna every last detail about the meteorites that had been found on the glacier.

By me, Jamie reflected sourly. I found the damned meteorites. That part he doesn't mention.

"Have any of them been definitely identified as Martian?" Joanna yelled back at him.

"Only two have matched comparisons with stones brought back from Mars by the automated probes," Hoffman hollered. "And those were found more than twenty years ago. None of the meteorites located recently have proved to be of Martian origin."

"Some of the stones found elsewhere in Antarctica have microflora living in cracks in their surfaces," Joanna shouted, shifting the subject to her field of expertise to keep the throat-straining conversation going and avoid thinking about being alone out there on the ice.

"Yes, I know," answered Hoffman. "A form of lichen that protects itself from the wind by living inside the surface cracks."

"They are close enough to the surface to catch sunlight for photosynthesis."

"And they also absorb warmth from the rock when it is heated by the sun, do they not?"

"Yes," Joanna yelled. "They get water from the frost that ices the rocks."

Jamie had heard all this before. And so had they, of course. He had been out on the glacier before, though, and they had not.

The chopper landed near the site Hoffman had chosen for the day's search, then took off again in a roaring whirl of snow and ice particles that turned the pristine sky into a kaleidoscope of sparkling rainbow colors. Jamie watched the bird dwindle off into the clear blue until the sound of its engines was lost in the moaning of the wind rushing down the glacier.

The three of them stood there against the crystalline sky in hooded, fur-lined, electrically heated parkas and leggings, face masks and goggles, thickly lined gloves and heavy spiked boots. They carried long-handled picks that doubled as walking staffs. A pallet of equipment, food, and emergency gear stood beside them, mounted on slick Teflon-coated skids that could traverse ice or deep snow with equal ease.

"Mars will be easy after this," Jamie said. He meant it to sound cheerful, but it came out otherwise.

Four hours later they were plodding across the broken rough ice, leaning heavily on their picks, the two men taking turns dragging the equipment skid behind them.

The wind poured mercilessly down the glacier in a raging torrent, howling like evil incarnate. Their electrically heated parkas and leggings barely kept them going against the buffeting, roaring wind that clawed at them like a furious beast trying to knock them over and suck the life warmth out of them.

Despite the heated suit Jamie felt the cold prying at him, working its freezing fingers in between his face mask and parka hood, worming past his gloves and up his sleeves. The air was so cold that even with the preheating that the face mask provided, Jamie's nasal passages were getting raw. Each breath hurt.

It would be better if we could use the space suits, he thought. Then we'd be totally encased in their insulated hard shells. But the suits weighed too much to be used on Earth.

For the hundredth time Jamie straightened up and wiped a gloved hand across his frosting goggles. The other two stopped when he did, wordless now, gasping with exertion. Jamie saw the little clouds of steam puffing from their masks. It took a lot of energy merely to keep moving in cold like this.

His two charges were just trying to get through the day. Jamie was searching for a bit of Mars that might have come to Earth. Show me a dark stone, glacier, Jamie pleaded silently. Just one. One that came from Mars. Don't hide it from me. Let me find it. Soon.

He knew that the glacier held its secrets deep within its icy bosom. There were ancient meteorites hidden out here, chunks of stone and metal that had fallen out of the sky long ages ago and buried themselves in the snow. But once in a while a stone worked its way up to the surface. Jamie scoured the ice field for such a meteorite and prayed to the glacier to be generous.

Don't hold your secrets from me, he said silently to the glacier. Show me the stones from Mars. They don't belong to you; give them up gracefully.

But the glacier was so *big*. It was a river that had been frozen for millions of years, wider and more powerful than any Amazon of liquid water. It flowed only a few feet per day, yet it was inexorable, unstoppable in its patient journey from the summit of Mount Markham down to the quarter-mile-thick crust of the Ross Ice Shelf.

In all the times he had been out on the glacier Jamie had never experienced such cold. Even with a face mask and goggles and heated parka the raw blustering wind was numbing him down to the bone. Little Joanna had slowed terribly; she seemed barely able to walk. Still, he knew if he called for the helicopter to evacuate them back to the base it would be noted by the administrators and marked against her.

Hoffman seemed to be in better shape, yet he had not uttered a word in the past hour. He and Jamie took turns leaning into the harness that pulled the equipment pallet, but it seemed to Jamie that Hoffman's turns were getting shorter and shorter.

"How are you doing?" he shouted over the wind.

Hoffman merely nodded from behind his mask and half raised one hand.

Joanna's voice wavered as if she were losing control of it. "I . . . am . . . all right." He could barely hear her over the wind.

"Is your heater turned up to max?"

"Yes. . . . Of course."

Why am I putting up with this? Jamie asked himself. Why should I suffer through this kind of agony when I'm not going to be picked for the mission anyway? Then he thought, Suppose I call for the chopper and say that Hoffman is getting too weak to continue? Put the blame on him.

But he knew he couldn't do it. He had never learned to lie convincingly. "Stay out of the retail trade," his grandfather Al had often told him. "And never play poker with strangers. Or anybody else, for that matter. Whatever's on your mind is in your face, Jamie. Some redskin!"

Joanna was a different matter. The daughter of Alberto Brumado had to make it through training. She had to be on the first team, everyone agreed. But why do I have to half kill myself to help *her* get to Mars?

Maybe more than half kill, he thought soberly. The sky that had looked as clear as a crystal bowl of pale ice blue was turning an ominous milky white. Already the summit of the mountain was lost in billowing mist. Squinting through his goggles, Jamie was certain he saw swirls of snow heading down the glacier's broad rugged highway toward them.

The thermometer strapped to the cuff of his parka showed that the temperature was dropping quickly. It was down to thirty-eight below zero; with the wind chill it must be more like eighty below or even worse.

"I'm going to call McMurdo for the chopper," he shouted at Hoffman and Joanna.

"No! Please!" she shouted back, her voice muffled by the mask. "Not for me. I will be all right."

"You're freezing."

She did not answer, but stubbornly shook her head. Hoffman said nothing; he simply stood there, gloved fists planted on his hips, obviously laboring to draw in breath. Jamie focused his attention on Joanna, a tiny miserable bundle inside the bulky hooded parka and goggled face mask.

Uncertain, a tendril of fear worming up his spine, he turned to look back up the glacier toward the approaching storm. Maybe an hour, he estimated. Maybe less.

Then he saw the stone, about the size of a man's fist, sitting dark and incongruous on the rough cracked expanse of the glacier as if it had been waiting for him, as if someone had placed it there for him to notice.

"Look!" He pointed.

He ran to it, nearly tripping on the broken jagged ice, leaving Hoffman by the equipment pallet, forgetting the exhausted freezing woman standing wearily beside the other geologist.

He knelt on the ice and stared at his discovery. Black, pitted like a missile's reentry nose cone, the rock was clearly a meteorite. Could it be from Mars? Jamie had picked up four other rocks in his treks across the glacier. They had all been disappointments, nothing more than ordinary "falling stars."

This one looked different, though. A shergottite, I'll bet. Blasted off Mars a couple hundred million years ago by a giant meteor strike.

God knows how long it wandered through space before it finally got caught by Earth's gravity well and plunged into this glacier. Probably been trapped in the ice for millions of years, waiting to rise up to the surface where somebody could find it. Me.

"Is it . . . ?"

Jamie turned to see Hoffman leaning over his shoulder.

"It's a Martian!" Jamie shouted.

"Are you sure?" The Austrian's teeth were chattering audibly.

"Look at it! Where it's not blackened it's pink, for god's sake!" he said, unable to hide the excitement he felt. "At the very least it's good enough to get us home." Fumbling in his parka's deep pockets he finally grasped the palm-sized radio and pulled it up to the mouth flap of his face mask. "I'm calling for the chopper. We've found something important. This rock is our ticket back to McMurdo."

No one could fault them for cutting short their time on the glacier. Not with a possible piece of Mars in their gloved hands and a roaring snowstorm coming down the mountain at them.

8

Nearly twelve hours later Jamie was walking tiredly from the geology lab toward his quarters, still feeling chilled inside. The storm that had been marching down the mountain range had enveloped the base at McMurdo Sound, howling outside the thickly insulated walls like an attacking barbarian army, piling snow up to the roof line. The base was snugly warm, though, as Jamie trudged slowly down the narrow low-ceilinged corridor toward his tiny cell of a room. Yet he still did not feel fully thawed out.

Joanna's room was near his and her door was open. He glanced in. Joanna was at her desk, her fingers flickering over her laptop computer's keyboard.

She looked up and saw Jamie.

"Please come in," she said. "I was waiting for you."

She got up from the desk chair and came toward him. Joanna still looked almost like a child to Jamie. Delicate little hands, big deep brown eyes. But in form-fitting coveralls her body was not childlike. He felt a stirring inside himself as he stepped through her doorway and stood awkwardly before her.

"I was writing a letter to my father to tell him what you did out there on the glacier," she said. "I wanted to thank you for it."

"What I did?"

Joanna smiled up at him and Jamie realized how sensuous her lips were.

"You could have called for the helicopter to pick us up hours earlier. You saw how poorly I was doing."

He did not know what to say. Suddenly his hands were as clumsy as if encased in boxing gloves. He finally settled on hooking his thumbs in the pockets of his jeans.

"If we had to be pulled off the glacier early," Joanna went on in her whispery voice, "it would have meant the end of my hopes to be on the first team. And Dr. Hoffman's, perhaps."

"Not necessarily," Jamie muttered.

"I appreciate your staying with me and protecting me the way you did."

He shrugged.

"It would break my father's heart if I was not on the first team," she said softly. "He wanted so much to go to Mars himself. If I fail him . . ."

Jamie wanted to take her by the shoulders and pull her to him and kiss her. Instead he heard himself saying, "They would have sent the chopper to us anyway, what with the storm bearing down on us."

"Yes. Perhaps." Her eyes were fastened on him.

"The . . . uh, meteorite looks Martian, all right," Jamie said. "Right ratio of inert gas isotopes. High pyroxene content."

Her brows went up slightly. "Organics?"

"Dorothy Loring is slicing some thin sections for the microscope."

Turning back toward her desk to shut down the laptop Joanna said, "I must get to the laboratory. She should have called me."

Jamie stepped back toward the doorway as she flicked through the file of miniature floppy disks on her desk, pulled one out, and slid it into the snug pocket of her coveralls.

Then she looked at Jamie as if she had forgotten he was in the room with her. "I do want to thank you for helping me. I appreciate it very much."

"De nada."

She came around the desk again and stopped half a step in front of him. "It was very important to me."

Looking down into her uplifted dark eyes Jamie brushed his fingertips against her soft cheek, uncertain, tentative.

Joanna flinched and backed away from him, her face reddening. "You mustn't do that!"

"I didn't . . . "

She shook her head. "We cannot get involved emotionally. You know that. They would never allow us on the mission if they thought . . . "

"I'm sorry," Jamie said. "I didn't mean to upset you."

"It's just . . . " Joanna almost wrung her hands. "I cannot get involved with anyone, Jamie. Not now. You understand that, don't you? It would ruin everything."

"Sure," he said. "I understand."

She wasn't talking about calling her father anymore. She wasn't worried about injustice or being Alberto Brumado's pawn. And there's no sense in her getting involved with a guy who's not going to make the team, Jamie told himself silently.

"I've got to get down to the lab now," Joanna said.

He stepped aside and let her pass, then went out into the narrow corridor and watched her hurry toward the laboratory.

At dinner that evening in the crowded dining room Joanna kept her distance from him. When the others congratulated him on having found a Martian rock that actually contained a trace of organic chemicals in it, Jamie muttered his thanks and told them he had been lucky.

"You realize, of course," said Hoffman, sitting across the table from Jamie, "that since I am the official geologist in this group and you are nothing more than a guide, that I will conduct the further examination of the meteorite. It is my responsibility now, not yours."

Dead silence fell across the table. Jamie stared into the Austrian's eyes and saw, deep beneath the arrogant exterior, a sort of pleading, like a drowning man reaching desperately for a hand to help him.

"I thought we would work together on it," he said tightly.

"Of course, you may assist me," said Hoffman.

Jamie nodded once, got up, and left the dining room. Get away before you break something. Go off by yourself, like a wounded coyote. He hurried down the dimly lit corridor back to his room and threw himself on his bunk, still fully clothed, feeling like six different kinds of fool while the blizzard raged on outside the snowbound base.

9

"I must speak with you, privately, in your official capacity." Joanna's voice was trembling.

Antony Reed looked up from the computer screen. She was standing in the doorway of the dispensary looking as if she would burst into tears in another moment.

"Come in," he said, rising from the desk chair. "Close the door and sit down."

Joanna was dressed almost formally, considering the lax standards of the base: tailored white blouse and snug whipcord jeans that emphasized her hourglass figure. She sat tensely on the wooden chair in front of the desk, biting her lower lip.

"I assure you that anything you tell me will remain strictly confidential between us," Reed said, leaning back in his swivel chair. It creaked slightly.

She was terribly upset, he saw. Nervous and fearful. He realized that Hoffman had gone after her at last. The Austrian has nibbled at the bait.

"What I have to say may have a bearing on our work, on the personnel selected for the mission," Joanna said.

Reed kept his face perfectly serious.

"I must have your promise that you will not reveal anything I tell you to the project administrators."

Leaning forward and placing his forearms on the desk, Reed said in his best professionally grave manner, "If what you are about to tell me actually does have a serious bearing on the mission, then you are placing me in an ethical dilemma."

She nodded and drew in a deep breath. Reed admired the way her blouse moved, even though it was buttoned up to the neck.

"I must be free to speak with you off the record," she said. "When I have finished we can decide what is important for the mission and what is purely personal. Is that all right?" Her voice was almost pleading.

Leaning back in the complaining chair again Reed said airily, "Yes, yes, of course. That will be fine. I want you to feel free to speak openly."

Joanna stared at the computer on the desk. Reed smiled, reached over, and turned it off.

"Now then," he said, "what seems to be the matter?"

She hesitated. Then, "A . . . a certain member of the group . . ." She went silent.

Reed waited for a few moments, then prompted, "A member of the group did what? Insulted you? Attacked you? What?"

Her eyes went wide. "Oh, nothing like that!"

"Really?"

She almost seemed relieved. "One of the men tried to make advances, but that was no problem. We have all learned how to deal with that."

"We?"

"All the women in the group."

"You're saying that some of the men make improper overtures to you?" Reed asked.

Joanna actually smiled. "Of course they do. We can handle that. It is not a problem."

"The men don't persist? They don't become threatening?"

She dismissed that idea with a feminine little shrug. "There is only one who makes a real pest of himself."

"Dr. Hoffman," Reed prompted.

"How did you know?"

"*Has* Hoffman bothered you?"

"He has tried. I was a bit concerned at first; he seemed so insistent."

"And?"

"I have learned to deal with him. We women help each other, you know."

Reed fought to keep himself from frowning. "What's your problem, then?"

Joanna's faint smile disappeared. She looked troubled once again. Glancing around the room before replying, she finally said, "It is Dr. Waterman."

"Jamie?"

"He has given up his chance to go on the mission in order to help me."

"As I understand it," Reed said stiffly, "he did not volunteer for that. Dr. Li ordered him to do it."

"Yes, I know," Joanna said. "But still—he is very kind, very helpful. Under other circumstances . . . "

"Good lord, young lady, you're not telling me that you've fallen in love with him!" Reed was aghast.

"No, no, of course not," she answered too quickly. "We have only been together a few days. But . . . " Her voice trailed off again; she looked away from Reed.

Feeling a puzzling confusion roiling inside him, Tony said, "It would be extremely unwise to become emotionally involved with a man you will probably never see again, once your tour here at McMurdo is finished."

"I know. I understand that."

"Then what is your problem?" Reed demanded.

"I feel terribly guilty that he is giving up his chance to make the mission because of me."

"I see." Reed relaxed, leaned back again and steepled his fingers. "Of course you do. It's a perfectly natural reaction."

"What should I do?"

He spread his hands vaguely. "Do? There's nothing for you to do. The decision to keep Waterman here was not made by you; you're not responsible for his fate."

"But I am! Don't you see?"

Pointing to the computer screen and smiling, Reed said, in his most persuasive doctor-knows-best manner, "My dear young lady, Waterman was picked to help you—and the others, I might add— because Li and the selection board had already decided he would not be included in the Mars team. Do you think for one moment that they would take someone already chosen for Mars and scratch him from the roster merely to help you here? No. Certainly not. Waterman's fate was already decided. You had nothing to do with it."

Joanna stared at him for a long wordless moment. Finally she asked, "You are sure of this?"

Nodding toward the silent computer once more, Reed said, "I *do* have access to all the personnel files, you know."

She breathed out a deeply relieved sigh.

Watching her blouse, Reed felt seething disappointment burning in his gut. Hoffman's so inept that he doesn't frighten her. And now she's allowed herself to form a romantic attachment to this red man from the wild west. This isn't what I had planned for her. Not at all.

S O L 2: MORNING

Standing out in the open, Jamie realized once more how much Mars reminded him of the rocky, mountainous desert of northwestern New Mexico. In the dawn's slanting light the cliffs to the west glowed red, just as they did at home.

But the sky was pink, not blue, and the rock-strewn ground was utterly bare. Not a twig or a leaf. Not a lizard or a spider or even a patch of moss to break the endless rusty reds and oranges of the desert. The sun was small and weak, too far away to give warmth.

Magnificent desolation. An astronaut had said that about the moon, decades ago. Jamie thought it more appropriate for Mars. The world he saw was magnificent, beautiful in a strange, clean, untouched way. Proud and austere, its desert harsh and totally empty, its cliffs stark and bare, Mars was barren yet splendidly beautiful in its own uncompromised severity.

Looking out to the horizon, Jamie felt an urge to walk out as far as he could, just keep on going forever across this magnificent landscape that was so alien yet so much like home. He snorted angrily to himself. Leave the mysticism behind you, he chided himself. You don't want to be the first man to die on Mars.

Yet it looked like a good place for dying—a dead world. On Earth life has crawled into every crevice and corner it can find, from pole to pole. Even in the dry Antarctic deserts there's life hidden inside the rocks. But this place *looks* dead. Dead as the moon. If any life at all exists here it should have changed the way the place looks.

Jamie recalled tales of creatures made of silicon and green-skinned Martians with six limbs. Don't judge without evidence, his scientific conscience warned. Be patient, said a deeper voice within him. The rules of life may be different on this new world.

He shook his head inside his helmet as if trying to clear away the

argument within. The suit had acquired that faintly acrid, not un-
pleasant odor of his own body now. We've personalized our suits,
Jamie thought, as he carried another bulky crate of medical supplies
from the lander to the airlock hatch of their dome, balancing it on
his shoulder as if it weighed no more than a sack of cornmeal.

"Look! There they are!"

It was Connors's voice, high with excitement. Jamie and the American astronaut were unloading the last of the supplies from the lander. Vosnesensky and Reed were carrying them from the airlock to
their proper storage places inside the dome. The two women had
been assigned to checking off the stores on the computer's inventory
lists. So much for equal rights, thought Jamie.

He straightened up and tried to follow Connors's pointing outstretched arm. The top of his helmet blocked his view for a moment,
but by tilting his head inside the helmet slightly, Jamie managed to
see the thin streak of a contrail blazing across the pink sky.

"Right on time," Connors said, holding his left wrist up in front
of his visor. "They'll be landing on schedule."

As if to confirm the observation, Vosnesensky's heavy voice came
through Jamie's earphones. "Team two is in reentry trajectory. We
must be finished off-loading by the time they land, in . . . fifty-eight
minutes."

Fifty-eight minutes later all six members of the first team stood
between their own lander and the inflated dome, watching the fiery
descent of the second lander.

Everything about the Mars expedition was done in pairs. There
were two landing parties, two backup teams who remained in orbit
around the planet, duplicates of every piece of equipment and mil-
ligram of supplies.

The expedition had been planned around the "split-sprint" mode
of operation, which meant (stripped of the technical jargon) that the
expedition took the quickest possible route to Mars and planned to
stay at the planet for a minimal length of time—two months. That
was the "sprint" mode. The scientists had fought against it with logic
and economics; they had failed in the face of the politicians' desire
for quick and spectacular results.

For while it was true that the sprint mode was more costly overall
than a more gradual approach that would permit a longer stay time
at Mars, the politicians knew that a quick mission would require
fewer years of wrangling and painful budgetary crises than a longer

one. Moreover, practically every politician involved in the Mars mission wanted to see humans on the red planet while he or she might still be in office to take the credit.

So the expedition sprinted to Mars.

The "split" mode simply meant that the expedition rode across the interplanetary gulf in two sets of spacecraft. The rationale was that if disaster hit one set, the other was self-sufficient and could complete the mission.

Now Jamie and the others stood waiting for the second half of their expedition to touch down on the dusty surface.

"There!" Vosnesensky blurted, and they all turned to see a dot in the sky hurtling toward them. Shapeless, formless, it was still too high to be anything more than a dark blur falling across the pink sky like a rock, dragging a bright flaming contrail behind it like a falling star.

My god, Jamie thought, that's what we looked like yesterday.

Then a streak of color streamed from the top of the speck and billowed into a trio of broad white parachutes. The lander slowed, coasted, swaying slightly, gliding toward the ground with the three huge chutes spread above it like angels' wings or the shade awnings of a desert tribe. But it was still falling fast, too fast. Jamie watched for several minutes, his heart in his throat, as the lander floated rapidly downward.

It grew and grew into an ungainly looking combination of saucer and teacup: the circular aeroshell drag brake topped by the cylindrical body of the landing vehicle. Jamie saw that the ceramic underside of the aeroshell was blackened and streaked from its burning flight through the upper Martian atmosphere.

Abruptly the parachutes separated from the lander and flapped away, lost angels wandering across the Martian landscape. The craft seemed to stagger in midair. Puffs of gray-white steam spurted from its control jets as the lander teetered and righted itself, hovering for an instant.

The retro-rockets fired fitful short bursts, blasting grit and swirling dust devils up from the ground as slowly, slowly the oversized saucer and teacup settled downward, cushioned by the hot rocket exhaust. Through his helmet Jamie could hear the intermittent screeching of the retros, like the staccato shrill of a frightened bird.

The lander was coming down more than a hundred meters away, yet a miniature sandstorm was pelting against his hard suit. He resisted the Earth-trained impulse to lean into the wind; there was no real pressure pushing against him in this thin atmosphere.

Finally the noise ceased, the sand stopped blowing, and the segments of the aeroshell drooped to the ground like wilted petals of a huge metal flower.

Jamie heard in his earphones, "That's it! We're down!"

There had been surprisingly little argument over the language to be used on Mars. For more than half a century scientists had used English as their common worldwide tongue. As had aircraft pilots and their ground controllers. A few of the politicians had put up something of a struggle, more for their own national egos than for any serious reason. The French had been especially difficult. Yet in the end they had to face the fact that the one language *all* of their prospective explorers understood was English.

Still, Vosnesensky spoke in Russian through his suit radio to the pilot of the second lander, Aleksander Mironov, while Ilona Malater and Tony Reed set up the hand-sized video cameras on their tripods.

Joanna Brumado, in her dayglo-orange hard suit, turned toward Jamie. "I suppose we are just the spear carriers."

"Waterman!" Vosnesensky's voice rang in Jamie's earphones. "Take the still camera and photograph the aerobrake structure."

Jamie said to Joanna, "One spear carrier."

"Brumado!" the Russian called. "Monitor the gas emissions from the landing craft."

He heard the Brazilian woman's laughter. "No spear carriers."

After slightly more than a quarter hour, the hatch of the landing vehicle popped open and the slim metal ladder slid down to the red dust. A figure encased in a brilliant red pressure suit appeared at the hatch. Must be the other Russian, Jamie thought as he snapped photos for the expedition's official history.

Six hard-suited figures trooped slowly down the ladder, one after the other, and gathered in front of the video cameras with their lander behind them. They too spoke solemn words about the triumph of the human quest and the glories of human intelligence and drive.

Jamie knew the six to be a Russian, an American, a Japanese meteorologist, a fellow geologist from India, an Egyptian geophysicist, and a French geochemist who was the only woman among the second landing team.

The politicians had worked frantically to please as many nations as possible—and to get as many as possible to help fund the quarter-trillion-dollar Mars Project. To their credit, where it was necessary for them to balance national pride against scientific needs, national pride did not win every round. But if an Israeli biochemist was selected to go to Mars, then it became absolutely necessary to send a follower of Islam along. It was imperative that both Japan and France be represented. And of course, there must be the same number of Russians and Americans.

Jamie's last-minute substitution for Father DiNardo had upset the Soviet-American balance, and while that could not be helped, it was not accepted gladly either in Moscow or, strangely, in Washington.

The first team started to help the second team unload their landing/ascent vehicle. More equipment would be sent later in the day by automated, unmanned one-way landers from the spacecraft in orbit. Vosnesensky was in charge of all the ground team, with Pete Connors his ostensible second-in-command. But Jamie heard a lot of Russian chatter in his earphones; the two cosmonauts were already talking to each other to the exclusion of the others.

Jamie was surprised, then, when Vosnesensky tapped him on the shoulder of his hard suit.

"Come to the communications center," the Russian said. "The expedition commander wishes to speak to you."

Without a word, Jamie hefted the crate of chemical analysis equipment he was already carrying and followed Vosnesensky into the airlock. After it cycled and they had vacuumed the red dust off their boots, they stepped inside the dome. Jamie put the equipment crate down just inside the hatch and unconsciously slid his helmet visor up as he walked alongside the Russian to the comm console.

His ears popped again. The air inside the dome was an Earth-normal mix of oxygen and nitrogen, pumped up to normal terrestrial pressure and heated to a comfortable temperature. The hard suits operated at almost normal terrestrial atmospheric pressure. Almost, but not quite. The transition from suit to "regular" air made itself felt in Jamie's inner ear. It was one of those minor maladies that no Mars explorer would even whisper about during training, for fear of being scratched from the team. Here on Mars, though, it was already annoying. And this was only the second day.

Dr. Li Chengdu, the expedition commander, was exceedingly angry with Jamie Waterman. The only visible sign of his anger was the slight throbbing of a vein in his forehead above the left eye. Otherwise his face was a mask of calm. The olive drab coveralls he wore were not quite standard issue: Dr. Li affected a stiff collar instead of the open-necked style everyone else wore. In the back of his mind Jamie wondered if that was supposed to be symbolic.

Puzzled, Jamie sat at the comm desk in front of the main display screen. The six other screens flanking it showed views of the unloading chores going on outside. Vosnesensky stood behind Jamie like a policeman guarding a prisoner about to be interrogated.

"Dr. Li," said Jamie, still in his blue suit and helmet.

"Dr. Waterman."

"You wanted to speak to me?"

Li took in a silent breath, nostrils flaring as if in distaste. "I have just received a most unhappy transmission from Kaliningrad, which was relayed from Houston."

Jamie tried to keep his face as stiffly unemotional as the expedition commander's.

"Your American mission controllers are quite upset that you did not speak the words they gave you for your first statement from the surface of Mars."

"Yes, I suppose they are." Of course they'd be upset. The Anglos in Washington always get upset when a red man doesn't follow their script.

"Why did you say what you did? And what does it mean? Apparently it has caused a sensation in the media in the United States."

With a slight shake of his head Jamie replied, "I had no intention of causing a sensation. I didn't know I was going to say that until I heard myself speaking. The words . . . they simply popped out of my mouth."

"What do they mean?"

"It's an old Navaho greeting. Like '*aloha*' among the Hawaiians or the Italians' '*ciao*.' Literally it means something like, 'It is good.' "

Li's stiff shoulders relaxed visibly. The throbbing vein eased. "Your government people are very angry with you."

Jamie tried to shrug inside the hard suit and found that it could not be done. He said, "What can they do about it? Send me home?"

"They can instruct me to remove you from the ground team and bring you up here!" Li's voice flared. "They can insist that I send Dr. O'Hara to the surface and keep you in orbit for the remainder of the mission!"

Jamie felt his guts lurch. "You wouldn't do that!" It was more of a question than a statement.

"They have not ordered me to do so. Not yet."

Thank god, Jamie breathed silently.

"However, they want a clarification of your words: a written statement from you as to what they mean to you and why you said them instead of what you had been instructed to say."

It suddenly struck Jamie as ludicrous. Sitting inside a space suit on a world a hundred million kilometers from Earth, he was being told that he had to write an apology for three words he had blurted unthinkingly. Or be punished like a truant schoolboy.

"You will write such a statement?" Li prompted.

"If I don't . . . ?"

"They will insist on removing you from the ground team, I fear. You must recall that your assignment to the landing team at the last minute caused some anxious moments in Washington and elsewhere. Please do not jeopardize your position any further."

Jamie remembered that frantic weekend of hurried telephone conferences and impromptu visits with his family. And Edith saying good-bye to him.

The expedition commander seemed to draw himself up into a taller, calmer, more regal posture. "My advice, for what it is worth, is to write a brief statement that explains how you were overwhelmed with emotion upon stepping onto the surface of Mars and lapsed into the language of your ancestors. No one can fault you for that."

"It's even the truth," Jamie said.

The Chinese allowed himself a fatherly smile. "You see? A soft answer turns away wrath."

Jamie nodded. "I see. Thank you."

D O S S I E R: JAMES FOX WATERMAN

Jamie was nine years old the first time he was sent back to New Mexico to spend the summer with his grandfather Al. His mother did not like the idea, but she and her husband had a summer of foreign travel ahead of them, lectures and seminars that would take the two professors across the Pacific to Australia, New Zealand, Singapore, and Hong Kong. They had little desire to drag their nine-year-old with them, and no intention whatever of turning down the all-expenses-paid junket.

So for the first time since he had been in kindergarten Jamie returned to Santa Fe. He learned to fish and hunt and to love his grandfather Al, even though he actually spent most of his days in Al's store on the plaza in Santa Fe. Al was a good grandfather but a better businessman. Anglo ladies cooed over the "little Indian boy" all summer long.

The very last week, while Jamie was already moping about his return to Berkeley, Al took him to one of the Navaho pueblos up in the mountains where he bought the pottery and carpets for which the Anglo tourists paid so dearly.

Most of Al's business that day was conducted at the trading post, a combination bar and general store with uncarpeted creaking floorboards, worn old wooden counters, warped shelves half bare, and a big ceiling fan that hardly moved at all. A half dozen older men sat at the bar, silent and virtually motionless beneath their drooping broad-brimmed hats, while Al bargained patiently, interminably in Navaho with the pueblo's head man. To Jamie the old men at the bar seemed as dusty and time ravaged as the room itself.

Bored with his grandfather's endless low-pitched haggling in a language he did not understand, Jamie went outside and sat on the sagging wooden steps. The late afternoon sun felt hot as molten lava, coloring the whole land copper red.

A scrawny cat slinked past his feet, gray and silent. A pair of mangy, mean-eyed dogs lay panting in the dust on the other side of the street beneath the shade of a cottonwood tree. Jamie could count their ribs.

Across the way, on the shaded porch that fronted an adobe house badly in need of patching, a little girl, maybe six or seven years old, was playing with a puppy, a joyful bundle of wriggling fur. Jamie thought about going over to her, but he did not know how to speak Navaho. The girl cuddled the puppy, petted it, crooning to it in her language.

She put the puppy down briefly, then picked it up by its tail. The pup yelped and snapped at her. She dropped the puppy and jumped to her feet. Then, breaking into English, she cried, "You bad boy! Bad! You always want make trouble, always fighting! I send you to principal. Get out of this classroom! Go to principal! I tell your mother on you!"

Even though he was only nine, Jamie immediately recognized that the girl was imitating an Anglo school teacher.

Her mother called from the cool darkness of the house, through its open door, and spoke sternly in Navaho to her. Jamie realized his grandfather was standing beside him now, laughing at the scene.

Scrambling to his feet, Jamie asked, "What'd she say, Al?"

"Aw, she just told her daughter not to hurt the puppy." He laughed. "Then she told her not to make jokes about her teacher in front of a white man."

"A white man?"

"You, son!"

"But I'm not a white man."

"Guess you look like one to her," said Al.

The following week Jamie was sent back to Berkeley, where his parents expressed great pleasure that their son had not turned into "a wild Indian."

MARS ORBIT

It was damned annoying to be a sage.

Li Chengdu stared at the blank comm screen and still saw James Waterman's stubborn face. An honest face, slightly square with broad cheekbones and just a hint of distant Asian ancestry in the shape of his eyes. Piercing black eyes that were an open pathway to the young man's soul.

I should not have lost my temper with him, Li scolded himself. I was angry because he is down there on the planet and I am forced to ride in this celestial tin can without ever setting foot on Mars.

There was more to it than that, he knew. Russians, Americans, Japanese—nineteen different nationalities living cheek by jowl a hundred million kilometers from Earth. If there isn't a mental breakdown before we return home I'll be surprised beyond words. Not even the Japanese were meant to live this close together.

The engineers had anticipated all the physical problems of the Mars mission, but they had studiously ignored the worries of the psychologists. No, rather, they had passed over all those worries by ordering the psychologists to pick "well-balanced" personalities who could remain stable even under the pressure-cooker conditions of this mission. Li did not know whether he should laugh or weep. Remain stable under these conditions! How does a man remain stable when he is supposed to deny himself sex for nearly two years? This mission should have been planned by Polynesians, not Russians and Americans. The two most prudish peoples in the world.

And now this American Indian has his government upset with his foolish words. That is something none of us had planned for.

At least the crowding had eased now that half the ship's complement had departed for the surface. Li leaned back in his softly yielding chair. Out of the corner of his eye he saw the ruddy curve of Mars float past in his compartment's round window. The orbiting

Mars 2 spacecraft was still tethered to its *Mars 1* twin, five kilometers away, the two of them still rotating about their common center to maintain a feeling of Martian-level gravity. If it became necessary to send one of the backup personnel down to the surface, he or she could go instantly. They were all acclimated to the gravity of Mars.

Li was grateful that their long voyage had not required them to live in zero gravity for any length of time. He always became nauseous in zero gravity; even thinking of unending months of it made him feel queasy.

Sighing heavily, he pushed his chair away from the comm console and stood up, almost six and a half feet tall, lean as a broom handle. The tightly buttoned collar of his coveralls hid the old scar on his throat, a reminder of the riots during his student days in Shanghai. The only decoration on the olive drab outfit was his name tag on the left breast and the shoulder patch of the First Martian Expedition.

Silly of the Americans to be troubled over a few words, he thought. Yet they have never fully resolved their problems with the Indians. Li frowned. No, they did not call them "Indians" anymore. Native Americans? Amerinds? Words are important, he realized, especially in a nation ruled by its media.

As commander of the First Martian Expedition, Li Chengdu had both absolute power and absolute responsibility. Two dozen human beings were under his charge, their very lives in his hands. Half of them, the envied half, were down on the surface of Mars. Waterman was not the first choice among the geologists, not even the second. But the young man is down there on the surface of Mars; his Tao is so powerful that it shapes and transforms the paths of all others who come in touch with him, even my own.

Those of us remaining up here, coasting in orbit, secretly consider ourselves second-rate. There is important work for us to do here in orbit, but except for the few who are going to probe the tiny moons, the scientists here would gladly commit murder for the chance to replace any one of the men or women down on the planet's surface.

I am being melodramatic, he sighed to himself. These are all adult human beings, the healthiest and most stable men and women who could be selected out of the thousands who sought positions on this expedition. The best of the best. They have their problems, naturally. We all face stresses and emotional tensions. It would be foolish to expect otherwise. My task is to reconcile these problems and make certain that they do not interfere with the performance of our mission.

But how healthy and stable was it for that American to speak Navaho to the world's media? How healthy and stable is it for anyone to want to fly off to another world, risking one's life for the thrill of setting foot where no one has stepped before?

Ah, said Li to himself, perhaps that is a form of madness that is divine. The human beast is an explorer, a wanderer, and always has been. Young Waterman's ancestors would never have roamed from Asia to America if it were not thus.

Dealing with two dozen such wandering souls while simultaneously trying to keep their overseers back on Earth placated—that requires the patience of a Confucius, the intelligence of an Einstein, and the guile of a Machiavelli. I am none of them.

Yet as far as these young men and women are concerned, as far as the mission controllers in Kaliningrad and Houston are concerned, I am all of those things and more. And so I must continue to appear to them. If for no other reason than to protect them from their politicians back on Earth. Even when I really want to pursue that slender young blonde who is running the cartographic cameras. Such a tempting smile!

Li sighed heavily. Damned annoying being a sage.

S O L 2: EVENING

"TOSH-ima," the Japanese corrected. "Not Tosh-EE-ma."

Jamie unconsciously bowed his head slightly, acknowledging the meteorologist's pronunciation. Toshima's voice was soft and he smiled as he spoke, but it was clear that he wanted his name pronounced his way. He seemed big for a Japanese: slightly taller than Jamie himself, thick-bodied, with a round flat-featured face.

The wardroom felt almost crowded with all twelve of them sitting together. They had pushed the three tables together and, after a long day of unloading supplies and equipment, were celebrating with a festive dinner.

Vosnesensky and his fellow Russian, Mironov, sat shoulder to shoulder at one end of the table, two squat fireplugs in gray coveralls. The American astronauts, Connors and Paul Abell, were on the Russians' left. The three women sat across from the Americans, and the other scientists had seated themselves around the rest of the table.

Jamie had spent more than an hour during the free time after they had finished unloading the second L/AV composing a conciliatory note for Houston. He had used Li's words as exactly as he could remember them: "I was overwhelmed with emotion upon stepping onto the surface of Mars and relapsed into the language of my ancestors." That ought to satisfy the pisspot sons of bitches, he thought as he transmitted his apology to the spacecraft orbiting above.

Now he sat at the improvised dining table flanked on one side by Seiji Toshima and on the other by Tony Reed.

"I've wondered why the Japanese weren't represented in the first landing," Reed mused as he picked at his tray of precooked beef slices. "After all, if it weren't for Japan's contribution of funding and electronics hardware we would never have gotten here."

Toshima looked up from his rice and fish at the Englishman. "Such decisions were made by the politicians. Japan is not so prideful that one day's difference matters to us. It is enough to be part of this expedition."

With a winking glance at Jamie, Reed teased, "Yes, but after all— even Israel and Brazil were represented before Japan."

"And even England," said Toshima thinly.

"Ah, but England," Reed countered, "represents the European Community."

Toshima bowed his head slightly.

"Then of course," Reed continued amiably, "there is the Navaho nation."

Jamie put down his plastic fork. "Tony, you know as well as any of us that the final decisions on who went aboard which ship determined the order of landing. Why make an issue of it?"

"Indeed," said Toshima, "it is sufficient for us to be here, regardless of which hour each one of us put his first bootprint on the ground."

Reed made a gracious nod and brushed back the stubborn lock of sandy hair that fell across his forehead. "I accept your superior wisdom. Excuse my English gamesmanship, please."

Reed broke into a conversation on his left and Toshima started talking to the Egyptian geophysicist on his right, leaving Jamie sitting alone and wishing that there was a burrito or even a supermarket taco on the microwave tray before him. He had not tasted real food since he had left Houston, more than ten months ago. The nutritionists who planned the meals for this expedition had paid careful attention to the varying national tastes of the Mars explorers—so they had thought. Jamie was eating their version of the Italian meals prepared for Father DiNardo: soybean paste attempting to look like veal cutlets; spaghetti that miraculously managed to be dry and mushy at the same time. And it was all so bland! DiNardo's damned gall bladder problems had ruled out spices, apparently. That's what you get for taking another man's position, Jamie told himself. Eat DiNardo's meals and be grateful you're here in his place.

He glanced at the three women, talking among themselves. Ilona's patrician face was animated, smiling as she spoke, her hands a flurry of gestures. Little Joanna looked almost solemn, as if hearing bad news. The other woman, Monique Bonnet, was nodding in rhythm to Ilona's gesticulations.

Bonnet was tiny, even shorter than Joanna, but as plump as a Provençal matron. She was older than the other two, her thick dark hair speckled with gray, laughter wrinkles at the corners of her eyes. Her face was round, with ruddy cheeks that dimpled when she smiled. She must have been a beauty when she was younger, Jamie thought. And thinner.

Liquor was strictly off-limits, as far as the mission regulations went. So naturally every member of the expedition had carried aboard a bottle or two among his or her personal baggage. Jamie, inserted at the last minute and flown unexpectedly from his quarters in Houston to the launching center in Florida, never had a moment to buy, borrow, or steal so much as a can of beer.

Vosnesensky rapped his knuckles on the table, making it rattle dangerously.

"I want to make it clear," he said, almost in a growl, "that this is the last occasion on which liquor will be tolerated."

Groans and grumbles down the table.

"We have much work to do and little time to do it. Liquor is strictly forbidden; it could be a safety hazard."

Vosnesensky was simply stating the mission rules, but no one felt happy about it.

"However, since this is the first night here on Mars for all twelve of us," he said, pushing himself to his feet, "I wish to propose a toast."

Relieved sighs and grins broke out around the table. Seven men and the three women raised glasses of whiskey, vodka, brandy, wine, and sake. Jamie lifted his water glass and noticed that whatever Vosnesensky had in his plastic glass was also clear.

"We have been through a difficult time," Vosnesensky said, his heavy features quite serious. With a glance at Ilona Malater he went on, "Nine months aboard the spacecraft created certain tensions, certain problems."

"At least no one got pregnant," Tony Reed whispered loud enough to generate a few giggles.

Vosnesensky glared at him. "Tomorrow our true work begins: the conquest of Mars."

Conquest? Jamie's mind flashed pictures of the white man's conquest of America. That's not what we're here for. Nobody's going to conquer Mars.

"The next seven weeks will test us," Vosnesensky was going on. "Make no mistake about it. Each of us will be tested to his limit. Or hers. Mars will test us all."

"Our arms are getting tired, Mikhail Andreivitch," quipped Mironov, grinning. "Is this a toast or a speech?"

Vosnesensky did not smile. Quite seriously he raised his glass even higher and said, "May each of us find on Mars what we are looking for."

"*Zah vahsheh zdahrovyeh!*" exclaimed Mironov.

"*Zdahrovyeh*," Vosnesensky echoed.

They all drank. Jamie's water tasted flat, sterile.

"I wonder just what it is that each of us is looking for," Tony Reed called from his end of the table.

"Good question," said Abell, the American astronaut, with a grin that creased his face from chin to hairline. He reminded Jamie of a frog: bulging eyes, round cheeks, and a wide grinning slit of a mouth. "Me, I'd like to find some beautiful Martian women who've been without men for a thousand years or so."

A few tolerant chuckles from the scientists. Ilona cast him a sultry look.

"No, seriously," Reed said. "I'm curious to know what each of us hopes to find on Mars."

Jamie grumbled to himself, Tony's taking his assignment as team psychologist too seriously.

"For myself," said Vosnesensky, placing a stubby-fingered hand against his broad chest, "I wish only that we can work in harmony and no one becomes injured so we all return to our homes in happiness."

Mironov added in a stage whisper, "And that you could weigh only thirty kilos even back on Earth!"

"I'm looking forward to flying the soarplane," said Pete Connors in his resonant caramel voice.

"I desire very much to see the great Olympus Mons with my very own eyes," said Ravavishnu Patel, the Indian geologist.

"Mount Olympus, the largest volcano in the solar system," agreed the Egyptian geophysicist, Abdul al-Naguib.

"I want to prove that a permafrost ocean exists beneath the surface of the ground," Ilona Malater said. "Theory predicts it does, but I want to find it for myself and map its extent."

"Life."

Joanna Brumado spoke the one word, and all other talk stopped. Everyone turned toward her. She looked embarrassed. Her heart-shaped face colored slightly.

"Of course life," said Monique Bonnet, sitting next to her. "Joanna is right. The most astounding thing we could find on this world would be life."

No, Jamie corrected silently. The most astounding thing we could find would be *intelligent* life. Or its remains.

LIFE

The Old Ones taught that miracles are not rare. The world is filled with them.

Life is a miracle so commonplace that it can arise wherever there is water and sunlight. Even in the desert life abounds, as long as there is a little water and sunlight.

Did life arise on the red world? Did Man Maker and the other gods of creation start their work there? If so, life may have begun there earlier than on the blue world, because the rocks of the red world's crust cooled sooner than those of the larger, warmer blue world. In the shallow seas that dotted the red world's surface, life could have taken shape and begun to reproduce itself. It would have been difficult, because the red world was always colder than the blue. Often the waters would have frozen and the living things in them would have died or gone into a long hibernation that was the next thing to death. Still, life is persistent.

The Old Ones taught that this blue world of ours is not the first world in which The People have lived. Our songs of the beginning tell how First Man and First Woman struggled upward from one world to another, from a world of darkness and cold to a red world where Water Monster tried to drown them in a raging flood because Coyote had stolen his baby. Finally they climbed to the fourth world and came out into the golden sunlight here at the center of the universe, among the mountains that mark the four corners of existence.

First Man and First Woman did not come alone. They brought the plants and animals and all good things with them. They were also accompanied by Coyote, the Trickster. Coyote, the force of chaos. Coyote, who always worked to ruin The People's search for order and harmony and beauty.

THE PROCESS OF DECISION

1

Jamie was in Galveston when the long-awaited, long-feared final decision was unmade.

Ever since he had joined the Mars Project, Houston had been as much of a home as he could claim. Although he had spent months on end in training sites all across the globe, nearly half a year in Antarctica, week after week in Florida, and even weeks aboard space stations orbiting the Earth, always he returned to Houston. And Edith.

Edie Elgin was the co-anchor of the seven and eleven o'clock news at KHTV in Houston. She had interviewed Jamie when he had first arrived at the Johnson Space Center. A dinner invitation turned into a relationship that both of them knew was temporary, at best.

"I'm not even thinking about marriage," Edith often told him. "Not until I get to New York and a job with one of the networks. Maybe not even then."

"I don't know where I'll be a year from now," Jamie said to her regularly. "If I don't make the Mars team I'll probably head back to California for a teaching job."

"No commitments," she would say.

"Couldn't make any even if we wanted to," he would reply.

Yet whenever he returned to Houston he returned to her. And although she never spoke of how she spent the time while he was away, she seemed always glad to see Jamie. They made a strange couple: the dark, taciturn, stocky half-Navaho and the blonde, vivacious, ever-smiling TV anchorwoman. She was recognized wherever they went, of course. And although she was known as Edie to everyone who watched television, to Jamie she was always Edith.

She claimed to be a natural blonde and one hundred percent

Texan, a cheerleader in high school, a beauty pageant queen at Texas A&M, where she had studied electronic journalism. She could not spell very well, but she could smile with perfect teeth even while announcing a disastrous earthquake or an airliner crash. There was a crafty brain behind the pretty smile; she knew opportunity when it arrived and she was wise enough never to let down her guard in the company of anyone even remotely connected with the news industry. With Jamie, though, she could be serious and tell him about her plans for her career. He could relax with her and forget about training and Mars and the men who stood between him and the assignment he cherished.

Jamie had just returned from three weeks aboard the *Mir 5* space station, working with Father DiNardo on the rock samples returned from Mars by the unmanned ships that had been landed on the red planet.

He had thought that DiNardo had been given the power to make the final decision as to who would back him up on the Mars mission. The Jesuit disabused him of that notion just before he had to board the shuttle that would return him to Florida.

DiNardo had asked him to come to the geology lab before he boarded the shuttle. The priest was waiting for him there, looking solemn, hanging weightlessly a few inches above the metal grillwork of the laboratory floor, his face so puffed up from the fluid shift that happens in near-zero gravity that he looked more like an Indian than Jamie himself. DiNardo shaved his balding scalp completely, yet there was a dark stubble across his jutting chin.

"The board of selection has made its decision," DiNardo said softly, the faintest hint of Italian vowels at the end of each word. From the tone of the man's voice Jamie knew the news was bad.

The two of them were alone in the space station's geology lab, hovering weightlessly in the apelike half-crouching position the human body normally assumes in microgravity. A carefully sealed glass-walled cabinet behind DiNardo held row upon row of reddish soil samples and small pink rocks from the surface of Mars. Jamie felt his stomach sinking.

"I am afraid," DiNardo went on gently, "that the choice has gone to Professor Hoffman."

Jamie heard himself ask, "And you concur?" His voice sounded harsh, tense, like a bowstring about to snap.

"I will not oppose the decision." DiNardo made a sad little smile.

"Personally, I would rather have you travel with me. I think we would get along much better. But the selection board must consider politics and many other factors. For what it is worth, the decision was the most difficult choice they had to make."

"And it's final."

"I am afraid that it is. Professor Hoffman will be the number-two geologist on the mission. He will remain in the spacecraft in orbit about Mars and I will go down to the surface."

Fuck the two of you, Jamie wanted to say. Instead he merely nodded, lips clamped together so hard that an hour later he could still feel the imprint of his teeth on them.

From Cape Canaveral Jamie had flown immediately to Houston, and from there he and Edith had driven to Galveston in her new, sleek, dark-green Jaguar. In her form-hugging jeans, tightly cuffed silk blouse, and racing-style sunglasses she looked like a movie star, especially with her blonde hair blowing in the breeze.

"It's a Ford Jaguar," she shouted over the rushing wind and the growl of traffic, trying to cheer his dark mood. "Got a Mercury six and transmission under the hood. Looks like a Jag, but I don't need an English mechanic riding in the backseat all the time!"

As they roared along Interstate 45 Jamie said barely a word. The Friday afternoon traffic was heavy, but Edith weaved through the trucks and the other weekenders as if the highway patrol would never even try to stop her. Jamie knew that this was the last weekend he and Edith would spend together. On Monday he would start packing his things. He wanted to be away from Houston, away from the space center, away from everything connected with the Mars mission. As far away as possible.

Where? Back to the university at Albuquerque? Back to teaching geology to students who would spend their lives searching for oil? Back to spending summers picking at ancient meteor craters while others were exploring Mars? Back to Berkeley and his parents?

Their hotel room in Galveston was high up in one of the towers that overlooked the Gulf of Mexico.

"It's a beautiful view, isn't it?" Edith said, reaching one arm around Jamie's waist as they stood together by the sliding glass doors that opened onto a narrow patio. She nestled her head against his shoulder.

"Until the next hurricane," Jamie said.

"Yeah. We cover the storm damage every year, and every year they build more of these high-rises."

Jamie turned back to the bed and began to pull the shaving kit from his dark-blue nylon travel bag.

"Which side of the closet do you want?" Edith asked.

"Doesn't matter."

"You're really down, huh?"

"Down for the count," Jamie said, taking the kit to the bathroom and placing it on the shelf above the sink without bothering to open it up.

She was at the doorway, more serious than he had ever known her to be.

"We got a release from the Mars program office that they'll announce the departure date Monday morning at a press conference in Geneva."

Jamie nodded. "And the crew list."

"You won't be going."

"I won't be going to Mars," he said.

Edith forced a shaky smile. "Well . . . you been saying all along that you didn't think they'd pick you."

"Now I know for certain."

The smile faded. "Now we both know."

They'll go to Mars without me and I'll disappear into oblivion, he said to himself, unable to speak the words aloud. I'll become just another university geologist, going nowhere, accomplishing nothing. He looked at his face in the mirror over the sink: anger smoldered in his dark eyes. All you need is some war paint, he said to the somber image.

Edith knew him well enough to realize he had no more words for her. She turned and went back to the sliding patio doors, tugged one open. It stuck halfway along its track.

"Damned rust," she muttered, slipping through the narrow opening and out onto the patio. "Air's pure salt out here."

Jamie crossed the carpeted room and leaned against the reluctant door, then pushed with all his strength with both hands, suddenly furious. It screeched and popped off its track as it slid all the way back. Jamie snorted and glared at it hanging lopsided from its top rollers. Then he stepped through onto the patio. Going out of the air-conditioned room was like going from ice cream to hot soup. He felt perspiration instantly dampening his armpits.

Edith ignored his explosion of brute force. "Looks pretty," she said, gazing out at the tranquil Gulf. "Between hurricanes, that is."

Grasping the railing beside her with both hands, Jamie tried to force his mind away from the pain and anger. "Ever seen the Pacific?"

"Just on tapes."

"The surf is incredible. This is a milk pond by comparison."

"You ever surf?"

"Not really," he said. "Never had the time for it."

"I like sailing. Got a friend with a Hobie Cat. They're fun."

Jamie took a deep breath of salt air. "The first time I saw the ocean, I must have been four, five years old. My parents had just moved to Berkeley from New Mexico and I thought the Bay was all the water in the world. Then they took me to the beach and I saw the Pacific. Damned breakers scared the shit out of me."

"What're y'all gonna do now?" Edith asked, forgetting her diction lessons.

Jamie kept his eyes on the calm water, the ripples of waves riding across the pastel green-blue water to foam briefly against the sand beach. From this height he could barely hear the hiss of the gentle surf.

"Look for a job, I guess."

"At the university or in private industry?"

"What the hell could I do in private industry that a kid ten years younger can't?" he snapped, then immediately regretted it. More calmly, "University. But not here. I don't want to be this close to the Mars mission. Not now."

"Up in Austin . . . ?"

"Maybe. California might be better. More likely Albuquerque." He turned to her. "I don't know. It's too soon."

"But you're gonna be leaving."

"Yes. I think so."

He realized that she was trying to hide the pain that she felt. Pulling her to him, Jamie held her tightly. Edith did not cry, but he could feel the tension constricting her body. He wished she would cry. He wished he could himself.

It was two in the morning when the phone call came.

The buzz of the phone jangled Jamie awake instantly, but for several blurry moments he did not know where he was. The phone shrilled again, insistently. He realized Edith was beside him, stirring now, mumbling into her pillow.

His eyes adjusting to the glow of the digital clock on the dresser, Jamie reached across her naked body and lifted the phone from its base.

"Hello."

"James Waterman?"

"Who wants to know?"

"Come now, Jamie, this is Antony Reed, in Star City. Do you have any idea how long it's taken me to track you down?"

"Christ, it's two in the morning here. What the hell do you want?"

"DiNardo's in hospital. A gall bladder attack. He'll need surgery."

Jamie sat up rigidly in the bed.

"What's happening?" Edith asked, awake now.

"Did you hear me?" Reed asked. It was the first time that Jamie had ever heard the Englishman sound excited.

"Yes."

"There's a godawful row going on upstairs. Brumado's flying in from the States, from what I hear. He wants to meet with the selection board and Dr. Li."

"So Hoffman's moved up to number one and I'll be his backup?" Jamie asked, surprised at the tremor in his voice.

"Can't be certain of anything right now," Reed answered. "The entire question is going to be reviewed this afternoon or Sunday."

"What is it?" Edith was excited now too. "Have they changed their minds?"

"Whatever you do," Reed was saying, "stay in close touch with Houston. You may have to fly out here on Monday. Or perhaps go straight up to the space station. We were supposed to start shipping up there tomorrow, but everything's been put on hold temporarily."

"Okay," Jamie said shakily. "Thanks for letting me know."

"Nothing to it, old boy. Most of us would much rather have you aboard than that prig Hoffman."

"Thanks."

"Good luck!" The line clicked dead.

"What is it?" Edith asked, sitting up beside him.

Jamie realized his hands were trembling. "Father DiNardo's been taken sick. He's going into surgery. It looks like I'll be going on the mission after all."

"Hot spit!" Edith dove out of the bed and began rummaging in her shoulder bag resting on the chair next to the curtained window. Jamie watched her slim naked figure as she bent over the bag, muttering to herself.

"Hah! Got it!"

She bounced back into the bed with a palm-sized tape recorder in her hand.

"What the hell?" Jamie wondered.

"This is an on-the-scene interview with geologist James Fox Waterman, who has just been informed that he has been selected to be on the team that flies to the planet Mars two months from now."

He laughed, but apparently Edith was completely serious.

"Dr. Waterman, how do you feel about being selected to be part of the first human expedition to the planet Mars?"

Jamie blurted, "Horny. Very horny."

He took the tape recorder from her hand and placed it on the night table beside her. The tape ran out long before they finished making love.

2

As the cab pulled up to the curb in front of his parents' home Jamie realized for the first time how undistinguished the house was. Genteel poverty was the facade for university professors, even those who had inherited old money.

He had hitched a ride in the backseat of a T-18 jet with one of the NASA astronauts who was dashing home to the Bay area for a quick weekend. Now, as he paid the cab driver and got out onto the sidewalk, he felt almost as if he had stepped onto a movie set. Middle-class Americana. A quiet suburban street. Unpretentious little bungalows. Kids on bicycles. Lawn sprinklers cranking back and forth.

He went up the walk, nylon travel bag in one hand, feeling a little unreal. How would Norman Rockwell paint this scene? Hello, Mom, just dropped in for a few hours to tell you that I'm off to Mars.

Before he could reach the front door his mother was there waiting for him, a smile on her lips and the beginnings of tears in her eyes.

Lucille Monroe Waterman was a small woman, pert and beautiful, who had been born to the considerable wealth of an old New England family that dated itself back to the *Mayflower*. The first time her family had allowed her to venture west of the Hudson River was the summer she had spent on a dude ranch in the mountains of northern New Mexico. There she had met Jerome Waterman, a young Navaho fiercely intent on becoming a teacher of history. "Real history," Jerry Waterman told her. "The actual facts about the Native Americans and what the European invaders did to them."

They fell hopelessly, passionately in love with each other. So much so that Lucille, who had not given much thought to a career, entered the academic life too. So much so that they were married despite her parents' obvious misgivings.

Jerry Waterman wrote his history of the Native Americans and it was eventually adopted as the definitive text by universities all across the nation. Success, marriage, the comfort of a dependable income, the insulated life of academia—all these mellowed him to the point where Lucille's family could almost accept him as their daughter's husband. And Jerry Waterman found that he wanted to be accepted. It was important to Lucille. It became important to him.

Lucille won her doctorate in English literature and then they had a baby: James Fox Waterman, the "Fox" being an ancient family name from Lucille's mother's side of the clan. Although he could not know it, Jamie was the grandson that brought about the true reconciliation of the New Englanders and their Navaho son-in-law.

Lucille clung to Jamie, there in the doorway of their Berkeley home, as if she wanted never to let him go. Then his father appeared, smiling calmly from behind his pipe.

No one would recognize Professor Jerome Waterman as the fiery young champion of Native American history. His hair was iron-gray and thinning so much that he combed it forward to cover his high forehead. His face showed what Jamie might be like in thirty years, fleshy, puffy from a sedentary life. Dark-rimmed glasses. Open-necked sports shirt with its manufacturer's logo embroidered discreetly on the chest. There was no more fire in Jerry Waterman's dark eyes. It had been a long time since he had been in a fight more strenuous than arguing with a dean over class size. He had won his youthful battles and over the years had become more like his former enemies than he could possibly admit to himself.

"I can only stay overnight" were the first words Jamie actually spoke to his parents.

"On the phone you said they were sending you to Mars?" His mother looked more frightened than proud.

"I think so. It looks that way."

"When will you know for sure?" his father asked.

They walked him into the book-lined library, where the bright sunshine was blocked from the window by a tall azalea bush that threatened to undermine the house's foundation one day.

"Monday, I guess. I won't have a chance to get away once they make their final decision."

The house was much as Jamie remembered it: comfortable, disordered, books and journals scattered everywhere, upholstered chairs and chintz-covered sofas that bore the imprint of his mother's and his father's bodies. Mama Bear has her chair and Papa Bear has his, Jamie remembered from childhood.

He sat on the edge of the library sofa, tense and nervous. Mama and Papa took their individual chairs, facing him.

"You really want to go?" his mother asked for the thousandth time in the past four years.

Jamie nodded.

"I thought that priest was the one they picked," said his father.

"He came down with a gall bladder attack. Too much wine, I guess."

None of them so much as smiled.

The afternoon and evening inched along. Jamie could see that his mother did not want him to go, that she was desperately trying to think of some argument, some reason that would keep him safely near her. His father seemed bemused by the whole matter; pleased that his son was at last finding some measure of success, but uncertain about the wisdom of the entire effort.

Over dinner his father said, "I've never been able to satisfy myself that Mars is worth all the money we're spending on it."

Jamie felt a wave of relief wash through him. It was easier to debate national policy than to watch his mother struggling to hold back tears.

They went through all the arguments, pro and con, that they had disputed back and forth with his every visit home. Without rancor. Without polemics. Without raising their voices or stirring their blood. Like a classroom exercise. As he discussed the question of Mars in calm debater's logic Jamie realized that his father had become the compleat academic: nothing really touched him anymore; he saw everything in the abstract; not even the obvious pain of his wife, sitting across the table three feet from him, could shake him out of the comfortable cocoon he had woven around himself.

My god, Jamie thought, Dad's gotten *old*. Bloodless and old. Is that the way I'm going to be?

It was not until long after dinner was finished, as he started upstairs toward the bedroom he had slept in since childhood, that his mother asked:

"Must you leave tomorrow? Can't you stay just a little longer?"

I can't take another day of this, Jamie knew. As gently as he could he told his mother, "I've got to be at the space center first thing Monday morning."

"But you don't have to leave so soon, do you?"

He hesitated. "I want to see grandfather Al."

"Oh." The one syllable carried a lifetime of grief and distaste.

His father overheard them and came into the hallway. "You'd rather be with your grandfather than with your mother?" he asked sharply.

Jamie was surprised at that; almost glad of it.

"He's the only grandparent I've got left. It doesn't seem right to go without saying good-bye to him."

Jerome Waterman huffed, but said nothing more.

3

Jamie had to be satisfied with a commercial flight from Oakland International to Albuquerque. Al was waiting for him at the airport. With a rental helicopter and pilot.

"What's this all about?" Jamie asked as he clambered into the little glass-bubble chopper.

Al was grinning broadly, his leathery face a geological map of happiness.

"You only got a few hours here, right? Thought we'd take a run up to Mesa Verde instead of sittin' around the house."

"Mesa Verde?" Jamie yelled over the whine of the copter engine start-up. "You're not going mystical on me, are you?"

Al laughed. "Maybe. We'll see."

The first snow of the season was already on the mountains and Jamie felt cold in his lightweight windbreaker as he and Al trekked through the well-marked trail from the helicopter landing pad to the rim of the canyon.

"I should have brought a couple of coats," Al muttered. He was in a worn old denim jacket and jeans.

"It's okay. The sun's warming things up."

The sky was cloudless blue. Big dollops of wet snow were melting out of the ponderosas and piñons, dropping like scoops of ice cream to splatter on the gravel trail. Jamie's high-tech Reeboks were getting soaked. Al wore his usual boots, tough and comfortable. And his drooping, broad-brimmed hat protected his head from the falling snow. Jamie, bareheaded, had to keep an eye on the trees and dodge the falls.

The air was thin up this high. Jamie heard his grandfather wheezing. He had seen the Anasazi ruins before, of course, but for some reason Al wanted him to see them once again before he took off for another world.

They reached the crest of the high ridge, walked along the edge for a few silent, puffing minutes, then stepped out from behind a stand of pine.

Across a bend in the ridge, a hundred feet down, the old ruins huddled in a cleft of the ancient solid stone. Even to this day the adobe brick dwellings were protected from the wind and snow by the overhanging rock. Reddish brown sandstone, Jamie knew. Almost the same color as Mars.

"Your ancestors built that village five hundred years before Columbus was born," Al said quietly.

"I know," said Jamie.

"Son, when you go to Mars, you'll be taking them with you. The Old Ones. They're in your blood."

Jamie smiled at his grandfather. "By god, Al, you are going mystical."

His grandfather's face was entirely serious. "It's important for a man to know who he is. You can't be in balance without that. You can't know where you're heading for if you don't know where you've come from."

"I understand, Grandfather."

"Your father . . . " Al hesitated. The old man had never called him his son as long as Jamie could remember. "Your father turned his back on all this. He wanted to be accepted by the whites so badly! He turned himself into an Anglo. I don't blame him. It's my own fault, I guess. I didn't teach him half of what I've taught you, Jamie. I was too busy then, with the store and all. I didn't take the time to raise him like I should have."

"It's not your fault, Al."

"I think it is. I wasn't as good a father to him as I've been a grandfather to you. I can see why he felt he had to take the path he did. But I want you to remember who you are, son. You'll be traveling where no one has gone before. You'll be facing dangers no one's ever dealt with. It'll go better for you if you remember all this, keep it in your mind always."

Looking out on the ancient adobe village, the square dwellings with their empty windows, the brick-walled circles of kivas where the men held their religious ceremonies in the heady smoke of precious tobacco, Jamie nodded to his grandfather.

"I knew you would go to Mars," Al said, his voice almost cracking. "Never had the slightest doubt that you'd go."

"I'll remember this," Jamie said. "I'll keep it in my heart."

Al reached into the pocket of his denim jacket. "Here," he said. "A reminder."

Jamie saw that his grandfather was offering him a carved piece of jet-black obsidian in the totem shape of a crouching bear. A tiny turquoise arrowhead was tied to its back with a leather thong, with a wisp of a white feather tucked atop it.

A fetish, Jamie realized. A protective piece of Navaho magic.

"That's an eagle feather," Al said, unable to suppress his shop-keeper's pride.

Jamie took the fetish. It was small in his palm, but weighty, solid, strong.

"I'll keep this with me every minute, Grandfather."

Al grinned, almost embarrassed. "Go with beauty, son."

4

Jamie made it back to Houston Sunday night and crawled into his apartment bed emotionally exhausted. While he slept his future was decided, more than ten thousand kilometers away, in Star City.

Alberto Brumado dozed in the limousine that had met his plane on its arrival in Moscow. Alone in the spacious backseat, jet-lagged by his supersonic flight from Washington, Brumado paid no attention to the lines of tall apartment blocks and low gray clouds that stretched eastward toward the true steppe country of Russia. For more than an hour the car sped along the wide concrete highway; traffic thinned away until there was little more than the occasional massive tractor-trailer rig, diesel engine belching sooty exhaust plumes into the air.

Past Kaliningrad they drove, past woods and lakes and over a railroad crossing, heading toward Star City.

The actual name of the community is Zvyozdniy Gorodok: literally, "Starry Town." But ever since the first cooperative Soviet-American space venture, the Apollo-Soyuz mission of 1975, a slight misinterpretation by a NASA translator turned it into Star City, and so it has been called by the western media ever since.

Once it had been a town, nothing more than a handful of apartment blocks and a dozen big concrete buildings that housed the cosmonaut training center, deliberately placed in the barren emptiness between a thick pine forest and a scattering of small lakes. Now, as Alberto Brumado's car drove past the guard post at the perimeter fence, it had grown into a sizable city. Scientists and astronauts from all over the world trained here for Mars. The world's media focused their attention here. A true city had grown around the clear blue lakes, homes for workers who served the training center, shops and open-air markets and entertainment complexes. Close by the main gate of the training center itself stood the Space Museum, a gracefully sweeping concrete form that captured the spirit of flight.

Brumado had learned the traveler's secret years earlier: sleep whenever you can. Now, as the limousine pulled up to the main office building at the training center, he roused himself from his nap, ready to step out and face his responsibilities, alert if not actually refreshed.

Dr. Li Chengdu came almost loping down the front steps of the building on his long legs to greet Brumado and guide him to the office that the Russians had set aside for his use. Dr. Li was wearing an expensive-looking running suit of maroon and slate gray. The white pinstripe down the legs made him look even taller and leaner than usual. His face seemed strained, grayish, almost ill. Perhaps it's that maroon top, Brumado thought. It's not good for his coloring. He himself was still in his Washington clothes: a dark blue business suit. He had removed the tie and stuffed it into his jacket pocket hours earlier. The shirt was limp and wrinkled from his long trip.

The office to which Li escorted him was big enough to contain a broad polished conference table, Brumado saw. Good. And its own lavatory. Even better. The second rule of the inveterate traveler: never pass a toilet without using it.

Three minutes later, his bladder emptied, his face washed, and his hair freshly combed, Brumado pulled out a chair from the middle of the conference table, ignoring the massive desk and the high-backed swivel chair behind it. Brumado felt he was here to help solve a sudden problem, not to impress others with the trappings of power.

Besides, he told himself, I have no real power here, no authority over these men and women. My strength lies in moral persuasion, nothing more.

Dr. Li was pacing the office from the draped windows to the head of the conference table and back again, more nervous than Brumado had ever seen him.

"Please sit here next to me," Brumado said mildly. "It hurts my neck to look up at you."

Li's thin ascetic face looked startled momentarily, then apologetic. He took the chair next to Brumado's.

"You seem very upset," Brumado said. "What is wrong?"

Li drummed his long fingers on the tabletop before answering. "We seem to have a virtual mutiny on our hands. And your daughter, sir, is apparently the ringleader."

"Joanna?"

"Once it became clear that DiNardo could not make the mission, your daughter—and others—demanded that Professor Hoffman be replaced as well."

Brumado felt confused. Joanna would never do such a thing. Never!

"I don't understand," he said.

"Your daughter and several other scientists here have refused to go on the mission if Hoffman is included. It is mutiny, pure and simple."

"Mutiny," Brumado echoed, feeling dull, stupid, as if his brain could not grasp the meaning of Li's words.

"We cannot announce the final selections for the mission, we cannot begin transporting the scientific staff to the assembly station in orbit, if they refuse to go." Li's voice was high and strained, nearly cracking.

Brumado had never seen Li like this, close to panic.

"What can we do?" Li asked, raising his hands in a gesture of helplessness. "We cannot tell Professor Hoffman that he has been removed from flight status because a cabal of his fellow scientists don't like him! What can we do?"

Brumado took in a deep breath, unconsciously trying to calm Li by calming himself. "I think the first thing I should do is speak to my daughter."

"Yes," Li said. "Certainly."

He sprang up from the chair, all six and a half feet of him, and nearly sprinted to the desk where the phone was. Brumado wormed out of his jacket and tossed it onto another chair. He was rolling up his shirtsleeves when Joanna stepped into the office. She too was wearing a softly comfortable running suit, butter yellow and muted orange. Brumado wondered idly what the Russians thought about this craze for American fashion.

"I will leave the two of you alone," said Li softly, nearly whispering. He scurried from the room like a wisp of smoke wafted away on a strong breeze.

Joanna came over to her father, bussed him on both cheeks, and sat in the chair that Li had used earlier.

Brumado studied her face. She looked serious, but not upset. More determined than fearful.

"Dr. Li tells me you are leading a mutiny among the scientists." Brumado found himself smiling at her as he said it. Not only did he find it difficult to believe such an outrageous story, but even if it were true he could not be angry with his lovely daughter.

"We took a vote last night," Joanna said in their native Brazilian Portuguese. "Out of the sixteen scientists scheduled to fly the mission, eleven will not go if Hoffman is included."

Brumado brushed his upper lip with a fingertip, a throwback to his youth when he had sported a luxuriant moustache.

"The sixteen includes Hoffman himself. Did he vote?"

Joanna laughed. "No. Of course not. We did not ask him."

"Why?" her father asked. "What is the reason for this?"

She made a small sigh. "None of us really likes Hoffman. He is a very difficult personality. We feel that it will be impossible to work with him under the very close conditions of the mission."

"But why wait until now? Why didn't you say something sooner?"

"We thought that Father DiNardo could keep Hoffman under control. Hoffman admired DiNardo, looked up to him. But the thought of having Hoffman without Father DiNardo—having him as the prime geologist for the mission—we realized we could not stand that. He would be insufferable. Unbearable."

Brumado said nothing, thinking: I'm not going into space with them. I'm not going to be cooped up inside a spacecraft for nearly two years with someone I can't stand.

"Besides," his daugher went on, "Hoffman was chosen mainly for political reasons. You know that."

"He is an excellent geologist," Brumado replied absently, thinking now about the difficulties he was asking his daughter to face. Two years in space. The stresses. The dangers.

"There are other geologists who have gone through training with us," Joanna said, leaning slightly closer to her father. "O'Hara is from Australia. He can move up. And there is that Navaho *mestizo*, Waterman."

Brumado's attention suddenly focused on his daughter's eyes. "The man who stayed on at McMurdo to help your group through your Antarctic training."

"And the following groups. Yes, him."

"And O'Hara."

"Waterman has done extensive work on meteor impacts. He even found a Martian meteorite in Antarctica, although Hoffman took the credit for it."

"Is he the man you want?"

She pulled back again. "I think he is the best-qualified person, isn't he? And everyone seemed to get along with him very well."

"But he's an American," Brumado muttered. "The politicians don't want more Americans than Russians. Or vice versa."

"He's an American *Indian*, Papa. It's not really the same thing. And O'Hara will make the Australians happy."

"The politicians wanted Hoffman to help represent Europe."

"We already have a Greek, a Pole, and a German to represent Europe. As well as an Englishman. If Hoffman goes on the mission there will be trouble," Joanna said firmly. "His psychological profile is awful! We have tried to work with him, Papa. He is simply unbearable!"

"So you took a vote."

"Yes. We have decided. If Hoffman is chosen there are at least eleven of us who will resign from the program immediately."

Again Brumado fell silent. He did not know what to say, how to handle this situation.

"Ask Antony Reed," Joanna suggested. "He has had more training in psychology than any of the others selected for the mission. It was his idea to take the vote."

"Was it?"

"Yes! I didn't do all this by myself, Papa. Most of the others cannot stand Hoffman."

Brumado got up slowly and went to the desk. Picking up the telephone, he asked the man who answered to find Dr. Reed. The Englishman opened the office door before Brumado could return to the conference table. My god, he thought, they must all be sitting in the outer office. I wonder if Hoffman is there too.

Reed seemed faintly amused by it all.

"None of us can get along with Hoffman," he said, smiling slightly as he sat relaxed in a chair across the table from Brumado and his daughter. "Frankly, I think bringing him along to Mars would be a disaster. Always have."

"But he passed all the psychological tests."

Reed arched an eyebrow. "So would a properly motivated chimpanzee. But you wouldn't want to live in the same cage with him, would you?"

"You've all been filling out cross-evaluation reports for the past two years!" Brumado heard his own voice rising with more than a hint of anger in it. He forced it down. "I admit that the reports written about Professor Hoffman have not been glowing, but there has been no hint that he was so disliked."

"I can tell you about those evaluation reports," Reed said, almost smirking. "No one ever expressed their true feelings in the reports. Not in writing. There is enormous psychological pressure to put a good face on everything. Every one of us realized straight from the outset that those reports would be a reflection on the person who wrote them as much as on the person they were writing about."

Brumado thought, We should have realized that from the beginning. These are very bright men and women, bright enough to see all the possibilities.

Reed continued, "To borrow a phrase from Scotland Yard, we understood that anything we wrote in those evaluation forms might be taken down in evidence and used against us."

With a shake of his head, Brumado said, "I still can't understand why you waited until this very last moment to bring your opposition out into the open."

"Two reasons, actually," said Reed. "First, we all expected that DiNardo could keep Hoffman under control. Our good priest seemed to have a calming effect on the Austrian, rather like old Hindenburg had on Hitler."

Joanna barely suppressed a giggle.

"Second, I suppose that none of us actually faced up to the awful possibility of spending nearly two years living cheek-by-jowl with Hoffman until this very weekend. With the final decisions made and DiNardo packing off to hospital—well, I suppose it suddenly dawned on us that Hoffman simply wouldn't do."

"How do I tell this to Professor Hoffman?" Brumado asked softly.

"Oh, I'd be willing to tackle that chore," Reed said at once. "I'd be almost happy to do it."

Brumado shook his head sadly. "No. It is not your responsibility."

He dismissed Reed and asked Dr. Li to come back into the office.

With Joanna still sitting beside him, Brumado said wearily, "I suppose there is no way around it. Professor Hoffman will have to be told."

Li seemed to have calmed down considerably. His mask of impassivity was in place once more.

"It is my duty to inform him," Li said.

"If you like, I will explain it to him," said Brumado.

With a quick glance at Joanna, Li murmured, "As you wish."

Hoffman looked as tense as a stalking leopard when he entered the office. He stood a moment at the door, eyeing Li, Brumado, and Joanna with unconcealed suspicion. Short, round-shouldered, his round pie face pale with tension. He was wearing a powder-blue cardigan sweater buttoned neatly over a shirt and tie striped yellow and red. His slacks were dark blue, almost black.

"Please," called Brumado from the conference table, "come in and sit down."

Li was standing at the end of the table, as far from the door as possible. Joanna still sat next to her father, turned toward Hoffman so that Brumado could not see her face.

As if stepping through a minefield Hoffman walked across the carpeted floor and pulled out the chair at the head of the table. He sat down.

"We have run into a difficulty," said Brumado, trying to smile disarmingly and not quite making it.

"They are all against me. I know that."

Brumado felt his eyebrows rise. "We must think of the good of the mission. That is our paramount duty."

Hoffman's face twisted. "I was chosen by the selection board. I demand that their choice be upheld!"

"If we uphold that decision the mission will be wrecked. More than half your fellow scientists have refused to go, I am sorry to say."

"More than half!"

Brumado nodded.

"This is an affront to the entire nation of Austria!"

"No," said Dr. Li, from the other end of the table. "It is entirely a personal matter. There are no politics involved here. It is all personalities."

"Yes, I see." Hoffman jabbed a finger toward Joanna. "She wants that American Indian by her side, so *I* am to be thrown off."

Brumado felt his jaw drop open.

"What are you saying?" Joanna demanded.

"I know very well how you and the Apache or Navaho or whatever he is . . . the two of you, at McMurdo . . ."

"Nothing happened between us," Joanna said. Turning to her father, "He's lying. There was nothing . . ."

Brumado raised his hand and she fell silent. To Hoffman he said, "I can see that there are stresses here and strained relationships that could cause a disaster for the mission to Mars."

Hoffman glared, his face reddening.

"I know it is an enormous sacrifice, but I must ask you to resign from the mission," Brumado said.

"Never!" Hoffman snapped. "And if you try to force me out I will tell the world's media that you have thrown me out in favor of your daughter's lover!"

Joanna looked stunned, stricken, speechless.

One of Alberto Brumado's traits was that the angrier he became, the more icy calm. Anger that would drive another man to tantrums or violence merely made him colder, keener, more deliberate.

"Professor Hoffman," he said, clasping his hands prayerfully on the tabletop, "if you ask me to choose between your claim and my daughter's denial, do you think for an instant that I would believe you?"

"They were lovers, I am certain of it."

"You have proven, merely in these few minutes, that it would be disastrous to include you on the Mars team."

"I will appeal to the board of selection! And to the media!"

As patiently as a physician detailing the risks of surgery, Brumado said, "The board of selection cannot and will not override the wishes of the exploration team. And if you go to the media we will be forced to reveal that most of the scientists on the team dislike you so much that they have refused to go on the mission if you are included."

Hoffman's nostrils flared. His eyes glittered with rage.

"Whatever happens, what do you think the effect on your reputation will be? How will your university react to such notoriety? Do you know what it's like to have the media hounding you night and day?"

The Austrian looked away from Brumado, glanced at Li, then turned his gaze toward the ceiling.

"I urge you," Brumado said, reasonably, placatingly, remorselessly, "to tender your resignation. For the good of your career. For the sake of your wife. For the sake of this mission. Please, *please,* do not allow pride or anger to ruin the human race's first attempt to explore the planet Mars. I beg of you."

Li said, "We can see to it that your university gets first priority in analyzing the soil samples and rocks returned from the mission."

"Or, if you wish," Brumado added, "we can help you to get an appointment at the university of your choice, and you can analyze the samples there."

"You are offering me a bribe," Hoffman growled.

"Yes," said Brumado. "Quite frankly, I would offer anything I could to save this mission."

"It is in your hands," Li said in a near whisper.

Brumado saw that the shock on his daughter's face had been replaced by something deeper than anger. Hatred, he realized. He put a calming hand on her shoulder and felt the tension that coiled within her.

Hoffman muttered, "My wife never wanted me to go to Mars."

"You can have a very prestigious position," Dr. Li coaxed. "Leader of the scientific analysis of the Mars samples."

"No announcements have been made about the final team choices," Brumado reminded him. "There will be no embarrassment for you."

Suddenly tears sprang from Hoffman's eyes. "What can I do? You are all against me. Even my wife!"

His head drooped to the tabletop, cradled in his arms, and he began to sob uncontrollably. Brumado turned toward Li, feeling like a torturer, a murderer.

"I will take care of him," Li said softly. "Please go now, both of you. And send in Dr. Reed, if he is still outside. Otherwise, ask the secretary to summon a physician."

Brumado pushed his chair back and slowly rose to his feet. His daughter still showed nothing but contempt for the sobbing man huddled at the head of the table. The mission is saved, Brumado found himself thinking. That is the important thing. The mission will go on despite this poor, wretched man.

5

It was still dark when the phone woke Jamie. He struggled up from a dream of ancient men trying to build a tower on the windswept top of a bare grassless mesa. The bricks kept melting away in the hot sunshine, the tower never rose higher than his own reach.

The phone buzzed insistently. Jamie finally opened his eyes, remembered that he was back in his own apartment again, alone, and groped for the telephone on the bedside table. The digital clock read 6:26 A.M. There was no hint of sunrise through the drawn blinds of the bedroom window.

"Dr. Waterman?" a man's voice asked crisply.

"Right."

"This is an official message from Kaliningrad. I am Yegorov, personnel section."

"Yes?" Jamie was instantly wide-awake.

"You are to report to the Johnson Space Center at eight hundred hours local time and receive your orders for immediate transportation to the Kennedy Space Center in Florida. From there you will board the space shuttle for transport to the orbital assembly facility."

"You mean I'm going to Mars?" Jamie shouted into the phone.

"Oh, yes. Did you not know? You have been selected as geologist on the first landing team. Good luck."

Jamie's first impulse was to give an ear-splitting war whoop. But instead he merely said, "Thank you."

He hung up, suddenly feeling hollow inside, empty, as if he had finally pushed through a door that had been locked against him and found that it opened onto thin air.

He got out of bed, showered, shaved, repacked his well-used travel bag, and drove out to the center. Sure enough, there was a team of grinning men and women at the travel office waiting for him.

"A plane will be ready for you at the airstrip in about half an hour."

"What about my car?" Jamie suddenly realized he had made no plans about the car, the apartment, his furniture. Absurdly, he wondered what to do with his magazine and journal subscriptions.

"We'll take care of all the details. Just sign these forms."

Jamie scribbled his name without reading the forms. Fuck it, he thought. They can have the car and everything else. Won't need it on Mars!

They drove him to the airstrip, the whole roomful of clerks piled into one gray agency station wagon, pressing against Jamie, wanting to be as close as they could be to the man who was going to Mars. Jamie did not mind the closeness, he was thankful for the ride; he did not trust himself to drive. The excitement was getting to him. Mars. Geologist on the first landing team. Mars.

Edith was standing at the entrance to the hangar, in jeans and a light sweater. Obviously not her working clothes. He suddenly felt ashamed for not phoning her.

"How'd you know?" he asked, travel bag in one hand.

She grinned up at him. "I have my sources. I work in news, y'know."

"I . . ." Jamie did not know what to say. The clerks who had driven him here, the airplane mechanics, there were too many people watching them.

Edith's grin turned rueful. "Well, we knew it wouldn't last forever. It was fun, though."

"I think the world of you, Edith."

"Only this world, though. Now you got another one to think about."

"Yes." He laughed, feeling shaky, unsure.

She twined her arms around his neck and kissed him soundly. "Good luck, Jamie. Best luck in two worlds to you."

All he could think to say was, "I'll be back."

She answered, "Sure you will."

S O L 3: MORNING

"Today's the big day, huh?"

Despite the fact that he had been a jet fighter pilot and an astronaut with more than twenty shuttle missions on his record, Pete Connors reminded Jamie of a high school football player moments before the opening kickoff. His dark brown eyes, usually sorrowful, now showed an excitement that most men lose after their teen years, a barely suppressed sense of adventure.

Connors, Jamie, and most of the others were suiting up for their first day of actual scientific work on Mars. Bright sunshine streamed through the clear double-walled plastic of the inflated dome's lower section; the weather forecast was for a typical late-summer day: clear skies, light wind, high temperature climbing up into the sixties after an overnight low of minus one hundred twelve.

"The big day," Jamie agreed, tugging on the sky-blue outer pants of his hard suit.

They dressed in layers. First the form-fitting underwear that was honeycombed with thin, flexible water tubes. The water carried away body heat and kept the wearer at a reasonable temperature inside the heavily insulated hard suit. Next came the fabric coveralls and then the hard suit itself, built to contain a normal terrestrial air pressure of roughly fourteen pounds per square inch inside even if there were nothing but pure vacuum on the other side of its metal and plastic shell.

You leaned against a locker and laboriously tugged the hard-suit pants over your hips. The torso shell stood on a rack so you could duck under it and slide your arms through the sleeves while pushing your head through the bright metal ring of the neck seal. Once inside the suit it was virtually impossible to bend over to pull on the boots. The explorers always dressed in pairs and helped each other with the boots and the backpacks that held the air regenerator, batteries, heater, pumps, and fans of the life-support system.

The first time Jamie had tried to don a hard suit, back on Earth, it had taken more than an hour and seemed like a particularly sophisticated combination of torture and humiliation. The first time he had tried it in Martian gravity, as their spacecraft approached the red planet, things had gone much more easily. Now, however, he was getting accustomed to the light gravity of Mars, and putting on the suit was becoming a chore again.

Eight of the team were preparing to go outside the dome, struggling into their suits like a short-handed football team getting into its padding and uniforms. Or like knights putting on their armor. Jamie wondered if King Arthur's men grumbled and swore while they suited up for battle.

Their dressing area was a line of racks and lockers where the suits were stored, with a pair of long plastic benches laid out in front of them. Built for Martian gravity, the benches looked to Jamie to be too thin to sit on safely, their slim legs too far apart.

But Connors thumped down on one, suit and all, to let Jamie help him into his heavy cleated boots. The others were doing the same, Jamie saw. The benches sagged slightly under the weight, but only slightly.

Boots zippered, Connors got up and stamped his feet on the plastic flooring.

"Good," he said, nodding from inside the suit. "Now let's get yours on."

Jamie sat warily. He noticed Ilona Malater standing beside Joanna, both of them fully suited except for their helmets, talking together softly and earnestly, like school chums or sisters. Biochemist and microbiologist. Jamie thought that of all the scientists brought to Mars the two of them had the most to gain. Or lose. If they found any evidence for life at all they would become international celebrities. But if they failed to find any evidence of life the whole world, perhaps even the scientific community, would always wonder if they had overlooked something.

Was that why the board picked all women for the life sciences? The third member of the bio team was Monique Bonnet, the French geochemist who had taken a cram course in paleontology, just in case they should discover fossils in the red sands or rocks.

The tall Israeli leaned closer to Joanna and said something that made her smile, then cover her mouth with a hand to keep from laughing out loud. They're looking at me, Jamie realized. All the others are already in their suits, waiting to go. I'm the laggard.

He was sitting on the bench, hands clenched on its back edge, with one leg raised up so that his foot rested approximately in Connors's groin. The women find that funny, Jamie thought, his face reddening.

"That's it, friend," said Connors.

Jamie put his leg down and got to his feet. The suit felt cumbersome, stiff. He clomped past the rack where it had hung, now looking like a pathetic dead plastic tree, and took his helmet from the shelf atop it. He started to put it on, more to hide his blushing than anything else.

"Gloves," Connors said. "You don't want to go outside without your gloves, man."

Flustered, Jamie yanked his gloves from the clip on the rack and tucked them into the pouch on his right thigh. He had carefully placed the fetish his grandfather had given him in the left thigh pouch. It was small enough so that no one noticed him doing it. Following Connors and the others, he walked toward the airlock and the next set of racks, where the backpacks waited.

"Got to remember to do everything by the numbers," Connors told him as he helped Jamie into the backpack.

"Right."

"It's not so bad now, everything's new, we're all real aware of what we're doing. But later on, a few days from now or a few weeks, when it's all so routine we don't even think about it—that's when you can make a mistake that'll kill you. Or kill somebody else."

Jamie nodded. He knew that Connors was right. Mission regulations insisted that one astronaut be part of the team whenever anyone went outside the dome. The astronaut served as safety officer; his responsibility was to make certain that all safety rules were strictly followed. His authority was absolute.

"What's your assignment for today?" Jamie asked as he turned to help Connors. "Or are you just going outside to watch us like a safety patrolman?"

Glancing back over his shoulder at Jamie, Connors said, "Sure I got a job. Decontamination and cleanup. I got to make sure all of us clean off whatever dust we pick up on our suits before we come back inside again."

Before Jamie could say anything, Connors added, "You know they'd make the black man into the janitor, don'tcha?"

For a moment Jamie felt startled, upset. Then Connors broke into a toothy grin. "My main task this morning is taping a TV show for the kids back home."

Jamie felt relieved. Connors had never shown the slightest trace of ill humor; he seemed always cheerful, not an angry bone in his body.

"I'm going to be Dr. Science on Mars. Show the local scenery, do a few simple demonstrations of the low air pressure and gravity. For educational TV. I'll be a media star all around the world!"

Laughing, Jamie said, "Good for you."

At last they were all ready. Jamie remembered to pull on his gloves and seal them to the metal cuffs of his suit. The backs of the gloves were ridged like an external skeleton of slim plastic "bones"; the palms and fingertips were clear plastic, hardly thicker than kitchen cling wrap.

Like the others, Jamie took the tools he needed for the morning's work and clipped them to the web belt at his waist. Rock pick. Scoop. Corer. Sample bags. He held in one hand the long telescoping titanium pole that could serve as a lever or extended handle.

"A true spear carrier."

Jamie turned to see Joanna standing beside him, a lovely butterfly trapped inside a glaring orange cocoon. Both her hands were filled with bulky silvered cases.

"You look like an encyclopedia salesman," he said.

She blinked, puzzled.

"Okay, listen up," Connors called to them. "We go through the airlock in Noah's ark fashion: two by two. Visors down, everybody."

Joanna had to put her instrument cases on the floor before she could deal with her helmet visor.

"Check seals and air flow." Connors's melodious voice now came humming through the helmet earphones.

The astronaut personally checked each of the scientists before starting them through the airlock. He and Monique Bonnet went through together, clean white and tricolor blue. Then Patel in his butter-yellow suit with Naguib, kelly green. Ilona and Toshima were next, the green of her suit a shade or two darker than the Egyptian's, while the Japanese meteorologist's softly peach-colored suit bristled with instruments and equipment that dangled from every conceivable type of belt and harness. Jamie thought that Toshima barely was able to raise his booted feet over the lip of the airlock hatch. If he ever trips and falls it'll take two of us to haul him back up to his feet.

Finally it was Jamie's turn, with Joanna. The two Russians, Abell, and Tony Reed remained inside. Mironov and Reed were assigned to monitor the scientists on the surface; the hard suits had instrumentation built into them that automatically reported on body temperature, heart and breathing rate, and oxygen/carbon dioxide ratio inside the suit. Astronaut Abell ran the comm console, maintaining contact with the expedition command in orbit while Vosnesensky watched everybody and everything with the eye of a Russian eagle.

With its visor down Jamie's hard suit served as a shell that protected him from the gaze of others. He was glad of it. He had been embarrassed minutes earlier, and now he felt his stomach fluttering and his palms getting damp. It was not fear so much as anticipation. He was about to step out onto the surface of Mars and begin the work that he had dreamed about for so many years.

Let me go in beauty, he found himself thinking. Let me find harmony and beauty out there.

The noise of the airlock pumps dwindled down until Jamie could only feel their vibration through his boots. The telltale light on the tiny control panel turned red, indicating that the chamber had been pumped down to the ambient pressure outside. He leaned on the control button and the outer hatch sighed open a crack.

Pushing it all the way open, Jamie waited until Joanna went through before he stepped out onto the sandy red, rock-strewn desert to begin his morning's work.

Like almost everything else about the mission, the selection of their landing site had been a political compromise.

The biologists had wanted to land near the polar cap, where beneath the layers of ice and frozen carbon dioxide there might be hidden pools of liquid water—and some form of life. Experiments conducted by unmanned landing probes, starting with the original Viking I and II back in 1976, had shown that there was unusual chemical activity in the Martian soil. Could life exist in that soil, if there was liquid water available?

The geologists could not make up their minds where they wanted to land, with an entire strange new world to sink their picks into. There were massive volcanoes to study, a rift valley longer than the distance from New York to San Francisco, regions where meteoric craters studded the landscape and made it appear as battered as the moon. There were areas that looked as if the ground were underlaid by layers of permafrost, oceans of water frozen underground. There were cliffs and highlands that undoubtedly bore the testimony of billions of years of weathering, and the huge Hellas Basin, a hole nearly a thousand miles wide and three miles deep.

The physicists wanted to study how energetic radiation and sub-atomic particles streaming in from the sun and stars interacted with the thin Martian atmosphere. They also wanted to probe the planet's interior, to determine why Mars had no planetwide magnetic field, as Earth does.

The Russians especially wanted to examine the two tiny moons of Mars and test techniques for extracting rocket propellants from their rocky bodies. The Americans wanted to visit the old *Viking I* lander and place a plaque on it honoring a dead scientist.

The resolution of these conflicting desires was a compromise that pleased no one. The landing site picked was just north of the equator at one hundred degrees west latitude, on the edge of the massive upland rise called the Tharsis Bulge. To the south was the badlands of Noctis Labyrinthus; to the west the mammoth Tharsis shield volcanoes. But their actual landing site was an undistinguished, gently sloping flatland that was considered relatively safe for the landings, about equally distant from the western end of the monumental rift valley known as Valles Marineris and the chain of volcanoes that crowned the Tharsis highlands.

A special team in the orbiting spacecraft would visit Deimos and Phobos, the two moons of Mars, so that the Russians could test their ideas. One of the American astronauts could fly the soarplane to the *Viking I* site, if conditions permitted. The ground team commander, cosmonaut Mikhail Andreivitch Vosnesensky, would decide if the conditions were right. And the flight would take place only if the expedition commander, Dr. Li Chengdu, granted his approval.

The explorers had two sizable ground vehicles for cross-country travel and two gossamer-winged soarplanes for covering longer distances.

Mission plans were specific and detailed. There would be brief excursions to the Noctis Labyrinthus badlands and to one of the Tharsis volcanoes. There would be extensive chemical tests of the Martian soil. There would be drilling to look for underground water. And of course, there would be the ongoing search for any sign that life might have once existed on Mars.

Of all the landing sites in all the regions of all the planet Mars, they had to pick this, Jamie grumbled to himself. Probably the dullest place they could find. A moderately cratered plain on an upland bulge, too far from the interesting line of volcanoes to even glimpse their sixteen-mile-high peaks above the horizon. Some sand dunes off to the west and the same old rocks that lay all across the surface everywhere you looked. The most interesting thing in this region would be the fracture ridges in the wild badlands to the south, but that's nearly three hundred kilometers away.

Ah well, he sighed inwardly. They picked this spot for a safe landing, not for its geological interest. Get to work.

Jamie began by collecting rock samples. The broad open plain on which they had landed was covered with rocks ranging from pebble-sized to boulders as big as a man. Probably thrown up when a good-sized meteoroid hit the ground. Or maybe an eruption of one of the Tharsis volcanoes, although they didn't look as if they had erupted so violently. Jamie's equipment back in the dome would tell him which it was, he felt sure.

"Please be sure to look for any odd color," Joanna's voice came to him through his earphones.

Jamie turned his head and saw only the inside of his helmet. He turned his entire body ninety degrees and there she was in her dayglo suit, a dozen meters away, with Monique Bonnet still close beside her.

"Any color in particular?" he half joked. "We've got a great assortment of reds and pinks here."

"Green would be nice," chirped Monique's lightly pleasant voice.

"Any color at all that seems out of the ordinary," Joanna said. "We are not particular. Not yet."

Just outside the dome's airlock Connors was setting up one of the TV cameras for his educational show. He had a little box of props at his feet. The others were stooped over as far as the suits would allow, intently searching the sandy soil like a squad of groundkeepers looking for litter. Or that famous painting, Jamie said to himself. *The Gleaners*. That's what we're doing, gleaning, trying to find scraps of food for our minds in this frozen desert.

Damned tough to see the ground inside the suit, Jamie grumbled silently. Hardly any flexibility at all. Whoever designed these aluminum cans wasn't thinking about the work we have to do while we're inside them.

Toshima was busily setting up a weather station about twenty meters from the dome, on the side away from the two landing vehicles. His peach-colored suit blended with the rust-red background much better than Jamie would have thought. He's camouflaged. That could be a problem. The suit colors had been picked to stand out clearly against the Martian landscape. Who the hell okayed peach?

Ilona was scooping up the loose sandy soil with a small shovel and pouring it into a box. She, Joanna, and Monique were going to try to raise an assortment of beans, squash, peas, and cucumbers inside the dome, using as much of the native Martian resources as possible—including water, if they found any. One of the goals of their research was to see how the lighter Martian gravity would affect plant growth and size. They expected to bring their small agricultural test facility back to the orbiting spacecraft with them and continue the experiment on the return flight to Earth.

They'll have to bake the oxides out of the soil first, Jamie knew. Otherwise it'll be like planting seeds in bleach.

He turned his attention to the rocks. There was certainly no shortage of them. Big blocks more than a meter wide, plenty of smaller stuff down to the size of pebbles. Many of the rocks looked pitted, etched by weathering. Couldn't be rain, Jamie thought. Hasn't rained here in a billion years, I'd bet. There was frost on winter mornings, though. The rocks expanded in the day's heat, such as it was, and contracted during the bitterly cold nights.

But that wouldn't pit them, Jamie thought. They ought to crack laterally and flake, not get pitted like golf balls. If they were volcanic, then the pitting could be from gases trapped inside the rocks bubbling out and escaping. Could they have been thrown all the way out here from the volcanoes six or seven hundred kilometers away? Or had they been blasted out of the ground by ancient meteor strikes and thrown clear of the atmosphere, reentering afterward like ballistic missiles?

He filled the two sacks he had brought with him with rocks of varying sizes, then realized with a start that he had been out for more than three hours. The sun was almost directly overhead, a strangely tiny and pale imitation of the sun he had known, shining weakly out of the salmon-colored sky.

Turning, he could no longer see the dome, although the blunt cylindrical tops of the two landers were still visible. In the distance he saw one of the unmanned spacecraft, its big cargo hatch gaping open, empty.

The horizon is shorter here, he reminded himself. Turn around, get yourself oriented properly.

"Waterman, you are out of range of the monitor cameras." Vosnesensky's voice sounded more annoyed than worried. "Can you hear me?"

"Yes, loud and clear."

"You are almost at the limit of safe walk-back distance. Come back toward the dome."

Jamie felt almost glad that he was being commanded to come back. It was one thing to be alone back home, in the mountains or desert scrubland. Out here, in this strange world without air to breathe or water to drink, Jamie had been almost frightened.

And yet—it felt good to be alone, away from the others. Solitude had been rare, nonexistent, over the past several years. Jamie stood as tall as his suit would allow and gazed out toward the beckoning horizon, his back to the dome and the others. Even inside the hard shell of his suit he strove to get a feeling for this Martian landscape, a sense of harmony with this strange new world.

Then he saw a patch of green.

T V   S C R I P T

During initial excursion on Sol 3 pilot/astronaut P. Connors will demonstrate on camera the following:

1. Colors of Martian landscape. Pan camera to show ground color and color of sky.

2. A Martian rock. Pick up moderate-sized rock, show it to camera. Explain that red color is from oxidation of iron-based minerals.

3. Temperature. Place thermometer on ground, show temperature (approximately 60–70 degrees Fahrenheit). Lift thermometer to eye level, show mercury dropping to zero or below. Explain that this phenomenon is due to low heat-retention capacity of thin Martian atmosphere.

4. Low air pressure. Open flask of ordinary water and let camera see that it immediately boils, even at temperature of zero or below, because of extremely low air pressure. Explain that same would happen to blood in body if not protected by pressurized hard suit.

5. Low gravity. Drop rock hammer to show that it falls more slowly than similar object on Earth, although faster than on Moon. (Contrast with earlier videotape of Astronaut Connors dropping same rock hammer when on Moon.)

6. Moon of Mars. If visible against daylight sky, show inner moon, Phobos, as it rises in west and crosses Martian sky in four hours. (It is not necessary to show entire four-hour transit. Use telescopic lens to show Phobos changing phase from "new" to "quarter" to "full." Tape can be edited to fit time allowed for broadcast.)

S O L 3: NOON

Jamie's first instinct was to blink and rub his eyes, but his gloved hands bumped into the transparent visor of his helmet.

He stared at the rock. It was roughly two feet long, flat-topped and oblong. Its sides looked smooth, not pitted like most of the other rocks. And on one side of it there was a distinct patch of green.

He walked slowly around it, stepping over other small rocks and around the larger ones that were strewn everywhere. There was no green anywhere else. If I'd come up on the other side of it I'd never have noticed the color, he realized.

One rock. With a little area of green on one of its flat sides. One rock out of thousands. One bit of color in a world of rusty reds.

"Waterman, I do not see you," Vosnesensky called.

"I've found something."

"Come back toward the dome."

"I've found some green," Jamie said, annoyed.

"What?"

"Green."

"Where are you?"

"What do you mean? What is it?"

Jamie scanned the area around him. "Can you see the big boulder with the cleft in its top?"

"No. Where . . ."

"I can!" Joanna's voice, brimming with excitement. "Just to the west of the second lander. See it?"

"Ah, yes," said Monique.

"This way," Joanna called.

Within a minute seven hard-suited figures appeared over the horizon just to the right of the cleft boulder. Jamie waved to them and they waved back.

Then he turned to the rock, his rock. Sinking slowly to his knees in the awkward suit, he leaned as close to it as he dared. He almost expected to see ants or their Martian equivalent busily scurrying around the ground.

What he saw, instead, was nothing but the powdery red sand and the rust-colored rock with a streak of green running down its flattish side. Christ, it looks like a little vein of copper that's been exposed to the air. But then Jamie remembered that there was precious little oxygen in the Martian air. Enough to turn a vein of copper green? How long had the vein been exposed to the air? Ten thousand years? Ten million?

He leaned back on his haunches, his back to the approaching scientists.

"Where is it?" Joanna asked breathlessly.

"You look as if you're praying," said Naguib's reedy nasal voice. "Has it made a believer of you?"

"Don't get too worked up," Jamie told them, looking up as they surrounded him and the rock. "I think it's just a streak of oxidized copper."

Patel, in his yellow suit, clumsily got down on all fours to peer closely at the rock. "Yes, I believe that is so."

Joanna flattened herself beside him. "It might be just the surface coating of a colony that lives inside the rock. Like the microflora in Antarctica, they use the rocks for shelter and absorb moisture from the frost that gathers on the rock's surfaces."

"I am afraid that it is nothing more than a patina of copper oxide," Patel said in his Hindu cadence and British pronunciation.

"We must make certain," said Monique, as calmly as if she were selecting a wine at a Paris bistro. Cool head, Jamie thought. Warm heart?

"We'll have to take it inside . . ."

"Don't touch it!" Joanna snapped.

"We can't examine it in any detail out here," Jamie said. "We've got to bring it inside the dome."

"It is a possible biological sample," Joanna said with unexpected proprietary fierceness.

It's copper oxide, thought Jamie.

Struggling to her feet, Joanna said, "I left my bio sampling cases when you called. They can maintain the ambient conditions inside them. If you bring the rock into the dome and it is suddenly thrust into our environment it would kill any native organisms that may be inside it."

Jamie nodded inside his helmet. She was right. Even though the chances were that the green streak was just a patina of copper oxide, there was no sense screwing up what might be the biggest discovery of all time.

"Please do not touch the rock," Joanna said. "Perhaps the rest of you could look around this area to see if any other rocks show such color. But do not touch them in any way. Do you all understand?"

Suddenly she was in charge. She wasn't whispering anymore. The lovely little butterfly had turned into a dragon lady. What had started out as a geology field trip had turned into a biology session, and Jamie was just one of the flunkies. He felt his lips pressing into a tight angry line.

But he knew that she was right, and within her rights. He climbed slowly to his feet inside the cumbersome suit.

"Okay, boss," he replied with exaggerated deference. "To hear is to obey."

Joanna did not notice any humor in his crack. She detailed Monique to stand guard over the rock and ordered the other four to scour the area for other green spots. Connors, in his white hard-shell suit, stood to one side like a policeman, observing without participating. Joanna headed back toward the spot where she had left her sample cases, almost skipping across the rocky desert sands.

"*Formidable.*" Monique's voice sounded amused.

Jamie asked, "Say, were any of us smart enough to bring a camera with him?"

"I have a camera," said Toshima.

Jamie said, "Could you take a series of snaps of the rock and the region around it, from every angle—complete three hundred sixty degrees?"

"Most certainly."

Jamie thought back to hunting trips he had taken with his grandfather Al. They would always snap photos of each other with their catch—deer, rabbit, even the gila monster that Jamie had shot with his twenty-two when he had been no more than ten years old. His mother hated to allow Jamie to go hunting, but his father could not stand up to grandfather Al's determination. "You can't keep the boy cooped up in a library all the time," Al would argue. "He ought to be out in the open." Then, when they were alone together up in the wooded hills, his grandfather would tell him, "They're trying to make you a hundred percent white, Jamie. I just want you to keep a little bit of yourself red, like you ought to be."

Jamie looked back at the rock, small enough to pick up and carry, especially in this light gravity. It'd make a great photo to send back to my grandfather, he thought. Me inside this damned suit with the rock for my trophy.

But he did not pose for Toshima's camera.

Joanna returned after nearly half an hour with Vosnesensky at her side toting the two hefty silver-coated specimen boxes plus a pair of long slim poles that looked to Jamie like fishing rods. He knew that they were marker poles, with tiny radio beacons at their tips. He grinned to himself: Joanna's even got the Russian working for her now.

"I wondered if I would ever have to use these," she was chattering. "I never thought I would need them on the first day of field work!"

The others had found no other spots of green in the hundred meters or so they had examined in all directions around the rock. The soil was crisscrossed now with the prints of their cleated boots, except for a sacrosanct half meter surrounding the rock. No one had dared to come any closer for fear of damaging or destroying some vital evidence.

Vosnesensky stopped and bent slightly forward, hands on hips, as if doing obeisance to the rock. In his bright red suit he looked to Jamie like a fat bell pepper with a hump on its back.

Joanna took charge. "Do not touch the rock. Before we do anything, I will need soil samples from the ground immediately around the rock and then underneath it."

"I can use the corer," Jamie said, reaching for the tool at his belt. "It attaches to the pole, so we can get samples from as deep as five meters."

"Good," said Joanna.

"That can also tell us if there is permafrost beneath the surface, no?" asked Ilona, sounding excited for the first time since they had landed.

He nodded; then, realizing no one could see the gesture through his tinted visor, he added, "Yes, that's right."

Vosnesensky commanded, "Pete, bring the video camera here. We must have a record of this."

The astronaut said, "Right," and headed back toward the camera he had left on its tripod.

"My still camera is almost out of film," Toshima said. "I will take the last few frames now and change rolls."

"No!" snapped Naguib. "Don't take the chance of high-energy

radiation spoiling the film. Here, take my camera. It has a full roll in it."

"Thank you," said Toshima.

Connors lumbered into sight again, dangling the vidcam in one gloved hand. When he was satisfied that both still and video photographers were ready, Vosnesensky ordered, "Proceed."

But no one moved until Joanna said, "I want four samples, one from each side of the rock, as far down as you can go." Then she added, "Please."

Jamie leaned on the pole and the corer bit into the ground. It buzzed through the first few centimeters easily enough but then the going got tough. Jamie pushed hard, breaking into a sweat.

"It's gotten like hardpan," he grunted.

"Or permafrost?" Ilona suggested hopefully.

Jamie pulled up the pole and let Patel, his fellow geologist, work the mechanism that neatly dropped the slim column of red dirt from the corer's sharp teeth into one of Joanna's sample boxes. Patel worked slowly, carefully, to make certain that the crumbly cylinder did not break apart.

Jamie noted that the column was striated. Different shades of red. Fluvial deposits, he guessed. There must have been an ocean here at one time. Or at least a big lake.

Four samples from the sides of the rock. Jamie had to stop his digging several times to let the fans of his suit clear away the mist that built up inside his visor. Despite his exertions, neither Patel nor any of the others made the slightest move to help him. Instead they peered at the samples and invented instant theories to explain their appearance.

They're all too entranced with what's going on to even think of helping, he told himself. Besides, they got an Injun to do the heavy work. Why should they bother with it?

"All right now," said Joanna, after four samples were resting in the first case. She sank slowly to her knees and bent over the rock.

Jamie got down beside her. "You'll need help lifting . . ."

"No!" she snapped. "I can do it myself. This is Mars, after all."

Jamie flushed with sudden anger and then felt sheepish. She's right. The damned rock only weighs a few pounds here. And she's not going to let anybody touch it but herself.

Toshima clicked away and Connors focused the vidcam tightly on the rock as Joanna reached out and grasped it at both ends, keeping clear of the green patch on its side. She tugged the rock up off the ground and placed it inside the other silver sample case as tenderly as a mother laying her newborn infant in its crib.

Jamie stared hard at the ground beneath the rock. Flattened and smoothed by the rock's weight but otherwise no different from the rest of the soil. What did you expect? he asked himself. A Martian rattlesnake coiled up under it?

"Now if you will please take a core sample from the ground that was beneath the rock," Joanna said as she sealed the lid of her sample case.

"How deep?"

"As deep as you can go," she said. "If you please."

Jamie did it. While they all watched in silence he dug the pole in as far as it could go. Gently, delicately, he pulled the core sample up . . .

"Look!" shouted Monique Bonnet.

"What?"

"What is it?"

"I thought . . ." She was almost breathless. "When you pulled out the stick, I thought I saw sunlight glinting off . . . something."

"Something?"

"What?"

"Was it water droplets?" Ilona asked.

"Perhaps," said Monique. "I don't know. It was gone in the blink of an eye."

Ilona dropped to her knees so hard that Jamie was afraid she would hurt herself or bang up her suit. She wormed her gloved hand down into the hole that he had dug and pulled it out swiftly. The sleeve of the suit was smeared with reddish dust and crumbling bits of rust-colored dirt.

"Look! *Look!*"

A half dozen tiny glinting drops of moisture were on her gloved fingers, like dew on the petals of a flower. Before any of them could say a word the droplets disappeared, evaporating into the thin cold Martian air.

"It's water!"

"It must be water!" Monique said, her voice vibrating with excitement. "Below the ground. Water!"

Naguib was laughing like a schoolboy. "We've discovered water! The first water found on an extraterrestrial body! It's only a few drops, but it's water! And *liquid* water at that!"

Jamie stood there leaning on the pole, all his physical tiredness from the digging evaporated just like the droplets from Ilona's glove. The others were practically capering, waving their arms and almost dancing in their hard suits, they were so thrilled.

All except Joanna, who remained kneeling before the hole that Jamie had dug for her like a worshiper at a strange altar, flanked on either side by her filled and carefully sealed sample cases.

And Jamie, who stood behind her with the pole gripped in both hands, standing like a Navaho warrior with his lance butted on the dusty ground, wondering what his colleagues would do if that green patch actually turned out to be real living Martian organisms.

D O S S I E R:
JOANNA MARIA BRUMADO

At the age of sixteen Joanna took her first lover and learned that her mother was dying.

An only child, she had spent all her life at home under the gentle, loving hand of a mother who never raised her voice yet ruled her household absolutely. When she was younger Joanna had adored her father, who traveled the world over and was enormously respected and admired. As she began to understand the urges flowing within her own body, though, she started to see her father with new eyes. She realized that women—even her mother's friends and students her own age—looked at Alberto Brumado with more than respect and admiration in their glances.

"Your father is handsome and very romantic," Joanna's mother told her. "Why shouldn't other women yearn for him?" And she smiled to show that she was not concerned about her husband's faithfulness.

"He loves us too much to care about anyone else," Joanna's mother assured her. Then she added, "His obsession is the planet Mars, not some student young enough to be his daughter."

Joanna had been born in São Paulo; her father had taught at the university there. But his quest for Mars eventually dictated that the family move to the capital, Brasilia, although they spent the hottest months of each year in Rio de Janeiro, like the politicians and their advisors.

Wherever they lived, Joanna did so well at the convent schools that her parents decided to send her to a prestigious preparatory school in the United States. She had pleased her father by showing an aptitude for science. She had pleased her mother by obeying her one unbendable rule: "Do not do anything that you can't tell me about afterward."

Joanna had intended to tell her mother about the tall fair-haired instructor who had taken her to bed. She was madly in love and bursting to tell her mother all about it. She waited a week and then could wait no more. She telephoned her mother.

To learn that her mother had been stricken with a serious heart seizure that very morning and taken to the hospital. Joanna forgot school and her lover; she hastily packed a bag and flew to Brasilia.

She could tell from her father's face that there was no hope for her mother. The doctors at first did not even want to allow her to see the stricken woman, fearing an emotional outburst that would hasten the end. With the same iron self-control that she now realized had been her mother's main strength, Joanna assured them that she would not upset her dying mother. They looked from her utterly determined face to her father, who nodded. "Let her see her mama," said Alberto Brumado in a broken, tear-strangled voice. "She may not have another chance."

Her mother looked very pale, very tired. Tubes ran from her slim arms to strange machines that chugged and beeped behind the bed. Another tube ran up her right nostril. Joanna thought they were sucking the life out of her mother.

She did not cry. She stood by the edge of the high bed and stroked her mother's hair, realizing for the first time how thin and gray it had become. Her mother opened her eyes and smiled up at her.

"Mama . . ."

"My lovely daughter," the woman whispered. "How beautiful you have become."

"Mama, I love you so much!"

"Don't worry about me, dear." Her voice was so weak that Joanna had to bend down to hear the words.

"I don't want you to die."

Blinking her dry eyes slowly, Joanna's mother whispered, "It is your father you must care for now. I can't protect him any longer. You must do it for me."

"Protect him?"

"His work. It is very important. To him and the whole world. Don't let him be distracted. Don't let anything stand between him and his work. Protect him. Help him."

"I will, Mama. I will."

"You've always been a good girl, Joanna. I love you very much."

"I love you, Mama."

"Protect your father. Remember."

"I promise, Mama."

Those were her mother's last words. Joanna kept her promise. She became her father's shield against any distraction that might interfere with his great, consuming goal. Especially any female distraction. Joanna attended college where her father taught. She traveled with him around the world. She kept house for him. She never took another lover.

They trooped back into the dome, suits and equipment smudged with red dust.

Despite their excitement over the green-streaked rock, Vosnesensky insisted that they follow mission protocol and carefully clean their suits and all their gear before stepping into the main section of the dome. The area just inside the airlock, where the hard suits and outside equipment were stored, served as the cleanup and maintenance section. Its partitions reached up to the curving dome itself.

"We will have to use the biological decontamination procedures if we have found native life forms," Vosnesensky grumbled as he pulled off his suit.

Jamie was vacuuming the dust from his boots with the angrily buzzing little hand machine thinking, You would take the greatest discovery in history and make a chore out of it, wouldn't you?

Tony Reed, standing just inside the door of the partition, his nose wrinkling at the acrid smell that filled the area, cast curious eyes at Joanna's sample boxes.

"In that case," he said, "we'd have to make this section airtight, with the sort of envelope they have in biology labs."

"That can be done," Vosnesensky said as he lifted the torso of his hard suit over his head.

Let's see what we've got first, thought Jamie.

As soon as she was finished dusting her suit Joanna lugged the cases to her small biology bench, where she had an isolation box and remote manipulators to work with. The Martian rock would be kept in a Martian environment while she examined it. Ilona and Monique went with her.

"Mother and daughters," muttered Naguib, watching them through the window in the partition as they marched off to the bio lab.

"Hera, Athena, and Aphrodite," said Reed, his eyes also fixed on them.

Jamie, finally free of his hard suit, felt too tired to go to his cubicle to remove the undergarments. He sat on the bench in front of his locker, hands on knees, head bent, silent. His left armpit felt raw, chafed. Suit's rubbing there, he realized. I'll have to pad it before I use it again. The pungent smell he had noticed on first taking off his helmet had dissipated now. Or we've all become accustomed to it, he thought. Maybe it's the dust.

"Dr. Malater must be Athena," Naguib said. "She's quite tall and athletic."

"Yes, and little Joanna is Aphrodite, wouldn't you say?" Tony murmured. "She's got the right figure for a sex goddess, hasn't she?"

"And Dr. Bonnet is older, so she must be Hera, queen of the gods."

Tony smiled at the brown-skinned Egyptian. "Rather a good fit, don't you think?"

Naguib nodded agreement, then added, "But wasn't it those three goddesses who started the Trojan War? We must be careful with them." He laughed.

Tony granted him a sly smile. "Careful, yes, by all means. But remember that goddesses can become angry if you don't worship them properly."

It was too much for Jamie. Reed and his slightly sneering way of looking at the world was more than he wanted to deal with at the end of this long, exciting, exhausting day. He hauled himself to his feet and headed for his privacy cubicle where he could strip off the rest of his clothes and then maybe go take a shower.

Before he got halfway there, though, Paul Abell intercepted him.

"Your turn before the cameras, friend." The American astronaut's frog eyes were wide and bulging, his smile curved almost from ear to ear.

"What do you mean?" Jamie asked.

"The media back on Earth. Looks like you're a very popular guy. They want to interview you, and mission control has set it up." Abell pointed. "The comm console awaits your pleasure."

Each of the explorers was expected to respond to the news media's demands for interviews "live, from the planet Mars."

With the distance from Earth growing larger every hour, it took nearly ten minutes for a radio or TV transmission to travel from one world to the other, so truly "live" interviews were out of the question.

How could you conduct an interview with a twenty-minute wait between each question and its answer?

The media producers had their solution: each explorer would receive a list of questions. The explorer would then answer those questions before the camera, one after the other. On Earth, the answers would be snipped apart so that a questioning reporter could be inserted into the appropriate spots. The result looked as if the reporter and the explorer on Mars were indeed talking to one another "live." Almost. There was little of the spontaneity of a truly face-to-face interview. But the world's audiences were accustomed to wooden performances from scientists and astronauts, or so the TV producers assured their executives.

Besides, these people were speaking from Mars!

Wearily, Jamie slid into the creaking plastic chair in front of the main communications screen, still in his thermal undergarment, like white longjohns covered with tubing. Abell sat off to one side, monitoring the equipment and grinning as if he enjoyed watching a scientist trying to field questions from the media.

It surprised Jamie when the screen lit up to show, not Li Chengdu up in the orbiting command spacecraft or even one of the mission controllers at Kaliningrad. He found himself looking into the sad gray eyes of Alberto Brumado.

Brumado had flown to Washington the morning after the tumultuous celebration in Rio. There was a public relations furor brewing in the States and no less than the Vice-President herself was making outrageous demands that one of the scientists be removed from the team of explorers on the surface of Mars.

He had spent two days calming the politicians, but he could not deny that the American media was in a hot-breathed frenzy over the fact that a Native American was among the Martian explorers and he had refused to speak the speech that the space agency public relations officers had written for him.

Brumado had met with the media as well as the politicians and discovered that, like sharks attracted by the scent of blood, the media were circling around the figure of James Waterman, ready to close in for the kill.

Brumado had one goal and one only: to make such a success of this first mission to Mars that the people of the world would demand further exploration of the red planet. He was not going to allow one man—foolish or stubborn or simply a victim of circumstances—to wreck what he had fought for thirty years to accomplish. He would not permit one man—red, yellow, white, or green—to turn public opinion against Mars.

Now he sat before a display screen in an office in Washington. Through the half-drawn blinds he could see the modernistic square facade of the Air and Space Museum, with thousands of people streaming through its front doors.

"Ready to transmit to Mars, sir," said the young woman sitting across the office. She had a headset clamped across her curly dark hair and a jumble of electronic gray boxes piled on the desk in front of her.

Brumado saw on the screen a man in white coveralls with a smiling frog's face. The NASA patch on his chest identified him as the astronaut Abell. He looked relaxed, perfectly at ease; his lips were moving. Brumado realized this transmission had taken place more than ten minutes ago, and the technicians had turned off the sound so that he would not be confused. They wanted him to begin speaking now, knowing that it would take almost ten minutes for his words and image to reach Mars. By then James Waterman should be sitting where the astronaut was.

Unconsciously, Brumado smiled as he began, "Dr. Waterman, this is rather awkward for me, for several reasons. First, I don't see you on the screen yet since it takes so much time to send messages back and forth. Second, I have to ask you for a favor. I recall that we met once during your training, and I regret that we did not have the chance to spend more time together and get to know each other better." Brumado hesitated, then plunged ahead. "I suppose you realize that you have caused something of an uproar here in the United States."

Jamie watched Brumado's neatly bearded face: kindly, a bit sad, his gray hair slightly rumpled. Just three lousy words, Jamie thought as Brumado talked to him. Three little words and there's an uproar back home.

". . . So what I have done is to sit down with the major networks and smooth things over as much as possible for you. They will not be satisfied, however, unless they have the chance to interview you. They have agreed to have one reporter ask the questions, and I have

reviewed the questions they have put on tape. We have no objections
to your answering any of them. They have your complete biograph-
ical file from the agency, of course, and there have already been
several interviews with your parents and other people you have
known in school and socially. So far, the coverage has been very
sympathetic, very favorable to you. But now they want to speak to
you."

Brumado pulled in a deep breath, then went on. "I know it must
sound almost ridiculous to you, where you are now and with what
you are trying to accomplish, but you must understand that you have
touched on a very sensitive nerve back here. Indian activists are
proclaiming you a hero. The Vice-President is quite angry with the
space agency for allowing you to become part of the Mars mission.
She thinks you are a troublemaker, although she used much stronger
language than that. I pointed out to her that I myself pushed to get
you assigned to the mission, but that only made her angrier, I think.
So—what to do?"

Jamie almost started to answer the question, then realized that
Brumado was not waiting for an answer. "We will transmit the media's questions to you immediately after I finish talking to you. We
want you to answer the questions as honestly and openly as you can.
The tape of your answers will be screened here in Washington by
the Space Council before being released to the media. The Vice-
President herself will make the decision to release your tape to the
media or not. I suggest you review the entire tape, listen carefully
to every question, and then go back and answer each one in turn."

Brumado seemed to hunch closer to the screen. His face took on
a more intense, more sorrowful look. "I must warn you that the
quality of your answers will determine whether or not you are allowed to remain with the surface team. I have spoken at length with
Li Chengdu and he is vehemently against your being replaced for
political reasons. But if the Vice-President insists upon it, we will
have no choice but to send you up to the orbiter and send the Australian, Dr. O'Hara, to the surface in your place."

Brumado leaned back again, then said, "Well, that's it. I regret
that this is happening, but we must try to deal with it as quickly and
honestly as we can. The interviewer's questions will follow immediately. Good-bye for now. And good luck."

The screen flickered momentarily, then the smooth smiling face
of a network anchorman appeared. Jamie recognized the face, but
could not recall the name. From somewhere in the dome Jamie could

hear music floating softly through the air: a Rachmaninoff piano concerto, no less. Dark and melancholy. Must be one of the Russians' tapes, he thought. Strange that Brumado didn't ask to speak with his daughter. Maybe he already did. Maybe Paul told him Joanna's busy in her lab.

The anchorman did not bother to introduce himself; perhaps he felt that he was so famous that no introduction was necessary.

"Dr. Waterman, I'm going to read off a list of questions we would like you to answer. As I understand it, your answers will be screened by the government before they're turned over to us. Please feel free to answer as completely as you want. Don't worry about time. We can edit any redundancies or coughs or sneezes out of the final interview."

His smile grew wider although his eyes seemed hard and intense, like a wolf's. Jamie remembered Edith warning him that a videotape could be edited to make an interviewee look good or bad, but he barely had time to think of that before the anchorman asked his first question.

"Your records from Berkeley and the University of New Mexico show no indication that you were involved in pro-Indian activism or any causes at all, other than student housing, even though you were president of the student council in your senior year at Albuquerque. Were you politically active in secret? If not, when did you become active?"

And so it went. Jamie followed Brumado's advice and went through the entire tape before trying to answer any of the questions. It was all the same: an attempt to get Jamie to take a stand on Indian affairs and against the U.S. government's handling of them. The Anglo even had the gall to bring up Wounded Knee and Custer.

Abell laughed out loud at several of the questions. When the tape was finished he showed Jamie how to rewind it and then stop it at the end of each question, so that he could give his response.

"And when did you stop beating your wife?" Abell asked gleefully. "He forgot to ask you that one."

Jamie leaned back in the flimsy plastic chair and stared at the empty screen, his mind churning. For many minutes he said nothing, remained absolutely still.

Finally Abell asked, "Are you ready?"

Behind him Jamie could hear the voices of the others and Rachmaninoff's dark melodies. Above him he saw the curve of the dome, darkened now against the encroaching cold of the Martian night.

Beyond that thin barrier was another world waiting to be explored.

He nodded to Abell. "I'm ready."

The anchorman's face came back on the screen, repeating his first question with that earnest little smile that was meant to convey sincerity. The face froze on the screen as Jamie answered.

"I've never been active in politics of any kind, on campus or afterward. I vote every election day, but that's about it. I consider myself to be an American citizen, just like you do. My ancestry is part Native American, part New England Yankee—a mixture of Navaho and *Mayflower*. To me, it's just the same as if all my ancestors came from some country in Europe, like yours did. I'm proud of my Navaho ancestry, but no more so than you're proud of your own heritage, whatever it may be."

Jamie took a breath, then went on, "I'm speaking to you from the planet Mars. This afternoon my fellow scientists and I discovered water here. That is far more important than the color of my skin or the nature of my political activities. For the first time in our exploration of the solar system we have found water in a liquid state on another world. You should be interviewing us about that, not over a few words I spoke at a very emotional moment in my life. All the others of our team spoke in their native languages when they gave their first words from Mars. I spoke in mine—spoke the only words of Navaho that I really know. And that's all there is to it. Now let's stop this bullshit and get on with the exploration of Mars."

He turned in his chair toward Abell. "That's it."

"You don't really expect them to put that last line on the air, do you?"

"I don't really give a damn."

Looking slightly worried, the astronaut punched up the anchorman's next question.

"No," Jamie said. "That's *it*. I've said all I have to say. Send it up to Dr. Li and on to Washington. I've got nothing to add to that."

Despite himself, Li Chengdu smiled as he reviewed the tape of Jamie's abbreviated interview. They will not like this back in Washington, but the young man has courage.

Li steepled his fingers and wondered how much trouble he would cause if he refused to remove Waterman from the ground team. Of course, Washington had not made that demand yet. But he had no doubt that they would once they saw Waterman's tape.

Yes, the young man has courage, Li said to himself. Do I have the courage to stand with him and defy the politicians?

They cannot reach out to Mars and replace me. But what might they do once we return to Earth? That is the interesting question. More than interesting. Perhaps my Nobel Prize hinges on this matter. Certainly young Waterman's entire career does. His career and his life.

EARTH

HOUSTON: It had taken Edith two days to make up her mind. Two days and all her courage.

When she had watched Jamie utter his Navaho greeting from the surface of Mars she had smiled to herself. Standing in the jam-packed KHTV newsroom that morning, she had no premonition of the uproar his few words would cause. One of her co-workers nudged her shoulder slightly as the picture on the screen focused on his sky-blue space suit.

"That's your significant other, isn't it?" the woman whispered to Edith.

She nodded, thinking, He used to be. Used to be.

Edith was surprised when the network news show that evening spent so much time on the fact that an American Indian was on Mars. The next morning, on her own, she called several of her contacts at the Johnson Space Center and found that there was considerable consternation among the NASA brass about Jamie's impromptu little speech.

"The guys upstairs are goin' apeshit," one of her informers told her. "But you didn't hear anything from me, understand?"

By the second day there were rumbles that the Space Council in Washington was reviewing the Indian's refusal to speak the words NASA had prepared for him. The Vice-President was up in arms, rumor had it. What *she* did was *news.* Everyone knew that she wanted to be the party's choice for their presidential candidate next year.

Edith reviewed tapes of boringly standard interviews with Jamie's parents in Berkeley and blandly evasive NASA officials. She went to sleep that second night thinking about what she should do.

She awoke the next morning, her mind made up. She called the station and told her flabbergasted news director that she was taking the rest of the week off.

"You can't do that! I don't . . ."

"I have two weeks' vacation and a whole mess of sick days I never took," Edith said sweetly into the phone. "I'll be back by Monday."

"Goddammit, Edie, they'll fire your ass! You know what they're like upstairs!"

She made a sigh that he could not help but hear. "Then they'll have to fire me and give me my severance pay, I guess."

She hung up, then immediately called for a plane reservation to New York.

Now, winging thirty-five thousand feet above the Appalachians, Edith rehearsed in her mind what she would tell the network news chief. I can get to James Waterman's parents. And his grandfather. And the people he trained with who were not selected to go to Mars. I know his story and I know the inner workings of the Mars Project. I can produce you a story of how this thing works, from the inside. The human story of the Mars Project. Not just shining science, but the infighting, the competition, the guts and blood of it all.

As she went through her mental preparation she thought of Jamie. He'll hate me for doing this. He'll absolutely hate me.

But it's my ticket to a job with the network. He's got Mars. He left me for Mars. Now I can use Mars my own way, for myself.

THE DEPARTURE

1

The personnel chosen for the Mars expedition were shuttled to the assembly station riding in low orbit a scant three hundred kilometers above the surface of the Earth. At that altitude, the ponderous bulk of the planet curved huge and incredibly beautiful, filling the sky, overwhelming the senses with broad expanses of blue oceans decked with gleaming white clouds, a world rich and vibrant with life glowing against the cold black emptiness of space.

Mars was a distant pinpoint in that blackness, a steady ruddy beacon beckoning across the gulf that separates worlds.

The assembly station itself was a composite habitat made out of a Soviet *Mir* space station linked to a reconditioned external propellant tank from an American space shuttle, bigger than a twenty-room house. The *Mir* part of the assembly station was attached to the shuttle tank about midway along the tank's long curving flank, looking like a tiny green gondola on a huge matte tan blimp. The Soviet hardware contained three docking ports for shuttles or the smaller orbital tugs.

Here the sixteen chosen scientists would live and work for more than a month before they departed for Mars, getting accustomed to one another and to their expedition commander, Dr. Li. And to the eight astronauts and cosmonauts who would operate the Mars spacecraft and be in command of the ground teams.

Hanging in the black emptiness a few hundred meters from the assembly station were the two long, narrow Mars spacecraft, gleaming white in the harsh sunlight, attended by swarms of orbital tugs and massive shuttles while tiny figures in space suits hovered around them, dwarfed to the size of ants, buzzing back and forth constantly, transferring supplies and equipment every day, every hour. Compared to the bulbous dull brown and green shapes of the assembly station the Mars craft looked like sleek racing shells.

In orbit the entire assemblage of vehicles and human beings was effectively in zero gravity, weightless. Jamie felt his guts dropping away the instant the shuttle rocket engines cut off. His inner ears were telling him that he was falling, falling endlessly. Yet he could see that he was strapped firmly in his seat down in the crowded middeck compartment of the shuttle, jammed in with five technicians on their way to a week's work. Their coveralls were stained and frayed from hard use; Jamie's were so new there were still creases on his sleeves.

All the scientist-candidates had spent at least a few days in orbit during their years of training. Jamie had also flown three flights on the Vomit Comet, the big jet transport plane that simulated zero g by diving from high altitude, then pulling up into a long parabolic arc that produced about half a minute of gut-wrenching weightlessness. He knew what to expect and he did not panic. Still he could feel his stomach churning and his head going woozy.

Jamie felt all the classic symptoms of space adaptation syndrome as he followed the veteran technicians past the shuttle's hatch, through the narrow metal chambers of the Mir, and into the more spacious receiving area of the huge shuttle tank. It was not like seasickness, not exactly. His head felt stuffy as his body fluids shifted within him, free of gravity's pull. He felt slightly nauseous, disoriented, almost dizzy. As if he had come down with a heavy dose of flu.

Medical personnel took him in tow, literally, and after a perfunctory examination cheerfully pronounced him normal. They gave him a slow-release medication patch to stick behind his ear and told him that all the Mars scientists were assembling in the main briefing area. Jamie started to nod, found that the head motion made him feel as if he wanted to upchuck, and settled for asking directions to the main briefing area.

He knew enough to go slowly up the central passageway, pulling himself along easily on the ladder rungs that studded all four walls, like a swimmer working his way along the hull of a sunken ship. It was difficult to think of ceiling and floor when up and down had no objective meaning. Jamie began to think of the passageway as a deep well with metal walls that he was climbing, floating weightlessly as he made his way in dreamy slow motion toward the top.

"Ah, there you are! You made it."

Jamie turned at the sound of the voice behind him and instantly wished he hadn't as his stomach lurched uneasily.

It was Tony Reed, smiling as if he had been born in zero gravity, gliding effortlessly along the passageway like a grinning dolphin.

Jamie tried to smile.

"Glad to see you here," Reed said, extending his hand as he rose to Jamie's level, "even though you do look a bit green."

"I'll adjust," Jamie said, hanging on to one ladder rung while his feet floated free.

"Of course you will. We're all delighted that Brumado talked the powers that be into giving you the geology slot."

Reed started off along the passageway again and Jamie pushed against a rung to keep up with him. "I'm still kind of dazed . . . it all happened so fast."

With his slightly crooked smile Reed said, "You can thank Joanna for it. She led the revolt against Hoffman."

"Joanna did?"

"Yes. Got her father to support it, actually. She can be quite the little jaguar when she wants to be."

There were others gathering at the far end of the long passageway, Jamie saw. And more coming behind (below?) them.

Lowering his voice, Jamie asked, "You mean Joanna was the one who forced Hoffman out?"

"She was the ringleader. We all had something of a hand in it. Once it was clear that DiNardo was gone, we suddenly realized that we were facing two years locked up with that Austrian martinet."

"He wasn't so bad," Jamie mumbled.

"Most of us thought he was, rather. And Joanna apparently wanted him off more than any of us." Reed's expression turned canny. "Or perhaps she wanted you to be *on* with us. I feel rather jealous, you know."

Jamie bit back a reply. They were too close to the others now to continue the conversation. He wondered how much truth there was in Reed's words and how much of what he said was joking exaggeration.

The scientists were not expected to do any work for the first few days in orbit; the mission planners had expected them to be suffering and useless for that long. But they could attend briefings. The psychologists even claimed that activities that required mental rather than physical exertion would take their minds off their queasiness.

Jamie followed Reed through a hatch set into the bulkhead that ended the long passageway. He found himself gliding weightlessly into a large open area, rising like a bubble into a cavernous chamber in the nose of the former propellant tank. The briefing center's dome-like interior had been painted with stripes of black and white that converged on the point of the nose cap. Jamie hovered in midair, blinked several times, and realized that the "wall" he had come through had become the "floor" of the briefing center.

The flat surface was studded with plastic foot loops, further defining it as the floor. The black and white stripes provided strong vertical orientation. With up and down clearly defined, Jamie felt somewhat better. He reached out a hand as he approached the curving wall and pushed himself lightly back toward the floor. Anyone can be an acrobat in zero gravity, Jamie realized. Or a ballet dancer.

Slowly sixteen queasy, faintly green scientists gathered on that floor, anchoring their boots in the foot loops, their bodies hunched forward slightly in what was called "the zero-g crouch," their arms floating weightlessly up around chest height. Like polyps attached to the sea bottom, Jamie thought, weaving back and forth in the currents.

Dr. Li, clad in sky-blue coveralls with a stiff collar, stood on a slightly elevated platform at one side of the circular area. Not that he needed a platform, with his height. In contrast, most of the astronauts and cosmonauts gathered around him were quite short, Jamie saw; American or Russian, most of the fliers had the sawed-off physiques of fighter pilots.

Li looked pretty green himself, Jamie thought. The expedition commander waited a few moments for the assembled scientists to quiet down. Then he began, in his thin, high-pitched voice, "Believe it or not, we are now going through the most difficult part of our mission."

"I believe it!" someone muttered loud enough for everyone to hear and laugh at.

"In a few days more we will become accustomed to microgravity. In a few weeks more we will transfer to Mars spacecraft, which will eventually be spun up to simulate terrestrial gravity—and then despun as we approach Mars to acclimate us to Martian level of gravity."

Li looked pallid, drawn. Yet his face was puffier than it had been on Earth, his eyes seemed narrower. It struck Jamie that if they maintained zero g all the way to Mars they could save tons of food; no one would have much of an appetite. But we'd be in no condition to work on the surface once we got there.

"In a moment I will introduce our astronauts and cosmonauts to you. Then we will break up into smaller groups to become better acquainted. However, first I wish to remind you of a very sensitive and very important point, a subject that you have all discussed individually with the physicians and psychologists. It is mentioned, but only briefly, in your mission regulations books."

Li took a deep breath. "I refer to the subject of sex."

Everyone took a breath, like a collective sigh wafting through the group. Jamie could not see the faces of the other scientists without turning his head—which would bring on a wave of nausea. But the astronauts and cosmonauts were facing the scientists, and Jamie saw a couple of grins and even a frown.

"We are all adult," said Dr. Li. "We all have healthy sex drive. We will be living together for nearly two years. As your expedition commander I expect you to behave in adult manner. Adult human beings, not childish monkeys."

No one said a word. There was no laughter, no giggling, not even a cough.

"Men outnumber women among us by four to one. I expect you men to behave sensibly and to keep the goals of the expedition above your personal desires. Dr. Reed and Dr. Yang, our two physicians, have medications that will suppress the sex drive. You can go to them in complete privacy and confidentiality if you need to."

Jamie wondered how much privacy and confidentiality there could be among twenty-five men and women locked inside a pair of spacecraft for nearly two years.

Li looked over his assembled team members, then added, "I want to make it quite clear that neither I nor mission controllers will permit sexual problems to interfere with success of this expedition. If any one of you cannot control his sex drive, he will be required to take medication. Is that clear?"

What about the women? Jamie wanted to ask. But he did not. The image of Edith flickered in his mind, but he found himself turning his head ever so slightly to look at Joanna, standing just off to his left in the row ahead of him.

"Very well then, I will now introduce the men who will pilot our spacecraft and be in command of our various teams once we reach Mars."

As Li began to introduce the astronauts and cosmonauts, Jamie wondered what would happen if a man made trouble and then refused to take the medication he was ordered to take. What can they do when we're millions of miles out in space?

2

After the introductions the group broke up into smaller units. Jamie joined his fellow scientists and the two men who had been appointed their pilots and commanders. They were assembling along the curving wall at one end of the platform where Dr. Li remained.

The scientists moved cautiously across the loop-studded floor, like men and women in a dream, or drunks who were trying to maintain their dignity and self-control. Jamie saw the astronauts and cosmonauts casually pushing themselves off the walls or the floor itself to glide effortlessly toward the little knots of scientists gathering to talk with them. Insolent grace, Jamie thought. It was a line from a story he had read years ago, in freshman English. One of the Russians floated by overhead, grinning wolfishly as he looked down at the lurching, wobbling scientists. Insolent grace.

Jamie made an effort to reach Joanna. He came up to her side and touched her on the shoulder of her coveralls. She jerked with surprise, then paled noticeably and put a hand to her mouth.

"I'm sorry," Jamie said in a low voice. "I didn't mean to startle you."

Joanna swallowed hard, the hint of tears in her eyes. "One moment . . . I will be all right . . ."

Jamie said, "I just wanted to thank you for helping me to get here. I'm very grateful to you."

Her face still pale, she replied, "It was necessary to remove Professor Hoffman. He would have been impossible."

"I'm very glad to be here," Jamie repeated. "For whatever part in this you played, *muchas gracias.*"

She smiled, faintly, and replied in Portuguese, "*Por que?*"

Then she turned away from him and went to stand beside Ilona Malater, tall and regal-looking even in plain beige coveralls. The scientists attached their feet to the loops on the floor with the clumsy care of newcomers. The Russian cosmonaut and American astronaut, both dressed in tan slacks and pullovers, hovered effortlessly before them.

The four scientists—geologist, microbiologist, biochemist, and physician—finally got themselves settled in the foot restraints and focused their attention on the astronaut and cosmonaut who would be their team commanders.

"I am Mikhail Andreivitch Vosnesensky," the cosmonaut introduced himself. "I am command pilot of the first landing team." He spoke English perfectly, without any trace of an accent, in a heavy voice almost in a bass register.

He looked to Jamie like Hollywood's version of a Russian. Short, thick torso and heavy limbs, dark reddish-brown hair, beefy face with skin so fair it was almost pink. He reminded Jamie more of a stubby character actor than a hotshot rocket jockey. I'll have to check his biography in the mission records, Jamie said to himself. While Vosnesensky's eyes were the clear bright blue of a summer sky, innocent, almost childlike, the expression on his chunky face was dour and brooding.

"And I'm T. Peter Connors," said the black American astronaut, with a good-natured grin. "My official position is pilot, safety officer, and second-in-command."

Connors's smile was charming, but his red-rimmed eyes looked somehow sad, wary. Not more than a centimeter taller than the Russian, Connors was much slimmer, sleeker. It made him look almost lanky compared to Vosnesensky. Like a racing thoroughbred standing beside a plow horse. His voice was not as deep as the Russian's, but richer, more resonant, like a singer's.

"I want to make one thing clear at the outset," Vosnesensky told the four scientists, almost growling. "I am not here to be your friend. I will be in command of your group from the instant we enter the *Mars 1* spacecraft here in Earth orbit until the instant we leave it, once safely back here in Earth orbit. Especially during the time we are on the surface of Mars my responsibility will be to see that all mission objectives are met and no one is hurt. I will expect my orders to be carried out without delay and without argument. Mars is not a university campus. We will maintain military discipline at all times. Is that clear?"

"Quite clear," answered Tony Reed.

"Any questions?"

No one spoke. No one even moved as they stood anchored to the floor by the foot restraints.

"Good," said Vosnesensky.

Connors added, "If you have any problems, we can always talk them over. We'll be in transit for more than nine months. That's the time to go over the mission plan in as much detail as we can and hash over any changes you want to make."

So they're going to be good cop and bad cop, Jamie thought. I wonder if they've planned that out or if it's just their natural dispositions?

The four scientists glanced uneasily at each other. Vosnesensky motioned to Connors and the two pilots glided off, heading toward the hatch.

"Well," said Reed once they were out of earshot, "it looks as if we got rid of Hoffman only to get the Russian version of a drill sergeant."

3

Jamie was surprised at how difficult it was for him to make the mental transition. His body became accustomed to zero gravity in a couple of days. But he still had a hard time convincing himself that he was really going to Mars, actually part of the first team.

It did not help when all the Mars mission members began sneezing and coughing and blaming it on him.

"The rest of us have been confined together for more than two weeks at Star City," Tony Reed explained, almost jovially. "You're the serpent in our garden; you've brought some new cold viruses with you that we haven't grown accustomed to as yet."

Jamie felt miserable, more from the accusing stares his bleary-eyed comrades gave him whenever they sneezed than from his own stuffed head and wheezing chest.

Like the first week of school, he told himself. Everybody catches everything. Yet it made him feel more the outsider than ever before. Even after the colds ran their course and everyone returned to good health Jamie still kept mostly to himself, alone and unhappy—until he remembered that he was going to Mars.

4

Space and time are two aspects of the same thing, dimensions of the universe. There was a keyhole in spacetime, or as the engineers of mission control phrased it, a window. The two Mars craft had to be launched out of Earth orbit through that keyhole, through that window, at a certain time and in a precise direction with exactly the proper velocity, if they were to reach the moving pinpoint of light that was their destination.

For twenty-three days the two dozen men and women of the Mars mission, plus their expedition commander, Dr. Li, checked and rechecked every piece of equipment stowed aboard the long sleek Mars spacecraft. While they did so, specialist teams of technicians and robots attached bulky ovoid tanks of propellants around the aft end of each craft. The spacecraft began to look like thin white pencils surrounded by clusters of matte-gray lozenges at their eraser end.

The propellants had been manufactured on the moon and catapulted from the airless lunar surface to rendezvous with the spacecraft waiting in Earth orbit. The mission to Mars required not only Earth's resources, but the mining and processing centers on the moon as well.

On the twenty-fourth day the Mars-bound personnel left the assembly station for good and transferred their personal gear to the spacecraft. Twelve men and women aboard the habitat module of *Mars 1*, twelve plus Dr. Li in *Mars 2*. No one made a single mention of the fact that there would be thirteen aboard *Mars 2*. None of the scientists or pilots would admit to being superstitious; still, no one spoke the word "thirteen."

Space-suited technicians attached the long tethers that connected the two assembled spacecraft. Manufactured in the microgravity environment of a space station facility, the tethers had a tensile strength many times greater than that of any material that could be made on Earth.

Once they were on their way to Mars, tiny cold-gas thrusters would spurt in a precisely programmed order and the spacecraft would begin to spin up in a stately, graceful rotation. The tethers would stretch to their full five-kilometer length, and inside the connected Mars spacecraft a feeling of normal gravity would return, while the universe outside would start to revolve slowly past their observation ports.

A cluster of astronomical telescopes and high-energy radiation sensors was carefully placed at the midpoint of the long tethers, where they would be effectively weightless and could maintain precise pointing accuracy for the astronomers who would operate them remotely from Earth.

Other thrusters would later de-spin the spacecraft enough to reduce the internal gravity to the Martian level. By the time they arrived at Mars the explorers would be fully accustomed to the low Martian gravity. On the nine-month flight back home the spacecraft would spin up to a normal terrestrial g once again.

The interior of the habitat module was like the interior of every spacecraft Jamie had ever been in: a central corridor flanked either by the closed doors of privacy compartments or the open benches and equipment racks of workstations.

Up forward was the command section where a Russian cosmonaut and American astronaut copiloted the spacecraft. Just behind it was a sort of passenger compartment with seats for all the personnel, which could also serve as an informal lounge or conference room.

There was no need for acceleration couches. The rockets that would propel them to Mars produced very low levels of thrust; they would hardly feel as much acceleration as during a jet airliner's takeoff. Lifting off from the ground and going into Earth orbit required a big jolt of thrust, several minutes of three g's or more. That had all been done by space shuttles and unmanned rocket boosters carrying cargo. Once in orbit, though, the rest of the solar system could be reached gently.

One part of the habitat module was different. A section toward the rear was devoted to an oblong window made of thick quartz. Once they got to Mars, this observation port would be studded with cameras and other sensors. For now, though, it made a fine picture window.

The hour they were scheduled to depart, Jamie found himself at the observation port, hovering easily in zero g, his slippered feet dangling a few centimeters above the foot restraints set into the metal floor. He saw the Earth sliding past, an enormously massive curve of deep luminous blue, then the duller green-brown of land and the hard gray wrinkles of a mountain chain, dusted with clutching skeletal fingers of white snow. Another ocean slid into view, the immense swirl of a tropical storm's seething clouds forming a gigantic gray-white comma over the water.

"Those are the Andes Mountains."

Joanna had come up beside him, floating noiselessly. He had not noticed, he had been staring at the world so intently.

"Come to say good-bye to Mother Earth?" Jamie asked her.

"Not good-bye," she whispered. "We will return."

"*Adios*, then."

She nodded absently as she slipped her feet into the floor loops, her eyes on the world they were about to leave.

"I still can hardly believe I'm here," Jamie said. "It's kind of like a dream."

Joanna glanced up at him. "We have a long and difficult journey ahead of us. Hardly a dream."

"It is for me."

She almost smiled. "You are a romantic."

"Aren't you?"

"No," Joanna said. "Women must be practical. Men can be the romantics. Women must think about the consequences."

"Departure in three minutes," came a Russian-accented voice over the speaker in the ceiling above them. *"Please take your assigned seats in the forward lounge."*

Jamie took Joanna by the shoulders and kissed her on the lips, lightly, swiftly.

"For luck," he said.

Joanna pushed free and floated away from him, her face frozen, unsmiling, her eyes wide and fearful. Without a word she turned and grabbed the edge of the hatch for purchase, then launched herself up the passageway toward the forward lounge.

Jamie waited a few moments, then went after her, moving more slowly. Then he saw Tony Reed hovering in the doorway to his cubicle, a sardonic smile on his lean face.

"I don't think the direct approach will work with little Joanna," Reed said.

Jamie said nothing. He pushed past Reed, heading forward.

The Englishman followed him. "I may have told you too much about our little cabal to get rid of Hoffman. Remember, my impetuous friend, that she *may* have wanted to have you picked for the expedition, but she *certainly* did not want Hoffman to come with us."

Jamie looked over his shoulder and said, "White man speaks with forked tongue."

Reed laughed all the way to the forward lounge.

There were no windows in the compartment. If necessary, this entire forward section of the spacecraft could be detached and flown by the pilots up in the cockpit into a reentry trajectory and an ocean spashdown. The procedure was for emergency use only; the mission plan called for the spacecraft to return to Earth orbit, where the personnel would transfer to shuttles for the final ride to Earth's surface. But a water landing was possible, if the need arose.

Jamie had barely floundered through the swimming course required by the mission planners. He wondered how the seven other
scientists strapping themselves into their cushioned chairs would
handle such an emergency. Or the four astronauts and cosmonauts
in the cockpit, for that matter. It would be fine irony to go all the
way to Mars and back and then drown.

"Departure in thirty seconds," came Vosnesensky's voice from the
cockpit. "I am putting an external camera view on the display
screen."

The compartment had a small screen built into its forward bulkhead. It flickered briefly, then showed the curving bulk of the blue-
and-white Earth sliding past. Jamie took the last remaining seat and
clicked the safety belt across his lap to prevent himself from floating
out of the chair. Reed had taken the chair beside Joanna.

"Five seconds . . . four, three, two, one—ignition."

The Russian's voice was flat calm. Jamie felt a surge of pressure
pushing him against the chair's back. Nothing startling; he had driven
sports cars with more acceleration. The picture of Earth on the display screen did not change discernibly.

But Vosnesensky's voice said, "We are off, on schedule. *Mars 2*
thruster ignition was precisely on time, also."

A clearly American voice broke in, "We're off for Mars!"

Not one of the scientists cheered. Jamie wanted to, but felt too
embarrassed. An image of Edith formed in his mind, the strangely
sad smile on her pretty face as they said good-bye for the final time.
No, not the final time, Jamie told himself. I'll be back. I'll see her
when I get back.

He did not notice Tony Reed staring at him, thinking, *I got rid of
that prig Hoffman and neither our Navaho geologist nor pretty Joanna
has even so much as thanked me for it. Perhaps I made a mistake.
She's interested in this Red Indian. As long as he's among us Joanna
won't even look at me.*

S O L 3: NIGHT

They did not eat together that night. Joanna and the other two women huddled by the biology bench, ignoring food as they tested the green-streaked rock. Tony Reed and a couple of the other men drifted by, but the women shooed them away.

Jamie picked at his meal, worrying more about the idiotic news media back home than the Martian rock. It's copper, he told himself. Got to be.

But suppose it isn't? A part of his mind *wanted* the rock to be life bearing. In fact, as he sat alone at the wardroom table methodically working his way through the bland microwaved meal, Jamie realized that if they had indeed found life it would surely divert the media's attention from this Native American business.

He got up and took his half-finished tray to the recycler, scraped the food into the slot in its top, and then stacked the tray and his utensils in the dishwasher's rack. Someone had put a swing-era tape on the sound system: a clarinet sweet as licorice worked through an old ballad.

Laughter rose from the far side of the dome; men joking together. He recognized Patel's high-pitched squeal. His fellow geologist had found something amusing. Whom was he sharing it with? Reed? Naguib? Toshima? From the sound of it they were all in one of the lab areas together.

Vosnesensky and the three other pilots were sitting around one of the communications consoles. Its screen showed a topographical map. Planning the first cross-country traverse, Jamie thought as he walked past them.

"Waterman, come and look at this," called Vosnesensky. "Latest photos of the badlands."

Jamie joined them and saw that the image on the screen was a map of contour lines superimposed on a photograph of the Noctis

Labyrinthus region, slightly less than three hundred kilometers to the south. He pulled a chair from the monitoring station next to the comm console and joined the little group.

Noctis Labyrinthus. The badlands. A real labyrinth of interconnected canyons and chains of craters, fault lines that ran for hundreds of kilometers like giant cracks crisscrossing the ground, slumped canyon walls with landslides that may have been caused by flowing water.

The labyrinth was at the western end of the titanic Valles Marineris, the Grand Canyon of Mars that extended more than four thousand kilometers, at places so wide that an observer standing on the lip of the seven-kilometer-deep canyon could not see the other side of it. Named after the *Mariner 9* spacecraft that discovered the giant rift, Valles Marineris was longer than North America was wide, and deeper than the Atlantic Ocean. Its western end butted into the enormous upswelling of the Tharsis Bulge, where ten-kilometer-high volcanoes sat atop a mammoth blister of rock the size of Europe.

Where the deeply carved Valles Marineris meets the dense rock of the Tharsis Bulge the badlands of the Noctis Labyrinthus spreads its fractured pattern of canyons. From orbit above Mars it almost looks as if the great rip in the ground was stopped and shattered by the uplifted bulge the way a battering ram might splinter against an iron door.

"We are deciding on the route for the first traverse," Vosnesensky said as Jamie sat down in front of the display screen.

Jamie looked at the four fliers. Vosnesensky seemed brooding and melancholy, as usual. Mironov was smiling the way a man does when he is bored or embarrassed. Connors was studying the map display intently, as if trying to memorize it. Paul Abell had a puzzled, quizzical expression on his pop-eyed face.

Tapping a fingernail against the screen, Jamie said, "I'd like to arrive here, at this point."

Abell said, "That's not exactly where Father DiNardo indicated in his mission plan, is it?"

"Not quite. I've been thinking about this traverse all during our flight here. This spot here is a branching point. I can look at three canyons from there." Leaning forward enough to reach the keyboard, Jamie punched up an enlargement of the region. "You see? There's slumping here; a landslide. And clear fracture lines . . ."

"Yes, yes," said Vosnesensky impatiently. "That is permissible. We can get you to that point."

"Good."

"I have decided to drive the rover myself," Vosnesensky said.

Jamie glanced at Connors. The American did not seem surprised. Jamie realized that he had been keeping his eyes focused on the display screen because he was angry. The astronaut's lips were pressed together in a grim tight line.

"I thought the mission plan called for Pete to drive the rover."

"I have changed the plan," Vosnesensky said flatly.

"Why?"

"This is no reflection on Pete. He will still command one of the other traverses and fly the soarplane."

"But why change the mission plan?" Jamie insisted.

Mironov's smile had gradually dwindled. He said, "This has nothing to do with politics, I assure you."

Which immediately made Jamie think that it was entirely due to national pride and competition. Or at least some form of rivalry between the Russians and the Americans.

Connors finally spoke up. "It's cool, Jamie. We talked it over. Mike just wants to take the first traverse himself." Forcing a humorless grin, the astronaut added, "It's part of Mike's god complex. He's afraid something'll go wrong if he's not there running the show himself."

Mikhail Vosnesensky made himself smile back at Connors. "I have no intention of flying the soarplane. You may have that honor entirely to yourself."

Connors nodded and turned back toward the display screen.

Jamie asked, "Do we start the traverse as scheduled?"

"In two days, yes."

"The only change," Mironov said, "is to substitute Mikhail Andreivitch as your chauffeur."

"Does Dr. Li know about this?" Jamie asked.

"He will be informed. I do not expect him to object," Vosnesensky said.

With a shrug, Jamie said, "Well, I guess it's okay then."

Mironov got to his feet and Vosnesensky lumbered up from his chair a fraction of a second after him. For a wild moment Jamie got the impression that Mironov was in charge, not Vosnesensky. Vaguely he recalled that the Russians used to have political officers among their men who worked at subsidiary jobs but were actually the real bosses.

As the two Russians walked away, Connors said earnestly, "Listen,

Jamie, the last thing I want is for a Soviet-American rivalry to break out here."

"But why'd he do it?" Jamie asked.

Leaning his forearms on his knees, Connors answered, "I think he really has a god complex. He thinks that if he's in charge nothing will go wrong. It's the first overland traverse and he's nervous about it."

Abell looked skeptical but said nothing.

"You don't mind being bumped?" Jamie asked.

Connors leaned back again, away from him. "Sure I mind! Shit, who wouldn't mind? But like the man said, there'll be other traverses. Let him take the first one; it's okay. I'll do the soarplane flying; he can't talk me out of that."

Abell grunted. "So our friend Mike gets to play god, but he lets you be the angel."

Connors tapped Abell on the shoulder and got up from his chair. Abell left with him. Jamie sat alone in front of the display screen, caring less about who drove the damned rover than he did about what they would find when they reached the intersection of those three canyons.

Finally he flicked the display off and got to his feet. Scanning the dome's interior, he saw that the women were still at the biology bench, but they were talking among themselves now, no longer bent over the equipment. The music had ended; the dome was quiet. Joanna looked tired.

Jamie approached them slowly, but they did not seem to notice him. They sat in the spindly Martian-gravity chairs earnestly talking among themselves.

"How's it going?"

Turning in her chair, Ilona gave him a bitter scowl. "It's inorganic."

"You were right," said Joanna. "It is nothing more than oxidized copper."

Even the normally cheerful Monique seemed downcast. "No organic material at all, neither in the rock itself nor in the soil samples. No long-chain molecules."

Jamie stood evenly balanced on the balls of his feet, as if ready to fight or flee, depending on the circumstances. They can give me the rock now, so I can determine its age and how long it's been sitting on the surface.

"But there's water," he heard himself say.

"Yes, permafrost," said Ilona. "Starting at about one meter below the surface."

Monique shook her head. "The water is frozen, not liquid. That makes it difficult to use for biological reactions."

"The soil is loaded with superoxides, as well," Ilona added. "Living cells cannot exist in such a corrosive environment."

"*Terrestrial* living cells," Jamie said. "This is Mars."

Ilona smiled thinly. "I can't imagine any kind of living cells existing in a pit of rusty iron."

"Anaerobic bacteria do so on Earth," Monique said.

"Without access to water?"

"Ah, yes, there is that."

Jamie looked into Joanna's eyes. He saw more than fatigue there; she looked defeated. Like a woman who had hacked her way through a jungle only to find that she had gone in a circle and was back where she had started.

"Well, it was just our first shot out there," he said. "None of us expected to find even copper, did we?"

Monique brightened. "There *must* be organic materials *somewhere* in the soil! After all, the unmanned probes brought back rocks that bore organics."

"The surface has been bombarded by meteorites for eons," said Ilona, as if trying to convince herself. "Some of those meteorites *had* to be carbonaceous chondrites!"

Nodding, Jamie agreed. "Maybe the impact sites of chondritic meteorites are centers where life processes began."

"If the organics in the meteorite are not destroyed by the heat of the impact," Joanna nearly whispered.

"Yes. They might be, mightn't they?"

"We must make impact sites a new priority on our list of objectives," Monique said.

Ilona turned thoughtful. "If life processes began at such impact sites they would have spread across the entire surface of the planet, wouldn't they? After all, life is a dynamic process. It doesn't stay in one place. It expands. It grows."

"Only if it can find the nutrients and energy it requires," said Monique. "Otherwise . . ."

"Otherwise it dies out," Joanna said in a low, drained voice. "Or it never even begins."

Jamie and the others fell silent.

"Even if meteorites bearing amino acids and other long-chain carbon molecules have been raining out of the sky for eons," Joanna went on, her voice so low he could barely hear her, "what do they encounter when they reach the surface? High levels of ultraviolet and even harder radiation, subfreezing temperatures every night, the soil loaded with superoxides, no liquid water . . ."

Jamie stopped her with an upraised hand. "Wait a minute. Even a small meteorite, like the one we found in Antarctica, would hit the ground with enough energy to liquefy the permafrost if the ice is only a meter or so beneath the surface."

"Yes," said Ilona. "But how long would the water remain liquid?"

"You saw what happened out there today," Monique said. "In this thin atmosphere the water boils away instantly."

Jamie nodded reluctant agreement.

"There is no life on Mars," Joanna said. "None at all."

"You're tired," said Monique. "We all are. A good night's sleep is what we need. Things will look better in the morning's light."

"Yes, Mama," said Ilona, grinning.

"But first let us put a little water on our seedlings, eh?" Monique said. "Then we can sleep."

Joanna tried to smile at her, but did not quite make it. Jamie realized that she had wanted to be able to tell her father that they had discovered life. No one else mattered to Joanna, only her father. She wanted to give him that triumph. Now she felt that she had failed.

He wanted to put his arm around her shoulders and tell her that it was all right, that if she hadn't made the great discovery there were still important and wonderful things to be done on Mars. Even if the planet were totally dead that information in itself could teach science vital knowledge about the needs and drives of life. He realized that he wanted to hold her, comfort her, lend her some of his own strength.

But Joanna had no room in her life for him. Her father owned her soul. Everything she did, she did for her father.

Jamie felt a smoldering jealousy for a rival who was a hundred million kilometers away, a rival he could not possibly fight.

WASHINGTON:
THE WHITE HOUSE

In bygone years the Map Room had been used by Franklin D. Roosevelt as a situation room where he could follow the course of World War II. Located on the ground floor of the mansion's central section, it was easy to get to from the Oval Office, even in a wheelchair.

Now the President used the room for his weekly private lunches with the Vice-President, a tradition neither of them cherished.

The first Hispanic to serve as President and the first woman to be Vice-President, the duo had inherited from the previous administration a Mars program that they would have canceled, except that it had gone too far to stop. Instead, they worked to win for themselves the credit for the first human landings on Mars while cutting expenditures for the program back to the bone. As political cynicism goes, theirs was almost trivial.

They made an odd-looking couple. The President was rotund and bald, with a dark moustache and large soft brown eyes. His skin was not so dark as to frighten non-Hispanic voters. On television he looked like a friendly smiling uncle or perhaps the easygoing guy who ran the hardware store. The Vice-President was wiry, ash blonde, and strident. When she raised her voice it took on the urgency of a dentist's drill.

She was incensed.

"Do you realize how this looks to the media?" she asked, waving a gold salad fork in the air.

The President glanced past her irate face to the portrait of Franklin Pierce hanging against the cream-colored far wall. The least-remembered of all the men who had lived in the White House. The President cherished Pierce's portrait: it served as a reminder and a spur. At least I can do better than he did.

"You're not even listening to me!"

The President returned his attention to his veep. She had never entirely outgrown her origins as a public schoolteacher in New Jersey. She was quick to anger, slow to forgive.

"I understand the situation," he said softly. "All sorts of people have been hounding me about this Native American business, too."

"Well, what are we going to do about it? If we let the media have that videotape interview he'll look like a goddammed saint. If we refuse to release it to the media we'll look like bastards."

The President winced at her choice of words. He was essentially a gentle man. He felt relaxed among the luxurious burgundy draperies and lustrous Chippendale furnishings of the Map Room. Even the huge Persian carpet soothed him with its glowing colors and intricate geometric designs.

"I saw the video," he answered. "The young man simply said he wasn't involved in politics. I don't see how that can hurt us."

"He's become a hero to the Indians," the Vice-President snapped. "And if we release that tape he'll become a hero to every minority group in the nation."

"But those are our own people . . ."

"Yes! Right! *Our* people. But if we let the media turn him into a hero, how long do you think it'll take Masterson and those other bastards to turn him into a front man for their own organization?"

The President shook his head. "I don't think so."

"Sure! You're retiring after next year. I've got to face all the primaries. It's tough enough being a woman without having to deal with a Native American who's been to Mars!"

"But he's not interested in politics," said the President.

"Then why did he start that Indian crap?" The Vice-President was fuming, her lunch lying before her untouched. "He'll be getting back from Mars just in time for the first primaries. I don't want him being used against me!"

The President, who understood something of politics, thought swiftly. "Suppose he becomes one of your supporters?"

She shook her head doggedly. "Masterson's in tight with the high-tech crowd. He'll grab this redskin before we can; you know that. Remember, *I* was the one who got the Space Council to vote *against* funding for further Mars missions until we get the results back from this one! Masterson will crucify me for that! And this Indian will help him. He's *already* helping him!"

Pushing his chair back slightly, the President gazed around the room for support. None of the portraits offered a bit of help, not even the one of FDR in his Navy cape.

"Well, what can we do about it?" he asked.

"Muzzle him," the Vice-President replied immediately. "Get him off the team on the ground there on Mars and put him up in one of the orbiting ships. That way he'll be ignored by the media. They're only interested in what's going on on the ground."

"But won't people think that we're hurting this scientist for political reasons?"

"We can find a reason to get him off the ground team. Not right away, of course. In a week or two. That will be plenty of time. The media might squawk, but I'd rather have them squawking now than a year from now when he gets back here."

"Do you think we can get away with that?"

"A year from now he'll be forgotten. Nobody's got an attention span that long."

The President smiled gently. "You do."

His Vice-President grimaced back at him. "In our business you need a long memory. And claws."

"And the video?"

"Tell the media he refused to be interviewed. Make him look like a stuck-up scientific type instead of a noble Indian trying to call attention to his people's plight."

The President nodded slowly. It might work. And this power-hungry woman sitting across from him might just make herself the first female President of the United States. She had the fire in her gut for it. And the claws.

IN TRANSIT:
BETWEEN WORLDS

1

During the long years of training, Jamie had traveled so much that he often awoke in the morning with the feeling that he had never really left Houston; some mysterious organization had merely changed the city outside his hotel window. The cities out there were gigantic stage sets and all the people in them were hired actors. Or perhaps very clever robots.

After several weeks aboard the *Mars 1* spacecraft coasting toward its distant destination, Jamie began to think that all spacecraft were stage sets, too.

They all looked alike from the inside. The space stations in Earth orbit, the shuttles that carried the Mars explorers to them, the Mars-bound craft themselves—their interiors were all almost identical. Cramped compartments, narrow passageways, the constant hum of electrical equipment, the glare-free, shadowless, flat lighting, the same smell of cold metal and canned stale air. The packed-in feeling that someone was waiting in line behind you, even in the toilet.

Now that the two spacecraft had been spun up, though, there was at least a feeling of gravity. One could walk down the central corridor, sit in a chair, sleep with the solidity of a mattress and blanket that did not float away when you turned over.

There was only one place on the *Mars 1* craft that was not claustrophobic: the observation port that looked out on the universe. Jamie found himself going there more and more often as the long wearisome weeks passed by. It would take more than nine months before they reached the red planet and established a safe orbit around it. Nine months of inactivity, living cheek by jowl like a dozen sardines inside an aluminum can. No, not a can, Jamie said to himself. A pressure cooker.

There was work for them to do, of sorts. And a strict schedule of physical exercises in the closet-sized gymnasium. But it was all perfunctory. Jamie put in his required hours on the exercise machines; they kept his muscles in shape, but his mind wandered—he was bored, moody, dull.

Every two or three days he received a call from DiNardo, recovered now from his surgery. The Jesuit reviewed the work going on in several terrestrial laboratories, further analysis of the rocks and soil samples returned from Mars by the unmanned robot exploratory vehicles. The various analyses differed only in the minutest details: the soil samples were sterile, although a few of the rocks contained traces of organic material, carbon-rich chemicals that might be the precursors of living organisms.

The chemicals of life might exist in those rocks, but that's about as exciting as looking at the bottles of aspirin tablets in a drugstore display case. They haven't found anything *alive* in the samples, not even an amoeba.

Nearly four months into the flight, Jamie suddenly asked, "How is Professor Hoffman? Is he involved in these analyses?"

It took several minutes for messages to travel the distance between the spacecraft and Earth. As he watched the little display screen of the communications console Jamie saw DiNardo's swarthy face register surprise, then something else. Guilt? The priest ran a hand over his shaved scalp before answering.

"Professor Hoffman has apparently suffered a nervous breakdown. He is in a rest home in Vienna for the present."

Jamie felt the same surprise flaring into guilt that seared his guts.

"I have visited him myself," DiNardo went on. "His doctors assure me that he will be fine in a few weeks or so."

I wonder how I'd have reacted to being yanked off the mission at the last minute, Jamie asked himself. He changed the subject back to geology and concluded his conversation with the priest as swiftly as he could.

He left the communications console up on the flight deck and rushed down the length of the habitat module toward the observation port. By common custom the section housing the port was considered private. Whenever someone entered it and closed the hatch that separated it from the rest of the module, no one else in the crew would enter. It was the one place aboard the Mars spacecraft where a person could be alone.

Jamie needed to be alone, to be away from all the others. Yet as he hurried down the narrow passageway he felt a sullen tide of anger rising within him. Not guilt. Not pity. Anger. They always have to take something away from you, he heard a voice in his mind complain. They can never let you have the whole cake; they always lick the icing off first. Or piss on it. So I'm on my way to Mars and Hoffman's in a funny farm. Great.

Then he remembered his grandfather years ago, when Jamie had been an eager young high schooler bursting to show off how much he had learned in his science classes. He had tried to explain to Al the laws of thermodynamics, throwing in terms such as "entropy" and "heat flow" and "thermal equilibrium."

"Aw, I know all about that stuff," Al had said.

"You do?" Jamie had been extremely skeptical of his grandfather's claim.

"Sure. Comes up every day in the store. Or when I play poker. What it boils down to is, you can't win, you can't even break even, and you can't get out of the game."

Jamie had gaped at his grandfather. Al had explained the concepts of thermodynamics as succinctly as he would ever hear.

"Main thing," Al said, grinning at his surprised grandson, "is to stay in balance with life. That way no matter what happens it won't throw you. Stay in balance. Never lean so far in one direction that a puff of wind can knock you over."

What it boils down to is that you have to pay for everything you get, and the price is always more than the value of the thing you're after. And you can't get out of the game. Even millions of miles from Earth, you can't get out of the game.

The hatch to the observation area was open. No one was there. Good.

The astronomers hated the spin that produced a feeling of gravity within the Mars-bound ships. It meant that their telescopes, even though placed outside the ships along the tethers connecting them, had to be mounted on complex motorized bearings that moved exactly opposite to the spin so that they could remain focused on the same distant speck of light for weeks or months at a time.

The spin had bothered Jamie, too, at first. The stars rotated past the oblong window in a slow steady procession instead of remaining fixed against the dark backdrop the way they did on Earth. But they don't really stay still on Earth, Jamie told himself. They rotate around the sky too slow for you to notice. Out here we've just speeded things up. We've made our own little world and it spins around every two and a half minutes instead of every twenty-four hours.

It felt cold in the observation section. He knew it was only his imagination, but the cold of that deep empty darkness out there seemed to seep through the window and chill him to the bone.

Someone was already there. As Jamie stepped through the open hatch he saw the tall, lithe form of Ilona Malater standing by the long window. She was staring out at the stars, her face solemn, immobile. In the faint light her honey-colored hair looked gray, her tan coveralls nearly colorless.

As Jamie approached the window he almost felt glad that someone else was there. His desire to be alone faded beneath his need for human warmth. He realized that Ilona was tall and slim enough to be a high-fashion model. Her aristocratic face had that magazine-cover haughtiness to it, as well.

"Hello," he said.

She whirled, startled, then relaxed and smiled. "Jamie. What are you doing up here?"

"Same as you, I guess."

"I thought this was my private hideaway." Ilona's voice was a rich, throaty contralto.

With a rueful grin Jamie said, "Me too." He hesitated, then offered, "I can go back . . ."

"No, that's all right." She smiled back at Jamie. "Perhaps I need someone to talk to more than I need solitude."

The only light in the area came from the faintly glowing guide strips on the floor. And the starlight. Barely enough to see her face, to catch the expression in her eyes. The electrical hum that pervaded the spacecraft seemed fainter here, muted.

"You heard about Hoffman?" Jamie asked.

"What has he done now?"

"He's had a nervous breakdown."

Ilona arched an eyebrow. "Serves him right, the pig."

"That's a hell of an attitude!"

"He was a womanizer. I imagine he's the terror of the female undergraduates wherever he teaches."

Jamie blinked at her. He had never thought of Hoffman as anything but a geologist who stood between himself and Mars.

"He tried to seduce every woman he met during training."

"He hit on you?"

Ilona laughed. "He tried to. I hit him back. I told him that if he could not satisfy his wife why did he think he could satisfy me? He never spoke another word to me."

Jamie thought it less than funny. There was a fierceness in this woman that he had never suspected, an anger seething within her.

Then it occurred to him. "He must have hit on Joanna too."

"Yes. Certainly."

That's why Joanna wanted him off the mission, Jamie said to himself. Not to get me aboard. Just to get rid of a man who bothered her.

He felt suddenly awkward. There was no place to sit except the chill metal floor, no one to turn to for support. He looked out the non-reflective window and saw nothing but the starry emptiness; the Mars 2 craft was out of sight, literally over their heads.

"Is Hoffman's breakdown what brought you up here?" Ilona asked.

Jamie nodded. "And you?"

"I had to get away," she said, her voice lowering. "I am becoming depressed."

"Why? What's wrong?"

"Mars is wrong. I am wrong. It was wrong to include a biochemist on this expedition. There is no life on Mars for me to study."

"We don't know that for certain," Jamie said. "Not yet."

"Don't we?" Ilona spoke the words with a weary sigh. Then she turned and stretched her arm toward a glowing ruddy point of light swinging past in the starry blackness.

"Look at the planet, Jamie. Think of all the rocks and soil samples and photographs we have studied. We get new photos and data every day from the orbiters they've put around the planet. Not a trace of life. Nothing. Mars is absolutely barren. Lifeless."

He turned from the red glow of Mars to focus on her sorrowing face once more. "But we've only had a few dozen samples. You're talking about a whole world. There must be . . ."

She laid a long manicured finger on Jamie's lips, silencing him. "You have heard of Gaia?" Ilona asked.

Jamie said, "The idea that the Earth is a living entity?"

Ilona gave him a scant smile. "That's close. Not bad for a geologist."

He found himself grinning back at her. "All right, what about Gaia? And what's it got to do with Mars?"

"The Gaia hypothesis states that all life on Earth works together as a self-regulating feedback system that maintains itself. No single species of life—not even the human race—lives in isolation. All species are part of the whole, part of the totally integrated living Gaia."

"I don't see what that's got to do with Mars," Jamie said.

"Life has spread itself all across the Earth," Ilona replied. "Down in the deepest ocean trenches there is life. The air teems with microorganisms, even up in the stratosphere there are yeast molds floating about. Even in the most barren Antarctic deserts there are rocks that hold colonies of lichens just below their surfaces."

"And Mars looks barren."

"Mars is barren. The probes have found nothing in the air. There is no liquid water. The soil is so loaded with superoxides it's like an intense bleach; no living organism could survive in it."

"Some of the rocks bear organic chemicals," Jamie reminded her.

"But if life existed on Mars it would not be confined to one place!" Ilona's husky voice was almost pleading now. "If there were a Martian equivalent of Gaia we would see life everywhere we looked, just as we do on Earth."

Stubbornly Jamie shook his head. "But Earth is warmer, Earth has liquid water everywhere you look, it's easy for life to grow and spread on Earth. Mars isn't that rich. Life would have a tougher time there."

Ilona shook her head too. "No, I don't believe that's the reason why Mars looks so bleak. The planet is truly barren. There is no life there and there probably never was. I have wasted the past three years of my life. Sending anyone involved in biology was a mistake."

She stood there framed by the oblong window, the slowly circling stars behind her. Ilona no longer looked haughty or regal. She looked depressed, disheartened.

Jamie shrugged and muttered, "I don't think you can give up before you've even started. No matter what you believe you can't really say anything definite until you've gotten there and looked for yourself. Mars probably has a few surprises in store for you. For all of us."

"Perhaps." Ilona sighed again. Then she wrapped her arms around herself and shivered. "It's always so cold in here! I should have worn my thermal underwear."

"I'm sorry I don't have a sweater or jacket . . ."

"It's my own fault," she said. "I acted on impulse, coming here in just these coveralls."

Jamie grinned at her. "That's against the rules. How many times has Vosnesensky drilled it into us: think ten times before you do anything."

"Vosnesensky." She growled the name, like a lioness snarling.

"What's wrong with Mikhail?" Jamie asked. "He doesn't seem like such a bad guy to me."

"He is a Russian."

"So what?"

"Half my family was murdered by Russians in nineteen fifty-six. My grandmother barely escaped the country. My grandfather was hanged. As if he were a criminal, the Russians hanged him."

"That wasn't Vosnesensky's fault. Russia's changed a lot since then. So has Hungary. It all happened half a century ago."

"It's easy for you Americans to forgive and forget. Not so easy for me and my people."

Jamie did not know what to say. There's nothing I can say, he realized. For several moments they stood facing each other while the stars arced around them and the background buzz of electrical equipment hummed its faint note like a distant chorus of Tibetan lamas droning a mantra.

Ilona shuddered. "It is cold up here." She moved closer to Jamie, pressed against him.

"We could go back," Jamie said. Yet he slid one arm around her waist. It seemed the right thing to do.

"No, not yet. I have been worried about you," said Ilona. Her voice was low, sensuous. Her face so close to Jamie's that he could smell the faint perfume in her honey-blonde hair.

"Worried about me?"

"You seem . . . withdrawn. Lonely."

He made half a shrug. "We're a long way from home."

"You avoid us."

"Avoid you?" Jamie felt stupid repeating her words, but she was catching him unprepared.

"Joanna and me. Katrin. You avoid us. Didn't you realize that?"

"We're not supposed to get emotionally involved with one another."

"Another rule, I know. But does that mean you can't sit next to us at meals? I've been watching you very carefully. You deliberately stay as far from us as you can."

A hundred thoughts raced through Jamie's mind. He muttered, "Lead us not into temptation."

"Are you in love with Joanna?"

"No! Of course not."

"Of course not," Ilona mimicked, smiling at him. "The rules forbid us to fall in love, don't they."

"Not just the rules," Jamie replied.

"You don't want to get involved emotionally, is that it?"

He nodded, thinking of Edith back in Houston, wondering suddenly where she was, who she was with now.

Ilona wrapped her arms around Jamie's neck. "When is the last time you made love?"

"What? I don't think . . ."

"I'll wager you haven't made love since the last time you went home to California, have you?"

"No, you're wrong."

"Certainly not since we arrived at the assembly station. Not since then."

Jamie's mind was telling him to disengage from her and get away but his arms were clasping Ilona close to him, holding her tightly against his body. Their lips were almost touching.

"I want to make love with you, Jamie. Right here and now. I want to make love with my strong silent friend here among the stars. I want your strength, your warmth."

She kissed him fiercely, then whispered, "The rules say nothing against fucking, Jamie. Fuck me, red man, fuck me."

Slowly, languidly, almost like a man hypnotized, Jamie pulled open the front of Ilona's coveralls; the Velcro seam split with the same noise as ripping fabric. As if in a dream he watched himself slide the garment over her shoulders and down her long arms. She wore nothing at all beneath the coveralls. The skin of her bare shoulders and slight breasts looked milky white in the starlight. All the long months of denial exploded in a sudden frenzy as Jamie pulled Ilona to the hard metal flooring, impervious to the cold, uncaring about Mars or Gaia or anything else except this eager tigress. The stars wheeled impassively about them.

2

The next morning at breakfast Jamie felt terribly embarrassed. He could not face Joanna at all, and found that it was difficult for him even to look into Ilona's face. She smiled at him, though, from across the narrow wardroom table as he sat down with his tray between Tony Reed and Tadeusz Sliwa, the golden-haired Polish backup biochemist.

Jamie hurried through his breakfast and headed quickly up toward the communications console, where he intended to contact the growing library at Houston and bury himself in reading more details about the odd, oxygen-rich chemistry of the soil of Mars.

"You seem to be in a hurry."

It was Tony Reed, striding up the narrow passageway behind him.

"I've got some reading to do," Jamie said.

"Afraid I have to conduct some official business with you, my friend."

Jamie stopped and turned around to face Reed. "Official business?"

"As the ship's resident physician, yes."

"I don't understand."

"Please come with me to my office," said Reed, smiling crookedly.

The ship's infirmary was situated just behind the exercise room. It was a cubicle no larger than any of the individual quarters for the personnel, cramped and crowded even with only two people in it.

Reed slid the accordion-fold door shut and carefully latched it in place. Jamie could hear the groaning squeal of the weight machine from the other side of the partition and the puffing grunts of whoever was working out with it.

"We missed you yesterday afternoon," Tony said, a sly grin on his face.

"I needed some privacy," he said.

"So did Ilona, apparently."

Reed squeezed past Jamie and sat on the edge of the built-in desk, folding his arms across his chest. He nodded toward the stool resting beside the locked medicine cabinet.

Jamie remained standing. He wondered who might be in the exercise room next door and how much he could hear through the thin partition wall.

Reed was practically leering. "You seemed to disappear right after she did. And then you both returned to us at about the same time."

"Hoffman's had a nervous breakdown," Jamie said. "I was pretty upset by the news."

"So you consoled yourself by taking your turn with our in-house sexual therapist."

"My turn . . . ?" Jamie's insides went hollow, as if he had suddenly become weightless.

The grin on Tony's face was positively evil. "Didn't you know? Ilona's decided to have her fun with each of the males aboard. Except for Vosnesensky and Ivshenko, of course. She hates the Russkies. I think she's doing what she's doing merely to drive our poor Russian leader and his backup insane with jealousy. It might work, too."

Jamie felt as if he were gasping for air.

"Now then." Reed cleared his throat and put on a more serious, professional face. "There's the matter of your sexual conduct."

Jamie frowned. "*My* sexual conduct?"

"I am required to give you standard lecture number double-ought one: sexual responsibility and its consequences." The grin had come back to Reed's face.

"Do you give this lecture to Ilona, too?"

"Yes, of course," He was smirking. "With some variations, of course."

"Every time?"

"Every time I can."

Jamie glowered at the Englishman.

"Seriously, James, I must warn you that if your sexual conduct threatens to create a problem aboard ship, it is my duty to report to Dr. Li—and to take certain steps."

"Make me take saltpeter?"

"Oh, we have much better stuff than saltpeter," Reed said. "Pharmacology has come a long way. The only trouble is, whatever suppressant we dose you with will shrink your gonads."

"Shrink . . . !"

"Can't be helped. They'll grow back to normal once the medication is stopped, of course. We won't castrate you, not even chemically."

Jamie asked, "What if I won't take the medication—assuming I'm going to be such a lecher that you'll want to dose me."

"Oh, you'll take it, one way or the other. I can always doctor your meals, you know. Or spike the drinking water. Just as I would do if you refused to take your vitamin supplements. It wouldn't be difficult."

Jamie heard himself mutter, "Son of a bitch."

"That's exactly what we're trying to prevent, actually," said Reed. Then he laughed out loud at his own little joke.

3

"I wish these bunks were just a bit wider."

"You don't like being so close?"

"My arm's fallen asleep."

"As long as nothing else on you has gone asleep."

"So what did you think of our wild Indian?"

"He was quite wild, once he got started."

"As good as I?"

She laughed softly. "As a famous film star once said, 'Goodness had nothing to do with it.' "

"That completes the roster, doesn't it? Except for the Russkies."

"I will not let them touch me!"

"Pity. Poor Mikhail Andreivitch looks as if he'll explode any day now."

"Let him. I don't care."

"And Ivshenko seems like a jolly chap. Perhaps if I accompanied you we could make a threesome out of it."

"You're already complaining about the bunks being too narrow."

"Um, yes, there is that."

"I will not approach the Russians. Let them stew in their own juices."

"But otherwise . . ."

"Waterman was the last holdout."

"And now he's fallen."

"What about you? How successful have you been?"

"Actually, Katrin and I had a little workout in the gymnasium again."

"But what about Joanna?"

A long silence.

"Well?"

"One has to be very circumspect with Joanna, you know. I believe she's still a virgin."

"Only three women on the ship and you've failed with one of them."

"I'm working on it."

"I've succeeded with every one of the men now."

"Except the Russians."

"Pah! You fuck the Russians if you're so worried about them."

"Hardly! It's little Joanna I want."

"Then you're going to have to try harder, aren't you?"

"You mean this isn't hard enough to suit you?"

"Hmm . . . well . . . I suppose it will do for now."

Hours later, alone and still sleepless, Tony Reed told himself that it was all a game, a pleasant way to pass the boring weeks while they were all packed together inside the spacecraft. We're harming no one. Except perhaps the Russians, but that's not my doing. Perhaps Katrin is accommodating them, a little Russo-German friendship pact.

He turned in the bunk, trying to find a more comfortable position. It's only a game, a delightful game. Yet a deeper voice in his mind reminded him that soldiers on their way to battle play a similar game. Fear is the spur, the voice said to Tony. You go through the motions of creating life because you are so terrified of impending death.

Nonsense, Tony replied to his inner voice. We're perfectly safe inside this spacecraft. We're protected by the work of the best minds in the world. There is a certain element of risk, of course. That's what makes it all so interesting.

The voice was not placated. Death is waiting a mere few centimeters from you, on the other side of this spacecraft's thin metal skin. Play your game, try to get the fear out of your mind or expiate it with bursts of lovemaking. But death is waiting for us all, and we are flying toward it.

S O L 6: MORNING

Strangely, Jamie felt more relaxed and free cooped up in the cramped rover with Vosnesensky than he had at their base camp's dome.

The rover was a segmented trio of aluminum cylindrical canisters, each of them mounted on spindly, springy wheels that trundled across the sandy, rock-strewn surface of Mars. One of the cylindrical segments held a fuel tank big enough to allow the rover to remain out in the field for a week or more. The middle segment held equipment and supplies. Up front, the largest of the three cylindrical canisters was pressurized like a spacecraft so that humans could live inside it in shirtsleeves. There was a bulbous plastiglass cockpit at its front end and an airlock at its rear, where it linked with the second segment.

The rover was designed to carry four comfortably, and could squeeze in twice that many in an emergency. Jamie had expected to feel tense, alone with Vosnesensky; two men from very different backgrounds, almost entirely different worlds. Yet their first day in the rover went smoothly enough, even though they hardly spoke to one another.

The Russian did most of the driving; Jamie did most of the outside work. They covered little more than a hundred kilometers the first day out, driving only during the daylight hours. The dull upland plain of their landing site quickly gave way to the rougher terrain of Noctis Fossae, crisscrossed with cracks and faults like the battlefield of two entrenched armies.

The badlands grew much more rugged, until they were threading through a jagged stony forest of rock spires that loomed high above them; rock pillars carved into eerie sculptures that reminded Jamie of wildly abstract totem poles. The wind's eroded away the soft stone and left these pillars of granitic stuff standing, he told himself. Then he realized that the gentle winds of Mars had to work for hundreds of millions of years to carve their magic this way.

For hours they drove through the towering spires of stone. Jamie sat fascinated, staring, waiting to see symbols of eagles or bears scratched into the rock.

The crevasses ran generally north-south, which made their southward journeying easier, but with the rocks that seemed to cover the ground everywhere, and the craters and spires and sand dunes, they seldom reached a speed of even thirty kilometers per hour.

Like driving a pickup on reservation land, Jamie said to himself as they rode jouncing through the desolate country. Except there are no roads at all. Not even a trail or an animal track.

They stopped virtually every hour. Jamie would go outside in his sky-blue hard suit to take rock and soil samples and plant an automated meteorology/geology beacon that would measure air temperature and pressure, humidity, wind velocity, and record heat flow coming up from underground, as well as any seismic activity. The beacon sent its signal to the pair of spacecraft hovering in synchronous orbit some twenty thousand kilometers above the equator. The communications equipment aboard the spacecraft automatically relayed the signals both to their base camp and back to Earth.

Despite the rover's pressurized interior both Jamie and Vosnesensky found themselves living inside their hard suits. The Russian went strictly by the mission rules that said he had to be suited up whenever Jamie went outside, in case an emergency arose. More often than not, the cosmonaut came out with Jamie. At first he busied himself with inspecting the rover's exterior: the wheels, the antennas, the way the iron-rich Martian sand powdered the finish of the rover's skin.

By the second morning, though, it seemed to Jamie that Vosnesensky came outside merely to have some human company and to enjoy the scenery.

"You say your New Mexico looks like this?" the Russian asked.

Jamie heard his voice in his helmet earphones. Bent stiffly over a waist-deep gully that exposed a seam of basaltic rock, he said, "Yep. Cliffs and arroyos—canyons. Clear skies. Not much rain."

"It must be very barren, then."

Smiling to himself, Jamie replied, "Compared to this it's the Garden of Eden."

The Russian fell silent.

Jamie straightened up and took the video camera from his belt. The gully ran all the way out to the horizon, almost as straight as train tracks except for some slumping here and there where the ground had slid down to partially fill it in. A fault line, Jamie recognized. The area's crisscrossed with them. But this one's been eroded by running water. Had to be. Or mass wasting, permafrost melting beneath the surface and undermining everything. But when? There's been no liquid water around here for hundreds of millions of years, most likely. Could a rill remain unchanged all that time?

He returned the camcorder to its clip on his belt and went to work chipping at the exposed rock ledge. Then he put the samples into a pouch and picked up the drill. As usual, the drill bit into the ground easily for the first meter or so, then hit resistance. Permafrost, thought Jamie. This whole region is sitting on top of a frozen ocean just a few feet below the surface. Once he had pulled the core sample from the drill bit and carefully deposited it in a sample case, he started back toward the rover.

Vosnesensky was standing there watching in his fire-engine red hard suit.

"Okay," Jamie said. "I'm finished here. All I've got to do is . . ."

He realized that the Russian had already taken one of his sensor beacons from the equipment bay in the rover's middle section. Jamie took it from him.

"Thanks, Mikhail."

He could sense the man's shrug. "I had nothing better to do."

"Thanks," Jamie repeated.

Minutes later they were back in the rover's cockpit, Vosnesensky in the left seat. They had both removed their helmets and gloves; their hard suits bulked in the cockpit's bucket seats like a pair of brightly colored armor-plated polar bears.

Vosnesensky steered between a boulder the size of a small house and a shallow circular depression that looked to Jamie like the weathered fossil of an ancient meteor crater. The Russian had small, almost delicate hands, Jamie noticed. He maneuvered the tiny steering wheel with nothing more than a fingertip's pressure.

"We should reach the canyons today," he said, "if we do not have to make more stops."

Jamie took the hint. "We'll stop only to fill in the net of beacons. Of course, if there's some important change in the landforms . . ."

Vosnesensky smiled slightly without turning his eyes away from his driving. "Of course."

Jamie tried to settle back and get comfortable, but the hard shell of the pressure suit was not meant to sit in. The damned armpit was still chafing despite the padding he had packed into it. He watched the landscape unrolling as they drove slowly toward the strangely close horizon. It bothered him, seeing the horizon so near. Almost frightened him down at the subliminal level where nightmares take root. Jamie felt as if they were driving toward the edge of a cliff.

"The horizon looks awfully close, doesn't it?" he said to Vosnesensky.

The Russian bobbed his head once. "The smaller the planet the shorter the horizon. It is even closer on the moon."

"I've never been to the moon."

"Much closer than here. And much more barren."

DiNardo had been on the moon, Jamie knew. I was called in so suddenly I never got farther off the Earth than the space stations until we started out for Mars.

He forced his attention away from the too-close horizon and concentrated on the land they were driving through. To anyone but a geologist the scenery would have looked dull, monotonous, barren. But Jamie's mind was leaping from rock to fault crack, crater to sand dune, trying to puzzle out the forces that had shaped this land, sculpted it into its present form.

"I have flown over New Mexico," Vosnesensky said, almost as if to himself. "In the *Mir 3* space station, while training for this mission."

"Then you saw how much it looks like Mars."

"I did not realize it at the time. I did not pay sufficient attention."

Jamie studied the Russian's face. He was dead serious, as always. Somber. Grim.

"Did you always want to be a cosmonaut?" Jamie asked suddenly. "Ever since you were a little child?"

Vosnesensky swiveled his head toward Jamie for an instant, then immediately turned back to look ahead. The expression on his face, fleetingly, was almost angry.

I shouldn't have asked, Jamie thought. He resents my prying into his personal history.

But the Russian muttered, "When I was very little, before starting school even, I wanted to be a cosmonaut. To me it meant everything. Gagarin was my hero; I wanted to be like him."

"The first man in space."

Vosnesensky nodded again, another single curt bob of his head.

"Gagarin was first in orbit. Armstrong was first on the moon. I told myself I would be first on Mars."

"And you were."

"Yes."

"You must feel very proud about it."

The cosmonaut glanced at Jamie again. "Proud, yes. Maybe even happy. But that moment has passed. Now I feel the responsibility. I am in charge. I am responsible for all your lives."

"I see."

"Do you? You are a scientist. You are happy to be here, to explore. You have a new world to play with. I am the man of authority. I am the one who must say no to you when you want to go too far, when you might endanger yourself or the others."

"We all understand that," Jamie said. "We accept it."

"Yes? Does Dr. Malater accept it? She hates me. She goes out of her way to annoy me every chance she gets."

"Ilona isn't . . ." Jamie's voice trailed off. He realized he had no defense for her.

"She is a Jewish bitch who hates all Russians. I know that. She has made it very clear to me."

"Her grandparents fled Hungary."

"So? Was that my fault? Am I to be blamed for things that happened in our grandparents' day? She risks the success of this mission because of a grudge that is two generations old?"

Jamie laughed softly. "Mikhail, I know people who have kept grudges going for two *centuries*, not just two generations."

The Russian said nothing.

"There are American Indians who're still fighting battles from colonial times."

"The Yankee imperialists took your land from you," Vosnesensky said. "They engaged in genocide against your people. We learned this in school."

"That happened a long time ago, Mikhail," said Jamie. "Should I spend my life hating all the whites? Should I hate my mother because she's descended from people who killed my ancestors? Should Pete Connors hate Paul Abell because his ancestors were slaves and Paul's were slave owners?"

"You feel no bitterness at all?"

The question stopped Jamie. He did not truly know what he felt. He had hardly ever considered the matter in such a light. Was Grandfather Al bitter? No, he seemed to accept the world as he found it.

"Use what's at hand, Jamie," Al would say. "When they hand you a lemon, make lemonade. Use what's at hand and make the best of what you find."

At length Jamie answered, "Mikhail, my parents are both university professors. I was born in New Mexico and went back there to spend summer vacations when I was a kid, but I grew up in Berkeley, California."

"A hotbed of radicalism." Vosnesensky said it flatly, as if reciting a memorized line. Jamie could not tell if the Russian were joking or serious.

"My father has spent most of his life trying *not* to be an Indian, although he'd never admit it. Probably doesn't even realize it. He earned a scholarship to Harvard University. He married a woman who's descended from the original *Mayflower* colonists. Neither one of them wanted me to be an Indian. They always told me to be a success, instead."

"They deny your father's heritage."

"They try to. Dad's scholarship came through a program designed especially to help minority groups—such as Native Americans. And the history texts he's written have sold to universities all around the U.S. mainly because they present American history from the minority viewpoint."

"Hmp."

"They were never active in Indian affairs and neither was I. If it weren't for my grandfather I'd be more white than you are. He taught me to understand my heritage, to accept it without hating anybody."

"But Malater, she hates me."

"Not you, Mikhail. She hates the *idea* of Russians. She doesn't see you as an individual. In her eyes you're part of an inhuman system that hanged her grandfather and forced her grandmother to run away from her native land."

Vosnesensky muttered, "That is not much help."

"Just like people who don't see individuals among the Indians, or even tribes," Jamie went on. "There's a lot of whites who still see 'the Indian' instead of individual men and women. They don't understand that some people *want* to live in their own way and don't *want* to become white."

"And you? How do you want to live?"

Jamie no longer had to think it over. "I'm the descendant of Indians. My skin is darker than yours. But if you take our brains out of our skulls, Mikhail, you wouldn't be able to tell the difference between them. That's where we really live. In our minds. We were born on opposite sides of the world and yet here we are together on a totally other planet. That's what's important. Not what our ancestors did to one another. What we're doing now. That's the important thing."

Vosnesensky nodded somberly. "Now you must give that little speech to Malater."

Jamie nodded soberly. "Okay. Maybe I will."

"It won't do any good."

"Probably not," Jamie agreed. "But there's no harm trying."

"Perhaps."

A new thought struck Jamie. "Mikhail—is that why you decided to come out on this traverse with me, instead of letting Pete do it? Just to get away from Ilona?"

"Nonsense!" spat the Russian with a vehemence that convinced Jamie he had hit on the truth. Ilona's hurting him, Jamie realized. She's really hurting the poor guy.

D O S S I E R: M. A. VOSNESENSKY

"Why can't you be reasonable, like your brother?"

Mikhail Andreivitch had heard that cry from his father all his life, it seemed. Nikolai was the older of the two boys, the paragon of the family. He studied hard at school and won excellent marks. He was quiet; his favorite pastime was reading books. His friends were few, but they were as studious and well mannered as Nikolai himself.

Mikhail, the second son (there was a younger daughter), sailed through school hardly even glancing at his textbooks. Somehow he got good grades; not quite as good as his older brother's, of course, but good enough to send him to the engineering college. Instead of studying, Mikhail listened to music, imported American rock mostly. The noise drove his father wild. Mikhail had lots of friends, girls as well as boys, and they all liked to listen to loud rock music and dress in blue jeans and leather jackets like bikers.

And he gambled. "The curse of the Russians," his father called it. His mother wept. Mikhail played cards with his friends and, sometimes, with older men who dressed well and had faces of stone. His parents feared the worst for him.

"You're turning your mother gray!" his father shouted when Mikhail announced he was going to buy a motorbike. He had worked for two years in secret, spending his afternoons in a garage helping the mechanic instead of attending classes. Somehow he had still managed to pass his examinations at school. Even so, two years' wages were not enough to buy the handsome machine he coveted. Mikhail had risked every ruble on a card game, vowing that if he won he would never gamble again. He won, mainly because he had been willing to take greater risks and had more money to put up than the other gamblers that night.

True to his self-imposed discipline, he never gambled again. He bought the bike over his father's objections and his mother's flowing tears. It did not matter to them that Mikhail could now drive from their apartment to his college classes without spending two hours a day on city buses. They only saw him zooming along the streets of Volgograd with pretty young girls shamelessly showing their legs as they rode behind Mikhail, clutching him tightly.

His mother was already gray, and his father almost totally bald. The old man had been a civil servant, one of the numberless apparatchiks who had been pushed out of the government bureaucracy in the name of *perestroika* and forced to find another job. Briefly he had worked as an administrator in one of the largest factories in Volgograd, but only briefly. He entered politics and soon was elected to a seat on the city council, where he settled down in comfortable anonymity for the remainder of his working life.

"Why can't you be reasonable, like your brother?" his father cried when Mikhail announced that he was going to take flying lessons. He had done well that school year, even winning academic honors now that he had given up the mechanic's job.

That was the summer Mikhail learned that he loved flying, and flying loved him. He was good at it, very good. He took to the air as naturally as an eagle, his instructor told him. He was actually in the air on his first solo flight when his older brother was killed in a senseless accident. A drunken truck driver smashed into the city bus he was riding. Fourteen injured and one killed. Nikolai.

Somehow his parents seemed to blame Mikhail for Nikolai's death. They raised no objection when he told them he had been accepted for cosmonaut training and would be leaving Volgograd. It was while he was in training that his mother quietly passed away in her sleep. When he went home for her funeral his father and sister treated him so coldly that Mikhail never returned.

Mikhail had not even been born when Yuri Gagarin made his epochal first flight in orbit. Vaguely, from early childhood, he recalled seeing blurry television pictures of the Americans on the moon. All through the long years of growing up he nursed the secret ambition of being the first man to set foot on Mars.

He told no one of his dream. Except once, when he was still a child, one dark autumn night while the first snow of the year gently sifted out of the sky to cover grimy old Volgograd with a clean coating of white, he spoke of it to his brother, half asleep in the bed next to his.

"Mars," his brother said dreamily, drowsily.

"I want to be the first man on Mars," Mikhail whispered.

"The first, no less." Nikolai turned in his bed. "All right, little Mickey. You can be the first. I give you my permission. Now let me sleep."

Mikhail smiled in the darkness, and when he dreamed he dreamed about Mars.

S O L 6: AFTERNOON

They arrived at the edge of the canyons in the middle of that afternoon, exactly where Jamie had wanted, at the juncture of three broad fissures in the ground that reminded him of arroyos carved out of the desert by wildly rushing waters.

But bigger. Gigantic. Like the Grand Canyon, except that there was no river down at their distant bottom. Jamie stood on the level ground where the three huge gullies joined together and he could barely see the other side. Peering down into their depths, Jamie guessed the canyon floors must be more than a kilometer below him, perhaps a full mile down, nothing but red-tinged rock cracked and seamed by eons of heating in the sun and freezing every night.

He felt suddenly small, insignificant, like an ant poised on the lip of a normal arroyo in New Mexico. For a dizzying moment he was afraid he would topple over and fall in.

The ground up here had fewer rocks strewn across it, as if it had been swept clean at one time and the rocks had only partially returned. Strange, Jamie thought. We're closer to the heavily cratered territory to the south, yet there's not as much impact debris here as farther north.

He returned his attention to the canyons, feeling an excitement trembling within him that he had never known before. The first man to look into a Martian canyon! There might be a billion years of the planet's history written into those rocks down there. Two billion. Maybe four. It was scary.

The canyon wall was a nearly vertical drop. The thought of climbing down that rock wall thrilled him and frightened him at the same time. The bottom was so far down! Yet he could see it with absolute clarity. The thin air had not the faintest hint of haze in it.

To his geologist's eye it seemed clear that this labyrinth of canyons had been caused by a splintering of the ground, a gridwork of faults in the underlying rock that had weakened the crust, cracked it. When water had flowed here, however long ago it was, it had followed along those cracks, widening and deepening them. Or more likely the permafrost beneath the crust melts from time to time and undermines the ground until it collapses.

"Is that the way it happened?" Jamie asked the silent arroyos in a barely vocalized whisper. "How long ago was it?"

The twisted gullies remained mute.

The more Jamie stared into the deep ravines the more he realized that there had been no great rushing flood here. Mars is a gentle world, he told himself. The ground doesn't quake. There are no storms. If there ever was a flood on this planet it didn't happen here.

He straightened up and looked across the huge gulf toward the other side of the canyon. Our ignorance is even wider, he knew. Every geologist on Earth could spend a lifetime here and still it wouldn't be enough to get all the information these tired old canyons have to yield. All I've got is the rest of today and tomorrow. Unless I can get Mikhail to change the excursion plan.

He turned to the Russian, who was standing between him and the rover, looking down into the canyon. The rover's bright aluminum finish was coated with reddish dust now, especially around the wheels and fenders. It made the vehicle look as if it were rusting.

Fighting down a tiny irrational fear that nagged at the back of his mind, Jamie called, "Mikhail, I've got to climb down to the bottom. I'll need your help."

The Russian, in his red hard suit, started walking toward Jamie. "That is an unnecessary risk."

Jamie made himself laugh. "I've done a lot of rock climbing. And in full gravity, too."

"It is an unnecessary risk," Vosnesensky repeated.

"Then why did the mission planners allow us to stow climbing gear in the rover? Come on, Mikhail, with the winch and all it won't be much of a risk at all. If you think I'm in danger you can haul me up whether I like it or not."

"The sun is setting. It will be too cold to work. Tomorrow you can have the whole day."

"I'm okay in the suit. We've got three-four hours before sunset," Jamie said. "Besides, the sun's hitting this side of the canyon now. Tomorrow morning this side'll be in shadow."

It was impossible to see the Russian's face behind the gold-tinted visor of his helmet. He was silent for a long time, obviously thinking, weighing the options. Finally he said, "Very well. But when I say to come up, you do not argue."

"Deal," said Jamie.

Jamie spent the next hour inching slowly down the sheer rock face of the canyon wall, stopping every ten meters or so to chip out samples. He wore a climber's harness over his hard suit, attached to the electrical winch at the canyon rim by a thin cable of composites stronger than steel. Jamie himself controlled the winch with a set of buttons built into the harness, although Vosnesensky could override him by using the controls on the winch itself or even hauling him up manually, if necessary.

The rock's not stratified, Jamie saw. Seems to be all the same, all the way down to the bottom. That puzzled him. One thick slab of undifferentiated stone? How can that be? He remembered a novel he had read years ago, a scene where an infantry division had been assembled on a parade ground that was described as solid iron one mile thick. Had that scene been set on Mars? Jamie could not remember.

This is different from the area around the dome. There's never been an ocean here to lay down silt deposits and have them turn into rock layers over the years. I'm looking at the actual mantle of the planet, the original material that made up the planet from its very beginning. One enormous slab of rock that must go down not just one lousy mile, it must be a hundred miles deep! Or even more!

Jamie dangled in midair, twisting slightly in the harness, staring at the reddish gray wall before his eyes. This stuff has been here since the planet was born, since it cooled off and solidified. It could be more than four billion years old! He was panting as if he had run a mile, as if he had just found the most precious diamond in the universe.

There was nothing like this on Earth. Mantle rock was always buried beneath miles of crust. Even the ocean beds were covered with sediments. You never saw exposed mantle rock on Earth. But Mars is different, Jamie said to himself. The old assumptions don't apply here.

It's not differentiated, he realized. That's why there's so much iron in the sand on the surface. The iron never sank into the core the way it did on Earth. It's spread all over the surface. Why? How?

Up above, Vosnesensky took an automated sensor beacon from the rover's cargo bin and busied himself setting it up. The anemometer immediately began turning, fast enough to surprise him. The air was so thin that even a stiff breeze was negligible. Toshima will be happy to have another station reporting to him, Vosnesensky said to himself as he turned on the isotope-powered telemetry radio.

Then he walked back to the winch. Planting his short legs as firmly as the machine's on the dusty red ground, he took hours' worth of video shots of the entire area.

Jamie took pictures too, with the still camera he carried in the equipment belt around his waist.

As he neared the bottom Jamie searched for signs of the actual fault line that had created the canyon. In vain. Eons of dust laid down by the winds that yearly billowed up into planetwide sandstorms had covered the canyon floor. Jamie smiled to himself, hanging in the climber's harness. Give Mars another billion years or two and the canyons will be all filled in.

He did not like to look up while he dangled in the harness. The rock wall loomed above him, much too high and steep to climb. The other walls were kilometers away, but the deeper down Jamie went the closer they seemed to squeeze in on him. It made him feel trapped, frightened in a deep unreasoning part of his brain. So Jamie busied himself chipping away at the rock as he descended and scanning the floor below for any evidence of the fundamental crack in the ground that had started this canyon. He never found it.

What did you expect? he asked himself. Something as obvious as the San Andreas Fault?

"Time to come up," Vosnesensky called. "Now."

Despite himself Jamie leaned back in the harness and looked up. For a dizzying moment he felt as if the rock wall were tipping over to fall in on him.

But he heard himself complain, "I haven't reached the bottom yet!"

"It is getting dark."

Swaying in the harness, Jamie realized that the shadows from the opposite canyon wall were almost upon him. He shuddered. Mikhail's right; I don't want to be down here in the dark.

"Okay, coming up," he said into his helmet microphone. He felt the harness tighten about him as the cable began pulling him. He held onto the cable with both gloved hands and tried to gain some purchase on the rock face with his boots as he rose. The winch did all the real work.

At last he reached the top. The sun was almost on the horizon. Even inside the heated suit Jamie shivered. The sky to the east was already dark.

Vosnesensky helped him remove the harness and equipment belt; then they started back toward the rover.

Jamie halted his companion with an outstretched hand.

"Wait a minute, Mikhail. We've been on Mars almost a week and we haven't really watched a sunset."

The Russian made a sound halfway between a grunt and a snort, but he stopped. The two of them stood there on the broad Martian plain, their hands filled with the climbing equipment, and watched the tiny pale sun touch the flat horizon. The sunset was not spectacular. No flaming colors of breathtaking beauty. The air was too thin, too dry, too clean. And yet . . .

The pink sky deepened into red, then violet, uniformly, evenly, the way the dome of a planetarium softly dims when its lights are turned down toward darkness.

"Look!" Jamie pointed as the sun dipped out of sight. A single lonely wisp of a cloud hung above the horizon, glowing like a silver ghost briefly. Then the sun disappeared and the cloud faded into the all-encompassing darkness.

"This is more beautiful than I could have imagined." Vosnesensky's voice was softer, gentler than Jamie had heard before.

"It sure is. I wonder . . ."

Jamie's words died in his throat. His heart began to pound. The sky was shimmering, glowing faintly as a spirit hovering above them, flickering colors so pale and delicate that for a breathless moment Jamie could not believe his eyes.

"Mikhail . . ."

"I see it. Aurora."

"Like the northern lights." Jamie's voice was hollow with awe, trembling. The lights pulsed and billowed across the sky, exquisitely ethereal pastels of pink, green, blue, and white. He could see stars through them, faintly.

"But Mars has no magnetic field," Vosnesensky said, sounding more puzzled than impressed.

"That's just it," Jamie heard himself reply. "Particles from the solar wind must hit the upper atmosphere all across the planet. The gases up there glow when the particles excite them. This must be going on everywhere, every night. We've just never stayed out long enough to see it."

"Wouldn't it be observable from orbit?" Mikhail was being more of a hardheaded scientist than Jamie.

"Must be pretty faint, looking down against the background of the planet itself. But if they know what to look for I'm sure Katrin Diels and Ulanov will be able to observe it."

The colors faded away. The lights died slowly, leaving the sky calm and dark. Jamie felt a shudder race through him, though whether it was fear or ecstasy he could not tell. Probably some of both. His pulse was still thundering in his ears. As far as the eye could see in any direction, there was nothing but utter darkness now. As if the world had vanished, as if he were standing alone in a universe all his own, unpopulated, unoccupied except for himself.

And the stars. Even through the tinted visor of his helmet Jamie saw the bright eternal stars looking down at him like faithful old friends, telling him that even on this strange empty world they were up there in their places, the guardians of universal order.

One of the stars was visibly moving across the sky. "Is that our ships in orbit?" Jamie wondered aloud.

Vosnesensky chuckled. "It is Phobos, so close it looks like a space station, going from west to east. Deimos is too faint to see unless you know exactly where to look for it."

Jamie recognized Orion and Taurus, with the cluster of the Pleiades in the bull's neck. Turning, he saw both the Dippers. The North Star isn't over the north pole of Mars, he remembered.

"Look there." Vosnesensky must have been pointing, but with nothing except starlight Jamie could not make out his form.

The Russian took him by the shoulder and turned him slightly. "Just above the horizon. The bright blue one."

Jamie saw it. An incredibly beautiful blue star shimmering low on the horizon.

"Is it Earth?" he asked, in a reverent whisper.

"Earth," replied Vosnesensky. "And the moon."

Jamie could not make out the fainter whitish star nearly touching the blue one. Vosnesensky insisted he could, but Jamie thought it might have been more the Russian's imagination than superior eyesight.

"We must get back inside the rover," Vosnesensky said at last. "No sense freezing to death while admiring the sky."

He turned on his helmet lamp, immediately destroying their night-adapted vision, and then touched the controls on his wrist to remotely turn on the lights in the rover. Reluctantly, almost angry at the cosmonaut, Jamie followed Vosnesensky back to the vehicle.

It took a surprisingly long time to get out of their hard suits in the confined space inside the rover's airlock. The excitement of discovering the aurora gradually dimmed away. By the time they were down to their tubed skivvies, sitting on folded-up bunks facing each other with a pair of microwaved meals on the narrow table between them, Jamie's pulse had returned almost to normal.

Vosnesensky hoisted his water glass. "A very good day," he said. "We accomplished much."

Jamie touched his plastic glass to the Russian's. "You'll have a good report to make to Dr. Li."

"Yes, after we eat."

"I'll feed the data tapes into the computer."

"Good. Then we call the base and see what they have been doing."

Jamie leaned forward over the narrow table. "Mikhail, I have a suggestion about tomorrow."

The Russian also hunched slightly forward, until their noses were almost touching.

"No more than a day or so to the east of here, if we drive steadily, is Tithonium Chasma, part of the Valles Marineris complex—much deeper and wider than . . ."

Vosnesensky was already shaking his head. "It is not on the excursion plan. It is too far for us to travel."

"It's less than six hundred kilometers from here," Jamie argued. "We could do it in twenty hours if we didn't stop."

"Drive at night? Are you insane?" There was no fear in the cosmonaut's sky-blue eyes, merely the unshakable firmness of a man who had already decided how many risks he was prepared to take.

Jamie said, "Let me explain the geological necessity."

Strangely the Russian broke into a lopsided grin. "Fine. You explain geology. I will clear the table."

As Vosnesensky got up and took their dinner trays to the storage rack where they would remain until the rover returned to the main base, Jamie folded the table and slid it back into its place beneath the bunk.

"The canyon walls here are undifferentiated," Jamie began to explain. "Just one big slab of iron-rich rock that's been worn away and exposed. That's unheard-of, Mikhail. There's nothing on Earth like that."

"So you have made a great discovery. Good."

"We've got to find out if the bigger canyons are like that! Is the whole canyon system that way? Three thousand kilometers of pure mantle rock? It can't be! It just can't be."

Vosnesensky was already sliding into the driver's chair and checking to see that their communications antenna was locked onto the spacecraft up in synchronous orbit.

"What do the satellite photographs show?" he asked.

The sloping transparent roof of the cockpit was so low that Jamie had to bend over as he stood behind the driver's chair. He could feel the cold of the Martian night seeping through the plastiglass even though Vosnesensky had drawn the thermal shroud for the night.

He answered, "Not enough detail, Mikhail. We've got to be there firsthand and see the rock formations close up. Take samples for analysis."

"It would take us at least two days out of our way. A full day or more to get there and the same to return to where we should be. We don't have enough food on board, and it would be an unnecessary strain on the air recycling system. And it would wreck the mission schedule."

"Come on, Mikhail! We can stretch the food. The fuel cells produce clean water and the air recyclers are good for months. You know that. And there's a full week between this excursion and the next one."

"Twenty hours of driving, even without stops."

"I'll help you with the driving," Jamie said, grinning. "I've driven pickup trucks over worse terrain than this."

The Russian turned in his seat and fixed Jamie with those clear blue eyes. "This is not New Mexico."

"That's right," Jamie replied. "This is Mars. And we're here to explore this new world. There's important scientific work to be done here, Mikhail. . . ."

"You scientists always want to break the rules."

"Damned right!" Jamie snapped. "We're here for the sake of science. To explore. To learn. To seek out the truth wherever it leads us."

"Pretty words," grumbled Vosnesensky.

"Men have died for those ideas!"

"Yes. That is exactly my point."

"We've come a hundred million kilometers—" Jamie was almost shouting—"What the hell is another day or two of travel?"

"It is not authorized. It is not on the excursion plan. The mission controllers back on Earth would disapprove."

"Fuck 'em! We're *here*, Mikhail. The reason we're here is to learn. We can't do that by sticking to plans written a year ago. They might as well have sent unmanned machines if they're going to make us behave like goddammed robots."

Vosnesensky took a deep breath, then exhaled slowly, like a man trying to control his temper. "We are not robots, but we are responsible to higher authority. The purpose of this mission is to start the exploration of Mars. If we displease those in charge, there will be no more missions and the exploration will end."

Jamie squatted down on his heels, one arm on the back of Vosnesensky's chair to steady himself. Forcing himself to sound more reasonable he said, "Mikhail, as far as I'm concerned all the politicians on Earth can take a flying leap into the Grand Canyon. What makes you think they're going to authorize more missions to Mars, no matter how obedient we are? We're here, now. *Now's* the time to find out as much about this world as we can. The more knowledge we acquire now, the harder it'll be for them to deny us follow-up missions after we return."

"You are skating on thin ice, Jamie."

"Maybe. I thought you Russians were all great gamblers," Jamie coaxed.

Vosnesensky stiffened visibly. "I am not here to gamble. Not with lives. Especially my own."

"But it's not that big a risk," Jamie urged, quickly switching tactics. "We can do it! We don't have to stick to the plans they wrote for us on Earth. The mission orders allow us some flexibility. We've got an opportunity here to make a fundamental discovery about the geological history of this planet."

"It is an unnecessary risk."

Jamie made himself grin at the Russian. "Look at it this way, Mikhail—if we kill ourselves you won't have to face Dr. Li or the mission controllers back at Kaliningrad."

Vosnesensky stared at him for a long moment, then burst into a peal of laughter. "You are a fatalist!" the cosmonaut said. "Just like a Russian."

"You'll do it?"

"It is not in the excursion plan."

"So we change the plan," Jamie said. "The rover's got the range and we've got enough supplies on board. If we get stuck, Mironov can come out with the other rover."

Vosnesensky's beefy face returned to its normal scowl. He said, "We cannot deviate from the excursion plan. It is not allowed."

Jamie felt himself tensing. With deliberate care, he slowly rose from his squatting position. "In that case," he said evenly, "mission regulations give me the right to go over your head and appeal directly to Dr. Li. I want to talk to Li."

Still frowning, Vosnesensky reached out across the control panel and flicked on the communications set.

"Speak to the expedition commander then," he growled. "Let him take the responsibility."

"To Tithonium Chasma?" Dr. Li was startled. "But that is a thousand kilometers away from your present position."

"Its western edge is less than six hundred kilometers from our present position," replied James Waterman.

Li sank back in his upholstered chair. He had retreated to his private quarters to take the expected check-in call from Vosnesensky, partly for his own comfort and partly because he felt he could deal with whatever problems arose more easily without the technicians and other team members crowding around him at the communications console of the spacecraft's command center.

His compartment was as luxurious as mission regulations allowed. Like all the other privacy cubicles aboard the two Mars spacecraft it was barely large enough to accommodate a narrow bunk, a tiny desk, and a single chair. Li's chair could tilt back, however, like an astronaut's acceleration couch. He often used it to sleep in, rather than the bunk, which he found uncomfortably short.

While other team members had decorated their cubicles with photos of their families or maps of Mars or even computer printouts, Li had taped an exquisite set of small silk paintings onto his walls. Mountains shrouded in mist. Beautiful birds perched on a graceful tree limb. A pagoda by a lake. Touches of home. Even if he died in space, he reasoned, he wanted the comfort of those paintings beside him.

But he did not so much as glance at them while he stared into the display screen that dominated his small desk. Waterman's broad, onyx-eyed face looked back at him. A face that could be very stubborn, Li realized.

"I wish to give you as much latitude as possible," Li said, "but adding three extra days to your traverse seems excessive to me."

He did not add that Vosnesensky was not even supposed to be on this traverse. The Russian should have remained at the base camp, as the mission plan called for. He was already exceeding his directives.

"It's necessary," Waterman replied. "For geological reasons."

Li almost let himself smile. Of course, for geological reasons. Naturally Waterman would have a sound scientific reason for pushing the limits. A born troublemaker.

Steepling his fingers in his lap, out of range of the comm unit's camera, Li waited for the geologist's explanation. Waterman looked eager, black eyes wide and sparkling, lips slightly parted, energy fairly shining from his dark-skinned face.

"We've calculated the rover's fuel reserves and they are more than sufficient to take us to the Tithonium region and back to the base, sir. Plus a generous allowance for reserve."

Li did smile, thinly. Waterman is thinking only of the technical side. To him, the political ramifications simply are not of importance. I wonder if he thinks of them at all.

"Dr. Li, you understand the principles of geology . . ." And without hesitation Waterman launched into a lecture about the rock formations on Mars.

Li listened with one ear while another part of his mind felt amused at the scientist's earnestness and the unthinking arrogance of this enthusiastic young man lecturing his elder.

The young fool simply does not understand that he is on terribly shaky ground politically. He honestly believes that science is all that matters. Li wished he could live such an uncomplicated life, have such unhampered enthusiasms, pursue knowledge without worrying about those who controlled the purse strings—and the honors.

On the other hand, he reasoned as Jamie continued his nonstop recitation, suppose he kills himself down there? He will become a hero, automatically. And cease to be a problem. He would most likely be killing Vosnesensky also, but that could not be helped.

Li shook himself when he realized where such thoughts were leading him. My task, he said sternly to himself, is to direct the exploration of Mars and allow the scientists to conduct that exploration with as little interference as possible. Waterman wants to go farther and faster than we have planned. The politicians will be angry if anything goes wrong.

It took him a moment to realize that Waterman had finished speaking and was gazing expectantly at him from the display screen. Like a child asking his father for permission to take a new step toward adulthood, Li thought.

He blinked his eyes twice, then heard himself reply, as if from some great distance, "Go ahead with your plan. I will expect you, Commander Vosnesensky, to call an immediate halt the instant you reach the critical point in your fuel supplies."

The camera down below swiveled back to Vosnesensky. "I have calculated the fuel reserves we need to get safely back to base and added a twenty percent emergency factor."

"When you reach that point you must return, no matter where you are or what you are doing. Is that clearly understood?"

"Yes, sir."

"Dr. Waterman?"

He heard Waterman's voice reply, "Clearly."

"Very well then, proceed." Li reached for the keyboard to end the transmission. He hesitated, though, long enough to add, "And good luck."

"Thank you!" The two men's voices rang back in unison.

E A R T H

K A L I N I N G R A D :   **In the early days of the Soviet space program, when secrecy born of Cold War fears dominated everything, the locations of space facilities were kept as concealed as possible. The major Soviet launching base, for example, was said to be at Baikonur, a city in the middle of the Kazakh SSR, a land where Mongol hordes and the fierce horsemen of Tamerlane once rode.**

    Actually the launch center is near the town of Tyuratam, more than three hundred kilometers southwest of Baikonur, on the main rail line from Moscow to Tashkent.

In those days of suspicion there was no public mention of Kaliningrad, the mission control center from which the earliest manned space flights were directed. Gagarin's pioneering orbit of the Earth, the thousands of man-hours of flight aboard a dozen space stations, and finally the first expedition to Mars—all were directed from the center at Kaliningrad, about six kilometers northeast of the outermost circular motorway ringing metropolitan Moscow.

The protocol for directing the Mars mission had been decided upon long before the various spacecraft had even begun to be assembled in Earth orbit. Knowing that there would be a communications lag of ten minutes or more between Mars and Earth, the mission planners placed full authority in the hands of the expedition commander, Dr. Li Chengdu.

There was no need for Dr. Li to check with mission command at Kaliningrad before making a decision. The day-to-day operations of the teams in orbit around Mars and on the planet's surface were his responsibility.

That did not mean, however, that he could not be overruled.

Having given his assent to Vosnesensky and Waterman's unscheduled dash to Tithonium Chasma, Dr. Li routinely reported the change in the excursion plan back to Kaliningrad. Routinely, in this case, meant that he waited until the end of his day, as usual, before filing his report. The rover team's diversion to Tithonium was given as item number seventeen of his customary daily report. Seventeen of twenty-two.

So it was slightly after four in the morning in Russia when his report arrived. The mission controllers worked three shifts, of course, but their directors—the men and women who made the real decisions—were soundly sleeping when Li's report began scrolling on the display screen of the chief controller for this shift.

He was a Russian who took his duties seriously. Sitting beside him at the console was his American counterpart, a perky redheaded engineer on loan from CalTech's Jet Propulsion Laboratory. Shoulder to shoulder, they read the report from the expedition commander on the display screen, the American woman slightly impatient with her colleague's slower pace at reading English. The mission control center was quiet and still at this hour. Even though all the stations were manned, there was little activity and less talk.

Until the American controller suddenly exclaimed, "He okayed it! Without checking with us?"

Eyes snapped wide and heads turned toward her.

The Russian chief controller said, "Dr. Li is within his authority . . ."

"The hell he is," said the American. Her green eyes were blazing fury. "The protocol specifically states that any major change in the schedule must be cleared with mission control first!"

"*Major* change," the Russian said mildly.

"You don't think a six-hundred-kilometer diversion of that rover team is a major change?" She yanked the telephone from its receptacle on the console and began pecking out a number. "How much fuel does that buggy hold, anyway? Aren't they putting themselves in danger of getting stranded?"

The Russian tapped the console keyboard, and the specifications for the Mars rover displaced Dr. Li's report on their display screen.

"It has a cruising radius of one thousand kilometers," he said. "More than half its mass is fuel. An enormous safety factor."

"Not if they're throwing in an unscheduled twelve hundred kilometers, it isn't."

"You are calling the chief mission director at this hour?"

"Hell no, I'm not that crazy," the American answered, a slight grin breaking through her anger. "I'm calling Houston."

The Russian smiled back at her. "Ah—and they will wake up the chief."

"Right. I may be quick-tempered but I'm not stupid."

HOUSTON: The chain of command on Earth was split, like everything else about the Mars mission, into two strands. While mission control was in Kaliningrad, there was a "shadow" mission control team at the old NASA center at Clear Lake, near Houston.

The center had been created in the early nineteen-sixties as a political plum for Texas. Originally designated the Manned Space Center and built nearly an hour's drive from downtown Houston, the center became the home of the astronauts, the place where all manned space activities were planned and directed. Eventually it was named after Lyndon B. Johnson. As Vice-President, Johnson had chaired John F. Kennedy's space council and pushed vigorously for the daring program to land Americans on the moon within the decade of the sixties.

But no matter how swiftly the engineers moved, the tides of history swirled faster. By the time the first astronauts set foot on the moon, Kennedy was dead and his successor, Johnson, out of office. The American space program, seemingly at the peak of success, was being gutted and virtually murdered, a victim of the Vietnam War that Johnson had escalated.

Yet the Johnson Space Center remained and even grew. As the hub of all manned space activities, it became headquarters for the hundreds of astronauts recruited to fly the space shuttle and its successors. Men and women trained there before they were allowed to ride up to the American space station *Freedom* or any of the foreign (or even private) space stations that orbited the Earth.

At first glance the Johnson Space Center looked rather like a university campus. Modernistic glass-walled buildings and green lawns, a relaxed atmosphere, young men and women strolling from one building to another or driving their cars along the wide tree-lined streets. At the main entrance, though, there rested a mammoth *Saturn V* rocket, a relic of the old Apollo era, lying on its side like a beached whale. And behind the tall towers of glass and steel were smaller windowless buildings that hummed with electrical power and the throbbing of pumps and motors.

In one of those windowless buildings the "shadow" mission control center was located. It was slightly after eight P.M. on a quiet, warm Texas evening when the inquiry came from Kaliningrad.

Here too, the top decision makers had left for the day and scattered to their suburban homes. The desks and consoles were thinly staffed by only a handful of men and women, most of them young and new to their responsibilities.

The man in charge, a middle-aged systems analyst, was munching on a bag of cheese-flavored tortilla chips when his "red" phone buzzed. With a mixture of pique and puzzlement clouding his fleshy face, he picked up the phone.

It was pure chance that the American controller in Kaliningrad was someone he knew personally. They had gone through several semesters together at CalTech.

"Josie, how are ya?" he said to the tense face that appeared on his display screen. "Those Russkies treating you okay?"

Almost a heartbeat's delay, as the electronic signal bounced off a communications satellite, before her answer came to him.

"Sam, we've got a problem here."

He lurched forward in his chair. "Whatsamatter?"

"Dr. Li has okayed an extension of the rover excursion without checking with mission control first."

"Jesus Christ!" He placed a chubby hand over his heaving chest. "I thought there was real trouble. Don't scare me like that, Jo!"

"This *is* trouble—it's a violation of the command decision–tree protocol."

"Aw, crap. If the goddam rover broke down or somebody got stranded out there, that's trouble. This is just paperwork."

She would not be put off. "You've got to get Maxwell and Goldschmitt on the phone. They've got to know about this right away."

"The hell they do."

"The hell they don't! Either you call them or I'm calling their Russian counterparts here in Kaliningrad."

Glancing at the clock displays on the far wall, "Christ, it's four in the morning over there."

"This is important, Roscoe."

"Don't call me Roscoe!"

"Call Maxwell and Goldschmitt. Do it now, before they get too far."

"They're probably having their dinners."

"Which would you prefer: interrupting their dinners or having them find out tomorrow that two of our ground team are off on an unauthorized toot because *you* didn't inform them in time to stop them?"

WASHINGTON: It was no coincidence that Alberto Brumado was attending the formal dinner where the Vice-President was the guest of honor. Brumado knew that this woman was in an excellent position to become the next president of the United States, and her views could very well determine when—or even if—the second expedition to Mars would be launched.

Brumado had met her many times before, and although they had drastically different opinions about the importance of space exploration they had become friendly in the polite, grudging way that political opponents often find necessary. Washington's social circle, after all, was too small to fight battles at cocktail parties and dinners. Better to smile and agree to disagree—in social settings.

So Brumado had no intention whatever of even mentioning Mars to the Vice-President. This was a social evening, a time to be charming and witty and build the amity that might smooth personal differences in the daylight hours of political business.

The Vice-President's after-dinner speech was a clear signal that she was seeking her party's nomination. She spoke of America's greatness, of the growth of the nation's economy, of how her efforts as leader of the urban revitalization task force were changing the face of cities from coast to coast.

"And the key to all this," she told her audience of dinner-jacketed men and gowned, bejeweled women, "the key is *synergy*, the way we have brought together people from many different walks of life and gotten them to work together, to add their energies to each other until the totality of their achievement is far greater than the mere sum of their individual efforts. Synergy works! And this administration intends to use synergy to solve the problems that still plague us. . . ."

Brumado listened carefully as he sat at one of the five dozen round dinner tables with nine strangers. She speaks about the economic contribution of high technology, she even mentions the success of orbital manufacturing, but she does not mention Mars or space science at all. Yet when the explorers return from Mars, he knew, she will be there to greet them in full view of the world's media.

It was a surprise to him, then, when one of the Vice-President's aides appeared at his side and bent over to whisper, "The Vice-

President would like to speak with you privately after her speech is finished. Would you follow me, please?"

Brumado folded his napkin neatly and placed it beside his half-empty coffee cup. Excusing himself in an inaudible whisper to the nine others at the table, he got up and tiptoed swiftly past the other tables in the darkened hotel dining room, following the dark-suited aide out into the kitchen.

Power is visible in small ways, Brumado understood. The kitchen staff usually would be busy cleaning up the six hundred sets of dinner dishes, clashing silverware and clattering pots while the speaker on the other side of the swinging doors tried to talk over their clamor. For the Vice-President, though, they sat and waited until her speech was finished. Brumado smiled at them as they whispered among themselves and glanced at their wristwatches. Overtime pay. Does it compensate them enough for spending an extra hour away from home?

At last the Vice-President finished and her audience applauded thunderously. Just enough time for the media crews to get tape on the eleven o'clock news.

She swept through the swinging doors, Secret Service guards in front and in back of her, so commanding a presence that the tired, bored kitchen help rose to their feet automatically.

Yet she was tiny, not much over five feet tall, a petite woman who worked hard to avoid gaining weight. Even so she dominated any room she entered. Her face glowed with energy, her eyes so deeply blue they seemed almost violet; their twin laser-beam glances could peel the hide off a rhinoceros. Her hair was a light ashy blonde, a shade that hid gray well, rich and thick yet cropped short enough to tell any woman who looked at her that she had no time for frivolities such as curlers and sets.

"There you are," she said as she spied Brumado standing in front of the long counter piled high with dirty dishes.

He fell in beside her as they paced toward the back of the kitchen and the doors that opened onto the loading docks and delivery access road.

"Right in the middle of my dinner," the Vice-President said, waving a flimsy sheet of paper, "this came in from Houston."

Brumado took the sheet from her without breaking stride and scanned it swiftly.

Looking back at the Vice-President he said, "Dr. Li apparently has no qualms about extending the rover excursion . . ."

"It's that damned Indian!" The Vice-President stopped at the doors and her whole entourage, Brumado included, stopped with her. Except for three of the Secret Service agents, who slipped through like wraiths to check the area outside.

"You mean Dr. Waterman."

"He's been a troublemaker from the first minute they landed! Why's he want to change the mission plan? What's he after?"

Brumado answered softly, "I'm sure he had valid scientific reasons. If . . ."

But the Vice-President was already shaking her head vehemently. "He's trying to upstage everybody else. He wants all the glory for himself. Thinks he'll come back here a hero."

"I have seen the tape you refused to release to the media," Brumado said, putting a little iron into his voice. "He does not seem to be interested in politics in any way."

"Not much! By the time he gets back home they'll be running him for the Senate. It's happened before. In New Mexico, too."

"You are worried that he might become politically active—against you?"

"I'm worried that my enemies will latch onto him and use him against me, just the way the liberal Republicans used Eisenhower against Taft."

Brumado bowed his head slightly, thinking furiously. If this woman becomes the next president she will certainly be against funding further expeditions to Mars. Especially if she believes that one of our scientists is being used by her opposition.

"You've got no idea how much pressure is building up around this Indian," the Vice-President was saying, her angry voice like fingernails on a chalkboard. "It's not only the Indian rights activists. It's the high-tech gang, too. They're forming alliances with the Hispanics and the ghetto blacks. It's the old Rainbow Coalition again, plus the techies, with a real honest-to-god Indian scientist hero to be their figurehead!"

Slowly, with an enormous weight inside him that made his words hesitant, Brumado asked, "Suppose . . . suppose . . . I could get Waterman to make a statement that would . . . support your candidacy?"

Her eyes flashed, then became calculating. "Why would he support me?"

"Because," Brumado had to struggle to get the words out, "because you will go on record as favoring further missions to Mars."

"I couldn't do that," she snapped.

"When the first expedition returns they will *all* be heroes. The public acclaim will be enormous. And there is no Vietnam War to take the public's mind off their success."

The Vice-President muttered, "They'll be coming back just in time for the primaries."

"You could capitalize on their success."

"You can get Waterman to make a statement supporting me?"

"Once you go on record as supporting further Mars missions."

The Vice-President had spent enough years in politics to understand that getting elected was the most important thing, and the way to get elected was to clear enemies away from your path. Sometimes this meant adopting their coloration—at least for a while.

She also understood that it was foolish to give a definite commitment right away. "I'll have to think about that. It sounds as if it might be workable."

"It will remove Mars as an issue during your campaign," Brumado said.

She nodded briskly. "I'll get back to you."

Then she stepped toward the doors, which a Secret Service agent pushed open for her. The entourage swept out onto the loading dock. Before the doors swung shut Brumado got a glimpse of a phalanx of limousines waiting where delivery trucks usually parked.

Then the doors closed and he was alone in the kitchen with the noisy, banging, yelling, clattering clean-up crew.

He smiled to himself. But the smile faded as he realized that he had just promised to "deliver" James Waterman for the Vice-President's election campaign.

That will not be an easy task, he realized.

NEW YORK: "But it doesn't make any sense!" Edith insisted. "Jamie's not the type to snub the media. He wouldn't refuse to be interviewed."

"Are you saying that the government's keeping him from talking to us? Muzzling him?"

"Yes! I'm certain of it!"

It was almost eleven P.M. Edith had waited for three days to see Howard Francis. As network news vice-president, he held the power of decision and she was determined to make him decide in her favor. Her days in New York had generated a frantic urgency in Edith. No longer the happily smiling former cheerleader, ex-beauty queen, anchorwoman for the local Houston TV news, she was in the Big Apple now, struggling with every weapon at her command to win a job with the network news organization.

Howard Francis's office was so high above the street that Edith expected to see clouds wafting past the window behind his broad gleaming desk. The walls were covered with photographs of Howard Francis with the great and near-great of politics, show business, and the news industry: smiling, shaking hands, presenting awards, receiving awards. The man behind the desk was almost as young as Edith herself. His suit cost more than Edith's weekly salary back in Texas. His necktie was fashionably loosened at his unbuttoned collar. He had the sharp-eyed features of a rodent, big teeth, and even a twitch when he got excited. Edith could see the tic contorting one side of his face.

Francis leaned his skinny forearms on his desktop and said to Edith, "Look—it's late and I haven't had dinner yet. I've got problems up to my eyebrows and a meeting with the corporate brass tomorrow morning at nine. Can you prove what you're saying?"

She made herself smile at him despite the sick feeling in her stomach. "Well . . . nobody in NASA is going to admit to it in public."

"Off the record?"

"I've got a lot of friends down at the Johnson Space Center," she said.

"Look," he said, "I've got whole teams of correspondents working for me in Houston and Washington and everyplace else. What can you do for me that they can't?"

"What about Jamie's parents?" she countered. "And his grandfather in Santa Fe? He's pure Navaho."

Francis shook his head. "The parents are *dull*. Maybe the grandfather, if he's really an Indian. That might be something. But later. First you've gotta prove to me that the government's muzzling your Indian. *That* would be news."

Edith kept her smile glowing for him. She was wearing her best silk blouse, creamy white, the top four buttons undone. Her skirt was short enough to show plenty of knee as she sat in the chair before his desk.

"Washington," said the network vice-president from behind his massive desk. "That's where the cover-up is going on—if there is a cover-up."

"Maybe I can get to somebody on the Space Council," Edith suggested.

"The Vice-President? Fat chance!"

"No, not her. But some of my contacts in Houston are pretty close to a couple of the men on the Space Council. I think I could get one or two of them to talk to me—prob'ly off the record, though."

"That'd be a start."

"Let me try that route. If it doesn't work I can go out to Santa Fe and talk to Jamie's grandfather."

The man nodded, his eyes on her blouse.

Edith decided to play her trump card. "And I could always contact Jamie on a personal basis. The project allows personal calls, and I'm sure he'd accept one from me. The officials don't have to know I'm a newswoman."

"The personal calls are private."

"Not if I tape it at my end," Edith said, turning her smile sly.

The man chewed his lower lip, face twitching furiously. Finally he jumped to his feet and stuck his hand out over the desk.

"Okay. Do it."

"I'm hired?"

"As a consultant. Per diem fee and expenses. If this works out, then you'll be hired. Fair enough?"

Edith rose from her chair and took his extended hand in hers. "You won't regret it," she said.

Howard Francis grinned at her. "I better not." Then he added, "Come on, let's get a bite to eat."

Edith agreed with a nod, remembering the old adage about not trusting a man who carried two first names.

I N T R A N S I T: STORM CELLAR

Halfway to Mars the sun suddenly turned deadly.

The mission to Mars had been timed for a period of low solar activity. Still, there was only the slimmest of chances that the spacecraft could carry their human crews through nine months in interplanetary space without running into a magnetic storm spawned by a solar flare.

Both on Earth and at the underground base on the moon, solar forecasters watched the sun in cramped narrow workrooms crowded with humming computers and video monitors. They saw a set of blotches take form on the shining surface of the sun, each of them bigger than the Earth itself. Their instruments detected weak radio emissions and bursts of soft X rays from the sunspot group. Completely normal.

Then the flare erupted. Nothing spectacular, to the eye. Just a brief flash of light. But the incoming radiation grew swiftly, ominously, its intensity rising a hundred times above normal, a thousand, ten thousand, in the span of a few minutes. Ultraviolet and X-ray sensors aboard monitoring satellites went into overload. An intense burst of radio noise sizzled in astronomers' receivers all around the Earth and shut down the radio telescope at the lunar base. It was a completely ordinary solar flare, no more powerful than a hundred billion hydrogen bombs all going off at once. Its total energy was less than a quarter second of the sun's normal output.

But the cloud of subatomic particles it blew into space could kill unprotected humans in seconds.

The solar forecasters' instruments automatically radioed a warning to the Mars spacecraft, more than seventy million kilometers away from Earth. The electromagnetic radiation from the flare, traveling at the speed of light just as the astronomers' radio signals did, hit the spacecraft at the same instant that the warnings arrived.

Alarms hooted down the length of both ships, startling the men and women at their tasks, jolting those asleep into a terrified waking. The first moment of adrenaline-drenched shock gave way to the reactions drilled into the Mars teams by years of training. Every man and woman on each of the two spacecraft dashed, sprinted, raced for the radiation shelters.

For the first wave of electromagnetic energy from the flare was merely the precursor, the flash of lightning that warns of an approaching storm. Following it by a few minutes or perhaps even a few hours would be a vast expanding cloud of energetic protons and electrons, particles that could slice right through the skin of the ship and fry human flesh in seconds.

In low Earth orbit astronauts are protected from solar flare particles by the Earth's magnetic field, which deflects the energetic protons and electrons flung off the sun and eventually pumps them down into the atmosphere at the north and south magnetic poles. Spectacular auroras can paint the skies for several nights in a row after a big solar flare. The geomagnetic field is bashed and buckled by the storm of incoming particles; for days it vibrates and twangs like banjo strings. Radio transmissions are garbled. Even underground telephone links can be scrambled.

On Earth itself the atmosphere absorbs any particles that power through the magnetic field, so that even the most energetic solar flare does not endanger life on the surface of the planet. On the airless moon, with its minuscule magnetic field, there is only one defense: go underground and stay underground until the storm blows over.

In interplanetary space the only defenses against a magnetic storm are those the spacecraft carry with them.

"Don't sweat it," said Pete Connors. "We all knew we couldn't make it all the way without running into a flare." He was trying to sound reassuring, but the expression on his long-jawed face looked quite serious, like a doctor discussing surgery with his patient.

"It's more like the flare is running into us, isn't it?" corrected George O'Hara, the Australian geologist.

The twelve men and women of the *Mars 1* crew were crammed onto the benches that lined the walls of the spacecraft's specially shielded radiation shelter. Everyone called it the "storm cellar." In this small compartment at the rear of the habitat module, the bulky propellant tanks attached to the spacecraft's outer hull provided a measure of protection against the lethal radiation spawned from a solar flare.

The two Mars-bound craft used their half-depleted propellant tanks to absorb some of the high-energy particles streaming out from the sun. In addition, the crafts' storm cellars were lined with thin filaments of superconducting wire. The first person to reach the radiation shelter—Pete Connors, as it turned out—punched the switch on the wall by the hatch to energize the shielding system.

The superconducting wire generated a strong magnetic field around the storm cellar, strong enough to deflect the lightweight electrons in the cloud of particles swarming past the spacecraft. But the heavier protons were the real danger, and the magnetic field was not nearly strong enough to deflect them.

Instead, the ship's defenses included a set of electron guns that charged the outer skin of the spacecraft to millions of volts of positive charge. In theory, the incoming protons would be deflected from the spacecraft by its megavolt positive charge, while the craft's magnetic field would keep electrons from reaching the skin and neutralizing the positive charge.

Small versions of the system had been tested aboard satellites flung into sun-centered orbits. Unmanned satellites.

"How long will we have to stay in here?" asked Ilona Malater. She was sitting between Tony Reed and the Greek biologist on the backup team, Dennis Xenophanes. Her long fingers clutched the edge of the bench so tightly her knuckles were white.

"Twelve hours or more," answered Ollie Zieman, the American astronaut who was Connors's backup. "Maybe a couple of days."

"My god!"

"No sweat," Zieman replied, almost jovially. "Radiation level in here is almost normal."

The shelter already felt crowded and sweltering with the smell of suppressed fear. Jamie leaned his back against the bulkhead, wondering if the magnetic field being generated by the superconducting wires mere inches away from his flesh actually had no effect on their bodies. According to the system's designers, the field was shaped so that the storm cellar was in the clear; the field extended outward in all directions, but the shelter itself was like a bubble in its middle.

Vosnesensky and his backup, Dmitri Ivshenko, were standing in front of the communications console built into the shelter's forward bulkhead, by the hatch. Mikhail had clamped a communications headset over his curly hair.

"Radio communication is difficult," Vosnesensky announced

loudly for everyone to hear, even though he kept his back to them. "We will use the laser system."

A magnetic storm can screw up radio waves, Jamie knew, but it shouldn't have any effect on a laser's beam of light. He felt a tightness in his chest, anxiety, even though they had trained for such emergencies. There's a semi-infinite number of subatomic particles out there just dying to get in here and kill all twelve of us, he thought. Like a cloud of spirits of the dead scratching and moaning outside the door.

"*Mars 2* is all right," Vosnesensky announced. "Everyone in the storm cellar with no trouble."

They've got the extra man, Jamie thought. Dr. Li makes it thirteen they have to squeeze into their shelter.

Pete Connors got up and went to stand between Vosnesensky and the other Russian. "All the ship's systems are working okay?" he asked loudly.

"Yes, yes." Vosnesensky pointed to the panels of lights that showed the condition of the rest of the ship. Most of the lights were green. "The equipment was built to withstand radiation. It is only we fragile creatures of flesh and bone who need protection."

Cheerful, Jamie thought. Very cheerful.

Fourteen hours later the radiation levels outside the shelter had not gone down discernibly. Jamie had dozed for a while, slumped back on the bench that lined the compartment's wall. Joanna and the Polish biochemist who was Ilona's backup had found enough room on the opposite bench to curl up and sleep. There were foldout cots built into the walls above the benches, but no one had bothered to use them.

Looking around with blurry eyes, Jamie saw that all four pilots were sitting up near the hatch and the comm console. The Christmas tree of monitoring panels still showed mostly green lights, although there were more red ones than before. Tony Reed was chatting amiably with Ilona and the Aussie geologist, George O'Hara, at the other end of the compartment, where food and drink dispensers were built into the rear wall.

Jamie pulled himself to his feet, feeling stiff and dull-headed. O'Hara was redhaired, rawboned, tall enough to need to stoop slightly unless he stood exactly in the midline of the compartment. Otherwise his head brushed the curving ceiling panels. He seemed an amiable enough sort. Jamie had not detected a trace of jealousy over the fact that O'Hara was to stay aboard the ship while he would be the one to go down to the surface.

"... in Coober Pedy the miners live underground most of the year," O'Hara was saying. "Too bloody hot to live up on the surface, so they've built a by-damn city down in the shafts and galleries. Swimming pools and everything."

Ilona was not impressed. "How much longer must we stay in here?"

"Don't be so anxious to go out," Tony said. "This is the best place in the entire solar system to be, right now."

"Except for Earth," said Jamie.

"Ah well," Reed admitted, "we can't have everything now, can we?"

"Reminds me of being stuck inside a bloody airliner," O'Hara said, grinning down at Ilona. "I remember once a couple years ago at Washington National, they had us buttoned up on the rampway and made us wait five bloody hours inside the bloody airplane before we could take off. Some mechanical problem they took their sweet time fixing. We drank all the booze on board and we still hadn't moved a fucking inch. It was like a zoo by the time we actually took off."

"I'm feeling as if I'm in a zoo," Ilona muttered. "In a cage."

"Steady on," Tony said in his best British stiff-upper-lip manner. But he looked tight to Jamie, tense, his smile forced.

"How much longer will it be?" Joanna's sleepy voice came from behind Jamie.

It was a rhetorical question. She pushed past them and went into the lavatory.

"Ever wonder why they always put the pisser next to the water fountain?" O'Hara asked no one in particular.

"Plumbing," Jamie said.

"Or recycling?" suggested Reed.

Jamie walked the length of the compartment, as much to stretch his legs and get some circulation going as to reach the pilots up by the comm console and equipment monitors. Katrin Diels, the German physicist, was deep in earnest conversation, a headset clamped over her blonde curls.

"When did the intensity peak?" she asked into the pin-sized microphone in front of her lips.

Jamie almost smiled at the fierce intensity on her snub-nosed freckled face. She was slight of frame, as butter blonde and blue-eyed as the people you would see in a travel poster advertising Oktoberfest. The pilots had made room for her and she sat on the end of the bench where she could operate the communications console.

She whipped the headset off and sprang to her feet.

"Good news, everybody!" she called out. "The lunar observatory reports that the storm's intensity peaked there almost an hour ago."

Smiles broke out. Heads nodded. Everyone murmured happily.

"According to the orbiting magnetosphere observatories," Diels continued, "the storm should be over in another twelve to sixteen hours."

Groans. "Another sixteen hours in here?"

Tony Reed raised his arms for silence. "Now don't complain. As long as the toilet works we should be perfectly fine."

Ilona was not amused. "Sixteen more hours. Ugh!"

"Try to relax," Reed urged. "Take a nap."

"Would you like to play a game of bridge?" asked the Greek biologist.

"Not with you," O'Hara snapped. "It's like swimming with a bloody shark."

Xenophanes laughed, but to Jamie it seemed strained.

Vosnesensky said, "We should not sit idly for another fourteen hours."

Ilona's lips curled into the start of a sneering reply, but before she could say anything Reed jumped in.

"What would you suggest, Mikhail Andreivitch?" the Englishman asked.

"A workers' council," the Russian replied. "We are all here. None of us has pressing duties to perform. Now is the time for a self-analysis session."

"A quality circle, like the Japanese?" asked Tad Sliwa, the backup biochemist.

"More like a self-criticism circle," said Ilona, "like prisoners in Siberia."

Vosnesensky's beefy face flushed slightly, but he did not reply to her. Ivshenko, lean in face and body, darkly handsome in an almost Levantine way, said, "Self-analysis can be a very useful way to examine interpersonal problems."

There was some argument, but Vosnesensky was determined and

none of the others really had any suggestion to offer as an alternative. So the twelve men and women sat along the benches facing one another.

"How do we start?" asked Ollie Zieman.

"I will start," Vosnesensky said. "This was my idea, so I will be the first volunteer."

"Go right ahead," said Reed, sitting across the central aisle from the Russian.

Vosnesensky glanced at Ilona, then turned his gaze to sweep the men and women on the bench opposite him. "I feel resentment from some of you. Resentment that I am in command. Resentment, perhaps, that a Russian is in command."

"That's rather natural, is it not?" asked Katrin Diels. "There is bound to be some resentment against any authority figure."

That started the discussion, and around and around it went. Jamie watched in silence, noticing that Ilona sat leaning back against the wall like a cat, her eyes following from one speaker to the next, her lips slightly curled in what might have been a smile. But she did not volunteer a word.

Like meetings of the student council, Jamie thought, remembering his undergraduate days. The ones who did most of the talking were the ones who were already in charge. The ones who needed to talk the most were the ones who stayed silent and kept their anger bottled up inside them.

After nearly an hour Jamie was startled to hear O'Hara say, "Well, if we're baring our souls and all that—I don't particularly like the idea that I'm going to be sitting up in orbit all during our stay at Mars while my esteemed colleague here," he jabbed a thumb in Jamie's direction, "gets to spend the whole seven weeks down on the surface. I don't think that's fair."

"I agree with you," Jamie heard himself say. "It's not fair." But, he added silently, that's the way the mission plan has been written and that's the way it's going to be.

O'Hara's gripe launched another hour's debate on why the mission had been planned the way it had been, and whether or not they could appeal to Dr. Li to change the procedure so that the backup teams could spend some time on the surface.

"It would be useless," Vosnesensky said flatly. "All these procedures were examined very thoroughly for years. One team stays on the surface and the backup team remains in orbit. That will not be changed. I know this for a fact."

"I agree with George," Ollie Zieman grumbled. "It's not fair."

"But more efficient," Vosnesensky countered, with the flat finality of a man who had decided the subject was closed.

"Why must the leader of each team be a Russian?" Ilona asked, her throaty voice purring, almost sleepy.

Everyone turned toward her.

"I mean, we have men and women of every nationality on this mission. Yet of the four teams, each group is headed by a Russian. A Russian *male*, at that."

For a long moment there was absolute silence. Jamie could hear the electrical hum of the ship's equipment and the quiet hiss of the air fans.

"I can answer that," said Pete Connors.

"Please do," Ilona said.

The black astronaut was sitting beside Vosnesensky, who had the other cosmonaut, Ivshenko, on his other side. Connors gave them a small grin, then turned back to Ilona.

"First," he raised a long finger, "the commander of each team must be a pilot. A man from the military, accustomed to giving orders and having them obeyed. Accustomed to receiving orders from higher authority and carrying them out. Without discipline we could all get killed. This is no weekend hiking trip we're on."

"You said a man," Katrin Diels interrupted. "Why not a woman?"

Connors made an elaborate shrug. "Guess they couldn't find any women with the necessary qualifications."

All three women hooted at him. Even most of the men laughed.

Once they calmed down, Connors resumed, "Second, the Soviet Federation has provided the boosters and the life-support equipment for this mission. Soviet cosmonauts have more experience in spaceflight than anyone on Earth; they've been doing long-term missions aboard their space station since 1971, for god's sake!"

"Because you Americans waited twenty-five years before you put up a permanent space station," Xenophanes said, practically sneering.

"Yeah, that's true," Connors agreed. "So when we started planning the Mars mission, the American government agreed that the team leaders would be picked from military pilots who had the most experience in spaceflight."

"Meaning Russians," said Xenophanes.

"That's the way it worked out."

Sliwa huffed, "The Russians outsmarted you at the very start of the program. They have always been clever at negotiations."

"I don't think you can say that Mikhail or Dmitri are here because some Russian politician outslicked his American counterpart," Connors objected.

Sliwa hunched his shoulders. Vosnesensky was glaring at the Pole.

Ivshenko glanced at his compatriot, then said, "The Soviet Union has made some sacrifices for this *privilege* of providing leadership. No Soviet scientist was selected for the ground team, even though we have many men—and women—who are highly qualified in the fields of planetary sciences."

"Same thing with the States," added Connors. "We have astronauts on all four teams, but no scientists on the ground team except for Jamie here."

They all turned toward Jamie, who forced himself to remain silent. I'm here by accident, he told himself. They all know that. And back in the States I'm only half American, whichever way you look at it.

"Perhaps we should change the subject," Reed suggested. "This kind of argument will get us nowhere."

Jamie was tempted to ask Reed to explain how he could sneak sex-suppressant drugs into their food or drink. But he thought better of it. No sense starting a real fight, he told himself. So he remained quiet while the others stared at one another, unable or unwilling to find a new topic for discussion.

"Well then, perhaps we should get some sleep," Reed said.

Vosnesensky nodded vigorously. "Yes. A good idea. In ten hours or so the radiation levels should be low enough for us to leave this shelter. Then we will have to check the ship's systems and all our equipment thoroughly to assess what damage the storm has done, and then repair it. We should sleep now."

It was an order, not a suggestion. No one argued, not even Ilona.

S O L 8: EVENING

Jamie and Vosnesensky had started as soon as the morning sunlight made the ground around them visible. All the previous day they had taken turns driving the rover at breakneck speed along the broken, rugged badlands country, heading north by east, away from the faulted canyons of Noctis Labyrinthus, away from their base camp. Breakneck speed, for the rover, was not quite forty kilometers per hour—almost the speed limit in a school zone.

Still they were exhausted by the time the sun had finally dropped behind the ragged horizon at their backs and the dark cold shadows of night overtook their vehicle. Two straight days of continuous driving, much of it detours around ridges too steep to climb or crevasses too deep to traverse, had sapped them physically and emotionally. They ate a sparse dinner in moody silence; then Vosnesensky checked in with Dr. Li and the base camp. Everything was going smoothly at the base, and to Jamie's continuing surprise and delight, Li still did not order them to turn around and return to the domed camp.

"The mission controllers haven't vetoed our excursion," he said, leaning back on the bench that would later unfold to be his bunk. Vosnesensky sat across from him, the narrow folding table between them.

"Not yet," said the cosmonaut, like a man waiting for the ax to fall.

Feeling something between guilt and embarrassment, Jamie said, "I'm sorry I had to go over your head about this."

Vosnesensky shrugged his heavy shoulders. "It was your right to do so." He looked into Jamie's eyes and added, "My responsibility was to stick to the mission plan until higher authority changed the plan. I was only doing my duty. I was not objecting on personal grounds."

A tendril of relief wormed along Jamie's spine. "Then you're not angry?"

"Why should I be? Do you think you scientists have a monopoly on curiosity?"

Jamie smiled broadly. "That's great! I was afraid I'd made you sore."

The Russian grinned back at him. "Not so. Once Dr. Li took the responsibility of allowing this change in the traverse, my objections vanished. I would like to see this Grand Canyon too."

Jamie slept soundly, dreaming of Mesa Verde and his grandfather.

They awakened after their third night aboard the rover at the first eerie light of dawn, the faintest pale pink brightening of the sky along the flat eastern horizon. Jamie pulled his coveralls over his briefs, then set up the folding table between their bunks and popped two precooked breakfasts into the microwave while Vosnesensky was in the lavatory. The Russian, already in his tan coveralls and soft slipper-socks, spooned down his steaming oatmeal while Jamie took his turn at the toilet.

As Jamie was washing up he heard Vosnesensky shout, "Jamie! Look at this!"

He ducked out of the narrow lavatory and saw that Vosnesensky was up in the cockpit. Squeezing past the table, Jamie hurried there.

Vosnesensky had pulled back the thermal shroud. The plastiglass bubble canopy was twinkling with faintly glistening little glimmers that winked on and disappeared like fireflies. Jamie felt his breath catch in his throat.

"Dewdrops," Vosnesensky said. "Morning dew."

"It condenses on the glass." Jamie reached out his fingers to touch the bubble. It was cold but dry inside. Even while he watched more tiny droplets appeared and flickered out, evaporating before his eyes, vanishing so quickly that he would have missed them altogether if others had not glimmered into brief existence. Like tiny diamonds they sparkled for a heartbeat and then were gone. After a few minutes they stopped completely. Jamie realized that he would never have suspected they had been there if he had not seen them himself. Mikhail caught them at just the right moment.

"There is moisture in the air here," the Russian said. "A little, at least."

"Frost," Jamie murmured. "Must be ice particles that form in the air at night. They melted on the warm surface . . ."

"And evaporated immediately."

"Where's the moisture coming from?" Jamie asked. Turning to the Russian, "Mikhail, how far are we from the canyon?"

"An hour's drive, perhaps a little more." Vosnesensky slid into the pilot's seat and punched up a map display on the control panel's central screen. "Yes, about one hour."

"Let's get going! Right away! I'll drive."

"I will drive," said Vosnesensky firmly. "You are too excited. You would drive like a cowboy, not an Indian." Then he chuckled deep in his throat at his own wit.

Jamie blinked at the Russian. Humor, from Mikhail? That's even more rare than morning dew on Mars.

Now the rover lurched and swayed as Vosnesensky threaded between rocks and over ridges, every ounce of his attention focused on his driving. He had the throttle full out and the segmented vehicle was making its best speed across the rusted desert. To Jamie, sitting at Vosnesensky's right, the rover was a large metal caterpillar inching its way across the Martian landscape. The dusty red ground was strewn with rocks, as everywhere, although craters seemed to be much fewer than farther west. Boulders as large as houses lay here and there, making Jamie itch to go out and investigate them.

But they stayed inside the rover, comfortable in their coveralls, and stuck to their low-speed dash toward the Grand Canyon of Mars. Jamie gripped the stone fetish in his pocket. There's moisture in the air in the morning, he kept repeating to himself. It must be coming from the canyon. Must be.

He worried in the back of his mind that Dr. Li's approval might be countermanded by someone in the chain of command on Earth. He wanted to be at their destination when such a signal came in— or so close that they could do some exploring before they had to obey the command to return to base. Mikhail seems to want it too, Jamie thought. In his own way he's as excited as I am.

"I have never met an Indian before," Vosnesensky said abruptly, without taking his eyes from his driving.

"I'm not much of an Indian," Jamie replied. "I was brought up to be a white man."

"But you are not white."

"No, not entirely." The rover jounced over a little rill, bouncing Jamie in his seat. "In the States we have people from every part of the world—all the nationalities of Europe, Asians, Africans . . ."

"I have heard about the problems of your blacks. We learned in school how they are held down by your racist system."

Jamie felt himself bristling. "Then why is the only black man on Mars an American? Why haven't the African nations joined in this expedition?"

"Because they are poor," the Russian answered, deftly maneuvering the rover around a new-looking crater about the size of a swimming pool. "They cannot afford luxuries such as space exploration. They can barely feed their people."

"Is this really a luxury, Mikhail? Do you think that reaching out into space is a waste of money?"

"No." Vosnesensky's answer was immediate and firm beyond the shadow of a doubt.

Thinking of the run-down pueblos and crumbling old adobe homes in New Mexico, Jamie mused, "I wonder. Sometimes I think the money could have been better used to help poor people."

The Russian shot him a quick glance, then returned to his driving. For long moments he said nothing and Jamie watched the dusty red land pass by, rocks, tired worn gullies, craters, little wind-stirred dunes. Off toward the horizon he saw a dust swirl, as red as a devil, spiraling into the pink morning sky.

"What we do helps the poor," Vosnesensky said. "We are not taking bread from their mouths. We are enlarging the habitat of the human species. History has shown that every expansion of the human habitat has brought about an increase in wealth and a rise in living standards. That is objective fact."

"But the poor are still with us," Jamie said.

A slight note of exasperation crept into the Russian's voice. "The Soviet Federation alone has spent thousands of billions on aid to poor nations. The United States even more. This expedition to Mars has not hurt the poor. What we spend here is a pittance compared to what they have already received. And what good does it do for them? They go out and produce more babies, make a new generation of poor. A larger generation. It is endless."

"So they're not going hungry because we're here on Mars."

"Definitely not. They lack discipline, that is their problem. In the Soviet Federation we pulled ourselves up from a backward agricultural society to a powerful industrial nation in a single generation."

Yes, Jamie replied silently, with Stalin in the driver's seat. He didn't care how many millions starved while he built his factories and power plants.

"But tell me, what was it like when you were growing up in New Mexico? It is near Texas?"

"Yes," Jamie said. "Between Arizona and Texas."

"I have been there. Houston."

"New Mexico is nothing like Houston." Jamie laughed. Then, "Actually, I did most of my growing up in California. Berkeley. That's where my parents taught, at the university. I was a kid when we moved there. But I spent a lot of my summers in Santa Fe, with my grandfather."

It had been a trying day. Jamie was almost seventeen, finishing high school, a vast disappointment to his parents because he had no clear idea of what he wanted to study in college.

His parents had flown with him to Santa Fe, where he was to spend the summer. His grandfather had just announced that he had secured a full scholarship for Jamie at the university in Albuquerque—if Jamie wanted it.

They were sitting in the dining room of Al's house, up in the hills north of Santa Fe, the evening meal long finished as they sat and talked across the big oak table littered with the remains of roasted goat.

The dining room was large and cool, with a slanted beamed ceiling high above the floor of gleaming ochre tiles. Through its broad window Jamie could see adobe-style town houses dotting the slopes that ran down to the city. Al owned most of them; rental condos for the skiers in the winter and the tourists who wanted to buy genuine Indian artifacts all year long. The sun was going down toward the darkening mountains. Soon there would be another spectacular New Mexico sunset painting the sky.

Jamie had gobbled every scrap of the *cabrito*, enjoying the spices that Al's cook had used so generously. His mother, who would eat *lapin* and even frogs' legs without a qualm, had barely touched her dinner. Jamie's father had eaten his portion easily enough, but now he unconsciously rubbed his chest, as if the spices had been too much for him.

"I'm sure you meant well, Al," Lucille was saying, with her sweetest, most persuasive little-girl smile, "but we had just assumed that Jamie would stay at home and attend Berkeley."

"Do the boy good to get a different slant on things," Al said, pulling a pack of slim dark cigarillos from his shirt pocket. "That's what schoolin's supposed to be all about, isn't it: gettin' an education? That means more than books and class work, don't it?"

Lucille frowned as her father-in-law lit up and blew a cloud of thin gray smoke toward the beamed ceiling. She cast a sharp glance at her husband.

With a slight cough, Jerome Waterman said, "Dad, the boy hasn't even made up his mind about what he wants to study yet, let alone about where he wants to go to school."

They're talking as if I get to make the decisions, Jamie thought. But they're not even asking me what I think.

His father was going on, "Considering his grades and the results of his aptitude tests . . ."

"Aw, bullshit on all that crap!" Al blurted. Then he turned his most flattering smile on his daughter-in-law. "Sorry for the language, Lucille. But I don't think those psychologists could find a skunk in their own clothes closet, let alone help a seventeen-year-old boy figure out where he wants to head in life."

"I will not have Jamie turned into an Indian," Lucille said firmly.

Al guffawed, a reaction Jamie had seen him use often in his store when he needed a moment to frame his thoughts before replying to a tough question.

"What do you think, Lucy? You think I want him workin' in a store, waitin' on tourists from Beverly Hills or New York? You think I want him wastin' away his life in some dumb-ass pueblo raisin' sheep and drinkin' beer the rest of his life?"

"He's shown an aptitude for science," Jerry said.

"Then let him study science! They got fine scientists at Albuquerque. All kinds of geologists and whatnot."

Geology. Jamie had spent long hours collecting rocks in the arid hills and arroyos. Al had taken him up to Colorado to see the Mesa Verde cliff dwellings, and out to Arizona for the Grand Canyon and the big meteor crater.

"Some of the finest scientists in the world are at Berkeley," Lucille was saying stiffly. "In the physics department alone . . ."

Al interrupted her. "Hell, here we are talkin' about the boy's future as if he wasn't even here. Jamie! What do you think about all this? What've you got to say?"

Jamie remembered the Grand Canyon. That vast chasm carved into the Earth. The colors of the different layers of rock, layer after layer. The whole history of the world was painted on those rocks, a history that went incredibly farther back than the span of time human beings had existed.

"I like geology," he said. "I'd like to study geology, I think."

More than an hour had passed since they had started off. Jamie was fingering the bear fetish in his coverall pocket as the rover climbed the slope of a ridge, laboring up a steepening grade that was strewn with smallish rocks and pebbles. The red soil seemed sandy, crumbly. Jamie could hear the electric motors that drove each individual wheel whining, struggling.

Vosnesensky slowed the vehicle to a crawl. Looking out ahead, Jamie could see only the approaching top of the ridge and the pink sky beyond it. Not a cloud in that sky, it was as clear and empty as the deep blue skies he had known in New Mexico.

"Can't we go any faster?" Jamie urged. "The moisture'll be all baked out of the air by the time we reach . . ."

Abruptly Vosnesensky tramped on the brakes. Jamie lurched forward, reflexively jabbing his hands out to the control panel. He started to complain, then gaped at what lay outside the plastiglass canopy.

"We are here," Vosnesensky said.

What Jamie had thought was the ridge line was actually the rim of the canyon. Beyond it there was a huge, vast, yawning emptiness. They were perched on the edge of a cliff that dropped away precipitously for miles and miles. Another few feet and the rover would have pitched over the rimrock and plunged down forever.

"Jesus Christ," Jamie breathed.

Vosnesensky grunted.

Jamie stood up in his chair, peering as far as he could into the depths of the enormity of Tithonium Chasma. It was dizzying, and knowing that this gigantic cleft was merely one arm of Valles Marineris, that the valley system stretched more than three thousand kilometers eastward, made his head swim even more.

Then he felt his heart clutch in his chest. "Mikhail—it's there. The mist . . ."

Frail gray feathers of clouds were wafting through the vast canyon far below, like a ghostly river that glided silently past their round staring eyes.

"The sunlight has not reached that deep into the canyon," Vosnesensky said.

"Yeah." Jamie pushed out of his seat and started back toward the airlock and the hard suits. "Come on, we've got to get this on tape before the clouds evaporate. There's moisture down there, Mikhail! Water!"

"Ice particles," the Russian said. He followed Jamie toward the suit locker.

"They melt into liquid water."

"And evaporate."

"And form again the next night." Jamie was struggling into the lower half of his suit. "The moisture doesn't go away. It stays in the valley—for a while, at least."

He had never put on a hard suit so quickly. After the lower half, the boots (it was much easier that way), then the torso, finally the helmet. Vosnesensky helped him into his backpack and checked all the seals and connections while Jamie quivered like a bird dog on the scent.

As he was grabbing for the video camera Vosnesensky said sternly, "Gloves! *Think* before you step outside. Go down the checklist no matter how excited you are."

"Thanks," Jamie said, feeling sheepish.

"In fact," Vosnesensky said, sliding his helmet over his head and fastening the neck seal, "the more excited you are the more you must force yourself to stop and go through the checklist point by point."

"You're right," Jamie said impatiently.

The Russian grinned at him, like a squat bear showing its teeth. "If you kill yourself here I will be in big trouble with Dr. Li and the controllers in Kaliningrad."

Jamie found himself grinning back. "I wouldn't want to get you in trouble, Mikhail."

"Good. Now we are ready to go outside."

It was not fair to call it a canyon. Jamie could not see the other side, it was beyond the horizon. The abyss named Tithonium Chasma was so vast, so awesome, that at first Jamie merely stared out from behind his tinted visor, numb with excitement and an overpowering feeling of reverence.

Unbidden, words from his long-forgotten childhood formed in his mind:

> These are the words of Changing Woman,
> wisdom she gave to the Holy People: The only

*goal for a man is beauty, and beauty can be
found only in harmony.*

"The camera." He heard Vosnesensky's voice in his helmet ear-phones. "The sunlight is beginning to evaporate the mist."

Jamie shook himself inside the hard suit and got to work. He panned the vidcam up and down the valley, then from the lip of the rimrock where they stood out to the mist-shrouded horizon. Wherever the sun touched the clouds dissipated, dissolved into thin air. Like the old myths of ghosts that vanish when the sun comes up, Jamie told himself.

"It's not right to call this a valley," he muttered as he worked the camera. "That's like calling the Pacific Ocean a pond."

Vosnesensky said, "If you will be all right here for a while, I will set up a sensor unit."

"I'll be okay," Jamie said. "I'll be fine."

For hours he watched the mists dissolving as the pale sun rose higher in the rose-pink sky. Down in the deepest recesses of the rocks there must be places where the mist clings, where the sunlight can't reach, Jamie said to himself. Little oases where there are droplets of liquid water and warmth from the sun's heating of the rocks. Little pockets down there where life might hang on.

By noontime he had used up three videocassettes and was inserting a fourth one into the camera. The mists were almost entirely gone now and he could see the rock formations standing like proud ancient battlements, marching off in both directions from the spot where he stood. The valley floor was so far below that he could only see the distant part of it, curving off past the horizon. Misty shadows still clung among the rocks down there.

"They're differentiated, Mikhail," Jamie said into his helmet microphone. "The rock walls here are layered. There was an ocean here once, or maybe an enormous river. Look at the layers."

Vosnesensky, standing beside him once more, said, "All the rocks look red."

Jamie laughed. "And on Earth all the trees look green. But there are different shades, Mikhail."

He pointed with a gloved hand along the line of cliffs. "Look out there. See, this top layer is cracked vertically, weathered pretty badly. But the layer under it is smoother, and much darker in color."

"Ah, yes," said Vosnesensky. "Now I see."

"And the layer under *that* is streaked with yellowish intrusions.

Maybe bauxite, or something like it. This region must have been a lot warmer once, a long time ago."

"You think so? Why?"

Jamie started to reply, then realized he was indulging in wishful thinking. "Good question, Mikhail. We'll make a scientist out of you yet."

He heard the Russian's deep chuckling. "Not likely."

Jamie squinted up at the sun. "Let's set up the winch. I want to . . ."

"Not down there!"

"Just the first three layers," Jamie said. "I know we can't get down to the bottom or anywhere near it. But I can reach that layer with the yellowish intrusions, at least. Come on, the sun's starting to hit this side."

"No lunch?"

"You can eat lunch after the winch is up. I'm too excited to eat."

In his stolid, immovable fashion Vosnesensky insisted that they both eat before breaking out the winch and climbing harness.

"Nutrition is important," the Russian insisted. "Many mistakes are made because of hunger."

Despite himself Jamie grinned. "You sound like a commercial for bran flakes, Mikhail."

Neither man bothered to take off more than his helmet and gloves once inside the rover. They each ate a hot meal perched on the edge of their facing half-folded bunks in their cumbersome hard suits. Vosnesensky brought the bottle of vitamin supplement pills from their little pharmaceutical cabinet.

"We forgot at breakfast," he said, handing the bottle to Jamie.

"Right." Jamie shook one of the orange-colored pills loose. "Wouldn't want to miss the Flintstones."

Vosnesensky scowled, puzzled. "It is no joke. Our diet lacks vitamins; we get no sunshine on our skins. The supplement is necessary."

"Besides," Jamie kidded, "it's written into the mission rules."

Jamie popped the pill into his mouth and washed it down with the last of the coffee in his mug. God, what I'd give for a cup of real coffee instead of this instant crap!

Then he saw that the sunlight was slanting into the rover through the canopy up in the cockpit.

"Come on, Mikhail, we're wasting time."

It took all four of their hands to work the harness over Jamie's backpack and crotch, then fasten it across his chest. With the Russian standing guard at the winch, Jamie lowered himself gingerly down the steep face of the cliff. Far, far below some tenuous threads of mist still clung to the rocks, gray and ghostly, slowly rising and sinking like long ocean swells or the breath of a sleeping giant.

There was no opposite wall of the canyon in sight, it was too far away beyond the horizon. Instead of the trapped feeling that had frightened him at Noctis Labyrinthus, Jamie felt as if he were working his way down the face of a mesa back home. Biggest goddammed mesa anybody ever saw, he said to himself as he peered down between his dangling feet toward the bottom, miles below. If this were New Mexico, the other end of this canyon would be in Newfoundland.

Jamie had to consciously force himself to turn his attention to chipping out rock samples. Still, as he started his work, dangling in the harness, he wondered about the world at the bottom of the solar system's largest canyon. We didn't expect mists in the summertime, didn't think there'd be enough moisture in the air for that. Down in the Hellas Basin, yes. But we didn't expect it here. Wish we could have taken samples of the stuff. Maybe it's ice crystals. But it doesn't look like an ice fog. How can you tell, though? The rules are different here; at least the conditions are. Down toward the bottom of the canyon there must be a completely different ecosystem from what we see up on the surface. Maybe the air's denser down there. Wetter. Warmer. Maybe there's life down there, hiding out in warm little niches the way our ancestors used to live in caves.

We should have set up base camp here, not out on that dumb plain. Then we could have spent our time exploring the canyon. This old rut in the ground has more to tell us than anyplace else on Mars.

Dangling in the harness, suspended a few meters from the lip of the canyon and many kilometers from its mist-shrouded bottom, Jamie thrilled that the cliffs here were completely different from those at the Noctis Labyrinthus badlands. There the cliff walls were a uniform slab of iron-red stone. Here the cliffs were layered, tier upon tier, as weathered and seamed as the mesas back home, rich pages of a petrified book that told the entire history of this world to those with the skill and patience to read it.

The topmost layer of the cliff, just under the caprock, had been almost soft; the rock there, crumbly, easily broken loose. On Earth it would have been weathered away by wind and rain in a geological twinkling. But here on dry, calm, gentle Mars it could remain for eons, undisturbed except for the slow erosion from the sun's warmth and the night's cold that eventually cracked it. Even so, there was no water in this layer, Jamie was willing to bet. Not even permafrost. If there had been, the water's expansion and contraction during the day-night cycle would easily have crumbled such friable stone.

The next tier was much tougher rock, its color a deeper red. More iron, Jamie guessed. Shergottite, like the meteor I found in Antarctica.

Jamie whacked away with his hand pick until he had several loose bits of the rock in his free hand. Chips and flakes fell clattering down, down beyond sight and hearing toward the canyon bottom so far below. As he slipped the rock samples into a collecting bag Jamie realized he was soaked with sweat from the exertion. The suit's fans were buzzing, sounding angry at him for pushing them so hard. He pulled in a deep breath of canned air as he carefully tucked the pick into its loop on his belt and then pulled out the ballpoint pen (guaranteed to work even in zero gravity) and labeled the sample bag precisely: date, time, exact distance from the rim. He got his depth, measured from the canyon's edge, by having Vosnesensky read off the tick marks on the winch's tether.

"Not much daylight remaining." Vosnesensky's voice sounded as remote and unemotional as a computer.

Jamie glanced up, then leaned a booted foot against the rock wall to turn himself around in the harness. His leg flared into a million pinpricks. Hanging in the harness, both legs had gone asleep. Jamie muttered and cursed to himself as he flailed his legs and wiggled his toes to get some circulation going again. He felt as if a whole colony of ants were gnawing at his legs.

"What is it?" Vosnesensky's voice was suddenly urgent. "Are you all right?"

"My goddam legs are asleep," Jamie answered.

"I will pull you up."

"No . . . it'll be okay in a minute or so. I want to get down to that third tier, where the yellow stuff is."

"Time is getting short."

"Isn't it always?" Jamie looked out across the vast chasm, saw the shadows creeping toward him. "We've got another hour, at least."

"One hour," said Vosnesensky, with implacable finality.

"Yeah. Okay."

Jamie pushed the sample bag into the pouch strapped to his right thigh, next to his fetish, then started to reach up to the keypad on his chest that controlled the winch. And froze.

His eyes caught a dark rift in the cliff wall a kilometer or more off to his left, a horizontal cleft with a flat floor and a slightly bulging overhang of rock above it. Like the cleft at Mesa Verde where the ancient ones had built their village of dried mud bricks.

And there were buildings in the cleft.

Jamie felt the breath rush out of him, felt his insides go hollow, drop away as if he had been suddenly pushed off the edge of the tallest mountain in the universe.

They can't be buildings, a part of his mind insisted. Yet as he stared he could make out square shapes, walls, towers. There was no haze to obscure his vision; the air was as clear as a polished mirror at this level.

Fumbling at his belt without taking his eyes from the vision, Jamie found the video camera clipped there and yanked it free. He banged it against his visor, his head jolting back in surprise, then held it steady and adjusted its telescopic lens.

His hands were shaking so badly all he could see at first was a blurry jumbled image. Fiercely, snarling inwardly, Jamie forced himself to a desperate calm, like a frightened man who knows he must aim his gun accurately or be killed.

The dark cleft in the rocks steadied and pulled itself into sharp focus. Deep inside it, well into the shadows of the overhang, Jamie saw the flat surfaces and crenellated outline of whitish rocks.

He was icy cold now. They're rocks, he told himself. Not buildings. Just a formation of rocks that look roughly like walls and towers made by intelligent creatures.

And yet.

Jamie cranked the lens to its fullest magnification, then squeezed the camera's trigger until its tiny beeping told him the cassette had been used up. Only then did he take the vidcam from his eyes.

"I'm coming up," he said, shouting even though the microphone built into his helmet was bare centimeters from his lips.

Vosnesensky sounded surprised. "Is something wrong?"

"No, Mikhail, nothing's wrong. Something's right."

"What? What did you say?"

It took more than fifteen minutes for the winch to lift him back to the rim of the canyon. Jamie had not realized he had traversed so far down. He spent the time trying to see more of the cleft, trying to convince himself not to let his imagination run loose, trying to stay calm and not babble once he got up there with the Russian again.

From the rim he could not see the cleft. As he shrugged himself out of the harness he said hurriedly to Vosnesensky, "Get into the rig, Mikhail. Quick! There's something down there you've got to see."

"Me? Why . . ."

"No time for discussion," Jamie urged as he slipped the harness over the Russian's fire-red backpack and started buckling it across his chest.

Puzzled, reluctant, Vosnesensky pulled the thigh straps tight and clicked them to the locking mechanism on his chest while Jamie reloaded the camera.

"What is it?" he asked. "What have you found?"

"A mirage, I think," Jamie said. "But maybe . . ."

Swiftly he described the cleft and the shapes inside it. Vosnesensky said nothing as he backed himself to the lip of the rimrock and stepped off.

"Wait!" Jamie yelled. He shoved the camera into Vosnesensky's gloved hands and fastened its tether to his equipment belt. "Use it as a telescope. But shoot the whole damned cassette. Keep shooting until it's all used up."

"Where do I look?" Vosnesensky asked as he descended. To Jamie he looked like an old-fashioned deep-sea diver lowering himself into the abyss.

Jamie kept rattling off instructions as the winch motor hummed thinly and Vosnesensky dropped lower.

"I see it!" For the first time since he had met the Russian, Vosnesensky sounded excited. "Yes, interesting formations of rock inside . . ." His voice trailed off.

"What do you think?" Jamie asked.

No answer for many minutes. Then, "It can't be a city. It looks like rock formations."

"Yeah." Jamie paced nervously back and forth along the canyon rim. Down below the Russian was silent.

Finally, "The tape is finished. I am coming up."

"Is it real?" Jamie asked as the winch labored, whining.

"Real, yes. But not artificial. It could not be."

"Never mind what it could or couldn't be. What is it?"

"Unusual formations of rock. But natural, not man-made."

"Martian-made."

"Not that either."

Jamie knew he should agree. It couldn't be artificial. It couldn't be a village created by intelligent Martians. It couldn't be the ancestors of his ancestors, the forerunner of Mesa Verde and the other cliff dwellings of the Anasazi. He knew it could not be.

But by the time Vosnesensky was standing beside him once more and pulling free of the harness Jamie was babbling, "We've got to get the rover to that spot on the rim, right on top of it, so we can lower down and look in there for ourselves. We're too far away to make certain from this distance and if there's any chance, any slightest chance at all, that we've found the remains of intelligent life, holy Christ, Mikhail, it's the biggest discovery in the history of the world!"

Vosnesensky remained strangely silent, like a stolid schoolmaster who is accustomed to sudden enthusiasms from his young students. Jamie kept on chattering and the Russian remained silent as they took the winch apart, stowed it in the rover's equipment module, and then clumped into the airlock.

Once inside the living section they took their helmets off. Jamie could see that Vosnesensky looked solemn, almost pained. His heavy jaw was covered with several days' stubble, making his face seem even grimmer than usual.

He realized he had been virtually raving. "Well, we can drive over there tomorrow morning, first light. Right?"

The Russian shook his head. "Not right. We have been ordered to return to the base."

"Ordered? By whom? When?"

"This afternoon, while you were down in the climbing rig. The order came over the command frequency; I heard it in my suit. Dr. Li himself specifically ordered us to return to the base camp. There has been an accident."

MARS ORBIT: DEIMOS

"It looks good enough to eat," quipped Leonid Tolbukhin. "Like a big potato."

Isoruku Konoye said nothing. The Japanese geochemist felt strangely tense as he and the cosmonaut approached the lumpy irregular blob of the Martian moon Deimos. To the Russian it might look like something to eat; to him it seemed like a huge brooding mass of darkness, evil and dangerous.

Mars has two moons, tiny chunks of rock named Phobos and Deimos, fear and dread, fitting companions for the god of war.

At first glance the moons of Mars do look rather like battered potatoes. Neither of them is round. They are too small to have been subjected to the forces that turn a lump of stone and metal into a spherical shape. Both are deeply pitted from meteorite strikes. Phobos is streaked with inexplicable striations, grooves that look almost as if its rocky surface had been scored by the claws of a titanic beast.

Deimos, the smaller of the two, is about the size of Manhattan Island: roughly ten by twelve by sixteen kilometers. It orbits just over twenty thousand kilometers above the surface of Mars. From the ground it looks like a very bright star that hangs in the sky for two and a half sols before dipping below the horizon.

Phobos is twenty by twenty-three by twenty-eight kilometers and orbits much closer to its planet, less than six thousand kilometers above the surface. It crosses the Martian sky in only four and a half hours, hurtling from west to east like an artificial satellite (which it was once suspected to be) and rising again about six and a half hours later.

It is believed that Deimos and Phobos were originally asteroids, perhaps members of the great belt of minor chunks of rock and metal that orbits between Mars and the giant planet Jupiter. Eons ago they drifted close enough to be captured by the red planet's gravitational field and fall into satellite orbits around it.

Thus, studying Phobos and Deimos can teach us much about the farther asteroids.

Most of the meteorites that have hit the Earth were originally asteroids. The Martian moons resemble the type of meteorites called by astronomers "carbonaceous chondrites." Such meteorites have been found to contain not only carbon compounds, but water, locked in chemical combinations called "hydrates" within the meteorite's rocky materials.

If the moons of Mars are rich in hydrates and carbon compounds, even though the water is not in liquid form, biologists will want to study the moons for signs of life or its precursors. Hydrates are immeasurably valuable to astronautical engineers, as well. They could supply life-giving water and oxygen. More important, water can be split into hydrogen and oxygen, which can be used for rocket propellants, which could cut in half the tonnages needed to be sent off Earth for any future missions to Mars.

The tiny moons of Mars, then, could become oases for space travelers where they can refresh life-support supplies and refuel rocket engines.

If they contain hydrates.

Which is why the Japanese geochemist and the Russian cosmonaut had left the *Mars 2* spacecraft to begin the hands-on study of Deimos.

Tolbukhin said into his helmet microphone, "Five minutes to impact. I am arming the penetrator." This was a rocket-powered grappling hook, designed to imbed itself into Deimos's pitted surface and anchor the two men safely. Without it to tether them, the explorers could go flying off the tiny moon with every step they took, Deimos's gravity was so negligibly low.

Still Konoye said nothing. He was no longer looking at the looming dark shape of Deimos. He stared instead at the enormous bulk of the red planet hanging overhead. He could not take his eyes off it.

The two men had left the *Mars 2* spacecraft an hour earlier, decked in hard-shell pressure suits and tubular metal frames of mobility units wrapped around their bodies. They looked like brightly colored fat robots stuck inside individual jungle gyms. The mobility units contained personal equipment, life-support systems, and the thrust motors and propellants that allowed them to fly from the orbiting spacecraft to the Martian moon named after the Greek word for *dread*.

Slowly revolving a few kilometers away, the tethered *Mars 1* and

Mars 2 spacecraft looked like miniature models, white and silent, lifeless and desperately far off.

To Konoye, Deimos was an ugly, irregular, dark-gray lump of crater-pitted stone blotting out the stars, covering half the sky. Enormous. Menacing. And Mars itself seemed terrifyingly huge, crushingly massive. In his perspective, the ponderous enormity of the red planet loomed above him, glowering overhead, pressing down, squeezing the breath from his lungs. The three immense volcanoes of the Tharsis Bulge and the even bigger caldera of Olympus Mons seemed to be staring down at him like the four monstrous wide round eyes of a demon, staring balefully.

The Japanese geophysicist had trained for this moment for more than three years. He had gone through all the simulations on Earth and experienced long weeks of zero gravity aboard the space stations in Earth orbit. He had prepared himself thoroughly to lead the first-hand study of Mars's two moons. Waiting for their turns behind him were a Russian geologist and an American geophysicist. But in this moment Japan was first.

Yet Konoye had not reckoned on that enormous expanse of red looming above him like a powerful, palpable force. This was no simulation. Mars hung over him and he could feel it squeezing down on him while its many-eyed demon glared at him, angry and demanding. Something in his childhood awakened and began screaming. Some long-forgotten nightmare tore at his mind. He had to get away. Get away!

Blindly Konoye fired the thrusters of his excursion unit. In panic he fled from the overpowering presence of Mars.

"Wait!" shouted Tolbukhin. "What are you doing?"

Konoye was jetting away from Mars, away from Deimos, away from the spacecraft in which he had lived for more than nine months. His gloved hands clamped rigidly on the thruster controls, like a catatonic or a man already in rigor mortis.

"Stop!" Tolbukhin yelled, so agitated he lapsed into Russian. "You fool, you'll kill yourself!"

But Konoye was fleeing, panic-stricken, unable to speak. The cosmonaut punched his own thrusters into life and jetted after him, even as his helmet earphones erupted in wild commands from the team in the *Mars 2* spacecraft monitoring their excursion.

Under the remorseless hand of blind nature Konoye had turned himself into a miniature asteroid. At full thrust the propellants in his tanks quickly ran out. In the frictionless vacuum of space he continued to fly away in the same direction, straight out into the endless void between worlds.

Tolbukhin could not catch him. Within a few seconds his training asserted itself—abetted by the frenzied shouts of the monitoring team in his helmet earphones. He reversed course and headed back for the safety of the *Mars 2* craft.

It took no more than two hours for the rescue team to reach Konoye in one of the emergency transfer vehicles they all referred to as "tugboats." The Japanese scientist still had several hours of air in his suit tanks. His heater and other life-support equipment were still functioning.

But he was quite dead. The autopsy promptly conducted by Dr. Yang aboard the *Mars 2* craft found the cause of death to be a cerebral hemorrhage. Tolbukhin shook his head when he heard the verdict.

"He died of fright," muttered the Russian. "He died of *deimos*, dread."

S O L 9: EVENING

"He died of natural causes, then," Jamie said.

Vosnesensky shrugged. "But would he have died if he had remained on Earth? Or if he had not gone on the EVA?"

Jamie shrugged back at the Russian. "We'll never know."

They were in the cramped confines of the airlock, slowly, laboriously pulling themselves out of their hard suits, tired from the day's work, depressed by the news from orbit.

"I still don't see why Li had to order us to return to base," Jamie grumbled. "Doesn't he understand what we've found here?"

"What have we found?" Vosnesensky smiled tolerantly. "An optical illusion?"

"Well . . . maybe," Jamie admitted.

"When we get back to the base we can ask the team in orbit for computer enhancement of the videotapes. If there is any chance that the rock formations are man-made . . . er, Martian-made—we will certainly return here."

"It's more than that, Mikhail. This canyon is an open book of the history of the planet. We should be *here*, studying what the rocks have to tell us. Joanna and the life-sciences people should be down there where the mists hang around all day. That's the best chance for life to be found."

Vosnesensky had peeled down to his water-tubed skivvies. Jamie was still in his hard-shell pants, leaning against the airlock bulkhead to tug off a boot.

The Russian looked at the red dust on Jamie's boots and sniffed loudly. "It smells different from the moon."

"What?"

"After a moon walk your shelter smells as if someone had shot off a revolver inside. The lunar dust that clings to your suit and boots has a burnt odor to it. This stuff—" he fingered the thin film of rusty powder on the sleeve of his empty hard suit "—this Martian dust smells different."

Jamie wrinkled his nose. "Now that you mention it—it smelled the same way back at the dome, didn't it?"

Nodding, Vosnesensky pulled on his hard suit's arm; it swung upward with the slight hissing sound of its slick Teflon shoulder joints.

"Smell."

Jamie sniffed at the metallic arm. Pungent. Harsh. Then he pulled one of his own gloves from the rack where he had tucked them. Somewhere deep in his memory the picture of an approaching thunderstorm formed itself, strange eerie afternoon light, the summer air heavy and still. Lightning flickering against approaching black clouds.

"Yeah. Strange smell. Almost like . . . could it be ozone?"

Vosnesensky rubbed at his eyes. "Yes, I think you are right. Ozone."

"The soil's loaded with superoxides," Jamie said.

"And in the high temperature inside here they are breaking down, baking out of the dust."

Jamie's own eyes were smarting now. The rover's airlock was much smaller than the clean-up area in the dome. "Maybe we ought to get out of the airlock."

"Not until we clean the suits."

Jamie finished pulling off his boots and wriggled out of the hard suit's pants. They vacuumed their suits thoroughly, yet the pungent odor remained in the airlock. Then he followed Vosnesensky through the hatch that led into the main compartment of the rover's forward section.

Blinking his eyes, Jamie said, "Wow, it feels like downtown Houston in there."

"The ozone will break down quickly enough," said Vosnesensky. "It becomes molecular oxygen. Harmless."

Scanning the shelves of equipment neatly stacked on either side of him Jamie muttered, "We have a GC/MS in here, don't we? They're not both back in the equipment section."

Vosnesensky pointed to the lowest shelf. "That is the quadrupole device. The magnetic one is in the equipment module."

"This'll do just fine." Jamie knelt down to pull the instrument from the shelf. The gas chromatograph/mass spectrometer analyzed the chemical composition of materials, virtually atom by atom. It was neatly packaged in a gray plastic casing, surprisingly light. The manufacturer's logo identified it as Japanese.

"I want to monitor the levels of ozone in the airlock. See how it decomposes, what else the soil might be outgassing."

"Good," said Vosnesensky.

"I'll set it up in the airlock and connect it to the secondary display screen in the cockpit. You set up dinner. I'm starving."

The Russian's dark brows knitted slightly. "You are giving me orders? I am the commander."

Jamie was already starting to open the airlock hatch, the spectrometer in one arm resting on his hip. He glanced back over his shoulder at the cosmonaut.

"I give the orders, Yankee. You set up the GC/MS while I prepare our meal."

"Right, boss," said Jamie, laughing.

Joanna watched the display screen as Vosnesensky and then Jamie Waterman made their evening reports. She was sitting on a spider-legged stool at the workbench in the biology lab, cocooned in the bulky equipment that surrounded her. She felt almost at home in the laboratory area; the microscopes and isolation boxes and racks of glassware made her feel more comfortable and protected here than in the bare narrow cubicle that served as her sleeping quarters.

She had patched her lab computer into the base's communications system so that she could see the excursion team's report in some privacy. Jamie's face looked serious yet happy. He was not really smiling, but there was an excitement in his eyes that she had never seen before as he described his day's observations.

"This is where we should have landed," he was saying, looking out from the screen as if he knew his eyes would meet hers. "There's moisture here and I'm willing to bet that the temperatures down at the bottom of the valley are significantly warmer than up here on the plain."

He went on, his eyes sparkling as he described the rock formations that looked to him so much like the adobe cliff dwellings of southwestern America.

"He's a handsome red devil, isn't he?"

Joanna whirled on the stool. Tony Reed was standing there, one arm casually leaning on the transparent plastic hood of an empty isolation box. He wore a black turtleneck shirt beneath his tan coveralls. One corner of his lips was curved slightly in a strange sardonic smile. Joanna stared at him for a wordless moment. It was almost as if Reed's face had been split in two: half his face was smiling, the other half not.

"Jamie makes a strong case for studying the canyon," she said. "The chances for finding living organisms, or even the fossils of extinct species . . ."

Reed moved closer to her, pulled up the other stool, and straddled it. Gesturing toward the screen he said, "Our Indian friend seems to think he's found the ruins of an ancient village. How preposterous."

Sudden anger flared within Joanna. "How do you know it is preposterous? How can we say anything about this world until we have explored all of it?"

Reed's smile widened. "I'm not a betting man, but I'd be willing to wager long odds that there are no ancient civilizations to be found on Mars."

"Yes, and a century and a half ago you would have bet that Schliemann would never find the ruins of Troy."

"My, aren't we fiery!" Reed laughed.

Joanna turned back to the computer, but Vosnesensky's heavy-featured, morose face filled the screen now. She clicked it off.

"You're right, of course," Reed admitted easily. "One mustn't jump to conclusions—either way."

Joanna accepted it as an apology.

"Jamie's doing good work, isn't he?" Reed asked rhetorically. "I'm glad we fought to get him onto the team."

"He is a great asset," Joanna agreed.

"Much better than Hoffman would have been, although I wonder how DiNardo would have fared here."

"What do you mean?"

Leaning both his elbows on the lab bench behind him, Reed appeared as relaxed as if he were in a London pub. "Well, DiNardo has this enormous reputation, you know. If he had seen what Jamie's seen out there at the Grand Canyon, I wonder if his prestige would have been big enough to get us to move the camp there."

"The entire base?"

Reed cocked his head slightly, sending a boyish lock of sandy hair over his forehead. "If Jamie's right and the canyon is the best place to look for life, then we should at least set up a secondary camp there, don't you think?"

Nodding slowly, Joanna said, "But we can't pick up this entire dome and move it."

"With that silly Japanese getting himself killed," Reed answered, "the mission controllers probably won't allow us to do anything that's even a millimeter off our official schedule."

"But the schedule was meant to be flexible! They cannot hold us to a preset routine, as if we were puppets."

"You think not? I can't help supposing, though, that if DiNardo were here we'd already be working out a plan to set up a camp on the floor of the canyon."

"That is what Jamie wants to do, is it not?"

"Rather. But he's in trouble with his own politicos back in the States, you know, over this Navaho nonsense he said when we landed. I doubt that his recommendations would be accepted by the powers that be."

Joanna studied the English physician's face. He was no longer grinning. He seemed completely serious.

"I can speak to my father about it," she said. "I am sure he already knows about the possibility—or he will, as soon as today's data reaches mission control."

"Yes, surely your father would be helpful. I was thinking more of DiNardo, though. If we can get his agreement that we should set up a secondary camp in the canyon, that would help enormously, I should think."

Joanna felt a thrill of excitement run through her. "Yes! Of course! They could not fail to agree with Father DiNardo."

"Hardly," said Reed.

"I will contact him myself," Joanna said. "And suggest to my father that he enlist Father DiNardo's aid, as well."

"Yes, that's the ticket."

"I will send a message now, this evening. Right away."

"Good show," said Reed. He straightened up and got off the stool. Leaning closer to Joanna he whispered, "We can accomplish a great deal, you and I, working behind the scenes."

"Oh, yes. Thank you. I am grateful for your help."

"Think nothing of it, dear lady."

But as he strolled casually away from the biology lab back toward his own cubicle, Reed thought: She's hot for Jamie, that's for certain. Now the game is to work things out so that he remains out there in the Grand Canyon and she stays here. A thousand kilometers or so between them ought to give me enough working room. I'll have her, sooner or later. All I need is patience. And a little help, which she herself will provide. How nice!

He actually whistled, tunelessly, as he strode past the wardroom where most of the others sat huddled together, discussing the day's events like a gaggle of schoolchildren. Reed ignored them and headed for his cot and his dreams.

Jamie and Vosnesensky sat in the rover's cockpit as they made their evening report. Once they were finished with their official duty, Pete Connors filled them in on the reactions to Konoye's accident. While he watched the astronaut's troubled features on the display screen in the center of the cockpit control panel, Jamie glanced at the secondary screen. The glowing curves of its graphic display showed that the ozone outgassing from the Martian dust in the airlock was now down almost to zero.

"The accident's got everybody pretty down," Connors was saying worriedly. "Dr. Li has been on the horn with Kaliningrad for hours now. God knows what they're going to do."

"But nothing went wrong with the equipment," Jamie said. "The cosmonaut and the rest of the team worked just the way they've been trained. Konoye just had a stroke."

"Or panicked for some reason and then suffered the stroke," Vosnesensky said, heavy with gloom.

Connors was also deeply somber. "Whatever happened, the politicians are going apeshit. It doesn't look good to have somebody killed. . . ."

"He wasn't killed," Jamie snapped. "He died."

"D'you think that matters in Tokyo? Or Washington?" Connors growled.

"No, I guess it doesn't."

Vosnesensky said, "We will start back at first light tomorrow morning, as ordered. In the meantime, I will transmit to you all the videotape and other data we have accumulated."

"Okay. I'll set up the computer to receive your transmission."

He's not even mentioning the cliff dwellings, Jamie realized. Not a word about them.

"Can I talk with Dr. Patel, please?" he asked Connors. "Is he there?"

"Sure."

In a few moments Connors's image was replaced by the round,

dark face of the geologist from India. Both the geologists on this mission are Indians, Jamie thought without humor. We can thank Columbus and his wacky sense of direction for that.

Patel's dark skin seemed to shine always, as if covered with a fine sheen of perspiration or newly rubbed with oil. His eyes were large and liquid, giving him the innocent look of a child near tears.

"I would appreciate it, Rava, if you'd get O'Hara to put the videotape footage we shot today through the image-enhancement program," Jamie said to his fellow geologist.

"Is there something in particular you wish me to examine?"

Jamie realized his fellow geologist had not bothered to listen to his oral report. Probably too busy gossiping with the rest of them about the accident.

"You'll see a formation in a cleft set into the cliff face," he said. After a moment's hesitation, "It—it almost looks like buildings erected there deliberately."

Those liquid dark eyes went even rounder. "Buildings?" Patel squeaked. "Artificial buildings?"

Jamie forced himself to state calmly, "The odds against them being artifacts are tremendous; you know that as well as I do." He took a breath. "But they sure remind me of the cliff dwellings I've seen in the southwest."

Patel blinked several times. Then he said, "Yes, of course. I will study the tapes most carefully. I will ask Dr. O'Hara to put them through the image-enhancement program. By the time you return here we will have the data thoroughly analyzed, I assure you."

Jamie said, "Thanks." In his gut he felt an irrational suspicion that they would distort the data, mess up the images, fix it so that the cliff dwellings he had seen would look like nothing more than weathered old rock.

He crawled into his bunk at last. Vosnesensky turned out all the lights except the dim telltales on the control panel up in the cockpit.

"Sleep well, Jamie," the Russian said, yawning as he stretched out in the bunk on the opposite wall.

"You too, Mikhail."

The soft night wind of Mars brushed past the parked rover, stroking its metallic skin mere inches away from Jamie's listening ears. He strained to catch a hint of a voice in the wind, even the moaning wail of a long-dead Martian spirit. Nothing.

No ghosts haunting the night here, Jamie said drowsily to himself. He felt disappointed.

DEATH

The red world was not only farther from Father Sun than the blue world. It was also much closer to the small worldlets that still swarmed in the darkness of the void, leftover bits and pieces from the time of the beginning. Often they streaked down onto the red world, howling like monsters as they traced their demon's trails of fire across the pale sky.

Small, cold, bombarded by sky-demons, its air and water slowly wasting away, if the red world bore any life at all its creatures must have struggled mightily to keep the spark of existence glowing within them.

Even so, death struck swiftly, and without remorse.

One of the biggest of those devil worlds drifted close enough to the red world to feel its pull. It was a huge mountain of rock roaming through the darkness of space, a thousand times bigger than the rock that caused the Meteor Crater to the south of the land where The People live. For a thousand thousand years it danced a delicate ceremony with the red world, approaching it and then slipping away into the outer depths of the emptiness. Like the ritual dancers of The People it moved to the rhythm of eternity. Each time it approached the red world it skimmed closer, each near-miss a temporary reprieve, a promise of what was to come.

Finally it plunged down into the red world, roaring like all the furies of hell as it smashed into the crust. Under that titanic violence the rocks turned liquid almost down to the very core of the red world. An enormous cloud of burning dust boiled high into the atmosphere and spread swiftly from pole to pole. The shock rang through the whole body of the poor tortured red world, lifting up the ground on the opposite side of the globe into a gigantic bulge. The very air of the red world was blown away almost completely.

Darkness covered the face of the red world. There was no day; only black night. The waters froze, later to be covered by the red dust sifting down through the pitifully thin air. The crust hardened over once again, but deep below, the rocks were still white-hot, liquid, seething. Volcanoes erupted for thousands of centuries afterward.

When the skies cleared at last, the red world was a scene of utter devastation. The seas were gone. The atmosphere was nothing more than a thin wisp of what it had once been. The ground was barren. Life, if it had ever existed on the red world at all, was nowhere to be seen.

EARTH

N E W Y O R K :   **Alberto Brumado squinted when the overhead lights were turned on; then his eyes adjusted to the brightness. How much of my life have I spent in television studios? he asked himself. It must be years, many years, if you add up all the minutes and hours.**

For the first time in his memory, though, he felt nervous about the impending interview. Not because it was American network television. Not because he would have to face a trio of experienced senior interrogators from the most prestigious newspaper, news magazine, and television network news department in the United States. He had fenced with such before.

The anxiety that rippled through his heart was that the interviewers smelled blood. The death of Dr. Konoye had brought the sharks out, circling, circling what they perceived as a wounded and bleeding Mars Project. There would be no gentility about this interview, no kid gloves. Brumado knew that he was in for a rough ordeal.

The technical crew had been uniformly kind, as usual. The matronly makeup woman smiled and chatted with him as she patted pancake on Brumado's browned face. While he was still in the barber-type chair, the harried-looking producer had come in. Standing behind him and speaking to Brumado's reflection in the big wall mirror, she assured him that all he had to do was to be natural, be himself, and the audience "will love you up." The young assistant producer, younger than his own daughter, had done everything she could to put Brumado at ease. Accustomed to smilingly evasive politicians and brash entertainment stars who hid their anxieties behind banalities, she offered Brumado coffee, soft drinks, even a Bloody Mary. Smiling tensely, he refused everything except water.

Now he was in the studio with the crew hiding behind their cameras and the electrician pinning the cordless microphone to his necktie just under his chin.

The show's moderator walked onto the brightly lit set, up the carpeted two steps to the chair next to Brumado's.

Extending a hand, he said, "Please don't get up, Dr. Brumado. It was good of you to come on such short notice."

"I want to dispel any doubts that may be in the public's mind about this unfortunate tragedy," Brumado replied as the moderator sat down. His microphone was already in place, hardly visible against his dark blue tie. He also wore a minuscule flesh-toned earphone like a hearing aid.

"Good, good," said the moderator absently, his eyes focused on the notes scrolling across the small display screen cleverly built into the coffee table in front of them so that it could not be seen by the cameras.

The three inquisitors arrived in a group, smiling, chatting among themselves. Two men and a woman whose ebony hair glowed like a steel helmet. Handshakes all around. Brumado thought of a prizefight. Now go to your corners and come out punching.

The floor director scurried in and out of the shadows among the cameras. The big clock beneath the monitor screen clicked down the final seconds, its second hand stopping discernibly at each notch on the dial.

The floor director pointed to the moderator.

"Good morning, and welcome to *Face the People*. This morning we are fortunate to have with us Dr. Alberto Brumado. . . ."

Brumado could feel his pulse quickening as the moderator introduced the three "distinguished journalists" who would be questioning him.

"At the outset," the moderator said, turning to face Brumado, "I'd like to ask this basic question: What does the death of Dr. Konoye mean for the Mars Project?"

Brumado slid into his fatherly smile as he always did at interviews. "It will have only a slight effect on the exploration of Mars. The mission was planned from the outset with the knowledge that exploring a distant planet can be dangerous. That is why there are backup members of the team for each scientist and astronaut. The team will be able to continue the exploration of Mars, of course, and even the work on Deimos and Phobos that Dr. Konoye was supposed to do. . . ."

"Are you saying that a man's death doesn't matter to you?" the newspaperman interjected, frowning like a gargoyle.

"Of course it matters to me," Brumado replied. "It matters to all of us, especially to Dr. Konoye's wife and children. But it will not stop the exploration of Mars and its moons."

"What went wrong, Dr. Brumado?" asked the woman. She was the TV reporter, dressed in a sleekly stylish red skirt and mannish white blouse.

"Nothing went wrong. Dr. Konoye suffered a stroke. It could have happened in his office in Osaka, I suppose. Or in his home."

"But it happened on Mars."

"It happened during an EVA," observed the magazine man. "Did that contribute to the cerebral hemorrhage? Was being weightless a factor?"

Brumado shook his head. "Weightlessness should have had nothing to do with it. If anything, microgravity is beneficial to the cardiovascular system."

"How could it be that he was accepted for this hazardous work when he had a cardiovascular problem?"

"He had no cardiovascular problem."

"The man died of a stroke!"

"But there was no history of a medical problem. He was thoroughly examined and tested, just as all the other mission crew were. He went through years of training and medical examinations without the slightest hint of a problem. He was only forty-two years old. Even his family medical records show no evidence of cardiovascular disease."

"Then how do you explain the stroke?"

"No one can explain it. It happened. It is unfortunate. Very sad."

"But you won't stop the mission or change its operation in any way?"

Brumado smiled again, this time to hide his growing anger. "To begin with, I have no official capacity in the Mars Project. I am merely an advisor."

"Come on now! You're known all over the world as the soul of the Mars Project."

"I am not involved in the day-to-day operation of the project. Nor do I have any official position. My influence ended, really, when the spacecraft left for Mars."

"Do you mean to tell us that if you went to the mission controllers in Houston . . ."

"Kaliningrad," Brumado corrected.

"Wherever—if you went to them and advised them to shut down the project and get those people back home to safety, they wouldn't listen to you?"

"I would hope not. If I gave them that kind of advice, I would hope that they would be wise enough to ignore it."

"You're not concerned about the safety of those men and women on Mars?"

Brumado hesitated just a fraction of a second, enough to remind himself not to let them lead him into statements he did not wish to make.

"You must remember that what has happened was not an accident, not a failure of a piece of equipment or even a shortcoming of our planning. The man suffered a stroke. He was a hundred million kilometers from Earth when it happened, but it would have been the same if it had happened in his bed."

Turning to look squarely into the camera that had its red light lit, Brumado went on, "Should we stop the exploration of Mars because a man has died? Did Americans stop expanding westward because people died on the frontier? Did the exploration of the world stop because some ships were sunk? If we stopped reaching outward for fear of danger we would still be squatting in caves, groveling every time it thunders outside."

The moderator gave a big smile and said, "We'll continue right after this important message."

The overhead lights dimmed. Brumado reached for the glass of water on the coffee table.

"Good timing. It's going very well," said the moderator. "Keep it up."

The second segment of the show was much like the first: the interviewers almost accusative, Brumado defending the Mars Project against their unsubtle insinuations of insensitivity or outright incompetence.

"And despite what's happened," hammered the newspaper gargoyle, "you really don't accept the idea that it's too dangerous out there for human beings?"

Brumado played his trump card. "One of those human beings is my daughter. If I thought she was in an unacceptably dangerous situation, I would do everything in my power to bring all the exploration team back to safety, believe me."

At the next commercial break the moderator asked, "Okay, we've got four minutes for a wrap-up. Is there anything we haven't covered that we ought to?"

Brumado replied mildly, "We have not said a word yet about what has been discovered on Mars so far."

"Okay. Fair enough." The moderator glanced at the three interviewers. They nodded without much enthusiasm.

The floor director pointed at the moderator and the red light on the camera aimed at him winked on again. Before he could open his mouth, though, the newspaper reporter jumped in: "What I'd like to know is, just what are we getting out of this mission? Have the scientists found anything on Mars that's worth five hundred billion dollars?"

Brumado put on his smile again. "That number is a considerable exaggeration of this mission's cost. And, of course, the costs are being shared by more than two dozen nations; the United States is not bearing the burden alone."

"Yes, but . . ."

"We have made significant discoveries on Mars." Brumado overrode him. "Very significant discoveries. The landing teams have been on the ground there for little more than a week, and already they have found water—the elixir of life."

"Buried underground, frozen," said the television newswoman.

"But no signs of life itself," the magazine reporter said.

"Not yet."

"You expect to find life on Mars?"

"I am more optimistic now than I was a week ago," Brumado said, his smile genuine now. "It would seem that there are extensive areas of permafrost. And according to the very latest report from the geologist who has trekked out to the Valles Marineris—the Grand Canyon of Mars—there are mists in the air each morning. That means moisture. And down at the bottom of that valley the temperatures may be considerably warmer than elsewhere. Life may exist there."

The newspaperman fixed Brumado with a glittering eye. "Now let's face it—you *need* to find life on Mars to justify this enormously expensive program. You've got to be optimistic, don't you?"

"I want the program to continue, of course. What this first mission has discovered is already more than enough to justify the next mission."

"Another five hundred billion?"

"Nowhere near that amount. Most of the costs of development

and facilities construction have already been paid. The second expedition will cost a fraction of the first. In fact, follow-on missions will amortize the costs we have already incurred and give us more value for the money we have already invested."

"And on that note," the moderator said, leaning forward between Brumado and the reporter, "we must take our leave. We've run out of time. I want to thank . . ."

Brumado leaned back in his chair and relaxed. Later he would review a tape of the show, but at the moment he felt he had gotten his points across well enough.

And they never once brought up the subject of the American Indian and his effect on the political situation here in the States. We can thank Konoye for that. He did not die in vain.

The overhead lights went off and Brumado allowed the electrician to remove his microphone. The three reporters made a few obligatory smiles and noises, then swiftly headed toward the small bar that had been set up at the rear of the studio.

"You've earned a drink," the moderator said to Brumado.

"Thank you. I could use one."

Brumado intended to use these informal few minutes to educate his interrogators. Without their knowing it, hundreds of media reporters had been subtly proselytized by him during social occasions such as this.

There was a younger woman already talking with the reporters, a pert blonde who had an outdoor, all-American look to her. She introduced herself as Edie Elgin, a newcomer to the New York scene—and a personal friend of James Waterman.

Brumado's internal defenses flared at Waterman's name.

"How is he?" Edith asked. "They haven't let me talk to him since he landed on Mars."

"You are a reporter?" Brumado asked.

Edith smiled her best Texas smile. "I'm a consultant with the news department. To tell the truth, Dr. Brumado, I'm looking for a job."

"You knew Dr. Waterman in Houston?"

"We were very close friends. And now they won't even let me talk to him."

Her smile warmed Brumado, melted his suspicions. "You don't want to interview him for the media?"

"I just want to talk with him for a few minutes, to see if he's okay and . . . well, to see if he still . . ." Edith let her voice dwindle into silence.

The mission administrators can't hold the man incommunicado, Brumado told himself. He smiled back at Edith. "I'll see what I can do."

"Oh, thank you! You're the kindest sweetest man in the whole Mars Project!"

WASHINGTON: Alberto Brumado liked the idea that a pretty young woman considered him kind and sweet. And influential. But he did not truly believe that he was a Very Important Person. "There are no indispensable men," he had often said. "If I had not led the effort for the Mars Project, someone else would have."

Yet both the Japanese and Soviet project directors easily agreed to come to Washington to meet with their American counterpart and Dr. Brumado—not only because they had an urgent problem to discuss, but because they actually desired to save Brumado from another long intercontinental flight. Hypersonic aircraft could cross half the globe in two hours, but the human passengers they carried suffered from jet lag all the same. The Russian and Japanese project directors decided, simultaneously and independently, to save their revered mentor from such fatigue.

Fresh from his television interview in New York, Brumado flew to Washington to meet them at the office of the American project director, in the old NASA headquarters building on Independence Avenue. As government offices go, it was not much: a room large enough to house an oblong conference table butted against a broad mahogany desk like the long arm of a T. The walls were covered with maps and photos of Mars and other photographs of rocket boosters lifting off on tails of flame and smoke. Behind the director's desk was a table covered with more personal photos showing the director with the high and mighty: presidents, ministers, even television personalities.

The American director of the Mars Project had once been an excellent engineer, many years ago. Now he was an excellent politician, crafty in the ways and means of surviving in the Washington jungle and keeping the lifeblood of money pumping into his project. He did not look like the archetypical "faceless bureaucrat," however. He wore utterly comfortable snakeskin cowboy boots below his rumpled gray business suit and a conservative blue tie. His fleshy face was florid, his hair thick and still fiery red despite the streaks of gray running through it. Behind rimless glasses his eyes gleamed with fervor; he still cared about what he was doing. Mars was not a program to him, it was a life's work.

"I 'preciate your coming here to my humble domain," he said to the others, with the trace of a south Texas twang in his gravelly voice that even years of testifying before Congress had not quite erased.

He was leaning back precariously in his chair on one side of the conference table, boots on the table and tie loosened from his collar. Brumado sat beside him. The Russian and Japanese project directors sat primly on the other side of the table.

Neither was smiling; both wore carefully tailored business suits with neatly knotted ties; but there the similarities ended. The Russian was bald, sallow faced, lean, and unhappy. He reminded Brumado of a melancholy movie actor from his youth who always portrayed émigrés pining for Mother Russia. The Japanese was a compact bundle of barely suppressed energy, his dark eyes darting everywhere, his fingers drumming nervously on the tabletop.

"As y'all know," said the American, his chins on his chest as he picked up a single sheet of paper from the table in front of him, "we have something of a problem with the ever-loving, blue-eyed Vice-President of the United States."

"I believe I should say at the outset," the Russian interjected, "that serious objections have been raised in the Soviet Federation about the wisdom of committing to a second expedition so soon."

The Japanese said rapidly, "The death of Professor Konoye has not dimmed Japan's enthusiasm for further missions. If anything, my people feel we must press on to honor his memory."

The ex-Texan glanced at Brumado, then at his fellow directors across the table. "Let's get one thing straight here: How do you all feel about the next mission?"

"I am in favor of it, of course," the Russian answered immediately. "I would go myself if they would allow me!"

The Japanese grinned. "Yes, of course."

"As I see it," Brumado said gently, "we have a sacred trust. Project Mars must not end as Project Apollo did. We *must* continue the exploration of the planet and its moons."

The American pushed his chair back. It screeched against the uncarpeted floor. "Okay," he said as he lumbered to his feet. "We're agreed as to what we want. Now we've got t' figure out how to get it." He walked around his desk and, bending down slowly, opened a panel and took out four glasses and a bottle of Kentucky sour mash. "Fuel for thought," he said, a bright grin spreading across his ruddy face.

Three hours later the bottle sat empty on the conference table and Brumado, who had hardly touched the one glass poured for him, was summarizing: "The Vice-President told me personally that she is willing to make a statement supporting the further exploration of Mars if we can get Dr. Waterman to make a statement supporting her candidacy."

"Better get her statement in writing," said the American, grumpily. "And get it down on paper *before* you let the Indian open his mouth."

"I'm not certain that Dr. Waterman would be willing to make such a statement," Brumado admitted.

"Then you'll have to convince him. Use your powers of persuasion. I'd do it myself," the former Texan said, "but if anybody up on the Hill found out about it they'd pin my balls to the wall and the Mars Project would go down the toilet in half a minute."

The Japanese turned to the Russian. "What would be the reaction of the Soviet Federation if the United States makes a strong statement of support for further missions?"

The Russian shrugged elaborately. "With both the U.S.A. and Japan lined up in favor, I think the forces of enlightenment in Moscow would gain enough strength to override the objections of the obstructionists."

The American hiked a shaggy eyebrow. "Does that mean yea or nay?"

They all burst into laughter. "Yes," said the Russian. "Positively yes."

Then all three of the project directors fixed their eyes on Brumado.

"It's up to you, then, Alberto old pal," said the American. "None of us can do it. You've got to convince this redskin that he's got to support the Vice-President."

"I hope he will," said Brumado.

"It's either that or the program ends when they return to Earth."

Brumado nodded his agreement. Then, "Has Waterman been kept from taking personal messages? Is he being held incommunicado while he is on Mars?"

The three project directors glanced uneasily at one another. The

Russian said, "Once the American government refused to release his interview tape we assumed that he was not to have any contact with the media."

"Far as I know," said the American, "he hasn't squawked. Hasn't even asked to send any personal messages, I don't think."

"No personal communications at all?" Brumado asked. "Not to his family, his friends?"

The Russian shrugged. "Apparently no one has tried to reach him, nor has he attempted to call anyone."

"Not even his parents?"

"Apparently not."

"Why do you ask?" said the Japanese director.

Brumado replied, "I ran into a young woman who says she is a friend of Waterman's, and she has been denied permission to speak with him."

The American leaned back in his chair again. "I don't see why she can't make a tape, like everybody else's friends and relatives are doing. Then Waterman can decide if he wants to answer her or not. That's the way we've been handling personal messages, what with the time lag and the busy schedule those guys have down on the surface of the planet."

"That makes sense," Brumado said. "I will tell her that."

S O L 1 3: MORNING

"The computer enhancements prove that your 'village' is nothing more than a natural formation of rock," said Ravavishnu Patel.

Jamie shook his head stubbornly. "The enhancements prove nothing of the sort."

"I'm afraid I must agree with Rava," Abdul al-Naguib said. "You are leaping to an erroneous conclusion."

The three men—two geologists and the Egyptian geophysicist—were sitting tensely on spindly stools in front of a computer display screen in the geology lab. The area was partitioned off from the rest of the dome, its shelves cluttered with bare rocks and transparent plastic cases that held core samples and stoppered bottles filled with red soil. A long table set against one partition held analysis equipment and computer modules, their display screens flickering orange and blue, showing curves and graphs of data from the global network of sensors that changed every few moments.

"Look," Jamie said to the others, "the computer enhancement of the videotape shows a nicely enlarged view of that formation. I'm not saying it's artificial; all I'm saying is that the enhancement really doesn't prove it's natural."

"But it cannot be artificial!" Patel insisted. "Even Father DiNardo back in Rome agrees it has to be a natural formation!"

Jamie gave him a stern look. "Rava, science doesn't work on opinions. We learn by observing, by measuring. For god's sake, when Galileo first reported seeing sunspots, there were priests in Rome who claimed the spots must have been in his telescope because everybody knew that the sun was perfect and without blemish."

Naguib smiled in a fatherly way. Older than either of the two geologists, he saw himself as the voice of mature wisdom in this emotional debate.

"We have observed," the Egyptian said patiently. "We have measured. The most powerful tools we possess tell us that the formation is natural, a formation of rocks and nothing more."

"The evidence says nothing of the sort," Jamie snapped. "You're looking at the evidence with a bias against it being artificial."

"And you are looking at the same evidence with a bias against it being natural," Patel countered.

"Which proves to me that the evidence is not conclusive," Jamie said.

Naguib asked, "But how could it be artificial? You are presupposing that an intelligent species once existed on Mars and built itself a village—in the same manner that your own ancestors built cliff dwellings? That is so unlikely that it beggars the imagination."

Patel added, "When you make a large claim, you must have strong evidence to back it up."

"Right!" Jamie said. "I agree! We have to go back to Tithonium Chasma and see that formation close up. Go right up to it and put our hands on it."

The Hindu geologist stared at Jamie as if he had uttered blasphemy. "Go there! And what of my excursion to Pavonis Mons? Do you think your make-believe 'village' is more important than the Tharsis volcanoes?"

"If that 'village' really is artificial, it sure as hell is more important than anything else," Jamie shot back.

"The next thing you know, you will want to go all the way to Acidalia to examine the 'Face'!"

Photographs from early spacecraft orbiting Mars had found a rock formation that resembled a human face when the sun hit it at the right angle.

"Maybe we'll have to," Jamie snapped. "But first I want to see if that 'village' is natural or artificial."

Naguib raised his hands in a gesture of peacemaking. "Everyone who has examined the enhanced video agrees that the formation must be natural. Just as the 'Face' is."

"Science doesn't work by counting votes," Jamie said, feeling anger rising inside him. "The only way to settle this question is to go back there and see for ourselves."

"It would wreck our schedule," Patel said. "It is entirely unnecessary."

"The hell with the schedule," Jamie said.

"The hell with your 'village'!" Patel shouted. "The hell with your fantasies!"

Jamie took a deep breath, trying to control his seething temper. Then, "Listen, both of you. Our job here is to seek the truth—and not be afraid of finding it. We've got to go back to the canyon."

"No," said Patel, anger simmering in his dark face.

"I'm afraid I must agree with Rava," Naguib said reluctantly. "Our mission here is clearly defined. We are the first scouts, our task is to make the preliminary reconnaissance. We have two other regions scheduled for overland traverses before our forty-nine days are finished. Others will come to study the planet in greater detail on follow-on missions. We are not here to swallow everything in one gulp."

Jamie looked at the two of them. Patel, worried that his excursion to the goddammed volcano might be in jeopardy. Naguib, willing to let others get the glory. Jamie thought that the Egyptian was old enough to become an administrator when they returned to Earth; his days as an active scientist are finished. He'll go back to Egypt and be a famous man, get a prestigious chair in a university and be solidly fixed for the rest of his life. What the hell does he care?

"What makes you so damned certain there'll be follow-on missions?" Jamie asked. "If the goddammed politicians have their way we'll be the *last* expedition to Mars as well as the first one."

Naguib and Patel looked at each other, dumbstruck, as if the idea had never occurred to them before.

Jamie grimaced and turned slightly on his stool. The display screen still showed the enhanced image of the rock formation: straight walls with some detritus at their base, set well back into the rock cleft, protected by the massive overhang of deep red iron-rich stone.

"Okay," he said calmly. "If you won't back me on this I'll just have to ask Dr. Li by myself."

The two other men groaned their displeasure.

Even over the whirring hum of the centrifuge Ilona Malater could hear the argument among the geologists growing into vehemence.

Ah, she said to herself, Jamie is showing some passion at last.

Joanna Brumado, a few feet away from Ilona at her workstation in the biology lab, heard the argument too. She looked worried, almost frightened as the men snapped at each other. She's frightened for Jamie's sake, Ilona thought. She cares about our Red Indian more than she is willing to admit. Perhaps more than she herself realizes.

Smiling inwardly, Ilona returned her attention to the whirling centrifuge and the work she was trying to finish. With the tedious, time-consuming care of the most conservative of chemists, she had spent the past several days tenderly baking the water out of half a dozen of the corings drilled out of the Martian ground. Only half a dozen, to start. The other core samples she left strictly alone, safe inside their protective boxes, as a control on her experiment.

The permafrost yielded its water easily enough. With Monique Bonnet's help, Ilona had tested the water, analyzed it with every instrument the laboratory had. It was water, all right: H_2O, heavily laced with carbon dioxide and minerals such as iron and silicon.

Jamie's changing, Ilona thought as she watched the arms of the bench-top centrifuge spin blurringly. We all are. Mars is changing us. Even Tony is different now; he tries to maintain his air of English imperturbability, but I can see that something deep inside him has changed. He's not the same man he was aboard the spacecraft. Something is eating away at him.

Is it Joanna? she wondered. Does Tony really care that much about bedding our Brazilian princess?

As if she sensed Ilona's thoughts, Joanna looked up from the work she was bent over, right into Ilona's eyes. For an instant Ilona felt flushed, caught red-handed. But just then the centrifuge finished its run and began to slow down, its thin shrill whine sighing to a fainter note, its arms slowly drooping as if exhausted from the work it had been doing.

Joanna slipped off her stool and came down the length of the lab bench to stand beside Ilona.

"Do you need any help?" she asked.

Watching the centrifuge slowly spinning down to a complete stop, Ilona answered, "Monique was supposed to be here by now."

"She's off tending to her plants. Some of them are beginning to sprout already."

"Yes. I know." The centrifuge stopped altogether. "If everything goes well, I'll be able to give her Martian water for her precious sprouts."

Joanna watched as Ilona detached a vial from the centrifuge and held it up to the overhead lights. The vial was divided into two sections; its top was clear liquid, the bottom section much murkier.

"You see? The water is clear now. I've separated out the dissolved minerals."

"It looks bubbly," Joanna said.

"Carbon dioxide, absorbed from the atmosphere. If all the permafrost could be melted, we'd not only cover half of Mars with water, we'd outgas enough CO_2 to make the atmosphere as thick as Earth's, almost."

Ilona decanted the clear water into a plastic beaker.

"Aren't you going to analyze it?" Joanna asked.

"The mass spectrometer is off-line again."

"I thought Abell . . ."

"Paul said he fixed it, but I don't trust the calibration since he's had his hands on it. I've got to go over it myself, and I haven't had the time for it."

Joanna said, "The geology lab has a mass spectrometer."

With a sudden smile, Ilona answered, "Good thought."

The men were still arguing, almost shouting, when the two women came around the partition and stepped into the geology lab. The argument snapped off into silence.

"We need to use your spectrometer for a few minutes," Ilona said. "Do you mind?"

Naguib said, "No. Of course not. Is that local groundwater you have there?"

"Yes."

"Unprotected?" Patel asked. "With no cover atop it?"

"It's only water, Rava. It can't hurt you."

Joanna added, "We have run it through every test we know; there are no organisms in it. It is completely sterile."

"Not now," said Patel. "You have exposed it to our air, to our microbes."

Ilona shrugged grandly, as if the Hindu's observation meant nothing whatsoever to her, and stepped over to the mass spectrometer sitting on the lab bench between an assortment of small stones and the thick sheaf of an operations manual. On the other side of the manual was a desktop computer, its screen blank.

"I've got to make a call up to Dr. Li," Jamie said, getting up from the stool on which he had been sitting.

"Don't go," Ilona said. "This will only take a moment or two."

Jamie hesitated, glancing at the other two men, then at Joanna.

"Please stay," said Joanna.

He stood uncertainly for a moment, then gestured Joanna to the stool.

Ilona's test of the water took longer than a moment or two. Monique Bonnet showed up, apologizing for spending so much time with her garden. "The legumes are beginning to unfurl leaves," she announced. No one but she seemed to care.

Tony Reed sauntered past the lab, saw the group, and asked, "What's going on? A cabal?"

Ilona looked up from the computer screen that now displayed the spectrometer's output.

"Come in, Tony. Come in. The medical officer should be here for this experiment."

"Experiment?" Reed asked, stepping inside the lab area. "What experiment?"

"We are about to sample the local wine," Monique said.

Reed saw the beaker of water sitting on the bench and immediately understood. "Nothing injurious in it, is there?"

Ilona replied, "As far as the mass spectrometer is concerned, it's nothing but water with some carbon dioxide dissolved in it and a barely detectable trace of a few minerals."

Reed went over and studied the display screen. "I've seen worse in London's water supply. Much worse."

"I can begin to use native water on the garden plants, then?" Monique asked.

"After the ultimate test," said Ilona. And she raised the beaker to her lips.

Utter silence as she sipped. She looked thoughtful for a moment, ran the tip of her tongue over her lips, then handed the beaker to Tony.

"See what you think," she said.

Reed took the beaker and made a show of holding it up to the light and then sniffing it, as if it were a fine wine.

"No bouquet at all," he said.

No one even smiled.

Reed sipped, gave the beaker back to Ilona, then said, "It tastes rather like seltzer, actually."

Monique took an eager taste. "*Mon dieu, it is like Perrier!*"

They broke into laughter. All except Jamie, Ilona noticed, who looked as tense as a caged panther.

"Martian seltzer," Reed said. "We can bottle it and sell it! What a sensation back on Earth!"

"At a million dollars an ounce," Naguib said, laughing as he took his sip, then passed the beaker as if it were communion wine.

"Perhaps we could finance the next expedition in this way," said Patel, after his taste.

The cup came to Jamie. He put it to his lips, handed it back to Ilona with a curt nod, and said, "I've got to get to the comm console. Excuse me."

At last some semblance of order had returned to the orbiting spacecraft, thought Li Chengdu. The scientific staff was back to its normal routine, the astronauts and cosmonauts had finished the thorough check of all the ships' systems demanded by mission control back in Kaliningrad. A purging ritual, Li thought. The death of Dr. Konoye was exorcised by checking each and every component of the two spacecraft, all their systems, supplies, and equipment. Konoye did not die of an equipment failure, but the controllers in Kaliningrad and Houston insisted on the meaningless checkout.

Now we are twelve, Li said to himself, instead of thirteen. That should assuage the superstitious among us. Which included himself. He realized that he had been vaguely uneasy whenever he had remembered that there had been thirteen men and women assigned to the *Mars 2* spacecraft.

Everything is back to normal now. The Russians and Americans have set up their equipment on Deimos to test their plan for baking water out of its rock. The explorations on the planetary surface are proceeding smoothly. The research teams here aboard the spacecraft have recovered from the shock of Konoye's death and settled back down to their work.

He sighed deeply. And James Waterman is back to causing trouble.

Li leaned back in his chair and fixed his gaze on the restful silk painting of misty mountains and graceful, slim, blossoming trees. Waterman wants to return to the Valles Marineris to investigate what he claims is a cliff dwelling. Patently absurd. They have not found even a trace of life and Waterman thinks there was once an intelligent civilization down there. Ridiculous.

On the other hand, it would help the politicians to forget about Konoye's death if we found something spectacular. The remains of an extinct civilization! That would be stunning.

Li frowned to himself. On the *other* hand, he thought, suppose I allow Waterman to lead a few scientists back to that site and they find nothing at all. The politicians would be furious. Suppose I allow them to go back there and one of them is injured. Or killed.

He sat bolt upright in the relaxing chair. No. That must not happen. Waterman must not be allowed to ruin this mission.

The intercom on his desk buzzed, its yellow message light blinking. Li reached out a long lean arm and touched its activating button.

"Dr. Li," said the voice of the astronaut on duty in the command module, "we are receiving a transmission for you from Dr. Brumado."

Li told the man to pipe it through to him.

Alberto Brumado's friendly, slightly harried face appeared on the desktop display screen. Li stepped over to the desk and peered down at the image. Then he realized that Brumado was talking about James Waterman and the Vice-President of the United States.

Li could feel the weight of responsibility lifting off his shoulders. He pulled his chair over and sat in it before the display screen, smiling like a Cheshire cat.

The lighting in the dome had been turned down to its low nighttime level. There were no voices to be heard, no tapes playing, only the faithful hum of electrical equipment and the faint keening of the wind outside the darkened dome.

Jamie paced along the dome's perimeter, his heavy slipper-socks noiseless against the thick plastic flooring, his eyes adjusted to the gloom, his mind churning the same argument over and over again.

You know it's a natural rock formation; it can't be buildings. Why are you so goddammed stubborn?

But it might be artificial. It just might be. What the hell do we really know about this world? How much would a Martian scientist learn about Earth if he landed in the Sahara Desert and looked around for a couple of weeks?

The chances of those rocks being actual dwellings are a zillion to one. Why are you alienating everybody? What are you trying to prove?

What are they afraid of? For Christ's sake, we're here to explore the planet, to find out what's really here. You can't do that by sticking to a schedule they wrote back in Kaliningrad.

"Jamie? Is that you?"

He looked around, realized he was next to the wardroom. Sitting there in the shadows was the tiny form of Joanna Brumado. The only light in the area came from the softly glowing guide strips along the floor and the steady red eye of the always-working coffee machine.

He padded to the table where she sat, her hands wrapped around a big steaming coffee mug.

"What are you doing up at this hour?" Jamie asked, sitting next to her.

"I could not sleep."

"So you're having a cup of coffee?"

"The Brazilian tranquilizer," she said. He could hear the smile in her soft voice even though her face was deep in shadow. "I need the warmth. It always feels cold in here to me. Especially at night."

Jamie wore a dark blue sweatshirt bearing the discreet rocket emblem of the British Interplanetary Society and softly faded jeans instead of the project-issued coveralls. In the dim light he saw that Joanna was in a bulky turtleneck sweater and corduroy slacks.

"Why can't you sleep?" he asked.

"I could ask you the same."

He wanted to laugh, but there was no laughter in him. "I asked you first. Besides, you know why I'm pacing the floor."

"You are waiting for an answer from Dr. Li."

He nodded, realized she probably could not see the gesture, and muttered, "Uh-huh."

"Are you so certain that what you saw really was a village?"

"Hell no! That's the whole point: I'm not certain at all. That's why we should go back and see it close up. Touch it. Smell it. Taste it, even. All the fancy instruments and equipment we use are just tools for giving us sensory information. Before we can decide just what that pile of rocks really is we need more information."

She took a sip of her coffee.

"But you haven't told me what's keeping you awake," Jamie said softly.

"Oh . . . many things. Loneliness, for one. I lie in my bunk and listen to the wind outside and remember that we are nearly two hundred million kilometers from home."

"Does that frighten you?"

"No, it just makes me feel—alone. It's strange. During the day we are busy and the dome feels crowded sometimes. But at night . . ."

"I know," Jamie said. "There's either too many people leaning over your shoulder or you're entirely alone. It's a weird feeling."

"You feel it too?"

He scowled in the darkness. "Joanna, I *am* alone. I'm the outcast here."

"No, that is not so."

"That's the way it looks to me. It's not just this business of the cliff dwelling. I'm a substitute, a last-minute replacement. None of the others really accepts me as part of the team."

He was surprised at himself for telling her so. For a long moment Joanna said nothing. In the shadowy lighting he could not even make out the expression on her face.

"I had thought," Jamie heard himself say, speaking very low, almost whispering, "that you wanted me on the mission because of what happened at McMurdo. Now I realize that you didn't want me here as much as you wanted to get rid of Hoffman."

"Jamie . . ."

"It's okay," he said quickly. "I can understand how you felt. I know that Hoffman bothered you."

She grabbed at the cuff of his sweatshirt and shook it slightly, like a schoolteacher trying to get the attention of a heedless student.

"Jamie, there were five other geologists that I could have recommended. They all had excellent qualifications. I asked my father to get *you.*"

"Because I helped you at McMurdo."

"Because of you, yourself. Because you are a talented, stubborn, sensitive, lonely man. Because you were kind to me instead of resentful. Because when I ran away from you, you let me run without pursuing me."

Suddenly Jamie felt confused. "I let you run . . ."

"What happened between us at McMurdo should have worked against you, if I had any sense. We are not supposed to form attachments, relationships. You know that! But still I recommended you, despite the danger."

"You feel danger?"

Joanna said, "You are an extremely attractive man, James Waterman. Perhaps when this mission is over and we are safely back on Earth we can begin to behave toward each other as ordinary men and women do. For now, we must put aside such feelings."

Jamie finally understood that her memory of McMurdo was his fumbling attempt to kiss her the evening after their first trek on the glacier. It meant a lot to her, he realized. And I thought it made her angry. She's taking it for granted that I'm in love with her.

Am I? He thought of Edith, smiling blonde and Texas beautiful and millions of miles away. Christ, I've had her tape sitting in my cubicle for two days now and I haven't even answered her. Joanna is completely different. Beautiful in a deeper way. Serious. Very serious.

Then he wondered, Does she know about Ilona? What would she think if she did?

Her hand was still clutching the cuff of his sweatshirt. Jamie covered it with his other hand.

"I guess you're right, Joanna. You were right at McMurdo and you're right now. We're a long way from home. Maybe someday we'll be able to face each other as normal people do and find out for ourselves what we really can mean to each other. But for now . . ." He ran out of words, finished with half a shrug that she probably could not see in the darkness.

"For now," Joanna finished for him, her voice so low he could barely hear her, "we can be friends. It will be good to have a friend, Jamie. Good for both of us."

"Yeah. Sure."

"It is the only way. We cannot form attachments now. Not here, not in this . . . fishbowl."

He nodded, not caring if she could see it or not.

Joanna asked, "Have you thought about what you will do when we return home?"

He almost blurted, This is my home. Here on Mars. Instead he replied softly, "Not really. Have you?"

She made a sighing sound. "My father has already been asked by the National Geographic Society to write an article about this expedition for their magazine. I suppose I will do most of the writing for him. I have been his ghostwriter for many years."

"That shouldn't take long."

"Then lectures, I suppose. The two of us. All around the world. And a book, of course."

"I guess I'll pick a university and spend the next few years analyzing the samples we bring back. And the data we're amassing."

"That could be a lifetime career."

"Maybe."

She fell silent.

"What about the next expedition?" Jamie asked. "Isn't your father going to push for a follow-on mission?"

"He is already. As I understand it, though, the politicians want to see what the results of this mission are before they commit themselves to another."

Jamie leaned toward her, sudden urgency burning in his blood. "Joanna, don't you see that it's important to go back to the canyon and check out those ruins? If we can go back with evidence that there was once a civilization on Mars, an intelligent species who built cliff dwellings . . . holy Christ, *nobody* could stop a second expedition. And a third, a tenth, a hundredth!"

He sensed her smiling in the darkness. "Ahh, but suppose we find that your village is nothing more than a natural rock formation? What then?"

Her voice was sad. Jamie had no answer for her.

S O A R I N G

Pete Connors felt relaxed for the first time since the expedition had left Earth orbit.

He leaned back in the cockpit seat and looked out at the pink and red landscape gliding by nearly ten miles below. The little soarplane was flying like a dream, as deftly responsive to his hands as a loving woman.

She was a tiny gossamer aircraft, as light as plastic ribs and Mylar skin could make her. The heaviest part of the soarplane was the miniature electric engine that drove her lazily purring propeller. The engine was powered by solar cells of plastic and silicon that hugged the curves of the soarplane's broad long wings, converting the plentiful Martian sunlight into electricity steadily, noiselessly, as she flew through the clean, bright, thin atmosphere of Mars.

The soarplane's official designation was *RPV-1*. There was an *RPV-2* stowed in the cargo bay of one of the unmanned landers, wings folded, patiently waiting its turn to fly. Connors had his own name for the plane, however. He called it *Little Beauty*. And that is the way he thought of her.

To him, *Little Beauty* was a thing of delight. Connors luxuriated in the feel of her controls in his hands, the broad beautiful expansive views of the passing Martian landscape he could see in panorama all around him.

One section of the view suddenly went blank. The video screen there hinged upward and Paul Abell's frog-eyed face appeared, high forehead wrinkled quizzically.

"Aren't you coming out for lunch?" Abell asked his fellow astronaut.

Connors shook his head. "Naw, I'm having too much fun with her. Could you make me a sandwich?"

Abell glanced at the control panel and the other video screens with their views of the distant Martian landscape. "Okay. But I want a turn with her, too, you know."

"Later," Connors muttered. "You can fly her on the leg back."

Abell looked doubtful, but he lowered the screen back down into its place. Connors felt alone again, as if he were actually soaring over Chryse Planitia, the Plain of Gold, instead of sitting inside the dome of the base in the teleoperator mockup of the soarplane's cockpit.

In an electronic sense Connors truly was flying his *Little Beauty*. He was linked so thoroughly to the remotely piloted vehicle that he felt every tremor of her slender frame, every slight gust of air buoying up her gossamer wings. Nearly a thousand kilometers separated plane from pilot, but Connors was as much in control of *RPV-1* as if the tiny plane actually were carrying him through the sky.

The engineers called it teleoperation, the technique of linking man and machine electronically even though they were not physically together. Thanks to teleoperation, an aircraft could range thousands of kilometers across Mars without the need to carry a pilot and all the life-support equipment that a human operator requires. The pilot could remain safely on the ground or in one of the orbiting spacecraft while the plane braved the unknown dangers of the unexplored planet.

Deep in his mind Connors felt almost the exact opposite of the symptoms of space adaptation syndrome. In zero gravity your ears screamed that you were falling while your eyes told you that you were safely bundled inside a spacecraft cabin. Flying *Little Beauty*, Connors's eyes told him he was soaring ten miles high, but his butt and all his other body senses reminded him that he was sitting on the ground.

Never mind. He smiled boyishly to himself. This is as good as it's going to get here on this rust ball. Good enough for now. Not bad for a minister's son. He remembered his first flights in the backseat of an ancient crop duster's biplane over the flat wheat fields of Nebraska. Everything square and neat, precise. The barren red ground below him now had never known the touch of human purpose.

Abell opened the hatch abruptly and stuck in a badly made sandwich as he asked again for a turn at the controls. Connors put him off and once more shut himself inside the cockpit.

Far down below he saw a shadow of darker red inching across the barren land. He banked the little plane slightly to get a better view of the ground.

A dust storm. Big one. Must be several hundred kilometers across its front. Connors knew that whatever his cameras saw was automatically relayed to the ships up in orbit and, through them, back to Earth. He made some mental calculations of his own, anyway, and spoke into the microphone of his headset. Toshima would appreciate all the information he could get; the Japanese meteorologist was trying to build a network of weather sensors all around the planet.

"Looks like a major dust storm blowing from northwest to southeast. Front's at least three-four hundred klicks wide." He checked his navigation screen, to his right on the control panel. "Location about longitude sixty, latitude thirty, thirty-one. Speed of advance must be fifty to a hundred kilometers per hour." Then he grinned and added, "Tether the camels."

In addition to its usual complement of sensing instruments, *RPV-1* carried beneath its belly a special payload, a tiny oblong aluminum box. Inside was a stainless steel plaque, small enough to fit into the palm of a man's hand. On it was inscribed:

DEDICATED TO THE MEMORY OF TIM MUTCH,
WHOSE IMAGINATION, VERVE, AND RESOLVE
CONTRIBUTED GREATLY TO THE EXPLORATION
OF THE SOLAR SYSTEM.

Connors had never met Thomas A. Mutch. The NASA scientist had been killed in a mountain-climbing accident only a few years after the first automated lander had set down on the surface of Mars, in 1976. That primitive lander, known originally as *Viking 1*, had been renamed the Thomas A. Mutch Memorial Station shortly afterward. The plaque had been made then, when Connors was still a kid just starting to buzz the farms of Cheyenne County, Nebraska.

Now he guided the remotely piloted *Little Beauty* to longitude 47°97′, latitude 22°49′ north, the location where the faithful old Viking still stood on its spraddling legs after more than thirty years. Connors was to land the little plane there and detach the box with the plaque inside it, then wait until morning to take off and return to home base.

There was one further line etched into the stainless steel plaque. It read: "Emplaced," with the space following it left blank. The date was to be filled in when human explorers finally reached the Viking lander, a feat that was not in the schedule for this first exploration mission.

Connors's face clouded slightly. He wished he were truly flying this plane, actually on board at its controls, really there so he could land her and bolt that plaque to the old spacecraft and scratch in the date.

There's no such thing as a private communication here, Jamie thought as he sat at the comm console. Vosnesensky was at his side, Tony Reed, Patel, Naguib, and Monique Bonnet standing behind him.

On the display screen in the center of all the communications equipment was the neatly bearded face of Alberto Brumado, his hair slightly tousled as usual, his smile just a little desperate.

For most of the day they had reviewed the arguments for and against returning to Tithonium Chasma to investigate Jamie's "village." Like all the others, Brumado had been against it.

"All the available evidence," he had said in his mild, fatherly way, "points toward its being a natural phenomenon. We cannot upset the mission schedule with another unplanned excursion."

That word *another* rankled Jamie. If it hadn't been for my insisting on going out to the canyon in the first place we would never have seen the village at all.

Then Brumado had surprised them all by saying, "I would like to speak with Dr. Waterman in private, if I may."

Jamie felt the others stir behind him. He glanced at Vosnesensky, who pursed his lips, his face glowering with suspicion.

But he said, "Of course," as if Brumado could hear him without waiting another dozen minutes. Turning to Jamie, the cosmonaut said, "You can speak with Dr. Brumado in your own quarters. I will see that no one else uses this frequency."

"Thanks, Mikhail." Jamie hurried back to his cubicle, thinking of how many hours of useful work had already been ruined in debate.

He pulled his laptop computer from the tiny desk and stretched out with it on his bunk. There was no way to scramble a conversation;

if anyone wanted to eavesdrop all they had to do was turn on their own unit to the same frequency. But the other scientists were heading for their various duties, already behind schedule, and Vosnesensky would guard the main comm console with the single-minded fervor of a cossack protecting his tsar.

So Jamie hoped.

Brumado's face took form on the laptop's small screen. For an instant Jamie felt almost ridiculous. Alone at last, he wanted to say.

Instead, "You can go ahead now, Dr. Brumado. No one else is on this frequency."

Then the minutes ticked by. It took more than ten minutes now for a transmission to span the widening gulf between the two planets; twenty-some minutes of lag in each two-way conversation. Jamie watched Brumado carefully; the man merely sat there looking into the screen, waiting with the patience of a true Indian. Maybe he's using his screen to display other data while he's waiting for my transmission to reach him, Jamie thought. But Brumado's eyes did not scan back and forth as they would if he were reading.

Jamie got up from the bunk, found the earphone attachment in his desk drawer and plugged it into the laptop. At least nobody could eavesdrop on Brumado's end of their conversation, he thought as he settled back on the bunk again.

I ought to answer Edith's message, he remembered. And send something to Mom and Dad. He had not expected his parents to try to contact him; they would expect him to call them, he knew. It always worked that way. Why should Mars be any different? And Al. What can I say to him that will mean anything? Having a wonderful time, wish you were here? Jamie grinned to himself. Al would play the tape in his store; the only shop on the plaza that gets messages from Mars.

At last Brumado came to life with a slow smile. "Thank you, Jamie. You don't mind if I call you Jamie, do you? Joanna told me that is the name you prefer."

"Sure, that's fine."

Again the wait. Jamie put Brumado's image into a small window in one corner of the little computer's screen and called up the mission schedule. He spent the time studying the schedule, looking for tasks that might be delayed or deleted altogether to make room for another traverse to the Grand Canyon.

"I must speak to you about politics," Brumado said at last. "Because of the long transmission lag, please bear with me and hear what I have to say. When I am finished you can tell me how my proposal strikes you."

Jamie nodded and muttered, "Okay," even though Brumado did not wait for a reply.

"I have spoken directly with your Vice-President," Brumado went on, "and several times more with her senior aides. She is willing to make a major commitment to the continued exploration of Mars—if you will make a statement supporting her candidacy for the White House in next year's election."

Jamie felt his eyebrows crawling toward his scalp. Me? Make a statement supporting her? Why me? Why do they think anything I have to say would be important?

"What she wants is a written statement from you," Brumado went on, "which she will hold until your expedition returns to Earth. At that time, when you are safely back home, she will expect you to make your statement public. In the meantime she will go on record as supporting further expeditions to Mars. I have suggested that she make a speech on the fiftieth anniversary of the first American satellite launch. I believe she will agree to that."

Jamie felt confused. All this because of the Navaho words I spoke when we landed? How in hell could this kind of maneuvering come out of three words?

Brumado had stopped talking. He was watching the screen expectantly.

Jamie took a deep breath. "I don't understand what's going on, or how things got to be this way. I sure want to see further expeditions come to Mars, but I don't see what my political support has to do with it."

In the two weeks they had been on Mars Jamie had been asked to submit to only the one media interview, on the second day after their landing. All the others in the landing party had been interviewed at least twice already. Jamie thought that national politics had been at the root of it: with two American astronauts on the surface of Mars, the project administrators did not want to upset the Russians by having a third American in the limelight.

Now he wondered if his reasoning had been naive.

Brumado began to look uncomfortable as Jamie's questions registered on his face. He ran a hand across his neatly clipped graying beard before replying.

"I'm glad this conversation is not being overheard," he said with a slow smile. "For the first few days after your landing the American media was in a furor about the fact that you were a Native American. A red man on the red planet: that was the *mildest* of their stories about you."

Jamie realized that the mission controllers had practically blacked out all news transmissions from Earth. For the first time he understood that Kaliningrad—and Houston—were censoring the news from home.

"The Vice-President is very sensitive to political nuances," Brumado was going on. "She thought that the radical branch of the ethnic activist groups in the States might use you as a weapon against her. She wanted you removed from the ground team."

But Dr. Li wouldn't let that happen, Jamie said to himself. The mission controllers wouldn't stand for such blatant political interference.

"I have tried to convince her that you could become an asset to her campaign for the presidency—if she will support further Mars expeditions instead of opposing them."

Jamie's head was spinning. Even before Brumado stopped speaking he said, "So you worked out a deal for me to make a statement supporting her, and then she makes a statement supporting continued exploration."

Brumado kept on talking about how difficult the Vice-President could make everything if she insisted on Jamie's being removed from the ground team. It would even make Australia happy, he pointed out, to have O'Hara sent down to replace Jamie.

Then at last he heard Jamie's words. He stopped short, muttered, "Wait . . ."

Jamie realized that Brumado had an instant-replay feature on his console, wherever on Earth he was. He watched Brumado's face as the Brazilian listened to his words.

"Ah. Yes. That is the deal. You send me a statement supporting the Vice-President. I hold it until she makes a public announcement of her support for further Mars missions. Then I give her people your statement. When you return from Mars you announce your support of her candidacy. Everyone gets what they want. Everyone is happy."

Not quite everyone, Jamie thought. Then he heard himself say, "There's one thing more. I want the schedule rearranged so we can go back to Tithonium Chasma before we leave. Otherwise no deal."

270

Alberto Brumado felt his jaw drop. He was accustomed to demands and counterdemands from the politicians, even from the academics who ruled universities. But to get one from this young pup of a scientist was something of a shock.

"Rearrange the mission schedule? But that would be impossible."

He watched Waterman's stolid broad-cheeked face as his words raced to Mars with the speed of light. It seemed to take forever.

Finally Waterman replied, "Either we go back to Tithonium Chasma and take a good look at that rock formation or there's no deal. I know that she'll demand that I be taken off the ground team and O'Hara brought down to replace me. Okay. If she does that I'll yell my head off once we've returned to Earth. I'll tell the media that I was removed from the ground team *because* I'm a Native American and she's against full political rights for ethnic minorities."

Brumado felt perspiration breaking out across his forehead. "You are putting me—the entire project administration—in a very difficult situation."

Waterman's reply, when it came, was, "That can't be helped. This is important, much more important than who gets elected next year. We've got to go back to the canyon."

"All right," Brumado said reluctantly. "I'll see what I can do."

He waited long, long minutes before he saw Jamie Waterman's answering smile.

The deal was done. Now to get the project administrators to agree to it and then implement it with the Vice-President's aides. And make certain that she has no way to back out of it.

Brumado ended his transmission to Mars and rose from his chair, weary, drained, more than a little fearful. Like an athlete who had given his last ounce of strength and now waited for the judge's verdict. There must be a second expedition sent to Mars. There *must* be. At least that. At the very least.

Glancing down at the blank gray screen of the communications console he realized that Waterman was both an asset and a liability. It's a mistake to get him involved in the politics of this thing. He does not think politically; all he is interested in is the science. He is aflame to make a great discovery on Mars. So much so that he could ruin everything.

Thank god we could speak in private, Brumado said to himself. With the time lag between us it was difficult enough to get anything agreed to. It would have been impossible if others had been listening in.

More than a hundred fifty million kilometers away, Tony Reed stared thoughtfully at the dead screen of his own laptop. He had gone from the dome's communications center to his infirmary, slid the accordion-fold door shut, and immediately tuned in on Jamie's conversation with Brumado.

As the team's physician and psychologist I have every right to know exactly what is going on, he had told himself. Secrecy be damned! They have no right to keep secrets from me.

Now he removed the plug from his ear and yanked out the hair-thin wire that connected it to his computer. So Jamie's forcing them to send him back to Tithonium Chasma. Good! It can't be soon enough.

S O L 1 4: AFTERNOON

Jamie had been unusually silent and moody at lunch, Tony Reed thought. Even for our stoic red man he's being awfully quiet and withdrawn.

Reed was sitting at his infirmary desk, mulling over Jamie's conversation with Brumado. The man has cheek, Tony thought, almost admiringly. Whatever inner demons are driving him, he has the gall to make demands on Brumado himself. And the Vice-President of the United States.

Smiling to himself, Reed thought, With any luck at all he'll be banished to the orbiting spacecraft and leave Joanna to me.

Humming tunelessly, Reed tapped at his computer keyboard, calling up the afternoon's schedule. Six of the seven scientists were supposed to be continuing the tedious business of mapping the depth and extent of the underground permafrost layer. Toshima, the seventh, would remain inside the dome working with his meteorology instruments. Reed had no responsibilities for outside work; one of the advantages of being team physician, he told himself.

Tony punched up his personal mission task schedule on the computer screen and saw that it was time for his weekly inventory of pharmaceutical supplies. With a barely suppressed moan of boredom he started by checking out the stocks of analgesics and vitamins. Next would come the uppers and downers. Have to be especially careful with them. Can't have these people depending on drugs.

Pock!

The sound startled him. What on earth was that? Reed cocked his ears, but heard nothing more than the usual hums of machinery and the distant muffled voices of the others. With a shrug, he turned his attention back to the task at hand.

Wearily he went through the computer's file on the analgesics. Every aspirin tablet must be accounted for. No one was allowed to take even one on his own; only the team physician could dispense the pills, and he had to keep a strict record of who received what.

Everyone took vitamins, of course. Reed slid the box of vitamin bottles out of its rack in the container bin and toted it to his desk. Four big bottles of five hundred each. Just one of the pills provided all the daily vitamin supplement a person required; carrying two thousand of them to the surface was typical mission overkill.

With a light pen Reed began to check the bar codes printed on the lids of each jar, like a supermarket clerk checking out groceries. Damned silly busywork, he grumbled to himself. Yet if the computer did not show a bottle-by-bottle check of the inventory, Vosnesensky would be up in arms. All mission tasks must be accomplished, as far as the Russian was concerned, no matter how trivial or boring.

Then a new thought struck him. If Jamie has his way and returns to the Grand Canyon he'll probably want to take Joanna with him. She's the mission biologist, after all. Damn him! Reed snarled silently. There's got to be a way to get this insolent red man separated from the Brazilian princess. Let's hope they banish him to orbit.

Pock! The same sound again, only fainter this time. What could it be? Reed asked himself as he unscrewed the first of the vitamin bottles. Might as well transfer them to the smaller bottles while I've got them out. Tony grumbled to himself about the efficiency experts who had planned the mission logistics; they had overlooked the fact that these giant-sized bottles did not fit in the galley shelves. He had to transfer the vitamin capsules by hand to smaller bottles that did. Utterly stupid nonsense.

Pock! Pock!

Reed jumped to his feet, knocking over the open bottle. Vitamin pills spilled across his desk, rolled onto the floor.

"Everyone into your suits!" Vosnesensky's heavy voice roared through the dome. "At once! Into your hard suits! *Now!*"

Cosmonaut Leonid Tolbukhin was on duty in the command center of *Mars 2* when the first pinging noise made him sit up rigidly in his chair. Cold sweat beaded across his upper lip.

My god, it must be me, he thought. I'm a Jonah, a jinx. First Konoye and now this.

But while his mind raced, his hands moved almost as fast. He flicked on the radar display and almost immediately, with the speed of a reflex action, he hit the alarm.

"Meteors! We're running into a swarm of meteors!" he yelled into the ships' intercom microphone, so excited that he said it in Russian.

Will Martin, the American geophysicist, happened to be at the comm console, in the middle of taping a long report back to Earth.

"What is it?" he shouted over the hooting of the alarm. "Speak English, dammit!"

"Meteors!" Tolbukhin shouted back. "Get into your hard suit at once!"

Vosnesensky was at the dome's command center, locked in an earnest conversation with Mironov and Abell about the logistics of the upcoming traverse to Pavonis Mons, while ostensibly monitoring the scientists who were outside with Pete Connors. He had not heard the first soft warning sounds of meteoroids striking the dome's exterior shell.

Both the dome and the orbiting spacecraft were double walled: the ships of metal, the dome of plastic. Although Mars's atmosphere was almost vanishingly thin by terrestrial standards, it still offered enough resistance to incoming meteors to burn most of them to ashes long before they reached the ground.

The greatest danger, according to the mission planners, came from meteors plunging almost straight in from overhead: they would have the most energy and be most likely to survive the blazing heat of their atmospheric ride and reach the ground sizable enough to do damage. Meteors coming in from lower angles would have to traverse a longer path in the atmosphere, burning every centimeter of the way. Therefore the dome's double walls were filled in along its top half with spongy plastic material that could absorb the energy of an impact.

Tolbukhin's warning blared in the dome's radio speakers, as well as throughout the orbiting ships.

Vosnesensky stopped in midword and bellowed, "Everyone into your suits! At once! Into your hard suits! *Now!*"

Only after he started running for the suit lockers by the airlock section did the Russian feel the fear that squeezed inside his chest like a cold fist.

Connors was the first to notice the tiny puff of dirt spouting out of the ground as if a rifle bullet had struck. The astronaut blinked, watching the dust settle slowly back to the ground, thinking, *Good thing that didn't hit any . . .*

Another puff sprouted ten meters away.

"Jesus Christ!" he yelled into his helmet microphone. "Meteors! Everybody back to the dome! Double quick!"

All six of the geology and biology scientists were spread across several hundred meters of the rock-strewn plain, trying to survey in detail the depth of the permafrost layer beneath the ground. The mapping work was slow, since they were doing it on foot. All excursions in the rovers were on hold until the mission controllers decided exactly where the rovers would be allowed to go.

Jamie was holding a digging pole whose toothed bit end drilled into the ground. He jerked to attention at Connors's shouted warning. The pole's bit stopped as soon as his gloved hands released the control stud, and the pole leaned lopsidedly out of the hole in the ground.

Jamie took in the locations of the five other scientists with a swift glance. Connors was to his right, halfway between him and the dome's airlock. Joanna was farther off, struggling with her corer.

"Now! Move it! Move it!" Connors was yelling so loud that it hurt Jamie's ears. "Come on! Into the dome!"

Jamie angled off toward Joanna, watching the other hard-suited figures start into clumsy motion like a small herd of brightly colored hippos. A spurt of dust erupted near her, but she did not seem to notice. He ran as fast as he could toward her, feeling like a galumphing tortoise while he fiddled with the radio controls on his wrist to turn down the volume of Connors's urgent voice.

He reached Joanna as she finally started to move toward the dome. Slowing to her pace, Jamie knew he could not speak with her because Connors was flooding the suit-to-suit frequency with his hollering. Instead, he reached out to touch her shoulder. He could not see her face through the tinted visor of her helmet, could not see how frightened she was. Then Jamie realized he himself was scared, sweating cold, innards shaking.

The ground was erupting into puffs of dust, as if a squad of riflemen had them under fire. Something banged at the back of his helmet, just a tap, really, but it startled him as if he'd been shot. He looked up and saw that the dome was dimpling here and there as meteoroids struck its surface. *Oh my god, if one of them breaks through . . .*

One did. Jamie saw the transparent fabric on the lower level of the dome pucker for an instant, and then a small geyser of spray erupted into the dry thin air, like a whale spouting.

"The dome's punctured!" somebody screamed.

The hole spread into a growing rip as moisture-laden air geysered out into the Martian atmosphere and the plastic fabric of the dome began to sag noticeably.

After that first moment of near panic Vosnesensky turned coldly calm. While the others rushed for their suits, he veered aside and trotted around the inner periphery of the dome, checking to see if the repair patches were in their proper places. He had checked the patches only a day earlier, part of his regular inspection routine. But now he checked them again, while a patter of *pock, pock* sounds rained gently over his head, almost drowned out by the fearful voices of Toshima and the fliers as they struggled to don their hard suits.

He never saw the dome punctured. The meteoroid that punched through both layers of the plastic was a nearly microscopic grain of dust. But Vosnesensky heard a different sound, like a sudden gusting intake of breath, the kind of sound a man makes when he's been stabbed in the chest.

He felt the breeze as the dome's air rushed toward the puncture. Books fluttered open in the wind; loose papers flew across the dome like a covey of frightened birds. The hissing noise grew louder, a moan, a rushing torrent of air.

Vosnesensky whirled and saw dozens of the lightweight repair patches lifting off the floor to be sucked up against the wall of the dome. They flattened there, edges fluttering madly as the air rushed past them to escape the dome. The plastic walls began to sag between the dome's stiff supporting ribs. The surface of the wall was ripping faster than the patches could cover it.

Ears popping, heart triphammering, Vosnesensky rushed to the spot, bent down to scoop up more of the repair patches, and slammed them over the widening hole. They slipped down, would not stay. They still fluttered, and Vosnesensky could hear the dome's air roaring now as it rushed into the near-vacuum outside. In a few minutes it would all be gone. The force of the escaping wind was tugging at him, trying to suck him through the wall and out into the deadly open.

Without a word or a call to anyone, he braced himself and began to struggle back toward the center of the dome, leaning against the wind, staggering like a drunk, threading his way painfully past the scientists' workstations, dodging chairs in the wardroom carelessly left scattered about the floor. His ears were screaming with pain, as if someone had jabbed icepicks into them.

The life-support equipment. Pumps that sucked in the dry cold air of Mars. Separators that culled the scanty nitrogen and even scantier oxygen out of the native atmosphere. More pumps to make the nitrogen/oxygen mix thick enough for humans to breathe. Cylinders of spare oxygen, in case of emergency.

He had to reach the oxygen. Vosnesensky went down the row of green, man-tall oxygen tanks, twisting their valves to the full open position, overpressurizing the dome as quickly as he could with pure oxygen. Force oxygen into the dome; replace the air being lost. It was a race, and he had no intention of losing. Higher pressure might even push the repair seals firmly against the hole. At the very least it would buy them a few more minutes.

Yet even over the hissing rush of the escaping oxygen he could hear *pock, pock.*

He clawed his way back toward the tear in the wall in a blizzard of papers swirling through the dome. By the time he got back to the place where the meteoroid had broken through, Abell was there in his white hard suit, spraying epoxy over the repair patches as calmly as a painter doing a living-room wall.

"I have turned on the emergency oxygen," Vosnesensky said, almost breathless, his chest aflame.

"Right," said Abell. It was standard emergency procedure.

The wind had died down. The shriek of escaping air had quieted. Vosnesensky was panting, but from fear and exertion, not lack of oxygen.

"Are the others in their suits?"

Abell turned toward him, a faceless robot in rust-stained white. "Uh-huh. You should be too, Mike."

"Yes, yes." Vosnesensky saw that the patches were no longer fluttering. They were glued flat to the curving wall. "What about the people outside?"

"They're coming through the airlock. Nobody's been hurt, far as I know."

"Good. Now, if we are not struck again . . ."

"You should get into your suit," Abell reminded him.

"Yes. Of course."

By the time Vosnesensky was fully suited up, though, he heard no more sounds of meteoroids striking the dome. He clumped awkwardly to the communications console and saw on the screen that Tolbukhin was still on duty up in orbit, and still in his coveralls. His armpits were dark with sweat.

Dr. Li stretched his long legs as far as he could, considering the pain, and wriggled his bare toes until the cramp in his left calf began to subside. Two hours in a space suit that had never fit his lanky frame properly was more than his body could endure.

He sighed as he tried to relax in the reclining chair. He sipped tea from the one delicate porcelain cup he had brought with him and gazed at the silk paintings on the walls of his quarters, waiting for them to work their calming magic.

No one was hurt, he repeated to himself for the hundredth time. All the emergency procedures had worked just as they were designed to; all the emergency equipment had functioned properly. We survived the meteor shower without even any damage to our equipment, except for one minor puncture in the dome that was quickly sealed and one strike on the *Mars 1* ship's main communications antenna, which the astronauts will go EVA to repair.

The odds against meteoroid danger had been carefully calculated on Earth; they were something on the order of a trillion to one. And this particular meteor shower had been a renegade, unknown and uncharted until it suddenly struck at them. At least we should not be bothered again for another hundred million years or so, Li told himself.

He almost smiled, realizing that he could claim discovery of a new meteor swarm, so small and insignificant that it had never even been noticed on Earth. But not so small and insignificant here. No, not at all. We are very vulnerable here, Dr. Li realized. Extremely vulnerable.

He had ordered that regular radar sweeps be made as they orbited around Mars. We cannot avoid meteors, but we may be able to give ourselves some warning time if another shower develops. And we can produce data on the density of meteoroids in the vicinity of Mars; that should please the astronomers back home.

He rubbed the back of his neck, still trying to relax after the long, terrible, terrifying day. No one was killed, he said yet again. No one even hurt, except for this damnable leg cramp. No equipment damaged, except for the antenna. The team on the ground survived without any problems greater than a single small puncture and a spilled bottle of vitamin pills.

Now to report it all to Kaliningrad.

It had taken hours to clean up the mess inside the dome. Mironov and Connors went outside to seal the rip in the dome's outer wall, while Vosnesensky and Abell checked every square centimeter of the inner wall for damage. They found none.

Now all twelve of the team were sitting in the wardroom, physically and emotionally spent after the adrenaline surge of their wild afternoon. The schedule said it was time for dinner, but no one thought about food. Instead, Vosnesensky had brought from his quarters the bottle of vodka he had not touched since their second night on Mars.

"For medicinal purposes," he said when Tony Reed arched a questioning eyebrow. The others immediately rushed to their quarters to ferret out their own stashed bottles.

The first toast was to Vosnesensky.

"To our intrepid leader," said Paul Abell, his hand raised high, "who ignored his own safety to turn on the oxygen tanks and save the dome from collapse."

"At great risk to his own life," added Toshima.

"And even greater risk to his own safety rules," Connors joked.

Vosnesensky frowned slightly. "We must modify the oxygen tanks so that their valves open automatically if the air pressure in here drops below a certain point."

"I don't think we've got the equipment even to jury-rig a setup like that," Connors said.

"I will check the inventory," Mironov volunteered. "Perhaps between our spares here and what's left up in the spacecraft we can do it."

Vosnesensky nodded, satisfied. But the scowl did not leave his face.

"Are you still in pain, Mikhail Andreivitch?" Reed asked.

The Russian looked almost startled. "Me? No. My ears feel fine."

"You're certain? I don't think your eardrums ruptured, but perhaps I should check you over again."

"No. I am all right. No pain."

They sat tiredly at the wardroom tables, slowly unwinding from the terror of the meteors. Joanna had offered Jamie a share of her half bottle of Chilean wine. "The last I have until we return to the space-craft," she confided. "I hid another bottle of champagne there for the day we start home."

Jamie sipped at the wine gratefully. He had put his helmet on the table in front of him. Its curving back held a long thin gouge, blackened as if a miniature incendiary bullet had grazed it. If it had been a little bigger, a little more energetic, it would have blown my head off, he knew. Jamie stared at the damaged helmet, his insides hollow. Just a little bigger . . .

"You are a fortunate fellow, Jamie," Vosnesensky called from the other end of the table. "A very lucky fellow."

Pete Connors said, "Well, the suits are built to take small meteorite hits. Jamie was in no real danger."

Not much, Jamie said to himself.

Vosnesensky made a rare grin. "I did not mean he is lucky to have survived. I know the suits can protect against such things. He is lucky to have been hit! Do you know the odds against being struck by a meteorite? Fantastic! Astronomical! I salute you, Jamie."

And the Russian raised his plastic glass again, while the others chuckled tolerantly.

"Perhaps you should place a bet on the next Irish Sweepstakes," Reed suggested.

Jamie shook his head. "No thanks. One stroke of luck like this is enough for me."

"To think of the odds," Vosnesensky kept muttering.

Mironov said, "Even long shots pay off, sometimes. What would you say were the odds against the only elephant in the Leningrad zoo being killed by the first cannon shell the Nazis fired into the city during the Great Patriotic War? Yet that is exactly what happened."

"They killed the elephant?" Monique asked.

"Exactly."

"No!"

"It is an historical fact."

"How long will we have to breathe pure oxygen?" Naguib asked. "I think it is giving me a headache. My sinuses hurt."

"A day or two," Vosnesensky said. "Virtually all of our nitrogen escaped. We must wait until the pumps accumulate enough nitrogen from outside to return the air mixture to normal."

"Let me take a look at you," Reed suggested.

Suddenly Naguib seemed reluctant, wary. "Oh no, it's nothing. Just a bit of a headache. Tension, most likely."

"Still," Reed said, "if you wake up with it tomorrow I'd better examine you."

Jamie fingered the gouge on the back of his helmet. It was not deep, nowhere near serious enough to threaten the helmet's integrity. He could wear it again if he had to. But he would use one of the spares instead. Katrin Diels had demanded that it be put aside so that she could examine it on the trip back to Earth. So had the mission controllers, once they learned of it. The hard-suit manufacturers would want to study the damage, to see how well the helmet had protected its wearer.

You'll be famous, Jamie said to the helmet. They'll put you in the Smithsonian. He thought of what the inside of the helmet would have looked like if the meteorite had gone all the way through. And shuddered.

"But I'm much too valuable to risk outside," Tony Reed was saying.

Looking up, Jamie realized that Ilona was teasing the Englishman.

"You haven't been outside the dome since our second day here, Tony," she said, smiling slyly at him. "One would almost think you're afraid to go outside."

"Nonsense!" Reed spat. "I am the team physician. I'm needed here, in my infirmary."

"Safely barricaded behind your pills and instruments," Ilona needled him. "And you even spilled all the pills, didn't you?"

"Only one bottle," Reed answered stiffly.

"Five hundred vitamin capsules, all over the floor."

"Only a few hit the floor! Most of them stayed on my desktop, which is clean enough to eat from, I assure you."

"Yes," said Ilona mockingly. "Certainly it is. Just be certain that you don't feed us the dirty ones."

The others were grinning, Jamie saw. Enjoying the entertainment. Usually Tony's the one who does the needling. He's damned uncomfortable when he's the victim instead of the attacker.

Joanna pushed her chair back and got to her feet. "I believe I will lie down for a while."

Grateful for a way to escape Ilona's scalpel, Reed asked swiftly, "Don't you feel well?"

"Oh, I'm just tired," Joanna replied. "I think I'll try to sleep."

"Without dinner?" Vosnesensky asked from down the table.

"I don't believe I could eat anything right now. Perhaps later."

The Russian glanced at Reed but said nothing more.

As Joanna left the table, Reed turned toward Jamie. "I think we should name this meteor swarm after Jamie, here. After all, it seems to be attracted to him. The James F. Waterman Meteor Swarm."

Rava Patel said seriously, "Dr. Diels and Dr. Li are attempting to plot out its orbit. The swarm is obviously the remains of an ancient comet."

"Obviously," said Reed.

"It will be quite difficult, however," Patel went on, "to plot its orbit with so little data. The swarm is so small that it does not return radar signals very well."

Reed's old smirk returned. "Perhaps we can stand Jamie outside again. The meteors seem to like him. Perhaps they'll come back if he's standing out in the open like a lightning rod."

"Or you could go out," Ilona said.

"Oh no, not me," said Reed. "Let Jamie do it. It would be the American Indians' first contribution to the science of astronomy, you see."

"Not the first," Jamie said.

"Oh? Really?"

"The Aztecs and Incas were fine astronomers. They built obser-vatories . . ."

"I don't mean them," Reed interrupted. "They were civilized, somewhat. I meant your people, Jamie. The savages of North Amer-ica."

All eyes had turned to him, Jamie realized. Tony's got the needle out of his hide by sinking it into me.

"My ancestors watched the stars," he said, measuring his words carefully.

Reed said, "Of course they did. In the desert where they lived, what else was there to do once the sun went down? But what did they accomplish, outside of some tribal mumbo-jumbo?"

Jamie hesitated a heartbeat's span, then answered, "They recorded the great supernova of 1054, for one thing. Carved the data into petroglyphs. Even decorated pottery bowls with accurate drawings of where and when the supernova appeared."

"Really?"

"Really." Jamie turned to the others. "The supernova of 1054 is the one that created the Crab Nebula; you can see it in a telescope today. The only other astronomers to observe the supernova were in China."

"Japan also," said Toshima.

Jamie nodded at him gravely. "Japan also. Nobody in Europe paid any attention, apparently."

"It was probably too cloudy that night," Reed said.

"The supernova was visible to the naked eye for twenty-three days," Jamie countered. "The Chinese records show that. So do the drawings my ancestors made. Even in England the sky must have been clear for part of that time, but nobody there bothered to look up. Either that, or they were too ignorant of the stars to notice a new one blazing away each night."

Ilona made a low whistle. Naguib chuckled softly. The others grinned and nodded.

Tony Reed got slowly to his feet and made a slight bow in Jamie's direction. "Touché," he said. "And now, if no one objects, I think I'll make myself a spot of dinner."

One by one the others got up and began to prepare their evening meals. Jamie sat alone at the table, staring at his damaged helmet, wondering why human beings had to inflict pain on one another to gain respect.

MARS ARRIVAL

For all the months that they had coasted across the dark emptiness between worlds, the members of the expedition had watched Mars steadily grow from a bright red star to a ruddy disc to a fully three-dimensional globe that hung before their eyes like a gigantic prize waiting to be seized.

Once the two spacecraft established themselves in orbit around the planet Jamie found himself spending hours at the observation port watching the strange world of rust and brick and almost bloody reds. The window bristled with instruments now, but peering between them Jamie could see Mars sliding past his feasting eyes slowly as the spacecraft turned in its stately revolutions. Jamie saw massive volcano cones projecting upward like the turreted eyes of lizards, staring at him impassively. The vast twisted gash of Valles Marineris called to him with memories of river-carved canyons back home.

He saw dust storms spring up and sweep across a quarter of the globe before dying away as mysteriously as they had started. Huge craters smashed out by ancient meteor strikes; some of them had blasted out the smaller meteoroids that had eventually made their way to Earth to be found on the Antarctic ice.

"Are you ready to go down there and start to work?"

Jamie recognized Ilona Malater's throaty voice even before he turned his head.

He nodded solemnly. "Aren't you?"

She gave a wintry smile. "After nine months in this concentration camp I'd be willing to run along the sand dunes in the nude."

Jamie laughed.

In the reflected reddish light of Mars Ilona's haughty face looked almost as coppery as Jamie's. Her short-cropped golden hair took on glints of fire.

"Have you remained celibate?" she asked, the corners of her lips curving upward slightly.

It was more of a challenge than a question, Jamie thought. He nodded once more.

"You must have interesting dreams," Ilona said.

He felt a surge of anger heating his face. "You know, Ilona, you have a reputation for being the local sex therapist."

Her smile widened. "And why not? Tony Reed assures me that no one aboard is carrying any communicable diseases worse than the cold you gave us all. Why not make life a little less tedious?"

"Less tedious, maybe, but a lot more tense."

"Really?" Ilona arched a brow. "I would think that sex lowers tensions among us."

"Not among the Russians."

"Oh, them! Let them jerk each other off."

Jamie huffed and turned away from her.

"You're such a prude, Jamie," Ilona said, still smiling. "I thought that once we made love you would relax, but you're not the kind who can take sex casually, are you?"

"*That's* why we're here," he shot back, jabbing a finger toward the observation window and the red bulk of Mars hanging beyond. "To explore that planet. Not for high-school fun and games."

"My god, you're so serious!"

"We're on a serious mission, Ilona. Very serious."

"I'm not hurting anyone. In fact, I think the tensions aboard this prison would have been a lot worse." Her eyes were dancing with amusement. "Tony agrees with me; he says my contributions to the team's morale have been invaluable."

"Tell it to Mikhail and Dmitri."

"Come on, now, Jamie. You could use some relaxation yourself."

"No thanks."

"Think of it as research," Ilona teased. "I think you don't really get to know a man until you see him with his pants down."

He stared at her for a wordless moment. Then, "Do Katrin and Joanna feel the same way?"

"You mean, are they doing what I've been doing?"

He started to reply, but heard voices drifting toward them from the passageway. Tony Reed and Joanna Brumado turned the corner and stepped into the observation area.

"I thought it was you, Ilona," Reed said amiably. "I'd recognize that sexy voice anywhere."

Jamie realized his eyes were fixed on Joanna. With an effort he pulled them away.

The four of them chatted about the landing they would make the next day, keeping their talk strictly on the business of the expedition. Reed seemed casual and relaxed, as ever. Joanna was serious, as usual, her dark eyes focused on Mars as if she realized for the first time that she was actually going to go down to the surface of that alien world.

Jamie felt almost like an automaton. He answered questions they addressed to him; he spoke the correct words and kept up his end of the four-way conversation. But his mind was racing, remembering the brief moments of wild animal heat he had shared with Ilona, remembering the sad, solemn expression on Joanna's face when he had kissed her, wondering why he could not relax and play with Ilona and forget about everything else.

"I must get back to my quarters," Joanna said quietly, almost timidly. "My father will be calling in another few minutes."

Tony Reed held out his arm for her. "I'll escort you there, if I may."

She glanced toward Jamie, then back to Reed. "Of course. Thank you."

Ilona watched them leave the observation blister, an enigmatic smile playing across her face. Once they were out of earshot she turned back to Jamie.

"The answer to your question is that Katrin has been much more discreet about her amours than I. And little Joanna, as far as I know, has been completely virtuous. Does that make you happy, Jamie?"

He nodded, trying to keep his face from betraying his emotions.

"But have you noticed," Ilona added devilishly, "that Tony follows her wherever she goes?"

Jamie blinked, surprised. "He does?"

"Watch him," she said. "He trails after her like a dog following a bitch in heat."

That sly, smiling bastard, Jamie thought. Who lectures him? Who doctors his food?

"Tony's not satisfied with me or Katrin," Ilona went on. "He wants the unobtainable."

And so do I, Jamie realized. So do I.

S O L 1 5: AFTERNOON

"This is kind of awkward, Edith," Jamie said into the camera.

He was sitting on the bunk of his privacy cubicle, the vidcam perched on the flimsy little desk opposite him, focused on his face. First thing in the morning, before his scheduled work hours, he had suited up and gone outside to take a few minutes' worth of panoramic shots of the rocks and dunes and distant mountains in the area around the dome. Now he sat on his bunk, wondering what he should say to Edith.

"Yesterday we had a bit of a scare. Things still aren't quite back to normal yet. A stray meteorite punctured our dome. Just a little puncture. We never even found the meteorite; it must've been so small it evaporated from the energy of the impact. But it leaked out some of our air and for a couple of minutes everything was pretty tense."

He looked upward. The dome was bathed in sunlight. The pumps and fans were throbbing their usual low notes. Jamie could hear voices and the cowboy twang of a country-and-western song from somebody's tape player.

"We're still breathing pure oxygen in here. We've got to tiptoe around and be extremely careful. In a pure oxygen atmosphere, the slightest spark could set the whole dome on fire. The separators are accumulating nitrogen from the air outside, but we won't be back on normal air for another day or two.

"There wasn't any damage, except for the puncture itself, which Vosnesensky and Paul Abell fixed inside of a couple of minutes. I was outside when it happened and another micrometeorite scratched my helmet. Oh yes, Tony Reed knocked over a whole bottle full of vitamin pills. He's getting kidded about being so clumsy."

Jamie turned off the camera with the remote control box in his hand and made a wide, long, exaggerated yawn. The pure oxygen atmosphere seemed to be affecting his ears. They felt clogged, as if they needed to pop. The yawn helped, but not much.

Turning the camera on again, he continued, "The meteors were probably the last remains of an old, ancient comet. Just a bunch of stray pebbles floating around the solar system that happened to drift right into our spot on Mars. Couldn't happen again in a million years."

Jamie hesitated for an instant. There was hardly any more news to tell her.

"I sure appreciated the tape you sent. And I'm glad you're moving up in the world. Going to New York must have taken a lot of guts. If there's anything I can do, like an interview or some background information about our work here on the surface, just send a request through the mission directors and I'll be happy to tell you whatever you need to know."

Jamie stopped the vidcam again, thinking, How much can I really tell her? How much would the mission directors let me tell her? He decided for now to stick to science and stay away from politics and personalities.

"It turns out that there's a lot more water beneath the ground than the earlier unmanned landers led us to believe. It's frozen, of course. We're sitting on top of an ocean of permafrost that probably extends all the way down to the Valles Marineris—the Grand Canyon of Mars, that is. Maybe farther, but we haven't crossed the canyon and investigated the other side."

Jamie described the brief traverse to the canyon and his hopes that he would be able to return there, skipping over the arguments and debates he had triggered. He carefully avoided mentioning the "village"; time enough for that when we've got definite evidence, one way or the other, he thought. Instead, he told Edith about the copper-green rock they had found. Then he ran out of things to say.

Fingering the remote control nervously, he finally flicked the camera on again. "I'm glad all that nonsense about my speaking Navaho has settled down. At least, I presume it has. We haven't seen much in the way of news here—mostly BBC stuff."

He clicked it off again, licked his lips while he thought of what else he could tell Edith.

"Well, I guess that's about it for now. We haven't found any signs of life yet, living or fossils, but maybe conditions down in the Grand Canyon will be more conducive. Monique Bonnet has a nice little garden growing out of Martian soil, using Martian water for it. I don't know what a few days of pure oxygen is going to do for her plants, though. We all go over and breathe on them now and then, to give them some carbon dioxide. It was nice of you to call me, Edith. I'll be talking with you some more, later on."

He turned the vidcam off for good, thinking, I can edit this tape for Al and for my parents and have mission control send it to them. That'll surprise them. Maybe my parents will even send me a message in return.

Seiji Toshima had listened to all the arguments raging between Waterman and the rest of the team without once opening his mouth. Their fight had nothing to do with him, and he had been trained from earliest childhood to refrain from interjecting his own opinions where they had not been specifically requested.

But now Waterman was asking, not for his opinion, but for knowledge. That was different. Toshima was happy to exchange knowledge with the American Indian. After all, that was the purpose of this expedition to Mars, was it not? To gain knowledge. And what good is knowledge if it is not exchanged with others?

Jamie Waterman sat on a spindly-legged plastic stool in the center of the Japanese meteorologist's laboratory. Toshima's area had been dubbed "weather central" by the team. It was the smallest of all the labs, as neat and gleamingly clean as if a squad of maintenance robots scrubbed and dusted the place every half hour.

The area looked like a showcase for an electronics shop. Where the other scientists' workbenches were cluttered with glassware and instruments, Toshima had a row of computers humming quietly, their display screens showing graphs and curves. At the far end of the row, where it bent in an ell shape at the corner of the partitions, was a scanner that could take videotape and digitize the images for computer storage.

Toshima sat in the other corner on a rickety-looking stool. He had given Jamie his best stool, the only one with a back.

Since the death of Isoruku Konoye, Toshima felt an unexpected weight of responsibility on his shoulders; the responsibility of honor, of upholding the proud name of Japan even here, on this strange world. He knew that most of the others belittled everything Japanese; he could see it in their eyes when they spoke to him, in the barely tolerant smugness of men like Antony Reed and the overly solicitous politeness of the Americans and the Russians.

Back on Earth, Japan was a power to be reckoned with. Without Japan's contributions of funding and technology the Mars Project would have died in bickering and cost-accounting among the Europeans, the Russians, and the Americans. Yet no Japanese was among the first group to land on Mars. And the only man to have been killed on this expedition had been the brilliant Japanese geochemist Konoye.

Seiji Toshima was the son of a factory worker, but within him beat the heart of a samurai. *I will uphold the honor of the Japanese people. I will make these aliens respect Japan. I will make the entire world recognize the contributions of Japan to the exploration of Mars.*

Suddenly he realized where his thoughts were leading. *This is unworthy,* he told himself. *We are scientists. Knowledge knows no nationality. I am part of a team, not a medieval egomaniac.*

"We can use the central processor," he was saying to Jamie Waterman, unconsciously bending over to pat the minicomputer that stood slightly more than knee-high in that corner of the lab. Waterman was a curious one; as withdrawn and inward as a Japanese, almost. A man who understands correct behavior, Toshima thought, yet is willing to do battle for his beliefs.

"Can you access the geological file from here or should I go to the geology computer and copy it onto a floppy?" Jamie asked.

"I should be able to access it," Toshima replied, his round flat face intently serious. Then he smiled slightly. "Unless you have put a special restrictive code on the file to keep it secret."

Jamie shook his head. "No. Not at all."

The meteorologist pulled a keyboard to his lap and flicked his stubby fingers over it. Jamie saw the display screen of the computer in front of him go blank for a moment, then show a full-color map of Mars made from a montage of photos taken from orbit.

Toshima muttered something in Japanese and the screen suddenly sprouted a weather map superimposed on the photo montage. Jamie recognized the symbols for a cold front, high and low pressure systems, and the irregular lopsided loops of isobars.

"That is the situation at this moment," Toshima said. "And here is the computer's forecast for tonight"— the symbols shifted slightly; the numbers representing temperatures plummeted by a hundred or more—"and tomorrow at noon, our time." Again the front advanced slightly. The temperatures shot upward. At their latitude they even rose above freezing.

A hint of pride crept into Toshima's voice as he added, "I can even show the wind speeds and directions for much of the planet."

"How?" Jamie asked, as vector arrows speckled the map. They showed the direction of the winds; the number of flags on their tails denoted the wind speed.

"The network of remote observation stations that has been placed around the planet," Toshima replied. "And, of course, the balloons."

The meteorology balloons were brilliantly simple, little more than long narrow tubes of exquisitely thin, tough Mylar filled with hydrogen. They were released as needed from the orbiting spacecraft, dropped into the Martian atmosphere in their tiny capsules, and inflated automatically when they reached the proper altitude. They floated across the landscape like improbable giant white cigarettes.

Dangling below each balloon was a "snake," a long thin metal pipe that contained sensing instruments, a radio, batteries, and a heater to protect the equipment against the cold.

By day the balloons wafted high in the Martian atmosphere, sampling the temperature (low), pressure (lower), humidity (lower still), and chemical composition of the air. The altitude at which any individual balloon flew was governed by the amount of hydrogen filling its long narrow cigarette shape. The daytime winds carried them across the red landscape like dandelion puffs.

At night, when the temperatures became so frigid that even the hydrogen inside the balloons began to condense, they all sank toward the ground like a chorus of ballerinas daintily curtsying. The "snakes" of instruments actually touched the ground and faithfully transmitted data on the surface conditions through the night as the balloons bobbed in the dark winds, barely buoyant enough to hover safely above the rock-strewn ground.

Not every balloon survived. While most drifted across the face of Mars for days on end, descending tiredly each night and rising again when the morning sunlight warmed them, some drooped too far and were torn by rocks. Some became snagged on mountainsides. One disappeared in the vast sunken crater of Hellas Planitia and could not be found even with the best cameras aboard the surveillance satellites orbiting Mars.

But most of the balloons carried on silently, effortlessly, living with the Martian day/night cycle and faithfully reporting on the environment from pole to pole.

"As you can see," Toshima said, with a barely perceptible nod toward the display screen, "the weather situation here in the northern hemisphere is quite stable, quite dull."

"Summertime pattern," Jamie muttered.

Toshima was pleased that the geologist understood at least that much about the Martian climate. Even in the southern hemisphere, where it was winter, the weather was also calm, disturbances weak. No major dust storms, not even a decent cyclonic flow to study and learn from.

"Can we zero in on Tithonium?" Jamie asked as he studied the meteorology screen.

"Yes, of course," said Toshima.

The twisted gash of the great rift valley seemed to rush up at Jamie until Tithonium Chasma and its southerly companion, Ius Chasma, filled the screen. For a moment Jamie ignored the meteorological symbols superimposed on the picture; he saw only the miles-high cliffs and the vast slumping landslides that partially filled in small areas of the huge canyon.

"There is an anomaly here," Toshima said.

The meteorologist had pulled his stool close to Jamie's chair. Their heads were practically touching as they examined the screen, Jamie looking at the gigantic handiwork of ancient fractures in the crust, Toshima examining the meteorological data with narrowed eyes.

"An anomaly?"

"I should have recognized it days ago, but with so much data coming in now . . . " He made a little shrug that was both an apology and an excuse. "We are even tracking the discarded parachutes from our landing vehicles as the surface winds blow them across the ground."

"What's the anomaly?" Jamie asked.

"Only two of the balloons have flown over this section of the Grand Canyon," Toshima said, tracing a fingertip across the image of Tithonium on the screen. "They both reported much higher temperatures in the air than our metsat gives us."

Jamie looked at him. "The meteorological satellite tells you the temperatures in the canyon are *lower* than the balloon instruments reported?"

"Correct," said Toshima.

"What kinds of sensors do they use?"

"Infrared detectors on the metsat, of course. That is the only way to obtain temperature data remotely. The balloons carry a variety of thermometers. They measure temperature directly."

"And the balloons say the air down in the canyon is warmer than the satellite data."

Toshima nodded, eyes closed, almost a little bow.

"Any other anomalies?"

He made a thin smile. "I had thought that the humidity data was unusable. It seemed to me that the sensors had saturated."

"Saturated?"

"They hit the top of their scale and jammed there for as long as they were in the canyon—a few hours, as it turned out. We have no way to control their direction or speed, you understand."

"Yes, I know."

Toshima looked away from Jamie, toward the image on the screen. "Now that you have reported seeing mists in the canyon, however, I think I can explain what is happening."

Jamie waited for him to continue.

"The humidity sensors are calibrated for the very minor humidity we have expected on Mars. If the balloons passed through the mists you reported, then they encountered a much higher humidity than the sensors were equipped to handle. The sensors became saturated."

"Okay, that sounds right."

"On the other hand, we have the matter of the temperature differences." Toshima smiled broadly. "Consider: the metsat infrared sensors are not seeing deeply into the canyon when the mists are there. The sensors see the mist and report its temperature."

Jamie understood. "And if the mist is made of ice crystals . . ."

"Or even water droplets," Toshima picked up, "it would appear much cooler to the infrared sensors than the air below the mist."

"The mists act as a kind of blanket, insulating the warm air at the bottom of the canyon!"

"Exactly. Yet the radar aboard the metsat penetrates the mist as if it were not there and gives us a true reading of the depth of the canyon. Until you reported the mists I had no idea they existed."

"So the balloons gave you a truer temperature reading than the satellites did," Jamie said, feeling the thrill of understanding tingling through his body.

"That is how I interpret the data," Toshima replied, grinning now with all his teeth.

"Okay, let's pump the geological data into this display," Jamie urged. He found it difficult to sit still, he was getting so excited.

Toshima pecked away at the keyboard, still on his lap.

"What are you seeking?" he asked.

"Heat," said Jamie. "Something's making that canyon warmer than the plains surrounding it. Warmer than we had any right to expect. Maybe it's heat welling up from the planet's interior."

"Ah! Hot springs, perhaps. Or a volcano."

"Nothing so dramatic as a volcano," Jamie said, eagerly watching the screen, waiting for the geological data to appear.

"There are very massive volcanoes on Mars," Toshima muttered, his fingers working the keyboard.

"A thousand kilometers away from Tithonium. And they've been dead cold for millions of years. Billions, maybe."

Toshima half whispered, "Now," and ostentatiously pressed the ENTER key with his stubby forefinger.

A thin train of bright red symbols sprang onto the screen.

"Can we back away from this close-up and see the region between our base and the canyon's rim?" Jamie asked.

"Of course," said Toshima.

There they were, the real-time readings from the sensors Jamie had planted on the ground during his traverse with Vosnesensky. The symbols formed a single track from their domed base to the Noctis Labyrinthus badlands, then out to the edge of Tithonium, and finally back to the base. Each cluster of sensors included heat-flow instruments. On Earth such sensors measured the heat welling up toward the surface from the molten magma deep below the crust.

"Not a helluva lot, is it?" Jamie muttered, straining his eyes at the tiny red numerals as if he could make them come alive by just staring hard enough.

Toshima said nothing. He sat with his hands folded politely on his lap.

"The planet's colder than a frozen potato," Jamie grumbled. "There's not enough heat coming up from its core to warm a cup of tea."

"No thermal flow in the canyon?"

Unconsciously kneading both thighs in frustration Jamie replied, "That's just it: we don't have any instruments down on the canyon floor. That may be the one place where some heat actually is flowing up out of the core, but we don't have any sensors down there to check it out!"

Toshima bowed his head slightly, this time to show understanding. "I see. We must put sensors on the canyon floor if we hope to understand what forms the mists."

"Not just sensors," Jamie said, his voice urgent. "We've got to get down there ourselves. Somehow, we've got to get a team down on the floor of that canyon."

Li Chengdu smiled thinly at the trio of images on his screen. This was such an important decision that all three project directors wanted to discuss it with him.

I can thank Waterman for this, Dr. Li said to himself. *If it were not for him everything would be going according to plan.*

"... we have therefore instructed the mission controllers," the somber-faced Russian director was saying, "to prepare a plan for a traverse of the Tithonium Chasma region, including—if possible— a direct examination of the floor of the canyon. Since it will take a minimum of two weeks to put such a plan into effect ..."

He's done it, Dr. Li thought as he listened with only half his attention to the Russian's droning voice. *Waterman has gotten them to shatter the mission schedule completely and agree to a traverse of Tithonium.*

The expedition commander eyed the other two project directors as the Russian continued his formal instructions. The Japanese director was trying his best to look impassive, but Li could detect a gleam of pleased excitement in his dark eyes. The American, veteran of Washington's political knife fights, had a benign little smile playing across his fleshy, florid face.

"... Father DiNardo will chair the ad hoc committee that will prepare the traverse plan. Dr. Brumado will attend the committee meetings as an ex officio member ..."

The Russian droned on and on, like an old Orthodox priest reciting some inflexible ritual.

How they must have connived! Li thought. *The American Vice-President has agreed to this change in the mission plan, obviously. Brumado must have swayed her somehow. She is no longer seeking to destroy Waterman; somehow Brumado has made the two of them allies. The man is a miracle worker.*

A traverse into Tithonium Chasma. We'll have to tear up the final four weeks' worth of the schedule and reorient everything for this. I'll have to curtail Patel's excursion to Pavonis Mons. The poor man will be apoplectic. He has spent half his life preparing to survey Pavonis Mons. That will have to be scratched now; we won't have the time or the resources to devote to it.

Even the work here in orbit will have to be redirected to support the Tithonium excursion. O'Hara will be especially upset—he has not been very secretive about his hopes that the American politicians would send him down to the surface to replace Waterman.

No chance of that now. Somehow Waterman has become the true leader of the ground team. He has stolen the lightning from the gods. He is even overshadowing me now.

Yet Li kept on smiling placidly at the images of the three project directors on his screen.

A traverse to the floor of the Grand Canyon! His scientist's mind was thrilled by the possibilities. Warmth and moisture. Perhaps life. Life! What a finding that would be. It would mark a new epoch in history.

Still the political side of his mind worried about the difficulties of changing the schedule, the dangers of moving so boldly into new territory, the risks that always haunted every step into the unknown.

Waterman, he thought. If it were not for him everything would be going smoothly and safely according to plan.

Li's smile broadened slightly. How dull that would be! Besides, if anything goes wrong he will take the brunt of the blame, not me.

E A R T H

Edith sat tensely on the edge of the upholstered chair. Howard Francis's apartment was much smaller than she had expected, little more than a studio. The so-called bedroom was nothing more than an ell in the one room, mirrored to make it seem larger. The kitchenette was an alcove with a sink, a microwave oven, and some cabinets.

The network vice-president was sprawled nonchalantly on the sofa, shoes off, tie gone, head lolling back, eyes half closed as he watched the big TV screen. The television set was the largest piece of furniture in the place.

Through the half-closed curtains of the apartment's only window Edith could see the darkened windows of the network news building. She felt nervous not only because the tape playing on the TV could determine the future of her career; she worried that her boss had insisted on looking at the tape here in his apartment rather than across the street at his office.

She had dressed as plainly as possible: a bulky sweatshirt and baggy old slacks. He had greeted her at his apartment door shoeless, collar undone, and a glass of white wine already in his hand.

Jamie's tape took less than ten minutes. When it ended the TV set automatically returned to the all-news channel.

Her boss muted the sound and turned his sleepy eyes toward her. Edith thought he looked like a drugged rat.

"Not much, is it?" he said lazily.

She felt genuinely surprised. "Not much? He's told us more about that meteor hit than Kaliningrad and Houston did, put together. And he showed us what's going on around their base. He's told us about what they've discovered . . ."

"The official reports have given us most of that. And better footage, too."

"Okay, but Jamie's telling us that he wants to go back to the Grand Canyon. That's not on the mission schedule. I checked."

He pulled himself up into a more erect sitting position. "Possible conflict with the mission controllers?"

"You bet!"

His eyes opened wider. "Maverick scientist battling against the brass. Russian brass, too. Maybe there's something there."

Edith smiled. "It's more than anybody else's got."

"Maybe. Maybe not. I don't want us to stick our necks out and get them chopped off. We need more than just this one guy's word."

"I can check with some of the people at Houston. And I can always get to Brumado . . ."

"I'll bet you can," he said, with a leering grin.

Edith jumped to her feet. "I ought to get on this right away."

"Tomorrow morning," he said, reaching out a hand to pull her down onto the sofa.

She avoided it. "Brumado's in Washington now, but not for long. I better get down there right away."

He frowned at her. "There's no planes this time of night, for Chrissake. Relax. Have some wine."

"You're paying me for making news," Edith said, keeping her smile in place. "Let me earn my living."

"You can earn your living . . ."

But she was heading for the door. "I'll rent a car and phone you from Washington with an exclusive interview with Brumado. And maybe even the Vice-President!"

Edith was out the door before he could pull himself up from the sofa. It never fails, she thought. Men always think with their balls.

Years earlier she had learned, the hard way, the first rule of survival: Don't go to bed with a man until you've gotten what you want from him. He wants sex. I want a permanent job, not this little consultant arrangement. He could bounce me out on my behind any time he wants to. Let me break the story about Jamie fighting the project directors. Then I'll get a full-time job and he can have sex to cement the deal. Maybe.

D O S S I E R: JAMES FOX WATERMAN

It was a neurotic assistant professor and a state police officer who made a student leader out of young James Waterman. The episode still haunted his dreams.

It had happened during Jamie's sophomore year at Albuquerque. He was a quiet student, a loner who attended his classes and did his work without socializing much with the other students. Most of his teachers, if they remembered him at all, recalled an intense young man with the coppery broad-cheeked face of an Indian who hardly ever said a word in class yet turned in quality papers. Jamie got very high grades in most of his classes, but no recognition from either his peers or the faculty.

He lived off campus with friends of his grandfather's, a Navaho family that ran a fashionable clothing shop on Albuquerque's Old Town plaza. Jamie drove back and forth on a secondhand motor scooter and earned a few dollars by helping out in the shop on weekends.

With hardly anyone noticing it, Jamie was almost a straight-A student. The *almost* was his sophomore-level course in Shakespeare.

Jamie had done well in his freshman English survey course; he had enjoyed his first encounters with the rich literature that began with *Beowulf* and extended across the centuries to Eliot and Ballard. He had balked at Kipling, at first, with his freight of "white man's burden." But the sheer marvelous adventure of the man's poems and stories had won Jamie over.

The sophomore course in Shakespeare was another matter. Assistant Professor Ferraro's idea of teaching was to stand atop his desk and read all the roles of the Bard's plays aloud to the class, declaiming dramatically and sawing the air with his gestures. It took only a week for Jamie to realize that the diminutive, middle-aged Ferraro was a frustrated actor who made all his classes into his personal stage.

By midterm Jamie was in trouble with Ferraro. The little man gave no quizzes, asked for no papers. He simply expected his students to watch his desktop performances with rapt attention. And then applaud. When Jamie asked why Othello—supposedly an intelligent leader of men—could fall so completely for the transparent schemes of Iago, Ferraro glared and told him to read the play until he understood it. When Jamie, genuinely puzzled, asked if Rosencrantz and Guildenstern were supposed to be homosexuals, Ferraro replied coldly: "I will not allow my class to be turned into a circus."

Of course Jamie spent most of his time on his other subjects: geology, chemistry, advanced calculus, history. But he felt he was as well prepared for the Shakespeare midterm exam as anyone else in the class. He had read the plays and watched the videotapes. He had looked up the critical analyses listed in Ferraro's syllabus. It was a jolt, then, when Ferraro read off the grades for the midterms and announced that James Waterman had received an F.

Shocked to the point where his insides were trembling, Jamie stayed after the class was finished to ask if he could retake the test. Ferraro refused flatly. Jamie saw the stack of blue books on the man's desk, and asked if he could see his, go over it with the professor, find out where he had gone wrong.

"You may not see your blue book," Ferraro said. Despite his thick-soled elevator shoes he had to crane his neck to look Jamie in the face now that he was standing on the classroom floor.

"But it's my test," Jamie said.

Ferraro placed a hand atop the pile of blue books. "These examination papers are the property of the university, not of the students. You may not take yours. I forbid it."

Then he turned grandly and started toward the door. His interview with Jamie was concluded, as far as he was concerned.

Suddenly furious, Jamie riffled through the stack of blue books and found his own. He quickly flipped through the pages. Not a mark on them. Not a notation. Nothing at all except the big red F scrawled on the cover.

"What are you doing?" Ferraro screeched from the doorway. "Put that down!"

Clutching the test book in his hand Jamie strode toward the little man. "You didn't even read my test! You just flunked me when you saw my name on the cover!"

"That test booklet is the property of this university!" Ferraro yelled, pointing a wavering finger at Jamie. "You can't take it out of this classroom! That's theft!"

Jamie brushed past the assistant professor, the test booklet tight in his fist, his teeth clenched in anger.

"I'll take this to the student council," he shouted back, over his shoulder. "I'll take this to the dean!"

And he strode down the hall, oblivious to the startled glances of the students, while Ferraro bellowed, "Thief! Stop thief!"

No one tried to stop Jamie. He went to his motorbike and drove back to the room he rented in the Navaho shopkeeper's home.

The state police officer arrived just as the family was sitting down to supper. The doorbell rang and one of the daughters went to answer it. She came back with drawn face and frightened eyes.

"It's a state trooper. He wants you, Jamie."

Wondering if he had committed a traffic violation of some sort with his bike, Jamie went to the front door. The state policeman looked about eleven feet tall in his uniform and mirrored sunglasses and broad-brimmed hat. The pistol in its holster at his hip seemed huge.

"James Waterman?" he asked in the voice of a robot.

Jamie nodded, his mind racing.

"We received a complaint that you have stolen state property."

"What?" Jamie's knees sagged.

The shopkeeper came up behind Jamie and laid a protective hand on his shoulder.

"Seems that you're accused of stealing some papers from the university," the trooper said. "You're on the edge of a deep hole, young fella."

"It's my test paper," Jamie mumbled. "My professor wouldn't give me back my own test paper."

The trooper slowly peeled off his sunglasses. His face instantly became human. "Is that what this is all about?"

Jamie nodded. "It's in my room. My midterm exam."

"This boy is no thief," said the shopkeeper. "He's a student at the university. Never been in any kind of trouble in his life."

"A test paper? Your own exam?" The trooper looked incredulous.

"I can show it to you. I took it to show to the student council tomorrow. He flunked me without even reading what I wrote."

The trooper blew out a breath from puffed cheeks. "All right. You get your ass back to the university first thing tomorrow morning and give that paper back to the professor you took it from. You understand me? First thing tomorrow. Otherwise he'll probably swear out a god-dammed warrant for your arrest and we'll have to post a goddammed APB on you."

"Yessir. First thing tomorrow."

The trooper put his glasses back on and headed down the stairs toward his powerful-looking car, muttering something about dangerous criminals and grand larceny.

After a sleepless night Jamie returned the test paper to the assistant professor. But not before making two photocopies of it. One he left with the dean of students, the other he handed to the president of the student council. Two tension-racked days passed before the dean called Jamie into his office. Ferraro was already there, sitting in a tight little glaring ball on a chair that looked two sizes too large for him.

From the comfortable swivel chair behind his broad desk the dean gestured Jamie to a stiff wooden seat in front of the desk. He was an amiable pink-cheeked beardless Santa of a man who had a reputation for avoiding trouble wherever it might arise.

"I think you owe Mr. Ferraro an apology," said the dean, with a friendly smile.

Jamie said nothing. Ferraro said nothing.

"Your blue book *is* university property, you know. Technically speaking, you had no right to take it."

Jamie's throat felt tight and dry. "I had a right to see what's in it. I had a right to discuss it with my teacher."

Nodding, the dean said, "That's why we're here. To discuss the contents of your test. Mr. Ferraro, can you explain where this young man went wrong in his ideas about Othello?"

Slowly it dawned on Jamie that the dean had no intention of dealing with his "theft." Ferraro mumbled through a series of excuses about Jamie's test; the gist of it was that Jamie had no appreciation for the work of Shakespeare.

After several minutes Ferraro ran out of words. The dean nodded again and put his smile back on. Folding his hands on his desktop, he said, "I think we have a failure of communications here. Let me propose a compromise. Mr. Waterman can get credit for finishing the course without attending the remainder of the classes. Will that make you both happy?"

Ferraro glanced at Jamie, then looked away.

"What grade will I get?" Jamie asked.

"I think a gentleman's C will do it," the dean replied.

Jamie shook his head. "That'll pull down my GPA."

The dean's smile turned waxy. "Your grade point average can survive a C, I think."

"Considering your failing mark now," Ferraro said, "you ought to be grateful for a C."

"I'm failing because you didn't read my test."

"That's a lie!"

"Now, now," said the dean soothingly. "Mr. Waterman, if you're unhappy with a C I'll allow you to retake the course next semester. That's as far as I intend to go."

Jamie accepted the C only until the next election of student council members. For the first time in his life he had a cause: his own cavalier treatment by the faculty and administration. He had to open up to his fellow students, learn how to smile and greet them, learn how to listen to them as well as tell them his own story. His "theft" became a campus cause célèbre and easily swept him to a seat on the council. He hated every moment of the campaign, hated the false smiles and fake good cheer, hated shaking hands with people who had ignored him only a few weeks earlier.

But he gritted his teeth and endured it. And won.

Once on the student council, Jamie found that there were much more important problems to deal with than Ferraro. Student housing, the quality of the cafeteria food, student access to computer time—these were real and pressing problems for all. He forgot about Ferraro. Almost. He became the hardest-working member of the council.

In his senior year Jamie was elected president of the student council. When he learned that his most trusted friend was suffering through Ferraro's course and that the midterm would again be on Othello, very quietly Jamie asked his friend to copy out his old Shakespeare blue book and hand it in as his own. The student received a B-plus. Jamie confronted Ferraro in his cramped, book-strewn office with the evidence. No one knew except the assistant professor, Jamie, and his student henchman.

Jamie's old C was upgraded to a B-plus. He graduated with honors. All his friends congratulated him, but Jamie took no pleasure in his victory. The memory still troubled his dreams.

R O M E

The meeting was raucous, almost chaotic. Six dozen of the world's top scientists, representing disciplines in geology, biology, physics, chemistry, and astronomy, were behaving like six dozen unruly children.

Father DiNardo ran a hand over his shaved pate as he tried to close his ears to the din of the arguing voices. Emergency meeting indeed, he thought. This meeting is becoming an emergency in its own right. Not even Brumado himself can keep order in this crowd.

The meeting was taking place in an auditorium graciously offered to the Mars Project by the Italian Institute of Aeronautics. Heavy drapes were drawn across the windows of the big chamber, but DiNardo knew Rome so well that he could practically see through the drapery. The railroad terminal was across the Via Praetoriano, and beyond that monument of nineteenth-century architecture rose the tired old seven hills, with the ancient Forum and Colosseum hinting at the glory that was Rome. The Vatican was all the way on the other side of the huge city, as far away from the Institute of Aeronautics as possible.

DiNardo longed for the quiet of the Vatican. Even with tourists streaming through St. Peter's, it would be quieter and more orderly than this near riot. But then, most of these men and women had interrupted their usual work to hurry to the Eternal City. DiNardo wondered how composed he would be if he had been suddenly called to an urgent meeting and had to spend nine or ten hours on an airplane and then more hours of sweaty rigor getting his baggage through customs.

He groaned inwardly as a florid-faced man, whose lapel badge identified him as a geologist from Canada, tried to outshout an intense young astronomer from Chile who had interrupted him.

Alberto Brumado, standing at the center of the long table that had been placed on the stage at the front of the auditorium, suddenly banged his fist on the table so hard that the six men and women flanking him on either side jumped with shock.

"You will both sit down," Brumado shouted into the microphone before him. "Sit down. Now!"

The room suddenly fell silent. The Chilean astronomer sank down into his chair. The florid geologist glared at him for a moment, then he sat down also.

Brumado ran a hand through his disheveled hair. "Our tempers are overcoming our good sense," he said, in a more normal tone. "We will take a fifteen-minute break. When we return, I suggest that we each try to remember that we are men and women of science, not politicians or street hawkers. I will expect a rational discussion, with the normal rules of order and politeness to be strictly obeyed."

Like sullen, guilty students the scientists filed out of the big auditorium. Leaders of their fields, all of them, DiNardo knew. World-class researchers. There were at least four Nobel Prize–winners in the group, by the priest's informal count. The best of the best.

He headed for the men's room, one flight down. He had to push his way past the crowd at the refreshment table, noting absently which nationalities were lining up for coffee, which for tea. The Americans went mostly for soft drinks, of course. With ice.

Sure enough, Valentin Grechko was already at one of the urinals. The Russian physicist had a reputation for drinking tea constantly and then racing for the toilet. DiNardo pretended to be finished as Grechko turned toward the sinks, zipping the fly of his dark blue trousers.

Grechko smiled with tea-stained teeth when he saw DiNardo. The two men bent over to wash their hands side by side. The priest saw in the mirror above his sink that he should have shaved before coming to this meeting. His jaw and skull were dark with stubble. Then he glanced at Grechko's face.

Director of the Russian Space Research Institute, Grechko was well into his sixties, his sparse hair totally gray. The jacket of his dark suit seemed to hang on him, as if he had recently lost weight. Is he ill? DiNardo wondered. The quizzical little smile that Grechko always wore was still in place; he seemed to be bemused by the world constantly. Yet he had clawed his way to the top of the Russian scientific hierarchy, a member of their academy and head of the institute that directed their space efforts.

As they shouldered their way out of the men's room Grechko asked, "You have recovered fully from your surgery?"

"Oh yes," said DiNardo, unconsciously running a hand across his side. "As long as I am careful with my diet I am in fine condition."

The Russian nodded. DiNardo noticed that their suits were almost the same shade. Except for my collar we might have gotten our outfits at the same place, he thought.

"Meetings like this give me an ulcer," Grechko muttered, getting into the tea line. "Not even Brumado can keep order."

"We have an enormous decision to make, whether to allow another excursion to the Grand Canyon or not. If we do, it will cut short all the other traverses."

"Or eliminate them altogether."

DiNardo asked, "How do you feel about it?"

"I have no strong opinion, scientifically speaking," said the physicist. He lowered his voice to the point where DiNardo had to lean close to hear him over the buzz of the crowd. "But I can tell you that our mission directors have already convinced the politicians to let the American go back to Tithonium."

"Really?"

Grechko nodded, his ever-present smile temporarily replaced by something close to a scowl.

DiNardo mused, "I wonder how the Americans feel about it?"

"There is Brownstein, we can ask him."

Murray Brownstein was taller than the Italian priest and the Russian physicist by several inches, yet his back was so stooped that he looked almost small, slight, in his gray jacket and off-white chino slacks. His face was California tan, his once-golden hair now graying and so thin that he combed it forward to cover as much of his high forehead as possible. Where DiNardo looked like a swarthy overaged wrestler and Grechko resembled a pleasantly puzzled old man, Brownstein had an air of intense dissatisfaction about him, as if the world never quite managed to please him.

He saw Grechko and DiNardo coming toward him and immediately flicked his eyes toward an empty corner down the corridor. Without a word the three men fell into step and walked away from the crowd at the refreshment table: Grechko with a glass of tea in his hand, Brownstein holding a can of diet cola, DiNardo empty-handed.

"What do you think of all this?" Brownstein spoke first as they reached the corner. His voice was low, tight, like a conspirator who was afraid of being overheard.

DiNardo made an Italian gesture. "Brumado has given our colleagues a chance to vent their anger, but now even he is growing short-tempered."

Brownstein said bitterly, "It's all a frigging waste of time. Our government's already made its decision."

"You are not pleased?" asked Grechko.

"I don't like scientific decisions being made in Washington and then rammed down my throat."

DiNardo said, "But perhaps the decision is a good one. After all, the canyon is an extremely interesting environment. If I had been allowed my own way, the teams would have been landed on the canyon floor."

"Much too risky for the first mission," Grechko said flatly.

"I disagreed then, and I disagree now," DiNardo said, without a trace of rancor.

"The science may be okay," Brownstein said. "It's the politics that rankles me. If we allow the politicians to override our decisions . . ."

DiNardo interrupted, "But that is why this meeting was called. So that we scientists could make our decision and then inform the politicians of it."

"Doesn't matter what we decide. That damned Indian is going to Tithonium whether we like it or not."

"You mean Dr. Waterman, not Dr. Patel."

"Yeah, right. Waterman."

"But if the sense of this meeting is opposed to changing the mission plan," Grechko said, "that will force the politicians to reconsider."

"No it won't. The Japs are going along with the new plan."

"They are?"

Brownstein nodded grimly. "Tanaka was in the same plane with me. He happened to be at CalTech when this meeting was called. He told me Tokyo has agreed with Washington to okay the Tithonium diversion."

"Without consulting their own scientists or mission directors?" Grechko seemed shocked.

"It's a done deal," Brownstein said. "All we're doing here is jerking off."

DiNardo raised his eyebrows slightly.

"Unless," Brownstein added, "we decide to make a fight of it."

"No," said the priest.

The two other men stared at him. Brownstein almost snarled, "You're willing to let some ignorant bunch of politicians tell us what to do?"

"In this case, yes."

Brownstein shook his head, more in anger than in sorrow. Grechko asked, "Why?"

"There are at least two very powerful reasons not to oppose this decision."

"Damned if I see even one," Brownstein said. "If we let the politicians win this one, next thing you know they'll be telling us how to tie our fucking shoes!"

"As a geologist," DiNardo said, with hardly a wince at the American's language, "I agree with Waterman. The canyon is the best place to go, considering the limitations of time, equipment, and supplies of this mission."

"And skip the volcanoes entirely?" Grechko asked. His little smile seemed to irritate Brownstein.

"If we are forced to make an either-or choice, I would say, yes, skip the volcanoes altogether. However, I believe we can at least make a preliminary reconnaissance of Pavonis Mons. A few days, at least."

"That's your professional opinion, is it?" Brownstein asked.

"Yes. As a geologist I agree with the politicians."

"You said there were two reasons," Grechko prodded.

"The second reason is political. Actually," the priest said, making himself smile at Brownstein, "a mixture of science and politics."

He hesitated until Brownstein asked impatiently, "Well, what is it?"

"I don't believe it is wise to try to fight the politicians when they have made a decision that is reasonably sound, scientifically."

Before either of the other two could say a word, DiNardo went on, "Besides, the most likely place for our team to find traces of life is in the canyon. I am willing to take the chance that they will find something there. Something that will force the politicians to agree to further missions."

Brownstein started to shake his head, but Grechko mused, "Certainly it would seem that the canyon is a better environment for life than the volcanoes. It's like comparing the jungles of Brazil to the mountains of Tibet, isn't it?"

"The Martian equivalent, yes," DiNardo agreed.

"I still don't like it," Brownstein muttered. "If we give in to the politicians on this one, we're opening a can of worms that'll ruin everything in the long run."

"Then we must not appear to be giving in to the politicians," said DiNardo. "We must convince our colleagues to *insist* on the excursion to Tithonium—while keeping as much of the earlier mission plan as possible."

Brownstein grimaced. "That's a tall order."

"It can be done," DiNardo said quietly. "I am certain that Brumado will be in favor."

Grechko's smile widened perceptibly. "Then *you* can get up on your feet and try to convince the rest of them."

DiNardo smiled back. "Oh no. I will convince Brumado. Then he will convince all the others."

"Spoken like a true Jesuit," said Grechko.

Brownstein snorted, but said nothing.

The crowd was beginning to stream back upstairs. The three men started back to the auditorium.

God grant me the strength to succeed, DiNardo said to himself. Then he thought, And God grant James Waterman good hunting on Mars.

S O L 2 2: AFTERNOON

Ravavishnu Patel stared at the broad, regal cone of Pavonis Mons. The volcano filled the horizon like a reclining Buddha, like a slumbering Shiva, destroyer of worlds—and their restorer.

"It's a shame Toshima is not with us." Abdul al-Naguib's soft voice broke Patel's nearly hypnotic spell.

The two men were leaning over the empty seats in the cockpit of the rover. Jamie and the cosmonaut Mironov were outside, placing geology/meteorology beacons on the rock-strewn ground.

"Toshima?" asked Patel, feeling slightly puzzled.

Naguib smiled. "It would remind him of Fujiyama, don't you think?"

"Oh. Yes, perhaps. Although this volcano is very much larger. And there is no snow at its top. And the slope is quite different."

"Different gravity field," Naguib said, as if that explained everything.

"Yes. Of course."

After a full day's travel, a night's stop out in the open plain, and a morning of jouncing over the roughening terrain, the rover was still more than a hundred kilometers from the base of Pavonis Mons. It was too big to be seen in its entirety close up. Only from this distance could they view the entire structure.

Like the volcanoes that formed the Hawaiian Islands, the giants of the Tharsis region are shield volcanoes, lofty cones surrounded by wide bases of solidified lava. Pavonis Mons was the central of three such volcanoes, and the closest to the explorers' domed base. The two others sat far over the curving horizon. Farther still beyond them was the most massive—and tallest—volcano in the entire solar system: Olympus Mons.

Pavonis Mons is a middleweight in comparison to mighty Mount Olympus. Pavonis's base is scarcely four hundred kilometers across, about the width of Ohio. Its peak is hardly ten miles above the uplifted plain on which the rover sat. At its top is a crater, a caldera, barely wide enough to swallow Delhi or Calcutta.

For all its size, though, its slope looked deceptively gentle. Not like the steep rugged peaks of the Himalayas; Pavonis Mons's flanks rose at a five-degree angle. Patel thought a man might walk to the summit easily, given a few days, and peer down into that yawning caldera. Was it truly dead? Or would he see fumaroles venting steam or wisps of other gases, preparing for the next eruption? The sky looked clear, cloudless. But what would he find if he could get to the top?

Patel shook his head, almost in tears, and said to Naguib, "To think that we will have only three days to spend there. Three little days! It would take months merely to make a preliminary survey."

This excursion to Pavonis Mons had been the first casualty of Jamie's insistence on returning to the Grand Canyon. The original mission schedule had called for a week's stay at Pavonis. That had been cut to three days.

Naguib gave him a fatherly pat on the back. "Even three years would not be enough. A man could spend his entire life studying this beast."

"It isn't fair!" Patel burst out, banging a fist on the back of the empty pilot's seat. "The entire reason for my coming to Mars was to study the Tharsis shields and now this . . . this . . . upstart . . ."

"Calm yourself, my friend," said Naguib. "Calm yourself. Accept what cannot be changed."

Patel pulled away and walked down the rover module as far as the airlock hatch. Then he turned back toward the Egyptian. The two men stood silently, facing each other along the narrow length of the module: the slim, liquid-eyed Hindu, his dark face shining as if sheened in sweat; the older, stockier geophysicist, graying at the temples, lines etched at the corners of his eyes and mouth.

"The next thing you will tell me is that this is the will of Allah," said Patel.

"I am an atheist," Naguib replied, smiling gently. "But I realize that our Navaho friend has prevailed with the mission directors, and the Americans have seized control of the mission plan. There is nothing we can do about it."

They heard the clumping of the two other men entering the airlock. Patel's slim hands clenched into fists, and for a moment Naguib thought that he would gladly murder Waterman.

While the three geological scientists were off on their excursion, the three biological scientists spent their spare time planning the coming trip to Tithonium Chasma.

They sat at the galley table, strewn with maps and photographs taken from the orbiting spacecraft. They had all watched Jamie's videotapes until they knew them by heart.

"Is it possible to believe that the formation could be a building of some kind?" Monique Bonnet asked.

Tony Reed, who had joined the three women when he saw them bringing their photos and papers to the galley, dismissed the idea. "It's projection on Jamie's part, a well-known psychological phenomenon," he said. "We see what we want to see. We hear what we want to hear. That's how palm readers make their money, telling their customers what they want to hear, no matter how outrageous it is. Something in Jamie's subconscious wanted to see cliff dwellings and, *voilà!* he saw them."

Ilona leaned back in her chair, reminding Reed of a tawny jaguar stretching on a tree branch.

"The formation truly exists. It is not imaginary. We will see for ourselves whether it is natural or artificial once we get there," she said, her husky voice sounding almost bored with the subject. "For now, we must decide which of us goes on the excursion with Jamie."

Joanna nodded agreement and turned to Monique.

"You go," said the French geochemist. "The two of you. I will remain here and tend the plants."

Ilona frowned at her.

"You don't want to go?" Joanna asked.

Monique made a gallic shrug. "You want to much more than I do. It makes more sense for our biologist and biochemist to go."

"But you are a part of our biology team, too," said Ilona, straightening up in her chair. "We will need your expertise to test the soil at the bottom of the canyon."

"You can bring samples back here to me."

"But what about fossils?" Joanna asked, looking worried. "You have the most training in paleontology. We might miss something."

Monique laughed lightly. "If there are any bones or skulls out there I'm sure you can find them as easily as I."

"Microfossils?" Reed asked.

She turned her dimpled smiling face to the Englishman. "Tony, I have scanned every soil sample that we have taken. I have cracked rocks open and put microtome-thin slices under the microscope. There are no fossils. No microbes, living or long dead."

Reed fingered his slim moustache. "Well . . ."

"But, Monique," said Joanna, "suppose we come across fossils at the bottom of the canyon but we don't recognize them as such? Organisms native to Mars. How would we know that we are looking at fossils?"

"How would I know?" Monique shot back. "How would any of us?"

Joanna cast an uneasy glance at her colleagues around the table.

Reed broke into a wide grin. "A classic problem, isn't it? How do you recognize something that you've never seen before?"

The three women had no answer.

Jamie could feel the hostility building within the cramped confines of the rover with every kilometer they covered on their way to Pavonis Mons.

Dinner that evening was virtually silent. Even Mironov, whose normal expression was a pleasant smile, had nothing to say, no jokes to offer. Patel, perched like a nervous bird on the edge of the bench across the narrow table from Jamie, would not look at him.

Naguib tried to ease the tension.

"Tomorrow we reach the fracture zone, at last," he said, mopping up the last bits of his meal with a thin piece of pita bread.

Feeling grateful, Jamie answered the older man, "Right. And we begin to get some absolute dates for the age of the lava flows."

Patel put his fork down. "We have three little days to do the work that was originally scheduled for a full week."

"I'm willing to work double shifts for those three days, Rava," said Jamie. "I know you . . ."

"You know nothing!" the Hindu snapped. "Nothing except your mad desire to go to the canyon again and make yourself the hero of this expedition."

"Hero?"

"Do you know how many years I have spent studying the Tharsis volcanoes? Not three. Not five. Not ten." Patel was trembling with rage. "Fifteen years! Since I was an undergraduate in Delhi! For fifteen years I have pored over photographs of those shields, studied the remote measurements made by spacecraft. And now that I am finally here, you have cut down my time to three miserable days."

Jamie felt no anger. He knew exactly what Patel was going through. He remembered how he had felt when Vosnesensky cut short his examination of the canyon and the cliff dwellings because of Konoye's death.

"You're right, Rava," he said slowly, his voice deep and calm and implacable. "Only three days. I'll do everything I can to help you learn as much as possible during our stay at Pavonis. But after three days we go back."

"So you can ride out to the canyon."

"Yes."

"And look for your absurd cliff dwellings."

"Look for life."

"Bah! Nonsense! Absolute nonsense."

"Rava, if I truly had my way we would stay here on Mars for a year or more. We would have new teams arriving. We would be exploring this planet on a rational scientific basis. But I don't have my way. None of us does."

"You have more of your way than I have of mine," Patel grumbled.

Jamie acknowledged the point with a dip of his head. "Yes, that's so. But if you want to come back to Mars someday and spend as much time as you like studying these volcanoes, then we've got to bring the politicians something that they can't ignore. They can't ignore evidence of life, Rava. And the most likely place to find life—even evidence of extinct life—is at the bottom of Tithonium Chasma."

"There are other places," Naguib said, "equally likely. Hellas, for example . . ."

"We can't reach that far on this mission," said Jamie. "It's halfway around the planet. The canyon is as far as we can get this time, and even that's stretching things."

"You can be perfectly rational, can't you, when you are getting what you want," Patel said.

"I'm not going to argue with you, Rava," Jamie replied. "I understand how you feel. I'd feel the same way if our positions were reversed."

"Yes, of course."

Jamie slid out from behind the narrow table and stood at his full height. Looking down at Patel he said, "If my jaunt out to the canyon had been scrubbed in favor of extending your stay at the volcanoes, I'd be sore as hell. But I'd accept it and try to do my best to make your excursion a success."

Patel turned away from him.

Mironov, his usual smile long disappeared, said quietly, "I suggest that we drop this topic of conversation. The mission plan is firm. We spend the next three days at Pavonis Mons and then return to the base. No further arguments."

Jamie nodded and headed up toward the cockpit. Naguib made a small shrug of acceptance. Patel grimaced and stared after Jamie, his dark eyes burning.

When Tony Reed tried to sleep he heard the night wind of Mars moaning outside the dome. The noise unsettled him. One little meteor hit, a bit of dust so small that they could find no trace of it afterward, had almost killed them all. Oh, it's very well for Vosnesensky and the others to boast that all the safety systems worked and we were never in actual danger. My left foot! We could have all been asphyxiated. No, we wouldn't have lasted that long. The blood and fluids in our bodies would have boiled. We would have popped like overcooked sausages, exploded like pricked balloons.

He shuddered beneath his light blanket.

I'm not a coward. Tony almost said it aloud. He pictured his father standing over his cot, glowering at him. I'm not a coward. It isn't cowardly to fear real danger. We're constantly on the edge of death here. Each breath we draw might be our last.

He squeezed his eyes shut and tried to force himself to sleep. Unbidden, the memory of his mother came to him: all the times she let him crawl into bed with her when a clap of thunder or some other noise had frightened him.

He wished his mother were here to comfort him now. Ilona had refused to come to his bed once they had landed on Mars. If he suggested it to Monique she would smile and pat his cheek and walk away, laughing softly to herself. He was certain of that.

Joanna. If only Joanna would come to him, comfort him. He needed her warmth here on this world of cold and danger. He longed to feel her arms enfold him in safety.

D O S S I E R:
ANTONY NORVILLE REED

Tony Reed was barely four years old, lying in a hospital bed feeling very small and very frightened. His father bustled in, bundled in a heavy dark overcoat and a muffler striped gray and red, his nose and cheeks pinkly glowing from the winter's cold that frosted the hospital windows.

"And how are you, my little man?" his father asked, sitting on the edge of the bed.

Tony could not speak. He was in no pain, but his entire throat felt frozen, numb. His father was a big man, physically imposing, with a loud insistent voice and a constant air of urgency about him. His father frightened him more than a little. The two of them had never been close. Tony, an only child, was never allowed to have dinner with his parents when his father was at home. Only when his father was gone could he sit at the big dining room table with his mama.

"They tell me you were crying all night," his father said sternly.

Tony could not answer, but tears sprang up in his eyes. They had left him alone in the strange hospital room, without Mama, without even his nanny.

"Now listen to me, Antony," said his father. "These people here in the hospital are my colleagues. They look up to me and respect me. It wouldn't do for them to think that my son is a coward, now would it?"

Slowly, reluctantly, Tony shook his head.

"So we'll have no more of this crying, eh? Chin up. Brave lad. Do what you're told and don't give the sisters any difficulty. Right?"

Tony nodded.

"Good! That's the spirit. Now look what I've brought you." His father pulled a small packet from his overcoat pocket. It was wrapped in bright gold paper.

"Open it up, go on."

Tony pulled at the paper ineffectually. His father's smile withered into an exasperated frown; he took the packet into his big, deft-fingered hands and swiftly removed the wrapping. Then he opened the slim box and showed Tony what was inside it.

A hand-sized telly! Tony goggled at it. Lifting it from the little box, he turned it over in his trembling fingers until he found the postage-stamp screen and the red power button. He pressed the button and the screen came to life instantly.

His father showed him how to pull the earphone from its all-but-invisible socket. Tony wormed it into his left ear.

The picture on the screen was of the red planet, Mars. The voice he heard was that of a young Brazilian scientist named Alberto Brumado, who was saying in a softly beguiling Latin accent, "Someday human explorers will travel to Mars to unravel the mysteries of its red sands . . ."

His father tousled his hair roughly and then left Tony watching the tiny pictures of Mars.

Tony's parents lived entirely separate lives under the single roof of their Chelsea home. As he grew up, Tony began to understand that his father kept a series of mistresses elsewhere in London. He changed them every year or so, like buying a new outfit of clothes for the spring. But he was never without a mistress for long.

His father paid Tony almost no attention whatever; the big gruff man always seemed preoccupied, busy, on his way out of the house somewhere. And when he did notice his son it was:

"Tennis? That's a damned silly game. When I was your age I was all for football. Now there's fun!"

No matter that Tony was slim and lithe where his father was bulky and powerful.

"Tennis," the old man fumed. "Game for foreigners and effeminates."

It was easy to get his graying mother's attention. She was a sweet, porcelain-white woman with the grace and beauty of a china doll. She looked frail, long-suffering, but Tony knew she could protect him from his cold yet demanding father. Everyone who met her loved her, and Tony loved her most of all. All he had to do to get her attention was to pretend to be ill. A cough or a sneeze would bring her fluttering to him. Before he was nine Tony learned how to fake a fever by holding the thermometer under the hot water tap. As he grew up he began to suspect that his mother knew all his little tricks, and forgave him unconditionally. He was the man of the house most of the time. He had his mother all to himself except when his father was home.

Tony had been secretly frightened at the thought of going away to university, but he quickly found that campus life was unalloyed joy. It was ludicrously easy to become the center of everyone's attention, the undisputed leader of his set. The other students seemed mostly dull, fit only to be the brunt of his practical jokes or the victims of his cruel wit. The more he humiliated them, the more they kowtowed to him, seeking his favor, turning themselves into lackeys to escape his annoyance.

It was something of a surprise to Tony that women fell for him so easily. They mistook his disguise of self-assurance and his utter self-interest for sophistication. Tony delighted in this reaffirmation that women could be manipulated more easily than men.

The only one in his class who did not bow to him was a stubborn, stolid son of a Manchester factory worker who ignored the campus's social life and stuck to his books with the single-minded intensity of desperation. He seemed as unimaginative and cautious as a peasant, yet he never fell for any of Tony's little schemes. He always detected the bucket of water balanced atop the half-opened door. He never fell for the compliant young ladies that Tony sent to tempt him. When he found his bed soaked in beer he patiently, uncomplainingly turned over the mattress and changed the linen and showed up in class the next morning as if nothing had happened.

Tony graduated second in his class. The peasant somehow took first honors. He infuriated Tony. Yet they had never exchanged more words than the common civilities in all the four years of college. Tony never saw him again after graduation, and he was glad of it.

"Travel to India?" His father was nearly apoplectic. "You're going to medical school, young man! You've been accepted at my old college and, by damn, that's where you are going and nowhere else!"

"But I don't think I'm ready yet . . ."

"Bah! I know you, you schemer. You're terrified that you might actually have to knuckle down and study. Frightened of hard work, that's what you are. Do you good, a bit of hard work. It's medical school for you, my boy. I won't listen to another word."

Thus Tony went to medical school. His father had been right; he was filled with trepidation. Once there, however, Tony found it was even more of a lark than the university. There were crib books and test cassettes for sale almost openly. Yet after the first few months Tony found himself becoming genuinely fascinated with the study of the human body. To his utter surprise he found that he enjoyed learning. He actually began to work hard at his studies. He wanted to excel.

And there was always Mars—hovering in the background of his thoughts, hanging just over the horizon of his existence. He would forget about it for long months, for years even, and then suddenly a news broadcast would show another rocket lifting off in a roar of flame and steam to carry a robot landing vehicle to the red planet. Or a guest lecturer would speak on the problems of medicine in the microgravity environment of a space station and mention in passing the similar problems to be encountered on a mission to Mars. Or Alberto Brumado, gray now but still sparkling with youthful zeal, would host a telly special about the origin of life on Earth and ask wistfully if it were possible that life had arisen on Mars too.

His father was shocked and angered when Tony refused to step into the family practice.

Red-faced, portly with years and too much living, sputtering with rage, his father roared, "I've spent my entire life building up this practice! You *must* carry it on!"

Tony smiled coolly, trying to hide the terror that his father's wrath always stirred inside him. "Father, there's nothing for it. I am not going to follow in your sacred footsteps."

"What's the matter with you?" his father roared. "Afraid of a little blood? Is that it? Surgery scares the liver out of you, eh? Damned sniveling coward!"

Tony stood his ground.

"By god, at your age I was sewing up wounded men on a hospital ship in the middle of the South Atlantic winter storms."

"You've told us of your glorious exploits in the Falklands War many times, Father."

"You're a coward! A damned trembling, shaking little coward!" The old man turned on his wife. "You've raised a coward for a son."

Tony felt his blood turn to flame. "Don't bully her!"

His father stared at him for a long moment, then with an exasperated grunt he stormed out of the room. Tony turned to his mother, sitting silently, patiently. They heard the front door open and then slam shut.

"You don't think I'm a coward, do you?" Tony asked his mama.

"Of course not, dear."

Two days later Tony applied for a post in the British government's space program. Within a fortnight he received notification that he had been tentatively accepted; he was to report to the training center for tests and evaluation. His father was not home when the letter came; there was no one in the house except Tony and his mother.

"They need physicians," he told her, still aching with wounded pride. "I may very well be selected for the Mars training team if Britain joins the program."

He had expected that she would be horrified, break into tears, beg him to reconsider. Instead his mother smiled and kissed him on the forehead and told him that whatever he wanted to do was what he should do.

In the end Tony was accepted by the Mars Project, a stranger bought the lucrative practice when his father retired, and his mother dragged the old man off to Nassau where he suffered an incapacitating stroke their first year in the sun, leaving him helpless and totally dependent on the loving care of his long-neglected wife.

Tony loved being part of the Mars Project. Most of the other trainees were either astronauts or scientists, dullard technicians or researchers so narrowly specialized that they knew practically nothing of the larger world of the arts and society. Tony enjoyed himself immensely, the sophisticated center of attraction and interest at all times. While others worried themselves into near hysteria over the selection process, Tony never doubted that he would be picked to go to Mars. If he feared the thought of riding millions of miles through space to an empty, harshly inhospitable world, he kept such apprehensions to himself. Only in his dreams did such terrors confront him, and then it was always in the shape of his father looming over him like a horrible devouring ogre, while his mother wept helplessly.

During his waking hours Tony made only one move that he would consider a mistake. He helped Joanna to get rid of Hoffman and bring the Navaho along with them to Mars. A blunder, Tony considered it in retrospect. The Navaho has become the center of everyone's attention. Even Joanna's. Especially Joanna's.

S O L 2 4: NOON

Aleksander Mironov hummed softly as he checked Jamie's backpack. The rover's airlock was crowded with just the two of them in it: Mironov in his fire-engine red hard suit, Jamie in his sky-blue, with a gray spare helmet to replace his meteorite-gouged original.

Mironov's visor was up, and Jamie could see that the Russian was smiling as he clomped back into his view. Mironov's face looked chunky, almost compressed in his helmet, as if stuffed into a container a half size too small. It was a broad-cheeked, snub-nosed face, slightly ruddy, sprinkled lightly with freckles, with pale blue eyes and eyebrows so fair they were barely visible.

"Gloves?" Mironov asked.

"Right here on my belt, Alex." Jamie tugged them on. Of all the equipment on the mission, the gloves were the most advanced piece of technology. Thin enough to be easily flexible and give the wearer a good feel for whatever he grasped, yet tough enough to protect the hands against the near vacuum of the Martian atmosphere.

"Visor down," Mironov said. Only after they had both sealed their helmets did he turn to the pumps and start them chugging.

"You look tired," the cosmonaut said over the suit-to-suit radio.

Surprised, Jamie said to the gold-tinted visor, "I feel okay."

"You were outside four hours yesterday, then you stayed up very late last night. You were outside all morning, and now you go again."

The pumps stopped. The indicator light turned red. Mironov pushed the hatch open.

"We've only got three days here," Jamie replied as they stepped through the hatch and down the short ladder to the rough, blackened ground. "We've got to make the most of them."

"Patel makes you feel guilty."

Jamie forgot himself and tried to shrug inside the suit. All he got for his effort was a fresh irritation under his armpit, where the suit chafed him.

"You must not drive yourself so hard," Mironov went on. "When you are tired you make mistakes. Mistakes can kill a man."

"I'll be all right. The others are pushing just as hard," Jamie said.

"I gave them the same lecture," said the Russian. His voice sounded more disappointed than distressed.

"And?" Jamie asked.

Mironov pointed a gloved finger toward the butter yellow and dark green figures of Patel and Naguib. "They ignored me just as you are ignoring me."

Patel and Naguib were already chipping samples of the dark basaltic rock that spread as far as the eye could see. Old lava flow, Jamie knew. Pavonis Mons had erupted over and over again, red-hot magma flowing in all directions. How long ago? The samples they were taking would give them the answer. They had decided to spend these three precious days at the base of the volcano's shield, collecting as many samples from as many different locations as possible. They would start to analyze them on the trek back to the base, they had agreed.

Yet none of the three scientists could resist testing the samples they had collected. Last night they had stayed up for hours, while Mironov reminded them of the mission schedule like an ineffectual camp counselor. They ran a dozen samples through the portable GC/MS in the rover's lab module.

The mass spectrometer told them that their samples were iron-rich basalts, no more than five hundred million years old, based on their ratio of potassium to argon.

"But the argon might have outgassed," Jamie warned. "Some of it may have escaped into the atmosphere."

"Much of it may be missing," Naguib agreed.

"Which means that the samples could be much older," said Jamie.

Patel, still refusing to meet Jamie's eyes, said to the Egyptian, "We will run more definitive tests back at the base, where we can irradiate the samples in the power reactor."

Naguib nodded and said, "Yes. If the remote handling system is working. It was down . . ."

"Pete said he'd have it running by the time we got back," Jamie said.

"Astronaut Connors!" Patel almost snorted. "He spends all his time flying the RPV instead of attending to maintenance."

"Pete will have the remote handlers working by the time we get back," Jamie insisted.

Finally they folded down their bunks for sleep: Patel and Naguib on the uppers, Mironov and Jamie below. Jamie fell asleep quickly, only to be awakened by a whining, almost sobbing sound from above. One of them's having a nightmare, he realized. He turned his face toward the curving wall of the rover and went back to sleep. His last conscious thought was that the metal skin of the vehicle felt cold; the freezing night of Mars waited outside, less than an inch away.

Over breakfast they had agreed that their best strategy was to work along the line of fissures and sinkholes that ran up one side of the volcano's massive base. They would go as far as they could up the gentle slope of the shield, with Mironov driving the rover behind them so they would not exceed the safe walk-back distance specified in the mission regulations.

All three of these volcanoes sit astride this big fault line, Jamie said to himself as he laboriously chipped away at the tough black basalt. Looking back toward the rover, he saw Mironov planting another beacon into the ground. It was not easy work; this was real rock, not the compacted sands they had found around their domed base. The thin layer of reddish dust that covered the rock was easily scuffed away. Jamie wondered why the wind did not remove it entirely.

Inside his hard suit Jamie could not feel any wind, and there were no clouds in the salmon sky to show air movements. Yet the meteorology instruments on their beacons showed a fairly steady breeze of more than forty miles per hour running up the long gradual slope toward the volcano's distant summit. At night the wind direction reversed to downslope and slowed to little more than twenty miles per hour.

Forty miles per hour would be a stiff gale on Earth, Jamie knew. But in the thin air of Mars there was no strength in the wind, not even enough to scour the last layer of sand off the rocks.

Jamie put his hands on his knees and let the suit's fans cool him down for a while. His visor was starting to fog over from his exertion. He waited, scanning the barren rocky waste that stretched all around him. Dead rock, as rough and bare as the worst badlands he had ever seen in New Mexico. Blasted and pitted by meteor craters, some as big as a football field, most nothing more than the dent a hammer might make on the hood of a car. There were cracks in the solidified lava, vents and fissures that twisted from one crater pit to another. The ground rose almost imperceptibly toward the volcano's high caldera, so far away that it was well over the horizon.

Strangely, not so many rocks were scattered around. The molten basalt must have pushed them downslope. Jamie pictured the black rocky field on which he stood as it must once have been: a broad surging stream of red-hot lava spewing from those vents to flow sluggishly down toward the plain, melting or bulldozing the rocks in its path.

Heat must be coming up from the interior along this fault line, Jamie reasoned. Molten magma flowing time and time again, building these big cones, spilling out to form the shields. Then what about Olympus Mons, some fifteen hundred kilometers to the northwest? It's not sitting on a fault, not that we can see. But it's probably younger than these three beauties. Could there be a hot spot down below that built Pavonis and its two companions, then migrated northwest to build Olympus?

Jamie realized his back ached from stooping awkwardly in the cumbersome suit. He straightened up, wondering, Does Mars have plate tectonics, like Earth? Wouldn't think so, the planet's so small that its core can't possibly have enough heat energy to move whole continents of mantle rock. But there was enough heat energy to build these volcanoes. Where did it come from? Is it still flowing?

He looked upslope, his eye following the rugged, dark landscape as it climbed into the pink sky. When's the last time you burped, Pavonis, my friend? Have you gone completely cold, or will you spread lava across this ground again one day?

Suddenly a flicker of motion in the corner of his eye startled him. It was gone by the time he turned his face toward it. A shadow flitting across the ground? Like a bird flying overhead . . . ?

Jamie looked upward and saw the silvery speck of the soarplane glinting in the sunlight high above. His heart was pounding from the sudden rush of adrenaline. It made him feel foolish. No Martian hawks circling up there; just Pete Connors trying to photo-map Pavonis's caldera. Hope it makes Patel happy.

"Voice check." Mironov's boyish tenor in his earphones startled Jamie. He looked around and saw that his shadow stretched long across the ground. The sun was getting close to the horizon.

"Patel here."

The rover was parked a hundred meters or so down the slope, between a meteor crater twice its size and a zigzag fissure that might once have been a lava vent. You were right, Rava, Jamie said silently. These volcanoes have so much to tell us, and we won't be here long enough to even begin to understand their story.

"Waterman okay," Jamie said. The voice checks were standard safety procedure when the scientists were out of visual range of the astronaut or cosmonaut in charge of the team. In this rough ground, Mironov could not possibly keep all three of his wandering team-mates in sight.

There was a long silence.

"Naguib?" Mironov's voice sounded sharp in Jamie's earphones. "Dr. al-Naguib, voice check please."

No answer.

"Dr. al-Naguib?"

"He was over by the fissure there." Patel pointed further upslope. "Perhaps the terrain is blocking his radio transmission."

Jamie heard low guttural muttering, Mironov cursing in Russian. Following the outstretched arm of Patel's yellow suit, Jamie called into his helmet microphone, "Let's take a look, Rava. Maybe he's in trouble."

"No, I do not believe so . . ."

"Stay where you are. It's my responsibility to find him," Mironov shouted. "I don't want two of you missing."

But Jamie was already striding upslope as fast as he could in the hard suit. The slope was easy and his boots gave him good traction, but the rough ground was treacherous.

"Rava," he called, "where did you see him last?"

The butter-yellow suit had not moved. "To your right," Patel's voice replied. "Perhaps twenty or thirty meters farther up."

Jamie worked his way around a conical pit, a meteor strike that looked shining new compared to the more weathered craters dotting the ground. He saw a fissure snaking across the black rock, wide enough for a man to fall into. How deep?

Very, he saw, as he bent awkwardly to peer into it. Black and deep as hell. He turned on his helmet lamp, but the beam shone only feebly into the steep crevasse.

"Dr. Naguib?" he called.

Still no reply. If he's stuck inside this fissure he ought to be able to hear my radio signal, Jamie said to himself. If he's conscious. If he's alive.

"Wait where you are!" Mironov called. "I am coming. I have the directional finder."

Jamie had to turn completely around to see the Russian bounding toward him in his fire-engine suit, a black box the size of a personal television set in one gloved hand. Patel was still frozen where he stood; his only motion had been to let his arm relax down.

A lot of good the directional finder will do, Jamie thought. If Naguib can't hear us and we can't hear him, there's no radio signal for the directional finder to zero in on.

"He must be on the other side of this crevasse," Jamie called to Mironov, unconsciously raising his voice, as if he had to shout to cover the distance between them.

Before Mironov could reply, Jamie took a few steps backward, then ran up and jumped across the fissure. In the low gravity it was easy, even with the cumbersome suit weighing him down.

"Wait!" Mironov bellowed. "I *order* you to wait!"

Jamie took a few more steps forward, swiveling his gaze back and forth as much as the helmet would allow. He's up here somewhere. Got to be. Out of our line of sight. Out of radio contact. That means . . .

The uneven ground seemed to stop suddenly off to the left, as if it dropped away steeply. Jamie headed that way while Mironov's puffing breath panted in his earphones.

"This way, I think," Jamie called, heading for the break. It was a ravine, he saw. Pretty steep.

And there Naguib lay, crumpled facedown at the bottom of a ten-meter drop. The ravine was roughly twenty meters across, a ragged irregular trench carved into the solid basalt. Naguib's deep-green hard suit sprawled at its bottom like a broken, discarded toy, legs spraddled, unmoving.

"He's here!" Jamie shouted, turning enough to see Mironov sailing across the crevasse. "Come on. We'll need a rope, a line."

Gingerly, Jamie started down the steep side of the crevasse. It was all in shadow, with the sun dropping toward the horizon, but there was still enough light to see rough places to clutch and precarious footholds.

"Go back to the rover and get the climbing winch," he heard Mironov call to Patel. The radio voice was noticeably dimmed once Jamie's helmet dropped below the rim of the ravine.

It seemed to take an hour to work his way down to the Egyptian. It was dark down at the bottom; he needed his helmet lamp to see the final few meters.

In his earphones, though, he heard Naguib breathing raggedly. He's alive. His suit hasn't ruptured.

Finally he reached the geophysicist's side. The backpack was badly dented. In the light of Jamie's helmet lamp it was difficult to see how serious the damage might be.

"Is he alive?" Mironov's voice was so loud it made Jamie wince.

"Yes. We'll need a line to haul him up."

"On the way."

Slowly, tenderly, Jamie turned Naguib onto his back. Damned helmet's banged up too, he saw. He peered into the visor, wiped at the red sand that had smudged it. Naguib's eyes were fluttering. His face seemed covered with blood. He coughed.

Jamie checked the backpack monitoring gauges on Naguib's wrist. Christ, he's out of air! He must be breathing his own fumes in there.

Quickly, with the automatic reactions bred by long hours of training, Jamie reached to the side of his own backpack and yanked out the emergency air hose. He looked at the telltales on his own wrist. Not much to spare; we've all been out so damned long the regenerator filters are just about tapped out.

Plugging the free end of the hose into the emergency port in Naguib's metal ring collar, he thumbed the release and let air flow from his own tank into Naguib's battered helmet.

The Egyptian took in a deep, sighing breath, his whole body arching slightly. Then he coughed.

"Easy," Jamie said. "Easy. Take it easy and everything will be all right."

Coughing like a man who had been underwater too long, Naguib managed to ask weakly, "Waterman? You?"

"Yes. Alex and Rava are rigging the winch. We'll have you out of here in a few minutes."

"I . . . slipped. Going down . . . the rock gave way and I started to fall."

"Can you sit up?"

"I think so."

Gently Jamie helped him up to a sitting position. With the hard suit it was like bending a length of stiff plastic pipe.

"How do you feel?" Jamie could not hear Mironov or Patel; he guessed that they had switched to another radio frequency.

"I think my nose is broken. I can't breathe through it."

"Ribs? Arms, legs?"

Naguib was silent a moment, then, "Everything else seems to be in order. I think I can stand now."

"Not yet. Just relax." Looking up, Jamie saw that the sliver of sky above the ravine was still bright. There was still some daylight up there, although night could enfold them in a matter of minutes, he knew.

Don't want to be out here with an injured man in the dark, he told himself, tapping on the control keys of his radio unit. His earphones erupted with Mironov's snarling, growling Russian as he struggled to get the winch in place.

"Alex," he called. The cosmonaut's voice cut off immediately, although Jamie heard him panting in his earphones. "Dr. Naguib seems to be okay, except that he might have broken his nose in the fall he took. His regenerator is ruptured, though. I'm sharing air with him."

Silence. Then Patel's voice, high-pitched, frightened. "We do not have very much air left in any of our regenerators. We have been out all afternoon."

"We can make do," Mironov said. "We will all share, once we get the two of you back up here."

The winch cable came snaking down with the climbing harness hanging like an empty vest. Jamie slung it around Naguib's shoulders and began cinching up the straps.

The Egyptian said, "My scintillation meter . . . it began flashing . . . there may be a vein of uranium exposed by this ravine."

"Is that why you climbed down here?" Jamie asked as he tightened the harness straps.

"I started down . . . then I fell. I must have blacked out."

"You'll be okay. Just save your breath. Don't need to talk now. Wait till we're back in the rover."

Slowly the two men at the top of the ravine winched the green-suited geophysicist up to them. Jamie heard Mironov order Patel to share his air with Naguib while the Russian worked the winch back down to the bottom. Jamie quickly slipped the harness on, shouted that he was ready, and let the winch motor pull him up.

Then they started trekking back to the rover, Jamie carrying the winch, Mironov and Patel supporting Naguib. The Russian was sharing air with him now, Jamie saw.

The sun was touching the horizon when they reached the crevasse that they had all jumped across earlier. The sky was already so dark in the east that stars were twinkling.

"We could go around it," Patel suggested, sounding as if he wanted to be contradicted.

"It would take too long," said Mironov. "The fissure is many kilometers in length. We must jump across."

"I'm not sure that I can," said Naguib.

"We will hold your arms," Mironov answered, "and all three of us will jump together. In this gravity it will not be difficult."

"I don't know if I can," Naguib repeated. "My legs . . ."

Jamie saw that Patel had released Naguib's arm and was stepping slowly, almost furtively, toward the edge of the crevasse. Mironov was sharing his air with the injured man. Jamie dropped the winch and came up on the Egyptian's other side. He took Naguib's free arm and lifted it across his own shoulders.

Softly he said, "You got us into this situation; you'll have to help us get out of it."

Patel began to object, but he heard Naguib chuckle deep in his throat. "True. Too true, James. I will do my best."

Jamie smiled inside his helmet. "Good. It shouldn't be any trouble. Come on, Alex, let's back up a bit and get a running start."

Patel leaped across first, without a word. Then Jamie and Mironov tried to carry Naguib across the fissure. Their first attempt was nearly a disaster. Naguib's strides did not match theirs, and the three of them nearly fell down trying to put on the brakes before they reached the edge. Jamie heard Mironov whispering curses to himself and the frightened panting of Naguib. The Russian's air hose popped out of Naguib's collar, so Jamie plugged his own in.

Vaguely Jamie recalled a myth about birds helping a Navaho hero to cross some impassable gulf. Or did he walk along a rainbow? We could use some help now, he said to himself.

Precious little daylight remained. The cold of night was seeping into Jamie, and he knew that Naguib must be even stiffer, colder.

They backed off again, with Mironov telling them to start on the left foot and keep pace. "I will count cadence," he said.

"Ahdyeen . . . dvah . . . tree . . . chyeetireh," Mironov counted off. "Ahdyeen . . . dvah . . ."

The three of them soared over the crevasse like a trio of armor-plated hippos and landed in a scuffing, skidding cloud of red dust on the other side. They managed to stay on their feet, just barely.

"Better than the Bolshoi Ballet!" Mironov beamed as they headed toward the rover, still propping up Naguib on either side.

"Too bad we didn't get it on tape," Jamie joked.

Naguib said nothing. Patel was up ahead, his helmet lamp on, a pool of light thrown against the dark ground as he headed for the safety of the rover.

Once through the airlock they sat Naguib down on one of the benches and helped him out of his hard suit, then Jamie cleaned up the Egyptian's bloodied face while Patel vacuumed the suits and Mironov went up to the cockpit to report to base.

"I don't think your nose is broken," Jamie said. "It's not even bleeding anymore."

"I banged it on my visor when I fell," Naguib said.

"You could have been killed," said Patel, his big eyes somber.

Naguib smiled weakly. "I was never much good at field work."

Mironov came back, unsmiling, grim faced. "Reed wants to speak with you," he said to the Egyptian. "He will prescribe medication."

Jamie offered to help him to the cockpit, but Naguib got shakily to his own feet. "I can make it," he said. "I think you are right—nothing broken."

Wordlessly Patel went to the galley and pulled out a dinner tray for himself. Mironov scowled after him.

"Nothing to be sore about, Alex," Jamie said to the cosmonaut. "Abdul's okay. Just a bloody nose, that's all."

Mironov snorted and glared at Patel.

Reed confirmed that Naguib's nose was probably not broken, and the four men pulled out the folding table and sat down for dinner.

"We have only two replacement backpacks in the stores," Mironov growled as they ate. "Please be more careful tomorrow."

"I thought there might be a vein of uranium exposed down at the bottom of that fissure," said Naguib, explaining and apologizing at once. "My scintillation meter registered high levels of radiation."

"Uranium?" Patel snatched at the idea. "If we could get a uranium-lead ratio we could date the lava field with great firmness."

Jamie said, "We haven't found any usable levels of radioactives anywhere else."

"*Something* is there, at the bottom of that ravine," said Naguib.

"Then we'll have to go back there tomorrow and get some samples," Jamie said.

Mironov hiked his almost invisible brows. "Go back?"

"With the winch, Alex," said Jamie. "And we can even lay the extensible ladder over the fissure that we had to jump across."

The Russian said nothing, but he looked across the table at Patel.

"Then it's agreed," Jamie concluded. "Rava and I will go back and get samples from the bottom of the ravine."

Abruptly, Mironov slid out from behind the table and strode up to the cockpit. They stared at his retreating back.

Patel blinked several times, then resumed their conversation as if nothing had happened. "A uranium-lead ratio could give us absolute dating for this particular segment of the lava flow . . ."

"Excuse me." Jamie pushed himself across the bench and got to his feet. Patel kept talking to Naguib.

Mironov was sitting in the driver's seat, his fingers flicking across the control board, checking all the rover's systems. Jamie slipped into the seat beside him.

"What's wrong, Alex?"

The Russian took a deep breath. From behind them, they could hear Patel's voice chattering away.

"Your fellow geologist would have let Naguib die out there, if he had his own way."

"What? Rava?"

"I told him to bring the winch. He carried it as far as the fissure, but he refused to jump over. He *threw* the rig across the crevasse and then started back for the rover."

Jamie fell silent, digesting the information. Rava must have panicked, he said to himself. And Alex is pissed as hell at him.

"But he did jump across afterward," Jamie said at last. "He came over and helped us out."

"After I threatened to break every bone in his scrawny body," Mironov grumbled. "His yellow suit is an appropriate color. I even had to force him to share his air with Naguib."

"He must have been pretty damned scared," Jamie said.

"He is not dependable. Not in an emergency. I will not allow you to go out alone with him."

Jamie shrugged. "Then you'll have to come with us, Alex. If there's really a vein of uranium down in that ravine—any radioactives at all—it's crucially important to us."

The Russian made a curt nod. "I will come. Naguib can stay inside and man the radio."

"Okay. Now try to calm down. Patel may have panicked, but being sore isn't going to help."

"Yes. I know. But I would still like to wring his neck."

Jamie tried to laugh. He patted Mironov on the shoulder and said,

"Carrying a grudge can be just as damaging as giving in to panic. Try to see things in perspective, Alex."

The Russian grunted.

Jamie got out of the chair and headed back to the table where Naguib and Patel were still chatting.

"Okay," Jamie said. "Tomorrow morning we go back to the ravine—Rava, Alex, and me."

"What about me?" Naguib asked as Jamie slid behind the opposite side of the narrow table.

"You stay inside and recuperate. You can analyze the samples we took today."

"And who put you in charge?" Patel snapped. "Who elected you the captain of this team?"

Jamie blinked with surprise. "It just seems like the logical way to proceed. Abdul's going to feel pretty stiff and sore tomorrow, I'm sure. That leaves you and me, Rava. And Alex."

Patel's nostrils flared. "Yes. Of course. You and me and our cosmonaut supervisor. And then the next day we return to the dome," he said angrily. "And that will be the end of our three days here."

Jamie leaned back on the bench, staring at Patel across the littered dining table, surprised at himself for expecting appreciation from his fellow geologist. Or even courtesy.

S O L 3 4: MORNING

Jamie awoke from the dream. For long moments he lay as still as death on his cot, gazing up at the plastic curve of the dome just starting to brighten with the new morning. At first he thought he was back in the rover, but then he recalled that they had returned from the excursion to Pavonis Mons a week ago. His sleep had been troubled by a strange, unsettling dream. It had not frightened him, exactly, but it had been disturbing.

He pulled himself up to a sitting position. Imagine dreaming you're back in school. With a shake of his head he reminded himself that he was safe from that. He was on Mars. And this was the day they would start out for the canyon.

The first pink light of dawn began to fill the dome as Jamie scrubbed and shaved, then grabbed a quick breakfast of hot oatmeal, steaming coffee, and the inevitable vitamin supplement capsule— alone in the wardroom until the others began drifting in to begin the day.

He said a few brief good mornings as he made his way toward the storage lockers where the hard suits were kept. The dome felt different now. No longer the same place it had been when they had first landed. It was more than the mere fact that a dozen men and women had been living and working here for thirty-four days. Nearly five weeks ago the dome had been strange, scary, a new and untried womb of plastic and cold metal. Now it was home, safe and warm, the smell of coffee wafting even out to the lockers. Nearly five weeks of working and planning, arguing and joking, eating and sleeping, had given the dome a distinct human aura. The floor was scuffed from their boot treads. Jamie could feel the emotions that drenched the very air. It's not the sterile dome full of equipment it once was. Not anymore. Our spirit fills this place now, he thought.

And today we leave this behind to go out to the canyon. No wonder I had an anxiety dream.

He passed the little greenhouse area where Monique Bonnet knelt beside the plant beds, nurturing them like a loving mother beneath the brightly glowing lamps. Even with the morning sun streaming in through the dome's curved wall they kept the full-spectrum lights on all during the daylight hours. The transparent plastic of the dome stopped most of the infrared in the sunlight and all of the ultraviolet.

"How's the farm?" Jamie asked.

Monique looked up from the big trays, rubbing a red smudge from her cheek. "Quite well. See?" She gestured to the little green shoots poking out of the pink sandy ground. "Before we return to Earth I will be able to make you *la salade verte.*"

"Still feeding them Perrier?"

"Of course. What else?"

Jamie smiled and Monique smiled back. She had taken over the management of the little garden, giving the plants Martian water and motherly care. Ilona and Joanna had left it mostly to her, despite the duties spelled out in the mission plan. Mars must agree with her, Jamie thought. Monique's figure looks trimmer than it did when we first landed.

Does she really look better or am I just horny? Jamie asked himself. He did not feel especially driven. Tony must be lacing our food with sex suppressants, despite what he says. Probably a good thing, he tried to convince himself.

Looking at the wide trays filled with reddish dirt and green shoots, Jamie realized: We could live on Mars indefinitely, if we had to. If we had brought enough seeds, we could have started a regular farm, using Martian water and pulling in oxygen and nitrogen from the air. We could grow enough food to survive in this dome, turn it into a real base. A permanent home.

The next mission. That's what we'll have to do. Bring enough seeds to start a self-sufficient farm. Use the local resources. We can do that. We know it now.

Attitudes among the explorers had changed over their five weeks on Mars. Jamie was still the outsider, the loner, but now it was because he was the tacitly acknowledged leader of the group. He was no longer the afterthought, the last-minute replacement. Most of the work being done by the eleven others was aimed now at making a success of the coming traverse to Tithonium Chasma.

Patel was still surly, angry that his excursion to Pavonis Mons had been cut short. He kept himself busy analyzing the samples they had taken during their brief foray. The dating they got from the uranium-lead samples did not agree with that derived from the potassium-argon measurements. Patel and Naguib were spending all their free time trying to find out why. Vosnesensky, at first dour and morose about the considerable change in schedule, had gradually warmed up to the idea. Over the past two weeks he had become almost jovial. There was a fun-loving man underneath all that responsibility, Jamie realized.

Toshima worked closely with Jamie, squeezing every bit of information they could out of the data that the geology-meteorology beacons were amassing about the canyon region. Connors, Mironov, and Abell took turns flying the RPVs through the canyon, mapping it down to a few centimeters' resolution.

Joanna and Ilona spent their time preparing for the biology experiments they would carry out in the canyon, below those mists, down on the valley floor where there was warmth and the hope of finding life. The two of them would ride the rover vehicle with Jamie and Connors, Monique would remain here at the base. Jamie wondered about having Joanna and Ilona together in the rover. Close quarters. They were friendly enough now, but what kind of problems might arise with both of them cooped up for ten days in the rover?

Jamie had spoken to Ilona about her bitterness toward the Russians. She had responded with a raised eyebrow and a haughty little smile.

"I'm serious, Ilona," he had said. "You've got to stop needling Mikhail. And Alex, too. It's got to stop."

"Is that an order, Captain?" Her eyes smoldered at Jamie.

"I wish I could make it an order," he replied. "I wish I had the power to change your behavior."

"You don't. No one does." Ilona took a small breath, almost a sigh. "Not even I have that power."

And then there was Tony. Something about the English physician worried Jamie. As the weeks had gone by Tony seemed to become— what? How to describe it? Sullen. Withdrawn. Maybe I'm just imagining it, Jamie thought. Tony looked the same: dapper, handsome, elegant even in project-issued coveralls. But he's not acting quite the same as when we first landed. He's quieter, he doesn't talk as much, and when he does the old zing has gone out of him. Something's wrong. Tony's become distant. Cold. Almost hostile.

Has Ilona been riding him again about his not going outside? Then he shook his head. Maybe it's me. Maybe I'm just imagining it. I'm so busy preparing everything for this traverse I just haven't had much time to spend with Tony. Or maybe he doesn't feel well.

"Do you need help?"

Jamie looked up to see Vosnesensky standing before him, a relaxed smile on his face. Mikhail shaved every morning, yet his dark beard was never completely erased.

"Thanks. I think I can manage."

Jamie had put on the tubed thermal undergarment when he had dressed in his own cubicle. Now he was worming his legs into the bottom half of his hard suit.

"Why are you going outside?" Vosnesensky asked, beginning to peel off his own coveralls. They had faded considerably from their original coral red.

"I haven't been out in more than a week," Jamie said. "All this planning for the traverse has turned me into an apparatchik."

"That is the price you must pay for leadership." Vosnesensky was grinning; he obviously meant it as a joke. Down to his briefs, he reached into his locker for his thermal undergarment.

"Well," Jamie half grunted as he tugged on his boots, "this leader is going to take his free hour this morning to just walk around the dome to admire the scenery. And think."

The old morose look came back into Vosnesensky's eyes. "You know that you are not allowed to go outside by yourself."

"Just a walk around the dome, Mikhail."

"It is not allowed."

"I need some time by myself."

"I am still the commander here," the Russian said, fastening the front of his thermal undergarment. He looked like a fireplug wrapped in overcooked spaghetti.

Still sitting on the bench, Jamie smiled up at him. "Yes, I know you're in charge, Mikhail. And you're right, the mission regulations say no one is allowed outside by themselves. Would you be kind enough to come out with me?"

The Russian grinned broadly. "Me? The group commander! You expect a man as busy as I am to drop everything merely to take a walk with you?"

"I would appreciate it if you did."

Leaning his butt against the locker to pull on the stiff metal leggings of his pressure suit, Vosnesensky bantered, "The group commander is much too important a person to go strolling out in the desert on the whim of one of his underlings. Much too important.''

Jamie got to his feet and stepped to the rack where the torso of his sky-blue suit hung empty and slack-armed, like a headless, legless display of armor.

"However," Vosnesensky said, raising a stubby finger in the air, "as one friend to another, I will be happy to go outside with you."

Jamie wriggled into the torso, popped his head up through the neck ring, and grinned back at the Russian. "As one friend to another, thanks."

"But only for the one hour," Vosnesensky said, more seriously. "We all have a busy morning ahead of us."

"Right."

In a few minutes more they were fully sealed into their suits. They checked each other's backpacks, called in to Mironov, who was at the monitoring console for the morning, and entered the airlock.

It was not until they stepped out onto the dusty red ground and Jamie looked up at the pink sky of Mars once again that he remembered that the color of his suit was not the color of the sky here; the nearest blue sky was more than a hundred fifty million kilometers from where he stood.

With Vosnesensky following a few paces behind, Jamie walked slowly around the dome's curving flank, out to the side where he could not see the landing vehicles and the litter of equipment and instruments surrounding them. This was his favorite vista, empty desert as far as the disturbingly close horizon, a wrinkled red line of cliffs out in the distance.

He blinked his eyes once and the view he saw was New Mexico, with scraggly thorn bushes and patches of scrub grass scattered across the sand and rocks. Another blink and it was Mars again, barren and cold.

Were you alive once? Jamie asked the world on which he stood. Will we find the spirits of your dead in the canyon? Are we the first to cross the gulf between us, or did your ancestors reach our world eons ago? Am I returning home?

The softly keening wind gave Jamie no answer. The spirits of Mars, if there were any, kept their secrets to themselves.

Jamie gave a heartfelt sigh. All right, then. I'll have to go out and find you. I'll have to see for myself what the truth is.

Finally he turned and smiled at the fire-engine red suit of Vosnesensky, even though he knew the Russian could not see his face through the tinted visor.

"All right, Mikhail. Let's go back inside."

"That is all you want?"

"You were right. There's a lot to do. We'd better go to work now."

Jamie could sense the Russian trying to shrug inside his hard suit. As they plodded back toward the airlock Jamie tried to remember the details of his dream. Something about school, something that bothered him. He put it down to anxiety and forgot about it.

Tony Reed had dreamed, too.

The English physician had gone straight from his sleeping cubicle to his infirmary, padding along the hard plastic flooring in a pair of woolen socks and nothing else except a frayed terrycloth robe of royal blue with the seal of his father's club sewn on its left breast.

Reed could not recall his dream, merely the fact that he had awakened in a cold sweat, thankful that the visions that had haunted his sleep had winked out like the picture on a television tube the instant his eyes had snapped open. He carefully shut the accordion-fold door of the infirmary and began preparing his morning pick-me-up.

"I love coffee, I love tea," he sang tunelessly to himself in a sub-vocalized whisper. "But I love you best of all."

The perfect morning drink. Enough amphetamine to start the day brightly, but not so much that it's harmful. Or noticeable. A touch of this and a touch of that. Just the thing to start another day on Mars. Blasted Mars. Dangerous Mars. Dull, bleak, dead Mars.

Reed held the small plastic beaker up to the light, made certain that the liquid in it was exactly at the level it should be, then quaffed it down with relish.

There! Now, by the time I finish my morning ablutions my hands will be steady enough for shaving.

He was the last to enter the wardroom that morning. No one remained there except Monique and Ilona.

"All the bees out being busy, I see," Reed said brightly as he headed for the freezer.

"I must go too," Ilona said, dabbing her lips as she got up from the table.

She took her tray to the recycling slot while Reed slid his into the microwave oven.

"Will you miss me?" he asked Ilona, low enough so that Monique could not hear.

Ilona looked almost surprised. "I will see you every day, when we make our medical report."

"That's not quite the same as being together, is it?"

She gave him a haughty smile. "We haven't been together like that since we landed here."

"Yes. A pity, too."

"Do you miss me?"

"Certainly."

"But I thought it was Joanna you were interested in."

Reed looked into her tawny eyes. "Ah, that was merely a pastime. A game."

"A game that you lost."

"The game isn't over yet," Reed said, miffed.

Ilona laughed. "If you can get her to bed with you after she comes back from being with our red man for ten solid days . . ."

Reed cut in, "And what will you be doing for the next ten days? And nights?"

She drew herself up to her full height, almost equal to Reed's. "I intend to be a good scientist and to behave myself properly. A field trip is no place for game playing, Tony."

"No. I suppose not."

"Definitely not."

She walked away, leaving the wardroom, leaving Reed standing there as the microwave beeped that his breakfast was ready and Monique tried to make it clear that she had not been eavesdropping.

They're both leaving me, Reed said to himself as he took his tray to the table. Ilona and Joanna. And the Navaho. They're all leaving me behind.

Monique smiled at him in her dimpling motherly way, then excused herself and left. Reed sat alone, picking listlessly at his food, feeling as abandoned and lonely as the time he had been left in the hospital to have his tonsils removed.

S O L 3 4: AFTERNOON

Pete Connors frowned at the rover's control panel as he said into the pin microphone of his headset, "The blamed fans still won't power up to one hundred percent."

Vosnesensky's face was on the display screen in the center of the panel. "How high will they go?"

"Eighty, eighty-two."

Sitting beside the astronaut, Jamie tried to keep the worried impatience tingling inside him from showing to the others. We can't put off the departure because the air circulation fans won't run up to max. That's no reason to delay the traverse.

Vosnesensky's eyes went down to the checklist in front of him. "Eighty percent is within tolerable limits," he said doubtfully.

"I don't think it's gonna cause any problems, Mike," said Connors. "The fans have always been kind of cranky."

"You can increase the oxygen ratio if necessary," Vosnesensky said.

"Right. Let's go with it. We're ready to roll."

Connors looked deadly serious, determined. Jamie thought that the man had lost weight since they had arrived on Mars. His face looks thinner, almost haggard. I guess we all do.

Ilona was standing behind Jamie's chair, her hands on the seat back. Joanna stood behind Connors, expectant tension drawing her lips into a tight line.

Come on, Jamie urged silently. Let's get this show on the road.

Vosnesensky's face pulled together in a morose little frown. He puffed out a deep breath, more of a snort than a sigh. "Very well," he said at last. "You are cleared to proceed."

Jamie let his own breath out as Connors nodded and replied, "Right. Here we go."

"*Dahsvedahnya*. Good luck."

"Thanks, Mike," Connors said. He licked his lips, then nudged the accelerator pedal. The rover surged forward. Jamie turned off the comm screen before Vosnesensky could change his mind.

"We're off," Ilona murmured.

"Next stop, Tithonium Chasma," said Connors, trying to sound cheerful.

Their excursion plan called for them to go directly to the canyon, stopping only at sundown and starting again at the next sunrise. There were to be no EVAs, no stops along the way to go outside and explore. Their goal was Tithonium Chasma and nothing less. Jamie wanted them to have as much time and as much food and water and other consumables at the canyon as they possibly could.

The impromptu maps that had been stitched together from the photos taken by the remotely piloted airplanes had shown that it might be possible to descend to the canyon floor along the slope of an ancient landslide that had partially filled in one section of the canyon's cliff wall. It would be tricky going at best. Most of the old landslides had slumped down below the canyon rim, leaving a drop too steep for the rover to handle. Some of the avalanches completely filled in the canyon floor and even rode up the southern cliff face.

This one, though, seemed usable, and was within the range of their rover. Not too steep, it extended from the lip of the cliff wall down to the bottom without totally covering the canyon floor. It was narrow, compared to most of the others, barely a kilometer wide. But that would be plenty of room for the rover. If the rubble was firm enough to ride over without getting bogged down. If the slope was gentle enough all the way to the bottom; the aerial photos could not catch all the details of every inch of the slide.

To Jamie it looked like a recent landslide, newer and fresher than the older, bigger ones that had gouged huge alcoves out of the canyon walls. Recent, he knew, meant that it might be only a few million years old.

"Looks like a nice day," Connors joked.

The sky was a delicate salmon pink and as cloudless as always.

Jamie cracked back, "I don't know. Might rain in another hundred thousand years or so."

"Damn! I left the umbrella back in Houston."

Joanna, still standing behind the driver's seat, said quite seriously, "Toshima said there have been an unusual number of dust storms farther north."

"How does he define unusual?" Ilona asked.

"Compared to satellite observations over the past ten years, I suppose."

"No storms this close to the equator, though," Jamie said.

"Not so far," Joanna replied. "But we do not know what causes the storms to start."

"Or stop," said Ilona.

Connors said, "Hell, we don't even know what starts storms on Earth, and the meteorology guys have been studying 'em since Ben Franklin's time."

They stayed precisely on schedule, stopped when the shrunken sun touched the red horizon, and called in their position to Vosnesensky back at the dome. Some of the old strangeness seeped into Jamie's soul as the four of them ate their precooked dinners. We're out in the middle of a frozen desert, surrounded by air we can't breathe at a temperature that can freeze our blood in seconds. How safe and homey the dome seemed now!

They sat on the padded benches that unfolded into bunks, two by two, the men on one side of the narrow table and the women on the other. Jamie took the first turn on the cleanup detail while Connors went back to the cockpit to check all the rover's systems before retiring for the night. The women slid the table into its niche below the bottom right bunk, chatting together, then took turns in the lavatory.

Once all four bunks were unfolded the rover's compartment became impossibly crowded. The two women took the uppers, leaving Jamie and Connors to slide into the lowers like a pair of sewer workers crawling into a tunnel. Jamie could hear Joanna and Ilona whispering together over his head like a pair of schoolgirls. No giggling, though. They seemed totally serious, whatever it was they were confiding to each other.

A sudden thought pulsed through him. Suppose Ilona tells Joanna about making out with me during the transit here! Damn! He did not want Joanna to know that.

Ilona wouldn't do that, he told himself. It doesn't make sense for her to talk about that. Why would she tell Joanna? It'd make a complete mess of our relationships here, cooped up in this aluminum can. She wouldn't do that. Ilona's smart enough to know she shouldn't.

But there's a strange streak in her, he realized. She has a weird sense of humor. Maybe she thinks it'd be funny.

Jamie strained his ears but could hear nothing except the wind sighing outside. The women had gone to sleep. Or at least stopped talking. It took a long time before Jamie fell into a troubled sleep, dreaming of school all over again.

Li Chengdu felt relaxed for the first time since they had taken up orbit around Mars.

We have weathered the political storms, he told himself. We are even doing some good scientific work. Despite the tragedy of Konoye's death, the Americans and Russians have proved that they can actually extract water from the Martian moons. The next expedition will be able to refuel here and replenish most of its consumables. There will be no more need to carry every gram of water and air and rocket propellant for the entire two-way journey. Things will be easier the next time. We will even be able to establish a replenishment depot on Phobos.

He eased back in his comfortable chair and watched Vosnesensky's heavy, dour face in his communications screen as the Russian made his evening report. The man's normal expression is a scowl, Li thought. I don't believe I have ever seen him so much as smile.

Vosnesensky was reporting that everything was proceeding normally. The traverse was going according to schedule; Waterman's team should reach the lip of the canyon before sundown tomorrow. Patel and Naguib were analyzing the lava flow samples that they had brought back from Pavonis Mons. Monique Bonnet was testing other rock samples from Pavonis for evidence of life. She had found some interesting microscopic formations in the samples, but no organisms, not even organic chemicals.

Toshima was fretting about a series of dust storms up north, almost at the edge of the melting polar cap. The Japanese meteorologist insisted that such storm activity at this time of the year was unusual and bore careful watching. Especially with a traverse team out in the open. Li Chengdu nodded absently. He agreed totally. The storms bore watching. But there was little else that could be done about them.

Finally Vosnesensky looked up from the notes he had been reading and said, "That completes my report."

Li said to the image on the screen, "Everyone is in good health?"

With a grunt and a nod the Russian answered, "Yes, it seems so. I can have Dr. Reed give you the data from his weekly examinations."

"That information is transmitted to our computer, is it not?"

"Yes. Automatically."

"Then I can access it if necessary without troubling Dr. Reed." Li hesitated a heartbeat. "Tell me, how is everyone emotionally? How do you assess the psychological aspects of your group members?"

Vosnesensky's beefy face showed surprise, then pulled into a thoughtful frown. "They all seem normal enough to me," he said after several moments. "There was considerable excitement just before the excursion team left, but everything has settled back to normal routine now."

That was precisely what Li wanted to hear. "Good," he said. "I am glad that they are happy in their work."

Mikhail Vosnesensky nodded glumly at Dr. Li's image on the comm screen. The expedition commander made a few more polite remarks, then bade the cosmonaut a good night.

Vosnesensky continued to stare at the display screen for long moments after it had gone dead gray. He had not lied to the expedition commander, not exactly. He had merely put the best face on the answer he gave to Li's question about morale. True enough, everyone seemed to be happy in their work. Yet that was not the entire truth.

There was something subtly wrong, Vosnesensky thought. He felt a tension in the air that had not been there a few weeks earlier. Nothing he could put his finger on, no obvious clashes or animosities. Nothing so blatant as Ilona Malater's malicious baiting or Patel's unhappy bleating about the schedule rearrangements.

But something was going on. Something.

Most of the group have lost weight. It's been especially noticeable over the past week or so. Reed says that's to be expected, though. And all that physiological data goes straight back to the medical experts on Earth. If it alarmed them they would have let us know by now, wouldn't they?

Or would they be afraid of frightening us, ruining our efficiency? After all, we only have a little over three more weeks to go.

Perhaps I should discuss it with Reed, he said to himself as he got up from the communications console. He's our doctor. And psychologist. Perhaps he can throw some light on the problem.

With a shrug of his heavy shoulders Vosnesensky decided to try to get a good night's sleep, instead. I can talk to Reed tomorrow if I still feel worried. Tomorrow will be soon enough.

S O L 3 5: EVENING

"Who would have thought," complained Ilona, "that one could get so tired merely sitting down all day?"

Long, darkly red shadows were stretching across the sandy barren landscape. Jamie saw that the sun would be setting in an hour or so.

"Doing nothing can be more exhausting than hard physical labor," Joanna agreed.

All day long the two women had been either sitting on the folded benches or standing behind the men in their cockpit seats as the rover trundled across the boulder-strewn wilderness toward Tithonium Chasma. Jamie had taken turns at driving with Pete Connors. His head ached from the unrelieved tension; even when he was in the right-hand seat he hunched forward in strained concentration, watching anxiously for rocks too big to clamber over or craters too steep to traverse.

The land they were traveling across was rough, uneven rust-red formations of low, flat-topped hills, with a rugged wall of mountains in the distance lining the horizon. Just like the Chinle Formation in Arizona, Jamie said to himself, shaking his head in wonder at the similarities between the two worlds. They had found dinosaur bones in those red rocks back home, he remembered.

"Anything wrong?" Connors asked.

Almost startled, Jamie pulled himself out of his reverie. The astronaut was grinning at him good-naturedly.

"You were frowning as if your shoes are too tight," Connors said.

"Just thinking about geology," said Jamie.

"Does it hurt?"

Jamie laughed and shook his head.

A few minutes later, Jamie asked, "Pete, what does the 'T' stand for? Why don't you use your first name?"

Connors's long face sank into a frown. "Tyrone," he muttered.

"Tyrone?"

"Don't tell anybody."

"Why not? It's a fine old Irish name."

Connors's grin returned, but somehow it looked almost sad. "The white kids in Nebraska didn't think so. Got me into a helluva lot of fights. Didn't look right for the minister's son to have skinned knuckles all the time. 'Pete' is a lot easier to live with."

I wonder how many extra battles he had to fight in the Air Force, Jamie thought. And the space agency.

They kept on driving as the distant, pale sun sank toward the red horizon. Connors was muttering into the microphone of the comm set clipped over his short-cropped hair. Jamie did not have his earphones on, but he knew that the astronaut was checking their position on the satellite-generated photo map and calling in to Vosnesensky at home base.

According to the display screen in the middle of the cockpit control panel they were less than five kilometers from the canyon. Jamie checked his wristwatch; about fifteen minutes of daylight remained.

Connors slewed the segmented rover almost ninety degrees off its course and eased it to a stop. The electric generator that powered the wheel motors hummed to a lower pitch.

"Okay, that's it for today," he said.

Before Jamie could ask why he had turned off course Connors called over his shoulder to the women, "Come on up and watch the sunset!"

They crowded into the cockpit and watched in silence as the strangely small sun sunk below a line of bluffs. The sky turned from pink to burning red, then went utterly black. Jamie strained his eyes for a glimpse of the aurora, but either it was too delicate to be seen through the tinted canopy or there was none. Maybe it's only there when the sun's active, he guessed.

None of them moved. No one said a word. Jamie felt the cold of the Martian night seeping through the plastic bubble of the cockpit. Slowly, as their eyes adjusted, a few of the brightest stars gleamed through the bulbous tinted plastic.

"That must be the Earth," Ilona said in her breathy sultry voice.

"Nope. It's Sirius," Connors corrected. "According to the ephemeris Earth is already below the horizon."

"We cannot see it at all?" Joanna asked.

"Not until she becomes a morning star. And we'll be on our way home by then."

Jamie stared out at the dark night sky. He could see only a sparse sprinkling of stars. The sky looked lonely, abandoned.

Connors reached up and pulled the thermal shroud over the plastic canopy. Then, "Could you let me squeeze past, please?" he said to the women. "I've got to get some aspirin."

"Headache?" Ilona asked.

"Yeah. Too many hours driving. It's a lot easier flying a plane."

"Me too," said Ilona. "I'll join you at the aspirin bottle."

Jamie wondered if Ilona was going to make a play for the astronaut. Not here, he thought. It's too crowded, there's too much at stake. Then he realized that his own temples were throbbing. It had been a tense day, driving constantly.

By the time they finished dinner, though, they all seemed to feel better. Connors regaled them with stories about his days as the "tail-end Charlie" with the U.S. Air Force's acrobatic flying team, the Thunderbirds.

" . . . so we pull out of the loop, wingtip to wingtip, and my goddam canopy pops off, *pow!* just like that. We're pulling four g's and battin' along close to Mach 1 and all of a sudden I'm in the middle of a regular hurricane right there in my cockpit!"

His black face was alive with expression, his hands twisting to show the positions of the airplanes. Both women were listening raptly, their wide eyes riveted on Connors. Jamie listened with half an ear and let his mind wander to the task they would face in the morning: finding a safe slope down the landslide to the floor of the canyon. Would the ground be firm enough to hold them? Would it be too rocky for the rover's wheels?

Li's people up in orbit had fired the last four of their geological probes into the canyon. Completely automated, the probes shed their atmospheric heat shields as they neared the ground and then drifted to soft touchdowns on billowing white parachutes. Only one of them had actually sunk its instrument-bearing anchor into the rubble of the landslide itself. The other three had missed it by ranges of a few dozen meters to a full kilometer.

That one probe's instruments reported that the landslide was firm enough for the rover to traverse. But it was only one spot on the slide. What if there were pockets of loose powdery soil? What if they got stuck halfway down? To come this close and then have to turn back would be sickening. . . .

He realized that Connors had finished his story and gone back to the cockpit for his final check-in with the dome before retiring for the night. Ilona had gone up there with him, sitting in the chair Jamie had occupied most of the day.

Joanna was sliding the table into its slot below the lower bunk, opposite Jamie.

"Are you all right?" she asked.

"Hmm? Yes, sure. I'm okay."

"You seemed to drift away from us."

"I was thinking."

She smiled slightly. "Not a bad thing for a scientist to do—on occasion."

"How do you feel?" he asked.

"Oh . . . tired. Worried, I suppose."

"Worried? About what?"

Sitting on the edge of the folded bunk beside Jamie, she said in her whispery voice, "Suppose we go all this way, suppose we get to the bottom of the canyon—and there is nothing there? No life."

Jamie shrugged. "That's why we're going all this way: to find out if there's life down there or not."

"But suppose we find none?" There was something in her eyes that Jamie could not fathom, something more than anxiety, deeper than a scientist's concern over the outcome of an investigation.

"If there isn't any life to be found down there," Jamie answered slowly, "that in itself is an important discovery. We'll just have to search elsewhere."

Joanna shook her head. "If there is no life beneath the mists, what can we expect from the rest of this frozen desert? We will have failed, Jamie. There will never be another expedition to Mars."

"Hey, don't get so down," he said, reaching out to grasp her shoulder gently. "It won't be your fault if Mars is lifeless."

"But we will have come all this way for nothing."

"No. Not for nothing. We're here to learn whatever it is that Mars has to teach us. That's what science is all about, Joanna. It's not a game, where you keep score. It's about building up knowledge. The negative results are just as important as the positives. More so, maybe."

The expression on her face was close to misery.

"We're here to seek the truth," Jamie said in an urgent whisper, "and not to be afraid of what we find, whatever it is."

Joanna did not reply.

"There's nothing to be afraid of," he repeated. "No matter what we find—or fail to find."

She turned away, got up from the half-folded bunk, and hurried toward the lavatory. Jamie realized she was crying. He felt sorry for her. And puzzled.

As he lay on his back in the darkened rover, listening to the soft wind of Mars just outside the metal skin, Jamie wondered why Joanna was so worried about what they would find in the canyon.

She's a biologist, he told himself. If she finds life on Mars her name will go into the history books. But if she doesn't she'll always wonder if she missed it. The whole world will wonder if there's really life here but she just didn't make the right tests or didn't go to the right place.

I've made her come here to the canyon. Maybe we should have tried to reach the edge of the polar cap. Plenty of water vapor there, that's for sure. But we landed too damned far from the cap. That'll have to wait for a follow-on mission.

Connors was snoring, six inches away on his bunk. Above him by only a few more inches was Joanna's bunk. He could sense that she was awake, tense and worried and frightened.

Frightened.

Jamie closed his eyes in the darkness and remembered the first time he had met Joanna Brumado. She had been frightened then, too.

All the trainees had been required to pass an ocean survival test. "There's a small but finite chance that your return to the Earth will end in an emergency landing at sea," said the grizzled old chief petty officer they had borrowed from a U.S. Navy aquanaut team. Although their return flight was planned to terminate at the space station in low Earth orbit, if something went wrong the command module of their spacecraft could be detached and enter the Earth's atmosphere to splash down in the ocean, much as the old Apollo spacecraft had done.

"You could be in a raft for several hours or even several days," the chief had said cheerily. "My job is to get you prepared for that contingency."

So they spent three days in an open raft several miles off the coast of the main island of Hawaii. Eight men and women, including the leather-skinned chief. Joanna had been one of them.

Jamie recalled how she spent the whole time sick and scared, her face white, her fists clenched so hard that her fingernails cut into her palms.

He had felt seasick too for the first few hours, bobbing incessantly on the dark, towering swells. In the trough of the waves they could see nothing but deep blue water and the pale sky. When they rose to a crest, the horizon slanted and weaved nauseatingly.

They each wore personal life preservers, puffy inflated vests that were too hot in the sun but not warm at night. The chief would not let them roll up their coverall sleeves or pants. They also had to wear floppy-brimmed hats. "Sunstroke," the chief said knowingly. No one argued.

"Be a helluva thing to go all the way to Mars and then drown coming home," said one of the trainees, a grinning tanned blond from California with the build of a weight lifter.

"Right now," said one of the other women, "I wouldn't mind drowning. It would be a relief."

The chief made each one of them slide over the raft's round gunnel and into the water for an hour at a time. "You won't sink, not with your flotation gear inflated. Only thing you gotta worry about is sharks."

Jamie spent his entire hour in the water worrying about sharks while the chief explained how to watch the water for their telltale dorsal fins. " 'Course, if one comes up from deep we won't see him until it's prob'ly too late. Not much you can do about that."

The water seemed warm at first, but as the minutes plodded by Jamie felt the heat leaching out of his body. I'm raising the temperature of the Pacific Ocean, he told himself. I hope the sharks appreciate it.

Joanna's hour came near sunset. She seemed rigid with terror, but she managed to swing her legs stiffly up on the water-slicked gunnel and slide almost noiselessly into the sea. She hung in the water almost like a corpse, legs unmoving, arms stretched out tensely, her eyes staring, her lips pressed into a tight bloodless line.

She drifted away from the raft time and again without making the slightest effort to swim back toward it. The chief yelled and bellowed at her, but each time he ended by hauling on the umbilical line to bring her closer.

As Jamie lay on his bunk in the darkened rover, the Martian wind calling to him, he saw Joanna once again alone in the cold black sea, terrified, enduring the chief's exasperated hollering and the embarrassed attention of the other trainees until finally the chief pulled her back aboard the raft. Shivering, Joanna wrapped a blanket around herself and crept to a corner of the raft. There she huddled into a fetal position without speaking a word to anyone.

Why would she endure such fear? Jamie asked himself. Why has she pushed herself to get through all the rigors of training and come here to Mars?

Then he remembered their foray onto the glacier at McMurdo and he finally realized what Joanna was truly afraid of.

She's scared of her father! She's afraid of disappointing him. She's more frightened of failing Brumado than she is of sharks or freezing or dying a hundred million miles from home. It's not her own failure she's afraid of. She's afraid of disappointing him.

He really does own her soul. He fills her entire life. What will she do when we get back to Earth? Especially if we don't have any evidence of life to show her old man?

He turned over and fell into a troubled sleep. He dreamed of Navaho hogans dotting the barren desert of Mars and of splendidly feathered gods descending from the heavens on pillars of fire. The most magnificent of all the gods looked exactly like Alberto Brumado, and he glared at Jamie with the angry glittering eyes of an eagle.

E A R T H

WASHINGTON: Harvey Todd was short enough to have been compared with Alexander Hamilton. Like Hamilton, he had never held an elective office in his life. He had a boyishly pleasant face, modishly styled sandy hair, and a reputation for being dynamic and ruthless. Not yet thirty-five years old, he had been involved in government since his college days, when he had made himself one of the tireless young men in the New Jersey campaign that had elevated a shrill schoolteacher into a congresswoman.

Now that congresswoman was Vice-President of the United States and Harvey Todd was her aide for science and technology. He was already spending most of his time preparing for next year's primaries.

He seemed at ease sitting across the small table from Alberto Brumado. The luncheon crowd at the Jefferson Hotel was quiet, subdued, as if each table full of people had its own secrets to whisper, huddling in the deep plush banquettes so that it was almost impossible to see who was sitting with whom.

Brumado sipped from his tulip-shaped glass of Portuguese *vinho verde*. He barely noticed its taste, so intent was he on what Todd was saying.

"I brought a copy of the speech." The Vice-President's aide pulled a tiny computer disk from his inside jacket pocket and placed it on the damask tablecloth. "I think you'll be pleased with it."

"She accepts the necessity of further missions to Mars?" Brumado asked, hunching forward slightly.

"Unequivocally."

"Wonderful." Brumado reached his hand toward the disk.

Todd covered it with his own hand. "Has the Indian written his statement supporting the Vice-President?"

"Not yet. He's been quite busy."

Sliding the disk back toward himself, "Well, when you can show me his written statement I can show you her speech."

"I see."

"I've scheduled it for the NASA anniversary, as you suggested. Your Indian doesn't have much time to get his statement to us."

"He will. As soon as he comes back from this traverse to Tithonium Chasma."

"Where?"

"The Grand Canyon of Mars."

"Oh, right, of course. The scientific jargon always throws me for a loop."

Brumado made an understanding smile.

Todd's boyish face held the searching, probing eyes of an opportunist. "You realize, of course, that if there's some calamity between now and the date of the speech, all bets are off. I can't have her backing a dead horse."

"I understand," Brumado replied slowly, "that no politician wants to be identified with a failure."

"On the other hand, if the mission should be a terrific success . . . if they find something alive up there, that would guarantee support all up and down the line."

"They are searching for life right now."

"It'd be a good idea if they found something. Even just a hint, let them send back word that they found something that makes it look like life existed there once. That might be even better than finding real live Martians."

"They will find what they find," said Brumado.

Todd grinned at him. "That's right. They're scientists, aren't they? They never slant their reports, do they?"

Brumado did not like the implication, nor the sly expression on the young man's face.

Leaning closer to the Brazilian and lowering his voice, Todd went on, "You know, if they do find something spectacular, like an ancient city or something, your Indian could write his own ticket."

"The Vice-President's support for further missions is what he wants."

With an impatient gesture Todd said, "I don't mean that. I mean he could work with me. He could even run for office."

"I'm sure that is the furthest thing from his mind."

Todd leaned back in his chair again and turned his gaze toward the ceiling. "You know, the Vice-President isn't going to get the

party's nomination automatically. She's going to face some stiff opposition from Masterson and his coalition."

"I am not very familiar with American politics," Brumado murmured.

The young man said almost dreamily, "You tell your Indian that
if he finds something really good up there he can write his own ticket
when he gets back. He could hold the balance of power at the national
convention, you know that?"

Brumado was not certain that he was hearing correctly. "Are you
saying that you would abandon the Vice-President if it seemed ex-
pedient?"

"Oh no, of course not!" Todd smiled like a cobra. "But after all,
the most important thing is for the party to nominate the man—I
mean, the candidate—who can win the election in November. Isn't it?"

Brumado was not staying at the Jefferson Hotel. That was far too
expensive for him. During these weeks in Washington he lived in
the Georgetown home of a friend who was away in South Africa on
State Department business. The house was a pleasant old red-brick
Colonial, beautifully furnished and staffed by a cook and butler.

Edith Elgin lived there, too. Almost.

As soon as Edith had shown up in Washington Brumado's internal
warning system began sounding alarms.

"Dr. Waterman replied to your message, did he not?" he had asked
Edith.

She had tracked him down at a congressional committee hearing
and walked with him out of the Capitol and along Maryland Avenue
toward the NASA headquarters building. The trees were still green
and in full leaf, the sunshine warm, the sky bright blue. Yet the
breeze had a tang in it, the first snap of autumn's coming chill.

"Oh yes, he surely did. It was a kind of impersonal message,
though." She laughed lightly. "More like a scientific report than a
message from a friend."

Brumado looked at her closely as they walked along. "You were
more than friends, I take it."

She returned his steady gaze. "Yes, we were. But we both knew
it would end when he left for Mars."

"I see."

They strolled along slowly. To passersby they looked almost like
father and daughter, although pedestrians in the Capitol Hill area

were accustomed to seeing older men with good-looking young women. Brumado wore a conservative gray pinstriped double-breasted suit, Edith a midthigh dark skirt, off-white blouse, and cardinal red blazer.

"I was wondering," Edith said, "if I might interview you—about some of the things Jamie told me."

"For your network?" Brumado asked.

"It would help me to nail down a permanent job."

They stopped at a corner traffic light. Brumado had seen Jamie's message to her. There were no private transmissions from Mars; project officials screened everything.

"You want to make a big story out of Waterman's desire to change the mission plan and make a traverse out to the Grand Canyon," he said.

She admitted it easily. "I can use Jamie's tape by itself if I have to. But I'd rather have you and maybe some of the project administrators telling your side of the story."

The light changed. Brumado gripped Edith's arm as they hurried across the street. He was thinking furiously. This woman could destroy everything. She could set the Vice-President back on the warpath.

"I have a proposition for you," he said when they had safely reached the other side of the intersection.

"A proposition?" Edith smiled at him.

"I propose a deal," Brumado said. "You can stay with me and get all the information about the expedition that you want—if you promise not to release anything until the team is safely back on Earth."

Edith frowned with puzzlement. "I'm not sure I understand . . ."

"You can become the unofficial biographer of the Mars mission. Go where I go. No doors will be closed to you. You will see everything and meet everyone."

"But I can't put any of it on the air until the mission's finished. Is that it?"

"That's it."

Brumado realized he was still holding her arm. He did not let go.

Thinking about Howard Francis back in New York, Edith said slowly, "I don't know if the network will go for a deal like that."

Smiling his warmest, Brumado coaxed, "They have dozens of reporters covering the mission. But they are all on the outside looking in. If you agree to work with me, you will be on the inside—no other reporter has been allowed such a privilege."

"But I wouldn't be able to file any reports . . ."

"Not until the mission is completed. Then you will be able to tell the entire story, from the inside. You will have information and interviews that no other reporter could possibly obtain."

She looked thoughtful. "I'll ask New York about it."

New York had leaped at the deal, of course. Howard Francis immediately saw visions of news specials that none of the other networks could duplicate. "And if we have to," he had told Edith, "we can always screw them and go on the air with something really big before the other correspondents even know what's happening!"

So for weeks now Brumado had practically lived with Edith Elgin, introducing her wherever they went as the project's unofficial biographer. The other networks complained; the print media howled. But Edith stayed with Brumado. They traveled together, ate together, spent every day together.

Except for his lunch with Harvey Todd. The Vice-President's aide had insisted that it be completely private.

Riding alone in the taxi back to Georgetown, Brumado wondered how long he could keep Edith silent. The deal between them had been simple enough when he had first proposed it. But now the situation was getting more complicated. One of the complications was the Vice-President. Another was Harvey Todd and his ambition to back the winning candidate, despite his ostensible loyalties. The most pressing complication was Edith herself. She was young, quite lovely, very desirable. Yet Brumado could not reach a decision about her. Would she go to bed with him or reject him? If he attempted to make love to her would that bind her to him more closely or drive her away?

He smiled to himself as the taxi threaded narrow, traffic-clogged Wisconsin Avenue. Perhaps if I do not try to seduce her she will go away. Perhaps she expects me to make love to her.

He shook his head. No. She is more intelligent than that. And more dangerous.

The taxi pulled up in front of the red-brick Georgetown house. Edith had a room at the nearby Four Seasons Hotel and a sumptuous expense account. She actually paid for most of their meals and all of her own travel.

Brumado chuckled to himself as he climbed the steps and fished in his pockets for the house key. Why not sleep with her? Everyone already thinks that I am. I might as well be hanged for a sheep as a lamb.

It was scary going down the slope.

"Easy does it," Connors muttered, his hands tightly gripping the rover's steering wheel, his booted feet playing the accelerator and brake as deftly as a concert pianist working the pedals of his instrument. A comm set was clamped over his head, one earphone with a pin mike crooked before the astronaut's lips on a slim curved arm.

Jamie felt as if he were driving too, sitting tensely in the right-hand seat, staring out at the steep incline of the landslide. It looked as if they were pointed almost straight down.

"Like landing the old space shuttle," Connors joked. "Drop a ninety-nine-ton brick from hypersonic to a soft touchdown in ten minutes. Nothing to it."

His insides pitching and reeling with every lurch of the rover, Jamie glanced back over his shoulder at the two women. They were strapped into the jumpseats that folded out from the bulkhead just behind the cockpit. Joanna was pale and sweating visibly. Ilona looked equally tense, but managed a tight smile.

All four were in shirtsleeves, wearing their regulation tan coveralls, although Ilona had wrapped a colorful scarf around her waist. There was no need for the hard suits until they were safely on the canyon floor and ready to venture outside the rover.

Jamie felt rivulets trickling down his ribs and beads of perspiration dotting his forehead and upper lip. His insides felt jumpy, twitchy.

The middle module of the rover had been reconfigured for this traverse. Instead of being merely a housing for instruments and equipment, it now was set up as a miniature laboratory where the three scientists could examine the rocks and soil samples they were to gather and make preliminary analyses. They could step from the forward module to the makeshift lab through the airlock. The logistics module was filled with methane fuel for the electronic generator and fuel cells, plus their other consumables: emergency oxygen, extra water, and food.

Connors seemed utterly cool, despite his deathgrip on the steering wheel. He slowly maneuvered around a crater looming ahead like a hole punched out by an artillery shell, working the rover between its raised rim and the dangerously close edge of the landslide. In the back of his mind Jamie noted that the slide was old enough to have been hit time and again by sizable meteoroids.

"Where's these mists you saw?" Connors asked. "Everything looks clear as a bell now."

"I don't know. Maybe they'll come up later."

"Funny thing about haze. From one angle everything can look clear, but if you're coming in from a different angle, with the sun in a different position, the haze can cover up everything, look like a smoke screen."

But there was no haze at all now. Jamie felt a tendril of fear worming through his mind. Maybe the haze Mikhail and I saw was a rare phenomenon, a once-in-a-lifetime thing. Maybe I've dragged us out here to chase a ghost that doesn't exist.

The slope was strewn with rocks and pebbles, though nothing as big as the boulders they had encountered up on the surface. Jamie could not see any accumulations of dust piled against the bigger rocks. Either the wind doesn't blow down here, he reasoned, or it blows hard enough to carry away any dust that's accumulated.

The rover's cleated metal wheels each had its own independent electric motor driving it, which gave the vehicle the best possible traction. Even so, now and again Jamie felt the ground sliding out from under them, heard a wheel motor whine suddenly before adjusting to the loose gravel beneath it.

Connors was muttering continuously under his breath, so low that even as close as he was Jamie could not tell if the astronaut was cursing or praying. Maybe some of both, he thought.

They passed the one geological probe that had landed on the slide. Its stubby white body stood out against the reddish ground and rocks like a garish advertising sign in the middle of the Sahara. Sure enough, the ground around the probe was firm and easy to drive across, its slope considerably flatter than the area they had just come through.

"Looks easier up ahead," Connors said.

Jamie saw that the ground was flatter and smoother. No craters in sight.

"Good," he said through gritted teeth.

A shadow flicked across the cockpit just as Ilona cried out, "Look!"

One of the RPVs flitted past them, low enough for Jamie to make out the glittering eyes of the camera lenses lining its belly. High above, he knew, the other RPV was soaring, watching the entire general area, piloted by Paul Abell. The low one scouted the terrain ahead. Mironov, at its controls, reported what he saw to Connors minute by minute through the earphone clamped to the side of his head.

"Should be getting to the end of it soon," Connors muttered, whether to Mironov or to the rest of them in the rover Jamie could not tell.

Just then the rover skidded, fishtailing in the inexorable slow motion of a nightmare, the forward section suddenly being dragged almost sideways by the jackknifing of the heavier middle and rear segments. Wheel motors screeched and something made a loud thumping noise. They bounced and jolted, Connors jamming the wheel hard over first one way, then the other.

"Hang on!"

Jamie braced his booted feet and started to reach out his hands to plant them on the control panel. The rover banged into another rock, slewed at a crazy angle, and finally crunched to a stop.

For long moments nothing could be heard inside the cockpit except the frightened gasping of four sweat-soaked people and the creaking and pinging of overheated metal.

Connors swallowed so hard they could all hear it. Then he said, "Must have been an old crater filled in with loose rubble."

"Or dust," Jamie heard himself say in a hollow voice.

"Felt more like sand, sort of."

"Are we stuck?"

Connors shook his head. "Might have to detach this section from the other two, but I think we can make it."

"Without the fuel tank and the lab?" Ilona asked.

"Lemme try first . . ."

As gently as a mother caressing her baby Connors touched his toe to the accelerator pedal. The electric motors hummed in a low register. Jamie felt the rover shudder, inch forward ever so slightly.

"Gotta get all three sections straightened out or we'll start sliding again," Connors muttered. "Like driving a semi rig . . ."

Slowly, slowly they crawled. The astronaut's long, serious face gradually evolved a tentative little smile. The electric motors whined to a higher pitch, the vehicle moved forward more assuredly, and Connors's smile widened until they were rolling confidently and all his gleaming teeth were showing.

"*Gracia a dios*," came Joanna's breathless voice from behind them.

Another few bumps, little ones, and Jamie saw that they were on level ground.

"That's it," Connors said happily. "We're on the canyon floor."

"Good work," said Jamie.

"Had a bad minute or two back there."

"Tell me about it!"

Their plan was to stop at the base of the landslide, go outside and take rock and soil samples, then traverse along the north face of the canyon cliffs until nightfall. They would take more samples first thing in the morning, then move forward again until they came to where Jamie had seen his "village." There they would see if they could climb up to the cleft where the rock formation stood. At the very least they could take more pictures of it and try to get a spectral analysis of the formation remotely, by using a laser to burn off a tiny amount of rock and photographing the spectrum of the cloud of gas that it gave off.

"I will take this first EVA with you," said Joanna, after they had eaten a quick cold meal.

Jamie was at the airlock hatch at the back end of the rover's command module. Connors had returned to the cockpit to check all systems and make his report to Vosnesensky.

"Ilona's on the schedule," he said.

"She does not feel well," Joanna replied.

Jamie glanced at Ilona. She was sitting on the edge of the folded-up bunk, pale and visibly trembling.

Jamie's own guts were still churning and he felt sweaty from the harrowing descent down the landslide. But Ilona looked really sick.

"Okay," he said to Joanna. "Suit up."

Making his way back to the midsection, Jamie leaned over Ilona. She looked up at him. Her eyes were watery, her face covered with a sheen of perspiration.

"Why don't you go up front and ask Pete to let you talk with Tony? I think you need medical attention."

"I'll be all right," she said, her voice weak. "I feel foolish."

"Call Tony; get his advice."

She nodded.

Jamie made his way back to the airlock. His own legs felt wobbly, achy. He put it down to the tension of the descent. Christ, I hope we're not all coming down with something. If any one of us has the flu, we'll all get it and that'll be the end of this excursion.

Joanna was halfway into her hard suit. Jamie began the laborious task of getting into his. It seemed to take an hour, but finally they were both suited up, backpacks connected, helmet visors fastened down. Connors came back into the airlock and checked them both. It felt unbearably crowded with three of them in there, even though Connors was in his coveralls.

"Stay within sight of the rover," the astronaut warned. "I'll be watching you from the cockpit, once I get my suit on."

Standard procedure. There must always be a backup person fully suited and ready to go out at an instant's notice in case of an emergency. It was bending the rules to have scientists go outside without an astronaut with them, but the change in procedure had been okayed by Kaliningrad—for this traverse only.

"We won't be out long," Jamie said. "Looks like plenty of rocks strewn all around here. Joanna can do the collecting while I dig a couple of boreholes."

"Just take it easy and don't strain yourselves," Connors said.

It was not until the astronaut had left the airlock that Jamie realized that Connors, too, had been sweating. As the airlock cycled down and the outer hatch popped open, Jamie wondered how Pete could be so absolutely cool at the wheel of the rover and perspiring now that they were safely on the canyon floor.

"Mikhail Andreivitch, I must speak with you in private." Mironov said it in Russian, in almost a whisper.

Vosnesensky looked up from the comm monitor where he had been sitting for the past hour, watching Waterman and Brumado working on the canyon floor.

Mironov's usually cheerful face looked very serious.

"What is it?" Vosnesensky asked, also in Russian.

Pulling up one of the flimsy plastic chairs, the cosmonaut said, "I don't feel well. I feel sick."

"Have you told Reed?"

"Not yet. I wanted to ask you if I should. It might not look right for one of us to be sick."

Vosnesensky's face contracted into a frown. "Then obviously you don't feel sick enough to see the doctor."

Mironov looked very unhappy. "I ache all over. I feel weak. It's as if I'm coming down with the flu."

"Let Reed examine you. We can't afford to have an infectious disease spread through the whole group."

"But what will they say back in Kaliningrad?"

Deliberately softening his voice, Vosnesensky said, "If you are ill it's not your fault. The worst that can happen is that Kaliningrad will order you to transfer to the orbiting ship while they send Ivshenko down here to replace you."

Mironov groaned. "That's what I was afraid of."

"If it must be done, it must be done. For the good of the mission." Vosnesensky reached out and patted him on the shoulder, grinning. "Besides, Dr. Yang has a much better bedside manner than the Englishman."

"You think so?"

"Once during training we had a very interesting discussion of Sino-Soviet relations, horizontally. I can vouch for her sympathy and tender care."

Mironov's hangdog expression brightened considerably. "Probably all I need is some aspirin, I suppose."

"See what Reed recommends. I know you don't want to leave the ground team, but if it has to be—well, there are some compensations."

The cosmonaut pulled himself up from the chair with an obvious effort, sighed deeply, and went off toward the infirmary. Vosnesensky turned his attention back to the comm screen. He ran a finger along the inside of his collar, then called up the environmental control display on his screen. The numbers showed everything inside the dome was normal, except for one of the air circulation fans, which had been turned off for maintenance. The dome's temperature stood just a hair below its usual twenty-one degrees Celsius. Strange, thought Vosnesensky. It felt warmer than normal.

Jamie felt totally exhausted. He sagged into the cockpit seat and reached for the communication switch.

"God, you look awful," Connors said.

"I feel lousy. Just about had enough strength to get out of the hard suit."

"You were outside too long."

"Maybe."

"A hot meal and a good night's sleep are what you need."

Jamie almost laughed. "You sound like my mother."

Grinning back at him, Connors said, "Come to think of it, I sound like my mother."

Jamie flicked on the comm system. Vosnesensky's dour face filled the tiny screen on the control panel.

"Christ, Mikhail, don't you ever take a break?"

The Russian grunted. "On our way back home I will be able to rest for nine months."

"You've got a point there," Jamie admitted. Sucking in a deep breath, he continued, "Okay, here's our preliminary report from to-day's EVA."

"I am ready. The tape recorder is on."

"We brought eight rocks aboard for testing. Dr. Malater and Dr. Brumado are sorting them out now in the lab section. Three of them have some sort of orange intrusions on them that we haven't seen before. There are also similar orange streaks running along the cliff wall here and there. We took scrapings."

Vosnesensky said, "Schmitt found orange coloration on the moon. Some form of glass, if I remember correctly."

"This isn't glass," Jamie said. "I'm sure of that."

"Then what is it?"

"I don't know. Some sort of sulfur compound, maybe. We'll have to put it through the analysis routine."

Vosnesensky gestured with one hand to indicate to Jamie to go on with his report.

"I took four borings down to depths of ten meters. There doesn't seem to be a permafrost layer here on the valley floor, or if there is one, it's deeper than ten meters."

"What about deeper borings?"

"We decided to do one deep boring on tomorrow's EVA, after we move to the second site. A deep bore takes more time, what with the heavier equipment and all; we just didn't have the time for it today. We won't travel so far that the two sites aren't geologically equivalent, so a single deep bore should do."

The Russian blinked slowly and nodded.

"Ilona and Joanna will send you videos of the rock samples. We took soil samples too, of course. Plenty of sandy regolith out here, a deep layer, more than two meters at this location. I set up a remote sensing beacon. The preliminary data we're getting from it show that the heat flow from below ground is significantly higher here on the canyon floor than it is up on the plain."

"Higher heat flow? Why is that?"

"Don't know. Not yet." Jamie forgot his fatigue as he spoke. "Everything we've seen so far indicates that Mars is cold inside; if it has a molten core the way the Earth does, it's very small and very deep. The core must've been bigger and hotter at one time, of course. Those Tharsis volcanoes can't be more than half a billion years old, at most. But the core seems to have cooled down almost completely. No evidence of continental drift . . . nothing that even looks like continents."

"Yet there is heat coming up from the canyon floor?"

"More than anywhere else we've investigated," Jamie confirmed. "Something under this canyon is warm. That's why there are mists and water vapor down here."

"What else?"

"Air density and temperature are consistent with what the remote probes have found. This whole canyon complex seems to have its own microclimate, warmer and with higher air pressure than the rest of the planet. Maybe the Hellas depression exhibits the same phenomena. We'll have to check that out."

"Not on this mission!"

"I know that. We'll need to come back. This is like exploring Africa, Mikhail. It's going to take decades, maybe a century or more, before we've got it all down."

Vosnesensky broke into one of his rare smiles. "One thing you do not lack, Jamie, is ambition."

Jamie felt startled. "Ambition? Me?"

But Vosnesensky was already framing his next question. "How do you feel? Do you want to speak with Tony? Is your health status good?"

Jamie hesitated. "I'm tired but otherwise okay. Ilona's under the weather a bit, but I don't think anybody else has any complaints. I'll ask each one individually; if there are any problems we'll call back."

"Be certain that you do."

Jamie signed off and cut the connection. Odd that Mikhail should ask about our health. The damned guy must be telepathic. Then he realized that Ilona must have spoken with Tony while they were outside. And Mikhail saw that Joanna took the EVA with me instead of Ilona. He's a suspicious cuss. Typical Russian.

M A R S   O R B I T

Li Chengdu frowned at the display screen. He was in the command module of the *Mars 2* spacecraft, sitting at the monitoring station behind the two pilots' seats. Tolbukhin and the American astronaut, Burt Klein, had turned their seats around to make a little conference circle.

Dr. Yang sat next to Li, pointing at the two lists displayed side by side on the screen.

"You see? Waterman and Brumado accomplished only half their scheduled tasks for the EVA."

Yang's fingernail was long and red and carefully manicured. Li wondered why the physician bothered to lacquer her nails. She was not an especially good-looking woman, he thought, rather plain in fact, with a pug nose and overly thick lips. Her figure was nondescript. Yet she adorned her tan coveralls with a bright gold-mesh belt and she wore a necklace and several bracelets that clashed together like miniature cymbals whenever she moved her hands. Her mouse-brown hair had been recently clipped; she wore it in bangs that came down almost to her eyebrows. And her face was made up with lipstick and eye shadow, no less.

Has she decked herself out for me? Li wondered. Or is she trying to impress our dashing cosmonaut and astronaut? Li sighed to himself. As long as she doesn't make any problems for me I won't interfere. But he found himself wondering if her toenails were lacquered, also.

"Their performance seems to be seriously degraded," Yang said, softly but insistently.

Li roused himself from his conjectures about her sex life. "They had a strenuous journey down to the canyon floor. Perhaps they need more rest."

Burt Klein agreed. "You can't expect them to stick to that schedule

Waterman set up. It's too crowded; there's not enough time to do everything he wants done."

"Perhaps," said Dr. Yang. She leaned close enough to Li to work the computer keyboard. She was wearing perfume. Jasmine blossoms?

A set of colored curves sprang up on the display screen.

"These represent the performance parameters of all the surface personnel, based on their own reports of tasks accomplished," Yang said. "You can see that everyone's performance is degrading."

Li fingered his moustache. "Yes, I see."

"Such a drop-off is normal," Tolbukhin said. "The same thing happens to personnel on the moon's surface and even aboard the space stations."

Yang nodded curtly, but she said, "They have been on the surface for five weeks and some drop-off in performance is to be expected, yes. But please look at how steeply these curves go down."

"Hm," said Li.

"The big decline started only a few days ago. If their performance continues to degrade at this steep rate they will all be helpless by the end of this week!"

Tolbukhin's snort told them what he thought of her fears. But Klein shifted in his seat uneasily.

For the first time Li felt troubled. "Might this be an artifact of the computer program? A coincidence, perhaps?"

Yang's painted face took on a stubborn hardness. "That is not possible. I used the standard evaluation program. The personnel here in orbit do not show the same deterioration; nothing like it."

"Hm," Li said again.

"Something is definitely wrong."

"More than the usual fatigue factors?" Klein asked.

"Much worse."

"What do you think it could be?"

Yang shrugged her slight shoulders. "It might be psychological. Or it might be physical. Or a combination of both."

Tolbukhin laughed at her. "You cover all the possibilities, and as a result you tell us nothing of value."

Li cast a sharply disapproving glance at the cosmonaut. Then he asked Dr. Yang, "Have you checked the physiological profiles that Dr. Reed has been sending up?"

"Yes. That was the first thing I did. They all look normal enough. The surface team is in good health."

"And the psychological reports?"

"They seem normal also, although it is easier to mask a problem there than with the physical examinations."

"Have you spoken to Dr. Reed about this?"

"Not yet. The mission regulations clearly state that I am required to inform you of this problem before contacting anyone on the surface team."

"Ah, yes. The regulations. Well, let us both speak with Dr. Reed. Immediately."

Tolbukhin raised a skeptical eyebrow. Klein looked worried.

S O L   3 6:   EVENING

"No, I have not seen any untoward deterioration of their physical condition," Tony Reed said to Li's image on his communications screen. He glanced at Vosnesensky, scowling at him. "Everyone here seems to be in reasonably good physical shape. Naguib's recovered from his bumps and bruises rather nicely."

Reed was sitting in the little cubicle of his infirmary. Off by the folding door, out of range of the TV camera built into the comm set, Vosnesensky sat on the examination stool like a menacing policeman, his arms folded stubbornly across his thick chest.

"Then how do you account for this deterioration in performance?" asked Dr. Yang, from behind Li's shoulder.

Reed made a bland smile for her. "I'll have to look into it. First thing I'll do is run a few snap physical checkups to make certain that there're no bugs infecting us."

"What is the team's psychological condition?" Li asked, his long sallow face etched with lines of worry.

"No major problems. Everyone seems to be happy with their work. Even Patel has settled back to his work and stopped grumbling."

Yang asked, "Why did Brumado accompany Waterman on the EVA instead of Malater, as the schedule called for?"

"Beats me," Reed replied, resisting the urge to look over at Vosnesensky again. "I'll have to ask them."

Li looked out from the screen in silence for a long moment, staring into Reed's eyes, the worry lines around his mouth and eyes slowly evolving into just the slightest hint of suspicion. Or so it seemed to Tony.

"This is very serious," he said at last. "The reports you have been sending indicate that nothing is wrong physically or psychologically with the surface personnel, yet their performance is degrading at an alarming rate. You must find out what is happening. If you cannot,

I will have to recall the entire team and cut the surface exploration short."

"No need even to think about that!" Reed flared. "If there's anything seriously wrong—which I doubt—I am perfectly capable of determining the cause of the problem and taking the necessary medical steps to alleviate it."

Li nodded, still looking suspicious, and said, "Please keep Dr. Yang informed on a daily basis. More than once a day, if necessary."

"Yes. Of course."

"Anything else?" Li asked Dr. Yang, turning slightly to address her over his shoulder.

"I would like to go down to the surface," she said abruptly. "To assist Dr. Reed."

Vosnesensky shook his head violently.

"That's not necessary," Tony said. "If there's a problem I can root it out. If I need assistance, rest assured I will ask you for it."

Li glanced at Reed, then at Yang, then focused his eyes on Reed again. Even through the comm screen Tony could feel the suspicion simmering in those almond eyes.

"To transfer personnel from orbit to the ground is a major undertaking. We have only two landing/ascent vehicles remaining. I must reserve them for any major emergencies that may arise."

"I assure you, it's not necessary," Reed said again.

"Conduct your examinations quickly," said Li. "This is a matter of great urgency."

"Yes, I understand."

"Very well. And stay in touch with Dr. Yang."

"I will. Surely."

Finally placated, though obviously not satisfied, Li ended the discussion and signed off. Reed stared at the blank display screen for long moments, his own shadowy reflection gazing back at him worriedly.

"Very good," Vosnesensky said. "You did well."

"Yes," answered Reed, "but I'm not so certain that I did right."

"We do not need another doctor here. It will only cause problems. You heard what Li said: already he is thinking of cutting the mission short."

"But, Mikhail Andreivitch, if we are becoming sick . . ."

"You are the team physician." Vosnesensky pointed a stubby finger at the Englishman. "You find out what is wrong and fix it. One doctor here is enough."

He turned and slid the accordion-fold door open, ending the discussion.

Left alone in his infirmary, Reed drummed his fingers on his desktop. Something was definitely amiss, he knew. Despite the physical exams, there is something incubating here. Vosnesensky would never have reacted like that a week ago. The man was so safety conscious it was almost ludicrous. Now he refuses to consider bringing Yang down here to assist me.

Are we all infected with something? Are we all going mad?

Vosnesensky walked scowling past the galley, straight to his own privacy cubicle. Only then did he let himself sigh wearily and sit on his cot. The air mattress sighed back at him. His legs ached. He felt edgy, almost angry.

Doctors, he grumbled to himself. The more they poke you the more they find that is wrong. We have caught a bug, some form of flu, and for that Li thinks of abandoning the mission altogether. Madness! Absolute madness.

"Are you sick?" Jamie asked.

Ilona looked up at him with bleary eyes. "I don't know what it is. My arms and legs ache terribly. I don't seem to have any strength . . ."

"What did Tony say?"

A guilty look flushed her face. "I didn't call him. I didn't want to take the chance that he might order us to return to the dome because of me."

They were in the lab module of the rover, Ilona sitting by the small diamond-tipped saw that they used to slice rocks into thin sections for examination. Jamie was standing next to her in the narrow aisle between the racks of equipment and the workstation counter tops. Joanna sat a few feet away, by the microscope, watching them intently.

"Maybe you should rest," Jamie said.

Ilona shook her head stubbornly. "No. It doesn't help. And there's work to do."

Jamie's own head was throbbing. He felt that Ilona should lie down, that he should call Tony Reed and report that she was sick. But he knew she would argue against it, and he hadn't the strength to start a fight.

"I'll be all right in the morning, I'm sure," Ilona said with a forced smile. "I need a good night's sleep, that's all."

"We all do," Joanna said. "I haven't felt this poorly since we all had those colds when we first came aboard the Mars spacecraft."

"You too?" Jamie asked.

"Perhaps there is something wrong with the air filters in here?" Joanna made the suggestion sound like a question. "Perhaps they are not taking enough carbon dioxide out of the air?"

Jamie's nod made his head hurt even worse. "I'll check it out." He started for the hatch, then turned back to Ilona. "Take it easy. Don't push yourself."

"Well, *something's* wrong, that's for sure," Connors said when Jamie got back to the cockpit. "I feel like somebody's been kickin' the shit outta me for the past six hours."

"I'd better call Tony," Jamie said. "This is getting serious."

But as Jamie reached for the radio switch on the control panel Connors grabbed his wrist. "Wait till tomorrow morning," the astronaut said.

Jamie gave him a questioning look.

"Never call the medics until you absolutely have to," Connors explained. "All those pill pushers know how to do is tell you to come back home so they can stick needles into you."

"But something's wrong, you said so yourself."

"You and I will check out the CO_2 system. That might be it. Then we'll have a good hot dinner and get a good night's sleep. If we still feel shitty tomorrow morning, then we can call for an ambulance."

Jamie reluctantly agreed.

Seiji Toshima felt that of all the men and women on this exploration team, he was the only one who truly dealt with the entire planet Mars.

Waterman and the others in the rover may be excited about their traverse to the canyon. Patel and Naguib were enraptured by their study of the giant volcanoes. The astronauts and cosmonauts maintained the dome's equipment while the English physician looked after their health and little Monique tended her garden and studied rocks.

I alone consider this world in its entirety.

He slowly swiveled his creaking plastic chair and surveyed his row of display screens. The entire planet was on view. Three screens showed the whole planet, pole to pole, as seen by the three observation satellites in synchronous orbit. The others showed data recorded by the satellites and roving balloons and the remote beacons that had been placed across the desolate sandy tracts of the red planet: air density, temperature, wind speed and direction, humidity, even the chemical composition of the air.

It was foolish of me, Toshima thought, not to realize that there would be enough humidity in Tithonium Chasma to form mists even in midsummer. He regarded this lapse as a failure of his own. It was *known* that the canyon floor is two to three kilometers below the surface of the surrounding plains. It was *known* from the probes that the air density down there was somewhat higher than elsewhere. *Of course* the air would be somewhat warmer and capable of holding more moisture. I should have foreseen that. I should have predicted it.

He did not dwell on the shortcomings of the past, however. On the largest of all his display screens, the one directly in front of the chair on which he sat, was his masterwork: a fully detailed weather map for the entire planet. Synthesizing all the data coming in to him, Toshima had drawn in the highs and lows, the cyclonic disturbances and wind-flow patterns, for all of Mars. At the touch of a keyboard button he could display the weather as it existed yesterday, or two weeks ago, or as he predicted it would exist tomorrow—or two weeks hence.

The longer-range forecasts were not as firm as the twenty-four-hour prediction, naturally. Even on a world as meteorologically dull as Mars, with no oceans and little humidity to complicate weather patterns, it was difficult to make forecasts more than forty-eight hours ahead. But he was learning, extending the predictive power of his vision further and further.

He rubbed his throbbing temples as he peered closely at his weather map. The dust storms swirling in the northern latitudes fascinated him. Driven by the energy released into the atmosphere by the melting polar cap, they appeared and vanished like ghosts. Unpredictable, so far. Toshima knew that in the spring season such storms could merge together, coalesce into a single gigantic storm that could blot out the whole planet for weeks on end.

He had no fear that these little storms would do that. What worried him was the cold front advancing southward across the broad sweep of Chryse Planitia.

As Martian weather systems went, that cold front contained considerable energy. Noontime high temperatures south of the front were still up into the midtwenties, Celsius. On the other side of the front they were below freezing, even at high noon. The front would pass the eastern end of the Grand Canyon complex during the night. Waterman and the others were more than a thousand kilometers west of there, but still Toshima worried about them.

He did not understand why he was worried. The rover was in no danger from the weather. The four men and women were prepared to face overnight lows of a hundred and fifty below zero. Why was a drop of thirty degrees worrisome?

Toshima felt an inner trembling take hold of him, almost like a sexual urge. There was something in the data before his eyes, something important that he did not recognize. He knew it. He could feel it within him. His subconscious mind was trying to tell him something, awaken him to a revelation, an important discovery. He bit his lips and squeezed his eyes shut, concentrating furiously. In vain.

His head pulsated with a dull pain. Again he kneaded his temples, then the back of his neck.

Opening his eyes again he took a deep breath, trying to calm the tension cording the tendons in his neck and cramping his shoulders. Turning slowly on his creaking stool he studied each of the display screens, one by one. The information is here, before my eyes, he knew. Yet he could not consciously grasp what his inner mind was trying to tell him.

Relax, said the long-forgotten voice of the monk who had guided him in childhood. Do not attempt to force your spirit, it will resist your efforts and cause you nothing but pain. Relax and empty your mind of all wants, all needs. Meditation is the key to understanding, the bridge to the great cosmic all.

Toshima closed his eyes once again, this time gently, without strain. He folded his arms across his chest, and let his chin droop to his chest. To a casual passerby it would look as if the Japanese meteorologist were taking a nap.

He tried to clear his mind by drawing up a picture of the divine Fujiyama, its exquisitely proportioned cone covered with snow against a clear blue winter sky. His thoughts drifted, slowly, languorously, from one past vision to another. He recalled the first time he had been in the U.S.A., in Boston, how cold the winter wind was at the airport, blowing in off the frigid water of the harbor. How cutting the wind was even in the city, at the hotel where the world meteorology congress was meeting.

The towers of Boston's Prudential Center created an inadvertent wind tunnel, he had been told. All the meteorologists marveled at the phenomenon. Even when the winds were calm elsewhere in the city, at the Prudential Center they screeched between the buildings so fiercely that they stirred whitecaps in the decorative ponds and fountains.

Toshima's eyes snapped open. Wind tunnel!

He rolled his little chair to the keyboard in front of his master map and began pecking furiously, headache forgotten. What will be the effect of a strong pressure gradient on the long narrow corridor of the Valles Marineris? How will the approaching cold front affect the winds in Tithonium Chasma?

It took a good part of the night, but finally Toshima had his answer. He checked it, then checked it again. Yes, the result was certain.

Again he trembled, this time with the exultation of victory. And the knowledge of fear. He had made a great discovery. It told him that Waterman and the others were in grave danger.

As the first light of dawn filtered into the dome, Toshima rose in bleary-eyed anxiety to awaken Vosnesensky.

"The people in the rover must be warned of this," he muttered to himself. "There is no time to waste."

THE LONG WINTER

The blue world was far luckier than its red companion. Closer to Father Sun, bigger, it held its deep oceans of water and protective mantle of air. Life flourished.

Not without interruption, however. Not without calamities. Great creatures took command of the seas, the land, even the air, only to die away completely into utter extinction. At times the hand of death swept the blue world so thoroughly that it was almost emptied of life completely.

Yet each time life struggled back, repopulating the blue world with new and different creatures.

Great sheets of ice marched outward from the poles; massive glaciers came grinding down from the mountains to cover the land with layers of ice miles thick. So much of the oceans' waters was turned into ice that the level of the sea sank. The blue world turned white and glittering under the pale sun of winters that lasted a hundred thousand years or more.

The cold reached the red world, too.

The red world had not yet fully recovered from that great cataclysm of long ago. Yet a broad new sea had arisen, gleaming water that covered almost half the planet. Enormous volcanoes reared their mighty peaks toward the stars and spread hot lava and steaming gases over the land. There was still energy deep beneath the red world's crust, the molten energy to build the tallest mountains of all time.

As always when there is water and energy, there was the chance for life to begin. Water and energy and time: those are all that life needs.

But then the cold began to do its deadly work. The great hemispherical sea froze and vanished into the ground. The volcanoes stilled. The red world began a long, long winter that has lasted to this very day.

S O L   3 7: MORNING

Jamie stood naked under the hot sun of Mars, sweat trickling down his ribs and legs as the gods gathered around him. His groin ached with the pleasurable anguish of yearning. His empty hands reached out longingly.

The land was as red as blood, the sky a blue so bright that it hurt his eyes to look upward. Across the sandy desert the gods were descending in their fiery chariots, one after another. Wherever they touched down, Martian rocks instantly changed into brilliant blooms of flowers. Soon the entire desert was carpeted with color, and even the craggy cliffs in the far distance shifted and melted into cities of adobe and wood. Jamie could see plumes of smoke rising from their chimneys.

The gods wore feathers and glittering beads. Their faces were those of totems: fox, eagle, dog, snake. Their bodies were magnificent, straight and tall as lofty pine trees, beautifully muscled and gleaming like burnished copper.

They gathered around Jamie solemnly, silently, encircling him until he felt like a small child in their superb presence. Jamie fingered the totem his grandfather had given him; the bear was his protector and guide.

"I have returned to you," Jamie said to the gods. "I have come back to your domain."

The gods said nothing. They stared wordlessly down at Jamie while the soft winds of Mars sang their morning song.

"From a great distance I have come," Jamie explained, pointing toward a single star that shone even in the daytime sky. "All the way from Earth."

The gods drew closer, looming over Jamie, making him feel small, weak, afraid. His knees trembled. He was sweating hard.

"You have brought all the white man's ills with you," said the voice of the gods. "You have brought death to our abode."

"No!" Jamie protested. "I bring life to you!"

"You bring death."

They raised their hands against Jamie. Each carried a mighty implement in his hand. For some it was a rattle fashioned from a giant gourd and painted in gaudy colors. For others it was a war club, daubed black and heavy with menace. They brandished the clubs, rattled the gourds. And vanished.

The gods disappeared, faded into oblivion, and the world around them lost all its life. The flowers, the blossoms, the beautiful adobe cities melted away and vanished, leaving only the empty desolation of Mars stretching as far as the eye could see.

The buzzing sound of the gourd remained, though—threatening, insistent, inescapable.

Jamie realized that it was the buzzer of the comm console. He opened his eyes, making the transition from dream to reality with the reluctance of a man leaving a warm fire to face a winter storm.

He was in the rover. Eighteen inches above his head stretched the gray bottom of Joanna's bunk. Even closer, to his left, Connors lay sprawled and entwined in his blanket. The astronaut's face was bathed in a sheen of sweat. His sleeping features looked drawn and pained.

The damned comm unit up in the cockpit was buzzing like a hive of hornets. Nobody else seemed to hear it. Jamie crawled carefully out of his bunk and padded in his stockinged feet to the cockpit. He shivered. His coveralls were soaked with cold sweat. His head thundered as if from a hangover.

Slumping into the right-hand seat, Jamie leaned a finger against the button that activated the communicator. With his other hand he started to wind the little wheel that pulled the thermal shroud off the canopy. It was still dark outside on the canyon floor. The only light in the cockpit came from the telltales on the instrument panel.

Seiji Toshima's round face appeared on the small screen. He looked as baggy-eyed and bleary as Jamie felt.

"I am sorry to awaken you so early," the meteorologist said, without preamble, "but I must warn you of a dust storm that may strike your region this morning."

"Dust storm?" Jamie muttered. "What?"

"Dust storm! Wind speeds of two hundred knots. Visibility reduced to near zero. Density of particles in air high enough to damage unprotected equipment! You must prepare!"

"Wait . . ." Jamie's head was buzzing. "Slow down. What are you talking about?"

"The canyon system acts as a wind tunnel," Toshima said rapidly. "The approaching cold front will send a wave of energy down the canyon and create a dust storm of great severity. You must be prepared for this! Unprotected equipment could be damaged. People out in the open could become disoriented. The dust could be thick enough to reduce vision severely. Even radio communications might be affected."

"But I thought the storms didn't come this far south at this time of the year," Jamie said as the impact of Toshima's warning began to sink in.

The meteorologist slowed down and explained his belief that the entire canyon complex could become a giant wind tunnel filled with blowing dust.

"I can keep you updated on an hourly basis," he said. "I have asked Ulanov and Diels in the orbiter to focus all instrumentation on the canyon area this morning. Fortunately, the spacecraft hovers over this hemisphere constantly."

Jamie could hear the sounds of the others getting out of their bunks behind him.

"I would advise against any EVA today that is farther than a few minutes' walk from your vehicle," Toshima said. "With wind speeds of two hundred knots a storm could be upon you before you know it."

"Shit," Jamie groused. "Suppose we move the rover farther west? We were going to anyway, and then dig a deep borehole and instrument it."

Toshima hiked his eyebrows. "The storm will overtake you no matter what your position."

"If the storm actually happens," Jamie said.

The Japanese meteorologist closed his eyes briefly. "Yes," he hissed. "If my forecast is correct."

Jamie leaned back in the seat, feeling exhausted already. "Okay. Thanks for the warning. Give us an hour to talk it over and have breakfast. Then we'll call you back."

Toshima looked away from the screen, then was pushed aside by Vosnesensky. The Russian looked grimmer than usual.

"Jamie, we have checked the situation with Dr. Li. Toshima's prediction is tentative, but serious enough to take . . . well, seriously."

"Yep. I understand."

"There is to be no EVA and no moving of the rover without checking with me first," Vosnesensky said.

Jamie nodded.

"Let me talk with Connors now."

It took an effort for Jamie to turn his head and look back toward the rear of the module. "He's in the john," Jamie said to the screen. "I'll tell him to check in with you when he comes out."

"Yes. As soon as he comes out."

It took nearly half an hour before all four of them were washed and dressed in their daytime coveralls. Jamie already felt too tired even to consider shaving. One advantage of Indian blood, he said to himself as he peered blearily into the mirror. Not much of a beard. When he came out of the lavatory he noticed that Connors had not shaved either. His beard was grizzled with gray; it made him look older.

They folded up the bunks in silence and sat on the benches, four steaming meals on the table between them, together with the usual bottle of vitamin supplement pills.

"Mikhail doesn't want us to move until they see if a sandstorm is actually developing," Connors said, picking at his reconstituted eggs and soy bacon.

"It's just as well," said Ilona. "I don't think we're in condition to do very much."

"You still feel that bad?" Jamie asked.

"Terrible. What about you?"

"Pretty punk. But I think we could at least go outside and do some more sampling. What about you, Joanna?"

She looked miserable: pale and red eyed. There were dark rings under her eyes. Ilona looked worse: gaunt, hollow cheeked. Jamie knew that his own face was sunken, bleary.

Connors said, "No way around it. We're gonna have to tell Reed about this."

Jamie nodded reluctantly. "What about drilling a deep core while we're stuck here?"

"No sense starting to unpack the power drill if we'll have to break it down and stow it away again when the storm hits. We're in no great shape for heavy work anyway."

"But if there's no storm we'll have wasted the whole damned day." Jamie realized he was starting to sound like Patel. For the same reason: precious time was being stolen from him, time he needed to do his work.

"We ought to know if the storm's going to happen in an hour or two," Connors said.

"Maybe," said Jamie. "And maybe Toshima's just going off the deep end."

"Want me to ask Mikhail?"

Jamie knew that Vosnesensky would simply repeat what he had already said: Stay safely inside the rover and take no risks.

Joanna was doggedly finishing her breakfast, spooning up the last of the frozen fruit dessert. "I can at least spend the day examining the rocks and soil samples we brought in yesterday," she said.

Ilona murmured, "I will assist you. I think I can manage that. The ones with the bright orange intrusions look interesting."

"Like Jamie's green rock?" Joanna forced a smile.

Ilona smiled back. "These are orange."

Jamie said, "I'd appreciate it if you'd analyze the core samples first."

"Not the rocks?"

He started to shake his head but the motion brought fresh pain. "There's heat coming up from below the surface and water in some form that makes up the morning mists. I think the core samples have more to tell us than colored rocks."

Joanna cocked her head slightly to one side. "If you wish," she said, sounding unconvinced.

"I'm going to call Reed," Connors said, sliding out from behind the table.

And I'm going to sit here like an idiot with nothing to do. The lab module was too small for three of them to work in it simultaneously. "I guess I'll clean up," he said.

The women went slowly back to the airlock and through it to the lab module. Connors was already up in the cockpit calling Reed. Jamie stood alone at the narrow table littered with the remains of their breakfast, feeling a dull ache in his joints and a sullen throbbing in his head.

It can't be the flu, he told himself. We would have come down with it months ago if it was flu or any other kind of infectious disease. It's something we've caught here, something from Mars. Can't be anything else.

He remembered his dream and shuddered.

.   .   .

He's let the cat out of the bag, Tony Reed said to himself as he studied the face of Pete Connors on his communications screen. Is it my imagination or has his complexion gone sallow?

The astronaut was perspiring lightly, that much Reed could easily see. His eyes were bloodshot, his speech a bit slower than usual. And he had reported that all four of the people in the rover were feeling sick. Vosnesensky can't hide that from Li. No matter how much Mikhail Andreivitch wants to cover this up, Connors has spilled the beans.

"And you say that all four of you are in the same condition?" Reed asked.

"Pretty much," replied Connors. "Ilona seems the worst off. Jamie's in the best shape—or at least he's not complaining as much."

The stoical Indian. He'd probably refuse to utter a peep even if he were being roasted at the stake.

"Any loss of appetite?" he asked aloud.

Connors frowned with thought. Then, "Doesn't seem to be. But we're all so damned tired, it's hard to tell."

"Hm, yes." Reed chewed his bottom lip momentarily. "And you're taking your vitamin supplements?"

"Yessir. I see that they all take the pills every morning."

"You've only been out two days," Reed muttered, "so it shouldn't be any dietary deficiency. . . ."

"It feels like we're all coming down with the flu or something," Connors volunteered.

"I see." Reed scratched his chin, fingered his pencil-thin moustache, ran a smoothing hand over his sandy hair. The same symptoms were showing up in the dome.

"It's difficult for me to do much for you remotely," he said to Connors. "I'm afraid it would be best if you started back before things get any worse."

"But we just got here! We're scheduled to be in the canyon for a week . . ."

"Not if you're all sick." Vosnesensky would have to see the necessity of it, Reed told himself. After all, as medical officer here I have the authority to order them back to base. Even if the Russian objects.

"Maybe if we all took a good shot of antibiotics?"

"I doubt that it would help."

"Give us another day, at least. We're not going anywhere today if that storm hits. Let's see what develops over the next twenty-four hours."

Reed considered the astronaut's earnest, anxious face. Connors was pleading with him. I am the team's physician. I should know what to do. I ought to be able to deal with this. If I order them back now Vosnesensky will be furious. He'll think it's a reflection on him, most likely.

"I've got to report this to Vosnesensky, you realize," he said.

"Yeah, I know."

"This transmission is automatically monitored by the orbiter. And Kaliningrad."

Connors nodded glumly.

Pursing his lips as though deep in careful thought, Reed at last offered, "I will recommend to Mikhail Andreivitch that you stay where you are for the next twenty-four hours. A dose of wide-spectrum antibiotic won't hurt you; I'll send specific written instructions over the computer link. Then we'll see how you feel tomorrow morning."

"Okay! Great!" The astronaut was as grateful as a puppy.

Reed terminated the conversation, then turned to his medical computer file and tapped out a prescription for the antibiotic. He pushed himself up from the chair slowly, reluctantly. I must face Vosnesensky, he told himself. Nothing for it but to beard him in his own den. Still, he dreaded the confrontation.

The Russian was in the wardroom, huddled over a mug of steaming tea, talking in low earnest tones with Mironov in their native language. They both looked sick to Reed's professional eye. Haggard, sallow complexions. Even their coveralls looked baggy and rumpled, not at all the neat aspect that they had presented only a few days earlier. Whatever it is, they've got it. And all the others, too. All except me. And possibly Toshima.

Reed felt absurdly normal: healthy and strong. Clear-headed and alert. He had even cut down on his morning amphetamine cocktail, to check whether or not his seeming good health was a chemically induced artifact.

The two Russians both looked up as Tony pulled out a chair and joined them.

"The team in the rover is down with it," Reed told them quietly, "whatever it is."

"Fatigue," Vosnesensky said immediately. "Psychological fatigue. I have seen it on long-duration missions in orbit."

"After only thirty-seven days?" Reed almost sneered.

"We have been in space for almost a year."

"Ah yes," Reed admitted. "True enough."

"The stresses of this environment . . . ," Mironov started, but his voice trailed off weakly.

"Mars is no more stressful than the moon or an orbiting space station," Reed said. "Rather less stressful, actually, I should think."

"Then what *is* it?" Vosnesensky growled. "What is happening to us?"

Reed shook his head. "Whatever it is, it's affecting everyone here with the same symptoms: weakness, pains in the limbs, headaches."

"It is the flu," Mironov said.

Cocking an eyebrow at him, Reed said, "How could we all come down with the flu nearly a year after leaving Earth? Influenza viruses don't lie dormant for that long. If it were the flu we would have seen it long before this." Unless it's a slow virus, Tony suddenly thought. Like Legionnaires' disease, or some such.

Mironov looked stubbornly unconvinced.

"But no one in orbit has it," Reed pointed out, arguing as much with himself as with the cosmonaut.

"The Martian flu," Vosnesensky half joked.

"It is patently impossible to contract a disease from a planet that is without any life of its own," Reed snapped, almost angrily. "There are no viruses here to infect us. Even if there were Martian microbes, they would not be adapted to our cells. Mars could be covered with all sorts of bugs, but they wouldn't bother us at all. Couldn't, actually."

"That is the theory of the doctors," Mironov mumbled gloomily.

"Perhaps this is not a disease at all," Vosnesensky said.

"Not a disease?"

"Coal miners get black lung," Vosnesensky said, "not from germs but from breathing in coal dust."

Reed stared at him. This cosmonaut actually has a brain inside that thick skull!

"Perhaps there is something in the Martian dust that is affecting us," Vosnesensky said.

"But we take great care to keep the dust out of our suits and out of our living habitat," Reed pointed out.

"The dust is very fine. Perhaps we do not take great enough care."

"I hadn't thought of that," said Reed.

Mironov said, "We could check the air in here, see how much dust is suspended in it."

"Yes," said Vosnesensky. "We must do that."

Reed was about to reply when Toshima came rushing up to the table. He was wide-eyed with excitement. If the "Martian flu" had hit him, he showed no evidence of it.

"The dust storm!" Toshima fairly shouted. "It has started!"

S O L 3 7: AFTERNOON

Grounded.

Jamie felt like an errant teenager being punished by his parents. The rover was in perfectly good shape, and even though he felt weak and headachy, he saw no reason why he should not be moving onward, closer to the "village" he had seen.

That's where we've got to go, he kept telling himself. Maybe I can even climb up there, once we get to the base of the cliffs where that cleft is. I'll bet there's even a natural path up the cliff face to that cleft and the formation inside it. Or maybe they carved steps out of the rock.

The day outside seemed perfectly clear, despite Toshima's insistence that a dust storm was howling down the length of the canyon and would soon engulf them.

There had even been the mists out there earlier in the morning, thin gray tendrils of haze that hovered in the early morning chill and slowly evaporated as the sun reached down into the canyon. Like ghosts that vanish when the light touches them, Jamie thought.

If the mists evaporate and then form again the next morning, he reasoned, either the moisture remains inside the canyon or it's renewed from some source of water vapor underground. Or in the cliff walls.

Christ! There's so much for us to look for and they've got us stuck inside this aluminum can!

For the fortieth time that morning he paced the length of the rover's command module, from the cockpit bulkhead past the little galley and the narrow passage between the folded-up bunks to the equipment racks and finally the airlock at the back end.

Connors called from the cockpit, "I think it's starting."

Jamie rushed the nine strides it took to span the module's length and ducked his head past the bulkhead. Through the cockpit's bulbous canopy the canyon outside seemed just the same as the last time he had looked.

Connors anticipated him. "Take a squint at the sky."

Jamie slid into the empty seat beside the astronaut so he could look upward. The pink sky seemed normal enough—almost.

"It's gotten ten percent darker in the past five minutes," Connors said, holding up a color comparison chart.

"There's really going to be a storm."

"Yeah."

"I'd better go back and tell the others."

"Might as well. We got nothing else to do." Connors slipped on his headset as he spoke and reached for the comm unit's switch.

Joanna and Ilona were sitting so close together in the lab module that their shoulders almost touched. The lighting was low, more from the glowing displays on the computer screens than from the dimmed overhead strip lamp.

Neither of the women looked up as Jamie stepped in from the airlock. They were both bent over something on the workbench.

"The storm is starting," Jamie said.

Joanna turned her head slightly to look at him over her shoulder. In the dimness he could not make out the expression on her face, only that she seemed terribly pale.

"The figures on the core samples are on the screen here," she said, tapping the computer humming beside her.

"Anything interesting?"

"See for yourself," she said, turning back to the work she and Ilona were doing.

Jamie frowned slightly at her abrupt manner. He leaned over, since there were no other chairs in the lab, and read off the figures on the screen.

Not much different from the values they had gotten from other corings, he saw. Except that there was no ice in the sample, no layer of permafrost.

Then where's the water coming from? Jamie asked himself.

He punched up a side-by-side display that compared the results of the core samplings taken near the dome with those from here in the canyon. Trivial differences, much less than Jamie had expected. Except for the water. There's less water here than up on the plain. Less! That doesn't make any sense.

The wind was keening outside. Straightening up, Jamie felt a kink in his back. He had been bent over longer than he had realized. The wind was really singing now. There were no windows in the lab module, no way to see what was going on outside.

Joanna and Ilona were still bent over their work. The diamond saw buzzed briefly, then whined as it bit through rock.

"I'm going up front to see what the storm looks like," he said.

"Good," said Joanna, without raising her head.

Curious, he asked, "What the hell are you working on that's so fascinating?"

"Go up front, Jamie, and leave us alone. We will call you when we are ready to talk."

Son of a bitch, Jamie grumbled to himself. Then he remembered how proprietary Joanna had become when they had found the green-streaked rock.

Half puzzled, half angry, he made his way back into the command module. Connors was still up in the cockpit, munching on a candy bar, headset still clamped against his ear although he had swung the microphone arm up and away from his mouth.

"Toshima says we'll be in this for the rest of the day," he announced glumly.

Jamie stared at the scene outside. The wind was howling like a squalling infant, high-pitched and thin. It had become quite dark out there, an eerie kind of fluctuating darkness, not like nighttime even though the lighting level was down to about its value just after sunset. Shadowy, like having a blanket thrown over your head. Menacing, somehow, deep down in the gut. Jamie could barely see the cliff face, less than fifty meters from the rover's nose. The sky was obliterated by darkness.

He slid into the cockpit seat and looked down at the display in the instrument panel's main screen. Connors had it showing a satellite view of the region. Jamie could see the canyon complex clearly, but the inside of the twisting labyrinth of canyons was filled to the brim with billowing clouds of reddish-gray dust. They looked soft, undulating like the waves of the ocean, thick enough to buoy up your body if you cared to sprawl on them.

"Vosnesensky's pissed because we don't have a cover to put over the canopy," Connors said. "He's afraid the dust will scratch up the plastic so bad we won't be able to see out of it."

"Is it? Scratching?"

Connors shook his head slowly. "Hard to tell, so far. Don't hear anything that sounds like scratching, do you?"

"The dust particles are microscopic in size."

"Yeah, but gritty."

"Nothing we can do but wait," Jamie said.

"How they doing back there?"

Jamie huffed. "They're so busy they don't even care about the storm."

"They'll miss the show."

He wondered again about the lack of water in the core samples. Something must be wrong. We're missing something.

"If we covered the canopy we wouldn't be able to see this," Connors said. His voice sounded tired.

"What about the cameras?"

"They're all on automatic. We'll get a complete record of the storm, unless the sand chews up the lenses too bad."

"We've got replacement lenses aboard, don't we?"

"Sure." Connors puffed out a weary sigh. "I wouldn't have the strength to put a cover over her anyway."

"Still feel bad?"

"Worse. How 'bout you?"

"Pretty lousy."

"Think we oughtta check in with Reed?"

"If he had anything to tell us he'd call," Jamie said.

"Yeah. Guess so."

Jamie leaned back and watched the dust storm billowing outside, tired and perspiring despite having done nothing all day. The gauges on the instrument panel told him that the wind was blowing a steady two hundred twenty-five kilometers per hour, with gusts up to nearly two-ninety. He could hear its high-pitched shrieking. Yet the rover was not rocked; it remained solid, without so much as a quiver. Jamie knew that the thin air of Mars packed very little punch. At almost three hundred kilometers per hour the wind had the force of a twenty-mile-per-hour zephyr on Earth.

Toshima called in and asked for the air temperature outside the rover.

"Goin' up," Connors reported, surprised. "It's up to just about ten degrees."

Jamie mentally converted the centigrade figure to fifty degrees Fahrenheit.

Toshima smiled toothily in the display screen. "Friction from dust particles heats the atmosphere. There could be lightning."

"Lightning?"

"It is possible. Be certain all equipment is protected."

Connors blew out an exasperated breath. "Everything's buttoned up, but the comm antenna's standing out there in the wind like a lightning rod."

"It is grounded, isn't it?"

"Sure, but how many amps will this lightning be packing?"

Toshima looked blank. Jamie realized that when he did not know the answer to a question he simply did not reply at all.

"Okay," Connors said, "I'm going to crank down the antenna in between transmissions." The astronaut glanced at the digital clock on the panel. "I will call you in forty-eight minutes, at exactly fifteen hundred hours."

The meteorologist nodded.

"If you've got an emergency call for us, send it over the voice radio or the computer link. Those antennas are flush to the roof. We can talk through the modems if we have to."

"I understand."

Connors signed off, then turned to the bank of switches on his left side. Through the shrill of the wind Jamie heard the faint click of a rocker switch, then the buzz of an electric motor overhead.

"That antenna's right over the cockpit. If it attracts a bolt of lightning we could get fried."

The electric motor's hum turned into a rasping growl.

"Kee-rap! It's stuck. Fuckin' dust must be packed into the joints." Connors flicked the switch up and down several times, his usual easygoing manner disintegrating into frustrated wrath. The motor whined and strained. With a shake of his head Connors said, "Stuck in the halfway position. Won't reach the satellite and still sticking up enough to attract lightning. Useless goddam piece of junk!" He pounded a fist against the panel.

"It *is* grounded, though," Jamie said, half a question.

"Yeah, but who knows how much juice a Martian lightning bolt might carry?"

Looking out at the dark clouds blowing past the cockpit, Jamie muttered, "Let's hope we don't have to find out."

"Wonder what the hell else the dust is screwing up."

Jamie felt his eyebrows rise.

"Like the wheels, maybe," Connors grumbled. "Maybe we'll have to walk back to the dome."

Jamie looked more closely at the black astronaut. It was not like

Connors to complain or be so bitter. The man's face was shining with perspiration. His cheeks looked hollow, his eyes sunken and bloodshot.

"Maybe we should take another dose of that antibiotic," Jamie said.

Tapping the digital clock display Connors said testily, "Not until seventeen hundred hours. Doctor's orders."

They both heard the footsteps at the same instant and turned in their chairs. Joanna was almost running up the length of the command module toward them. Her heart-shaped face was haggard, but she was smiling the biggest smile Jamie had ever seen on her.

"We have it!" she said, almost breathless. "Living organisms! In the rocks!"

Fast as Connors's flier's reflexes were, Jamie scrambled out of his seat first. His throat was so tight he could not say a word, but he pounded down the module after Joanna and ducked through the airlock hatch, Connors right behind him.

Ilona was half slumped over the optical microscope, its intense light the only illumination in the lab module. Profiled against the bright white light she looked totally spent, exhausted like a woman who had just given birth.

She smiled up at Jamie. Wanly.

"Inside the rocks," Joanna said, her voice a reverent whisper. "Just as you said back at McMurdo. . . ."

Jamie found himself staring at Ilona. She looked terribly weak.

"It is something like terrestrial lichen," Joanna was explaining, ignoring her coworker. "They have a hard silicate shell to protect them from the cold, but the shell is water permeable. And there are windows in it that allow sunlight through." She was almost babbling. "We think the windows are transparent mainly in the infrared, but they obviously let visible wavelengths pass through them too, to some extent. Their internal water is apparently laced with some form of alcohol, a natural kind of antifreeze. They must go dormant at night or whenever the temperature drops so low that even their antifreeze crystallizes, then they become active again when the temperature rises enough for their antifreeze to liquefy. It is definite! It is real! Look for yourself!"

Ilona managed to move her chair slightly so Jamie could bend over the microscope. He saw a mottle of colors, purplish circular things interlaced with threads of a lighter bluish tone.

"I thought they were orange."

"They are," Ilona said softly. "We stained them for the microscope."

"They take up dyes the same way terrestrial tissues do!" Joanna was still excited, exultant. "They polarize light the same way terrestrial organisms do! They must be based on the same kind of nucleic acids and proteins!"

"It's too soon to say that," Ilona corrected in a whisper.

Jamie was still peering into the microscope. Martian organisms. Living creatures of Mars.

"They are like the crustose thalli of Antarctica," he heard Joanna say into his ear. "Do you see the outer cortex and then the clusters of algae?"

"The purple things?"

"Yes." She even laughed, shakily. "The purple things. They are alive, Jamie."

He straightened up and gave Connors a chance to squint into the microscope.

"It is life, Jamie," said Joanna, tired but triumphant. "It is merely a form of lichen and it must remain dormant almost all the time. But it is alive and native to Mars."

"We've done it!" Despite her exhaustion there was joy in Ilona's voice. "We've found life on Mars."

"I guess you have," said Jamie. His insides were trembling. He felt awed by their discovery.

Connors grinned at the women. "You guys'll get the Nobel Prize for this."

"Yes, yes," Joanna said. "I suppose we will. But what does that matter? Nothing matters now. We have found what we came for! Whatever happens from now on, it does not matter."

Ilona suddenly sagged against Jamie's shoulder for support. Jamie felt her going limp, collapsing. Outside, the dust storm sang its own melody.

E A R T H

W A S H I N G T O N :   Edith was standing beside Alberto Brumado when the phone call came.

They had just returned to the red-brick house after dinner in Georgetown. Edith knew instinctively that the man was going to make his play for her. What she did not yet know was how she would react. Brumado was kind, intelligent, gentle, and even suave in a sort of bashful, boyish way.

What would he be like in bed? she wondered. And she found herself also wondering, Is Jamie bedding his daughter?

But the telephone interrupted Brumado as he was pouring two snifters of Osborne brandy. He crossed the bookshelf-lined living room and picked up the phone.

"Yes, this is he. . . . Oh, hello, Jeffrey, how are . . ." Brumado's face went white. "*What*? She did? It's certain?" He lapsed into a string of rapid Brazilian Portuguese. Then, realizing it, he switched back to English, breathless. "Yes, yes, yes. I'll be right down. As soon as I can get a taxicab. Yes. Thanks! Thank you for calling! I'll be there, surely!"

If he hadn't been grinning from ear to ear Edith would have thought some disaster had hit the Mars explorers.

He looked across the room to her. "They've found living organisms on Mars. My daughter made the discovery!"

Edith yelled a Texas war whoop and ran to him and threw her arms around his neck. He held her around the waist and they kissed the way strangers do on New Year's Eve.

Then, "I've got to get a taxi. We're expected at NASA headquarters."

"I've got to tell my boss!" Edith said.

"All the media will be informed," Brumado said, pecking at the phone with a trembling hand. "They're calling a news conference for midnight."

While he paced the oriental carpet, impatiently waiting for the taxicab, Edith phoned the network vice-president at his apartment in Manhattan.

"You have reached . . . ," an answering-machine tape started.

Edith felt a moment of exasperation, then started laughing. When the beep sounded she shouted into the phone, "This is Edie Elgin. I'm in the nation's capital with Alberto Brumado and as soon as a cab can get here we're goin' to NASA headquarters. *They've found life on Mars,* buddy! And you weren't home to take the call!"

Edith then phoned the network news office. The news director was at home, and the woman in charge at this hour of the evening had never heard of Edie Elgin.

"I'm a consultant to the vice-president's office," Edith explained.

"So?"

"I've got a story. I've got to get on the air from the Washington office here. Top priority."

"What's this all about?"

"It's the biggest news break in the history of the business, honey!"

"Really?" The woman's voice dripped suspicion.

Suddenly Edith hesitated. They'll take it away from me, she realized. I'll tip them off and they'll call in the managing editor and the evening news anchor bastard and I'll wind up in the cold.

"Can you give me the news director's home number?" she asked.

"No." Flatly.

"This is important, dammit!"

"If it's that important you'd better tell me what it is."

Edith took a deep breath. "Okay," she said sweetly. "Just remember this call tomorrow when they fire y'all."

She hung up the phone and turned to Brumado. "Is the taxi here? Do I have a minute to go to the bathroom?"

In the hour and a half between their arrival at NASA's headquarters building and the official start of the news conference, Edith used up four spools on her miniaturized tape recorder, talking to the men who had gathered together to drink champagne and smoke cigars. She was not the only woman at the impromptu party, but she was the only member of the media among the Mars Project people.

The news conference filled the building's largest auditorium, even at midnight. Television crews elbowed one another for choice spots up front. The lights were blindingly bright, but nobody seemed to mind. Phalanxes of microphones and tape recorders were propped up on the long table at which the grinning NASA people assembled, shaking hands with one another, glowing with self-vindication. They sat Alberto Brumado in their midst.

Edith took a folding chair set up by the side wall, next to an emergency exit. She smiled to herself. She had her story, and she would continue to gather in all the details of the human side of this fantastic night. Even if she had to finish the job in bed with Brumado. That might not be such a bad way to end a night like this, she thought.

Although stodgy gray-haired NASA administrators officially broke the news to the goggle-eyed reporters, it was Alberto Brumado who ended up doing most of the talking. The soul of the Mars Project had his hour in the limelight. His smiling, triumphant face and voice were broadcast all across the world.

Life on Mars.

While Brumado answered the reporters' myriad of questions and bantered happily with them, no one noticed that the physician in charge of the medical section sat at the very end of the table of NASA officials, looking tired and grim. No one asked him a question. No one paid him any attention at all. Which was just as well, because he had made up his mind to remain absolutely silent, no matter what. He was not the kind of man to rain on the organization's parade.

S O L   3 7:   EVENING

Dr. Yang Meilin gave a disdainful snort at the data on her display screen. Pushing her chair away from the tiny desk, she got to her feet and opened the accordion-fold door of her infirmary.

Dr. Li was up in the command section, of course, in the middle of a three-way conversation with the excursion team down at Tithonium Chasma and the mission controllers at Kaliningrad.

So they have found life on Mars, Dr. Yang said to herself. And they are all sick, perhaps even dying. Could there be a connection? No, that cannot be, she said to herself.

The passageway was empty, silent except for the hum of machinery. Everyone in the craft is packed into the command module, Yang realized. No one is paying any attention to this medical emergency. No one is paying any attention to me.

When she reached the command module, Dr. Li was at the comm console. Every one of the display screens was lit up. Alberto Brumado himself was beaming happily from the main display, while the other screens showed bigwigs in Kaliningrad, Houston, and what appeared to be Tokyo. Men, all of them. The TV link to the excursion team was out due to the storm, but Joanna Brumado was on the radio, trying to answer the volleys of questions.

She is beautiful, Yang thought, and the daughter of Alberto Brumado. Now she has found life on Mars. The center of everyone's attention, everyone's desires. I am nothing but a nondescript physician, the bearer of unhappy news. No wonder they want to ignore me.

Does Brumado know that his daughter is ill? Yang thought not. The mission controllers knew, of course, but so far they regarded the malady that was affecting the entire ground team as nothing more serious than a bout of flu.

It is more than flu. Yang was sure.

What if there *are* Martian organisms in the air? Viruses or microbes so tiny or so different that they escaped notice when the air was tested. What if they *can* infect human cells?

She shook her head, a motion that set her severely straight bangs whisking back and forth. Nonsense! Alien organisms cannot affect terrestrial cells. Their metabolisms would be completely different.

And yet, from the little that she had been able to glean about the lichenlike creatures Brumado and Malater had discovered, they were remarkably similar to terrestrial organisms. They must do a DNA workup, Yang thought. And a thorough chemical analysis.

A Martian plague. The very idea was too outlandish even to consider seriously. It was as unlikely as . . . as—she felt a tremor race through her body—as unlikely as being hit by a meteoroid.

Then she realized that she was standing in the hatch of a spacecraft orbiting the planet Mars, standing on tiptoes to peek over the shoulders of the crowd clustered around their leader, who was being congratulated now by the directors of the Mars Project for successfully finding the first extraterrestrial life forms ever discovered by humankind. What can be considered outlandish? she chided herself. What might be likely or unlikely?

How happy they all looked. Even Li, the human scarecrow who never allowed himself to relax, was smiling joyfully at the multiple screens facing him. They were all congratulating each other, man to man, like an overaged athletic team that had just won an unexpected victory, confident that this discovery would assure their futures.

But not if the people on the ground die. That will terrify everyone. And they *are* dying. Despite Reed's assurances, the data showed that something was debilitating all the men and women on the surface of Mars. They are growing weaker. They are dying.

It had been a momentous day. Despite their fatigue and pain the foursome in the rover had spent the entire afternoon on the radio with the dome, with Li and the other scientists in the orbiting ships, with the mission controllers in Kaliningrad and then Houston, and finally with the project directors in Moscow, Washington, Tokyo, and six other capital cities on Earth.

"You might know this is the one time the goddam TV link is down," Connors grumbled.

The TV antenna was still jammed in its halfway-down position, useless. But the backup radio voice links worked, even though the interference of the dust storm made the transmissions relayed from orbit sound faint, blurred with crackling static.

Joanna had used the computer modem and the attached fax machine to squirt every bit of data—and all the photomicrographs— she and Ilona had gleaned from the lichen. Ilona herself was resting in her bunk; after she had practically collapsed in his arms, Jamie had unfolded the bunk and insisted that she try to sleep.

It was well after sundown before all the radio calls were finished. They would still have been talking, but Jamie begged off, claiming that they had to eat and rest so they would be fresh the next morning. Dr. Li had quickly taken the hint.

"I will handle all communications until you are ready for the morning's work," he said.

They had made no mention of their illness to the project brass in the various capital cities. Neither had the mission controllers, who knew as much about their condition as Li did. No one wanted to tarnish the triumph of the moment.

Now the four of them were gathered around the rover's narrow table, seated as usual, the two men on one bench, the two women opposite. Ilona seemed slightly better for the few hours' sleep she had obtained; still, she looked pale and drawn. Joanna too looked sallow, tense, her eyes shadowed, her cheeks hollow.

Connors was relentlessly cheerful, as if he dared not show anything but good humor. Yet it seemed to Jamie that his movements were slower than usual, forced, his breathing heavy.

"We've got to have a toast," the astronaut said, sliding out from the bench and heading toward the refrigerator built into the galley bulkhead. "A toast to the discovery of extraterrestrial life."

Jamie felt dull, achy. Connors's phony enthusiasm irritated him, but he kept silent.

"Damn! There's nothing in here to toast with," Connors muttered, scanning the inside of the fridge.

"Is there any orange juice?" Joanna asked.

"Yeah. Still got a half a quart of it."

"Let's use that, then," said Jamie.

"Orange juice?"

"Pretend there's vodka in it."

So they toasted in orange juice. Weakly. To Ilona and Joanna. To the discovery of life on Mars. To the unequivocal fact that Earth is not the only world that harbors life. To the Nobel Prize that the two women would share.

"Oh, I do not think they would award the Nobel for this," Joanna said.

"Are you kidding?" Connors insisted. "For the discovery of extra-terrestrial life?"

"There is no category among the Nobels for it," Joanna pointed out. Then she added, musing, "Unless the Swedish Academy wants to stretch their definition of medicine and physiology."

"Or chemistry," Jamie said.

"Maybe they'll make a new category," Connors suggested hope-fully.

Ilona gave him a wan smile and said, "You don't know the Swedes, Peter."

They picked at their dinner trays. The meal went slowly. The aftereffect was setting in, Jamie realized. The reaction, the letdown after the high excitement of discovery and success.

So we've found life on Mars, he thought. I'll bet by tomorrow there'll be a flood of Martian jokes on TV.

His legs ached as if he'd been running cross-country all day. He felt weak. Leaning his head back against the padded bulkhead Jamie wondered how sick they really were, and how soon they would recover. It seemed to him that they were all getting worse, not better.

The comm unit up in the cockpit buzzed, making Jamie's insides jump.

"Must be Vosnesensky," Connors guessed. "I'll get it."

The astronaut's breath was fetid. What the hell did he eat tonight? Jamie asked himself. And why can't he turn off that damned buzzer? The noise grated like a dentist's drill.

Jamie got up too and wordlessly began stacking up the dinner trays. He noticed that none of them had finished more than half their meal, yet the jug of orange juice was entirely gone. Plenty of toasting, he told himself. Good thing we didn't have any vodka to spike it.

Joanna got up to help. Ilona slumped back on the bench, eyes half glazed. She's in real trouble, Jamie thought, studying her pale face. Outside, the wind was still keening, calling, like the beckoning spirit of a departed loved one.

Are we going to die here? The sudden idea startled Jamie. But then he thought, What of it? This isn't a bad place to die. We've accomplished what we came here for. Maybe Mars will demand our lives in return for giving up its biggest secret. A fair payment, life for life.

But Mars is a gentle world, he told himself silently. It may look harsh and forbidding at first, but it's really placid and gentle. Then another part of his mind answered grimly, Until your air runs out. Or your suit ruptures. Then you'll see how gentle this world is.

Connors came back to the table as Jamie was sliding the trays into the storage rack.

"Mikhail says we're going to have a news conference tomorrow morning. Multinational hookup. Every goddam reporter on Earth wants to talk to us. I'll have to go outside first thing and straighten out the video antenna. They want to *see* us."

"Oh god, not like this," Ilona moaned.

"Tell them we can't fix the antenna," Jamie said.

Connors started to shake his head, thought better of it. "Got to try, man. Besides, I'll have to go out tomorrow anyway to see how much sand's piled up against us and whether there's any other damage to the rover."

"That means I go out too," Jamie said.

"No. It'll be okay if you just suit up. If there's any emergency you can pop out inside of a minute."

"But the regulations . . ."

"Regulations permit an *astronaut* to go EVA solo, as long as there's a backup suited up and ready for trouble. It's just you poor little scientists who can't go out on your own."

Connors was trying to be jovial, but Jamie felt himself snarling inwardly at the astronaut.

"Oh yeah," Connors added. "Reed wants another set of tests: temperature, blood pressure, pulse rate, and—the best comes last—more blood samples."

"Not again," Ilona protested.

"Now that we know there's Martian life here, maybe we've caught Martian bugs," Connors said. "That's something new to worry about."

"I'll go first," Joanna said, struggling to get out from behind the table.

"I'll help you," said Jamie.

There was no such thing as privacy aboard the rover, but at least they could conduct the medical tests in the lab module while Ilona and Connors remained in the command section. The lab felt intimate with just the two of them in it. Only the single strip of overhead lights was on, throwing muted shadows over the equipment they had used earlier, softening the lines etched into Joanna's pallid, uneasy face. The wind sang its high, shrill note outside, but here in the lab alone with Joanna it was almost cozy.

Jamie made her sit down as he rummaged through the medical cabinet for the blood pressure cuff, thermometer patches, and hypodermic syringes. He carefully took her temperature, blood pressure, and pulse. All a little higher than normal.

As he was swabbing the crook of her arm for the blood-sampling needle, Jamie said, "I hadn't thought about it before, but if there are Martian lichen then there must be other Martian organisms, too."

Joanna nodded solemnly as she pumped her arm up and down. "Yes. Lichen may seem like a lowly form of life to us, but they are highly organized compared to protozoa and even alga colonies."

Jamie hated needles. It almost made him sick just to watch someone, anyone, being stuck with one. It was an effort to keep his hands steady as he jabbed the hypodermic into the swollen vein in Joanna's arm on the first try. She flinched slightly.

"Then there really are Martian microbes," Jamie said as he drew her blood. "Germs and viruses and all."

"There must be. The lichen cannot be the only form of life on the planet. There must be at least a primitive ecology."

"Then why haven't we found any?" He slowly eased the plunger back.

Joanna was watching the syringe fill with dark blood. "Either they don't exist outside the canyon, or we did see them but did not recognize them as microbes."

Pressing an adhesive bandage on the tiny wound, Jamie took Joanna's wrist and made her fold her arm.

"You mean all those tests on the air and soil samples and rocks you did . . ."

But Joanna was already off on another tack. "Jamie, on Earth there are deposits of iron oxides that were produced by ancient bacteria. Do you think it is possible that the iron oxides on the surface here are the result of biological activity?"

He blinked at the new idea. "All the dust, all across the planet?"

"From millions of years ago. Hundreds of millions."

"That could explain why the iron is still on the surface," Jamie mused aloud. "Why it didn't all sink toward the core; why the planet's not differentiated the way Earth is."

Then he looked into her dark weary eyes. "It could explain a lot of things, maybe. I never thought about the possibility of biology affecting the geology here."

"It is possible, perhaps," she said.

"Perhaps."

Then he realized he was holding a syringe full of her blood in his upraised hand. Carefully, Jamie injected the blood into a stoppered tube in the automated blood analyzer. It sat on the far end of the lab bench, stainless steel and glass vials, smaller than the coffeemaker back at the dome and still gleaming new. They had not expected they would need to use it.

"How do you feel?" he asked as he pecked out Joanna's name and the time on the medical computer's keyboard.

She tried to smile. "I will live. I think."

Her breath smelled bad too. Jamie guessed that his own was not sweet. Stepping slightly back from her, "What the hell is it? What's making us sick?"

"Tony will find it," she said softly. "He is an excellent physician."

"Yeah. They'll end up calling it Reed's Martian Fever."

"But we don't have fever," Joanna pointed out gently.

"Yes you do," he said. "Low-grade, but your temperature's above normal."

Jamie entered the data from her tests into the lab's computer, which automatically modemed the information up to the orbiting spacecraft and back to the dome. He turned on the analyzer; except for its green light glowing it gave no hint that it was working. Silently its findings about Joanna's blood sample would also be relayed automatically through the computer link.

Without getting up from her chair Joanna plucked at Jamie's sleeve.

"Now I'll do you."

He looked down at her. "Do you feel well enough . . . ?"

"I won't bleed you to death, Jamie," she said. "I am still capable of doing simple tasks like sticking a needle into your arm."

Reluctantly, Jamie rolled up his sleeve.

As she wrapped the pressure cuff around his arm Jamie applied one of the temperature-sensing patches to his own forehead.

"The question is," she said, almost to herself, "do the lichen represent the best that Mars can do, or are they the survivors of more complex life forms that have become extinct?"

Jamie leaned his rump against the edge of the workbench as she read off the digital display of his blood pressure.

"Maybe that rock formation really was a village?" he asked.

"We have not seen any other evidence for *intelligent* life, Jamie. I am merely suggesting . . ."

"There's that face carved on the rock up in the Acidalia region."

"Oh, James! Surely you don't believe that!"

He shrugged. "Now that we know that there's life on Mars, who knows what to believe?"

"That there were once intelligent Martians?" She was reaching for a fresh hypo.

Looking away from the glinting needle, Jamie said, "The planet's had billions of years. Time enough for intelligence to evolve—and then get wiped out when the climate changed."

Joanna shook her head as she tied the rubber tubing above Jamie's elbow. "But there is no evidence, no remains of civilization, no ruins."

"All covered up by the dust storms." He pumped up his arm. "Except for my village up there in the cliff. Maybe there are more . . . *ouch!*"

"I'm sorry." She had missed his vein. It took her three tries before she got blood.

Jamie said, "This changes everything for you, doesn't it?"

"What do you mean?"

"Finding life. You're a famous woman now. You'll be more famous than your father."

She blinked several times. "I had not thought about that. Once we get back . . ."

"We won't be able to settle into normal lives after all. At least you won't."

"Nor you," Joanna said. "If it had not been for you, we would never have gotten here."

"You've fulfilled your father's greatest expectations," Jamie said, as gently as he knew how. "You don't have to be afraid of him anymore."

"I am not afraid of my father!"

"I mean, he'll have to let go of you now."

She looked into his face for a long moment, troubled, uncertain. "I will have to let go of him, too, then."

"Yes." Jamie nodded even though it hurt his head. Neither of them smiled.

Ilona and Connors took their turn in the lab module together while Joanna went to the lavatory and prepared for bed. Jamie, too restless even to think about sleep, made his way up to the cockpit. The storm shrilled continuously outside, making the night blacker than any he had yet experienced on Mars. He peeked through the thermal shroud, saw that there was nothing to see, then let it snap back into place.

He felt no fear of the billowing dust racing past. To Jamie it was more like soft cottony clouds enwrapping them; he had no sense of gritty sand particles that could scratch and grind metal. I could walk out there if I had to, even at the height of this storm, he told himself. It might even be fun.

When will it end? he asked himself. Maybe I should call Toshima and ask for his forecast. Then he thought, Why bother? It'll end when it ends, no matter what the meteorologist says. Fingering the comforting smooth stone of the bear fetish in his pocket, Jamie told himself it was foolish to try to press things. Especially when you have no power over them. Wait out the storm. Wait out all the storms.

He felt tired, utterly tired, yet too keyed up to crawl into his bunk. Like a kid the night before Christmas. So damned tired he can barely keep his eyes open, yet too excited to go to sleep.

Connors and Ilona are spending a long time in the lab. Is she up to her old tricks again? Well, if Pete can get it up when he feels as bad as he looks, then more credit to him. And Ilona—he almost laughed—she's like the good old Post Office: neither rain nor storm nor dark of night will stop her.

He rubbed a hand across his bristly chin. Maybe I ought to shave. If we get the antenna fixed and we're on TV tomorrow I ought at least to try to look respectable. On the other hand, maybe I'll look worse shaved than with a four-day growth. Maybe. Li won't want the media to know we're sick. Brumado must know about his daughter and the rest of us, but we sure as hell don't want the media to pick up on it. They'll go nuts. Martian fever. Everything we've accomplished will get buried the instant they suspect one of us has so much as the sniffles.

He realized that there are people on Earth who would be afraid of any Martian life. The idea of life on other worlds destroyed their comforting self-esteem, attacked their religious beliefs, shattered their view of the universe. Or worse. The UFO nuts must be going crazy! They'll be expecting a Martian invasion, at the very least. The thought startled Jamie. Saddened him beyond measure.

Absently, his mind churning, Jamie leaned across the control panel and turned on the rover's headlamps. Peeking through the thermal shroud again, he saw a softly diffused grayish light that revealed nothing, just a dimensionless glow like a thick, billowing fog. The Martian wind sang its endless song, although he thought it sounded a tone deeper than before. Is that good news or bad? he wondered.

They're going to make us turn back tomorrow, he knew. Without getting near the cliff village. They're going to say we're too sick to go on and make us head back for the dome.

Jamie knew that it was the right thing to do. Four lives depended on it. Yet as he peered out at the pearly gray clouds wafting past the rover's canopy he wondered if there were some way he could get them to agree to pushing forward instead of retreating.

I could walk it, he thought. I could walk there from here and get to see it, climb up the cliff and put my hands on it. I could do it.

And then die. There's no way to get back again; the suit can't keep you alive for that long. But I could at least get there and see it for myself. It wouldn't be a bad place to die. Maybe that's the meaning of my dream.

Tony Reed could not sleep either.

He had retired to his cubicle, of course, as had the seven others living in the dome when the lights had automatically dimmed for the night. Vosnesensky insisted on keeping exactly to the mission schedule except for dire emergencies, and Mikhail Andreivitch was becoming more of a stickler than ever, grouchy and brooding, as the illness took hold of him.

As soon as he heard the Russian's deep snoring, like a farm tractor rumbling back and forth, Reed got up from his bunk and tiptoed in his bulky slipper socks back to his infirmary. The dome felt cold in the darkness. Reed dared not turn on the overhead lights as he padded past the silent workstations. He reached the infirmary and, sliding its door shut, groped around his desk to his chair and reached for his desktop computer as he sat down. He found its power switch by touch and turned it on. The little screen glowed orange like a cheery fire.

They're dying, Reed knew. They're all dying and they're looking to me to save them. And I don't know what to do! He scrolled through the data from the latest medical checks. Nothing new. Nothing he could see that offered the slightest clue as to what might be infecting them.

Tony shook his head as he stared at the screen. He himself felt fine: a bit tired, eyes burning from overwork, but otherwise fine. None of the symptoms the others had. How can that be? he asked himself. We all eat the same foods, breathe the same air. Yet they're all sick, every one of them, in the rover and here in the dome. And I'm not.

Leaning back in his spindly plastic chair, Reed half closed his eyes and steepled his long fingers on his chest. Think, man, he snarled to himself. Use the brain up there inside your skull and *think*.

Proposition one: Both the team in the rover and the crew here in the dome have come down with it, whatever it is. Therefore it cannot be an infection from the life forms that the rover team has found.

Yes, true. But can it be an infectious organism in the air? Even though theory says Martian parasites could not possibly attack visitors from another planet, might there be some sort of highly adaptable virus in the air? We know that there is life on Mars. What if there are organisms floating in the air?

Reed shook his head, trying to dismiss the idea. We've sampled the air. Monique has tested it with every piece of equipment she has. Vosnesensky has checked the air purifiers. They've found nothing. And the air in here is Earth-normal, not Martian. Any Martian organisms would be killed by the high levels of oxygen.

And yet—we don't have an electron microscope. A virus could slip past Monique's tests, especially since we don't know exactly what to look for. Maybe they *like* oxygen. And we aren't consistent; we're very careful not to contaminate Martian soil or air samples with our bugs, aren't we? If the bigwigs actually believed their theory, why would they worry that we might possibly infect Mars?

It just doesn't make any sense, Reed told himself. If it's a native Martian organism infecting us, why haven't I been infected? Why am I healthy while all the others are dying?

For the first time he could remember, Tony Reed felt guilty. And inadequate.

He also felt terribly afraid. But that was an emotion he had experienced all his life.

Dr. Yang Meilin slept, but not well. She was troubled by a dream. A nightmare. She was an intern once again in her native city of Wuxi. The great famine had the entire province in its grip. The streets were so littered with the dead that people wore perfumed gauze masks to keep the stench of decaying flesh from their nostrils.

Dr. Yang was at the hospital, in a ward jammed with squalling babies. Emaciated limbs and bloated bellies. Yet even though the babies were being fed with the supplies sent by the International Red Cross, they were still dying.

She was making love with the handsome doctor from Beijing, but she could not give herself to him totally because she could hear the painful crying of the babies through the thin curtains they had pulled around the bed. The doctor returned to Beijing the next morning without even bidding her farewell. And the babies continued to whimper and shriek. And die.

They are not dying of malnutrition, Dr. Yang knew. And even as she said that to herself her dream changed, shifted, mutated: the babies were astronauts, the hospital ward was the dome on the red surface of Mars.

She felt totally helpless. Why are they dying? It is my responsibility to save them, to help them, to keep them alive and return them to health. It is my responsibility to remember. Remember.

She sat bolt upright in her bunk aboard the *Mars 2* spacecraft, instantly awake.

But she could not remember what the dream was trying to tell her.

EARTH

WASHINGTON: Staring out her hotel room window, Edith held the phone tightly against her ear.

"You're fired, Edie," said Howard Francis's angry, rasping voice.

The first thought that went through her mind was, There goes the expense account.

"But why me?" Edith asked. "I tried to get you . . ."

Francis's voice screeched, "You had the fuckin' story an hour and a half before anybody else and you just sat on it! We could've been on the air before all the other networks, even before CNN, if you had done your job right!"

"I tried to get y'all. I tried to get through to the news director, but some shitty little tramp wouldn't let me."

"She was the assistant news director, for Chrissakes! You shoulda told her!"

"She would have cut my throat."

"So what? The *network* would have been first on the air with the biggest story of all time!"

Fuck the network, Edith thought. Aloud, she said, "I tried to tell her how important it was. She just wouldn't believe me. I bet even if I told her what it was, she would have thought I was just some nut."

"Oh, my god, Edie, my own ass is in a sling around here. I'll be lucky if they don't fire me!"

"That'd be too bad," Edith said, her voice brittle with anger. I hope they fire all you assholes, she added silently as she hung up.

Later that morning, when Alberto Brumado picked her up on his way to NASA headquarters, Edith told him her sad news.

"Well," he said, glancing around the quietly opulent hotel lobby, "I suppose you could move in with me."

Edith felt her brows go up.

Brumado smiled his boyish smile. "There is a guest suite on the top floor of the house. You can have complete privacy. I did not mean to suggest anything more."

Edith gave him a smile in return. "I appreciate it, Alberto. I sure need a place—until I can find a job."

"Perhaps I can help you there, too. I have many acquaintances among the media people."

Edith marveled at how smart Brumado really was, understanding that the media people he knew were acquaintances, not friends.

S O L 3 8: MORNING

Jamie awoke well before dawn. The wind had stopped! He lay flat on his bunk, listening. The storm must be over. There was no sound of the wind, no sounds in the darkened rover at all except Connors's fitful snoring and the faint rustling of Joanna turning on her bunk just above him. And the ever-present background hum of electrical power and air fans.

Slowly, silently, he slid out of the bunk and padded in his socks and coveralls to the cockpit. He pulled back the thermal shroud. Still black night outside. There was no discernible moonlight on Mars; its two satellites were too tiny to shed much light on the planet's surface. Jamie switched on the rover's headlamps. The air was clear. He could see the cliff wall out there standing gray and rugged like the ghost of some ancient grandfather.

Quickly he turned the headlamps off, closed the shroud, and crept back to his bunk, satisfied that the storm had indeed ended. He crawled beneath the thin blanket and soon fell back to sleep.

He dreamed of Joanna, the two of them walking across the desert wearing ordinary street clothes. He could not tell if the desert was on Earth or Mars. A city shone on the horizon, white and sparkling in the hot sun. But no matter how long they walked the city came no closer. They trudged along for hours, tired, thirsty, sweaty, but the gleaming towers remained nothing more than a hope in the distance. They became weaker and weaker. Joanna collapsed in his arms, suddenly naked. They both sank to the burning sand, dying, too weak to go any farther.

Jamie had his fetish in his hand, but the little stone bear melted beneath the awful heat and flowed between his fingers.

He was reaching for it, scrabbling in the sand to recover it, when he awoke and realized he was pawing at the sheet that had become tangled between his legs.

Sheepishly Jamie got out of his bunk and headed for the lavatory before any of the others awoke. For the first time since they had left the dome, he shaved. The razor seemed to be slicing flesh, even though it drew no blood. No blood left in me, Jamie thought wearily. The lotion stung when he splashed it on, but the sharpness of the pain was almost welcome after days of the dull, sullen, glowering ache that had been dogging him.

"Thanks," Jamie muttered to his freshly shaved image in the lav's metal mirror. "I needed that." The face that looked back at him was gaunt, red eyed, with hollows beneath the high cheekbones. You're turning into a paleface, Jamie said to it.

Joanna seemed wearier, too, and Ilona barely managed to pull herself out of her bunk and make it to the lavatory. After a glum breakfast Jamie accompanied Connors outside despite the astronaut's mild protests.

"There won't be a media conference until the antenna's fixed," Jamie pointed out. "So there's no reason for me to stay inside."

He got the impression that the astronaut was too weak, too much in pain, to argue. Jamie himself felt ragged, and tired. The night's sleep had done nothing to restore his strength. The achy feeling that had assailed him for two days now was worse; every muscle in his body felt strained.

Morning mists hovered as they stepped out from the airlock. Tendrils of cold gray fog drifted by, slowly as departing spirits. Where does the moisture come from? Jamie asked himself again. It's being replenished every day. It evaporates when the sun touches it, and then more mist forms the next morning. How? Why?

Connors ignored the mist. "Looks like we've got some digging to do."

The rover was piled almost roof high with sand on its windward side, nearly buried in dust so fine and loose that it blew up in powdery clouds when the two hard-suited men stepped in it.

"Good thing the hatch is on the sheltered side," Jamie said.

"I don't think the sand's heavy enough to keep the hatch closed," Connors said, as they walked through the powdery drifts, tossing up plumes of dust with each booted step. "We could've pushed it open with no sweat, I betcha."

Maybe, Jamie said to himself.

Connors clambered slowly, awkwardly up the ladder set into the command module's side just behind the cockpit canopy and began to examine the microwave antenna.

"Just what I thought," Jamie heard in his earphones as he waited at the ladder's base. "Goddamn dust wormed its way under the gasket seal . . . oh shit, I can't believe I did that!"

"What? Are you okay?"

"Yeah. Just dumb, that's all. I tried to blow the dust out of the gasket."

Connors was grumbling to himself. Then Jamie realized, "With your helmet on!"

"Fogged up the faceplate real nice."

"Turn up the blower."

"Already have. It's clearing up."

Connors came down and went to the outside equipment compartment on the lab module for tools: a fine wire brush and a shovel. In a few minutes he had the antenna mount clear of dust.

Over the suit radios, they asked Joanna to check the TV link. They saw the antenna arm unfold; then the dish turned slowly until it locked onto their spacecraft orbiting over the equator. Joanna reported that she had contacted the dome without difficulty.

"Vosnesensky says the news conference will start in another hour, if we can be ready by then," she reported.

"No sweat," said Connors.

Jamie grunted to himself. In fact, he was perspiring heavily inside his suit and was certain that Connors was too.

"You go in now," the astronaut said to Jamie. "I'll go around the other side and dig out one of the wheels, see if we can get away without digging out the others."

"I can help."

"Naw, it's okay. This stuff is so fluffy you can blow it away with a whisk broom. If I need help I'll ask you. Maybe we'll have a digging party after the media conference, all four of us."

"You're sure you'll be okay out here?"

"I'm no hero, Jamie. If I need help I'll yell, don't worry."

Reluctantly Jamie went back inside. It took much longer than usual to vacuum the dust off his suit. Leaving his helmet in the airlock, he tramped the length of the command module to the cockpit. Joanna was in the pilot's seat, speaking into the display screen. Jamie recognized the face of Burt Klein, the American astronaut on *Mars 2*.

Klein grinned at him. "You guys have your antenna back on track," he said.

Jamie mumbled an acknowledgment, then turned to the voice link with Connors. "Everything's fine. We've got Mars 2 on the screen."

"Great," said Connors, puffing. "I've got our right front wheel almost cleared."

Looking from Joanna's tired face to Klein's healthy unclouded image on the little display screen Jamie realized how sick the four of them must be. His skin's almost pink, Jamie thought.

Dr. Li came on the screen and began giving instructions about the news conference that would begin within the hour. He asked Jamie to bring Connors inside before the conference started. Jamie checked his wristwatch against the digital clock on the cockpit control panel, then asked Joanna to take over the comm link. Klein came back on and Joanna chatted with him almost as if they were old friends discussing the weather.

Jamie saw that Joanna had put on a fresh set of coveralls, coral pink, and had applied makeup to her face. She's trying to hide the pallor, he realized, trying to look good for the media. And for her father.

Making his way back toward the airlock in the bulky hard suit, Jamie passed Ilona. She sat on one of the benches, looking exhausted. She too had put on makeup and had even wrapped a bright flowered scarf around her coverall collar. But she still looked terribly pale and weak.

Jamie tried to be cheerful. "Ready to be famous?"

She smiled faintly. No amount of makeup could hide the strain in her face, the redness of her eyes. But maybe she could get past the cameras okay. The big story today is supposed to be the discovery of life on Mars, not our physical condition.

The two-way transmission lag between Earth and Mars was now more than twenty-five minutes, so a live give-and-take interview was impossible. Instead, the media reporters and the mission controllers had worked out a different protocol. Twelve reporters had been selected from the swarms that had descended on Kaliningrad, Houston, Washington, and other capitals the instant the news of life on Mars had been released. Each of the twelve was in a different location on Earth. Each would ask a question, to be answered by one of the Mars explorers. There would be no follow-on questions. Alberto Brumado, in Washington, would fill in the time between question and answer with commentary and chat among the mission controllers, project

administrators, and politicians assembled in Kaliningrad and elsewhere.

Many politicians had come to place themselves before the cameras, eager to bask in the glow of the great discovery and allow the
world's media to interview them on global TV.

Jamie wondered if Edith would be among the questioners. Not
likely, he decided. She's just started with the network; she's not high
enough on their ladder for this.

The two women sat in the cockpit seats, with Jamie and Connors
standing behind them. The hour had barely been enough time for
Connors to dig out one of the rover's wheels and then drag himself
back inside. He had taken off only the top half of his hard suit, and
stood beside Jamie with his boots still on and his lily-white leggings
spattered with red dust that exuded the stinging odor of ozone, despite his efforts to vacuum them clean.

Vosnesensky was at the comm screen in the dome, Dr. Li up in
orbit. The people on Earth could speak with any of the units of the
Mars expedition that they wished to converse with.

Brumado came on the screen before the conference officially
began. He congratulated his daughter, and Joanna sent him a loving
thank-you. Jamie was almost jealous of the warm smile she offered
her father. When her message finally reached him Brumado gave no
indication that he was shocked or even worried by his daughter's
appearance; she had put up a smiling front without once mentioning
their physical condition.

He's probably too excited to even notice, Jamie thought. Maybe
we're all too worked up about how lousy we feel. If it doesn't show
on television, how bad can it really be?

The order in which the reporters asked their questions had been
picked at random by the mission control mainframe computer in
Kaliningrad. Everyone thought that was a fittingly scientific way to
handle the problem of priority. The reporter selected to be first was
Hong Kong's foremost media personality, a strikingly beautiful
woman with skin like porcelain and almond eyes that had inspired
poetry.

"First, I wish to congratulate you on the most significant discovery
in the history of the space age," she said in flawless British English.
Her voice was a silvery soprano; she almost sang out the words. "My
question is: Which of you actually made the discovery, and how did
you feel when you first realized that you had found life on Mars?"

Joanna turned doubtfully in the chair toward Ilona, sitting beside her. The face of the Hong Kong woman was replaced with Brumado's, who would fill in the time until their response reached Kaliningrad. The sound volume automatically went down to a barely audible level.

"I can answer that," Ilona said, forcing a smile. "Dr. Brumado was the first to realize that the forms she was examining in the microscope were alive. She is our biologist, and it is she who actually made the discovery."

Joanna said, "Dr. Malater was with me. We were working together on the samples we had gathered that morning. I merely happened to be the first to examine them in the microscope, but we worked together on the collection and preparation of the samples. You would have to say that we discovered them together."

Ilona took over again, her husky voice more than an octave lower than Joanna's. "As for how we felt—it was the most exciting moment of my life. Better than sex."

Pale as she was, Joanna flushed. "It was very thrilling," she agreed. "I think that at the first moment neither of us could believe it. Then, when we finally convinced ourselves that it was real, that the specimen in the microscope was actually a life form, we looked at each other and could not say a word."

"Which is very unusual for me," Ilona blurted.

"We realized that this was one of the most momentous discoveries in the history of science. I felt . . . what is the word in English? Awed. Yes, that is right. It was an awesome moment. Truly awesome."

"I felt like dancing," Ilona said.

Jamie added silently, But you were too tired and weak to try.

"We must all remember," Joanna added, more seriously, "that it was not merely Dr. Malater and I who made this discovery. Dr. Waterman was the one who recognized that this rift valley would be the most likely place to find life. The other scientists and astronauts—without them we could never have reached this place. All the men and women of this great expedition, all the men and women supporting this mission back on Earth, they have each played their role in this discovery. We are a team, a team that reaches across more than two hundred million kilometers of space and embraces two worlds. Each of us has played an important part."

Jamie said to himself, She's her father's daughter, all right. There's a future for her in the politics of science.

The questions were mainly superficial. Connors was asked by a bored-looking Frenchman how it felt to be the only black man on Mars. The astronaut grinned a one-word answer: "Terrific!" But once the screen showed Brumado talking with one of the opportunistic politicians, Connors muttered, "Fucking pissant."

When Jamie's turn came he was asked by an American reporter how it felt to be vindicated in his battle to change the mission plan and make the traverse to the Grand Canyon.

Wishing that Edith had possessed the clout to make it to the news conference, suddenly lonely for the sight of her blonde cheerful smile, Jamie replied to the pinch-faced man: "There was never a battle. We had a mission plan, but it had been made up on Earth long before we got here. Fortunately, the mission controllers and the expedition commander, Dr. Li—as well as Cosmonaut Vosnesensky and my fellow scientists—all saw the wisdom of altering the plan so we could take advantage of what we found here on the ground. We had the flexibility to change the plan, to take advantage of new discoveries."

Jamie realized that there was another tremendous advantage to being on Mars: the interviewers could not interrupt you. Nor could they stop you from going on at length and giving the complete answer that you wanted to give.

"Another thing," he said, forgetting his tiredness for a moment. "It's more than just simple lichen that we've discovered. Life doesn't exist in one species alone; we know that from Earth. There's got to be a Martian ecology here, a chain of living organisms. Certainly there must be organisms that are lower down on the chain of life than the lichen we've found. But the interesting question is, are there organisms *higher* on the chain? Or were there such higher organisms at one time in the past?"

He glanced down at Joanna, who was smiling encouragement at him. Connors patted his shoulder.

"Here in this Grand Canyon we discovered a rock formation that might not be natural. It's a long shot, of course, but there may have once been intelligent Martians. We have the opportunity—the responsibility, really—to come back to Mars with expeditions that are equipped to stay for much longer so they can tackle some of these questions."

Jamie enjoyed seeing Brumado's eyes sparkle when his little speech finally reached Earth.

The next reporter threw away his prepared question and asked, "Do you mean that there might have been intelligent creatures on Mars?" His eyes were wide with incredulity.

"Yes," answered Jamie firmly. "Might have been. We don't know if there actually were. The chances against seem very high, but—we just don't know enough about Mars to say, one way or the other."

The display screen picture broke up momentarily as every one of the reporters tried to get in a question about intelligent Martians. Brumado restored calm only by shouting over their voices the name of the next reporter picked by the computer.

All of the following questions were about "real, live Martians." Most of them were directed at Jamie, who felt that their questions were generally trivial and terribly repetitious. He remembered a friend of his, a lawyer, who always replied to questions he felt to be redundant with a curt, "Asked and answered."

Joanna interrupted him once to say, "I want to make certain that everyone understands exactly what we have found here on Mars. We have discovered living organisms, somewhat the same as terrestrial lichens. We have not found any evidence at all for the existence of intelligent Martians, even intelligent Martians who might have become extinct ages ago."

Jamie nodded agreement. "That's right. My speculations about intelligent Martians are nothing more than speculations, based on a rock formation that we've seen from a distance."

At last Brumado announced that each of the twelve chosen reporters had been heard from. "Now we must break away to the White House. The President and Vice-President of the United States have a few words to say to our explorers."

The screen flickered, then showed the President smiling from a deep leather-covered wing chair by a marble fireplace and mantle. A portrait of Thomas Jefferson was visible behind him.

"I want to add my congratulations and best wishes to you on Mars," said the President in his warmest manner. "You have made a magnificent accomplishment and everyone in the nation, everyone in the world, is thrilled by your discovery."

The view on the screen widened to show the Vice-President, wearing a kelly green pants suit that offset her blonde coiffure nicely, sitting in a smaller armchair across the empty fireplace from the President. A bronze bust of Jefferson stood on the table to the right of her chair.

"I want to offer my personal congratulations to you all, and to assure you that this administration will do everything in its power to support the further exploration of Mars." She lowered her eyes modestly for a moment, but her voice remained sharp and strong as she added, "And if the people of this great nation choose me to lead them in the next administration, we will support continued missions to Mars as well as the economic development of cislunar space."

Connors huffed. "I wonder if she knows what cislunar means?"

"One of her aides does," Jamie said. "That's good enough for now."

Brumado's face came back on the screen, announcing that the President of the Soviet Federation would now say a few words.

The two-way radio buzzed. Jamie leaned between the two women, turned off the sound on the TV altogether, and flicked the answering switch.

"Li Chengdu here." The expedition commander's voice issued thinly from the radio speaker. "I am afraid that there is a long line of politicians waiting to appear on television. It would be more useful if you prepared your vehicle to leave the valley rather than watching their orations. We will tape everything here so that you may see it when you have the time."

Jamie turned to glance at Connors, who nodded agreement. "Yessir," he said. "We'll contact the dome when we're ready to move."

"Very good."

Ilona got up slowly from the right-hand seat and straightened to her full height and stretched her back, catlike. "Call me if they get down to the Israeli prime minister."

Jamie laughed and reached for the switch to turn off the radio.

"One further question." Li's voice froze them all. "What is the status of your physical condition?"

Glancing at their tired, wan faces, Jamie replied, "Whatever it is, we've all got it. Aches, weakness—it's slowing us down."

"I have decided to send Dr. Yang down to the dome. She will arrive within a few hours to assist Dr. Reed. It is imperative that you return to the dome within forty-eight hours so that you may be given medical attention."

"But what is it?" Jamie asked. "What's wrong with us all?"

For a long moment there was no sound from the radio speaker except the faint crackle of static. Finally Li said, "We do not yet know. But based on the rate of deterioration of your health, it is urgent that you reach the dome for treatment quickly. As quickly as you can.''

Jamie started to ask what would happen if they couldn't reach the dome in the next forty-eight hours. But he held his tongue. He did not really want to hear the answer.

EARTH

The Vice-President's smile disappeared the instant the last of the camera crew left.

It was unusual for the media corps to swarm into the Vice-President's office, but this had been a very unusual day. A news conference from Mars. And that damned Indian had weaseled out of his end of the bargain.

She glared at the two aides who remained in the room. Her media secretary was at the little cabinet that served as a bar. Harvey Todd, her aide for science and technology, was fidgeting nervously as he slowly paced in front of the curtained windows. He's got a lot to be nervous about, the Vice-President said to herself. She got up from the small sofa where she had dealt with the reporters and stalked to her desk. It was a tiny, delicately curved desk of gleaming dark rosewood, beautifully proportioned to the Vice-President's own slight frame.

Her media secretary handed her a frosted glass of vodka citron as the Vice-President sat herself in the maroon swivel chair behind the desk.

The Vice-President took one small sip of her ice-cold drink, then said to Todd, "Well?"

He looked startled. He was the small, nervous type, his hair thinning despite the fact that he was barely into his thirties. He looked soft, but inwardly he was sharp as a razor; he carried degrees from Princeton in political science and management. His favorite author was Niccolò Machiavelli.

He swallowed hard and tried to smile. "I thought the conference went very well, didn't you?" he asked the media secretary, a note of desperation in his voice.

She nodded but did not smile.

"That goddammed Indian never said a word about backing me,"

the Vice-President snarled. "I went out on the limb for him and he just talked about frigging *Martians!*"

"Well, he is a scientist . . ."

"Bullshit!"

The media secretary sat herself on the sofa that her boss had just vacated and crossed her legs primly. "We have his written statement," she said. "You can release it whenever you choose to."

"He should have said he was going to support me," the Vice-President insisted.

"I'm not sure that this particular hookup was the right time to make such an announcement," Todd said timidly, rubbing a forefinger across his round chin.

"What the hell did they teach you at Princeton?" the Vice-President fairly screamed. "What would be a better time, with the whole frigging world watching on TV? An endorsement from Mars, for god's sake! What could make a bigger impression on the voters, you jelly-brained imbecile?"

The media secretary headed for the bar. Todd tried to return his boss's angry stare but failed; he turned away and focused instead on the painting he had arranged to have hanging in the office: an original Bonestell starscape.

"I can think of a better time for him to announce his support," said the media secretary as she poured straight bourbon into a tumbler full of ice cubes.

"You can?"

"When they land back on Earth. *Everybody* will be watching that. And you won't have to compete with Martians for the media's attention, either."

The Vice-President's angry expression softened into a thoughtful scowl. She sipped at her drink. Todd cast an utterly grateful look at the media secretary. She smiled at him and mouthed silently, You owe me one.

S O L 3 8: AFTERNOON

"What'd I tell you?" Connors puffed. "Light as feathers."

The astronaut and Jamie were shoveling away the red dust that had piled up against the rover's side. Jamie thought that the stuff was so light they could engage the electric motors and the wheels would churn right through it. But Connors insisted that they take no chances, or at least as few as possible. So the two of them dug, despite their weariness, despite the pain that shot through their arms and legs, despite the growing nausea that was surging through Jamie's gut in hot sickening waves.

The morning mist was almost entirely gone, merely a few wavering tendrils clinging to spots along the cliff wall where the sun did not reach. The cliffs themselves stood towering over them, immense rugged fortifications that blotted out half the sky and marched beyond the horizon both to their right and to their left.

The orange streaks of the lichen stood out sharper than ever against the red rocks. Jamie wondered if the lichen colonies on the ground had some method of shaking off the dust that now covered the canyon floor to a depth of several inches. We won't be here long enough to see, he knew. And we don't have a remote TV camera to set up here and watch them for us, dammit.

The dust billowed up as their shovels bit into it, rising in strangely soft, slow clouds that drifted dreamlike on the gentle wind wafting down the canyon. Jamie saw that Connors's suit was covered with the rust-colored dust almost up to his armpits. He looked down and saw that his own blue suit was similarly splashed with rust.

"One good thing," Connors was panting, "about this stuff.... It doesn't ... cling to your ... visor."

Jamie nodded inside his helmet.

"On the moon ... damned dust sticks ... it ... gets charged ... with static ... electricity."

"Save your breath," Jamie said.

"Yeah . . ."

The two women were inside battening down the lab module for the trip. Their precious specimens of lichen were already safely protected in insulated containers. Ilona had worried that the lichen might die for lack of sunlight until Joanna pointed out that they obviously could lie dormant for long periods without light when sandstorms covered the rocks for days or even weeks on end.

"I think . . . that's . . . good enough," Connors panted as Jamie dug around the rearmost wheel on the logistics module.

"Think we've got . . . enough traction?" Jamie was gasping too.

"Yeah. . . . Looks okay."

"Let's try it."

They trudged back to the airlock, utterly weary, and clambered inside. Jamie would have left his shovel outside, but Connors insisted that they stow both shovels in their proper place in the outside equipment bay of the lab module. Pete hasn't lost his sense of detail, at least, Jamie thought. Must be his astronaut training.

It took more than an hour for them to squirm out of their suits and vacuum them clean, even with Joanna and Ilona helping them. Ilona was not much help; she was very weak. We must look pathetic, Jamie thought. I'm glad Mikhail isn't here to see us.

"Get some food into you," Joanna said, looking ashen herself.

Jamie's insides were boiling. "I don't think I could keep anything down."

"Energy bars, at least. The glucose will do you good."

Ilona slumped on the bench in the midship area, her eyes barely open.

Connors pulled the refrigerator open. "Maybe some juice. . . . I feel like I've got a hangover. A bad one."

"Juice will raise your blood sugar," Joanna said. "That will be good."

The orange juice was entirely gone. There was no other juice in the capacious refrigerator except tomato. Connors grabbed the plastic container and pulled off its cap. Raising it to his lips he took four big gulps, then handed it to Jamie.

Thinking that if whatever was ailing them was infectious it didn't matter now, Jamie drained the container almost to the end.

"There are juice concentrates in the freezer," Ilona called weakly from where she sat.

"Do we have enough water?" Jamie asked.

"Yes, we should," Joanna said. "I'll see to it."

Connors shambled off toward the cockpit. But he got no farther than the benches halfway there. He sagged onto the bench opposite Ilona.

"My . . . legs . . . Jesus, they . . . won't carry me."

Jamie pushed past Joanna toward the astronaut, driven on a sudden spurt of adrenaline. Connors's eyes looked frightened. Joanna's, terrified.

"What's the matter, Pete?"

"Can't . . . I just feel . . . so damned weak . . ."

"Okay. Okay. Just sit there. Get your strength back."

"But we got . . . to get started."

"I can drive."

"You?"

"I can do it. I know how."

"Yeah . . . but . . ."

Jamie made a smile big enough for them all to see. "Just like driving pickups in New Mexico. No sweat."

Wishing he truly felt that confident, Jamie made his way to the cockpit and slid into the driver's seat. He had been trained to operate the rover as a backup, of course, and he had watched Vosnesensky and Connors for enough hours. He had even driven the rover under their skeptical eyes.

Can you do it all alone? Jamie asked himself. Hell yes, he replied silently. I've got to.

Taking his time, going deliberately slowly, carefully, Jamie checked out the control panel from one end to the other. Then he touched the switch that started the drive motors. Beneath his seat the electric generator whined to a higher pitch. Funny how you never notice the damned thing humming away until it changes its tune, Jamie said to himself. Or stops altogether.

"Here we go," he called over his shoulder. Ilona made a weak smile back at him. Joanna was sitting beside Connors, holding a plastic cup in one hand. She's turning into Florence Nightingale, Jamie thought. Will Pete be okay? Will Ilona make it? God, they could both die. We could all die.

The rover lurched forward, slewed slightly to the left, then straightened as Jamie eased off the accelerator and held the steering wheel firmly.

"We're moving!" he yelped. "We're on our way."

Not a sound came from the three behind him.

Then Jamie thought, We're heading in the wrong direction. The cliff village is the other way; we're leaving it behind.

Despite his own pain and the terrible weariness that was sapping the strength from his body, Mikhail Vosnesensky grimly donned his hard suit. Abell and Mironov helped him, but neither of them looked any better than Vosnesensky felt.

It is the dust, the Russian told himself. It has to be. Outwardly he had dismissed the idea of some weird Martian infection as too preposterous even to consider. Yet deep in his heart he feared the possibility that they had all been poisoned by some alien bug for which there was no cure.

Although Dr. Li said it was not necessary for him to be outside when the lander arrived, Vosnesensky quoted regulations until the expedition commander reluctantly bowed acquiescence.

I may be sick, Vosnesensky told himself, but I still know my duty. The regulations call for a cosmonaut to be suited up and ready to assist the landing party once they touch down. There is a good reason for this rule and as long as I can stand on my own two legs I will not allow any rule to be broken.

So he tottered weakly out through the airlock hatch and stood waiting, a fire-engine red figure standing stolidly on the rusty soil of Mars. Exactly on schedule the L/AV streaked across the pink sky and deployed its parachutes. They billowed into perfect white hemispheres dangling the cup-and-saucer lander beneath them. At the precise moment the chutes detached the retro-rockets fired. The lander, with cosmonaut Dmitri Iosifovitch Ivshenko at its controls and astronaut Oliver Zieman beside him, touched the sands of Mars about two hundred meters away.

The lander had one passenger only: Dr. Yang Meilin. And a cargo of pharmaceuticals packed in hard plastic boxes.

In less than half an hour the diminutive Dr. Yang was deep in conference with Tony Reed in the dome's infirmary.

Hard to tell what's going on behind those slanted eyes, Reed said to himself as he showed her the data from all his tests of the ground team.

"The people in the rover seem to be the worst off," Reed was saying aloud. "Although god knows that most of the people here in the dome are in bad-enough shape."

"How did you permit this to happen?" Dr. Yang asked. Her voice was silky, low. But still the question startled Reed.

"Permit it?" His voice sounded shrill, defensive, even to himself. "How can anyone combat a disease unless he has a clear diagnosis?"

"You have no idea of what is affecting your comrades?"

"None," he snapped. "Do you?"

Her face was a perfectly impenetrable mask. "I cannot say until I have performed some tests."

Reed pushed back his stubborn lock of sandy hair. "Then I suggest we get started on your tests."

"Yes. I notice that you do not seem to be troubled by this illness. Therefore I will use you as a baseline control, if you have no objection."

"None whatsoever."

"Good," said Dr. Yang. Then, matter-of-factly, "Roll up your sleeve, please."

Reed obediently bared his left arm, thinking, You come down here all fresh and businesslike, certain that you'll discover whatever it is that I've overlooked. Perhaps you will. Perhaps you'll be luckier than I've been. Or smarter. It's my own fault. I've missed something, I've done something wrong. Or failed to do something I should have. And she knows it. They all know it. They all blame me.

As Dr. Yang deftly slipped a needle into his vein, Tony insisted silently, But it isn't me. It's this blasted alien world we're on. We have no business here. We're out of our depth. I'm out of my depth. I should never have come to Mars. None of us should have. Mars has defeated me. Mars has defeated us all.

Jamie thought his vision was blurring, but then the stinging made him realize that sweat was getting into his eyes. He blinked and rubbed his eyes with one hand, keeping a firm grip on the wheel with the other. The rover was churning along at a steady thirty klicks per hour, heading for the landslide that they had come down two days earlier.

Maybe we can make it before sundown, Jamie thought. If we can get all the way up the slope and onto the plain again before sundown, we can just keep going all night long. I'll slow her down, of course, but the lights are good enough to keep us on the move. No need to stop for the night. We can even follow our own tracks, the tracks we made coming out here. If they haven't been covered up by dust. If we can get to the top.

Connors slid into the right-hand seat. Jamie shot him a glance. The astronaut looked spent. He sat as if his bones could not hold him up, his head almost lolling on his shoulders.

"How's it goin'?" Connors's voice was hoarse.

"So far so good."

"How far to the slide?"

Jamie gestured with his chin toward the map displayed in the control panel's central screen. "Half an hour, maybe a little more."

"We got a shot at getting to the top in daylight, then."

"Yep."

"Good."

"How are the women doing?" Jamie asked.

"Ilona's asleep. Joanna's watching her. She don't look too good herself, though."

"Asleep? Or passed out?"

Connors tried to shrug. "Hard to tell."

"And what about you? How do you feel?"

"Like a piece of shit that's been stomped on by a herd of elephants. How 'bout you?"

"Not much better. But this go-mobile is easy to drive. It's almost relaxing."

"Just don't fall asleep at the wheel."

"Not much traffic to worry about."

"Yeah, but some of the potholes in the road can swallow you up."

Despite Connors's awful appearance, Jamie felt better with the astronaut sitting beside him. He pressed the accelerator a little harder and watched the digital speedometer climb to thirty-five; just over twenty miles an hour. He kept hearing Li's voice telling him, "It is urgent that you reach the dome for treatment quickly. As quickly as you can."

The ground seemed to be rising. At first Jamie did not notice it, but then he realized that their ride was getting bumpier.

"I think we're almost . . . Hey! There it is!"

Through the canopy they saw the dark red slope of the ancient landslide rising off to their left like a stairway to heaven. The cliffs that towered before them were masked by the beautiful, gentle grade that ramped all the way up to the caprock and the plain that led back to their dome.

Connors's dark face broke into a toothy grin. He turned in his seat, but said nothing. To Jamie he muttered, "They're both asleep back there."

"It's okay. We'll be up this slope and heading for home before the sun goes down."

The grade was studded with rocks and boulders. Jamie could not see the tracks they had made on their way down; the dust storm had covered even the deep ruts where the rover had gotten temporarily stuck in loose sand.

"Don't get into that loose stuff again," Connors said.

"Not if I can help it."

"Slow her down a little, but keep moving forward."

"Yeah."

The astronaut licked his lips. Jamie knew he wanted to take over, to drive the rover himself. Yet Connors stayed in the right-hand seat. To switch drivers now would mean stopping the rover, and neither of them had any intention of coming to a stop on the pebbly gravel of this ancient avalanche.

"You're doin' fine," Connors muttered. "Just watch that depression on the right."

Jamie skirted the edge of what looked to him like an old crater that had been partially filled in with sand. He turned around its flank, maneuvering past a boulder almost as big as the rover itself.

"Good. Good," Connors mumbled. "Keep it goin'."

It all happened in slow motion. The rover was making steady progress up the slope. Jamie could feel the gritty, bumpy texture of the surface beneath its wheels transmitted through the steering column to his hands. He was perspiring heavily, sweat stinging his eyes, Connors's backseat driving in his ears, neck stiff with tension, arms aching with the effort of steering the lumbering vehicle.

Jamie felt the nose dip as if it had started down a steep incline. Automatically he leaned on the brakes, but the big blunt-nosed rover plowed into a lake of fine loose sand, throwing up a rust-red bow wave of dust that covered the canopy.

"Look out!" Connors yelled too late.

As inexorably as fate, with all the slow-motion horror of a nightmare, the rover dug itself into the loose sand like a burrowing mole. Jamie felt the wheels churning uselessly, spinning them deeper into the sand-filled pit.

"Stop! Stop everything!"

Jamie was already disengaging the wheel drives when Connors shouted it. The canopy was spattered so heavily with clinging red dust that they could barely see outside.

The rover slid to a stop. Jamie felt his heart thudding in his chest, heard its thunder in his ears. He looked across at Connors, who was staring outward, mouth hanging open, gasping for breath.

"I don't think the rear module is in the stuff," Jamie said. "I'm going to try to put its wheels in reverse."

"Yeah. Maybe it can pull us out of this."

The generator whined and they could hear the faint screech of wheels spinning without traction. Jamie shut them down before the bearings burned out.

"We're stuck," he said.

Connors's bloodshot eyes were wide with fear. "Yeah. Looks that way."

S O L 3 8: SUNSET

Vosnesensky was the last one to be tested.

The Russian was in no mood for having a medic punch holes in his skin. Connors had just reported that the rover was stuck halfway up the landslide. They would need a rescue effort. But how? And who? Dr. Li refused to allow anything to be done until he had consulted with mission control in Kaliningrad. Meanwhile night was coming on and the four people in the rover were as sick as dogs.

Not that the people in the dome were much better off. Toshima had suddenly collapsed at his workstation; they had had to carry him to his bunk. Patel, Naguib, even Abell and Mironov were not much good for anything except sitting around and moaning. Monique Bonnet, who had been playing the cheerful, motherly nurse for the past two days, was dragging herself around, hollow eyed with exhaustion.

"And how do you feel, in general?" Dr. Yang asked as Vosnesensky sat on the little white stool in the infirmary.

The Russian glowered at her. "I have important work to do," he said. "We have a crisis . . ."

Yang was barely taller than Vosnesensky even though he was seated and she was standing. But she stopped him cold with a snap of her almond eyes.

"You will not be able to do anything about your crisis if your medical condition continues to worsen," she said. She did not raise her voice, but there was cold steel in her words. "Now please answer my questions and do as I tell you."

Vosnesensky glanced at Reed, who was leaning against the patient's couch in the corner of the tiny infirmary. Reed seemed to be in good health, his face pink. At least that damned superior smile of his was gone; he was frowning with puzzled frustration.

"The sooner you cooperate the sooner we will be finished," Yang said.

Vosnesensky capitulated. "What must I do?"

"Roll up your left sleeve and tell me how you feel. *Exactly* how you feel."

The Russian pulled in a deep breath as he unbuttoned the cuff of his coverall sleeve. "I am weak, my legs ache, I have no appetite."

"Have you ever felt this way before?" Yang held a hypodermic syringe in one hand, its needle glinting in the overhead lights.

"Not that I can remember."

"Are you coughing or sneezing? Does your chest hurt?"

Vosnesensky shook his head, then winced. The needle went in smoothly; Yang found a vein on her first try.

"Any rash on your body?" she asked.

Watching the syringe fill up with dark blood, Vosnesensky replied, "No. Not that I have noticed."

Yang pulled the needle out and slapped a plastic bandage on the puncture. Reed watched in silence, his arms folded across his chest. The diminutive Chinese physician asked Vosnesensky to strip to the waist. Wordlessly the Russian pulled down the top of his coveralls and slipped his undershirt over his head.

Yang looked at his back. "No rash," she muttered.

"Is that significant?" Vosnesensky asked.

"Perhaps." She looked across the small cubicle toward Reed, then murmured absently to Vosnesensky, "You may go now."

"Thank you." The Russian tugged on his coverall top and scurried from the infirmary despite his aching legs, carrying his undershirt in one hand.

Jamie fingered his bear fetish through the hard suit's gloves. Thin and flexible as they were, the gloves still robbed him of the true feeling of the stone's polished warmth.

He was standing on the lab module's roof in the last slanting rays of the dying sun. He and Connors had barely been able to push the airlock hatch open; then the astronaut had slumped to the floor of the airlock, too weak to move any farther. Jamie had left him sitting there in a pile of loose dust that had drifted in, while he clambered up the ladder set into the rover's side to survey their situation.

He had not dared to step out into the sand itself, for fear that he would sink through the powdery dust so deeply that he would not be able to extricate himself.

The mission rule book doesn't cover this, Jamie had told himself as he slowly, carefully climbed the ladder. He had gone up as if mountain climbing, three points attached at all times. Move one gloved hand to the next rung. Grip it, then move the other hand. Grip, then one booted foot. Make sure it's firmly seated on the rung, then pull up the other one. The dust frightened him. He pictured himself drowning in it like a man caught in quicksand.

Now at last he stood up on the roof. If you have any power to help at all, he said silently to the fetish, now's the time to get it working.

"What's it look like?" Connors's voice came through his helmet earphones.

"Not good," Jamie replied, surveying the scene. "She's buried up over the fenders, all except the last half of the rear module. Not enough traction to pull us out."

Connors said nothing, although Jamie could hear his ragged breathing.

"How're you doing?" he asked.

"I'm fine. Just can't get up on my fuckin' feet, that's all."

Jamie's head was swimming with dizziness. His body ached all over and he felt so tired that it was tempting just to stretch out right there and go to sleep. The canyon was so wide that he could actually see the sunset; the cliffs on the other side were too far away to be visible, tall as they were. He watched the sun for a moment, saw it touch the rocky horizon, felt the shadows of deathly freezing night reaching toward him. Inside his suit he shuddered, almost like a dog trying to shake off water.

He looked down at the tiny stone bear in the fading light. The leather thong holding the miniature arrowhead and the feather had been lovingly tied by his grandfather. An eagle's feather, Jamie thought. Symbol of strength. I could sure use some now.

Into his helmet microphone he said, "I might as well come down. There's nothing I can do up here and the sun's going down."

Tucking the miniature stone bear back into the pouch on the right leg of his hard suit, Jamie started slowly down the ladder. By the time he had painfully made his way back into the airlock it was dark outside. Connors was sitting in the heaped sand, his white hard suit coated with the red dust.

Jamie tried to sound cheerful. "You look like a snowman playing in a pile of rust."

"I feel like a goddammed snowman—in July," Connors grumbled.

Slowly, like two arthritic old men, they shoveled most of the sand outside and then closed the outer hatch.

"Gotta clean off the suits," Connors muttered.

"We've got to get you on your feet first," Jamie said.

It seemed like hours of tugging and pushing, but finally Connors was standing again and they went through the motions of vacuuming the dust off their suits. The suits were still stained rust-red, though, as they struggled out of them. The airlock smelled of ozone so heavily that Jamie's eyes burned and watered.

Finally they staggered through the inner hatch and half collapsed on the midship benches. Both women were up in the cockpit, Joanna with a headset clamped over her thick dark hair.

"Vosnesensky wants to talk to you," Joanna called back to them, her voice hoarse, labored.

Ilona muttered, "The Russian pig won't trust a woman with his important messages."

Jamie felt his temper snap. "Jesus Christ, Ilona, knock off the anti-Russian crap! We're in a bad enough fix without your bullshit!"

She smiled languidly at him. "What difference does it make? We are all going to die here no matter what I say, aren't we?"

Joanna clutched at her arm. "No! We are not going to die! Jamie won't let us die."

He looked into their faces as he painfully made his way toward them in the cockpit. The illness had changed them. Ilona was no longer the haughty, imperious beauty who flouted all the rules. Her cheeks were sunken, her eyes ringed with dark circles. She had a look of near panic in her face; the smell of death was on her. Joanna's eyes were burning, blazing. She still looked like a bedraggled little waif, but now there was something in her eyes that Jamie had never seen before: a strength, an endurance he had not realized was in her. Perhaps Joanna had not known it herself. She focused those eyes on Jamie, urgent, demanding.

"No, I won't let us die," Jamie said in a half whisper. He added silently, Not without a fight, at least.

A growing feeling of helplessness was beginning to overwhelm Dr. Li.

"Kaliningrad insists that a rescue flight is out of the question," he said.

The expedition commander wanted to stand and pace, wanted to work off the nervous energy sizzling inside him. But in the low-ceilinged confines of the command module he had to content himself with sitting in one of the narrow padded chairs with his knees poking up ridiculously, clenching and unclenching his fists as he spoke.

"But they're stuck down there!" Burt Klein said.

Li shook his head. "Kaliningrad says the last lander is to be used only in the direst emergency."

"The fact that four of our people are in danger of dying is not a dire emergency?" asked Leonid Tolbukhin sourly.

The cosmonaut and astronaut had quickly volunteered to pilot the expedition's last remaining landing vehicle to the canyon to rescue the four stranded in the rover.

"We could sit her down within fifty yards of the rover," Klein said confidently, "and then bring them straight back here. Nothing to it."

"A piece of cake," Tolbukhin confirmed, the British idiom sounding strange and deliberate in his deep Russian voice.

"Kaliningrad says no. You two are the only pilots left here in orbit."

"Bring Ivshenko and Zieman back here," Tolbukhin suggested. "Then Burt and I can go to the canyon."

"Sure!" Klein said. "You'll still have two L/AVs and four pilots at the dome. That'll be plenty to bring the others back when the time comes."

Li's face was a picture of misery. "Ivshenko and Zieman cannot return here without Yang. We cannot leave both our doctors at the dome. What good would it do to bring the traverse team up here if there is no physician here to treat them?"

Tolbukhin nodded reluctantly.

"There is something more," Li told them. "The medical staff at Kaliningrad has brought up the question of quarantine."

"Quarantine?"

Li felt miserable as he said, "Since we do not know what is infecting the ground team, they fear that whatever it is might infect us here in orbit if we return the ground team here."

"Holy shit," Klein muttered. "They want us to leave them down there?"

Tolbukhin grasped the larger implication. "That means they will not allow us to return to Earth if we have not found the source of the disease."

"Yes," admitted Li. "We ourselves might be quarantined in Earth orbit."

"If we live long enough to get back that far," the Russian said.

"The alternative is to leave the ground team and return to Earth without them."

"That'd kill them!" Klein snapped.

"Yes. But to rescue them and bring them back up to orbit with us might kill us all."

For long moments neither the astronaut nor the cosmonaut spoke a word.

Finally Klein said, "Well, you've got to do something."

Li knew he was right. The weight of responsibility was squarely on his shoulders. Let the four in the rover die, or risk the lives of everyone—including those in orbit—by allowing the last of their pilots to ride to the rescue on the last of the landing/ascent vehicles. Abandon the ground team altogether or risk catching their disease and killing everyone.

Li felt the weight of two dozen lives on him. The weight of two worlds.

When the last of the physicals was finished Tony Reed asked Yang Meilin, "What do you expect to find?"

She shot him a sharp glance from the chair on which she sat. "The cause of this epidemic."

Reed had barely budged from the corner of the infirmary where he had watched her examine all the people in the dome. Now he made a puzzled shrug.

"Vosnesensky thinks it might be Martian dust that we're inhaling," he said.

Yang's almond eyes watched him unblinkingly from beneath her straight bangs. "Do you believe that?"

"No, I don't. We've tested the air here in the dome. It's cleaner than the air in London, by far."

She got up from the chair, a tiny Chinese woman with a nondescript figure and an utterly forgettable round, flat-featured face— except for those eyes. Reed thought they looked at him accusingly. Why not? Why shouldn't she blame me for this calamity? It is my fault, my responsibility. I was put here to protect the health of these men and women. Some protector!

"Well," he asked, "what do you think?"

She shook her head slightly. "I cannot tell. All the data from the tests we have just done are being analyzed by the medical computer aboard *Mars 2*. Until we get its results I cannot go further."

Reed gave an exasperated sigh. "It won't do any good, you know. The first thing I did when they started coming down with this malady was to run all the medical records through the computer diagnostic program. It just burped out nonsense."

"Perhaps now, with more data . . ."

"I doubt it. The computer can only tell you what it already knows, and we're facing something new and unprecedented here."

"Perhaps not. It may be something ordinary but unexpected. That is the great strength of the computer: it is not clouded by human expectations or emotions. It analyzes all the symptoms and reports which medical conditions fit the data."

"Yes," Reed sniffed, feeling real anger surging up inside him. "I'll tell you what the damned computer will give us. It will suggest that the malady might be a variation of influenza—which it isn't, because we've found no influenza viruses in the blood workups; or malaria—which is ridiculous because the nearest mosquito is two hundred million kilometers from here; or radiation poisoning—which it can't be, because the dosimeters show that every member of the team is well within tolerable limits; or a vitamin deficiency—which is ludicrous because I see to it that everyone takes their bloody vitamin supplements."

Yang said, "Perhaps a slow virus? Perhaps an infection such as Legionnaires' disease?"

"I thought of that," Reed snapped. "The symptoms don't match."

The Chinese doctor murmured something too low for Reed to hear. Ignoring her, he went on:

"The marvelous computer analysis will also suggest the possibility of salmonellosis, tuberculosis, or typhoid fever—in decreasing probabilities, of course."

He stopped, out of breath, seething with a rage that he had not realized was in him.

"Why are you angry with me?" Yang asked, her mask of impassivity gone. She looked shocked, hurt.

Tony stared at her, his insides jumping, his hands clenching into fists. He took a deep breath, then stepped back to his desk.

"I'm sorry. I apologize. It's not you. I suppose I'm angry at myself, really. This thing—I can't for the life of me figure out what it is!" He banged a fist on the flimsy desktop.

"That is why we need the help of the computer program."

Reed cast her a cynical smile.

"Not to tell us what the disease may be," Yang explained, "but to rule out definitely what it is not."

"I don't believe it can even do that."

Yang tried to smile. "Was it not one of your English writers who said that once you have ruled out the impossible, then whatever is left—however improbable it may seem—must be the truth?"

Reed blinked at her. "Arthur Clarke?"

As politely as she could, Yang replied, "I believe it was Conan Doyle."

EARTH

KALININGRAD: In a windowless conference room in the mission control complex, twenty men and women from six nations thrashed out the problem that assailed them from nearly two hundred million kilometers away.

The oblong conference table was littered with scribbled sheets of paper, crusts from sandwiches, charts and viewgraphs, Styrofoam beverage cups, ashtrays heaped high with smoldering butts. Some of the people around the table slouched miserably, heads in their hands, jackets long pulled off and shirtsleeves rolled high. A few paced pointlessly along the length of the stuffy, smoky room.

They had long ago shouted themselves hoarse without arriving at a conclusion.

At the head of the table sat the chief of mission control, a lean red-headed Russian with a saturnine pointed beard and red eyebrows like inverted vees. He tapped a long fingernail on the imitation wood of the tabletop. In the exhausted silence of the room every head swiveled toward him.

"We cannot merely sit here without making a decision. Human lives are at stake. The success of the entire mission is at stake!"

One of the women, a Swede, coughed slightly, cleared her throat, then said: "Our alternatives are clear—allow the traverse team to die or take the risk of killing more members of the expedition in an attempt to save them."

"We can't just let them die!" said another woman.

"But a rescue attempt might fail and there will be more deaths," countered a Japanese male.

"Half the reporters in the world are pounding on our doors," someone commented sourly. "We've got to do *something*, and do it now!"

"We should never have permitted an excursion into the canyon," a Frenchman complained. "Not on the very first mission. It was not in our original plan. We bowed to blatant American political pressure. That is what has put us in this chamber pot."

"But Brumado's daughter is one of the people who are stranded. We can't let her die! Who's going to face *him* and say that we decided to let his daughter die?"

"I am convinced," said a chubby, balding Russian, "that the only thing we can do is to bring up the people in the dome right now, get them up to safety in the orbiting ships, and then send the last lander down to the canyon to take up the four in the rover."

"And abort the expedition two weeks earlier than the schedule calls for?"

"Schedule?" an American shouted. "Schedule? What the hell difference does the damned schedule make? We're talking human lives here!"

The chief controller pressed both his hands together, almost as if praying. "I am afraid that your suggestion is the only reasonable course of action that we have open to us. Even though it is not entirely free of risk."

"It means that the people in the rover will have to wait at least another two days before the lander can be sent to them."

"I doubt that we can close down the operations at the dome and bring all those people up with their equipment and specimens in just two days. The schedule calls for a full week to shut down the dome."

"This is an emergency! Leave the equipment and specimens. Bring up the people and get on with the rescue, for god's sake!"

"Leave everything?"

"Retrieve it on the next mission."

"There won't be another mission. Not if we have to abandon this one, run away from Mars like thieves in the night."

"That's the most stupid metaphor I've heard yet!"

"Just because you're a woman doesn't give you the right to . . ."

"*Silence!*" roared the chief controller. "I will not have us squabbling like children in a schoolyard. We will abort the mission. We will bring up the people in the dome as quickly as possible and then send the last of the landers to pick up the traverse team in the canyon. Anyone who wants to go on record as being against that decision should raise his or her hand. Now."

Not a single hand went up.

"And it is also agreed," the chief controller added, "that none of the expedition members will be allowed back to Earth unless and until this medical problem is solved. They will remain quarantined in Earth orbit.''

"If they get that far," someone said in a stage whisper.

WASHINGTON: Edith could tell from Alberto's face that something had gone very wrong.

"What is it?" she asked.

They were in the kitchen of the Georgetown house, just finishing breakfast before heading to Capitol Hill. Brumado had a date to testify before a congressional subcommittee holding hearings on the next fiscal year's budget for space. The kitchen overlooked a lovely garden bounded by a red-brick wall. Most of the flowers were gone this late in the season, except for the hardy little impatiens lining the curved brick walkway with pink-and-white blooms that nodded in the soft morning breeze.

"What is it?" Edith asked again.

Brumado was at the telephone by the sink. His face was ashen. "My daughter . . . the traverse team . . . they are stranded in the canyon. Their rover vehicle has bogged down."

Edith got up from the glass-topped table, her breakfast instantly forgotten. "They have the backup rover, don't they? They can pick them up . . ."

But Brumado was shaking his head. "They're sick. All of them on the ground team. Something has made them all very sick and weak."

"Jamie too?"

"Yes. Him too."

Edith felt her own breath catch in her throat. She swallowed hard, then asked, "What're they going to do?"

"NASA has offered to fly me to Houston, the mission control complex there."

"But what about Jamie and your daughter?"

"I must testify to the subcommittee," Brumado was muttering absently, like a man in shock. "They asked me not to reveal any of this. Not yet."

"But Jamie?"

Abruptly he seemed to realize she was standing in front of him. "Edith, I must have your word that you will not break this news to your network."

"Hey, I don't have a network anymore. I'm unemployed, remember? But what about Jamie? Is he . . ."

440

"I don't know!" Brumado snapped. Edith realized that he was fighting to maintain his self-control. She saw tears glimmering in the corners of his eyes.

"Maybe you ought to cancel the subcommittee appearance," she suggested.

"No," he said, more gently. "No, I can't do that. It would raise suspicions."

"You could have a cold, for god's sake."

"And then fly off to Houston?" He smiled without humor. "Half the subcommittee would be on the next plane. Or their aides, at least."

"Yeah, maybe," Edith admitted.

"Will you promise me not to call anyone, not to break the story?"

"Can I go to Houston with you?"

"Yes. Of course."

"Okay."

"You promise not to contact anyone about this while I am testifying this morning?"

"We have a deal, don't we?"

But Edith was thinking, In Houston I can see how bad it really is, how tough a spot they've put Jamie into. An eyewitness account of Alberto Brumado watching as the team on Mars tries to rescue his daughter who's stuck a thousand kilometers from their base. And sick. I could write my own ticket with that.

Sick from what? What's happened to them? To Jamie?

Inwardly she made up her mind to keep her silence only until she was certain that they were doing everything they could for Jamie and the others. I've got to find out how they got into this mess. The minute I find out whose fault it is, then all deals are off.

This could be even bigger than finding life on Mars: four explorers trapped and sick a thousand kilometers from safety. *That's* a real story! You don't have to be a scientist to get excited about that.

Tony Reed smiled bitterly as the computer screen scrolled the list from the medical program's analysis.

"Just as I told you," he said to Dr. Yang. "The idiot machine has nothing new to tell us."

Sitting beside him at the infirmary desk, Yang Meilin scanned the short list as a woman lost on the desert would search the horizon for an oasis.

"The answer is here," she said, barely loud enough for Reed to hear her. "I am certain of it."

The anger that Tony had felt earlier was gone now. Yang was not going to upstage him. She was just as bewildered and frustrated as he was. He felt almost sorry for her. Sorry for both of them. The two great medical experts, he said to himself, as stymied as a pair of chimpanzees. Says worlds for the selection board, doesn't it?

"I have a feeling," Yang said, pressing one hand flat against her middle, "that we have seen the answer, but we do not yet recognize it."

Reed let a thin sigh escape. "Feelings are one thing," he said almost gently. "What we need are facts."

"The one clear fact that we have," she said, "is that everyone here on the ground is ill, except you."

Tony felt a pang of guilt. "Yes. That's what's so damned puzzling about all this, isn't it?"

"What are you doing that the others are not?"

He shook his head. "Not a damned thing, as far as I can tell. I breathe the same air, I eat with them. . . ."

"Something in the food?"

Leaning back in his chair, Tony replied, "I can't imagine that there is something in my meals that is protecting me from whatever the others have come down with. Or conversely, that their food is tainted in some way and mine just happens not to be."

"Vitamin deficiency is on the computer's list."

"Yes, I know." Some of the old exasperation was creeping back into Tony. "But we've checked that out time and again. They all take their vitamin supplements, just as I take mine. It can't be that."

"You take the same pills they take?"

"Yes, of course."

"Every day?"

"Yes."

Yang lapsed into silence and turned her eyes back to the screen, as if she thought that by staring at it hard enough the answer would come clear.

Something nagged at Reed's consciousness. Something peripheral, subliminal. As if they had touched on the answer without knowing it. As if . . .

It can't be the vitamins, he told himself. I take the same dietary supplements that the others do every day. I watch them all swallow them down with their breakfasts every morning. The four in the rover are out of my sight, of course, but I check with them every day.

Could it be radiation poisoning? Something so subtle that the dosage meters aren't equipped to detect it? After all, everyone else has been outside the dome much more than I have. I've stayed in here while they've been out doing their work.

That couldn't be it. There's no strange radiation on Mars. Naguib and the others have been measuring the radiation environment since we landed. And the unmanned probes were measuring it for years before we arrived here.

Still the unconscious thought pecked at him. Something about the vitamins.

Reed closed his eyes and envisioned his morning routine. He came to the infirmary and took his own vitamin pills, then went to the galley and made certain that there were enough there for all the others and that they took theirs with their breakfasts. He no longer mixed his morning cocktail; he wanted his head absolutely clear of drugs during this emergency. He personally watched everyone swallow their pills each morning, except for the occasional early bird who finished breakfast before he got to the galley. Since this malady had struck, there had been no one up and stirring earlier than Tony, not even Vosnesensky.

His eyes suddenly shot to the cabinet where the vitamin bottles stood. Each bottle held five hundred of the ovoid orange pills.

And locked in his medicine chest was a smaller bottle, the one he took his own pills from.

"Oh no," he groaned.

Yang jerked from her self-absorbed study as if Reed had slapped her. "What? What did you say?"

"I don't take my vitamin pills from the same jar as the others."

She looked hard at him. "Does that make a difference?"

"It shouldn't . . . except—"

Yang Meilin watched him expectantly. Tony could *feel* the anticipation radiating from her tense body.

"That first jar there," he pointed to the glass-fronted cabinet, "was open when the meteor strike punctured the dome. The other jars have never been opened; they're still in their original seals."

Tony felt his face flush deeply with guilt. When the meteoroid had punctured the dome and all the alarms had gone off, that one big jar had been sitting open on his desk. He had knocked the bottle over in his rush to get out of the infirmary and into his hard suit. Afterward, when the emergency was over, he had picked up the pills scattered across his desktop and replaced them in the same bottle, discarding only those he had found on the floor.

Nothing wrong with them, he had told himself. Then he had transferred the pills to the smaller bottles that fit into the galley shelves.

His own supply of vitamin supplement was already in a smaller bottle, safely sealed in his medicine cabinet along with his amphetamines and other drugs. That medicine cabinet was not only locked; it was airtight.

"Their pills were exposed to pure oxygen," he muttered.

Yang put a hand to her lips.

"Yes," Reed said, putting the scenario together as he spoke, "the dome was pressurized with pure oxygen for almost thirty-six hours. It took a couple of days before we pulled enough nitrogen from the air outside to make an Earth-normal mixture in here again."

"Pure oxygen . . ."

"Pure oxygen will destroy ascorbic acid," Reed said absently, as if recalling some obscure test question from a college examination.

"The pills they are taking have no vitamin C in them."

"Right. They've all come down with scurvy."

"Scurvy!" Yang immediately grabbed the computer keyboard and typed furiously for a few moments. The machine hummed to itself, while Tony writhed inwardly in mental agony. *My fault. Every bit of it is my own stupid fault.*

"It correlates," Yang said, eyeing the new data displayed on the computer screen. "They all show the symptoms of scurvy."

Reed sat back in his chair feeling as weak and hollow as if he had come down with the affliction himself. *Scurvy. And it's all my fault. If only I had seen it earlier. Of course it had to be that. The oxygen, the pills . . .*

He looked up and saw that Yang was striding through the infirmary doorway.

"Where are you going?" Tony called to her as he scrambled from behind his desk.

"Wardroom," she answered over her shoulder. Little though she was she marched like a trained soldier, arms swinging, boots clacking on the plastic floor. Tony hurried to catch up with her.

"Looking for anyone in particular?" he asked.

"The ground team leader. Vosnesensky."

"Ah. Yes, of course."

"You have bottles of vitamins that have not been unsealed?" Yang asked. "Not contaminated by oxygen?"

"Yes," he answered. "Fifteen hundred of them, in three sealed bottles."

Monique Bonnet was at the wardroom table with Paul Abell and Mironov, all three of them slumped wearily.

"Where is the group leader?" Yang asked.

Monique gave an exhausted sigh, then replied, "I believe he is at the communications console."

Yang headed off for the comm console without another word, Reed trailing right behind her. *She must be hell on wheels in a hospital,* the Englishman thought. *God help the man or woman who gets in her way!*

Vosnesensky looked as if he were ready to drop off to sleep. He sagged in the chair; his face looked puffy, red eyed, bleary. Connors's black features in the communications screen looked no better; worse, in fact.

"I require your cooperation," Yang said without preamble.

Vosnesensky turned in his chair, started to push himself to his feet, then gave it up and simply sat there looking at the Chinese physician, almost eye to eye.

"You must begin taking large doses of vitamins, now, immediately."

"Vitamins?" Vosnesensky was saying dully. "But we take vitamins. We take them every day, on the regular schedule."

"They are contaminated," Yang said.

Vosnesensky's eyes shifted to Reed.

"It's true, Mikhail Andreivitch," said Tony. "They were bathed in oxygen after the meteor hit. They're practically useless."

"But what has that to do . . . ?"

"Scurvy," said Yang.

"Scurvy?"

"That's right," Reed said. "You've all come down with scurvy from lack of vitamin C."

Silently he added, Because of me. Because I panicked. Because I didn't want to see the truth. I'm a murderer. That's what I am.

"**Vitamin deficiency?**"

The words woke Jamie. He had been sleeping dreamlessly when Connors's voice, shrilly high-pitched, cut through to his conscious mind.

Untangling himself from the thin blanket, Jamie slithered out of his bunk and padded in his stockinged feet forward to the cockpit. The rover felt shivering cold. Connors was talking to Vosnesensky. Both men looked utterly drained, but there was a strange grin on the Russian's image on the screen.

"We have scurvy," Vosnesensky said, almost as if it were a joke.

"Scurvy?"

"It is definite. Yang's tests were analyzed during the night. Our vitamin pills have been poisoned—no, that is not the correct word. The vitamin C in the pills has been deactivated because it was exposed to oxygen after the meteorite hit. Without sufficient vitamin C we have all come down with scurvy."

Jamie slumped into the right-hand seat. "You mean like old-time sailors who've been at sea too long?"

"That's why they called the Brits 'limeys,' " Connors said, his voice still echoing disbelief. "Because they carried limes and other fresh fruits aboard their ships once they figured out what caused scurvy."

"Scurvy," Jamie mumbled. "Scurvy."

"According to Dr. Yang it will take several days before the symptoms go away," Vosnesensky said.

"What about us?" Connors asked.

The Russian's grin disappeared like a light winking off. "So far, Kaliningrad has forbidden a rescue flight from orbit. Not until they make a decision."

"We're stuck here until they make up their minds?" Connors said it as if it were equivalent to a death sentence.

"And our illness will get worse, not better. We can barely stand on our feet, as it is," Jamie said.

"There is the backup rover," Vosnesensky said.

"But who's going to drive it?" Connors asked. "You're all just as sick as we are."

"I will."

"You can't do that," Jamie said. "You're too sick to risk it."

Vosnesensky's grin reappeared, faintly. "I will drive the rover. I will gobble vitamin capsules by the kilogram. I will arrive in your vicinity in no more than thirty-six hours."

Despite his exhaustion, Jamie understood the reason behind Mikhail's smile. "Ivshenko and Zieman are at the dome now. You'll take them with you. They're both healthy."

The Russian bowed his head slightly in acknowledgment. "Yes, I will bring Ivshenko with me. We will ride to your rescue like the Seventh Cavalry in your western cinemas."

Connors muttered, "Wasn't that Custer's outfit?"

Vosnesensky had not made up his mind until he had seen their faces. Connors looked gaunt, dying. Waterman's broad cheekbones were jutting out, the flesh of his face was pulled taut, his eyes were red and watery.

There is nothing else to do, Vosnesensky told himself. I will pilot the rover to them and bring them back here to the dome. I will carry a supply of vitamins and food for them. Ivshenko will go with me, and Zieman will remain here. It is all within mission regulations; no safety measures will be broken.

His mind made up, he called Dr. Li up in *Mars 2* and informed him of the decision.

Li looked startled. "You are in no condition to make such a traverse."

Vosnesensky said stubbornly, "Ivshenko is. And I am quite capable of sitting in a chair and steering the vehicle. We will detach the middle section and take only the command module and the logistics module. I will be in constant communication with Dr. Yang and Dr. Reed. I will take whatever medications they prescribe."

"Kaliningrad will refuse to permit it," Li's image on the screen said. "They have decided that the eight of you in the dome are more important than the four in the rover."

"The four in the rover have the specimens of Martian organisms with them," Vosnesensky pointed out.

Li shook his head. "The decision has been made to evacuate you from the dome first, and then to see if it is possible to rescue the traverse team."

"In that case," Vosnesensky said, "I will go without Kaliningrad's permission. Or yours."

Li's eyes widened. "Do you realize what you are saying?"

Feeling all the enduring strength of Mother Russia surging through his veins, Vosnesensky said, "Certainly I do, Dr. Li. But you must realize what you are saying. As expedition commander your responsibilities are huge, heavier than I would want to bear. But I would not willingly allow Kaliningrad or god almighty to write off four of my comrades."

"The safety of your remaining team members is the most important issue now."

"Perhaps so. I am merely the leader of this ground team. I do not have to worry about the mission controllers or the politicians above them. My responsibility is to the men and women here on the surface of Mars. All of them, including the four stranded out there in the canyon."

"You would be risking your life and the lives of whoever you take with you," Li said.

"Ivshenko will be happy to volunteer, doctor. I will see to that, never fear. We will observe all the safety regulations."

"I cannot grant you permission for this!"

"Yes, I understand. That is your responsibility. Mine is to my comrades."

"Let me discuss it with Kaliningrad."

Vosnesensky almost laughed. "By the time the mission controllers finish arguing we will all be ready for our pensions—or our funerals. No, this must be done now, not two days from now."

Li licked his lips. In the comm screen he suddenly looked to Vosnesensky like a startled rabbit staring at him, ready to dart to safety. For long moments the two men stared at each other wordlessly.

Finally Li said, "Good luck."

Vosnesensky gathered the eleven men and women together in the wardroom and announced his decision.

"Ivshenko and I will drive the second rover to the canyon and pick up Waterman's team. We will be gone for three days—four, maximum."

The others said nothing. Standing in a loose semicircle before the cosmonaut, they looked at one another uneasily, feet shifting, eyes questioning.

Finally Dr. Yang said, "You are not in physical condition to make such a journey."

"It is my responsibility," Vosnesensky said. "Li and the mission controllers want to evacuate us back to orbit before trying to rescue the excursion team. I have decided otherwise. I must go. Me, myself."

"But you are still ill," said Yang. "The effects of scurvy will linger for many days. You will be weak and debilitated. . . ."

"Dmitri Iosifovitch will do all the work; I will merely take the glory."

They laughed, nervously.

"I'll go with you," said Tony Reed.

"You? No."

"I must," Reed insisted.

"There is no need for you to come," Vosnesensky said. "It is an unnecessary risk."

Reed stepped up to confront the Russian. "It is my responsibility to go," he said quietly, "just as it is yours."

Vosnesensky shook his head stubbornly. "We will not need a physician on board the rover. You will be in touch with us over the comm link."

"Don't you understand?" Reed burst out. Turning to face the others, "Don't any of you understand? It's my fault! The reason you all got sick is my fault! My doing! I fouled up the vitamin pills. Then I failed to see what was happening to you."

It was the most difficult thing Antony Reed had ever done in his life. The others stared at him in surprise.

"I've *got* to go with you," Tony pleaded, turning back to Vosnesensky. "Jamie and the others . . . they'll need a doctor once we get there."

Vosnesensky's mouth was open, as if he wanted to reply but did not know what to say. The others began to look embarrassed, uncertain of what to do.

"He should go," Yang said firmly. "He is right. The four in the rover will need immediate medical attention once you reach them."

Vosnesensky stroked his broad chin. "I see."

"So will you," Yang added.

The Russian grinned weakly. "My personal physician?"

Yang did not smile back. "If you insist on making this traverse in your condition, you will need a physician with you."

"Very well," Vosnesensky said reluctantly.

"Thank you!" said Reed. He saw the look on Vosnesensky's face, on all their faces. He had expected anger, or perhaps disgust at his stupidity. Instead they all seemed sympathetic, even the sickest of them. They don't blame me, Reed realized with a surge of gratitude that nearly buckled his knees. They don't blame me!

For the first time in his life he had admitted a shortcoming, accepted the consequences for his own actions, bared his guilt to the men and women around him. He had thought it would be more painful than slicing open his own guts. And it was. But he had survived the pain. Like a man facing suicide he had confronted the worst he could imagine and come through it alive.

Vosnesensky sank gratefully into the nearest wardroom chair. His legs were so weak he could not stand any longer. A good thing that I will be able to sit all the way out to the canyon, he told himself. I only hope I will be able to drive the damned rover without collapsing like a weak old woman.

Jamie was sitting in the cockpit again, Joanna beside him. Connors was stretched out on his bunk, moaning softly in his sleep. Ilona was also trying to sleep, on the bunk above the astronaut's. None of them had possessed the strength to fold the cots back. They had eaten their gloomy breakfasts sitting on the edges of the lower cots, heads bent low to avoid bumping the uppers.

"Vitamin deficiency," Jamie mused. "Of all the things that could have gone wrong with this mission, we come down with scurvy. Talk about Murphy's Law."

Joanna seemed barely awake. But she said, "Knowing what the problem is, somehow it does not seem so bad. It was the unknown that frightened me."

"It can still kill us, whether we know what it is or not."

She smiled wanly. "You won't let us die, Jamie. I know you won't."

Why is she putting this load on me? he wondered, half angry. But aloud he said to her, "There's not much any of us can do now except wait."

Joanna's weak little smile widened slightly, as if she knew something that Jamie did not.

The comm unit buzzed. Jamie flicked the switch and Abell's frog-like face appeared on the control panel screen. He looked just as sallow and gaunt as the four in the rover, his sunken cheeks making his protruding eyes seem to pop out even more than usual.

"There's a message coming in for Joanna from Kaliningrad," Abell said. "Is she up and about?"

"I am here," Joanna said, leaning enough from the pilot's seat so that Abell could see her even though the miniature camera built into the control panel was aimed at Jamie.

"Oh, good. I'll tell them up in *Mars 2* to pipe it right down to you."

"How are you doing?" Jamie asked.

Abell swung his head back and forth. "Reed's pumping so much vitamin C into us that I feel like I'm turning into an orange grove. I can shake my head without getting woozy, but I still feel like canned dog food."

Jamie realized that he felt like *used* dog food. And that Abell refrained from asking how he felt.

"Dmitri and Ollie are outside rerigging the spare rover. Mikhail's straw-bossing them over the TV link and making their lives miserable. He's too weak to go out there himself so he's giving them hell every inch of the way."

"How long before they get under way?" Jamie asked.

"Another hour. Two at most. Mikhail's taking Dmitri with him. Ollie's sore as hell."

"No sense risking more skins than you have to," Jamie said.

"Reed's coming, too."

"Tony? Going outside?"

"Yeah. He says you'll need a medic by the time they get to you."

That's a comforting thought, Jamie said to himself.

Abell said, "Okay. I'll tell them to shoot you the message from Kaliningrad."

The screen cleared briefly, flickered; then the image of a tired old man took form. His red hair was rumpled, his sharp little Vandyke beard messy, his shirt collar unbuttoned. He identified himself as the chief of mission control.

"My message is for Dr. Joanna Brumado, and it is of a personal nature. It is a question, actually, that Dr. Brumado must answer for us."

Jamie swiveled the little ball-mounted camera on the control panel toward Joanna while the mission controller hesitated, as if waiting for him or expecting a reply. Then he took a deep breath and plunged onward:

"Dr. Brumado, this question concerns your father. As you know, he has been quite close to the day-to-day operations of our mission. Naturally, he has been informed of your . . . predicament. He is already heading for Houston. I have given strict orders that no one outside mission control is to know about the problem we are now facing until the situation has been resolved. This is to forestall the media from sensationalizing the situation, you see."

Jamie thought, I sure as hell see that they don't want the media to know the fix we're in. They'd be buried alive by reporters.

"However," the chief controller went on, "apparently your father is being accompanied by a representative of the American news media, a young woman television reporter. We have not been able to learn her affiliation, although we have her name." The Russian looked down, obviously reading from a piece of paper. He pronounced stiffly, "Edie Elgin."

Joanna frowned. Jamie felt a jolt of surprise. Edith? With Brumado?

The chief controller looked distinctly uncomfortable. "Your father will want to speak with you, of course. Apparently this newswoman with him wants permission to tape your conversation for possible broadcast—after this crisis is resolved. The tape would not be released, of course, without the permission of the Mars Project administrators. And your father's permission also, of course."

She's hooked up with Brumado, Jamie realized. Son of a bitch! And she wants to make a tape of their conversation. What a cold-blooded piece of genius that is! If we die she'll have terrific footage of the last tender moments between father and daughter. If we live, it'll still be great human-interest material for her.

And she hasn't asked to contact me. She doesn't give a damn about me. Why the hell should she? She's got Brumado now.

The chief controller was asking Joanna, "Will you be able to conduct a brief conversation with your father—allowing for the time lag between transmission and reception of messages, of course."

Joanna glanced at Jamie, then seemed to draw herself up taller and straighter in the cockpit seat.

"I appreciate your solicitude toward my father and myself, and I thank you for it. But please do not bother to arrange a special transmission for us," Joanna said, more firmly than Jamie had ever heard her speak before. "I repeat: do *not* set up a link with Houston. I want no special privileges. If you have chosen to maintain a news blackout about this problem we are facing, then please do not consider me to be an exception."

Jamie cut off the transmission switch. "Wait a minute," he said. "Doesn't your father have a right . . ."

Her red-rimmed eyes flared at him. "I am not a little girl who must talk with her papa when she is in trouble. I want to be treated just the same way you and the others are treated."

"But he's Alberto Brumado," Jamie said. "It's not you that they want to give special treatment to; it's him."

Joanna tried to shake her head. The effort made her grip the edge of the control panel with a white-knuckled hand. "No. I would not be able to keep my strength in front of him. I would break down and cry. I will not have that put on videotape."

"Oh. I see. I guess."

"Jamie—if we . . . if it becomes certain that we are going to die here, then there will be plenty of time to speak to my father. Each of us will tape messages for our families, I am sure."

"I guess so." *And Edith will get it all for the goddammed prime-time news.*

"But not now. I have not given up hope. You have not given up hope, have you?"

"Hell no," he said, with a fervor that he did not truly feel.

"Then turn the transmitter on once again."

Jamie did. Joanna took a breath, brushed her hands unconsciously through her tousled hair.

"I appreciate your offer," she said calmly, with great dignity, "but my decision is that I want to be treated exactly like the others. I expect you to keep my father informed of our situation—and the newswoman with him. Thank you very much."

She's as sore about Edith as I am, Jamie saw. The realization gave him no comfort at all.

Dmitri Iosifovitch Ivshenko was at the controls of the backup rover, a crooked grin on his pinched face. *He is happy to be on the ground doing something useful instead of sitting up in orbit,* Vosnesensky thought.

Reed sat back on one of the midship benches. Vosnesensky wondered about the Englishman. *He is here with us out of a sense of* guilt; he wants to atone for the accident with the vitamins. Will he be a positive help to us or will he just get in our way? He doesn't know how to drive the rover. He has no real experience in EVA. I doubt that he has been outside the dome more than a few hours, total, since we landed. What good will he be in an emergency?

The Russian turned in the cockpit seat and looked over his shoulder at Reed. The physician seemed lost in thought, dazed almost, as he leaned back on the bench, both hands gripping its edge.

Vosnesensky shook his head, then immediately regretted it. He still felt woozy and terribly weak. Having my own private physician aboard has done nothing to improve my health, he grumbled to himself.

Vosnesensky turned his attention back to Ivshenko. Studying the fellow, he realized for the first time that Ivshenko looked decidedly un-Russian. He was as lean as a willow and his hair was a thick curly thatch of midnight black. His eyes were coal dark too. A thin aquiline nose and even thinner lips. His complexion was pale, bloodless white, although Vosnesensky thought that he would tan to a deep brown if he could get some sun on him.

He is younger than I am, Vosnesensky thought, envying the energy that radiated from the cosmonaut's taut, wiry frame. Younger and healthier. Vosnesensky's head thundered; his arms and legs ached miserably. If Reed is right, these vitamin doses ought to be helping, but I certainly don't feel any better. Perhaps worse.

"Tell me, Dmitri Iosifovitch," Vosnesensky said aloud, his voice sounding harsh and strained even in his own ears, "where did you get such good looks?"

The younger man glanced at him, almost startled, then quickly turned back to his driving.

"My mother is Armenian, if that's what you mean," Ivshenko replied.

"Ah, I wondered. I thought perhaps you had some Turkish blood in you."

Ivshenko's nostrils flared. "No. Armenian."

"I see," said Vosnesensky. "And how is your love life, up there in orbit?"

Ivshenko's grin returned. "Adequate, comrade. Quite adequate. Especially when that German physicist gets bored with her work."

"Diels? The blonde?"

"She is teaching me things about physics that I never knew before."

"The quest for knowledge is never-ending," Vosnesensky agreed.

"A worthwhile goal."

Vosnesensky started to laugh, but it made his chest hurt. He ended up coughing.

"You are in pain, Mikhail Andreivitch?"

"It's nothing. Just a little agony."

"Do you want to turn back?"

"No!" Vosnesensky thundered. "We go onward. No matter what happens, we go onward."

Hours passed. They stopped the rover briefly and changed seats so that Vosnesensky could drive. Ivshenko watched him carefully, though. The younger cosmonaut had no great desire to allow his older comrade to get them both killed.

"At sundown you can take over again," Vosnesensky said, feeling perspiration beading his face, trickling along his ribs, plastering the back of his coveralls against the seat.

"You will sleep then?"

"I will try."

"The safety regulations forbid operating the rover unless a backup driver is awake and prepared to take over in case of an emergency. And operating at night . . ."

"I know the regulations quite thoroughly," Vosnesensky snapped. "I helped to write them. This is an emergency situation; we will bend the rules a little."

"A little," Ivshenko murmured.

Jabbing a thumb over his shoulder, "If you get lonely while I sleep you can have our physician to keep you company."

Ivshenko made a sour face.

Across the rubble-strewn plain they drove, south by east, the dwarf sun lowering toward the rugged horizon, throwing long blood-red shadows from every rock on the barren desert. To Vosnesensky the shadows looked like the lean claws of dead men's hands reaching for him.

Back in the midsection of the command module Tony Reed felt every bump and dip of the rover as he sat gripping the edge of the bench with both hands. This is madness, he told himself. Why did I ever talk myself into coming out here? Penance? This is carrying expiation for one's sins a bit too far, really.

But he stayed silent, uncomplaining, trying to hold down the fear that was building up inside him. We're out in the middle of the empty Martian plain in this piddling little vehicle. If anything goes wrong, anything at all, we're all dead men.

Up in the cockpit the comm unit buzzed. Ivshenko turned it on and Dr. Li's long sallow face appeared on the screen. His mouth curved downward, his eyes looked weary, defeated.

"I have spent half the day arguing with Kaliningrad," Li said, his voice hoarsely rasping. "The mission controllers are adamant."

Vosnesensky grunted, but kept the rover moving forward.

"They insist that the crew in the dome must be evacuated to orbit, and only afterward can an attempt be made to rescue the team in the rover."

"Have you told them that we are already on our way to the canyon?"

Li slowly shook his head. "No. I told them that we do not agree either with their assessment of the situation or their decision."

"Yet they still insist?"

"Yes."

"So what do you intend to do?"

The expedition commander tugged nervously at one end of his moustache. "It is my duty to command you to turn around and return to the dome so that you can carry out the orders from mission control."

"Very well," Vosnesensky said. "You have done your duty." He reached across the control panel and turned off the communications unit. Then he slowed the rover to a halt.

Ivshenko was looking at him worriedly. "You're going to turn around?"

Heaving a great pained sigh, Vosnesensky said, "Don't be an idiot. You drive for the next two hours while I nap. If we go all night we could reach the canyon rim by midday tomorrow."

Oliver Zieman stared at the comm screen.

He sat alone in the command section of the dome; most of the others were down sick. Dr. Yang was in the infirmary, running still more tests. Zieman scratched his head, thinking furiously. He had not expected a crisis of command.

Dr. Li's image on the screen looked pained, tortured. He must be spending all his time right there in the command module, Zieman thought. He must be living there night and day. He looks almost as bad as the scurvy cases.

"We have a very difficult situation on our hands," Li said to the

astronaut, "and I want to be certain that you are fully aware of all
the implications."

"Yes, sir," said Zieman, almost eagerly.

"Mission control has issued an order to abandon the dome and
return the entire base crew here to orbit," Li said.

"But the rover team . . ."

Li raised a long slim finger to silence the astronaut. He continued,
"Kaliningrad reasons that we must think of the health and safety of
the greatest number first. They are prepared to abandon the base and
evacuate everyone in the dome."

Zieman swiftly thought, That means I'll have to pack them aboard
the L/AVs myself. Eight of us, counting me. Can't fit that many in a
single L/AV. Who in hell's going to pilot the second vehicle? Mironov
and Abell are in no shape for it, and Dmitri's off with Vosnesensky
and Reed.

"After the contingent from the dome is safely in orbit," Li was
saying, "and we have all the astronauts and cosmonauts here, we
can use the final landing/ascent vehicle to attempt to rescue the four
in the rover."

"Then you want Vosnesensky to turn back," Zieman said.

"I have ordered him to do so. He has refused."

Refused! A burning jet of fear shot through Zieman. A man can't
refuse to carry out orders! That's crazy! The whole mission could
fall apart if we don't follow orders.

Li waited a moment for his words to register with Zieman. Then
he said, "Vosnesensky has tied my hands. I cannot order the evac-
uation from the dome with only one healthy astronaut present there.
I cannot send Tolbukhin and Klein down to you because that would
use the last remaining lander. It would mean abandoning the team
in the rover altogether."

"Yeah. Right." He still felt stunned that Vosnesensky had dis-
obeyed orders. Of all the people on this mission! Vosnesensky, the
straightest of the straight arrows.

"If Ivshenko were with you it would be possible to lift all personnel there in two of the vehicles," Li said, stating the obvious.
"Since he is off with Vosnesensky, I cannot order the dome evacuated."

"Yessir. I understand," said Zieman.

"That means you will be in charge of the personnel in the dome
until Vosnesensky returns."

Zieman nodded wordlessly, thinking, If he returns. If.

S O L 4 0: MORNING

Just as he had expected—no, as he had *known*—there was a stairway cut into the sheer wall of the cliff, leading up to the city built in the giant cleft high above.

Jamie stood in the brightly warm sunlight of New Mexico even though the sky was a delicate Martian pink. He slid his helmet visor up, knowing he no longer needed his hard suit to protect him. He was coming home, his true home, where two worlds met and blended in the unity and balance that he had unconsciously sought since childhood. For the first time in his life Jamie felt in harmony with the world, with both his worlds, with all the worlds.

He climbed the stairs slowly, almost unwilling to end the happiness, the peacefulness of this moment. Yet he knew that at the top his people would be waiting to welcome him. Like an ancient priest of the Old Ones climbing the temple stairs in solemn dignity, Jamie moved his booted feet from one stone stair to the next. He saw that the steps had been cut into the living rock long ages ago; their stone surfaces had been worn smooth and saddle-backed by countless generations of climbing feet.

Piece by piece his protective hard suit disappeared as he climbed. His helmet vanished first, and he could drink in the clean cool air of the true world. Then his boots, the torso shell, the leggings. By the time he reached the top he was naked and possessed nothing except the bear fetish that his grandfather had given him hundreds of millions of kilometers ago.

Sweat trickled along his flanks, his legs, ran down his face. The air was cool but the sun warmed him, filled him with its life-giving energy.

He was nearing the top of the stairway. He could hear the breeze sighing, hear fully leafed trees up there calling to him. He looked down at the fetish in his hand and the bear smiled at him. Only a few steps more, my son, said his grandfather's voice. Only a few steps more.

Jamie reached the top. The city was there, just as he had known it would be. Magnificent. Straight clean walls of fresh adobe brick. Tier upon tier of houses rising to the top of the cleft where the overhanging rock sheltered them like the protective arm of god.

"It is good," Jamie said. "Ya'aa'tey."

His grandfather appeared before him, young and strong and naked as Jamie himself. "It is good," his grandfather said.

All the people poured out of their homes, thronging into the central plaza where Jamie stood with his grandfather, smiling, singing, carrying wreaths of flowers that they put over Jamie's head. The women were beautiful, the men strong and handsome.

Yet Jamie turned to his grandfather. "I can't stay. The others—they need me."

"I know," said the old man. "Go in beauty, my grandson."

Jamie's eyes snapped open.

The dream had been so vivid, so real. He dug his hand into the pocket of his coveralls and felt the fetish resting there, a warm comforting lump of stone. Only then did he allow himself to relax in his bunk and take stock of the new day.

His entire body ached with a dull sullen pain that sapped his strength. His head throbbed, pulse thumping in his ears like a drum slowly beating out the cadence of death. Next to him Connors moaned softly in his troubled sleep, his breath whistling slightly.

Quietly, Jamie slid out of his bunk. His legs were almost too weak to hold him up. For long minutes he gripped the edge of Joanna's bunk, uncertain that he could squeeze past the bunks and make it to the lavatory. She was huddled in a fetal position. Ilona lay facedown, unmoving. For a moment Jamie feared she might be dead, but then he saw the slow rhythm of her breathing.

He pushed past the bunks, grabbing at the hand grips set into the bulkheads to make his way to the lav. In the polished metal mirror above the tiny sink his face stared back at him, gaunt, unshaven, hollow eyed. Slowly, with the deliberate care of a drunk or an old, old man, Jamie washed his face and hands. When he brushed his teeth the brush came away bloody. The teeth even felt loose in his gums. He peeled off his night coveralls and pulled on his day pair. Not much between them, he realized. They were both wrinkled and smelly.

The others did not begin to awaken until he had mixed himself a glass of instant orange drink and a mug of steaming coffee. They got up slowly, looking as exhausted and pain wracked as Jamie himself felt. Gaunt faces, red eyes, hands trembling, legs almost too weak to hold them up.

They barely said a dozen words to one another. Mumbles. Grunts. Sighs that turned into gasping, labored breathing.

Jamie slid past them, the coffee mug in one hand, and forced himself to the cockpit. Sliding into the right-hand seat, he punched up the comm unit and put in a call to the dome.

Paul Abell's face appeared on the screen. He was smiling—weakly, but smiling. His cheeks and chin looked freshly shaved, slightly red. His bulging frog's eyes were clearer than Jamie remembered them.

"Good morning!" Abell was almost cheerful.

"How are you?" Jamie's voice was a scratchy croak.

"Yang's vitamin doses seem to be helping," Abell said brightly. "Got a good night's sleep. I feel better this morning than I have in days. Not one hundred percent yet, but better."

"That's good."

Abell pointedly did not ask how Jamie felt. He could see.

"Heard from the Russkies yet?"

"Who?"

"Mikhail and Ivshenko. They ought to be just about at the canyon's edge by now."

"No. No contact yet."

"This morning, for sure," Abell said.

"This morning," Jamie echoed.

"Be careful now," Vosnesensky muttered. "The horizon is so close that you could become confused."

Ivshenko, driving the rover, shot him a dark glance. "Mikhail Andreivitch, I have had as many hours in the simulators and in training exercises as you, have I not? I drove this beast most of the night, did I not? Why do you constantly . . ."

"*Stop!*" Vosnesensky bellowed. Ivshenko tromped his booted foot on the brakes so hard that they would have both pitched into the canopy if Vosnesensky had not insisted that they wear the safety harnesses. Tony Reed, standing behind Vosnesensky's seat, lunged into the chair back with a painful grunt.

The Grand Canyon of Mars stretched out in front of them, its rim a bare twenty meters from the rover's nose. Ivshenko gaped, jaw slack, chest heaving.

"Good god!" Reed gasped.

"That is what I was trying to warn you about," Vosnesensky said calmly. "What appears at first to be the crest of another ridge is actually the edge of the precipice."

"You . . . you should have said so."

Vosnesensky chuffed out a weary sigh, like a teacher disappointed with a pupil.

The canyon was filled with mist, billowing gently in the morning sun, looking almost thick enough to walk on. From inside the cockpit they could not see the bottom of the canyon; it was far too deep for that even if the air had been perfectly clear. To their right and left the cliff walls marched off beyond the horizon, red rock battlements, rugged with untold eons of weathering, tall and proud. Looking straight across the canyon, Vosnesensky thought he could make out the jagged outline of the opposite wall, faint and wavering in the hazy distance. So far away.

"I don't see the landslide," Reed said.

"Nor do I. We must have drifted off course during the night. I will take a navigational fix. Dmitri Iosifovitch, you contact the base and tell them we have reached the canyon—without falling into it."

Ivshenko muttered to himself as he leaned over slightly to reach the comm unit switches. He did not see the slight grin on his commander's face.

Within a quarter hour they had pinpointed their location with a fix from one of the navigation satellites deployed around the planet and were on their way to the lip of the landslide, some five kilometers westward.

Vosnesensky felt almost relaxed as he rode in the right-hand seat. Ivshenko had driven most of the night, slept a few hours, and now was driving again. He seemed fresh; his reflexes were sharp. Mikhail himself felt little better than he had since the scurvy had hit him; he was still weak, still achy; he had barely slept at all during the night.

The body affects the mind, he said to himself as they creaked along at twenty kilometers per hour across the boulder-strewn red landscape. When the body hurts, the mind becomes tired, easily confused, quick to despair. I must remember that. I must keep my thinking clear, no matter how my body feels.

"I think I see it."

Ivshenko's words snapped Vosnesensky out of his musings. He followed the pilot's pointing finger with his eyes and saw, through the morning haze, what appeared to be a wide semicircle cut into the cliff edge, with a rusty-red pile of dirt slumping down from its rim toward the bottom of the canyon, far below.

"Yes, that must be it."

While Vosnesensky checked the navigational display, Ivshenko said, "You don't expect to go down that slope, do you?"

"We have come to rescue the team in the other rover," Vosnesensky said. The nav screen showed that they were in the right area. The trapped rover was sitting roughly two thirds of the way down the ancient avalanche.

"Comrade cosmonaut," Ivshenko said, "what good would it do for us to trap ourselves alongside them?"

"What do you suggest?" Vosnesensky growled, feeling a sudden impatience with his cohort.

"I suggest," Ivshenko put an ironic emphasis on the verb, "that we stop at the lip of the canyon and let them walk to us. That is the safest thing to do."

"And if they are too weak to make it?"

The cosmonaut bit his lip. Vosnesensky waited for his answer, thinking, If he says that we should go back to the dome without going down there and getting them, I'll throw him out the airlock without a suit.

"If they are too weak to make it," Ivshenko said slowly, "then I suppose we will have to go down on foot and help them."

"We?"

"Dr. Reed and myself," Ivshenko said. "You should remain here in the rover, Mikhail Andreivitch."

Vosnesensky felt his heart expand. He broke into a huge grin. "Well spoken, Dmitri Iosifovitch! Brave words! But I can think of something much better."

Tony Reed thought, I should hope so. No one's going to get *me* to go out there!

S O L 4 0: NOON

Jamie turned the ridged little dial on the binoculars; the rippled expanse of sand swam into sharp focus.

"It must be an ancient crater that's been filled in with dust," he said, as much to himself as the others clustered in the cockpit.

"Why doesn't the wind blow the dust away?" Joanna asked.

He put the glasses down. She was sitting next to him, in the right-hand seat, her face pale, her hair tangled and matted. Her breath stank. Mine does too, Jamie told himself. Everybody's does.

Connors, looking more ragged than ever, sat on the floor between the two seats. His coveralls were rumpled and dark with sweat stains. Ilona stood behind him, leaning wearily on the seat backs. She looked bedraggled too; like Joanna, she had not had the strength to brush her hair. Sick and weary as they were, though, they were all eager to catch the first glimpse of Vosnesensky's rover.

"I don't think there's enough power in the wind to clean out the crater. The air's too thin, even when it blows at two hundred knots. The crater must have steep walls. Probably made by a meteorite coming in from almost straight overhead."

"The wind can gradually fill up the crater with dust," Joanna surmised, "and once it is full it remains full."

"Right," said Jamie. We're talking millions of years here, he added silently. Nothing goes quickly on Mars. Come back in a million years and the rover will still be sitting here, most likely.

He raised the binoculars to his eyes once again. If the oddly rippled sand represented the area of the crater, then it was more than a kilometer across. Jamie could see its boundary clearly, a wide circle where the little wavelets of red sand ended and the ground was more heavily littered with rocks and boulders.

He remembered arguing with Naguib about the frequency of such dust-filled craters. The Egyptian called them "ghost craters" and believed they peppered the landscape even where the ground looked relatively smooth. Jamie had disagreed. But Abdul was right; we've fallen into a ghost crater. I should have noticed the difference in the ground, Jamie berated himself. I should have avoided this area. If only I had been sharp enough . . .

"There they are!"

Joanna pointed eagerly, her wan face suddenly wreathed in a smile.

Following her extended arm, Jamie saw the rover nosing over the crest of the slope like a fat silver caterpillar with a big gleaming bulbous head inching their way.

"Greetings, fellow travelers!" Vosnesensky's voice was harshly rasping in the control panel speaker. To the four of them it sounded like an angel's sweet melody.

Jamie glanced down at the comm screen. The cosmonaut looked weak, strained, sweating as he sat at the controls of the second rover and guided it down the slope of the ancient landslide with excruciatingly deliberate, patient care. Tony Reed was hunched behind him, his face drawn, pale, nervous. Both men were in their coveralls.

Putting the binoculars to his eyes again, Jamie saw a figure in a brilliant red hard suit plodding slowly toward them on foot in front of the rover, poking at the ground in front of him with a long pole the way a blind man gropes along unfamiliar territory, the way a mountaineer feels his way across a snow-choked crevasse.

Ivshenko trailed a tether from his waist, connected to the nose of the rover, more than twenty meters behind him. The vehicle was inching along, but getting closer every moment. Trust Mikhail to use every safety precaution, Jamie thought. Does he think Ivshenko's going to float away? For an absurd moment it looked as if the cosmonaut was towing the ponderous rover.

"They're coming," Ilona said in a choked whisper. "They're coming to save us."

"Three cheers for our side," said Connors weakly.

Jamie remained in the cockpit and watched their rescuers approaching. More than an hour went by as the rover trundled closer, agonizingly slow, with Ivshenko out front testing the ground. A blind man leading an elephant, Jamie thought.

"Now be careful," he said to the cosmonauts. "You see where the ground starts to break up into a series of little sand ripples?"

Vosnesensky's image in the display screen nodded its head. Ivshenko said from inside his helmet, "Yes, it is about fifty meters in front of me."

"That's where the crater rim is, I'm pretty sure," Jamie said. "It's filled with this very loose sand, more like dust. You'll have to take the rover around it. Otherwise you'll get stuck too."

Vosnesensky was peering at it suspiciously. "It seems quite wide."

"I know. But you can work your way around it, can't you?"

"Going down, perhaps. I wonder about going up again."

Ivshenko's voice said, "It might be best to stop the rover at the edge of the loose soil and let me go through the area on foot. Then we can connect a safety line and winch them across to our rover."

"Can all four of you get into your hard suits?" Vosnesensky asked.

"Yes," said Jamie. "I think so."

"I hesitate to risk getting the second rover stuck, too."

"I understand. We can get into suits and you can winch us across the soft stuff—if we can set up a line from your vehicle to ours."

"Very good. That is what we will do."

Dr. Li Chengdu had never in his life felt so hesitant about making a report. This could ruin everything, he knew. It will reflect poorly on my ability as a leader; it will devastate the mission control team. If the politicians and the media find out about it, it will destroy our chances for further missions to Mars.

Yet he had to report on the scurvy and the chain of events that had led to it. There was nothing else that Li could do except tell the facts to the men and women who directed the mission. There is no way to cover it up, Li realized. Nor would it be proper to do so. Even to think of a cover-up is criminal. No matter what affect this has on my career or the careers of others.

Scurvy. Everyone on the ground team nearly killed by scurvy because they had overlooked the fact that pure oxygen had deactivated their crucially needed vitamin C supply. The politicians will jump to the conclusion that the traverse team got stuck in their rover because the scurvy sapped their strength and their judgment. And now Vosnesensky, of all people, is disobeying orders and trying to rescue them.

Vosnesensky. Wait until the mission controllers sink their teeth into that morsel! What a mess. What a confounded, convoluted, unequivocal disaster.

Li knew he had to tell the facts to Kaliningrad. Still he hesitated.

Pacing his private cubicle in three long-legged strides, back and forth, back and forth, he passed his desktop computer a dozen times without even thinking of starting to file his report.

Even if I wanted to hide the facts it would be impossible. They will know soon enough that we are not evacuating the dome, as ordered. He agonized for hours. *How to put the best face on this disaster. How to tell the news in a way that will not destroy any chance for future missions to Mars. How to admit my own inadequacy without ruining my chances for the future.*

That is the important thing. How to tell this terrible news in a way that will not destroy our chances for the future. That is the vital thing.

Virtually all of the reports from the ground team were made orally and transcribed into hard copy automatically by the computers in the spacecraft and back at Kaliningrad. Li alone regularly wrote out his reports and transmitted them in written form. *But what can I write now? What words can soften this news?*

Like a caged cheetah he paced back and forth, seeking a way out and finding none. Finally, in an agony of reluctance, he sat at his little desk and began pecking on the computer keyboard with his long manicured fingers.

Dmitri Iosifovitch Ivshenko had the physique and the personality of the typical cosmonaut. Slight of build, lightning-fast reflexes, and enough youth to have survived being a fighter pilot and then a test pilot. Drinking all night, sobering up on oxygen in the morning, breakfasting on a cigarette and then throwing up behind the hangar before climbing into the cockpit of some supersonic jet. Yet once in the cockpit he became cool and calculating, capable of sizing up a situation in an instant and doing the right thing at precisely the right moment on a combination of instinct, training, and blindingly fast thought processes. He did not consider himself to be a bold pilot; the bold ones died young. Ivshenko was a cautious pilot who flew dangerous aircraft. When he transferred to the cosmonaut corps he was almost bored with the Newtonian predictability of each space mission.

He was not bored now. He was not particularly worried, either. Merely careful. *No need to rush,* he reminded himself as he cautiously poked his pole into the sandy ripples a meter in front of his boots. We are here to rescue those four wretches, not to get stuck alongside them.

Dust stirred up where he prodded the ground. The pole sank in a few centimeters, then seemed to hit firm soil. Ivshenko nodded inside his helmet and took a step forward, dragging his safety tether behind him.

"How is it?" Vosnesensky's voice rasped in his earphones.

"Soft, like sand. Not good traction."

"Be very careful."

"I am always very careful, Mikhail Andreivitch."

"Then be *doubly* careful."

"Yes, sir, comrade group commander." Ivshenko chuckled to himself and took another step forward.

His foot slid out from under him. His body half turned as he grabbed at the pole with both hands but it too was sinking into the sand, suddenly the consistency of talcum. Clouds of pink dust billowed softly as Ivshenko felt himself slipping, sliding forward, his boots suddenly without purchase, sinking into a sea of soft red sand.

He did not call out. Even as he sank down into the clinging dust he let go of the useless pole and tried to twist his body around and reach back toward the last bit of firm ground. But inside the cumbersome hard suit he could barely turn a few degrees as he floundered, arms flailing, legs kicking. It was like sinking into gooey mud. Ivshenko imagined himself being sucked down into quicksand.

With those rapid reflexes and his ability to size up a situation quickly, Ivshenko stopped his struggling even as he heard Vosnesensky bellowing in his earphones: "What's wrong? What's happening?"

He felt something firm beneath the heel of his left boot and tried to balance all his weight on it. But the boot slipped off it and he continued to sink slowly, inexorably, into the fine red dust. It rose up to his chest, up to his armpits, to the lip of his helmet.

"I am sinking," he reported glumly. The visor of his helmet was spattered with rust-colored dust. His arms were spread across the surface of the sand like a swimmer trying to float. He was afraid to move them for fear of sinking faster.

Vosnesensky swore in Russian.

"I'm sinking!" Ivshenko repeated, louder, his voice pitched higher. The talcumlike sand was crawling up the faceplate of his helmet.

Vosnesensky hesitated only a moment. It would be dangerous to try to back up on this slope, he knew, but Ivshenko's tether was attached to a simple ring fastener on the nose of the vehicle. There was no winch to pull him up.

"Sit down," he snapped at Reed as he punched the control panel buttons that put all the wheel motors into reverse.

Reed slipped into the right-hand seat, his eyes goggling at the scene in front of them. Ivshenko's helmet had disappeared into the sand almost entirely. He was yelling something in Russian, but his radio voice was breaking up, garbled with static.

"Pull me up, dammit!" Ivshenko shouted into his helmet microphone. He was completely drowned in the red dust now. And still sinking. It was bottomless.

Then he felt the tether take hold. Like a parachute blossoming over his head. Ivshenko felt the same rush of gratitude and joy.

"Good! Good! Pull me back."

He knew Vosnesensky would inch the rover backward with infinite care, infinite caution. That's fine, Ivshenko said to himself. I have twelve hours of air, maybe more. Take your time, Mikhail Andreivitch. Take all the time you want, but keep pulling me up.

His head rose above the sand and almost instantly he could hear a babble of voices: Reed, Vosnesensky, the four in the other rover, all talking at once.

"I'm fine," he said to them all. "Keep pulling."

His shoulders came free of the dust. He could wave his arms at them all. Then his left boot seemed to catch on the same projection of underlying rock that had almost stopped him when he was sinking.

"Wait, I'm caught . . ."

But the tether kept pulling him. His left leg was pinned somehow. He tried to twist it free as he called on Vosnesensky to stop for a moment.

The tether was made of the same lightweight, high-strength carbon fiber composites as those that linked the spacecraft together. The underground rock was as hard and durable as granite. The rover continued to grind slowly backward despite Ivshenko's yowls, stretching him as if he were being racked.

It only took a few seconds. Ivshenko felt his knee pop, a searing bolt of pain stabbing the length of his leg. He screamed a curse at the universe as the tether suddenly went slack.

Vosnesensky bellowed into the cockpit radio, "What's the matter with you?"

"You've just broken my leg, that's all," Ivshenko answered in a
voice sharp with misery.

"How . . . ?"

"Never mind! Pull! I'm starting to sink again."

It cost him excruciating pain, but Ivshenko dislodged his leg from
the projection of rock while he snarled at Vosnesensky. He felt the
tether tighten again. His leg throbbing terribly, he lapsed into a grit-
ted-teeth silence as the rover pulled him out of the sand pit.

For long minutes he lay on the firm ground, panting, squeezing
his eyes shut against the pain.

In the cockpit, Tony Reed stared at the prone red-suited figure,
his heart pounding in his ears. "What's happened to him?"

"He said his leg became caught on something," Vosnesensky answered dourly. "When we pulled him, the leg snapped."

"What are we going to do?"

"We've got to go out and get him!"

"Go out? You can't!"

"I will suit up," Vosnesensky said.

"You're in no condition to go outside," Reed insisted. "You
haven't had more than two hours' sleep since we left the dome."

"I must." But his first try at getting up from the cockpit seat was
a failure. His legs were too weak to support him. The Russian tried
again; the best he could do was to stand shakily for a moment and
then collapse back onto the seat.

"Don't look at me!" Reed said, near panic. "I can't go out! I . . . I'm
not trained for EVA work."

"Stop arguing," Ivshenko's voice came over the radio speaker,
weak, gasping. "I can make it to the hatch . . . I think."

The cosmonaut began crawling along the ground, pulling himself
with his hands, dragging his useless left leg.

"If his suit ruptures . . ." Vosnesensky let the thought hang. Turning, sweaty-faced, to Reed he commanded, "Get into your hard suit,
doctor. Now."

"But I . . ."

"You need not go EVA," Vosnesensky said, his voice heavy with
distaste. "But our comrade will need someone to help him into the
airlock. You can do that much, can't you?"

Reed's insides were fluttering, his hands trembling. "Yes, of
course," he said, desperately trying to calm himself. "Naturally. I
can help him out of his suit and tend to his leg."

"An angel of mercy," Vosnesensky snarled.

From the cockpit of the stranded rover, Jamie and the three others had watched and listened to Ivshenko's ordeal. With growing horror they saw their would-be rescuer sink into the sand, heard his shouts for help, watched the second rover carefully back up and pull the cosmonaut free, flinched at his scream when his leg went.

Now Jamie watched grimly as Ivshenko crawled painfully toward the rover's airlock hatch. And he knew there was nothing left, no hope of their being rescued. Unless he did it himself.

S O L 4 0: AFTERNOON

It took almost two hours for Jamie to struggle into his hard suit. Exhausted and weak from his illness, he knew that he had to make the trek to the second rover carrying a lifeline that would at last bring his three companions across the ghost crater of treacherous sand to the safety of the rescuing vehicle.

Vosnesensky had objected strenuously.

"You are too sick to do it!" the Russian had insisted. "I am the only one remaining who has even half his normal strength . . ."

Jamie shut him down with an upraised hand. "Mikhail," he said softly to the cosmonaut's image on the comm screen, "if you get stuck out there too, then we're all dead. If I get stuck, we still have Pete or even one of the women to try to get to you."

"They are all in worse condition than you are!"

"You've got to stay with your vehicle," Jamie said flatly, unemotionally, as if he were reading instructions from a printed form. "That is self-evident. The regulations are perfectly clear, and they're entirely right, too."

Vosnesensky scowled. But he no longer argued.

"I'm strong enough to make it around the perimeter of the crater," Jamie said. "I'll carry a line that we can use to bring the others across the lake."

"Lake?"

"The crater full of sand."

"It is more like a bog than a lake," Vosnesensky grumbled.

"Whatever. That's how we'll do it," said Jamie.

Vosnesensky muttered something in Russian.

"How's Ivshenko?" Jamie asked.

The cosmonaut's face went even darker. "Reed is taking care of his leg. Apparently it is not broken, but the knee is badly dislocated. He cannot walk. He can't even stand up without support."

"So it's up to me."

Now, after two hours of sweaty struggle, Jamie dogged down his helmet on the neck ring of his suit, trying to keep his doubts at bay. A couple of kilometers, he told himself. Two-three klicks, at most. I can do that. Yet his arms felt almost too heavy to lift; his legs were rubbery.

Connors had wanted to help him into the hard suit, but he was too weak to stand for more than a few minutes at a time. Joanna and Ilona assisted him, tight-lipped and silent, while Connors read off the checklist.

"Not bad," the astronaut quipped, "having two gorgeous women help you dress."

He was sitting on the edge of his own bunk, the checklist trembling in his hand, trying to keep a smile on his sweaty, weary face. Through the open hatch of the airlock Jamie could see that Connors was having trouble breathing; his chest heaved painfully, his mouth hung open.

The two women were not much better off. They moved slowly, listlessly. Their faces were drawn and pale. How many mistakes are they making? Jamie wondered. Are they killing me because they're too weak to know what they're doing?

The climbing harness, its tripod stand and winch mechanism, and its massive drum of cable was set against the airlock's side bulkhead. As he slid the harness over his shoulders and fastened it across his chest Jamie thought ruefully, We won't be using this to climb the cliffs and see my village. I'll never get to see whether it's a real village or not.

Finally he was fully suited, his backpack cinched tight and checked out, his harness ready to be connected with the cable. All systems working, unless they had overlooked something.

"Okay," Jamie said, already feeling the enormous weight of the suit, the backpack, the responsibility on his wobbly legs. "Clear the airlock."

Joanna reached up and touched his cheek. "Shut your visor first," she said tenderly. "And may god go with you."

God? Jamie thought. He remembered that his fetish was still in his coverall pocket. Buttoned up inside the hard suit he could not reach the pocket to touch it. It's there, he told himself. I'm not going without it. It's there where it should be.

Ilona cast him a wan smile as she and Joanna backed out of the airlock compartment. Jamie pulled the hatch shut after a desultory wave to Connors. Once the hatch was sealed he reached out a finger to push the control button that started pumping the air out of the chamber.

And saw that he had not put on his gloves.

His stomach lurched. Four of us checking out everything and the damned gloves are still tucked in my belt pouch. What the hell else have we screwed up?

He pulled the gloves on and sealed them to the suit cuffs. Then he started the pumps. In what seemed like mere seconds the light on the little square control panel went red. Jamie unconsciously drew in a deep breath. His chest felt strange, rasping, the way it did sometimes in the chill mountain air of winter.

The outer hatch popped open a few inches, then stopped. A trickle of reddish sand seeped into the airlock chamber.

It's going to be a battle every step of the way, Jamie realized. Just be careful. Be damned careful.

He pushed the hatch all the way open, leaning against it with his weight to force it back against the sand. The powdery rust-colored stuff poured in around his boots, billowing up into feather-light clouds of dust as he moved. Despite the low gravity the climbing rig's stand and reel of cable felt as if they weighed tons. The cable reel especially. It was meant to be rolled along the ground, not lifted.

There's no way to carry it in one hand, he told himself. I'm going to have to make a couple of trips.

Grasping the folded tripod stand, Jamie reached with his free hand for the ladder rungs studding the rover's flank just outside the hatch. Methodically he made his way up to the roof of the forward module and set the tripod down there.

"Jamie, are you all right?" Joanna's voice asked.

"I'm up on top of the cab," he reported. "I've got to figure out how to get that damned reel up here. It weighs a ton."

He heard a mutter of voices, indistinct. Then Connors came on, weak, almost breathless. "Connect the cable to the winch motor . . . latch it so it won't turn . . . then you can . . . power it up to you," the astronaut said.

Jamie grimaced inside his helmet. "I guess I would have thought of that eventually. Thanks, Pete."

"Nothing to it."

Everything seemed to go so slowly. Jamie spent half a lifetime winching the reel up to the rover's roof, then clomping down to the tail end of the vehicle and carefully climbing down onto the firm ground back there. Fumbling, sweating, cursing to himself, he set up the tripod stand and bolted it to the equipment attachment points built into the side of each of the rover's modules. Then he once again hooked the cable to the winch motor built into the stand. This time he unlatched the reel so that it could turn freely.

"Okay," he panted, breathless now himself. "I'm ready to start my little walk."

"Good luck, man," said Connors.

"*Vai com deus,*" Joanna replied.

Again with god, Jamie thought. Which god? The nasty old man of the Hebrews? The pacifist Christ? Or Coyote, the trickster? He's the one who's been working against us here on Mars. The old trickster. He must be howling with laughter at us, stuck in a stupid dry mud hole.

Vosnesensky's voice cut into his thoughts. "Did you say you are starting toward us?"

"Yes, Mikhail. I'll be moving to your right, around the perimeter of the crater's edge."

"I don't see you."

"You will in a few minutes. . . . I'll be there in an hour or so," Jamie said, knowing he was being wildly optimistic. Even with the cable drum resting firmly on the ground now and unreeling easily, he felt as if he were dragging the entire rover and all its contents with each step he took.

"It would be good if you got here before the sun went down," Vosnesensky said.

The thought startled Jamie. He turned halfway around and saw that the tiny, wan sun was already nearing the distant rocky horizon.

"I'll try," he said into his helmet microphone. "I sure don't want to be out in the dark if I can avoid it."

Dr. Li had started to write his report to Kaliningrad. He had wanted to be precise in his words, exact in the information he gave to the mission controllers. Knowing that the news that the ground team had contracted scurvy would hit like a thunderbolt and immediately be relayed up the chain of command to various national directors and then to the politicians, Li knew he had to be extremely careful in whatever he decided to say.

Hours later he still sat in his private quarters staring at the glowing computer screen. It was empty. He had not written a single word.

The only news from the ground was that Ivshenko had crippled his knee.

With a sigh of exasperation, more at his own failure of nerve than anything else, he tapped at the keyboard to get a status report from the ground team. Seiji Toshima's round face appeared on the screen.

After a few Japanese bows and hisses, the meteorologist explained that he had the comm watch for the moment. Zieman was manning the link with Vosnesensky, in the second rover.

Li wanted to inquire about Vosnesensky's rescue attempt, but instead he heard himself say, "Can you put me through to Dr. Reed, please?"

The only indication of surprise from Toshima was the barest instant of hesitation before he replied, "Yes, sir. Of course."

It took a few minutes but at last Reed's face appeared on his screen. The Englishman was sitting in the rover cockpit, the expression on his face wary, guarded.

"I would like to have a medical report," Li said.

Reed ran a finger across his moustache. "Well—Ivshenko's knee will need to be drained once we get back to the dome and I have the proper facilities for it. Vosnesensky is progressing well enough, but he's exhausted and quite weak. It takes several days to recover from scurvy, even with high doses of vitamin C."

"And the others?"

"Difficult to say. Waterman apparently feels well enough to walk from his rover to ours, although he seems to be moving awfully slowly."

Li ran out of questions. He sat in front of the display screen, trying to find a polite way, a way that was not painful, to bring up the subject he really wanted to discuss.

"I am in the process of making my report to Kaliningrad," he said at last.

"Yes," Reed responded.

"I intend to give you full credit for deducing the nature of the illness and its cause."

The Englishman seemed to stiffen. "And full blame, I should think, for not being clever enough to deduce it sooner."

"There is no blame . . ."

"Responsibility, blame, it's all the same thing, isn't it? I was the responsible man, the medical officer. I fouled up. That's the simple truth of it."

"No one could foresee that a meteor strike would have such consequences."

"No?" Reed almost smirked. "Then what are you going to put into your report, that it was an act of god?"

"It was an unforeseen chain of events," Li said.

The Englishman shook his head. "That won't wash. A mission such as this can't admit to an unforeseen chain of events. The controllers in Kaliningrad and Houston want everything planned and spelled out in the finest detail. Unforeseen events are not allowed. For god's sake, that's why they're called *controllers*, isn't it?"

"I do not want you to be the scapegoat."

"How can you avoid it?"

The answer came to Li as he spoke. "By emphasizing that you discovered the cause of the malady and have taken the necessary steps to cure it."

"And deemphasizing that my clumsiness caused it, and it took me weeks to realize what had happened? No matter how you write your report, that fact will stand out like a lighthouse beacon. As it should."

"You are too hard on yourself."

"Not as hard as Kaliningrad will be. My career in the Mars Project is over. Or it will be, once we get back. We both know that."

Li studied the Englishman's image on his screen. Reed had changed; it seemed as if he had aged. There were lines around his mouth that he had never noticed before. And yet, he did not appear to be angry, or even particularly unhappy. Reed seemed strangely satisfied with the idea that he would be blamed for the illness. He seemed almost relieved to think that he would never be permitted to return to Mars.

E A R T H

H O U S T O N :   **"It must be bad," said Alberto Brumado. "Very bad. Joanna refuses to speak to me. Something must be terribly wrong."**

For the first time since Edith had met him, Brumado looked his sixty-some years. His face was lined with worry; his boyish grin had been replaced by a somber, fearful frown.

She sat on the bed next to him. "Do you think the project people aren't telling you the whole story?"

They had taken adjoining rooms at one of the dozen hotels lining the road that passed the Johnson Space Center, neither Brumado nor Edith even thinking ahead far enough to consider who would pay for her room. As they had checked in, Edith had noticed that the lobby was filling up with reporters and camera crews. They sensed that something was happening, a big news story was about to break. Somebody was leaking information.

Brumado wrung his hands. "Joanna is trapped in the rover and they are all ill. Apparently they have come down with some sort of vitamin deficiency disease."

"Holy lord!" Edith breathed. "How bad off are they?"

"That is what I do not know. I wanted to speak with Joanna, but she refused to talk to me."

"Refused? Why?"

"I don't know!" he shouted.

Edith's mind raced. Jamie must be sick too, then. Stuck out there in the wilderness and sick. Maybe dying. And all those newshounds gathering down in the lobby. Like buzzards circling over a wounded deer.

"And the project still wants to keep a blackout on the news?" she asked.

Brumado nodded, his face a portrait of misery. "My baby is dying out there and she won't even speak to me."

"Alberto—the blackout won't work. The reporters already know something big is stirring. It's only a matter of time until somebody spills their guts, and then you're going to have a three-ring circus here."

His deep dark eyes focused on her, as if seeing her for the first time. "You want to break the story, is that it?"

"If I don't, somebody else will."

"Our agreement—that doesn't matter to you anymore?"

"This is my big chance, Alberto. And yours."

"Mine?"

"You're the soul of the Mars Project. Everybody calls you that, right? Well, now's the time for you to get in front of those cameras and tell the world what's happening up there on Mars. Tell it your own way. You've got to be the spokesman for the project now. You've got to be the link between them and the rest of the world."

"I can't . . . the project administration would never allow it. They have their own media relations staffs, their own spokespersons . . ."

Edith shook her golden curls. "It's got to be you, Alberto. Everybody in the world knows you and trusts you; they been watching you on their TVs for more'n thirty years. You're as respected as ol' Walter Cronkite, for lord's sake. You've got to be the one who faces the media."

He got up from the bed and paced to the curtained window.

"You can tell the world what's happening, Alberto. Tell it your way, the right way. Otherwise those reporters are going to get bits and pieces from leaks and hints and they'll put their own suspicions and guesswork on the air. It'll be a fiasco, a grade-A numero-uno disaster for the Mars Project. Every enemy the project's ever had will be on TV screamin' and yellin' their heads off. You know how they work. If you don't get in front of the cameras, and damned soon, they will."

"But my daughter . . ."

"Do it for her!" Edith snapped. "You want her to die up there while people down here are saying that exploring Mars was all a big mistake? A big waste of money?"

"I don't know if I can do it."

"Nobody else can."

His back was still to her. He pulled the window drapery open a little. "My god, there are three TV trucks down on the parking lot— and another one pulling in."

"Somebody's already leaking the word," Edith said.

Brumado turned back toward her, his face grim, doubtful. "I could call Kaliningrad. If they have no objection to your plan . . ."

"Whether they do or not, you've got to do it. You're not officially part of the project. They can't control you."

He looked as if he were going to object, but instead he went to the telephone.

"I'll go downstairs and tell the guys in the lobby that you'll talk to them," Edith said.

Brumado looked up at her, hesitated a fraction of a second, then nodded unhappily.

Edith went out into the corridor, heading for the elevator. It's the right thing to do, she kept telling herself. Whether or not it helps me, it's the right thing to do. And maybe I can get through to Jamie. Maybe they'll let us talk to them once we break the story.

S O L 4 0: SUNDOWN

The thermometer on the instrument cluster built into Jamie's left sleeve read forty below zero Celsius. He almost smiled. The one place where the Celsius and Fahrenheit scales agree: forty below is forty below on either system. Cold, no matter which way you read it.

The sun had just touched the jagged horizon, throwing immensely elongated shadows across the broken, rocky ground. Jamie saw his own shadow reaching out incredibly, stretching far out in front of him. But nowhere near far enough.

He had been pushing forward around the rippled sand that betrayed the dust-drowned crater. When he turned to see the tiny lifeless sun he also saw his rover, two thirds sunk in the red dust, disappointingly close. He had been trudging around the ghost crater's perimeter for more than an hour, yet it seemed that he had hardly begun his trek to the second vehicle.

The cable stretched from the connection on his harness backward toward the partially buried rover, most of it resting on the ridged surface of the sand. The farther I go around the crater, the more cable's going to be lying on the sand, Jamie said to himself. That shouldn't cause any problems. I don't think it will. Shouldn't be any problem at all. The cable won't sink into the damned sand. Even if it does we can winch it taut if I get to Vosnesensky's rover. Not if. When. When.

He kept walking. Even when he turned backward he kept his legs moving toward his goal: that second rover where Vosnesensky and Reed and Ivshenko were waiting for him.

It was getting dark. And cold. Jamie's legs felt rubbery, weak. Cold saps your strength. Got to keep going.

He walked at the slow, steady pace he had learned from his grandfather when they had hunted mule deer up in the mountains. "Just get your rhythm right," Al would say, "and you can walk all damned day, no trouble. It's all in the rhythm. Don't hurry. Don't rush. The deer won't run very far. You can walk him until he's exhausted and ready to drop at your feet."

Yeah. Right, Grandfather. If you're healthy. If you've been getting all your vitamins. If you're breathing real air and it's not forty below zero and dropping fast.

It was getting too dark to see the ground. Jamie reached up and turned on the lamp atop his helmet. Don't want to step into the sand by mistake. Wonder how golfers would like it here on Mars? Sand traps two kilometers wide. No water hazards. Maybe we ought to bring a set of clubs here the next time. Might start a demand for tourism. Take your vacation on Mars. Climb the solar system's tallest mountain. Drink a glass of Martian Perrier. Put your bootprints where no one has stepped before.

"Jamie! Did you hear me?"

He snapped his attention to Vosnesensky's demanding voice. "What? What did you say?"

"I asked if you had turned on your helmet lamp. It is becoming quite dark."

"Yes, it's on."

"Can you see the ground well enough to guide yourself?"

Jamie looked down. He was trudging along the hard-packed stony soil. A dozen paces to his right the rippled sand began.

"Yep. I can see okay."

"Good. Good."

Then Jamie realized what Vosnesensky's call meant. The Russian could not yet see Jamie's light. He was still too far away from the rover to be seen. He had miles to go.

They chattered back and forth, Jamie, the two cosmonauts, even Connors and the women. Jamie listened to the tension in their voices even when they tried to joke and banter. They're scared. They're all scared. And I am too.

It was fully night now. Jamie heard the soft breeze of Mars sighing past him. Gentle world, he told himself. If only you weren't so damned cold. Why did you make it so cold, Man Maker? Or why did you make us so weak? Did Coyote trick you into it?

"Talk," Vosnesensky said. "Speak, Jamie. Let us know that you are all right."

"It's getting . . . too damned cold . . . to talk much," he said. He was panting now. His legs felt stiff, hurting.

"Turn up the heater in your suit to maximum."

"Did that already."

"Make certain."

"Right."

The heater dial was already turned to max, Jamie knew. He tried it again and the dial would turn no further. Too bad we don't have a thermostat control for the planet. Stop the temperature from dropping any lower. Be a nice touch.

He kept plodding along, one foot after the other. One step at a time. I can outwalk any mule deer in these mountains. I can walk all the way around Mars if I have to. Show me how, Grandfather. Lead me.

Jamie remembered the fetish, stuck in his coverall pocket. He wished he could worm his arm free and reach into the pocket for it. He knew its power would warm him, bring him strength.

The cable suddenly pulled taut, yanking Jamie off his feet. He toppled over backward and hit the ground with a thud.

"Holy shit," he muttered.

"What?"

"What is it? What's wrong?"

Vosnesensky in one ear, Joanna in the other.

"Cable's stuck," Jamie said. He struggled up to his knees, tugged on the cable. "Christ, it feels as if . . ." he had to take a gulping breath ". . . as if the winch motor's frozen."

"That should not happen," Vosnesensky snapped.

"Right. Tell me." Jamie pulled on the cable again, leaning his full weight against it. It gave a little, stuck momentarily, then suddenly freed up. He staggered backward ludicrously, arms flailing to regain his balance, a string of obscenities he had not used since undergraduate days flowing from him.

"Jamie!" Joanna's voice was pitched high with anxiety, almost a scream.

"Okay . . . I'm okay . . . ," he gasped. "It worked loose again."

"The motor of the winch is self-heating," Vosnesensky said, as if to prove that what had happened had not happened.

"Right," said Jamie. He looked down at the ground to get his bearings, then started out again, keeping the sand a dozen paces to his right.

Sure, the motor's self-heating. Down to what temperature? Fifty below? A hundred below? A hundred fifty? Jamie did not want to look at his thermometer again. The numbers would be meaningless. It was cold. He could feel his life warmth seeping out into the thin keening night air. Numbers. Numb. Cold and freezing and numb.

His feet felt as if they no longer belonged to him. Cold and numb. He kept plodding forward; at least his legs obeyed the dogged commands of his brain. He leaned into the harness, dragging the cable behind him. If the winch motor goes I'm really stuck. Damned cable weighs too much for me to drag all the way without a motor helping me.

He heard a humming sound in his earphones, almost rhythmic, droning.

"What's . . . that?"

" 'The Song of the Volga Boatmen,' " Vosnesensky's voice answered solemnly out of the darkness. "It has been used for ages by men pulling barges up the Volga river. I thought it would help you."

"Sounds like . . . a funeral dirge."

Vosnesensky stopped his humming. "If you do not appreciate my music, then let me hear you speak. I want to hear you."

"No breath for talking."

"Make breath! I want to know that you are conscious and making progress."

"You can hear my gasping, can't you?"

"Yes, but I—wait! I can see your light! Jamie, you are getting close enough for me to see the light from your helmet lamp! Where are those binoculars? Yes! It is your helmet lamp! You are getting closer!"

Vosnesensky was being ridiculous. What other light could he possibly see out on this frozen empty slope?

"Keep moving, Jamie." Tony Reed's voice. "Don't stop now."

"Don't stop now," repeated Vosnesensky, with even more fervor in his voice.

"What're you . . . going to do . . . if I stop? Come out . . . after me?"

"If both my legs worked," Ivshenko said, "I would gladly come out to greet you."

Jamie shook his head, knowing that they could not see his gesture even if they were standing beside him in the full warm light of noon. Ivshenko can't walk and Mikhail can't even stand up, from what he had heard.

"Jamie," Joanna called, "talk to me, please. Tell me about your home in New Mexico. I have never been there."

"Not my home. I don't have . . . any home. Not in New Mexico . . . not anywhere. Except here. Maybe here. Mars is my home."

"Tell me what we will do once we return to Earth, then," she said.

"I'll tell you about Coyote."

"Coyote?"

"The trickster. Always causing trouble."

"Yes," Joanna said. "Tell me."

"You know . . . the patterns of the stars? The constellations?"

No answer. Jamie kept plodding forward, panting, until he heard Joanna in his earphones. "Go on."

"First Man and First Woman . . . put the stars in their places," he said. "They had . . . all the stars . . . in a blanket. Wanted to put them . . . in the right places . . . in the sky. Harmony is beauty. Order and . . . harmony."

The cable was sticking again; it was harder to pull it along. Jamie leaned all his weight into the harness.

"What happened then?" Joanna asked.

"Old Coyote came by . . . saw what they were doing. He grabbed . . . the blanket . . . swung it around and around . . . then he hurled the whole blanket . . . full of stars . . . into the sky. That's . . . what made . . . the Milky Way."

"Oh!" said Joanna.

"Coyote ruined . . . the harmony of the sky. He's always . . . messing things up."

"A cosmological myth," Vosnesensky said.

"Kind of." Jamie wondered how Coyote had tricked Man Maker into making Mars so cold. So utterly damnably cold. Then he realized that Coyote had tricked him, had tricked all of them, into coming to this dead world. This world of death.

But it's not dead, a voice in his mind said. You found life here.

Jamie blinked sweat from his eyes. Strange to find life on a world where we're all going to die, he thought. Strange to be sweating while you're freezing to death.

He staggered forward another few steps, then sank to his knees. His legs refused to move any farther. His arms felt as if encased in ice. Far in the distance he could see the tiny running lights of Vosnesensky's rover. Close enough to see. Close enough to reach.

Jamie tried to push himself to his feet, but he hadn't the strength to do it. Cold freezing numb. He crawled on his hands and knees, hearing the voice of his first mission instructor warning, "Even the smallest tear in your gloves, the tiniest leak in a seal or a joint, will kill you within minutes out on the surface of Mars."

Totally spent, he sprawled on the hard rocky ground. With a last supreme effort he managed to turn himself on his side and tried to struggle up into a sitting position.

He failed.

Lying on his side, half propped up by the bulky backpack and harness, Jamie looked up at the cold solemn stars glittering in the darkness. He thought he saw Coyote up there, laughing next to the Hunter.

"I'm sorry," he gasped. "I can't go . . . any farther. I'm done . . ."

"Jamie!" Joanna shrieked. "You must go on! You *must!* For me! For all of us! Please!"

"I tried . . ." The pain was ebbing away. His entire body was becoming numb, floating in nothingness like the Buddhist nirvana.

He heard Joanna sobbing and the muttering of voices in his earphones.

"Listen . . . ," he said, his voice sounding weak, far away, even to himself. "Tell them . . . it doesn't matter. Doesn't matter . . . that I died. That all of us die. Everyone dies. Not important. We've learned so much . . . and there's so much more . . . to find out."

"You must not die, Jamie! You must not!"

He felt no pain. A profound sense of acceptance spread over him, as if he had always been meant to be at this place. He remembered his grandfather telling him of Chief Seattle, who had said long ago that the Earth does not belong to man, but man belongs to the Earth. We belong to Mars, too, Jamie realized. Now we do. Now we do. And to the sun and all the worlds, all the stars. That's why we want to see it all, explore it all. It's our heritage. Our birthright. It's worth dying for.

I understand, he said silently, marveling at the clarity of his vision. Finally I understand who I am.

The whole universe of stars hung up in the darkly glittering night sky and gazed down at the small frail figure of a man lying helpless and alone on the frozen windswept slope of an ancient avalanche on Mars.

From far, far away he heard voices, but they meant nothing to him. They faded into the silence of eternity.

He understood now that Man Maker and Life Taker are one and the same, just two different aspects of the single creator. I'm ready, Jamie said silently. I've done the best I could. Now I'm ready for you. He heard Coyote laughing in the crystal darkness of the frozen night.

S O L 4 0: MIDNIGHT

Something was droning faintly in his ears. It was all dark, he could see nothing. His body felt numb, encased in ice. But there was that soft humming sound coming from somewhere.

His eyes were gummy. Too tired even to try raising his head or moving his arms, Jamie used every atom of his willpower to force his eyes open. A blurred confusion of grays swam before him. He blinked several times. It was the curved ceiling of the rover. The hum was the steady background throb of electrical power. He was lying on his back on one of the bunks. A bottom bunk, he saw, still blinking, focusing. The top bunk was pulled up and locked into its stowed position.

Vosnesensky appeared over him, his beefy face strangely gentle, tender. His wrinkled green coveralls looked too big for him, as if he had lost weight.

Jamie tried to say something but his throat was too dry. All that came out was a cracked groan.

"Rest, my friend," Vosnesensky whispered. "Do not try to exert yourself. Here . . ."

The Russian lifted Jamie's head and brought a steaming mug to his lips. "Easy . . . just a sip."

It felt scalding hot on Jamie's tongue. And good. Hot tea, heavily laced with lemon concentrate. He took several sips. It felt warm all the way down.

Vosnesensky laid Jamie's head back down softly on the bunk, then looked at him silently with dark solemn eyes. Jamie realized the Russian was sitting on the opposite bunk, not standing. From up in the cockpit he heard Ivshenko's voice speaking in English: reporting to the dome, or maybe straight to Dr. Li.

"You went out," Jamie croaked. "You went out and got me."

The Russian shook his head. "Reed went out."

"Tony? Tony brought me in?"

Vosnesensky nodded.

Jamie lay there, realizing that they had pulled him out of his hard suit. He wormed a hand into the pocket where the bear fetish was; it felt solid, warm, comforting. Tony went out and got me, he said to himself. Tony's not trained for EVA, but he went outside in the dark and dragged me in.

He heard the clumping thumps of boots and then Reed came into his vision, still encased in his yellow hard suit, except for the helmet. He looked like a man at an amusement arcade posing behind a cardboard cutout figure.

"You're very lucky, James," the Englishman said softly. "No frostbite. We got you in time."

"You saved my life."

Reed's face flushed slightly. "Couldn't let you freeze out there, could we?"

"Our physician has become a hero," Vosnesensky said. But he did not smile.

"It took a lot of guts to go out into the night," said Jamie. "Mars has given you courage."

Reed glanced at Vosnesensky. "No heroics. Mikhail Andreivitch would have strangled me if I hadn't gone out," he said. "I was saving my own life, actually."

"I don't believe that. It took a lot of courage. A coward would have stayed in here no matter how Mikhail threatened."

"You were practically here," Reed said. "You collapsed less than a couple of hundred meters from the rover. We couldn't sit here and let you die. That would have killed the other three in your group, as well, wouldn't it?"

"But still . . ."

Vosnesensky scowled down at Jamie. "After what you did, in your condition, our physician's little journey is insignificant."

Jamie smiled back at him. "Except for one small detail—without that little journey everything I did would have meant nothing at all."

Reed suddenly looked terribly uncomfortable. Vosnesensky shrugged and slowly pulled himself to his feet, leaning heavily on the metal supports of the upper bunk.

"You should try to sleep," Vosnesensky said.

"Yes," Reed agreed swiftly. "Rest. You've earned it."

"Dmitri is in contact with Connors and the women. Once the sun comes up I will ride the cable to their vehicle and help them into their suits. Then we will winch them across to us."

Jamie nodded, his eyes already closing.

"Good," he said. "Good."

His last conscious thought was that Reed seemed a reluctant hero. God knows what Mikhail threatened him with. But Tony came through. That's the important thing. Tony came through when it counted.

The chief controller sat behind his desk, alone in his Kaliningrad office except for the head of the British contingent. Outside the room's one window a cold, dreary rain was spattering, the first taste of autumn and grim winter.

The display screen built into the paneled wall had just turned off. For the past fifteen minutes the two men had watched and listened to the tape of the latest report from Dr. Li. The expedition commander had read from a prepared script and kept his face an immobile mask that revealed no emotion whatever.

Now the screen had gone blank. Li's tape was finished. The snow outside blanketed the usual noises from the street. The office was absolutely silent.

The chief controller tugged absently at his ragged Vandyke. "Well," he said in English, "what do you think?"

The head of the British team for the Mars Project was a Scottish engineer who had risen through the technical ranks to become an administrator. He was a slightly built man with graying dark hair and a crafty look in his eyes even when he was relaxing socially.

"It's a serious blow," he said. "The physician should have caught the symptoms earlier and taken steps to avert the problem."

"He found the answer, finally," said the chief controller.

"Aye, but he came close to killing them all."

The chief controller muttered, "How can we keep the media from finding out about this?"

"You cannot," the Scot said flatly. "Not with Brumado talking to all those reporters in Houston."

"Then we will have to keep this information from Brumado."

"Are you prepared to keep the entire team incommunicado for the rest of the mission? Be reasonable, man. It cannot be done."

The chief controller shook his head. "We'd have to keep them all quiet for the rest of their lives, wouldn't we?" He tangled his fingers in the abused Vandyke again.

"I know what you're thinking. It's one thing if the politicians learn of this in private. We can explain it to them reasonably and make them see that it was an unavoidable accident. But if the media get hold of it and ballyhoo it, the politicians will have to react to what the media is saying, not what we tell them."

"Exactly. That will mean the end of the Mars Project. There will be no return mission."

" 'Tis a thorny problem."

The chief controller stared out the window at the falling snow. "It's too bad we can't keep them all on Mars permanently."

The Scotsman smiled grimly.

By the time Jamie awoke it was fully light. Ivshenko was up in the cockpit; Vosnesensky had already suited up and gone through the airlock to winch himself across the treacherous lake of sand to the mired rover. It was the grating buzz of the winch motor that had pulled Jamie up from his sleep.

Once he realized Jamie was awake, Reed brought him a tray of hot breakfast with six gelatinous capsules resting beside a plastic cup filled with orange juice.

"Reed's recipe for recovering your health," the Englishman said when Jamie looked up at him questioningly. "Enough vitamins to lift a horse into orbit."

Jamie still felt weak and aching, but better than the day before. He realized that it was not his physical symptoms that had eased; rather, the terrible fear he had kept bottled up within him was gone. The body will heal, he knew, once the mind has been convinced that healing is possible. The real agony is in the mind, always.

He took a deep breath. The pain in his chest was gone. The turmoil in his mind had cleared away, too. Everything looked different, clearer than he had ever seen it before. As if he had looked at the world through a veil. Until now.

For the first time in his life Jamie felt an inner serenity, a certainty. He felt as sure and solid as the ancient mountains. This is what Grandfather Al told me about. I've found my balance, my place in the scheme of things. I know who I am now. I know where I belong. What I went through out there in the darkness has changed everything. Once you accept death nothing else can harm you. I can face anything now. Anything. He smiled inwardly. Not this time, Life Taker. Not yet.

"I want to thank you again, Tony. . . ."

Reed's brows knit together. "There's been enough of that. I'd prefer that you drop the subject, if you don't mind."

Jamie sat up and accepted the tray from Reed's hands. "Where's Mikhail?" he asked.

"Off to help your stranded comrades."

"By himself? Is he strong enough?"

"He got seven solid hours of sleep," said Reed. "He feels much better this morning. The vitamins are taking effect in him."

Ivshenko called back to them from the cockpit, "Mikhail has made it to their rover. He is helping Connors into his suit."

"I'd better get into mine," Reed muttered. "I'm assigned to greeting our guests at the airlock hatch."

"I'll help," said Jamie.

"You rest," Reed said firmly. "You've done enough. We can handle the remainder."

Reed went back to the airlock. Jamie gulped down his reconstituted eggs and lemon-laced tea, then made his way forward. Ivshenko grinned at him as he ducked into the cockpit. The cosmonaut's left leg was encased in a rigid plastic cast that stuck out awkwardly. Jamie was careful not to bang it as he slipped into the left-hand seat.

Through the bulbous canopy Jamie could see the winch line stretching tautly to the mired rover, on the far side of the dust-drowned crater.

"Connors is fully suited up," Ivshenko said.

"What about Joanna and Ilona?" Jamie asked as he clamped on a headphone set.

"Dr. Malater is apparently too sick to get out of her bunk without help. Dr. Brumado seems somewhat better than that, but not much."

"Maybe I ought to go back there and help them."

"You stay here," Ivshenko said firmly. "Mikhail Andreivitch gave strict orders. He will get the job done."

Jamie felt his body tense with something between frustration and guilt. He wanted to be helping, to be active, not sitting like a spectator. But a part of his mind told him, You're in no shape to go outside again. You've done your share. You can't do it all. Let the others help. The tension eased away.

Reluctantly, he accepted the situation and sat there in the cockpit, listening to the chatter among the people in the other rover. Joanna refused to go without her sample cases, the boxes that contained the precious specimens of Martian lichen. Jamie listened to their argument over the intercom radio link. Joanna's voice was weak, exhausted, breathless. Yet her will was stronger than the toughest steel. She absolutely refused to leave the rover without the sample cases.

Vosnesensky abruptly dumped the problem in Jamie's lap. "Waterman, you are the scientific leader. What do you recommend?"

Ivshenko glanced across the cramped cockpit to Jamie.

"The reason we came all this way was to see if life exists here," Jamie said. "Can't you attach the cases to the cable and send them here along with the people?"

A long pause, then Vosnesensky muttered, "Very well."

"Thank you," Joanna's voice said, as if from a great distance away.

The rover's exterior camera was aimed forward, along the taut cable that stretched between the two vehicles, and cranked up to maximum magnification. In the display screen set into the center of the control panel Jamie saw the half-buried rover's airlock hatch swing open. There stood Joanna, encased in her dayglo orange hard suit, with Vosnesensky's blaring red suit beside her. The cosmonaut helped her into the climbing harness, then attached it to the winch line.

"We are ready," Jamie heard in his earphone. "Start the winch."

The motor began whining. Joanna was pulled off her feet and began moving toward Jamie, dangling in the harness, her boots trailing bare centimeters above the rippled sand. Behind her, Vosnesensky attached four bulky boxes to the cable: the bio cases, with their samples of the Martian lichen safely inside them.

Joanna was absolutely silent as she rode across the treacherous lake of sand. Jamie heard Vosnesensky and Connors talking over the intercom, grunting and panting with the exertion of getting the half-conscious Ilona into her hard suit. Joanna's suited figure rode past him, her gloved hands gripping the cable, but her feet dangling as if she were unconscious. Or dead.

She's all right, Jamie said to himself. She just doesn't know how to hang on properly. She's forgotten what they showed us in training about riding the safety cable out of the shuttle if there's a malfunction on the launch pad. She'll be okay.

Still, it seemed like an hour before he heard the airlock hatch sigh open behind him. Jamie twisted in the cockpit seat to see Joanna step wearily into the module, encased in her bright suit, with Reed in his yellow suit supporting her like a solicitous robot helping one of its own kind. The pair of them clumped as far as the midship area, where Joanna half collapsed on one of the folded-up benches.

Jamie pulled himself out of his seat and stumbled aft toward her, surprised at how weak he still was.

"Can you take care of her?" Reed's voice was muffled from inside his helmet. "The sample cases are on their way and Mikhail's already yelling at me to take them off the cable."

"Sure, I'll take her," Jamie said, his voice shaking.

He helped Joanna lift off her helmet. She smiled at him feebly. Gently, he moved her to a half-reclining position, her back against the rover bulkhead, then tried to pull off her dust-spattered boots. The tang of ozone almost felt good, reviving, like smelling salts.

"I think I can manage the rest," Joanna said, once he had tugged her boots off.

Jamie sagged down onto the bench beside her, then turned her halfway around so he could reach her backpack.

"I'll help you."

"I was afraid . . . you had died out there."

"So was I."

"It was a very brave thing you did."

He tried to laugh. It came out more like a groan. "Bravery is the other side of fear, I guess. I was afraid we were all going to die."

"You saved us. You saved me."

"Tony saved me. Tony and Mikhail. There's enough heroism to go around for everybody."

He unclipped the last of the backpack connectors and lifted the bulky pack off her. It felt heavy, heavier than Jamie had remembered. Reaching across, he put it down on the opposite bench. Then he began to help unseal the suit's hard-shell torso.

"Please, Jamie," Joanna said. "I can do it for myself now. You should be ready to help Ilona. She is really in bad condition."

He nodded. "Okay."

Before he could get up from the bench, though, Joanna reached a hand to his cheek and pulled his face to hers. She kissed him tenderly.

"Thank you," she whispered.

He clasped one hand around the nape of her neck, feeling the silky softness of her thick dark hair, and kissed her.

Before he could think of anything to say they both heard thumping sounds from the airlock.

"Ilona," Joanna said. "She'll need help."

Jamie got up and went to the airlock hatch. Ilona was barely conscious and totally unable to stand on her own feet under the weight of her hard suit. Jamie and Reed laid her out on the bench opposite Joanna and removed her helmet and backpack.

She looks half dead, Jamie thought. Her eyes were vacant, glazed, bloodshot, with deep black circles beneath them. Her cheeks were hollow, gaunt, her breath fetid.

But she forced a little smile as she looked up at Jamie. "A man should never . . . see a woman . . . first thing in the morning."

"This morning doesn't count," Jamie said.

"All right . . . but just . . . this once."

Connors and finally Vosnesensky rode the cable across the sand-filled crater. By the time the sun was at high noon, they were all out of their suits and Vosnesensky was at the controls in the cockpit, grinning hugely.

"Now we return to the dome," he said. "And from there to orbit in a few days."

"And from orbit, back to Earth," Connors said, perched on one of the benches.

Ivshenko was up in the cockpit with Vosnesensky. Jamie was sitting on the bench between Joanna and the astronaut. Reed was standing beside the galley, his back to the airlock hatch. They had pulled down the lower bunk on the opposite side so that Ilona could lie on it. She seemed to be asleep as the rover lurched into motion.

"You saved our necks, man," said Connors.

"Not me," Jamie said. "Tony . . ."

But Joanna interrupted him by laying a hand on his thigh. "You saved us. And not only us. You saved our Martian specimens."

Jamie looked down at her urchin's face, drawn and pale. Is that why she kissed me? Because I saved her damned lichen?

E A R T H

Alberto Brumado smiled tiredly into the dazzling lights. He thought he knew how exhausted the explorers on Mars must feel; he felt the same way. He had lost track of how many hours he had been sitting before the lights and cameras and reporters, answering their questions, feeding them the news of the stranded team as it became available to him.

The little lobby of the hotel had quickly proved too small for Brumado's impromptu news conference, so they had moved—reporters, camera crews, lights, and all—to the largest conference room in the hotel and quickly jammed it to the walls and out into the corridor beyond its wide double doors.

The Mars Project officials at the Johnson Space Center had been furious, at first, that Brumado was talking off the cuff to the media. But after the first few hours, and hurried phone discussions with Washington and Kaliningrad, the project bigwigs had offered Brumado their own spacious conference hall at the Johnson Center.

None of the media people wanted to shut down and move to Johnson, not while they had Brumado live, giving a bravura marathon performance. So, swallowing their resentment, the Johnson people began passing information to Brumado as it came in from Mars.

Brumado was sitting on a folding chair behind a little table, up on the makeshift dais that had been quickly erected at the far end of the room. Perspiring, hair tousled, suit rumpled, tie long gone from his collar, he took another sheet of paper from Edith's hand, scanned it quickly, then smiled up at the cameras.

"They are safe," he said, the three most wonderful words he had ever spoken. "Dr. Waterman carried the cable line to the second rover and cosmonaut Vosnesensky has brought the others to their vehicle. They have started on their way back to the dome."

He could not see the pack of reporters beyond the glare of the TV lights, but he heard them sigh audibly, then break into spontaneous applause. Brumado felt surprised at that; then he wondered if they were applauding the good news or his own performance. The good news, of course. Joanna is safe. She will live. He stood up on weak, trembling legs and raised both his hands.

"If you will excuse me, I would like to take a break now. The public-information people at Johnson can take over, if you would be kind enough to go there."

They applauded again, startling him anew. This time he realized it was for him. Alberto Brumado smiled boyishly and realized he needed to go to the toilet very badly.

Edith, standing off to one side of the dais, knew that Brumado would immediately want to speak to his daughter. She intended to be there when he did. It would be her chance to see Jamie.

He's safe, Edith said to herself. And a hero. She felt proud of him. And of Alberto, who had turned this near disaster into a global media triumph.

It was only then, after more than twelve nonstop hours, that Edith began to think about how this event could be used to further her own career.

S O L 4 5: MORNING

Everyone feels so damned happy to be leaving, Jamie thought. Why don't I?

They had packed their specimens and computer disks aboard the ascent modules of the L/AVs. All the lab equipment and what remained of their supplies had been carefully covered and sealed, to be left inside the dome with the furniture and life-support equipment, ready to be used by the next explorers—if there was to be a second Mars expedition.

Jamie felt as if he were leaving a home he had lived in all his life. He remembered the hollow, almost frightened feeling in the pit of his stomach the day he and his parents had left Santa Fe for their new home in Berkeley. He had been five years old then. Funny the things you remember, he thought.

The dome echoed now with emptiness. He felt sad, despondent about it.

"Message coming in for you," Ollie Zieman told him, startling Jamie out of his reverie. The astronaut was manning the communications console until the last L/AV was ready to lift off.

Jamie followed him to the comm center and sat in front of the main console. He was surprised to see Edith's face on the screen.

She looked very tired, as if she had not slept for days. But happy.

"Jamie, I've been trying to get through to you for five days now. The project people have finally let me send a personal message to y'all. We—Alberto and me—we've been on the air almost nonstop, trying to do what you guys call damage control for the project. Alberto gave them a blow-by-blow account of your rescue, and I saw to it that *his* version of what happened to y'all got out on the air before anybody else had a chance to say diddly-squat."

Jamie grinned at her image. No matter what she was doing with her private life, Edith had become part of the Mars team.

"Now, they only gave me a minute of their precious transmission time, so all I got time to say is—I'll be waiting for you in Washington when you get back. I'll be the full-time regular space correspondent for Cable News, and I expect to get a private and exclusive interview with you. Don't matter who else you been talking to, if you get what I mean. I want to interview you. Understand me?"

She looked out from the screen expectantly. Jamie glanced over his shoulder at Zieman, who busily pretended not to have been eavesdropping.

"Okay," Jamie said, knowing it would take more than twelve minutes for his words to reach Edith. "A complete and exclusive interview. Like the one we did in Galveston when I found out that I'd been selected for the landing team. Maybe you can arrange to meet us at the space station. Zero gravity can be a lot of fun."

He sensed another person standing behind him. Turning in the chair, he saw it was Joanna, looking at him with a strange, quizzical smile playing on her lips. She held up the fingers of both hands to him. Nine fingers. We'll be in transit for nine months, Jamie translated her silent message.

Joanna walked away, still smiling. And Jamie realized that she was telling him that the trip back home was going to be very different from the voyage outward.

"It is time to suit up," Vosnesensky said.

For the last time, Jamie said to himself. One final hour or so in the hard suits and then we'll be aboard the spacecraft and ready to start for home. Everyone headed for the airlock and the racks of hard suits waiting for them.

Zieman and Dr. Yang went with Tony Reed, the diminutive Chinese physician walking in front of the Englishman, the husky astronaut behind him. Like a prisoner under house arrest, Jamie thought. They're already blaming him for the scurvy outbreak. They'll want a scapegoat back on Earth and they've decided it's going to be Tony.

Reed looked pale and withdrawn, but when he saw Jamie coming up beside him his old crooked little smile returned. "My god, James, you look positively morose. Don't you want to go home?"

"Sure I do." But Jamie knew it was only partially true.

"You want to continue exploring Mars, don't you?" Reed said. "Don't you?"

"No thanks," Reed said fervently. "I've had enough of this dust bowl. I'm looking forward to England and rain and flower gardens."

Jamie thought of the desert where his Navaho ancestors lived. How much like Mars it is; yet how different.

"If you're feeling so melancholy," Reed jibed, "then perhaps you ought to stay here."

"I wish I could," Jamie admitted.

Reed hiked an eyebrow.

"How are you doing, Tony?" Jamie asked.

"I'm fine. Don't worry about me."

Jamie said, "I'm going to have a long talk with Dr. Li, once we get back into orbit. And with the mission controllers."

"On my behalf?"

"Right."

"Don't bother."

"I damned well will bother," Jamie said, with quiet intensity. "I'll take it all the way up to the project directors, if I have to."

"Don't be silly," said Reed. "And don't give me that 'you saved my life' business again."

"But they're going to make you the scapegoat for everything that went wrong with the mission!"

Reed's smile turned bitter. "What of it? The mission needs a sacrificial lamb, doesn't it? One man killed in orbit. The entire ground team nearly killed by a stupid mistake. You can be the mission's hero, James. I'll be the goat."

"That's not right. It's not fair."

Reed's smile turned sour. "Perhaps you'd better stay, then, my heroic friend. That's the only way you're going to get to explore more of this miserable ball of rust. Once we get back home and they start dissecting all the mistakes we've made, there will never be another expedition to Mars. Never."

Jamie saw that the others had gathered around them, faces questioning. Even Vosnesensky looked doubtful, scowling worriedly. They had reached the row of lockers where their dust-spattered hard suits waited like the battered armor of knights who had sought the Holy Grail.

Jamie turned around to face Reed. Calmly, quietly, he said, "There will be no scapegoats among us. Not among us. We're a team. Even when we get back to Earth we're still a team. Without heroes and without goats."

"I wish that could be true, Jamie," said Reed, with real yearning in his voice.

"It will be."

"It can't be. The project directors will never trust me again. I'll get a polite handshake and be mustered out into private practice. And think of what's waiting for Mikhail. Our noble team leader fractured every rule in the regulations and thumbed his nose at Li and the mission controllers. Mikhail's career is finished."

Vosnesensky grunted. "So I will retire. I have achieved my dream. I was the first man on Mars. I will not return. I don't think anyone will come back to Mars. Tony is right. There will be no more expeditions."

"For how long?" Jamie demanded. "For my whole lifetime? For a hundred years? A thousand? I don't think so. But even if it happens that way, what of it? We'll come back to Mars one day, just as surely as the sun rises."

"Really?"

"Yes! Because we have to. The human race has to. We're explorers, Tony. All of us. Even you; it's what brought you here. It's built into our blood, into our brains. That's what science is all about. Human beings have to learn, have to search and seek and explore. We *need* to, just like a flower needs water and sunlight. It's what made our ancestors move out of Africa and spread all across the Earth. Now we're spreading all across the solar system and someday we'll start to move out to the stars. You can't stop that, Tony. Nobody can. It's what makes us human."

Reed backed off a step, then lifted his chin a notch higher. "Very pretty speech, Jamie. But most of the human race doesn't give a damn about Mars or anything else except their own squalid little greeds. They're going to close down the Mars Project, Jamie. They're going to kill it."

"They'll try, I know. They'll do their best to shut us down. And I'll do mine. Because I'm not going to rest until they send another expedition back here. If I have to do it with my bare hands, I'll bring us back to Mars."

Jamie stuck his hand into his coverall pocket and pulled out his bear fetish. He reached up and put it on the rack beside his gray helmet.

"And to prove it, I'm going to leave this little fellow here to greet me when I return."

They all stared at the fetish. Jamie had not allowed any of them to see it before.

"My grandfather would say it has powerful magic," Jamie told them. "But the real magic is in us. We make things happen. We're coming back to Mars—all of us who want to."

Reed huffed. "A gesture."

"A symbol," Jamie corrected.

"Speaking of gestures," Ilona said, stepping through the group to stand between Jamie and Vosnesensky, "I had intended to do this in private, once we were aboard the spacecraft."

She took from her breast pocket the dog-eared photograph that had been taped up over her bunk. Staring solemnly at Vosnesensky, Ilona methodically tore the photo into small pieces.

"Mikhail, I have wronged you and all the Russians on this mission. I apologize. You saved our lives, and it was wrong of me to hold a fifty-year grudge against you personally."

Vosnesensky, totally surprised, shifted from one foot to another. "Well . . . I suppose . . . ," he stammered.

Ilona threw her arms around his neck and kissed him so soundly that Vosnesensky's face turned as red as his hard suit. Everyone laughed. Even Reed.

Jamie looked at the other members of the Mars team. One by one, from Abell's grinning frog face to Ivshenko, leaning heavily on a pair of stainless steel crutches. Mikhail was right, he thought. Mars has tested us. Each and every one of us. None of us is the same person we were when we arrived here.

His gaze ended with Joanna, standing slightly aside from all the others, strong and proud. Her eyes gleamed back at him.

It's going to be an interesting trip home, Jamie thought. Very interesting.

S O L 4 5: NOON

One after the other, the three ascent modules lifted from the surface of Mars on tongues of shimmering flame. Their rocket engines blew miniature sandstorms across the landscape as they shrieked like departing demons, leaving the lower half of each L/AV sitting empty, incomplete, on the red dusty ground.

Quiet returned to Mars. The wind sighed as though sad to be alone again. The planet turned as it had since its beginning. Here and there in special niches on the bitterly cold little world, life abided, soaking up the sunlight and whatever pitiful moisture it could find.

Night fell and the pale distant sun rose again. More nights and days passed in their turn and nothing changed on the red surface of Mars. At last on one bright morning a new double star burned briefly in the pink sky and then was gone. The two linked spacecraft that had orbited the planet, a strange twinned artificial moon from another world, began the long journey back toward Earth.

Mars was alone again. Nothing of the inquisitive visitors from Earth remained. Except their scattered equipment, dead and still now, and their domed base, waiting for the next explorers. Inside the dome, sitting crouched on an empty rack, waited a miniature stone likeness of a bear that carried a tiny flint arrowhead and an eagle's feather, tied by a leather thong that had been lovingly knotted.

The wind of Mars stroked the dome gently, waiting also.

High up on the flat top of a mesa where the Old Ones had built themselves a city a thousand years ago, Edith Elgin and Al Waterman walked beneath the bright blue sky. They both wore strong, comfortable boots, sheepskin jackets, and broad-brimmed hats.

"They're on their way back," Edith told Jamie's grandfather. "They'll be here by the springtime."

Al nodded and squinted up at the brilliant sky. "I hope I'm still around by then."

Edith looked at him sharply. "Why? Are you sick?"

"Not yet," he said. "But there's this feeling in my bones, you know."

"Jamie told me you had a mystical streak in you."

Al laughed. "Yeah, I guess I do."

They walked along in silence for a while. The wind gusted hard, lifting the collars of their coats against their necks. All that remained of the ancient city was a scattering of adobe bricks almost hidden by the wild waving grass.

"You know," Al said, "he's gonna want to go back there soon's he can."

Edith nodded. "Maybe. It's going to be a tough fight to get everyone to agree to another mission."

"Naw, not as tough as you think. Jamie's found his path; he's turned into a hero. Nobody will be able to stop him from goin' back to Mars. Not even the President of the United States, whoever it might be next year."

"You think he's that strong?"

"Sure." Al peered at her, his eyes questioning. "He'll make a lousy husband, you know, away for years at a time."

Edith said nothing.

"Maybe he'll marry one of the women scientists," Al said.

"Or maybe," Edith smiled her brightest smile, "maybe a really smart newswoman could get herself a spot on the next expedition and go out to Mars with him."

Al grinned back at her. "Now that would be something, wouldn't it?"

"Yes," said Edith. "That would be just about perfect."

Mars waited.

The giant volcanoes thrust their massive cones high into the thin atmosphere. The long rift valley sheltered its stubbornly rugged patches of lichen. The strange rock that bore the likeness of a human face abided patiently, as it had for untold millennia. The ocean of water frozen beneath the ground waited for a warmer time when it could release its vital moisture and renew the red world once more.

The dead cities carved into ancient cliff sides held their secrets, waiting, waiting for the children of the blue world to return and discover them.

Mars waits for us.